THE YEAR'S 25 FINEST
CRIME & MYSTERY STORIES
Fifth Annual Edition

THE YEAR'S
25 FINEST
CRIME & MYSTERY
STORIES

Fifth Annual Edition

Edited by the Staff of
Mystery Scene

With an Introduction by Jon L. Breen

Carroll & Graf Publishers, Inc.
New York

Copyright © 1996 by the staff of Mystery Scene
Introduction copyright © 1996 by Jon L. Breen
Head notes by John Helfers

The permissions listed on the following pages constitute
an extension of this copyright page.

First edition September 1996.

Carroll & Graf Publishers, Inc.
260 Fifth Avenue
New York, NY 10001

Library of Congress Cataloging-in-Publication Data are available.

ISBN 0-7867-0361-X

Manufactured in the United States of America.

PERMISSIONS

This book is dedicated to Janet Hutchings

CONTENTS

Introduction
THE MYSTERY IN 1995

It's tempting to call 1995 the Year of the O. J. Simpson Trial, which occupied the nation's attention for most of that year before finally concluding in a controversial verdict of not guilty. But the full impact of this hard-fought case as an inspiration for mystery fiction (and there will be such an impact) probably won't be felt for a couple of years. Whatever you believe about the justice of the verdict, the murders of Nicole Brown Simpson and Ronald Goldman will inevitably join Lizzie Borden, the Lindbergh kidnapping, and the John F. Kennedy assassination as one of the classic American true-crime cases. In fact and in fiction, like it or not, we'll never hear the end of it.

I prefer to call 1995 the Year of the Fan. I'm not only referring to voracious readers but to active enthusiasts of the sort who plan and run conventions, publish and contribute to amateur and semi-pro periodicals, write book reviews and letters to the editor, compile and contribute to reference works, establish small publishing companies devoted to their favorite genre, offer encouragement to writers via mail or face-to-face, exchange information and recommendations with other fans, and become specialist book dealers.

While science fiction has had an active fandom for sixty years or more, mystery fiction fans (aside from Sherlockians) have not been a visible body for much more than a quarter of a century. The birth of mystery fandom is usually traced to the founding in the middle sixties of a couple of fanzines—Len and June Moffatt's *The JDM Bibliophile,* devoted to the works of John D. MacDonald, and Allen J. Hubin's *The Armchair Detective*—and to the first Anthony Boucher Memorial Mystery Convention (Bouchercon) in 1970. In the years since, the volume of publications and conventions has grown beyond all expectations, thanks mostly to people who did what they did not for profit or glory but out a love for the genre.

The inspiration for this elegiac note is the usual one: a sense of loss. The toll of prominent mystery fans in 1995 was cruelly large: Ellen Nehr, whose energy, commitment, and profound depth of knowledge of the field resulted in the monumental *Doubleday Crime Club Compendium* (1992), among other achievements; Jim McCahery, longtime fanzine publisher and contributor who cracked the ranks of professional mystery novelists in the last years of his life; and Bob Samoian, *Mystery and Detective Monthly* contributing editor and almost legendary collector, who was surely among the most widely loved individuals in the mystery world. All these people will be remembered both for their achievements and for themselves.

The explosion of publication in the crime/mystery genre continues unabated. For the first three-quarters of the year, M. S. Cappadonna's Checklist column in *The Armchair Detective* listed about 320 new hardcover novels. Project that over a full year and you top the 400 mark, which suggests an upswing of mystery publishing. Figure in a paperback original total that must top the century mark, and you have over 500 new mysteries in print, possibly a record.

BEST NOVELS OF THE YEAR 1995

In 1944, I chaired the Edgar committee and was surprised when the committee's choices didn't meet with universal acclaim. When the nominees were announced for 1995, I checked out the winner and a couple of others and was puzzled by what I found. There's plenty of good mystery fiction being published, and there's no reason to expect much unanimity of opinion of what is best. While the Grand Master award voted to Dick Francis by the Mystery Writers of America is obviously well-merited, and if anything overdue, I was surprised by the record third best-novel Edgar for *Come to Grief* (Putnam), which was dependably readable and had its moments of brilliance but on balance was surely one of Francis's weaker books. (In my view, it wasn't even the best horse-racing mystery of the year.) Another nominee, John Dunning's *The Bookman's Wake* (Scribners), is bound to delight collectors and dealers with its wealth of book lore but has the common contemporary fault of excessive length. It was hard for me to imagine a reader less enthralled with the subject matter than I not to become patient with it. The nominee by Peter Lovesey, on the other hand, struck me as worthy Edgar fodder. (See below.)

Anyway, with the usual disclaimer (and declaimed even more loudly than usual this time) that nobody including me can speak with real authority about the whole year's output, here are the fifteen novels of 1995 that most impressed me.

Robert Barnard, *The Bad Samaritan* (Scribners). Charlie Peace investigates a case involving a vicar's wife who has suddenly lost her faith. Barnard never fails to entertain.

Max Allan Collins, *Blood and Thunder* (Dutton). This re-creation (with fresh solution) of the Huey Long assassination ranks with the best of the Nate Heller historical private eye novels.

Barbara D'Amato, *Hard Christmas* (Scribners). In another of the author's trademark "backgrounder" mysteries, journalist Cat Marsala encounters murder among a family of Christmas tree farmers.

Susan Dunlap, *Sudden Exposure* (Delacorte). The series about Berkeley, California cop Jill Smith combines solid detection with an incomparable sense of place.

Jack Finney, *From Time to Time* (Simon & Schuster). Is this sequel to the classic time travel novel *Time and Again* really a mystery, or is it better defined as fantasy or science fiction? I don't care. The author, who died in 1995, was one of the greatest of popular storytellers.

Robert Irvine, *Pillar of Fire* (St. Martin's). Salt Lake City's Moroni Traveler's eighth case, involving a Mormon cultist faith healer and a small town ravaged by bomb-testing fallout, takes a fine series to new heights.

Stuart Kaminsky, *Hard Currency* (Fawcett Columbine). Russian cop Rostnikov visits Castro's Cuba, while his colleagues are having their own problems back in Moscow. How can the prolific author write so well in so many different modes?

Peter Lovesey, *The Summons* (Mysterious). The third novel about nostalgic ex-cop Peter Diamond proves its author can live in the present as engagingly as in the past.

John Lutz, *Death by Jury* (St. Martin's). Long-running St. Louis private eye Nudger is at the top of his form in this one, which shows his creator can handle trial action as well as all the other elements of the mystery.

Stephen Marlowe, *The Lighthouse at the End of the World* (Dutton). If I had been on a 1995 awards committee, I think this intricate, beautifully written, and boundlessly creative riff on the life of Edgar Allan Poe is the novel I'd be pushing for top honors.

Joyce Carol Oates, *Zombie* (Dutton). A mainstream literary figure who has been increasingly identified with varieties of crime fiction in recent years produces one of the finest and most frightening explorations of the mind of a serial killer ever committed to paper.

Bill Pronzini, *Blue Lonesome* (Walker). Only a few books in the author's long and distinguished career impressed me as much as this Woolrichian story of a driven man's quest for a phantom lady.

Ruth Rendell, *Simisola* (Crown). The latest about Chief Inspector Wexford offers the customary tricky plot and social insights, with an especially interesting view of British race relations.

Kate Ross, *Whom the Gods Love* (Viking). Should the Regency-based adventures of Julian Kestrel be recommended to historical readers? Certainly—but even more so to traditionalists who value the clue-planting and games-playing of the Golden Age of Detection.

Steven Saylor, *The Venus Throw* (St. Martin's). The cases of Roman sleuth Gordianus the Finder were good from the start, but with each volume, they seem to get even deeper and more astonishing.

SHORT STORIES

The more people talk about the shrinking outlets for mystery short stories, the healthier the market for anthologies and single-author collections seems to be. In the latter category, two of the pioneering female private eyes had their short cases collected in 1995, Sharon McCone in Marcia Muller's *The McCone Files* (Crippen & Landru, P.O. Box 9315, Norfolk, VA 23505-9315) and V. J. Warshawski in Sara Paretsky's *Windy City Blues* (Delacorte). Walter Satterthwait's African stories were gathered in *The Gold of Mayani* (Buffalo Medicine Books, Box 1762, Gallup, NM 87305), while other small presses produced collections by Ed Gorman, *Cages and Other Stories* (Deadline, P.O. Box 2808, Apache Junction, AZ 85217), and Janwillem van de Wetering, *Mangrove Mama and Other Tropical Tales of Terror* (Dennis McMillan, 2421 E. Speedway Blvd., Tucson, Arizona 85719). Kate Wilhelm's *A Flush of Shadows* (St. Martin's) gathers five novelettes about the husband-and-wife team of Constance Leidl and Charlie Meiklejohn, some bordering on fantasy and science fiction and some more mundane. Collected for the first time (at least in the U.S.A.) were Colin Dexter's stories in *Morse's Greatest Mystery and Other Stories* (Crown), and Joyce Porter's in *Dover: The Collected Short Stories* (Foul Play/Countryman). A forgotten series from the early thirties by the celebrated Margery Allingham was rediscovered in *The Darlings of the Red Rose* (Crippen & Landru).

Among the multi-author anthologies, it was a banner year for retrospective gatherings with strong editorial notes: Mike Ashley's *The Mammoth Book of Historical Detectives* (Carroll & Graf), Peter Haining's *Murder at the Races* (Chartwell), Bill Pronzini and Jack Adrian's *Hard-Boiled: An Anthology of American Crime Stories* (Oxford University Press), and Paula L. Wood's *Spooks, Spies, and Private Eyes: Black Mystery, Crime, and Suspense Fiction of the Twentieth Century* (Doubleday). Among the other reprint anthologies were several thematic gatherings from the backfiles of *Ellery Queen's Mystery Magazine* and *Alfred Hitchcock's Mystery Magazine: Murder Most Medical* (Carroll & Graf), edited by Cathleen Jordan and Cynthia Manson, and two edited by Manson alone, *Mystery Cats 3* (Signet) and *Murder by the Book* (Carroll & Graf). Among the flourishing original anthologies were *Vampire Detectives* (DAW) and *Murder Most Delicious* (Signet), both edited by Martin H. Greenberg; the Valentine-themed *Crimes of the Heart* (Berkley), edited by Carolyn G. Hart; *Malice Domestic 4* (Pocket), introduced by Hart and ghost-edited by Greenberg; *Cat Crimes Takes a Vacation* (Fine), edited by Greenberg and Ed Gorman; and *Sherlock Holmes in Orbit* (DAW), edited by Greenberg and Mike Resnick.

REFERENCE BOOKS AND SECONDARY SOURCES

It was an extraordinary year for crime-writer biography. Douglas G. Greene's *John Dickson Carr: The Man Who Explained Miracles* (Penzler) was a meticulously well executed account of one of the giants of the Golden Age, while Robert Polito's Edgar-winning *Savage Art* (Knopf) was the best secondary souce yet on a quite different but equally fascinating figure, Jim Thompson. The first volume of *The Letters of Dorothy L. Sayers* was published in Great Britain by Hodder and Stroughton, with St. Martins's American edition following in early 1996. B. J. Rahn collected essays on another Golden Age great in *Ngaio Marsh: The Woman and Her Work* (Scarecrow); Lawrence Block chatted with book dealer/ scholar Ernie Bulow in *After Hours* (University of New Mexico Press); and the updated edition of Robin Whiteman's *The Cadfael Companion: The World of Brother Cadfael* (Mysterious), an encyclopedic guide to the late Ellis Peters's famous series, constituted its first American publication.

Mystery buffs looking for tips on what to read next could turn to *The Crown Crime Companion* (Crown), in which the Mystery Writers of America membership endeavor to pick the hundred best mystery novels of all time, or the second edition of *The Armchair Detective Book of Lists* (Penzler), probably the most comprehensive listing of awards winners and other best lists ever compiled. Readers obsessed with who-really-dun-it can't be without *Hawk's Author Pseudonyms II: A Comprehensive Reference to Modern Authors' Pseudonyms,* a much improved and expanded second edition of a volume that lives up to its subtitle and inevitably emphasizes authors of genre fiction. (Author and publisher is Pat Hawk, 1740 Sunshine Lane, Southlake, TX 76092-9543.) The most disappointing, became error-ridden, reference of the year was Jay Pearsall's *Mystery and Crime: The New York Public Library Book of Answers* (Fireside).

SUBGENRES

I. Private Eyes. Among the sleuths for hire in good form during the year were Harold Adams's Carl Wilcox in *The Ditched Blonde* (Walker); Peter Corris's Australian Cliff Hardy in two cases new to American readers, *Beware of the Dog* and *Wet Graves* (both Dell); Dick Lochte's New

Orleans-based Terry Manion in *The Neon Smile* (Simon & Schuster); John Lutz's Floridian Fred Carver in *Burn* (Holt), albeit not in quite as good form as St. Louis stablemate Nudger (see the list of fifteen); and Parnell Hall's Stanley Hastings moonlighting as screenwriter in *Movie* (Mysterious). And we also had strong cases for three characters who are not exactly private eyes but often act like them: Jonathan Kellerman's child psychologist Alex Delaware in *Self-Defense* (Bantam), Robert Campbell's Chicago politico Jimmy Flannery in *Sauce for the Goose* (Mysterious), and Andrew Vachss's underground child advocate Burke in *Footsteps of the Hawk* (Knopf). A real oddity (and astonishingly successful) was Australian Dorothy Porter's lesbian private eye novel in verse, *The Monkey's Mask* (Arcade).

II. Formal Detection. The formal puzzle, constantly subject to premature burial by some commentators, lives on in the work of writers like Jean Hager, with *Seven Black Stones* (Mysterious); Jennifer Rowe, with *Stranglehold* (Bantam); M. D. Lake, with *Grave Choices* (Avon); Ellen Hart, with *For Every Evil* (Ballantine); K. K. Beck, with *Cold Smoked* (Mysterious); H. Paul Jeffers, with an Edgar-awards mystery, *A Grand Night for Murder* (St. Martin's); and Carolyn G. Hart, with a book festival case, *Mint Julep Murder* (Bantam). Also on the scene was a British cop who seems to fit here better than in the procedural category: Colin Dexter's Inspector Morse in *The Daughter of Cain* (Crown). Though I've been getting impatient with Sharyn McCrumb's series about the irritating Elizabeth MacPherson, I must admit the Agatha-winning *If I'd Killed Him When I'd Met Him . . .* (Ballantine) presents the forensic anthropologist with a dandy poisoning mystery. I thought the late E. X. Ferrars's admirably tricky Andrew Basnett novel *A Hobby of Murder* (Doubleday) must surely be her final novel, but it was followed later in the year by *Seeing Is Believing* (Doubleday)—with a publisher's promise of more to come!

III. Police procedurals. My first encounter with a Dutch cop famous in his own country, Baantjer's *DeKok and the Brothers of the Easy Death,* was enjoyable enough to make me seek out and buy (grave confession for a reviewer!) as many as I could find of the fourteen-or-so other titles in the series currently available from Intercontinental Publishing, P.O. Box 7242, Fairfax Station, VA 22309. Other series cops I enjoyed in my admittedly spotty procedural reading were Neil Hockaday in Thomas Adcock's *Devil's Heaven* (Pocket) and Charlie Resnick in John Harvey's *Living Proof* (Holt).

IV. Historicals. This subcategory is getting stronger every year: The titles by Collins, Marlowe, Saylor, and Ross on my list of fifteen are only a sample. The prolific P. C. Doherty was busy under several names—*An Ancient Evil* (St. Martin's), about the Canterbury pilgrims, is one notable example. Robert Lee Hall continued to make a credible fictional sleuth of Benjamin Franklin in *Murder by the Waters* (St. Martin's). Anne Perry's *Cain and His Brother* (Fawcett Columbine) is a below average (but still estimable) entry in the Victorian William Monk-Hester Latterly series. Walter Satterthwait involves Houdini and Conan Doyle in the stylish country-house mystery *Escapade* (St. Martin's). W. W. Lee continued her concise Old West mystery series in *Cannon's Revenge* (Walker), while William L. DeAndrea started a new one with *Written in Fire* (Walker). E. J. Gorman considered a more recent historical event (the death of Marilyn Monroe) in *The Marilyn Tapes* (Forge), which includes one of the more interesting fictional depictions of J. Edgar Hoover. The latest in a series set in the present but obsessed with the past, Richard A. Lupoff's *The Cover Girl Killer* (St. Martin's), sets Hobart Lindsey and Marvia Plum on a case involving the paperback world of the early 1950s and the Spanish Civil War.

V. Humor. If MWA, like its British equivalent CWA, gave an annual award for best humorous mystery, Donald E. Westlake would be able to field a ball team of Edgars—I mean a baseball team; he may already have enough for a basketball team. In *Smoke* (Mysterious), he makes fun of the tobacco companies while running farcical changes on the classic invisible man situation. Also good for more than a few laughs were Alan Russell's second hotel detective mystery, *The Fat Innkeeper* (Mysterious) and Barry Willis's parodic short novel *The Strange Case of the Lost Elvis Diaries* (Waynoka Press, P.O. Box 40856, Memphis, TN 38174-0856).

VI. The Lawyers. Some of the best fictional lawyers were in action, among them Butch Karp reopening the Kennedy assassination in Robert K. Tanenbaum's *Corruption of Blood* (Dutton), Gideon Page in Grif Stockley's *Illegal Motion* (Simon & Schuster), Cass Jameson in Carolyn Wheat's *Fresh Kills* (Berkley), and Gail Connor in Barbara Parker's *Suspicion of Guilt* (Dutton). Among the good nonseries lawyer books were Jay Brandon's *Local Rules* (Pocket); Perri O'Shaughnessy's *Motion to Suppress* (Delacorte), the best first mystery I read in 1995; and Patricia D. Benke's *Guilty by Choice* (Avon), which admirably sticks to the legal issues and eschews the rather obvious woman and/or child in jeopardy situation it could easily have fallen into. Even the Harlequin Intrigue line of romances got into the legal fiction act with a pair of novels by M. J. Rodgers about the Seattle firm of Justice Inc.: *Beauty v. the Beast* and *Baby v. the Bar,* entertaining through nuttily plotted and somewhat shackled by romance novel conventions.

VII. Celebrities. Former New York mayor Edward I. Koch's mystery debut, *Murder at City Hall* (Kensington), also marked the return to the novel lists of collaborator Herbert Resnicow for the first time since 1990. The Coley Killebrew novels of retired jockey Bill Shoemaker continued with *Fire Horse* (Fawcett Columbine); though the credit to ghost/collaborator Dick Lochte seen in the first book in the series is absent here, the style is unmistakably the same. Other celebrities signing new mysteries included Steve Allen, Louis Shaffer, Ron Ely, and the late Elliott Roosevelt, who we are told "left behind several manuscripts" when he died in 1990.

OTHERS MENTIONED IN DISPATCHES

Did any other writers of note have new books in 1995? How about this list?: Catherine Aird, Linda Barnes, Lawrence Block, Simon Brett, Edna Buchanan, Michael Connelly, K. C. Constantine, Amanda Cross, Loren D. Estleman, Nicolas Freeling, John Gardner, Jonathan Gash, Michael Gilbert, Sue Grafton, Martha Grimes, John Grisham, Joan Hess, Reginald Hill, Faye Kellerman, P. D. James, Elmore Leonard, Ed McBain, Charles McCarry, Charlotte MacLeod, Margaret Maron, Barbara Michaels, Robert B. Parker, Julie Smith, and Julian Symons.

A SENSE OF HISTORY

Though the mystery field remembers its roots better than some literary genres, the sheer volume of new material sometimes threatens to obscure even the best writers of the past. Carroll & Graf continued to honor the classics with reprints of Anthony Boucher's *The Case of the Seven of Calvary* (1940), Christiana Brand's *Fog of Doubt* (1953), and Margery Allingham's *Black Plumes* (1940). The sadly discontinued Otto Penzler imprint brought a reprint of Ellery Queen's *The French Powder Mystery* (1930) along with H. W. Bell's Sherlockian essay collection *Baker Street Studies* (1934). Mignon G. Eberhart's first two novels, *The Patient in Room 18* (1929) and *While the Patient Slept* (1930), were issued in handsome new trade paperback editions by the University of Nebraska Press.

For several years, Bantam has been reissuing the Nero Wolfe series and other mystery novels by Rex Stout in a uniform edition with new introductions, usually by other mystery writers and sometimes by celebrities from outside the field. In 1995, their publishers embarked on similar projects with Charles Willeford and John D. MacDonald. Dell began its Willeford series with *Miami Blues* (1984), the first Hoke Moseley novel, introduced by Jon A. Jackson and followed with the other three Moseley novels early in 1996, introduced by James Lee Burke, Elmore Leonard, and Donald E. Westlake. Fawcett Crest reissued MacDonald's first Travis McGee novel, *The Deep Blue Good-Bye* (1964), with a new introduction by Carl Hiassen and an afterword by Maynard MacDonald—but when the second volume, *Nightmare in Pink* (1964), was reissued early in 1996, the same accompanying material was recycled.

What could honor the past more than to bring into print a previously unknown novel by a revered writer? Gary Lovisi's Gryphon Publications (P.O. Box 209, Brooklyn, NY 11228) published the first edition of the late William Campbell Gault's notable Hollywood novel (a nonmystery), *Man Alone,* unpublished after its writing in 1957 for reasons unrelated to its quality.

AWARD WINNERS FOR 1995

EDGAR ALLAN POE AWARDS
(Mystery Writers of America)

Best novel: Dick Francis, *Come to Grief* (Putnam)
Best first novel by an American author: David Housewright, *Penance* (Foul Play/Countryman)
Best original paperback: William Heffernan, *Tarnished Blue* (Onyx)
Best fact crime book: Pete Earley, *Circumstantial Evidence* (Bantam)
Best critical/biographical work: Robert Polito, *Savage Art: A Biography of Jim Thompson* (Knopf)
Best short story: Jean B. Cooper, "The Judge's Boy" (*EQMM,* August)
Best young adult mystery: Rob MacGregor, *Prophecy Rock* (Simon & Schuster)
Best juvenile mystery: Nancy Springer, *Looking for Jamie Bridger* (Dial)
Best episode in a television series: Theresa Rebeck, "Torah! Torah! Torah!" (*NYPD Blue*/Steven Bochco Productions/ABC-TV)
Best television feature or miniseries: Chris Jerolmo, *Citizen X* (HBO)
Best motion picture: Christopher McQuarrie, *The Usual Suspects* (Gramercy Pictures, PolyGram Bat Hat Harry, Blue Parrot)
Grand master: Dick Francis
Robert L. Fish award (best first story): James Serafin, "The Word for Breaking August Sky" (*AHMM,* July)
Ellery Queen award: Jacques Barzun
Raven: The Library of America for their publication of the collected writings of Raymond Chandler

AGATHA AWARDS

(Malice Domestic Mystery Convention)

Best novel: Sharyn McCrumb, *If I'd Killed Him When I Met Him . . .* (Ballantine)
Best first novel: Jeanne Dams, *The Body in the Transept* (Walker)

Best short story: Elizabeth Daniels Squire, "The Dog Who Remembered Too Much" (*Malice Domestic 4* [Pocket])

Best nonfiction: Alzina Stone Dale, *Mystery Reader's Walking Guide: Chicago* (Passport)

Lifetime achievement: Mary Stewart

AWARD WINNERS FOR 1994

ANTHONY AWARDS
(Bouchercon World Mystery Convention)

Best novel: Sharyn McCrumb, *She Walks These Hills* (Scribners)

Best first novel: Caleb Carr, *The Alienist* (Random)

Best true crime: David Canter, *Criminal Shadows* (HarperCollins)

Best short story: Sharyn McCrumb, "The Monster of Glamis" (*Royal Crimes* [Signet])

Best anthology or short story collection: Tony Hillerman, ed., *The Mysterious West* (HarperCollins)

Best critical work: John Cooper and B. A. Pike, *Detective Fiction: The Collector's Guide,* 2nd edition (Scolar)

Best film: *Pulp Fiction*

Best TV series: *Prime Suspect*

SHAMUS AWARDS

(Private Eye Writers of America)

Best novel: Sue Grafton, *"K" is for Killer* (Holt)

Best first novel: Dennis Lehane, *A Drink Before the War* (Harcourt Brace)

Best original paperback novel: Ed Goldberg, *Served Cold* (West Coast Crime)

Best short story: Brendan DuBois, "The Necessary Brother" (*EQMM,* May 1994)

Lifetime achievement award: John Lutz and Robert B. Parker

DAGGER AWARDS

(Crime Writers' Association, Great Britain)

Gold Dagger: Val McDermid, *The Mermaids Sing* (HarperCollins)
Silver Dagger: Peter Lovesey, *The Summons* (Little, Brown)
John Creasey Award (best first novel): Janet Evanovich, *One for the Money* (Hamish Hamilton)
Best short story: Larry Beinhart, "Funny Story" (*No Alibi* [Bouchercon])
Best nonfiction: Michael Beales, *Dead Not Buried* (Robert Hale)
Last Laugh: Laurence Shames, *Sunburn* (Macmillan)
Dagger in the Library: Lindsey Davis

MACAVITY AWARDS

(Mystery Readers International)

Best novel: Sharyn McCrumb, *She Walks These Hills* (Scribners)
Best first novel: Jeff Abbott, *Do Unto Others* (Ballantine)
Best nonfiction or critical work: Dean James and Jean Swanson, *By a Woman's Hand* (Berkley)
Best short story: (tie) Deborah Adams, "Cast Your Fate to the Wind" (*Malice Domestic 3* [Pocket]); Jan Burke, "Unharmed" (*EQMM*, December 1994)

ARTHUR ELLIS AWARDS

(Crime Writers of Canada)

Best novel: Gail Bowen, *A Colder Kind of Death*
Best first novel: Sparkle Hayter, *What's a Girl Gotta Do?*
Best true crime: Michael Harris, *The Prodigal Husband*
Best short story: Rosemary Aubert, "The Midnight Boat to Palermo" (*Cold Blood V*)
Best juvenile: James Heneghan, *Tom Away*
Derrick Murdoch Award (for outstanding service to the mystery genre): Jim and Margaret McBride

HAMMETT PRIZE

(North American Branch, International Association of Crime Writers)

James Lee Burke, *Dixie City Jam* (Hyperion)

ERRATA: Last year's annual mistakenly awarded the Agatha Award for best nonfiction of 1994 to William L. DeAndrea's *Encyclopedia Mysteriosa*. The actual winner was *By a Woman's Hand* (Berkley) by Jean Swanson and Dean James. The following Crime Writers Association Awards for 1993 were inadvertently left out: John Creasey Award (best first crime novel): Doug J. Swanson, *Big Town* (Little, Brown); Last Laugh Award (most amusing crime novel): Simon Shaw, *The Villain of the Earth* (Gollancz). The author extends apologies to the writers and organizations involved.

THE YEAR'S 25 FINEST
CRIME & MYSTERY STORIES
Fifth Annual Edition

Of "She Rote," John Harvey writes, "One of the things I enjoy doing in the few Resnick short stories I've written is finding out a little more about characters who have appeared in previous novels." The ninth novel featuring Resnick is currently being written, and may possibly feature Ray-o and his uncle Terry. Either way, his stories of city life and crime in England are attracting interest in larger circles with every book.

She Rote
JOHN HARVEY

She wrote Ray-O on her arm, scratching the letters with the blunted point of a compass she'd borrowed from one of the girls in Maths class. Scratched them and then gone over the outline in blue biro, painstakingly slow.

She rote SARAH 4 RAY-O one hundred and twenty-seven times in felt-tip on the inside of the toilet door. Only the persistence of two of the older girls, anxious to get in and light up, stopped her writing it one hundred and twenty eight, one hundred and twenty-nine, one hundred and thirty.

She wrote a letter to the problem page of Just Seventeen: *"my boy friend wont use a condom he says theres no need cos I'm only 13. Please will you tell me if this is true. I need to no."*

But by then it was too late; by the end of the month she was bleeding but not enough, not the right kind.

Ray-o was nineteen, rising twenty. His real name was Raymond, Raymond Cooke, but everyone called him Ray-o. The longest job he'd held down before going with his Uncle Terry had been in the wholesale butchers, down by the abattoir on Cattle Market Road. Hefting carcasses from the hooks of the conveyor belt, emptying tubs of tripes and offal into the incinerator bins; blood under his fingernails, gristle in his hair; the smell of it insidious on his skin.

Terry had saved him from all that. "How 'bout it, Ray-o? How d'you fancy working for me?" His uncle had taken a lease on a shop in Bobber's Mill, just to the north of the bridge. Secondhand stuff,

3

that's what they'd be selling. Refrigerators, cookers, stereos, the odd bit of furniture—there was always a call.

"There's a couple of rooms over the top, an' all. Could live there if you want. Shan't charge you no more'n you're paying now. What d'you say? You and me, workin' together, eh?"

Raymond hadn't needed asking twice. A chance to get away from that poxy little room he had in Lenton, turn his back on all the shit and guts he'd been up to his elbows in. And besides, Terry, he was like a father to him really, more than his own father, that was sure; a father and a mate, both at the same time. Terry would take him out drinking, buy more than his fair share of pints, have a laugh about women, you know, doing it, having it away. "Now then, Ray-o, how d'you fancy sinking your teeth into that lot? Need a pair of flippers and a bleedin' snorkel!"

And Terry knew what he was talking about—ever since that cow of a wife of his had left him, he had new girl friends all the time. Raymond didn't know how he did it: forty if he was a day. And that one he was going with now, Eileen, she couldn't have been much older than Raymond himself. Great looking, too. Really gorgeous. If ever she came round to the shop, Raymond couldn't look at her without blushing.

OFF-DUTY, Mark Divine and Kevin Naylor were propping up the bar in the Mason's Arms, a little removed from their normal stalking grounds, but Divine had half a mind he might set eyes on one of his snouts who'd been avoiding him. Three pints and a couple of shorts down the road, so far he had had no luck.

"Another?" Naylor asked, hoisting a crisp new twenty in the barman's direction.

"Go on," Divine said. "Why not?"

Naylor's wife, Debbie, was off to her mum's, hatching plans for her sister's wedding; underskirts enough to bandage a battalion and more sequins than *Come Dancing*. Divine's on-again, off-again relationship with a staff nurse from the Queen's was decidedly off-again, and all he had to go home to was a video of *Baddiel and Skinner's Fantasy Football League* and the remains of last night's king prawn biriyani, adhering to its aluminum container in the fridge.

"This," Divine said, at the end of a copious swallow, "tastes like piss."

"Yes," Naylor said, licking the residue of froth from where he was considering growing a moustache. "Agreed."

Over to the far side of the room, in what would, before these democratic days, have been partitioned off as the public bar, a group of a dozen or so lads were in increasingly party mood. A good score of jokes, sexist, of course, ribald laughter, angry words, a bit of informal karaoke, spilt beer, a few choruses of *Happy Birthday,* a slight accident in the passageway outside when one of them didn't make it all the way to the bogs.

"Nice to see," Divine said.

"How's that?"

"People enjoying themselves."

Naylor nodded. He had personally felt the collars of at least two of them in the past eighteen months, one a suspected burglary, the other of being in possession of a controlled substance. Neither case had gone to court.

"Hey up!" Divine said, nudging Naylor in the ribs. "Catch a look at that."

The young woman who had come into the bar had long red hair, shading towards chestnut, and it hung loose past the collar of the oversize beige raincoat she was wearing. Aside from the hair, and the brightness of her lipsticked mouth, what marked her out most clearly was the police-woman's cap she wore at a jaunty angle on her head. A moment to take in the room and then she strode purposefully to where the lads were sitting.

"You don't think there's been a complaint?" Naylor said.

"Not yet."

First the table, then the whole pub fell quiet.

"Which one of you is Darren Matthews?" the young woman asked, not a tremor in her voice.

A few shouts and jeers, pointed fingers and sniggering behind hands and the aforementioned made a passable attempt at getting to his feet, pale face and tie askew, speech slurred. "Who wants to know?"

Before you could say Robert Peel, the woman had her raincoat unfastened and whisked away; she had obviously done this before. She was wearing police uniform skirt and tunic, black tights and three-inch heels. "Darren Matthews," she said. "You're nicked."

In the resulting uproar, Divine caught the barman's attention and got in another couple of whiskies, doubles. Someone had switched on the pub stereo and Janet Jackson was breathing encouragement to the woman, as, on the table now, she danced and swayed in front of the birthday boy's face, removing her uniform piece by piece as she moved. With a semblance of unison, the others around the table clapped encouragement.

"Debbie do that for you this year, Kev?" he asked.

"Did she, heck as like. Set of socket wrenches and a pair of Paul Smith socks."

The redhead stepped out of her skirt and revealed a pair of handcuffs tucked into the elastic of high-sided silk briefs with *Go to Jail* in tasteful red lettering over the crotch.

The object of her attentions did his best to make a bolt for it, but his mates grabbed him and pushed him back down.

"Only kind of arrest that poor sod's about to have," Divine said, "is of the cardiac variety."

With a professionalism that many of Divine and Naylor's colleagues would have envied, the woman cuffed Matthews' wrists to the arms of the chair. So many were on their feet then, crowding round, it was difficult to see exactly what happened next, but what flew in the air above their heads was clearly Matthews' trousers.

"Jesus!" Divine exclaimed, shifting along the bar for a better view. "She's only going to do the business."

"She's never."

"Want to bet?"

Naylor grabbed Divine by the arm. "Then we're leaving."

"You're bloody joking!" He could no longer see the swaying head of red hair and he guessed she must be down on her knees.

"You want to get in there and put a stop to it?" Naylor demanded.

"No, I bloody don't."

Naylor pulled at the front of Divine's shirt. "Then we're out of here. Now, Mark, now."

Divine drove with almost exaggerated care; he didn't want to get pulled over and be ordered to blow into a plastic bag. "What d'you reckon she gets for that?" he asked. "Side from a nasty taste in the mouth."

Naylor shrugged. Ever since leaving the pub, he'd been hoping against hope Debbie would be back from her mum's by the time he got in. "Fifty, hundred."

Divine whistled appreciatively. "Only need to do that a few times, pull in more than you or me."

"You fancy it then?"

"What? Spot of the old Chippendales? Why not? Might as well make some use of that old uniform, eh?" He laughed. "You read about that bloke, did this act dressed as a copper, strip-o-gram, like. Poor bastard only got three years, didn't he? On account these women he stripped for complained how he'd—what was it?—humiliated and degraded them."

"Maybe he had."

"Yeh? Shame they hung around long enough for him to get his tackle out of his Y-fronts, then, might not've been so fucking degraded if they hadn't."

Nodding, not really listening, Naylor glanced at his watch. He'd get Divine to drop him off at the Paki shop on the corner, pick up a bottle of that Chardonnay Debbie liked, glass or two to put her in the mood.

TERRY WAS NOT QUITE ASLEEP when he heard the key in the lock, a smile on his face as soon as he recognised Eileen's footsteps on the stairs.

"Hello, love. How'd it go?" Reaching up for her as she leaned across him, brushing the top of his head with a kiss.

"Fine. Yeh, it was fine."

"Good tip?"

"Sixty. Not bad."

Terry pulled her down towards him. "Maybe we should celebrate."

"Not now. I want to take a shower first, clean my teeth."

"Okay, sweetheart. Whatever you say."

But by the time she had come back again, Terry had begun to doze off, so that when she slipped under the covers beside him, what he did was slide himself against her gently, one arm covering hers, the pair of them slotted together like spoons. It was what he liked most: what he missed those nights she stayed away.

FROM HER ROOM ALONG THE LANDING, Sarah had heard Eileen come in too; had lain there listening to the litany of doors—bedroom, bedroom, bathroom, bathroom, finally the bedroom once more. Sometimes, if she tip-toed across the floor, opened her own door just a crack and listened long enough she would hear her dad cry out and know that they'd been doing it. The same sound that Ray-o made, she knew what it meant.

Ray-o. Sarah lifted the covers over her head and said the name out loud. Ray-o. Ray-o. Ray-o. Abruptly, she stopped, realising that she had been shouting and even muffled like that she might be heard, if not by her dad or Eileen, then by her grandmother in the room adjoining hers. Ray-o. If only they knew. . . . She remembered the first time she'd gone with him, ages she'd been, deciding which skirt to wear, which top, using this article she'd torn from a magazine to get her make-up just right.

Ray-o had met her in the rec and they'd sat on a bench near the kids' swings, drinking cider and smoking Raymond's Silk Cut. After a bit, he'd said how it was getting cold and taken her up to his room. All his mates, the blokes he shared with, had been out. She remembered a smell of sour milk and something else which seemed to come from Raymond himself. When he kissed her he pushed his tongue so far into her mouth she almost choked.

"Wash that stuff off," he said. "Here." Offering her a cloth.

"What stuff?"

"That muck you've got all over your face."

When she'd finished, he took the cloth back from her and wet one corner of it with spittle, the way her mum had used to do when she was little; carefully, he wiped away the eye shadow that had smeared her cheek.

"Ray-o," she said quietly.

"What?"

"Nothing." She'd read somewhere it was a mistake to tell a boy you loved him too soon.

"That's all right then." He started to take off his clothes and she thought that she should do the same.

When she was stretched back on the bed, one arm across her face to shield her eyes, she felt him touching her, her breasts and down between her legs. He hurt a little but not much.

"Here," he said. "Here."

He was kneeling over her, his thin sticking out, hard and thin. His balls were tight in wrinkled skin. "Here." He took her hands and placed them on him, sliding them back and forth. After a while he closed his eyes, pushed her hands away and did it for himself. She didn't know what was more surprising, the way his stuff sprayed across her or the shout that was more of a scream. Concerned, she asked him if it hurt. He lifted the cloth coloured by her make-up from the floor and wiped himself then gave it to her to wipe the stickiness away.

"Ray-o," she said.

"What?"

"I love you. Honest." She couldn't help herself. After all, he hadn't done it to her for the first time; that proved he respected her, right?

Without really wanting to, Sarah ran her hands gingerly over her stomach, the swell of her belly. She was larger each day now, she'd swear it, though when she was standing straight it wasn't as if she even showed. Her clothes she wore loose and shapeless, just in case. Careful to lock the bathroom door. Ray-o. She couldn't understand why her dad had flown off the handle when he'd seen Ray's name written on her arm. Crack! The back of his hand across her face so fast she'd scarcely seen it coming and the next thing she knew she'd been picking herself up from the floor. "You stupid little cow! What d'you want to do a thing like that for?" And when she'd said it didn't mean anything, only that she liked him, he'd hauled her off the floor and shaken her until her eyes seemed to rattle in her head. "Flesh and blood, you horny little cow! He's your own flesh and fucking blood!"

Well, he wasn't. He was only her cousin. In the bible, cousins did it all the time. She'd read it at primary school.

Through the wall Sarah could hear her gran's low, reverberating snore.

MORE MONTHS PASSED. The first frost caught Resnick by surprise. Opening the front door to retrieve the bottles (yes still bottles) the milkman had left on the step, his feet nearly went from under him. Then he saw that the leaves that had collected in the lee of the wall were rimmed with white along their brittle edges; Dizzy's coat, when he ran his fingers along it, bristled cold and dampish to the touch.

Back in the kitchen, coffee ground and ready; he warmed the milk for all four cats before pouring it into their bowls. While the rye bread was toasting, he sliced Jarlsberg cheese and pulled the rind away from several rounds of Polish salami. The local weather forecaster was predicting a further drop in the temperature of five to ten degrees, but clear and sunny skies. One of the pullovers he had neglected to take to the cleaners had a bronze stain all down one side; the other was coming unravelled beneath the left arm. In the back of the drawer he found a sleeveless cardigan and he put this on over his pale blue shirt and beneath the brown tweed jacket he'd bought seven or eight years before, at a shop which now sold charity Christmas Cards and next year's calendars with twelve different picture of Madonna or Ryan Giggs.

The previous night he'd been listening to some Gerry Mulligan—the California Concerts from the early fifties—and he fancied hearing a handful of the tracks again, but there wasn't time. He had arranged for Graham Millington to give him a lift into the station, and, sure enough, there was the sergeant now, punctual as ever, sounding his horn.

"Cold enough to frighten brass monkeys," Millington said, as Resnick climbed into the car.

"Happen we'll be busy, Graham. Take our mind off the weather."

Millington stubbed his Lambert and Butler out in the ashtray between the seats and set the car in gear.

BUSY WASN'T THE WORD FOR IT. Aside from the ongoing investigations in which all the officers in Resnick's team were involved, the cold night had fostered a flurry of activity through the early hours. Amongst the items stolen from the good burghers of the city were seven fur coats, including two minks and one sable, two cases of five-star brandy, three electric blankets and a state-of-the-art gas fire with full three-dimensional coal effect, neatly removed from its marble fireplace home. And this was without the usual plethora of jewellery, CD collections and VCRs, most of which would, even now, be exchanging hands as part of the system on which the invisible economy depended. How else were people supposed to get pissed, book holidays in Spain, buy something decent for the kids, score weed, pay the tally man, eke out child support, place a bet or put a little aside for a rainy day? If they didn't win the lottery, that is.

"Then there's this, boss," Divine said. They were sitting round the CID room, tea getting stewed, blue cigarette smoke frescoing the ceiling. "British Telecom van broken into, two gross of new DF50 fax machines gone missing."

"Soon to be a lot of those around on discount, then," mused Millington. "Shouldn't mind one myself."

"All right," Resnick said, getting to his feet. "Let's keep our eyes peeled. Known fences, secondhand dealers, car boot sales, any of these fly-by-night merchants sailing along by the seats of their pants. Graham, we've got a list, let's parcel it out. And while Lynn's off on that course, you'd best put a few my way as well."

FOR SOME REASON, Raymond had caught himself thinking about Sara: not his cousin Sarah, Sarah with an *h*, but the Sara he used to go out with a couple of years before. The one who had been with him when . . . well, some of what had happened back then Raymond didn't like to remember. That little girl who'd gone missing and then all that business with the Paki copper as got knifed . . . but Sara, he didn't mind thinking about her. Nice, she was. Pretty and posh, sort of posh. Clever, too. Never able to understand what she'd seen in him, Raymond, and after a month or two, neither had Sara herself. She'd written him this letter, full of words he didn't properly understand—except he knew what they meant. She was dumping him, that was what. Raymond had tried to talk her out of it, get her to change her mind, but it hadn't been any good. "I'm sorry, Ray, but I'm afraid my mind's quite made up." And she'd walked off to where one of her customers was waiting to pay for a large bag of mixed soft-centres, head stuck in the air in that toffee-nosed way she had.

He hadn't been good enough for her, that's what it was. Of course, she hadn't come straight out and said it, Sara, not in so many words. She wasn't like that, better brought up. Whereas his cousin Sarah, she was pathetically grateful if you as much as looked at her, never mind anything else. Always hanging round though, that was the trouble. Wouldn't leave him alone. Not even indoors; in her house, his Uncle Terry's house. There they'd been, one day, Raymond feeling her up on the settee, thinking Terry was clear and instead he'd come breezing in, nearly caught them at it. "I shouldn't like to think, Ray-o," Terry said after Sarah had scarpered upstairs, "that you were taking advantage of me."

After that, of course, Raymond had backed off and told Sarah to do the same. Stop mooning after him, finding excuses to come to the shop, looking at him all the time like he was God's fucking gift—though from Sarah's point of view, most probably he was. Raymond couldn't see anyone else fancying it, scrawny little tart with a bony arse and tits like doorbells. Mind you, having said that, he thought she might have been putting on a bit of weight lately. All that ice cream and chocolate she was stuffing herself with, Raymond thought, making up for the fact that he wasn't giving her any. He was near the back of the shop, chuckling about that, when the street door opened and Detective Inspector Resnick walked in.

Raymond recognised him right off and the blood flew to his face. Half-turning a clumsy step away, he sent a clock radio crashing to the floor.

The plastic top splintered clear across and the radio started playing Jarvis Cocker's *Underwear.*

"Raymond, isn't it?" Resnick said, letting the door swing to behind him. "Raymond Cooke."

Down on one knee, mis-hitting the control buttons and switching on the alarm instead, Raymond mumbled yes.

"So, what you up to these days?" Resnick asked, flicking idly through a shoebox of secondhand CDs. "Keeping out of trouble?"

"Yes."

"And you've got a job?"

"Yes, here. I work here. My uncle, he . . ."

"Uncle Terry?" Resnick asked. "Terry Cooke?"

"Yeh."

"His place, then?"

"Yes."

"And you, you're what? Helping him out?"

"No, no, like I said, I'm here all the time. Live here, too. Upstairs." Raymond pointed towards the ceiling, past a couple of slightly battered kiddies' mobiles and a string of plastic onions that could have done with a dust.

"Nice," Resnick said. "Handy."

"Yeh."

"Of course . . ." Resnick had taken one of the CDs from the box now and was studying the writing on the back. '. . . not so handy for the park, the rec, watching little girls on the swings."

"I don't . . ." Breath caught high in Raymond's throat and for a moment he thought he wouldn't be able to breathe.

"Don't what, Raymond?"

"I'm not . . ."

"Yes?"

Raymond steadied himself against a tumble drier, cleared his throat, found a screwed-up tissue in his pocket and blew his nose. "I've got a girl friend," he said. "Going steady."

"That's nice, Raymond," Resnick said pleasantly. "Anyone I know?"

"No, no. Shouldn't think so, no."

"You're not . . ." Resnick looked upwards. ". . . living together?"

Raymond shook his head. "Thinking about it, you know."

Resnick reached out suddenly with his free hand and, as Raymond flinched, flicked something from the shoulder of the youth's leather jacket. "Treat her well, I hope, Raymond?"

"Yeh, yes, of course."

Raymond gulped air and Resnick stepped back and glanced at the CD in his hand. "How much?"

"Fiver."

"Good condition is it? I mean I'm not going to get it home and find it doesn't play?"

Raymond shrugged. "Far as I know it's okay."

"You've not heard it then?"

"Jazz, isn't it?" He shook his head. "Look, you can have it for four. Three-fifty."

"You're sure? Only I wouldn't want to get you into trouble with Uncle Terry."

"He doesn't mind. What I do in the shop here, it's up to me."

"Responsibility."

"Yeh."

Smiling, Resnick gave him a five pound note and waited for his change. "You wouldn't have anything in the way of fax machines, I suppose? You know, the kind with the telephone. Integral."

Raymond's face brightened. "Terry did say something, yes. I reckon we'll be getting some in, the next couple of days. You could always call back. You know, if you were passing."

Resnick hesitated for a moment at the door. "All right, Raymond, I might. Maybe you could even put one aside."

SARAH HAD SHUT HERSELF IN THE BATHROOM, the cabinet where her dad kept his aftershave and deodorant, his spare razor blades and his condoms, pulled over against the door. There were days—most days—when she could forget what was happening to her, happening to her inside, but this wasn't one of them. Sometimes the pain was so sudden and sharp, she had to bite her bottom lip to stop the screams; sometimes she almost went as far as thinking she would call her gran, ask her to help, but she knew she wouldn't do that. Not really. What she wanted—if she couldn't have Raymond—were friends to turn to, girl friends to ask for advice, but none of the girls at school would give her as much as the time of day.

After a while, she didn't know how long, set heard her gran going down the stairs, on her way to the early evening bingo. Her dad was already out, had been most of the day, she didn't know where. Squatting in the bath, Sarah bore down on the toothbrush she had placed across her mouth and bit it clean in half.

MILLINGTON WAS LAUGHING as Mark Divine set down fresh pints between Resnick and himself. "And that's what he said? Come back in a couple of days and I'll have one here ready?"

"More or less."

"Daft twat!"

Resnick nodded. The more he thought about the way Raymond had reacted when he'd walked into the shop, the more he thought the lad might have something to hide, something he might like to ease off his chest. He doubted if it were anything as straightforward as a few BT fax machines.

"Turn him over, shall we?" Millington asked. "What d'you think?"

Resnick set down his glass. 'Why not? Take Mark here and Kevin; pay them a call. Out of shop hours. But, Graham . . ."

"Yes?"

"This Cooke youth, Raymond, let's not drop him in it, not with the uncle. Let him stay clear."

"Plans for him, have you?"

"Maybe." He shrugged heavy shoulders. "Stay on his good side for a while, that's all."

Millington tapped the last Lambert and Butler from the packet; no sense in buying any more now till the morning, not with the wife how she was about him smoking. "Just as you like."

They went in with a warrant two days later; still not light. They had the door down before Raymond, deep asleep, could stumble down the stairs to let them in.

"Your uncle here?" Millington asked sharply.

Standing there in boxer shorts and an Oasis T-shirt, one hand cupped across his balls, Raymond just shook his head.

"Call him. Then get yourself back up there out of the way."

The DF50s were in the store room on the first floor, below where Raymond slept. Two dozen, neatly boxed. All in all, they hauled away a van load of stuff, mostly electrical; nice job that would be for someone, checking them against the stolen goods inventory.

"Course," Millington winked, "you've got the paperwork on all this lot."

Beside him on the pavement, hands deep in pockets, no time to grab a topcoat, freezing bloody cold, Terry Cooke didn't say a thing.

SARAH SAT THERE IN HER ROOM, curtains closed tight. She didn't know if it were day or night. Her eyes were open and then her eyes were closed. The pain came and then it went. Slowly, she reached from the side of the bed down into the drawer and lifted the baby with both hands. So small and light. So cold, Carefully, she unbuttoned her blouse and pressed him to her chest, the spongy top of his head soft against the nub of her breast.

SEEING IT ON THE TABLE where it had been left, poking out from the pages of last night's *Post,* Resnick realised he had never got around to playing his bargain price CD. *Charlie Parker: from Dizzy to Miles.* Pouring himself a glass of the bison grass vodka he had won in a raffle at the Polish Club, he took the CD from its case, set on the machine and pressed play.

It began with two of the tracks Parker had recorded with Max Roach and Miles Davis in 1951, but through some quirk of programming, the third tune didn't appear till some way into the disc. One of those unison statements so beloved of boppers to begin and then Parker takes off in surprisingly light, long fluid phrases before giving way to the choppy sound of Miles' muted trumpet; a chorus of so-so piano which Parker can't wait to end before he's muscling back in, stronger now, more aggressive, grabbing the piece by the scruff of its neck and hurtling it into four bar exchanges with the drums. Three minutes and six seconds later, abruptly, it's over. *She Rote.*

Settled back in his chair, Resnick smiled: well worth three-pounds-fifty of anybody's money.

THE GRANDMOTHER FOUND THE BABY the next morning, searching through Sarah's drawers for an old jumper to unpick for wool. He had been wrapped in several layers of clothing and set snug against the drawer's edge, buttons across his eyes.

HER DAD FOUND THE NOTE IN THE KITCHEN, propped up between the stacks of plates near the back door.

Dear Dad,
I am riting to let you no you dont have to worry about me. I shall be OK. I'm sorry but I took the money from where you keep it in your room beside the bed and also from Grans bag. Im telling you this cos I didnt want you to blame Eileen or Ray-o.
Im sorry for what Iv done—and about the baby.
Love,
Sarah
xxxxx

Nancy Pickard is a Macavity-, Agatha-, and Anthony-award winning author who just seems to get better with every story she writes. Her long-running novel series features Jenny Cain, director of a philanthropic organization in a small New England town trapped in a recession. Pickard is a past president of Sisters in Crime, and her short fiction also appears in *Careless Whispers, Murder, She Wrote,* and past *Year's 25 Finest Crime and Mystery* volumes. In "Valentine's Night" she takes a dark look at a holiday that isn't always moonlight and roses.

Valentine's Night
NANCY PICKARD

Oh, yes, there really is such a thing as a blue moon.

It is an actual scientific phenomenon, caused by this and that, or something or other, but who cares about that?

That's merely science.

All that really matters is that on certain fantastical nights, some fortunate folks—who lean back on their heels and squint their eyes just so—may actually see a fabulous, delectably deep blue aura around the moon, be it full, waxing, waning, or even gibbous.

It's so strange, so beautiful, so ... moving, somehow, that they can't stop feasting on the sight of it. They want to pluck it from the sky, to revolve it in their hands, to bring it to their nose and sniff its moonly blue fragrance, and finally to gobble it down, with blue and yellow light dribbling down their chins, as if the moon were a luscious peach bathed for that one extraordinary night in fairies' blueberry juice. It makes people greedy, a blue moon does—at least that's what some folks (not scientists) say. They claim that it makes some folks want more than they already have, more than they ever dreamed—or admitted—they'd ever need. In other words, it makes some folks crave their deepest, most secret desires. And when those desires are frustrated? Watch out! A blue moon, or so it's said, is a powerfully hungry moon, and hunger—as everybody

15

knows—is not centered in the stomach or even the mouth, but rushes, instead, straight from the heart.

It was on such a night, the very night of Valentine's Day, that Marianne Griff—who was normally a nice, steady, levelheaded sort of woman— figured out where her husband really was.

And it wasn't where he'd said he'd be!

No, where Ned Griff really was that night was a long way from where he had said he'd be, but only a few tempting and dangerous blocks away from home.

AT SIX O'CLOCK THAT EVENING, when the unwelcome knowledge tore Marianne apart like dynamite exploding in her hands, the moon had only just begun its rise in the Valentine's sky, and it wasn't even blue, not yet. Perhaps that is why Marianne was forced to endure so many hours of ordinary human misery.

"Cincinnati," was what Ned had told her. "With Christy."

Well, of course, with Christy. Marianne had easily accepted that fact. Law partners frequently traveled together. It was commonplace, wasn't it? Marianne was, herself, an account executive with a telephone company; she knew she could trust herself to travel platonically with men, so it was easy for her to trust her husband to travel innocently with women, on business.

Yes, it was true that Christy was beautiful—a shiny brunette with a body sculpted by personal trainers. Oh, and yes, Christy was youngish, with seven fewer Valentine's Days than Marianne had notched in her own belt. Oh, and brilliant, to have made full partner in her early thirties. Christy Phares was, indeed, frighteningly good at cross-examining plaintiffs' witnesses in civil courtrooms. Marianne had seen her in action, and she'd felt impressed and proud, on general feminist principles, on behalf of all women.

Get 'em, Christy! She'd thought at the time.

Christy had sat at the table on the defendant's side of the courtroom, face forward to the judge (a man), with her back straight, the palms of her hands disarmingly flat and splayed upon the table, her legs crossed at her silky knees but not at any provocative angle. In the courtroom, Christy had looked alert, sleek in her black suit, like a panther with nothing to fear in this jungle, her claws sheathed, her nostrils delicately flared, her muscles relaxed but ready to spring.

Marianne's husband, Ned, had sat at the same table, but never touched his partner, never jotted a note to her, or even lifted an eyebrow in silent dialogue. They had looked the very picture of the perfectly prepared law partners. The phrase "a matched set" had occurred to some observers, though not to Marianne. The fact that Ned was every bit as handsome and muscled and well-groomed as Christy, or that every man in the courtroom had fantasized a vision of the naked breasts beneath the black suit, was irrelevant and immaterial to Marianne. The law was all: magnificently neuter. It never occurred to Marianne—also for good feminist reasons—to suspect that Ned found less beauty in the law than he did in the lawyer seated next to him. (Even if it had just possibly crossed her mind, for one teeny second, she would have quickly shooed the treacherous thought away as being disloyal to her husband and traitorous to women.)

"We'll be at the convention hotel," he'd told her.

That made sense to Marianne; she'd doubted nothing.

But then, when she was in the bedroom changing out of her business clothes into a comfortable old gray sweatsuit, she noticed the brochure for the bar convention poking out from under some of Ned's papers that he'd left on top of the chest of drawers. Curious to see who the star-spangled speakers would be this year, Marianne drew the pamphlet—*the stick of dynamite*—toward her.

The first speaker, scheduled for 8 A.M. Saturday, February eighth, was . . .

Now the dynamite was lit.

Marianne never did learn the identity of the keynote speaker for the Ohio Bar Association Convention. Her gaze had fallen back onto the date. The eighth? For a moment, she felt confused: this was Valentine's Day, February fourteenth, wasn't it?

The flame ate the wick, drawing closer to the charge.

Yes—she glanced over at the king-sized bed—there was the Valentine's card Ned had left on her pillow this morning. It was one of those modern amusing ones that were very nearly hostile in their humor, nothing sentimental or even nostalgic about it. Still, she'd been happy to receive it. He'd signed it: *"Me."* She looked into her living room and glimpsed the dozen pink carnations in a clear glass vase on her coffee table. Yes, they'd been delivered to her office today, all right, with a note: "Guess Who?"

The eighth?!

Boom.

The intuition arrived in a blast of searing pain that made Marianne feel as if she'd splashed hot grease onto her chest.

What? she thought.

And then: *No!*

To prove to herself that it wasn't true, she walked on jellied knees to the bedside telephone to dial, with trembling and suddenly freezing fingers, the convention hotel. Crazy, she thought, to feel so frightened of the phone, the very instrument she sold in such huge and profitable numbers to other people. She wished now—as it rang once, twice, in Cincinnati—that it had never been invented (her own salary and profit sharing notwithstanding). The hotel operator graciously consented to look up the number and ring the room of guest Edward Griff. Marianne waited, wishing all the while that when Alexander Graham Bell had yelled, "Watson! Come here! I need you!" Watson had not replied. If only Bell had then thought, Oh, the hell with the damn thing, and given up on his invention that had changed the world. And was about to change her world. . . .

"I'm sorry, there's no Mr. Griff registered."

Marianne longed for the pony express, which would take days to reach Cincinnati and return with the terrible news of loss and heartache. At the very least, a telegraph might have taken hours.

She pleaded: "Are you sure?"

But no. Bad news came much more quickly in this century than it ever had before, giving you no time at all to arrange your emotions, your face, your voice, your future. . . .

"Yes, ma'am. Thank you for calling Marriott."

With one hand, Marianne gently hung up the telephone; with her other hand she pressed her chest, where all the pain was radiating like heat from a charcoal briquette, and she fell onto Ned's side of the bed and buried her face in his pillow. The scent of his shampoo was like a blow to her abdomen, kicking sobs up into her chest from deep inside of her. Soon she was gasping, weeping. So melodramatic, she thought, from some cynically observing part of herself. I'm dying, she thought, from another part of herself that was a good deal closer at hand, and suffering. I'll kill him! I'll kill her! I love him! I hate him! Caught painfully in a vise whose one side was steaming passion and whose other side was coolly ironic detachment, she felt exposed, absurd, primitive, raw and vulnerable and uncivilized and deeply, unfairly wounded.

For the next five and a half hours, until nearly midnight, Marianne paced the house she'd shared with a husband—a liar!—for fifteen years. Upstairs, downstairs, the basement, every room. She touched every wall and every piece of furniture, walking, walking, as if she could walk the pain off like a hangover, as if she could exhaust it out of herself, wring it out like a good sweat. She thought: It isn't true, it isn't, it is. She wept, she swore.

She took scissors and cut his Valentine's Day card into the shape of a heart, which she then cut—with jagged edges—down the middle. She taped both sides to the dresser mirror right where her face was reflected. Now she saw a broken heart surrounded by streaked blond hair with a reddened nose between the jagged edges and a forty-one-year-old neck and body below.

She panicked, she tried to meditate, she tried to read, she prayed, she screamed, she tried to reason herself back into sanity, she attempted to evolve right then and there into a better, higher sort of person, she tried to defend Ned against her own accusations, she tried to wait, to understand, to find another explanation.

She tried, she tried, she tried!

All to no effect, of course, perhaps because the moon had not yet risen to its fully royal blueness.

Finally, five minutes before the mark of midnight, the moon did appear outside her living room window.

Oh! It was fuzzy all around with a sort of incredible blue color!

Marianne stopped in her tracks, startled, staring. The sight of the moon reminded her that this day of Ned's unfaithfulness, of his wicked betrayal, was Valentine's Day.

Of all days! The schmuck!

That single awful, ironic, sentimental, full realization struck the final shattering blow to her sadly pummeled heart. She stared at the moon—it was almost half, lying on its back in the sky like a beautiful golden fat lady in a hammock, bathed in a blue spotlight.

Marianne felt, in that moment, desperate.

She felt as if the blood inside her broken heart was spilling into the huge cavity behind her ribs, and that now the blood was lying there, helplessly pulsing at the sight of the moon, right in time to the breathing of the lady in the hammock. Marianne felt the rhythm of the moon sucking at the living pieces of her heart, tugging at her breastbone, pulling at her blood like heat drawing spilled pieces of mercury. Like an irresistible magnet, that cruel and gorgeous moon drew her out of her home and then into her car. It pulled her along the dark streets to the house where she suspected her husband lay that Valentine's night with his lover.

The golden fat lady in her hammock reached for the front fender of Marianne's car to pull her along the road to Christy's house.

THIS BEING FEBRUARY, there was snow everywhere.

It was cold in the car, almost immediately, when she turned the engine off, and she sat bundled in coat, hat, gloves, boots, and muffler, breathing frost into the air inside her car. There, one house down, was the two-story, red-brick house where Christy lived with her husband, Adam Phares.

A married woman!

Illuminated by the snow and the moon, the house seemed bright among the other homes on the block, as if helicopters had their spotlights beamed at it.

There! There's where the illicit couple is hiding!

Coupling, Marianne thought, and the word was a stab into her own side. That's where they're coupling. She looked over at her passenger's seat: God only knew why, but before she left her house she'd grabbed the vase of Ned's carnations. She'd set them on the car seat and then buckled them in, as if they were a child. It was an irrational act. So was coming here.

"But I have to have proof, don't I?" she asked the moon, plaintively.

Maybe she was being ridiculous. Oh, she liked that idea very much, and she let it warm her. Maybe she was the one who was betraying Ned, by being suspicious of him. Maybe she should be ashamed of herself for jumping to such an evil conclusion, maybe she could look forward to cringing with secret humiliation whenever she looked back on this awful night. Oh, yes! She'd happily trade that little private mortification for the more public one she'd been imagining: being left for a younger woman. So banal; could it possibly be worth all this heartache?

The earth swung in its orbit, passing the moon behind a cloud, then out again on the other side. Perfidious, nomadic moon! Silently, it seemed to swing into Marianne's vision, its blue halo catching the corner of her eye, snagging her attention so that she turned her head, the exact forty-five degrees that was needed to direct her attention to . . .

Ned's car.

It was parked across the street from Christy's house in the parking lot of a condominium complex, sneaked in between a red BMW and a vintage Mustang, as if it belonged there. Maybe it wasn't his. There were nearly as many Mercedes in the city as there were lawyers. Maybe. But no, the light of the snow from below lit the personalized license: L EAGLE (short for legal eagle). And the moon shone revealingly on the dark (sinister) gray finish of the car.

No mistake: it was Ned's incriminating car.

The moon looked bluest at that very moment when Marianne's heart pulsed so hard she thought surely it would jerk from her chest and hop down the snowy street without her, plop by bloody plop.

"Oh, God," she groaned, mostly from the pain of finding out she was right, but also from the problem of trying to use a tissue to wipe her nose while she still had gloves on. The worst of her pain was centered just inside the warm curve of her left breast. She pressed her fingers there, and leaned into them. *Oh . . .*

The unrelenting moon pulled Marianne's hand away from her wounded breast—like a shot bird, she was—and placed the fingers on the handle of the car door, which opened. The moon tugged her out into the street and pushed her hands to close the door with a muted *click*. It shoved her hands into the pockets of her overcoat and pulled the breath from her mouth in a white mist. It made her stand alone under a street lamp for a moment, staring helplessly, furiously, at Christy's house.

And then the moon—the plump, soft invisible tugging hand of the fat lady in the hammock—touched Marianne's chin and nudged it to the left, drawing her attention to another car.

This one—an ivory Infiniti—was parked at the curb.

She saw a man seated in it, and he was also staring at Christy's house. The moon caught his chin and turned it toward her.

It was Christy's husband, Adam Phares.

Simultaneously, he and Marianne gasped, and then flushed with the embarrassment of being caught in the act of having their hearts broken. And then the moon, merciless creature, placed its fat blue hands on the woolly lapels of Marianne's coat and jerked her right into the passenger seat of Adam's car.

"I'll kill the son of a bitch," were his first words to her.

"Just Ned?" she retorted, in a shaky voice. "What about your wife? Where did she tell you she'd be this weekend?"

"I told her I'd be in New York."

Marianne thought about that, and then exclaimed: "You *knew*?"

"I was only suspicious. *Now* I know."

"How long do you think it's been going on?"

He shook his head. "What difference does it make if it's more than one night?"

Marianne slumped down in the seat. "It doesn't." Wearily, feeling defeated, she turned her head toward him. "So what are you going to do?"

"Make sure," he said, lingering over each word, nailing them into the night. "You want to come with me?"

"Where?" And when he nodded in the direction of the house, she exclaimed: "Over there? You're kidding!"

"It's my house—" He looked distracted. "I'm sorry, I can't remember your name."

"Marianne."

"I'm Adam."

She knew that, but they'd only met at office parties. She couldn't remember what he did for a living, she didn't know anything about him, except that apparently his wife was cuckolding him with Marianne's husband.

"Marianne," he repeated. "It's my house. I can do anything I want to."

"But what—"

"I want to see them together."

He picked up a thirty-five millimeter camera from the console between them and held it up. "*Catch* them together."

"Oh, my God, are you sure—"

"They're *lawyers*, Marianne."

"Right." She nodded, immediately grasping the harrowing prospect of divorcing an attorney. "Okay, then I'm coming, too." As he stuck the little camera into the right-hand pocket of his overcoat, an even more frightening idea occurred to her. "But what if they hear us and think we're burglars and call the police? Do you keep guns in the house? What if they mistake us for burglars and shoot us?"

"So they call the cops, so what?" Adam Phares tightened his lips, as if to draw them in from the cold. "So they shoot us." He added, angrily, dully, "So what?"

Then they'd be sorry, Marianne thought, before she corrected herself. No, they wouldn't. She bit her lips to restrain the sob that wanted to burst from her mouth.

The moon, having done its mischievous job, ducked behind a cloud and wisely stayed there.

"CAN'T YOU SNEAK MORE QUIETLY?" she hissed, behind Adam, as they approached the bushes in front of the back bedroom window. She'd hoped the snow would muffle their approach, but no, the ice crunched like peanut brittle. Plus, Adam seemed intent on bulling his way like a defensive end charging a quarterback: his arms swinging wide of his coat, his head jutted out ahead of his body, his boots taking giant strides, he seemed oblivious of the noise he was making. She felt as if they were alerting the neighborhood, much less the lovers. "Adam, wait!"

She ran, crunchingly, after him, catching him by his coattails and jerking him back toward her. "We'll never catch them if they hear us coming first!"

It was reassuring to her that he was behaving as irrationally as she felt that she was.

They covered the rest of the distance like cautious rabbits in the snow. Adam led Marianne smack up against a windowsill toward the rear of the house, and they stood side by side, peering in, standing on top of dead and frozen marigold plants.

The lovers hadn't bothered to close the curtains.

They'd even thoughtfully left a light on in a bathroom, and that, plus the light from the moon and the snow, illuminated them like lovers on the cover of a book.

Marianne stared at the tumble of blankets on the huge bed inside.

At first, she couldn't make out any human forms, but then a fold in white sheets revealed itself to be a slim and shapely female arm, pale and crooked at the elbow so that the forearm lay on top of a larger pile of blankets that revealed themselves to be a curve of male chest and shoulders. Finally, Marianne could make out the tousle of two dark heads in the shadows of the pillows, two heads sleeping so close together they looked like one, a giant's.

The giant on the bed didn't stir.

"Must be exhausted," Marianne muttered, spitefully.

"What?" Adam whispered.

She didn't answer, but pointed, instead, at something inside.

"What?" he asked again.

"The mirror," she told him.

There was a mirrored double closet door directly to the side of the sleeping lovers and directly across from their spouses standing outside the window in the snow. Marianne and Adam could look in the mirror at themselves looking in at Christy and Ned. Marianne moved her own head slightly, to superimpose it on top of Christy's head: now it was she who was sleeping beside her husband. Feeling reckless, Marianne turned her face and puckered her lips: her image seemed to kiss the man on the bed.

"What are you doing?" Adam hissed, and when she shifted her glance from the mirror to him, she discovered that her lips were pointed in his direction.

"Embarrassing myself," she said.

Suddenly he put his left arm around her shoulders in a strong, abrupt motion that let her know he was trying to comfort her. "I'm sorry," he said.

"Me, too," she whimpered, and she tucked her right hand into the left pocket of his overcoat. "They look . . . happy."

"Wonderful."

She laughed a little at his sarcastic tone, but she couldn't stop staring at the bed, and neither, it appeared, could Adam. Maybe it wasn't so much that Christy and Ned looked happy—Marianne couldn't, after all, even see their faces—but that they looked warm, cozy, loving. Those adjectives added up to happiness in Marianne's personal dictionary. She and Ned hadn't slept entwined like that since before they were married, not unless one of them was a little drunk. Even after they made love, there were only a few brief moments of embracing, then a quick, rather astringent kiss, and then they turned their backs to one another, each moving to opposite sides of their bed to sleep. But Marianne knew what Christy would be feeling—if she were awake—with Ned's arm underneath her head, how big and masculine and firm Ned's upper arm and shoulder would feel, and how much heat his body would be giving off. Marianne imagined she could feel some of that heat radiating all the way outside, melting some of the snow where she was standing.

Suddenly, Adam raised his right hand and touched his glove to the storm window. Snow that had been stuck to his glove filtered down to their boots. His fingers were splayed against the glass. It was a hurt and forlorn gesture that made Marianne's heart ache for him. She pulled her hand out of his pocket and snaked her arm around to his back and patted him two or three times, as if to say, "There, there."

After a moment, she had to admit to him, "My feet are freezing."

"Okay, come on." He grabbed her right hand in his left and pulled her away from the window. Together, like linked burglars, they made their way the rest of the distance around to the back of the house.

Adam used his key to open two locks almost without any noise.

Marianne held her breath as he pushed open the door.

"We'll track snow," she warned.

"It'll melt. They'll think they did it."

She entered the darkened kitchen of her husband's lover, stepping right behind her husband's lover's husband.

THERE WAS ONLY A LIGHT on the stove and the brightness of the night outside, but once their eyes adjusted, they could see perfectly well.

"Take your coat?" Adam asked her.

She almost smiled as she took it off and handed it to him. Christy's husband had nice hospitable instincts, even under pressure. Removing her coat seemed to Marianne to be the most daring thing she'd done so far, because it might keep her from making a clean, fast getaway. She felt as if she'd taken the big step off the high cliff.

"Boots?" he asked, looking undecided.

Boldly, she nodded and they both removed their boots and then lined them up facing the door, as if they could jump into them in a second, like the Lone Ranger onto the back of Silver. Marianne even took off her hat and unwound her muffler and put it all, including her gloves, on top of her coat, which he'd placed on a high stool.

They looked around the kitchen, which was messy with the signs of a dinner having been recently prepared and nothing cleaned up or put away.

"She never cooks for me anymore," Adam complained.

"He never did cook for me," Marianne retorted.

It appeared that the happy couple had fixed a Valentine's dinner together, and a good one: pasta still clung to the edges of a big silver pot, and you could see where butter and bits of parsley and other goodies had been stirred in a sautéeing pan. The oven door had been left wide open, and it revealed a greasy broiling pan with a butcher knife and a sliver of steak fat still on it.

The smell of garlic permeated the air.

Adam lifted a dried string of pasta from the pot and nibbled morosely on it, while Marianne walked to a doorway and looked into the next room, which turned out to be a dining room. She crooked her finger at Adam, who came over to stand beside her. Together, they gazed in at a dining room table set elegantly for two: white china with gold bands on it, heavy silver service, candles galore, and a silver decanting rack for the red wine.

"She'll be sorry," Adam said, sounding gruff and satisfied. When Marianne gave him a quizzical look, he explained: "Christine can't tolerate red wine. Gives her migraines."

Marianne said: "I hope she throws up."

"She will, you can count on it."

"Good. Any chance it'll kill her?"

"Probably not," he said glumly, and walked back into the kitchen. He opened the refrigerator. Marianne watched him remove an orange-and-black carton and take a clean glass from a cupboard, then pour orange juice into it. He then bent over and opened the cabinet doors under the sink and began to remove various cans and bottles.

Curious, Marianne went over to watch what he was doing.

Adam took a bottle of window cleaner and sprayed some of the contents into the orange juice. He looked at Marianne. "She drinks a glass of orange juice whenever she has a hangover. I've tried to tell her that tomato juice is more effective, but she always knows better." He set the window cleaner down and picked up a can of abrasive bathroom cleanser and shook some of it into the juice.

"Won't she taste it?" Marianne asked, feeling oddly detached.

"She'll think it's the hangover."

Marianne reached around him to pick up a plastic bottle that contained ammonia, and she poured a dollop of that into the orange brew.

"You'd think it'd bubble or something," she said.

He grunted. "It will, inside her."

Marianne laughed, and then he did, too. When they had emptied a little of everything into their witch's potion, he carefully poured it all back into the orange juice carton, and then he washed out the glass and put it into the dishwasher.

"Now it'll be diluted," Marianne said, feeling disappointed.

"No, there's not much left in the carton," Adam assured her as he returned it to the refrigerator. They looked at each other and smiled, and then they turned to appraise the contents of the kitchen again. Adam seemed to be drawn to the huge butcher knife lying sideways across the meat broiler. He slid it out of the oven and held it up in the air so that for a moment he looked to Marianne like a medieval warrior.

He glanced over at her. "What'd you think?"

She shook her head. "No, you'd be sure to get caught."

"You think?" He walked over to where there was a butcher-block table, and without warning, he violently plunged the knife into the wood, groaning with his effort. Then he backed away, and he and Marianne watched the handle of the knife quiver in the odd light in the night kitchen. She had gasped when he did it, but now she was mesmerized by how deeply the knife had penetrated the table.

Adam broke the charged silence. "Is he a good lover?"

Marianne shrugged. "If you love him."

He stared at her. "Don't you?"

"Don't I what?"

"Love him?"

"After tonight? How could I!"

"It's been done before," he said wryly. "I'm more interested in before tonight. Did you love him before tonight?"

"I thought I did. Now I don't know. Do you love her?"

Adam grasped the still-moving knife handle and tried to pull it out. It wouldn't come loose. "What's love got to do with it?" he said, and then gestured to her. "Come on."

In the dining room, Adam looked at the table and said, 'Somebody's been sitting in my chair."

"And eating your porridge."

They didn't have to say the next line out loud: "And sleeping in your bed."

There was an opened gift box of designer chocolates on the table, with several pieces missing. And there were a dozen perfect pink roses in a chic black vase. And there were two Valentine's Day cards lying on the table.

Marianne took a piece of chocolate, stuck it in her mouth, and picked up the cards to read. They were as sentimental as the one that Ned had given her was not; they were as gooey as the chocolate. The handwritten extra message on one of them, in the handwriting that wasn't Ned's, said: "Darling, I love you more than life itself." Marianne handed the card to Adam, who read it and then said: "Let's find out if she means it."

Marianne felt a sudden chill of coldness, a splash of jarring realty. She swallowed the chocolate, which felt like a marble going down. This was no game they were playing. Poisoned orange juice in the refrigerator. Butcher knife in the table. With her heart trip-hammering, she watched as Adam disappeared back into the kitchen. When he returned, there was a lump in his suit coat pocket—unlike her, he hadn't changed out of his work clothes—that he was patting with his hand.

"Adam," she said, weakly. "I don't—"

She didn't what? She didn't know.

"Come on," he said, and she followed him, like a puppy being trained. On her way out of the dining room, she picked up a couple more pieces of the chocolate.

It was easy to follow the clues to the next stage in the illicit couple's evening: a trail of discarded clothing started at the beginning of a hallway and led to an open door. Marianne and Adam found, in order: a woman's belt, man's belt, woman's blouse, man's shirt, woman's skirt, woman's shoes, hose, garter belt, black bra, black panties, and finally, a man's trousers. At the last item, Marianne knelt down. She pulled Ned's wallet from his right rear trouser pocket and removed from it the photograph of herself and the one of them together.

Adam tapped her shoulder.

When she looked up, she saw that he was holding down to her his own wallet-sized photograph of Christy. Marianne slipped it into one of the empty slots in her husband's wallet. She also pulled out all the cash and then emptied his front pockets of change.

She held the money up to Adam, offering him some, or all.

He took the bills, went back to his wife's hosiery, and stuck the money down inside one of the legs.

Nasty, Marianne thought, and smiled to herself. She put the change back in his pocket, for lack of any better—or quieter—idea of what to do with it. Now Ned might suspect that his lover had stolen his money and even had the nerve to substitute her own photo for his family pictures. He wouldn't like that, the overconfidence of it, even if he decided, as he would, that it was only a joke. And *she* really wouldn't like his idea of humor: sticking cash in her stockings, as if she were some hooker. And they could each deny it until their faces were as blue as the moon, but who else could have done it, as they were all alone in the house at the time!

As an extra fillip, Marianne stuck the two chocolates deep in the left rear pocket of Ned's trousers.

There!

She smiled up at Adam, feeling almost satisfied now.

But he was staring into the bedroom beyond her, ignoring her childlike pleasure in their petty vengeance. And he was reaching toward the right-hand pocket of his suit coat.

As he walked past her, Marianne grabbed at his coat, frantically, but it only served to pull her off balance, so that she had to scramble to keep from crashing onto the floor of the hallway. For a panicked instant, she wondered if that would have been best: maybe she should scream, warn them. . . .

Adam stepped to the door of the bedroom, and pulled out his camera.

Marianne sank against a wall in relief so flooding she thought: This must be how pregnant women feel when their water breaks. Oh, God, she'd thought it was a gun. She tiptoed to a bathroom down the hall and used it. When she returned, Adam was still standing in the doorway, the camera at his side. She took her place beside him, his companion voyeur.

There they were, sprawled, blanket coated, sleeping off the booze and lust. (Marianne refused to call it love.)

Adam leaned over and spoke right into her ear. His breath tickled her as he said: "Your husband's better looking than I am."

Into his ear, Marianne responded: "She's better looking than I am." (Particularly now, Marianne thought, knowing how red her nose and eyes must be, after the cold and so much crying.)

He leaned over again. "Yeah, but we're much nicer."

She hadn't expected that, and muffled a snort of laughter behind her hands. When she looked at him again, he was smiling at her, but his brown eyes were glistening. For the first time, she really saw him: an attractive man, possibly a little younger than she, with a broad forehead and a long, slim nose and nice eyes. It was true, he wasn't as handsome as Ned was. And she wondered if the other was true: was he really any nicer?

"I'm so tired," she confessed.

He nodded and took her hand and led her down the hall.

Silently, in total understanding, they both lay down—fully clothed—on the white chenille cover on the double bed in the guest bedroom down the hall. They held hands, each of them staring at the ceiling.

"Did you get the pictures?"

"Yeah."

"Good. I guess."

Just as she was starting to go to sleep, he said, "She's not really prettier than you are. She's just smoother. It's like she licks herself down every night, like a cat." He sounded so serious, Marianne thought, as he said these awful things about his wife. "When she sees herself in a mirror, she nearly purrs."

To keep it even, Marianne said, "He's all clothes and haircut."

Adam turned his head on his pillow, toward Marianne. "Your face is much more interesting than hers ever will be. Yours isn't just pretty, it also has character."

"After tonight, it sure will."

Her tone was sarcastic, but he'd made her feel a little better.

He was almost asleep when Marianne said: "Is she your best friend?"

"I guess not."

They both fell asleep, feeling comforted by the hand they held.

IN THE MORNING, they awoke to the unmistakable sounds of their spouses making love to one another in the next room. At first, Marianne thought she would weep with the terrible sorrow and longing she experienced. But when Adam pounded his fist into the mattress, Marianne felt sheer fury. Finally, they found themselves laughing at the moaning, the groaning, at the "Oh, God"'s and the "Oh, Yes"es, until they were helplessly clinging to each other, stifling each other's hysteria.

And then they heard their spouses get up from the bed.

Gather their clothes, get dressed.

"Is this your idea of a joke?" demanded Christy, from the hall.

"I didn't do that!" Ned protested. "I'd never do that."

"Well, who the hell did? Nobody else has been here! Jesus, I can't believe you'd insult me like this!"

"Christy!"

"Damn, don't yell at me, I have a migraine."

In the other bedroom, Marianne clutched Adam and whispered in horror. "Oh, my God!"

He sat up, and she saw the wild look on his face.

"Try orange juice," they heard Ned say.

"No. Adam always says that tomato juice is best."

"Oh, well, if Adam says it—"

"I believe I can make my own decision about what to do for my own hangover," was Christy's cold response to that.

Adam lay back down, grinning.

"'But our coats!" Marianne hissed at him. "Our boots!"

He pointed to a chair, where Marianne saw all their belongings piled up, and he whispered back: "I woke up in the middle of the night and brought it all in here."

"What woke you?"

"The sound of Christy throwing up in the bathroom."

Marianne buried her face in the sleeve of his suit coat and grinned, despite the tears in the corners of her eyes.

The edgy, angry voices of the lovers moved out of the hall, into the dining room.

But in a few minutes, Christy's voice was coming back at them, saying, "... just get it the hell out of my chopping block! What do you expect me to believe, that I walked in my sleep and stuck it there? Honest to God, Edward, I never dreamed you'd have this childish kind of practical-joke humor. I have to tell you that I am *not* amused . . ."

And her footsteps sounded in the master bedroom, followed by the sounds of slamming drawers and doors.

From the vicinity of the front door, Ned called out: "Do you want to ride with me, Christy?"

"No!" she called back. "I'll drive my own car!"

"I love you!" he yelled, angrily, at her.

"Love you, too!" she yelled back, sounding furious. And then they followed that with loud good-byes, and he slammed the front door behind him.

"Ass!" Christy said, in the next room.

She slammed her way out the back door shortly after that.

It was Marianne's turn to shoot up in bed.

"Oh, my God," she said. "Our cars are outside."

But Adam was starting to laugh again. He pulled her back down on the bed. "That's okay. She'll steam out of the driveway so fast, she'll never see mine. And he'll never think that out of all the gray Accords in the world, that one could possibly be yours."

Marianne turned toward him. "Should we feel sorry for them?"

He thought about that. "I guess we can afford to be charitable."

They gazed at each other, and then said, at exactly the same time: "Nah." They burst out laughing in a fit that continued until Marianne fell into one last crying jag. Adam held her sympathetically, tactfully, until it ended. Then they got up, gathered their belongings, straightened themselves up, and left the house by the front door.

Before they left, however, Adam gathered up the dozen beautiful pink roses and swept them into his arms, making a lovely, if dripping, bundle of them. He presented them, with a gallant bow, to Marianne.

"Will you be my Valentine?" he asked her.

She took the flowers and cradled them. Feeling suddenly shy, she said to him, "Well, maybe next year."

ADAM PHARES WAVED his camera at her as he drove off.

Marianne waved the roses at him. Then she took the carnations, opened the car door, and dumped them in the slushy street. She placed the roses carefully in the vase, made sure it was still securely buckled in, and headed home.

Behind her, the moon, nearly invisible now, looked pale and ordinary in the morning sky. The fat lady was gone. Nobody, seeing it right then, would have guessed it had ever been blue.

Sharyn McCrumb lives in the Virginia Blue Ridge Mountains, and uses that area as a basis for her beautifully written novels of mystery in the backwoods. Her novels have been nominated for just about every award imaginable, including the Anthony and Agatha awards, and she won the Macavity for *If I Ever Return Pretty Peggy O*. She has been a member of Sisters in Crime, Mystery Writers of America and the American Crime Writers League. Her most recent novel is *She Walks the Hills*. "The Matchmaker" is on a different level from her usual writing, exploring an unusual personal dating service.

The Matchmaker
SHARYN McCRUMB

"You don't look like the head of a dating service," said Carl, nervously licking his lips.

The large woman behind the desk smiled and fingered a lock of greasy brown hair that dangled over her glasses. "You were expecting someone more like a game-show hostess, Mr., er ..." She consulted the manila folder in front of her. "Mr. Wallin."

Just as she said this, the woman looked up from Carl's file, and Carl had to pretend that he hadn't been wiping his sweaty palms on his slacks. "Did I expect glamour?" He shrugged. "I guess so. I've never been to one of these dating places before."

"Naturally not, Mr. Wallin," said the director blandly. Her expression suggested that all the clients said that, and that nothing could interest her less. "Please sit down. I am Ms. Erinyes."

Carl blinked. "Is that Spanish?" His dating preferences tended more toward northern European ancestry.

"It is Greek. Ancient Greek, as a matter of fact." Her jowls creased into a smile. "Now let's talk about you.'

"I thought you people matched couples up by computer," said Carl, frowning.

Another smile. "And so we do, Mr. Wallin, which is why I don't look like a centerfold. I started this company with personality-matching

31

software of my own design. So you see, my specialty is not romance or even the social niceties. I am a psychologist and an expert in computer technology."

Carl nodded his understanding. That made sense. Now that he thought about it, this Ms. Erinyes reminded him of a couple of people in his night class: the intellectual nerds. The ones whose whole lives revolved around computers. Even their friends were electronic pen pals. Of course, Carl didn't have any friends, either, but he still felt himself superior to the hackers. The one difference between Ms. Erinyes and his ungainly classmates was that she was female. There were no women in the class. Too bad; then he might not have needed a dating service. But, after all, the community college course was in electronics. Carl thought it was fitting that there were no women taking it.

With a condescending smile at the lard-assed misfit behind the desk, Carl flopped down in the chair and leaned back. "So how come you wanted to see me? I filled out the opscan form, just like the girl out there told me to, but I thought some of the questions were pretty off-the-wall. Like asking me to draw a woman. What was the point of that? Does it matter that I can't draw?"

Ms. Erinyes had her nose back in the manila folder again. She was looking at Carl's drawing: a stick figure with scrawled curls and a triangle for a skirt. The penciled woman had fingerless hands like catchers' mitts, and no mouth. Her eyes were closed.

"The questions? Consider it quality control, Mr. Wallin," she said without looking up. "Computers aren't perfect, you know. Sometimes we like to check our results against good old human know-how. After all, love isn't entirely logical, is it?"

Carl wanted to say, "No, but sex is," but he thought this remark might count against him somehow, so he simply shrugged.

"Now let's see . . . Your medical form came back satisfactory, including the blood test. Good. Good. Can't be too careful these days. I know you appreciate that."

Carl nodded. The medical certification was one of the reasons he'd decided to come to Matchmakers.

"I see you had a head injury a few years ago. All well now, I hope?"

Carl nodded. "Fell off my motorcycle. Lucky I had a helmet on, or I'd have got worse than a bad concussion."

"I expect you would have," murmured Ms. Erinyes, dismissing motorcycles from the conversation. "Now, let's see . . . You are five feet nine," Ms. Erinyes was saying. "You weigh one hundred and fifty-eight pounds. You are twenty-eight years old, nominally Protestant, never married. You have brown hair and green eyes. Regular features. I'd say average looking, would you?"

"I guess," said Carl. It didn't sound very complimentary.

"And do you have any pets?"

"No. I like things to be clean and neat. I never could see what the big deal was about animals." He smiled, remembering. "My grandmother had a tomcat, though. We didn't get along."

Something in his voice made Ms. Erinyes look up, but all she said was, "I see that you were raised by your grandmother since the age of two."

"What does it matter?" Carl Wallin was annoyed. "I thought women would be more interested in what kind of car I drive."

"A nineteen seventy-seven AMC Concord?" Ms. Erinyes laughed merrily. "Well, some of them will be willing to overlook this, perhaps."

Carl's lips tightened. "Look, I don't make a lot of money, okay? I work as a file clerk in an insurance office. But I'm going to night school to learn about these stinking computers, which is what you have to do to get a job anymore. I figure I'll be doing a lot better someday. Besides, I don't want a lousy gold digger."

"Nobody does. Or they think they don't. We have to wonder, though, when sixty-year-old gentlemen come in again and again asking for ninety-eight-pound blondes younger than twenty-eight." She grinned. "We tell them to skip the question about hobbies and substitute a list of their assets."

"I don't need a movie star."

"Well, that brings us to the big question. Just what kind of companion are you looking for?"

"Like it says on the form. A nice girl. She doesn't have to be Miss America, but I don't want anyone who—" He groped for a polite phrase, eyeing Ms. Erinyes with alarm.

"No, you don't want somebody like me," said Ms. Erinyes smoothly, as if there had been no offense taken. "I assure you that I don't play this game, Mr. Wallin. I just watch. You want someone slender."

"Yeah, but I don't want one of those arty types either. You know, the kind with dyed black hair and claws for fingernails. The foreign film and white wine type. They make me puke."

"We are not shocked to hear it," said Ms. Erinyes solemnly.

Carl suspected that she was teasing him, but he saw no trace of a smile. "She should be clean and neat, and, you know, feminine. Not too much makeup. Not flashy. And not one of those career types, either. It's okay if she works. Who doesn't, these days? But I don't want her thinking she's more important than me. I hate that."

For the first time, Ms. Erinyes looked completely solemn. "I think we can find the woman you are looking for," she said. "There's a rather special girl. We haven't succeeded in matching her before, but this time . . . Yes, I think you've told me enough. One last question: have you always lived in this city?"

Carl looked puzzled. "Yes, I have. Why?"

"You didn't go off to college—no, I see here that you didn't attend college. No stint in the armed forces?"

"Nope. Straight out of high school into the rat race," said Carl. "But why do you ask? Does it matter?"

"Not to the young lady, perhaps," said Ms. Erinyes carefully. "But I like to have a clear picture of our clients before proceeding. Well, I think I have everything. It will take a day or two to process the information, and after that we'll send you a card in the mail with the young lady's name and phone number. It will be up to you to take it from there."

Carl reached for his wallet, but the director shook her head. "You pay on your way out, Mr. Wallin. It's our policy."

HE STARED AT THE NUMBERS on the apartment door, trying to swallow his rage. Being nervous always made him angry for some reason. But what was there to be anxious about? His shirt was clean; his shoes were shined; he had cash. He looked fine. A proper little gentleman, as Granny used to say when she slicked his hair down for church. But he didn't want to think about Granny just now.

Who did this woman think she was, this Patricia Bissel, making him dress up for her inspection, and dangling rejection over his head? That's all dating was. It was like some kind of lousy job interview: getting all dressed up and going to meet a total stranger who *judges* you without knowing you at all. He clenched his teeth at the thought of Patricia Bissel, who was probably sneering at him right now from behind her nice safe apartment door with the little peephole. His palms were sweating.

Carl leaned against the wall and took a few steadying breaths. Take it easy, he told himself. He had never even seen Patricia Bissel. She was just a name on a card from the dating service. He had thought that they were supposed to send you a couple of choices, maybe some background information about the person, but all that was on the card was just the name: Patricia Bissel.

It had taken him two days to get up the nerve to call her, and then her line had been busy. Playing hard to get, he thought. Damned little tease. Women liked making you sweat. When he had finally got through, he'd talked for less than a minute. Just long enough to tell her that the dating service had sent him, and to let her hem and haw and then suggest a meeting on Friday night at eight. Her place. It had taken her three tries to give the directions correctly.

She hadn't asked anything about him, and he couldn't think of anything about her that he wanted to know. Nothing that she could tell him anyway. He'd decide for himself when he saw her.

He was one minute early. He liked to be precise. That way she would have no excuse for keeping him waiting when he rang the bell, because they had agreed on eight o'clock. She couldn't pretend not to be ready and keep him hanging around in the hall like a kid waiting to be let out of the closet. Like a poor, shaking kid waiting for his granny to let him out of the closet, and trying so hard not to cry, because if she heard him, she'd make him stay in there another half hour, and he had to go to the bathroom so bad ... She had to let him out ... in.

The door opened. He saw his fist still upraised, and he wondered how long he had pounded on it, or if she had just happened to open it in time. He tried to smile, mostly out of relief that the waiting was over. The woman smiled back.

She wasn't exactly pretty, this Patricia Bissel, but she was slender. To the dating service people, that probably counted for a lot; real beauties did not need to use such desperate means to meet someone. Neither did successful guys. Maybe she was a bargain, considering. She was several inches shorter than he, with dull brown hair, worn indifferently long, and mild brown eyes behind rimless granny glasses. She offered a fleeting smile and a movement of her lips that might have been hello, and he edged past her into the shabby apartment, muttering his name, in case she hadn't guessed who he was. Women could be really dense.

Carl glanced around at the battered sofa beneath the unframed kitten poster and the drooping plants on the metal bookcase. He didn't see any dust, though. He sat down in the vinyl armchair, nodding to himself. He didn't take off his coat and gloves because she hadn't offered to hang them up for him. She probably just threw things anywhere, the slut.

Patricia Bissel hunched down in the center of the sofa, twisting her hands. "You're not the first," she said in a small voice.

Carl looked as if he hadn't heard.

"Not the first one the dating service has sent over, I mean. I just thought I'd try it, but I'm not sure it'll do any good. I don't meet many people where I work. I'm a bookkeeper, and the only other people in my office are two other women—both grandmothers."

Carl tried to look interested. "Did your coworkers suggest the dating service to you?"

She blushed. "No. I didn't tell them. I didn't tell anybody. Did you?"

"No." What a stupid question, he thought. As if a man would admit to anybody that he had to have help in finding a woman. Why, if a man let people know a thing like that, they'd think he was some kind of spineless bed-wetting wimp who ought to be locked in a dark closet somewhere, and—

She kept lacing her fingers and twisting them, and she would only glance at him, never meeting his eyes. She was so tiny and quiet, it was hard to tell how old she was.

"You live here with your folks?" he asked.

"No. Daddy died, and Mama got married again. I don't see her much. But it's okay. We weren't ever what you call close. And I don't mind being by myself. I know I could have a nicer place if I had a roommate to chip in, but this is all right for me. I don't mind that it isn't fancy. A kitten would be nice, though." She sighed. "They don't allow pets."

"No," said Carl. He thought animals were filthy, disease-ridden vermin. They were sly and hateful, too. His granny's cat scratched him once and drew blood, just because he tried to pet it, but he had evened that score.

Patricia was still talking in her mousy little whine. "Would you like to see my postcards? I have three albums of postcards, mostly animals. Some of them are kind of old. I get postcards at yard sales sometimes . . ." The whine went on and on.

Carl shrugged. At least she wasn't going to give him the third degree about himself, asking if he'd gone to college or what kind of job he had. As if it were any of her business. And she couldn't very well sneer at his car, considering the dump she lived in. And so what if his clothes were K mart polyester? She was no prize herself, with her skinny bird legs and those stupid old-lady glasses. Those granny glasses. What made her think she was so special, going on about her stupid hobbies and never asking one word about him? What made her think she was better than him?

"I have one album of old Christmas cards and valentines," she was saying. "Would you like to see that one? I keep it here in the coat closet."

She edged past him as she got up to get the postcard album. Her wool skirt brushed against him like the mangy fur of a cat, and he shuddered. Her whining voice went on and on, like the meowing of an old lady's cat, and the closet door creaked when she pulled it open. Carl smelled the mothballs. He felt a wave of dizziness as he stood up.

She was standing on tiptoe, trying to reach the closet shelf when Carl's hands closed around her throat. It was such a scrawny little neck that his hands overlapped, and he laced his fingers as he choked her. He left her there in the dark closet, propped up against the back wall, behind a drab brown winter coat.

Before he left the apartment, he wiped a paper towel over everything he had touched, and he found the dating service card with his name on it propped up on the bookcase, and he took that with him. His palms weren't sweating now. He felt hungry.

CARL WAS NOT SO NERVOUS this time. It had been several days since his "date," and there had been no repercussions. He had slept well for the first time in months. The old stifling tension had eased up now, and he smiled happily at Ms. Erinyes. He had been here before. He tilted the straight-backed chair, his mouth still creased into a semblance of a smile.

Ms. Erinyes did not smile back. She was concentrating on the open folder. "I see you are applying for another match from our dating service, Mr. Wallin. Didn't the first one satisfy you?"

Carl wondered whether he ought to say he hadn't found the woman to his liking, or whether he was expected to know that she was dead. The newspaper item on her death had been a small paragraph, tucked away on an inside page. Police apparently had no clues in the case. He smiled again, wondering if they'd ever show photos of the crime scene anywhere. He'd like to have one to keep, to look at sometimes when the nightmares came. He thought of mentioning it, but perhaps Ms. Erinyes had not seen the death notice.

Carl realized that there was complete silence in the room. He had been asked a question. What was it? Oh, yes, had he liked the previous match arranged for him? Finally, he said, "No, I suppose it didn't work out. That's why I'm back."

The director set down the folder and stared across the desk with raised eyebrows and an unpleasant smile. "Didn't work out. Oh, Mr. Wallin, you're too modest. We think it did work out. Very well, indeed."

Carl kept his face carefully blank, wondering if it would look suspicious if he just got up and walked out. Slowly, of course, as if he couldn't be bothered with such an inefficient business.

Ms. Erinyes went on talking in her steady, slightly ironic voice. "Perhaps it's time we revealed a little more about Matchmakers to you, Mr. Wallin. Most of the time, you see, we are just what we say we are: a dating service, matching up poor lonely souls who are too afraid of AIDS or con artists to pick up strangers on their own. People don't want to risk their lives or their life savings in the search for love. So we provide a safe referral. Ninety-nine percent of the time that is all we do; ninety-nine percent of the time, that is quite sufficient. But sometimes it is *not* enough. Sometimes, Mr. Wallin, we get a wolf asking to be let loose among the sheep."

"Con men?"

"Occasionally. We can usually spot them by their psychological profiles. And of course we do a criminal record check. I don't believe I mentioned that to you."

"So what? I've never been arrested."

"Quite true. You are a different kind of danger to our little flock." Carl shook his head, but Ms. Erinyes tapped his folder emphatically. "Oh, yes, you are, Mr. Wallin. Our questionnaires are carefully designed to screen out abnormal personalities, and we are very seldom mistaken."

"There's nothing wrong with me," said Carl. He wanted to walk out, but something about the fat lady's stare transfixed him. She was a tough old bird. Like his grandmother.

"There's quite a bit wrong with you, I'm afraid. Not that we're blaming you, necessarily, but on this particular scavenger hunt, you come up with every single item: abuse in childhood, alcoholism in the family, lower middle class background, illegitimacy, cruelty to animals. Oh dear, even a head injury. And the answers you gave on our test questions were chilling. I'm afraid that you are a psychopath with a dangerous hatred for women. There's no cure for that, you know. It's very sad indeed."

"What are you talking about?" said Carl. "I never—"

"Just so," said Ms. Erinyes, nodding. "You never had. We know that. We checked your criminal record quite thoroughly. But the tendency is there, and apparently it is only a matter of time before the rage in you builds up past all containment, and then—you strike. An unfortunate, untreatable compulsion on your part, perhaps, but all the same, some poor innocent girl pays the price of your maladjustment. Usually quite a few innocent girls. Ted Bundy killed more than thirty before he was stopped. But how could we stop you? The deadly potential was there, but, as you pointed out, you had done nothing."

Carl glanced at the closed door that led to the receptionist's office. Was anyone listening behind that door, waiting for him to make a fatal confession? He had to stay calm. He hadn't been accused of anything yet. Besides, what could they prove with all this crap about psychology? There were no witnesses; no fingerprints. He had made sure of that. The girl had no friends. It had taken two days to find her body, and the police had no clue. Carl's palms were sweating.

The director had taken a piece of paper out of the manila folder labeled WALLIN, C. It was Carl's drawing of the stick-figure woman with no mouth. "Not a very attractive opinion of women, is it, Mr. Wallin? I'm afraid there's no way to alter your mind-set, though. We could not cure you, but we had to stop you. That's the dilemma: how do we prevent you from slaughtering a dozen trusting young women in your rage? That is always the difficult part—making the sacrifice, for the good of the majority. We don't like doing it, but in cases like yours, there's really no alternative. So, we found a match for you."

Carl sneered. "Her? Miss Mousy? I'm supposed to be a dangerous guy, and you pick her as my ideal woman?"

"Precisely. It was not a love match, you understand. Far from it. Although, I suppose it was 'till death do us part,' wasn't it?"

Carl did not smile at the witticism. He thought of lunging across the desk, but Ms. Erinyes simply nodded toward the corner of the office, and he saw a video camera mounted near the ceiling. He had not noticed it before. Still, they had no evidence. Let the stupid woman talk.

"It was definitely a match," Ms. Erinyes was saying. "Just as we get the occasional killer for a client, we also get from time to time his natural mate: the victim. Patricia Bissel was, as you say, a mouse. Shy, indifferent in looks and intelligence—and, most important, she was suicidal. Her childhood was quite sad, too. It is unfortunate that you could not have comforted each other, but I'm afraid you were both past that by the time you met. Patricia Bissel wanted to die, perhaps without even being aware of it herself. Did you mention any of her accidents to you?"

Carl shook his head.

"She fell down the stairs once and broke her ankle. She ran her mother's car into a tree, when she was sober, in daylight on a dry, well-paved road. Twice she has been treated for an overdose of medication, because—she said—she had forgotten how much she'd taken."

"She *wanted* to die?" said Carl.

"She was quite determined, I'm afraid, and through her own fatal blunders, she would have managed it or—worse—she would have found someone else to do it for her. If not a psychotic blind date picked up on a bar, then an abusive husband or a drunken boyfriend. Since the accidents had failed, but the suicidal impulses were still strong, we concluded that cringing, whining little Patricia was going to make someone a murderer. Why not you?"

"Maybe she needed a doctor," said Carl.

"She'd had them. Years of therapy, all financed by her long-suffering mother. Medicine can't cure everybody, Mr. Wallin. Nice of you to care, though."

Her sarcasm was evident now. Carl's eyes narrowed. He was beginning to feel himself losing control of the interview. The tension was seeping back into his muscles, knotting his stomach, and making him sweat more profusely. "You can't prove a thing, lady!"

Ms. Erinyes' sigh seemed to convey her pity for anyone who could be so obtuse. "Did our brochure not assure you that we had years of experience, Mr. Wallin? Years." She withdrew a half-letter-size envelope from his folder, and took out a stack of photographs. "We are not a shoestring operation, Mr. Wallin. You have been observed by a number of Matchmaker employees, who took care that you should not see them. Here is a nice telephoto shot of you entering Patricia Bissel's apartment building. A concealed camera snapped this one of you knocking on the door of her apartment. Didn't the number come out clearly? And there are the two of you in the doorway, together for the first and last time."

Carl stuck out his hand, as if to make a grab for the pictures.

"Why, Mr. Wallin, how rude of me. Would you like this set of prints? The negatives and several other copies are, of course, elsewhere. You do look nice in this one. No? All right, then. Where was I? Oh, yes, the police. So far they have no leads in the Bissel case, but I think that if pointed in the right direction—*your* direction, that is—they could find some evidence to connect you to the murder."

Carl had the closet feeling again. He knew that he must be a good boy and sit quietly, or else the feeling would never go away. "What are you going to do?" he asked in his most polite voice.

Ms. Erinyes put the pictures back in the envelope and slid it into Carl's folder. "Ah, Mr. Wallin, there's the question. What shall we do? We've spent the past week looking into your background, and there is no doubt that you have had a rough life. Your grandmother—well let's just say that some of your rage is entirely understandable. And it's true that Patricia was self-programmed to die. So for now, we will do nothing."

Carl exhaled in a long sigh of relief. He could feel his muscles relaxing.

The director shook her head. "It's not that simple, Mr. Wallin. You understand, of course, that this cannot continue. You have no right to take the lives of people who don't want to die. So we will keep the evidence, and we will watch you. If you ever strike again, I assure you that you will be caught immediately."

Carl returned her stern gaze with an expressionless stare. The director seemed to understand. "Oh, no, Mr. Wallin, you won't try to harm any of us here at the dating service. For you, it has to be passive, powerless women."

She stood up to indicate that the interview was over. "Well, I think that's all. You won't be coming here again, but we will keep in touch. You were one of our greatest successes, Mr. Wallin."

Carl blinked. "What do you mean?"

"You were going to be a serial killer, but we have stopped you. Oh— one last thing. We will keep your description in the active file of our computer. If anyone should come in with your particular problem—the urge to kill—and you happen to fit his or her victim profile . . ." She shrugged. "Who knows? You may find yourself matched up again."

"The Judge's Boy" was the 1995 recipient of the Edgar Award for best short fiction. This is not the first award for Jean B. Cooper, who lives in Columbia, South Carolina, with her husband and two children. The story was also a finalist in the Mystery Writers of America short story contest to celebrate their fiftieth anniversary. Recently her play *Truth, Beauty and FDR* premiered at Piocolo Spoleto in Charleston. The southern influence can clearly be seen in this story of life and crimes coming to a slow boil on the Carolina coast.

The Judge's Boy
JEAN B. COOPER

A thought will jump out at you from behind a door; a memory will rise from the wet napkin under your drink. Everything comes back. Dreams, too. This is a good dream, I'll say to myself: naked woman, a curving outstretched form negative against the light coming through a window shade; the room going gold. There is always a woman. Always a woman. Maybe it was the Judge who told me that, along with all the other crap he put in my head when I would listen. Then the dream is gone, and it's the face of the Judge I see.

When I dream, it's not really about the Judge. I see him in my waking hours. I'm driving down 17 and turn off on a Carolina river road that's nothing more than a carriage lane, and there's His Honor the Judge leaning against a live oak, rolling a cigaret. I'm tooling through Cottageville to Edisto Beach, going to drink beer, catch a fish, get this low country fog out of my brain, and standing under the rusted tin roof of an abandoned tobacco house in the middle of a field is the image of the Judge, exhausted by his own evil.

The Judge is dead. I know he's dead. I was there when they took his body five years ago. It's just the old ways of this sad moist land that keep him before me. It's the religion ringing from the small spare clapboard churches that spring up like ghosts in the marsh as I take the narrow turns at high speeds trying, maybe, to outrun my guilt, or to find some final pardon.

There is always a woman. Now I know when he said it to me (have always known, but the game, see, is to pretend it's dim and slipping away from me, falling off me like old clothes, ancient skin, and me, Ray Ford, emerging new and unscathed).

He said it when we were on the porch of my grandfather's house, a dingy wood framed cottage that sat at the edge of a pond. A sandy road led to it, and I'd been mildly interested in the cloud of dust I saw coming at me down that road. A visitor. And me just returned to the empty house only the night before. Then I recognized the car, big and black. A 1974 Mercedes. The Judge himself. Of course he would know I was ... back. I almost said "home," but it wasn't home anymore.

The Judge had come out of the car like a thundercloud building, one dark billow at a time, his enormous feet in glossy black wing tipped shoes; next his heavy legs, lifted ponderously; then his dark suited self, round and rumpled. He wiped his forehead with a handkerchief and gingerly managed the three cement steps to the porch.

"Ray," he said, "I got some business I need you to take care of for me." Like we had been talking to each other at full tilt for hours. Like I had not been gone for ten years away at school, away at work for a law firm I hated. Like the cane bottomed rocker was warm from him having sat in it all morning. He seemed to remember his manners then. "Well, it's good to see you, son."

We shook hands. Over his wide shoulder I glimpsed his driver, a big solemn black man, Durrell James. "All I have is coffee," I said.

"I don't want no coffee. I got a little business I want you to take care of for me."

"Maybe your man, Durrell, there, would like something to drink."

Judge let a slow yellow gelid smile part his lips, but the eyes never left mine. "Don't do nothing for Durrell. Let it be."

In our years of growing up, Durrell James and I had never been friends, vying as we had for the attentions of the Judge. We had more than once gone at it as boys. There was one fight when Durrell had held a knife at my throat, but the Judge had walked in on us. You know there are some frogs that can go underground and live out of sight in the mud. That's what is out there in the swamp. Waiting. Hate and jealousy can be like that. I looked at Durrell. He was staring straight ahead intent on marsh grasses.

I decided to be nonchalant in spite of the bile and maybe a wave of fear rising in me. "What in the world could an out of work lawyer possibly do for the Honorable Galen D. Pringle, Retired?"

"I don't have time to joust with you, Ray. I will remind you only about who it was taught you everything you know, and I ain't talking about them silly-billies in Virginia, either. What you can do is this: I want you to find somebody for me."

"Find somebody?"

"Yes."

"You want me to find somebody for you?"

He sank into the unpainted rocking char and sighed to let me know how I wearied him. He decided on a different approach. "Me and your dead grandaddy used to take john boats all over this place. I loved your grandaddy like a brother, but you, Ray, have always been a pain in the ass. Which is why you can't practice in somebody else's law firm. Got to be on your own. Well, that's okay. It's how I did it. But don't give me grief this morning. I'm old, and I'm hot. Do this one thing for me."

He knew before my car turned onto the road that would take me back that I was coming. He knew that I had told one of the top firms in South Carolina they could stuff it, and I'd walked out. Such were his sources. And because he knew me, he knew I would do what he asked. He was probably discussing it with Durrell as they rumbled down my forlorn road. Not one to waste a motion, the Judge had grown fat and slow through excesses of life's pleasures and with economy of activity. He had paid for my education at UVA. He had fed and clothed me and watched over me, according to his lights, because my mother was dead, my father was long gone, and because he and my grandaddy had roamed the backwaters in john boats in sweet, languid days. Days, the Judge said, of his last remembered happiness. So he wanted me to find somebody.

"Whom shall I find for you?" I slung the bitter coffee into the bare dry yard.

He did not look at me, but handed me a wallet-sized photograph of a black girl of indeterminate age, except to say young. She might have been fifteen or twenty-five. Her hair was pulled back tight and smooth. Her oval defiant eyes looked at the camera like she might climb through it. Her full mouth had no trace of a smile. "Who is this?"

"A girl worked for me. Tablue . . ."

"Durrell's little sister?"

"Yes. But not little anymore. A thief and who knows what else."

I held the picture, recalled a skinny little girl, Tablue James, but it was the Judge I was watching. He was a wily old cuss, and if he wanted to find this girl, he could have a sheriff on her, the people in these hamlets, farmers, everybody looking for her. Even Durrell.

He shifted his bulk in the chair, flicked nonexistent lint from his trouser leg. "Don't be thinking why can't Durrell or somebody else be finding Tablue for me. This is a sensitive situation. Durrell does not understand sensitive."

I looked again at the man in the car. No, Durrell could not be expected to have sensitivity. What Durrell had was hands like slabs of meat and a neck thick as a tree trunk. "Why is she important to you?" I rested my back against the porch post and prepared for one of the Judge's lies.

"She's not important. It's what she took that's important. She took my money."

I tried not to smile.

"I put her in my office, to give her a break, and what does she do, but make off with cash from my safe!"

I could see by the pain in his watery eyes that his heart was broken. Parting with cash money for which he received absolutely nothing in return was a mortal wound to him. "I still don't see ..."

"She took two hundred thousand dollars!" He spat the words at me. They sounded like water on a hot pan. "You think I want people knowing I had that kind of money on me? Durrell don't even know it. And you better not tell him, either."

Things were clearer. The Judge had known the right people, done the right things and had himself put on the family court bench, which is not a position in and of itself that is a money-maker, but it has its bennies: you hang in there, don't muck up too much, and you just might get into a juicier position. The word is if you can go along and get along, you'll be around a long time. The Judge could do that. He'd made a pile when the South Carolina coastline started developing. Cheap property overnight going through the roof. Somebody here and there dropped a word or two to Judge Pringle, and he knew what to buy and when to buy it. But he had gone to some trouble to let everybody believe he was almost broke all the time. Driving old cars, wearing cheap suits and eating blue plate specials at a grill in Walterboro, the county seat. The Judge in town for court. The Judge in tragic dramatic form. He'd seen *To Kill a Mockingbird* too many times, and probably would have given his left eye to shoot down a dog in the street.

He motioned for me to come closer. I did. He smelled of bourbon and some sweet after shave. "Ray, I know where she is."

I looked at him. He had broken capillaries around his nose branching out onto his florid cheeks. How old was he, seventy? "Where is she?"

"She thinks she's so smart." He looked into the middle distance whether for effect or for real, I do not know. He shook his head sadly. "There is always a woman." Then finally, "She's on Melinda."

The Judge owned Melinda Island. His only real estate deal that did not pan out into big bucks. He'd started to develop it, but the native islanders raised such a stink about it, that he dropped it rather than be confronted by the NAACP or whatever investigative news program decided to take him on. The Judge did not wish to be investigated by anyone at any time. "How do you know she's there? Why wouldn't she just hightail it out to Canada, the Bahamas, wherever?"

He stood up. Suddenly he did not seem angry or agitated. "I just know, that's all. You go over there and get her for me. She'll remember you. You bring her back to me. It's not even a day trip, Ray. Do this one last thing for me. What with emphysema, gout, and whatall, I won't make it to the end of the year. All debts will be paid between you and me."

The Judge had been dying for the last thirty years from some imagined protracted malady or other. In his heart of hearts he really believed he would live forever. "What makes you think she'll come with me?"

He got into the back of the car and was closing the door, "You'll charm her, Ray, just like you've always charmed everyone." Durrell gunned the big car and threw sand back into my face.

A BAD DEED IS BEST DONE QUICKLY. That's not quite Shakespeare, but it's close enough. I set out the next morning for Melinda Island. It's isolated. They don't even have mail delivery. Every now and again someone of the few families who live there will boat over to French Island, pick up mail and some sundry things, then go back. You can forget Melinda Islanders even exist. In fact, they wish you would. I took the ferry across to French Island, rented a small outboard, and docked in Melinda about lunch time. There's only one place to eat there: Loobie's Shack. Loobie is one of three white people that live on Melinda. The other two are his sister and her husband. Loobie's name is Lou B. Dunn. He retired from the navy in Charleston and opened this bait and tackle shop and makes a mean cheeseburger. His beer is so cold. I remembered it from my high school days when the Judge would bring me over so he could walk his beautiful, but poor island to mourn what might have been. Loobie sneaked me beers then. Loobie told me things he thought I might need to know: how to fish for sheepshead,; how to cure a hangover. Loobie had said to me things men say to each other as cautionary tales: Ray, watch a man's hands. If a man's gonna hurt you, he'll use his hands.

When I walked into his place, he recognized me, even after ten years.

"Ray!" His grip was firm as ever. He pulled a dripping beer out of his case. "What brings you here?"

We were both ten years older. His military buzz cut was frosty now, but he was still Loobie in a dirty tee shirt, frazzled khakis, and an apron tied at his big belly. I didn't see a health department rating sign up anywhere, but I breathed in air saturated with crab, beer, hot grease, and salt water. It was good.

"I'm looking for somebody."

"Is that right?" He chewed on his cigar stub. "Who's that?"

I figured he knew. But I played on anyway. I showed him the photo. "Tablue James. The Judge wants to talk to her."

"That sonofabitch." Loobie took a hand towel and zapped a fly with it. "Why don't he come hisself?"

We both knew why Judge Pringle would not come to Loobie's. Loobie had told him during the first stages of the Judge's real estate plans that if he set foot in Loobie's establishment, the Judge would be gut shot.

"He's getting old." I let Loobie consider that for a beat then I said, "He could have sent Durrell."

"Durrell." Loobie's voice was filled with loathing. Most people steered clear of Durrell James. He was born a menace and lived to prove it. How he avoided jail is still a mystery, even with the Judge on his side. "You know what they say about him, Ray? I don't know if it's true, but they say he beat up a girl over in Georgetown, and then because she wasn't dead, he set her on fire."

I said, "He's quite a guy, huh?"

"Let the Judge send Durrell. I'll cut that sonofabitch from stem to stern. I'll hang him out for the sea gulls to pick at. Wouldn't nobody on this island, including his own people, give a rip about it. He's terrorized too many of them for too long."

I turned the beer up. Loobie was mean as death, but he was old and probably slow. Durrell was maybe twenty-nine and didn't know the concept of remorse. Me, I'm the kind that'll either outwit you or sneak up on you. I am, in those things, like the Judge, and it hurts me to admit it. "I'm here because the Judge wants to talk to Tablue."

Loobie got a beer for himself. "None of my business. You want to see that girl, suit yourself. It's a small island. You won't get no help."

That was true. Most of the people knew my connection with Judge Pringle and those who did not outright hate him, at the least mistrusted him, and would not give up Tablue.

"She ever come by here?"

"Everybody comes by here. Hell, Ray, even you're here." Loobie reached with astonishing speed, caught another worrisome fly with his hand and shook it silly in his massive fist.

The rain started about half an hour later. It was steady, beating on Loobie's broad glass front window and his tin roof. He had two booths in the long part of his L-shaped hovel. I slid into the one on the left, sat facing the door, and ate some boiled shrimp. The wind had picked up a little, making the screen door slap. Every time it did I looked up and saw nothing, just more rain on the window. I dozed off a couple of times. Then out of the rain there she was. Tablue James.

She shook the water from her jacket, and hung it on a peg by the door. There was only the insistent drumming of the rain, Loobie's hand coming out with a cup which Tablue took, and she headed straight for me. Her dress was black and short, more like a tee shirt but with the neck cut low. I watched her coming; I couldn't help it. Ten years had grown into long legs and hollows and swells you can't take your eyes off of. She wore no shoes. I stood when she stopped at the booth. She didn't even look at me, but sat in the booth and put her coffee cup on the table.

I said, "Don't the shells hurt your feet?"

She took a sip of the coffee and turned her bronze eyes up at me. "You look the same. Bigger, though."

"You remember me?" I'd been trying since the day before to recall Tablue James, but all I could manage was a skinny little kid standing inside her mama's door when the Judge and I would drive out to the ramshackle house to pick up Durrell. And Durrell never said anything about his family.

"You the Judge's boy."

There was just the slightest emphasis on the word 'boy." I said, "I'm Ray Ford. I worked for the Judge when I was a kid."

"My brother, Durrell, he hates your guts."

"Yes, well, Durrell is good at that."

Tablue broke into a wide grin. She had a small space between her top front teeth. It was not unattractive. It was like a little door and you might want to go in there. She said, "He's good at some other things, too." Her grin disappeared. "Why you here?"

I wanted to get it over with. At least that's what I was telling myself. "The Judge wants you to come back with me."

"I bet he does." She took a napkin from the dispenser on the table and dabbed at the water on her chest and arms. "And you came to get me. You still work for Judge Pringle? A grown man like you still an old man's errand boy?"

"He says you are a thief. He says he did you a favor and you took advantage of him. Said you stole some money."

Her eyes widened. I thought for an instant she might slap my face like an offended woman in those old black and white movies. Instead she slumped against the back of the booth and shook her head.

I said, "You mean you didn't take the money?"

She was studying the contents of her cup. "Oh, I took the money. I cleaned out his office safe. What gets me is he told you he did me a favor? That's what he said?"

"More or less."

She let out a long sigh. "A favor."

Up at the front, the door continued to bang with the wind, and a fog had gathered, even inside of Loobie's, where it mingled with cooking fumes and steam. The weathered walls were damp. The light was low now. There was a heavy thunderstorm out there. I hoped I had tied up the rented outboard well enough.

She broke into my worry. "The Judge does that for people, doesn't he? Did you a favor or two?"

It was not a secret. The Fords had always been backwater people, and who my daddy was never came to light. My mother took that information to her grave. I was eight years old, and they pulled my poor mother out of the creek where the car she had just learned to drive had landed after she took a curve too fast. I was left to Grandaddy Cleatus Ford, a man aged and failing when I was born, and not able to care for an eight year old boy. Judge Galen Pringle, with his powers as a family court judge, took on my care. It was a favor, but to Cleatus Ford, not to me. I said to Tablue, "I worked for what I got from Judge Pringle. Durrell did, too. There were many times we would have preferred fishing for shad or crappie to shoveling out the Judge's horse stalls or washing his car, cutting his grass. We were just kids. I'm not here to talk about me. I'm here to ask you to make everything right with the Judge, to come back with me."

Tablue picked up my beer bottles with long slender fingers. "In this weather? No, settle back, Ray. Let's have a talk."

I watched her walk to the front, saw her slender profile as she leaned over Loobie's counter and got two beers. Tablue moved like water coming back to the booth, like an inexorable wave rolling toward shore. From her toes to her sleek head she was liquid and lovely. Yet I felt something wasn't right. I didn't mind she was a thief. I'd lived in big cities, had lunch and kept society with all manner of thieves daily. But still about Tablue there was something. She sat, and I dismissed that nagging feeling to the effects of the spell of being back in South Carolina lowlands again after a long absence. You forget the magic and the mystique of this haunted place. Time is different here, amorphous and intoxicating in its own way. I'm not even sure how long we sat there with the fresh drinks before she said, "I'm not going back."

"He could put the law on you."

"Could. But ask yourself, why hasn't he?"

I had asked myself that on the way to Melinda. I figured:

1. he wants to keep quiet about the money
2. he wants Tablue spared embarrassment
3. he doesn't want the hassle of the law

Maybe. But then I had said to myself: She's got something on him.

"You've got something on him."

Her eyes sparkled and narrowed. She laughed, but without mirth. She was about to say something, but changed her mind. Then: "Your name is Ray. Like in sunshine? Your mama name you that?"

I had not thought about my mother like that for so long that the question caught me off guard. "I don't know. I guess so." I was trying to remember.

"Ray, tell me about your mother."

"She's dead."

"I know. I'm sorry. So is mine. But tell me about your mother anyway."

The rain came driven sideways at the window in Loobie's and there was a tight cold howl in the wind. I took a long pull on the beer and a long look at the dripping glass window, vapor condensing because of the heat in the cafe. Down here something is always becoming something else. My mother's face almost came to me, pulled up from those far away days when her voice was a grace note through Grandaddy's little house. I could remember walking down that road to the house, feeling the warm sand between my toes. My mother was beside me. The sun was hot on my neck. My hand was in hers. She's talking, because I recalled her soft words. . . .

Under the table I grabbed Tablue's ankles and held them, squeezing. "Stand up now."

Tablue's face was blank. Our eyes locked. She stood. It's her feet. I had noticed, but had not seen. She was missing her little toes, from each foot the little toe gone. I looked down at them and felt the tiny hairs on my neck lift. That walk down the sandy road, my feet, my mother's feet. My mother was missing her little toes.

"Ray, the Judge likes to own things," Tablue said.

You condition yourself. You force yourself to avoid emotions: fear, sadness, loneliness. The one thing as a man you will allow yourself to have is anger. I was having a feast of it, felt it filling me until I thought my eyes would plop out onto the table and look back at me.

Tablue said, "You don't look so good."

She got up and came back with a soft drink. This time she sat in beside me. I felt her press up against me, heard her voice go inside my ear and grab me somewhere low and deep. "'Baby, I'm in it up to my nose, and I need your help. These people here on Melinda can help just so much. I got to get away."

I sipped the drink. "Nobody's keeping you, Tablue." I shook my head to loosen the memory of my mother walking.

"The Judge is a powerful man. You got to come out of the dark. It's time you saw what's real."

"Tablue, what do you have to say to me?" I did not look at her while she spoke.

Her mother had told her. There'd been talk about it for years. The Judge and my mother. I knew mama'd gotten pregnant at fifteen and whoever the father was had taken off. But Tablue said, shortly after I was born, from the fields her people would see the Judge's car snaking through the countryside, my mother in there with him.

Tablue lit a cigaret, picked a piece of tobacco from her tongue. "They say your mama, she was gone leave him. He took her toes. Not too long after that she had the wreck. My mama was there when they pulled her from that water. He was there, too, the Judge. Mama said he liked to died on the spot, was clawing at the car door for her."

"Yeah? You have a lot of information. You're not trying to tell me that old man is my father." I never would have believed that.

"No. I don't know. Maybe."

"Where do you fit into this, Tablue?"

She got up and sat across from me again. Her mood had changed. We were no longer confidantes. There was a childish quality to her voice. "I'm no angel. You been gone a long time. But look around you. What is in this place for me? The Judge, he puts me to work in his office, and one thing leads to another."

"So. You and the Judge." It was an image I could not manage. Tablue, in her early twenties, and the Judge. I'd had enough for one day. "I'm done with this. Get Durrell to help you. He is, after all, your big brother."

This time her laughter was quick, loud, and hoarse. I saw Loobie look back at us. "Who you think held me down when Judge took my toes?"

That I could believe. "You've got two hundred thousand dollars of the Judge's money. That'll get you away from him and from your brother. Just leave. It's what I'm going to do."

"You can't go anywhere in this storm. That's three miles of bad water out there now." She leaned across the table to me and said, like she'd just thought of it, "Tell you what. You come home with me. I fix you nice fish stew, hush puppies, or griddle cakes."

It's a misery to realize that everyone who knows you thinks you're stupid. What had I done or not done to give them that impression? I'd been raised in the inlets, marshes, and swamps by a man whom I always knew was despicable. Children know when things aren't right. Children see what goes on, and eventually they put it all together no matter how it breaks their hearts. Buried deep into my psyche were my mother's missing toes and glimpses of the Judge's hand on her shoulder, her hip. I dredged up quick whispers between them. Now the Judge had sent me for Tablue. Now Tablue invited me home.

"You want to cook my supper, Tablue?"

"Why not?"

Why not, indeed? "You do look good in that black dress."

She smiled broadly. "I dressed for you."

"I know you did. Does the Judge like black?"

She almost lost it a little, but she was good, I'll give her that. "No, Honey," she cooed. "He likes white."

THE CLOUDS WERE BRUISED AND LOW, but the rain was lighter. The wind was at about 16 knots. We walked a mile under broad dripping oaks. The worn house where she was staying was dark and silent. Tablue walked ahead of me, stepped lightly onto the porch and opened the door. She went in. When I did not follow, she came back out. "Ray?"

I went in.

There was no dignity in what we did. It was just something to do, something to kill a rainy night. I lay beside her afterward in the shadowed room. Finally the rain had stopped. The moon broke through the clouds in a tide of truth. Its light shone golden through the window and spilled over Tablue's sleeping body.

There were only a few hours left. The storm had prevented his coming, but now with the weather right, Durrell would come. It was almost firstlight when I heard what I'd been listening hard for. Tablue slept on. There it was again. He was so sure of himself, he was coming through the front door. I eased from the bed and pressed my back against the cool wall behind the door. Durrell entered, crouched, ready to spring. I caught him over the back of his head with a brick I'd found by the back porch. He went down. I hit him again.

On the bed Tablue sat frozen, her mouth open. "Is he dead?" she said.

"I don't know." I felt for a pulse. "No, he's alive."

Her words shot at me. "Kill 'im."

"What?"

"Do it! You don't, he's gone come for you sure."

I went outside and came back with Tablue's clothesline. I tied Durrell's hands and his feet. Tablue sat in her bed smoking, furious with me, and not knowing what her next move should be.

I said, "Durrell put you up to taking the money." She was silent except for desperate drags on her cigarette. Her big eyes watched me, tried to fathom how much I knew. "Durrell put you up to it, and you and he were going to what . . . leave?"

"Durrell is tired of driving the Judge's car. What's it matter to an old man like that anyway, sick as he is? Rolling in money he'll never use. Durrell and me, we had some of it coming. That crazy man took my toes off!"

"With Durrell's help."

Her cigarette flared hot as a laser. "I haven't forgot that. Why you think I'm doing what Durrell told me to do?"

"Why do you think he has two cans of kerosene outside the house?" She looked at her cigarette and stubbed it out. "I take it Durrell didn't say anything about that to you, did he? What did he say, 'Just get cozy with Ray Ford, little sister, and let Durrell handle the rest'?" I'd found the cans when I'd gone for the clothesline. They were meant just as much for Tablue as they were for me. She could see that. Durrell was a loner. He had never needed a partner even if she were his sister.

Tablue got out of bed and walked over to her brother. She kicked him. He did not stir. But soon he would. Maybe I'd cracked his thick skull, but Durrell James was like the rent: he'd just keep going on, just keep getting up. I left them there in that halflight. They could fight it out, do what they would with the money.

Down by Loobie's I untied my boat and started out across the water toward French Island. Halfway across the inlet I heard a muffled noise.

Gulls squawked overhead. Looking back at Melinda, I saw a black plume rising to blend with the mother of pearl morning clouds. A lick of red flame showed. Tablue had made her move. And she just might get away with it.

THE JUDGE LIVED IN AN ANTEBELLUM HOUSE badly in need of renovation. I pulled my car into his circular gravel drive and let myself in the front door. It was almost midday, but the interior of the house with its fourteen foot ceilings was cool and dark as a tomb. After a thorough search of the downstairs, I found him upstairs in his bedroom alone. My heart had raced, wondering whether I'd find some of Durrell's handiwork, but in his big, high bed the Judge lay.

When I entered, his eyes opened, and his hand flopped on the counterpane. His bedside table was littered with upset prescription medicine containers. Some pills lay on the floor. When the Judge spoke, I could barely hear him. "Ray. That Durrell." I moved to his bedside. His face seemed to have fallen in on itself. He had a bad color to him. It looked to me that after all his years of complaints, something had finally got to him. But he was still the Judge, and he was trying to gather enough of himself into this one place. He pushed up onto his pillows. It was a mighty effort. I watched. "Ray." The old man licked his dry lips. His eyes went to his empty water glass. I stood still. "Ray. Durrell took my money."

"I know."

"I swear I'm dying."

"You just might be."

"Durrell took my medicine and put it over there on the mantelboard." I looked across the room. On the mantelboard sat a prescription bottle. "It's my heart. You hand me them pills. I'll put one in my mouth and might pull out of this thing."

I did not move.

He closed his eyes. For a long moment we stayed like that. He then opened his eyes again and said, "Hand me the pills, boy. You know you want to do it. You've always had a sense of the heroic."

I SAT OVER BY THE WINDOW, listened to the doves in the myrtle trees, listened to his breath come out in short rasps. My old grandaddy knew two things: the backwaters and the Bible. It was he who tried to drill into me the Gifts of the Spirit. I'm low in most of them except patience. I can wait. I'm the most patient man there ever was. It took a while for the Judge to die. It was evening with the sun going down in a flood of orange behind a stand of pines when I took one last look at the body of Judge Galen Pringle. What had he done to my young ignorant mother? He wasn't my father. We did not look anything alike. I straightened his bed clothes. I set all his medicine bottles, including the longed for bottle on the mantel, back into position on his nightstand. I called the doctor whose name appeared on the bottles.

I STILL LIVE HERE in this low country. I'm Ray Ford, the Judge's heir. I own the old house. I own Melinda Island. I practice a little law, and I go fishing with my friend, Loobie, who swears that Tablue's house just up and burned that day and the islanders had let it. One of Tablue's cousins had taken her over to French Island. She has not been seen since. Driving these back roads, I do have visions of the Judge. Tricks of the mind. They don't bother me. One of these days, if you believe my grandaddy's religion, I'll have to answer for what I did not do for the Judge. Meanwhile, the fish are biting, the beer is cold, and the dreams of the absent Tablue are fond and familiar.

One of the most memorable figures in modern crime fiction is that of the Nameless Detective. Just like his title, he is a man about whom the reader knows everything but his identity. Even more incredible is the fact that Nameless has appeared in sixteen more novels since his first, *The Snatch,* in 1969. Despite the lack of a first name, Nameless is as endearing a character as has ever been created. But strong writing is not the only thing his creator, Bill Pronzini, is known for. He has also coedited more than fifty anthologies in the Western and mystery genres. Here Nameless makes another appearance in his hometown of San Francisco and addresses many of the problems of today's modern city.

One Night at Dolores Park
BILL PRONZINI

Dolores Park used to be the hub of one of the better residential neighborhoods in San Francisco: acres of tall palms and steeply rolling lawns in the Western Mission, a gentrifying area up until a few years ago. Well-off Yuppies, lured by sweeping views and an easy commute to downtown, bought and renovated many of the old Victorians that rim the park. Singles and couples, straights and gays, moved into duplexes that sold for $300,000 and apartments that rented for upwards of a grand a month. WASPs, Latinos, Asian Americans . . . an eclectic mix that lived pretty much in harmony and were dedicated to preserving as much of the urban good life as was left these days.

Then the drug dealers moved in.

Marijuana sellers at first, aiming their wares at students at nearby Mission High School. The vanguard's success brought in a scruffier variety and their equally scruffy customers. As many as forty dealers allegedly had been doing business in Dolores Park on recent weekends, according to published reports. The cops couldn't do much; marijuana selling and buying is a low-priority crime in the city. But the lack of control, the wide-open, open-air market, brought in fresh troops: heroin and crack dealers. And where you've got hard drugs, you also have high stakes and violence. Eight shootings and two homicides in and around Dolores Park so far this year. The firebombing of the home of a young couple who tried to form an activist group to fight the dealers. Muggings, burglaries, intimidation of residents. The result was bitterly predictable: frightened people moving out, real-estate values dropping, and as the dealers widened their territory to include Mission Playground down on 19th Street, the entire neighborhood beginning to decline. The police had stepped up patrols and were making arrests, but it was too little too late: They didn't have the manpower or the funds, and there was so damned much of the same thing happening elsewhere in the city.

"It's like Armageddon," one veteran cop was quoted as saying. "And the forces of evil are winning."

They were winning tonight, no question of that. It was a warm October night and I had been staked out on the west side of the park, nosed downhill near the intersection of Church and 19th, since a few minutes before six o'clock. Before it got dark I had counted seven drug transactions within the limited range of my vision—and no police presence other than a couple of cruising patrol cars. Once darkness closed down, the park had emptied fast. Now, at nine-ten, the lawns and paths appeared deserted. But I wouldn't have wanted to walk around over there, as early as it was. If there were men lurking in the shadows—and there probably were—they were dealers armed to the teeth and/or desperate junkies hunting prey. Only damned fools wandered through Dolores Park after nightfall.

Drugs, drug dealers, and the rape of a fine old neighborhood had nothing to do with why I was here; all of those things were a depressing by-product. I was here to serve a subpoena on a man named Thurmond, as a favor to a lawyer I knew. Thurmond was being sought for testimony in a huge stock-fraud case. He didn't want to testify because he was afraid of being indicted himself, and he had been hiding out as a result. It had taken me three days to find out he was holed up with an old college buddy. The college buddy owned the blue and white Stick Victorian two doors down Church Street from where I was sitting. He was home—I'd seen him arrive, and there were lights on now behind the curtained bay windows—but there was still no sign of Thurmond. I was bored as well as depressed, and irritated, and frustrated. If Thurmond gave me any trouble when he finally put in an appearance, he was going to be sorry for it.

That was what I was thinking when I saw the woman.

She came down 19th, alone, walking fast and hard. The stride and the drawn-back set of her body said she was angry about something. There was a streetlight on the corner, and when she passed under it I could see that she was thirtyish, dark-haired, slender. Wearing a light sweater

over a blouse and slacks. She waited for a car to roll by—it didn't slow—
and then crossed the street toward the path.

Not smart, lady, I thought. Even if she was a junkie looking to make
a connection, it wasn't smart. I had been slouched down on my spine; I
sat up straighter to get a better squint at where she was headed. Not
into the park, at least. Away from me on the sidewalk, downhill toward
Cumberland. Moving at the same hard, angry pace.

I had a fleeting impulse to chase after her, tell her to get her tail off
the street. Latent paternal instinct. Hell, if she wanted to risk her life,
that was her prerogative; the world is full of what the Newspeakers call
"cerebrally challenged individuals." It was none of my business what
happened to her—

Yes, it was.

Right then it became my business.

A line of trees and shrubs flanked the sidewalk where she was, with a
separating strip of lawn about twenty yards wide. The tall figure of a
man came jerkily out of the tree shadow as she passed. There was enough
starlight and other light for me to make out something extended in one
hand and that his face was covered except for the eyes and mouth. Gun
and ski mask. Mugger.

I hit the door handle with my left hand, jammed my right up under
the dash, and yanked loose the .38 I keep clipped there. He was ten
yards from her and closing as I came out of the car; she'd heard him
and was turning toward him. He lunged forward, clawing for her purse.

There were no cars on the street. I charged across at an angle, yelling
at the top of my voice the only words that can have an effect in a
situation like this: "Hold it, police officer!" Not this time. His head swiveled in my direction, swiveled back to the woman as she pulled away
from him. She made a keening noise and turned to run.

He shot her.

No compunction: just threw the gun up and fired point-blank.

She went down, skidding on her side, as I cut through two parked cars
onto the sidewalk. Rage made me pull up and I would have fired at him
except that he pumped a round at me first. I saw the muzzle flash, heard the
whine of the bullet and the low, flat crack of the gun, and in reflex I dodged
sideways onto the lawn. Mistake, because the grass was slippery and my
feet went out from under me. I stayed down, squirming around on my belly
so I could bring the .38 into firing position. But he wasn't going to stick
around for a shootout; he was already running splayfooted toward the trees.
He disappeared into them before I could get lined up for a shot.

I'd banged my knee in the fall; it sent out twinges as I hauled myself
erect, ran toward the woman. She was still down but not hurt as badly
as I'd feared: sitting up on one hip now, holding her left arm cradled in
against her breast. She heard me, looked up with fright shining on the

pale oval of her face. I said quickly, "It's all right, I'm a detective, he's gone now," and shoved the .38 into my jacket pocket. There was no sign of the mugger. The park was empty as far as I could see, no movement anywhere in the warm dark.

She said, "He shot me," in a dazed voice.

"Where? Where are you hurt?"

"My arm. . . ."

"Shoulder area?"

"No, above the elbow."

"Can you move the arm?"

"I don't . . . yes, I can move it."

Not too bad then. "Can you stand up, walk?"

"If you help me. . . ."

I put an arm around her waist, lifted her. The blood was visible then, gleaming wetly on the sleeve of her sweater.

"My purse," she said.

It was lying on the sidewalk nearby. I let go of her long enough to pick it up. When I gave it to her she clutched it tightly: something solid and familiar to hang onto.

The street was still empty; so were the sidewalks on both sides. Somebody was standing behind a lighted window in one of the buildings across Church, peering through a set of drapes. No one else seemed to have heard the shots, or to want to know what had happened if they did.

Just the woman and me out here at the edge of the light. And the predators—one predator, anyway—hiding somewhere in the dark.

HER NAME WAS ANDREA HULL, she said, and she lived a few doors up 19th Street. I took her home, walking with my arm around her and her body braced against mine as if we were a pair of lovers. Get her off the street as quickly as possible, to where she would feel safe. I could report the shooting from there. You have to go through the motions even when there's not much chance of results.

Her building was a one-story, stucco-faced duplex. As we started up the front stoop, she drew a shuddering breath and said, "God, he could have killed me," as if the realization had just struck her. "I could be dead right now."

I had nothing to say to that.

"Peter was right, damn him," she said.

"Peter?"

"My husband. He keeps telling me not to go out walking alone at night and I keep not listening. I'm so smart, I am. Nothing ever happened, I thought nothing ever would. . . ."

"You learned a lesson," I said. "Don't hurt yourself any more than you already are."

"I hate it when he's right." We were in the vestibule now. She said, It's the door on the left," and fumbled in her purse. "Where the hell did I put the damn keys?"

"Your husband's not home?"

"No. He's the reason I went out."

I found the keys for her, unlocked the door. Narrow hallway, a huge lighted room opening off it. The room had been enlarged by knocking out a wall or two. There was furniture in it but it wasn't a living room; most of it, with the aid of tall windows and a couple of skylights, had been turned into an artist's studio. A cluttered one full of paintings and sculptures and the tools to create them. An unclean one populated by a tribe of dust mice.

I took a better look at its owner as we entered the studio. Older than I'd first thought, at least thirty-five, maybe forty. A sharp-featured brunette with bright, wise eyes and pale lips. The wound in her arm was still bleeding, the red splotch grown to the size of a small pancake.

"Are you in much pain?" I asked her.

"No. It's mostly numb."

"You'd better get out of that sweater. Put some peroxide on the wound if you have it, then wrap a wet towel around it. That should do until the paramedics get here. Where's your phone?"

"Over by the windows."

"You go ahead. I'll call the police."

". . . I thought *you* were a policeman."

"Not quite. Private investigator."

"What were you doing down by the park?"

"Waiting to serve a subpoena."

"Lord," she said. Then she asked, "Do you have to report what happened? They'll never catch the man, you know they won't."

"Maybe not, but yes, I have to report it. You want attention for that arm, don't you?"

"All right," she said. "Actually, I suppose the publicity will do me some good." She went away through a doorway at the rear.

I made the call. The cop I spoke to asked half a dozen pertinent questions, then told me to stay put, paramedics and a team of inspectors would be out shortly. Half-hour, maybe less, for the paramedics, I thought as I hung up. Longer for the inspectors. This wasn't an A-priority shooting. Perp long gone, victim not seriously wounded, situation under control. We'd just have to wait our turn.

I took a turn around the studio. The paintings were everywhere, finished and unfinished: covering the walls, propped in corners and on a pair of easels, stacked on the floor. They were all abstracts: bold lines and interlocking and overlapping squares, wedges, and triangles in primary colors. Not to my taste, but they appeared to have been done by a talented artist. You couldn't say the same for the forty or so bronze, clay, and metal sculptures. All of those struck me as amateurish, lopsided things that had no identity or meaning, like the stuff kids make free-form in grade school.

"Do you like them? My paintings?"

I turned. Andrea Hull had come back into the room, wearing a sleeveless blouse now, a thick towel wrapped around her arm.

"Still bleeding?" I asked her.

"Not so badly now. *Do* you like my paintings?"

"I don't know much about art, but they seem very good."

"They are. Geometric abstraction. Not as good as Mondrian or Glarner or Burgoyne Diller, perhaps. Or Hofmann, of course. But not derivative, either. I have my own unique vision."

She might have been speaking a foreign language. I said, "Uh-huh," and let it go at that.

"I've had several showings, been praised by some of the most eminent critics in the art world. I'm starting to make a serious name for myself—finally, after years of struggle. Just last month one of my best works, *Tension and Emotion,* sold for fifteen thousand dollars."

"That's a lot of money."

"Yes, but my work will bring much more someday."

No false modesty in her. Hell, no modesty of any kind. "Are the sculptures yours too?"

She made a snorting noise. "Good God, no. My husband's. Peter thinks he's a brilliant sculptor but he's not—he's not even mediocre. Self-delusion is just one of his faults."

"Sounds like you don't get along very well."

"Sometimes we do. And sometimes he makes me so damn mad I could scream. Tonight, for instance. Calling me from some bar downtown, drunk, bragging about a woman he'd picked up. He *knows* that drives me crazy."

"Uh-huh."

"Oh, not the business with the woman. Another one of his lies, probably. It's the drinking and the taunting that gets to me—his jealousy. He's so damned jealous I swear his skin is developing a green tint."

"Of your success, you mean?"

"That's right."

"Why do you stay married to him if he has that effect on you?"

"Habit," she said. "There's not much love left, but I do still care for him. God knows why. And of course he stays because now there's money, with plenty more in the offing . . . *oh!* Damn!" She'd made the mistake of trying to gesture with her wounded arm. "Where're those paramedics?"

"They'll be here pretty quick."

"I need a drink. Or don't you think I should have one?"

"I wouldn't. They'll give you something for the pain."

"Well, they'd better hurry up. How about you? Do you want a drink?"

"No thanks."

"Suit yourself. Go ahead and sit down if you want. I'm too restless."

"I've been doing nothing but sitting most of the evening."

"I'm going to pace," she said. "I have to walk, keep moving, when I'm upset. I used to go into the park, walk for an hour or more, but with all the drug problems . . . and now a person isn't even safe on the sidewalk—"

There was a rattling at the front door. Andrea Hull turned, scowling, in that direction. I heard the door open, bang closed; a male voice called, "Andrea?"

"In here, Peter."

The man who came duck-waddling in from the hall was a couple of inches over six feet, fair-haired, and pale except for red blotched cheeks and forehead. Weak-chinned and nervous-eyed. He blinked at her, blinked at me, blinked at her again with his mouth falling open.

"My God, Andrea, what happened to you? That towel . . . there's blood on it . . ."

"I was mugged a few minutes ago. He shot me."

"*Shot* you? Who . . . ?"

"I told you, a mugger. I'm lucky to be alive."

"The wound . . . it's not serious . . ."

"No." She winced. "What's *keeping* those paramedics?"

He went to her, tried to wrap an arm around her shoulders. She pushed him away. "The man who did it," he said, "did you get a good look at him?"

"No. He was masked. This man chased him off."

Hull remembered me, turned, and came waddling over to where I was. "Thank God you were nearby," he said. He breathed on me, reaching for my hand. I let him have it but not for long. "But I don't think I've seen you before. Do you live in the neighborhood?"

"He's a private investigator," Andrea Hull said. "He was serving a subpoena on somebody. His name is Orenzi."

"No, it isn't," I said. I told them what it was, not that either of them cared.

"I can never get Italian names right," she said.

Her husband shifted his attention her way again. "Where did it happen? Down by the park, I'll bet. You went out walking by the park again."

"Don't start in, Peter, I'm in no mood for it."

"Didn't I warn you something like this might happen? A hundred times I've warned you but you just won't listen."

"I said don't start in. If you hadn't called drunk from that bar, got me upset, I wouldn't have gone out. It's as much your fault as it is mine."

"*My* fault? Oh sure, blame me. Twist everything around so you don't have to take responsibility."

Her arm was hurting her and the pain made her vicious. She bared her teeth at him. "What are you doing home, anyway? Where's the bimbo you claimed you picked up?"

"I brushed her off. I kept thinking about what I said on the phone, what a jerk I was being. I wanted to apologize—"

"Sure, right. You were drunk, now you're sober; if there was any brushing off, she's the one who did it."

"Andrea . . ."

"What's the matter with your face? She give you some kind of rash?"

"My face? There's nothing wrong with my face. . . ."

"It looks like a rash. I hope it isn't contagious."

"Damn you, Andrea—"

I'd had enough of this. The bickering, the hatred, the deception—everything about the two of them and their not-so-private little war. I said sharply, "All right, both of you shut up. I'm tired of listening to you."

They gawked at me, the woman in disbelief. "How dare you. You can't talk to me like that in my own home—"

"I can and I will. Keep your mouth closed and your ears open for five minutes and you'll learn something. Your husband and I will do the talking."

Hull said, "I don't have anything to say to you."

"Sure you do, Peter. You can start by telling me what you did with the gun."

"Gun? I don't . . . what gun?"

"The one you shot your wife with."

Him: hissing intake of breath.

Her: strangled bleating noise.

"That's right. No mugger, just you trying to take advantage of what's happened to the park and the neighborhood, make it look like a street killing."

Him: "That's a lie, a damn lie!"

Her, to me, in a ground-glass voice: "Peter? How can you know it was Peter? It was dark, the man wore a mask . . ."

"For openers, you told me he was drunk when he called you earlier. He wasn't, he was faking it. Nobody can sober up completely in an hour, not when he's standing here now without the faintest smell of alcohol on his breath. He wasn't downtown, either; he was somewhere close-by. The call was designed to upset you so you'd do what you usually do when you're upset—go out for a walk by the park.

"It may have been dark, but I still got a pretty good look at the shooter coming and going. Tall—and Peter's tall. Walked and ran splayfooted, like a duck—and that's how Peter walks. Then there are those blotches on his face. It's not a rash; look at the marks closely, Mrs. Hull. He's got the kind of skin that takes and retains imprints from fabric, right? Wakes up in the morning with pillow and blanket marks on his face? The one he's got now are exactly the kind the ribbing of a ski mask would leave."

"You son of a bitch," she said to him. "You dirty rotten son of a—"

She went for him with nails flashing. I got in her way, grabbed hold of her; her injured arm stopped her from struggling with me. Then he tried to make a run for it. I let go of her and chased him and caught him at the front door. When he tried to kick me I knocked him on his skinny tail.

And with perfect timing, the doorbell rang. It wasn't just the paramedics, either; the law had also arrived.

PETER HULL WAS AN IDIOT. He had the gun, a .32 revolver, *and* the ski mask in the trunk of his car.

She pressed charges, of course. She would have cut his throat with a dull knife if they'd let her have one. She told him so, complete with expletives.

The Hulls and their private war were finished.

DOWN IN DOLORES PARK—and in the other neighborhoods in the city, and in cities throughout the country—the other war, the big one, goes on. Armageddon? Maybe. And maybe the forces of evil *are* winning. Not in the long run, though. In the long run, the forces of good will triumph. Always have, always will.

If I didn't believe that, I couldn't work at my job. Neither could anybody else in law enforcement.

No matter how bad things seem, we can't ever stop believing it.

"When Your Breath Freezes" was one of the seven finalist stories for the Mystery Writers of America's fiftieth Anniversary contest. Kathleen Dougherty's novels have been described as "explorations of the dark underbelly of the mind." She has worked as a sales manager for an artificial intellience company and as a research associate in pharmacology. This story doesn't draw on any of those experiences, simply because it doesn't need to. Instead, it looks at rationalization, fear, and the human psyche, surrounded by an Arctic wasteland.

When Your Breath Freezes
KATHLEEN DOUGHERTY

There are seven of us.

I am Sister Ellen: the youngest, the ugliest, the least devout, the most fragile. I need the vast silences of northern Alaska and the imposed silence of this cloister. The souls of these women are quiet, their musings as distant as the Chukchi Sea. The nuns have taken me in for the winter, an act of charity, a charity they might well regret. But they don't know about my special ability, my accursed gift. If they did, they'd shun me as others have. Their unspoken thoughts, though, are safe from me. Nothing could compel me again to peruse the mind of another. What you see there are the ugly shapes of nightmares.

Under my white robes, the color for a novice, are a pair of expedition-weight long johns, the fabric a heat-retaining, sweat-wicking synthetic; then a pair of wind-blocking pile pants. We have no television, no radio, yet we have the latest in underwear.

Off come the sturdy black shoes and on go the insulated knee-high boots. I unpin the white novice's veil from my hair and hang the veil on a wall peg. I slide a black ski mask over my head, position the mouth and eye holes. I like wearing the mask; its blank anonymity hides my facial scars. There is only one mirror here, in the infirmary. I have little use for mirrors.

I wrap my neck with the wool scarf knitted by Sister Gabrielle. I think

63

tenderly of her gnarled hands, twisted by arthritis, the black yarn, and the slow clack of the needles. She had embroidered "Ellen" on a cloth tag. My fingers worked a stretch cap on top of the ski mask, then I shrug on the anorak with its thick pile of yellow fleece lining, its rich fringe of fox fur around the hood. The drawstring snugs the hood low on my forehead and up over my mouth. The fur tickles and has that dusty aroma of animal skin.

Last are the glove liners and the padded mittens with Velcro wrist bands. Even before I open the heavy wooden door, I imagine I hear the cows lowing, though that's not possible. The wind's voice whips away sound and, deceptively, mimics the wail of a cat, a distant locomotive, an unhappy ghost.

I flick on the outdoor lights and step beyond the door, pulling it closed behind me. The frigid air steals my breath. Outside all is the white of an unusually bitter February. Though midmorning, there are hours before dawn bleaches the sky. My teeth chatter. It is colder than death out here.

The north wind pauses in its cold rush. I spit. The saliva crackles, freezing in midair, and shatters like glass on the walkway. Cold, very cold, even by the standards of northern Alaska. More than seventy below. Gusts sweep snow pellets, hard as gravel, across the covered walkway to the barn. That wooden structure, like the convent, appears to sprout from the mountainside.

During the Yukon gold rush, miners hewed these caverns, clawing from granite the shelters that shielded them from brutal winters. The south-facing walls are wood; north-facing walls and much of the ceiling are the smoothed underbelly of the mountain. Snaking into the earth from those north walls are tunnels; a few lead to steaming pools of hot springs, potable—though slightly sulfurous—water. After the Second World War, the exhausted claim was purchased by the Immaculata order, and this remote land, once brimming with the harsh voices and greed of prospectors, became the refuge of silent nuns.

The gale blasts against my long skirts and I cover the walkway in a graceless stagger. The barn door sticks, its hinges cranky with cold. I wrench open the door and step inside to rich aromas: cow hide, dung, hay, bird droppings, wood smoke. The miners had used the large room as a barracks. Humid air fogs a tunnel entrance, one which leads to the hot springs, where the nuns take paying guests during the brief summers.

The barn houses two cows, a mangy good-for-nothing goat, and a chicken-wire enclosure with a dozen hens and an irritable cock. The hens set up a comical squawking and fluttering, shocked to their very cores every few hours when I come to tend the wood stove. The cows regard me with their calm brown eyes, aware that it's morning and hoping for fresh fodder. These are, as far as I've seen, the only cows in Alaska, a gift from a rancher in the lower forty-eight. He'd stayed here last summer, Leonidist said, soaking in the convent's hot sulfur springs, and was convinced he'd been miraculously healed of gout.

Pine logs dropped into the wood stove make the coals flare. The stove stands in an isolated hollow scooped from the mountain. The flue disappears into the rocky ceiling.

I milk the cows and the sullen goat, gather eggs from the hens. I slap the cow's haunches, urging them up and down the center aisle. They don't like the enforced exercise, but their shanks tend to develop abscesses. Sister Fiske, a paramedic and our only source of medical expertise during these frozen months, prescribed aerobics. The cows want only to share into their food bins and meditate golden hay into existence. Their resistance makes the stroll hard work and I wonder about the medical benefits for any of us. After half an hour, I stop, panting. Their bony heads study me quietly, a pitying look which makes me smile.

I muck out the stalls and coop, spread down fresh straw, and rake the soiled material to the far entrance. I switch on the outdoor lights. This part gets tricky. If drifts have built up in the past hours, a path will have to be cleared. That means shoveling for two minutes, dashing into the warmth of the barn and scaring the heck out of the chickens, shoveling another two minutes, and so on.

To my delight, the door swings open easily and the path to the garden appears clear. I rake the straw outside and drag the mound a few yards when a snow-dusted rock catches my eye. A mound of black, a large stone that hadn't been there before ... and with awful clarity the form resolves into that of a huddled person. My chest tenses with shock. I am kneeling next to the shape without memory of moving closer.

She is curled into the fetal position. The ebony veil, hard and shiny, has frozen into place, covering most of the profile, but there's enough exposed to see the broad jaw, the deep etch of lines from nose to mouth, the dark brown mole with its two stiff hairs stark against ashen flesh. Frost has made a mask of the features, smoothed out the web of wrinkles on her full cheeks, lessened the downward draw of persimmon lips. It is Sister Praxades, our cook, who refuses—refused—to bake white bread. In the kitchen with her black sleeves rolled up over dimpled forearms, she taught me to knead whole-grain dough. She smelled of flour and yeast and discontent.

With my right glove and liner off, I touch her throat where, in life, the carotid artery throbs. Her neck is frozen solid, hard and unyielding.

Her pudgy hands and feet are bare, pale as alabaster. How can this be? No one would willingly tromp barefoot in Alaska's winter.

My thought are slow lizards, too long in the cold.

My right hand signs the cross over the body. I mentally begin an Act of Contrition, but retreat to the barn when the air hurts my lungs. Chickens cackle and the goat bleats while I finish the prayer for Sister Praxades, an inadequate charity for a woman who had been more than tolerant of a newcomer.

Tears burn my cheeks. I, who have so little opportunity for love, loved her.

There had been seven of us.

Now there are six.

REVEREND MOTHER THINKS in German, a language I don't comprehend. Snatches of words, swirling in her mind-winds, fly out: *schnee, tot, unschuld, verlassen.* She is in her late forties, the youngest except for me, yet authority is a mantle she wears with ease. Her bearing is military, her oval face composed, her gray eyes sharp. Only now her gaze reveals disquiet upon my panicked report of Sister Praxades's death. Reverend Mother's face shutters down; her thoughts whirl. Rosary beads rattle within the folds of her black robes. Her pale lips shape the English words, "Jesus, Mary, Joseph," a favored indulgence of this order. Each nun says this prayer so often that the rhythm becomes one with each inhale and exhale. When the rare words seep from their minds, that is what I sense: JesusMaryJoseph.

Reverend Mother orients on me. Her lapse of control is over. Her fingers sign, *You—lead me—Praxades.* Even now Reverend Mother does not break the quiet meditation.

Her hand halts me as I turn. She shapes sentences fast, too fast, and I shake my head in confusion. She places a long index finger to her lips, then signs, *No tell—others.*

Why not tell the others? They'll know Sister Praxades is missing. I gesture for permission to speak, my sign language inept. Reverend Mother slices her hand in the negative, a command that reminds me of my position here. The shock of finding Sister Praxades has made me exceed my bounds. Flushing, I bow my head in apology, nod compliance, and we exit her office. It is up to Reverend Mother, not the distraught pseudo-novice "Sister" Ellen, to decide when to tell the nuns. If she waits until after the Angelus, before the noon meal when contemplation officially ends, Sister Praxades will not be any less dead for the delay.

In the hall Sister Leonidist, standing on a foot stool, scrapes tallow from a wall sconce. Candle glow highlights the postmenopausal down of her cheeks and chin. Thick red eyebrows shadow her sockets, making her pale blue eyes seem large and black. Leon the Lion, my pet name for her in my head, is the one I'd have gone to first to share the terrible discovery. She performs a modified curtsy from her perch in respect of Reverend Mother as we pass. I look longingly over my shoulder at Leon. She grins and winks, pretends to stick a finger up one wide nostril.

At the side door, before Reverend Mother dons her anorak, she removes her black headdress. Her hair is a flattened, short gray-brown, and its thinness somehow diminishes her authority. I focus on the splintered wood planks, embarrassed. It is disrespectful to see her so. After a moment, she nudges me, not unkindly. It is time to go out into the cold.

ONE VOICE: *"Dominus vobiscum."* The Lord be with you.
Five voices: *"Et cum spiritu tuo."* And with your spirit.

It is noon and the hours of silence end. Reverend Mother observes us from the lectern. Her hands clutch the frame on either side of the Bible. Her knuckles whiten. She is, I know, gathering strength to talk about Sister Praxades. The nuns do not speak. Their minds are suspended in a sea of expectation; no gleanings travel from their consciousness to mine, not even the Jesus, Mary, Joseph prayer. Leon catches my attention with a raised bushy eyebrow and looks pointedly at her lap. She signs: *Cook sick?*

The others may think that. We are not allowed in our cells except to sleep or to rest if we're ill. How I wish Sister Praxades were on her pallet, tucked under quilts, resting away a fever instead of curled miserably outside, the door of her mind forever frozen closed. I hope that whatever malady caused her to wander in the snow also prevented the cook from suffering.

My vision blurs and I drop my gaze to the pine table. In front of me and the four seated nuns are blue ceramic bowls of potato soup, our lunch. In the kitchen I simmered the potatoes in chicken stock—no wonder those fowl squawk with such alarm—and added cream, butter, salt, pepper, and a dash of crisp Chardonnay. As Sister Praxades taught, I tasted and added more butter, cream, tasted and added more spices, tasted and added more wine . . . and still the broth seemed bland.

Rich yellow butter dots the soup's surface, my poor attempt to duplicate the dead woman's craft. Only the bread, a thick, sweet rye, can be trusted. The large, round, crusty loaves were baked by the cook yesterday.

Reverend Mother's sharp inhale pulls my attention to the lectern. Her lips pressed together. "Sister Ellen found Sister Praxades outside this morning. Sister Praxades is dead." The bald statements straighten every spine, including my own.

"No," cries Sister Gabrielle, an old friend of the cook, eldest nun, knitter of woolens for the likes of me. Her misshapen hand fists, hits the table, and spoons jump. Her anguish bolts to my heart. She cries again: "No!"

"Sister Gabrielle," comes the cautioning, authoritative voice of Reverend Mother.

The old nun's mouth gapes, showing too-even dentures. Tears diffuse down cheeks as creased as parchment. She hunches over the table, gasping with hushed sobs, and a thread of saliva descends from her lips. Sister

Fiske, the medic, sits next to the stricken woman. Her chin lifts, her eyes narrow behind magnified glasses. A sharp, disapproving line creases between her brows and her mouth thins, a compassionless look from a woman who frets about the abscesses of cows.

At a nod from Reverend Mother, Fiske rises, accompanies the crying Gabrielle into the stone corridor. The old woman's voice muffles in decrescendo. After a moment, the thin creak of the chapel door reveals their location. And in this room ... silence. Leon stares at her lap. Sister Xavier, our housekeeper, an angular woman with a jaw as square as a box, fingers a soup spoon. She rarely speaks even when conversation is allowed.

Reverend Mother sighs deeply and bows her head. She says, "Why did you doubt?" Stress has made her German accent noticeable. Their shared emotion builds critical mass and penetrates my carefully erected barriers.

Each is deeply, piercingly ashamed.

REVEREND MOTHER RESTRICTS me to the kitchen with my bowl of cooling soup while she conducts a private meeting with the others in the dining room. At the pine counter where Praxades taught me to shape loaves of whole wheat, I force myself to finish my lunch. Food is never wasted. Each tight swallow emphasizes my hurt: grief for the cook and, to my chagrin, the wound of being excluded from the nuns' discussion. I don't belong here, I chide myself. Why should Reverend Mother behave as though I'll stay beyond the spring thaw?

After I eat and feed more coal to the stove, the temptation to eavesdrop wins. I press my ear against the swinging door to the dining room. Not even hushed conversation seeps through the wood. Pushing the door open a crack—my toes still on the kitchen floor so there isn't technical disobedience—I see the five blue bowls on the table, still full. The nuns are gone.

Determined to be a help and to demonstrate a charity I'm not exactly feeling, I busy myself in the pantry, planning dinner. Surveying the shelves, my gaze touches opaque brown vials, medicines that Sister Praxades took on a complicated schedule. The names on the labels don't mean anything to me; once she showed me the collection on her chubby palm, pointing out one for blood pressure, another for cholesterol, and so on.

I pop the cap of one bottle and spill out beautiful azure capsules into my hands. Whatever her medications were supposed to do, they hadn't done their job last night. Sighing, I return the pills to their container and scoop the half-dozen prescriptions into my pocket. Fiske will want these returned to the infirmary.

I decide on tuna casserole, a dish I'm unlikely to ruin. I gather the canned fish, mushroom soup, noodles, and a stale bag of potato chips.

The planks squeak under my thread and I see Praxades of last night, after dinner, sashaying and spinning her robes in exaggerated mockery of Sister Fiske, floorboards complaining under her weight. Mimicry was her gift and no one, myself included, was exempt, but Fiske was the cook's specialty.

At the sink I twist the crank of the opener around the tuna can and indulge the sweet sorrow of memories. Oddly enough, Praxades was liberal while the much younger Fiske was conservative. Praxades wanted a satellite dish and television so she could learn recipes from Julia Child; she wanted a subscription to *Gourmet* magazine, deliverable by bush pilot when weather allowed. In the common room, the arguments between Praxades and Fiske were high entertainment. Fiske struggled to control her indignation, I'll give her that. However, Praxades was a master of provocation. The cook's suggestions would become more and more extreme: the nuns should forgo habits and wear fleece slacks and shirts, the L. L. Bean catalogue had them in black.

Last night the cook's trump card, so to speak, enraged Fiske to unusual heights. Praxades suggested that evenings be passed by rousing games of stud poker, using holy cards as chips. The silent Sister Xavier grinned. Leon always looked happy, as though her features were incapable of any other expression. Fiske sprang to her feet, hands clenched by her sides, her complexion red; she'd flung her book to the floor. She sputtered, "You ... you .. you sacrilegious old fool, you disgusting—"

"Enough," interrupted Reverend Mother, a regal lift to her chin. "Sister Praxades, hold your tongue. Sister Fiske, you allow the cook to bait you every evening. Both of you must learn control and tolerance." However, Reverend Mother's eyes held a glitter of amusement; not, I'm sure, because of Fiske's fury but because of the cook's inane ideas.

Smug satisfaction brightened Praxades's plump face. Fiske retrieved *The Lives of the Saints,* touched the cover to her lips in apology—to the book, which must have been blessed—and returned to her chair, hands trembling. I felt the heat of her hate for the cook, an emotion as searing as any that had touched me in the cities. It is Lent, weeks of sacrifice in preparation for Easter, but she definitely wasn't offering up her aggravation to the Lord, Fiske even lacked the control to school her expression. She darted a withering, mean look at Reverend Mother, then dropped her gaze to her book. Her face was murderous.

The fork in my hand stops scooping out the tuna. An uneasy resonance jingles in my mind. Had Fiske looked surprised at Reverend Mother's dire announcement? I recall only Fiske's disapproving expression over Gabrielle's outburst.

Perhaps Fiske had nothing to be surprised about.

Fiske, while not a physician, plays the part of one by doling out medications. In my habit's pocket, my fingers clutch the containers of pills. No one would know if they had been tampered with. No one, that is, except for Fiske.

No, I think, please. Not here.

Not again.

REVEREND MOTHER IMPOSES an afternoon of silence in memory of the cook. When I enter her office and request permission to speak, she signs, "later." Minutes afterward, swaddled in my anorak, I tromp through the barn, chickens squawking in terror, and exit by the rear door. If Praxades was disoriented by medication, probably Fiske had to lead her outside. Snow squeaks like plastic pellets under my boots. Wind whips up millions of grains as fine as baby powder, shoving me nearly off my feet. My polarized lenses fog. I push the goggles above my eyes with awkward mittens and squint. The body is gone. While I was sequestered in the kitchen, the nuns moved the cook.

The day's dilute glow is muted by dark-bellied clouds, and though I search, crouching near the ground, crabwalking the path, there's no evidence that anyone has been here: not the dead cook, not the nuns, and—as I look at ground near my boots—not even Sister Ellen. The harsh land of winter has wiped away the traces. A spasm of shivering makes my jaw muscles tremble. I straighten. Abruptly a gale whites out the world and my name floats through the whirl: *"Ellen."*

I pivot, pulse galloping, half-expecting to see Praxades levitating from the ground. That movement is a dangerous mistake. The wind increases, howling and spinning drifts, shoving so hard that I stagger. The mad swirl of snow is blinding. Panic shoots through my very core, more invasive than the cold. Which way is the barn? How long have I been out here? Two minutes? Three? Already my fingers are deadened, ice freezing together my eyelashes, narrowing my view to thin, blurry slits.

I must move. My feet stumble, forcing my body against the wind, and again I hear my name, swallowed by the squall, but definitely from my left. If I'm hallucinating, if hypothermia is creating a false call, then I'm dead. I fight, moving to my left for an eternity of seconds; finally arms grab and pull me into the thick smell and chicken cackles of the barn. Violent shivers drop me to my knees on the straw. The door latch clunks closed. My rescuer drags me to the heat of the wood stove.

My gloves are pulled off, then the liners, and my frozen fingers are clasped in hands so warm they burn my flesh. When the ice melts from my lashes, I'm staring into the kind, silent face of Sister Xavier. I know her the least, yet I know this: She will perform extra penance for the sin of breaking silence when she called my name.

IN THE INFIRMARY, I proffer Sister Praxades's medicines. Fiske's cold fingers remove the bottles from my palm.

I speak, violating the imposed quiet. "Why would Sister Praxades go outside?"

The woman is still a moment, studying me, and the intensity of her stare and the knowledge of my scars make my cheeks warm. Then she shrugs, a who-knows gesture. That motion is a lie. I feel her dissembling, controlling body language. She walks across the rough brick floor, twirling her robes in the way that Praxades mocked. For a moment the mirrored cabinet bounces her image at me, then her double swings away as she opens the cabinet. I follow. "The cook was fine last night. What would make her do such a thing?"

Fiske ignores me, reads the label on one vial, and places it on a shelf cabinet. In my cell, under my pallet, is a list of the prescriptions and one pill from each container. Feeble evidence. The thought strikes me that if Fiske decides to remove any other thorn in her side, by persisting like this, I'm making Sister Ellen the next likely target. Fiske's pinched face last night rises to mind, her seething fury at the cook . . . and, now I recall, toward Reverend Mother.

Anger, however, isn't an omen of murder. "What do you think caused her odd behavior?" I ask, observing her profile as she shelves the remaining vials. "The mix of drugs she'd been taking?"

Her lips curl slightly in contempt. This impugning of her medical care prompts her to talk. "Not at all."

During the next pause, I expect her to announce that Praxades was befuddled by a stroke or low blood sugar. Instead, she closes the wall cabinet. I'm careful not to look into the mirror. Fiske says, "Separation from God."

"What?"

"That's what killed your precious Sister Praxades."

She turns in a flair of robes and for a moment a silly picture forms, a ballet of nuns in long black habits. I catch her by the arm. With slow disdain, she rotates her head to fix a dark gaze on my hand. I don't let go. "She . . . you're saying she died from, what, weak faith? *That's* your clinical diagnosis?"

She raises her eyes to meet mine. Behind thick lenses her irises glint as though forged of hard, shiny metal. "No, Sister Ellen. That's my spiritual diagnosis."

Our gazes lock. I almost do the thing that I vowed never to do again under any circumstances: invade the mind of another.

If I forcibly examine her thoughts, she will know. They always knew. The last time I used this accursed ability, I destroyed everyone around me.

Fiske stares, a smirking, superior look. It strikes me that she knows all about me, but that's impossible. Her hands shape the words *Look, Files, Top, Ellen.* With a nod she indicates the tall file cabinet.

I release Fiske. She strides away, footfalls slapping the brick floor, and exits the infirmary. As I look at the file cabinet, my stomach clenches in sudden, inexplicable fear. I, of all people, understand that some things are better left alone. Yet minutes later I have scanned the thick files bearing my name. Everything is there: the *Journal of the American Medical Association* study about a woman with provable telepathy; the Duke University professor's interview in *People* magazine and a photo of me hooked to an EEG machine; the *Newsweek* and *Time* articles about my assisting with various murder investigations nationwide; the *New York Times* report about how Gardini the Magician, a debunker of so-called psychics, finally paid a quarter of a million dollars to a bona fide mindreader.

Dozens of newspaper and magazine articles cover the famous psychic's last murder case: Psychic's Husband and Brother Guilty of Business Partner's Murder. Then the same grainy photograph shows up in report after report: my disfigured features after the men my brother hired attacked me with acid. Long before that, though, everyone I came into contact with was leery of me. And weeks before acid ate away my features, I decided never again to snare thoughts from another's mind. After plastic surgeons had done the best they could with flesh that scarred so badly, I sought anonymity, a location where my history and notoriety might be unknown, where I might find, if not peace, at least isolation.

I thought that the nuns hadn't questioned me about my past or my scars due to their otherworldliness. Now I see that they had no need to interview me.

I stand in front of the infirmary mirror, holding the heavy file and gazing at my wretched reflection.

DURING DINNER, while heads bend over a surprisingly tasty tuna casserole, first Leon, then Reverend Mother read passages from the Bible. Dinners are a time to fortify our bodies and our spirits. Reverend Mother, now at the podium, chooses the verses describing Jesus walking on the sea. The expressions of Leon, Xavier, Reverend Mother, and Gabrielle—especially Gabrielle—are serious and downcast. Fiske, to my eye, appears artificially solemn. I swallow a second helping of casserole, eager for the meal to end so that I can interrogate Leon over the dishes. After a minute, the only sound of fork against plate is my own. I look up. Fiske, Xavier, Gabrielle, and Leon are rapt with attention on Reverend Mother. She reads:

"But when he saw that the wind was boisterous, he was afraid; and beginning to sink he cried out, saying, 'Lord, save me!'

"And immediately Jesus stretched out His hand and caught him, and said to him, 'O you of little faith, why did you doubt?' "

Reverend Mother closes the Bible, kisses the gold-embossed cover, and returns to her place at the table. Everyone resumes eating, but something has happened which I've missed. The heavy cloud of their mood has lifted. On a psychological level, the dim dining room is bright.

IN THE CAVERN, Leon and I wear headlamps to light our way to the spring. The earth-generated heat keeps the temperatures from dropping below fifty, yet the high humidity is chilling. The damp mist blurs her shape and when our buckets accidentally clang together as we walk, my pulse jumps. She appears comfortable with how the cook died. She explains that Sister Praxades was moved to a mining shaft north of the barn. After leaving the corpse, they barricaded the entrance. When the ground thaws and, with the approval of the medical examiner—from two-hundred-mile-away Lygon—and Praxades' relatives, a burial plot will be prepared. Until then, her body will remain frozen and will be safe from the occasional arctic fox.

Her chipper tone nonpluses me. She might be discussing the disposal of the goat. We reach the pool and kneel down to draw water. I ask, "Why can't we have a memorial service now?"

"To mourn her would be to question God's will."

I set my full bucket down impatiently; water sloshes over the lip. "Leon, *talk* to me."

The desperation in my voice must have moved her. She sets her pail next to mine and says, "Of course I miss Sister Praxades. She brought this place alive. She made us laugh." Through the steam I see her grin. "Well, everyone except Sister Fiske," Leon amends. "Ellen, look at it this way. If you died, would you want those you love to feel grief, to suffer over losing you?"

I wouldn't. Still, I'm troubled by the acceptance of the cook's death. Even the elderly Gabrielle appears adjusted to her friend's absence, though perhaps that's not true. She might be numb with grief.

Leon places her hand on my shoulder. In the steam, her headlamp creates a bright halo. "Perhaps it's easier for us. Our beliefs treat death as a natural part of the soul's journey. It wouldn't make sense for us to behave as though Sister Praxades is gone forever."

I wish I believed in the immortality of the soul. "What if Fiske messed with Praxades's medication?"

Leon is quiet a moment. I know I've surprised her. "I guarantee that Sister Fiske is innocent of everything except anger. She's devoted to safeguarding our health, not endangering it."

Leon could probably find good in Judas. We trudge back through the tunnel toward the living quarters. An aura radiates from her, and in that aura three words ring over and over: JesusMaryJoseph.

*   *   *

I ASSUME THE DUTIES of the cook, though joy has evaporated for me. The others appear inexplicably cheered, except for Reverend Mother, who wears a preoccupied expression as though straining to hear a faint voice just beyond the audible range. A snowstorm blankets the grounds with one foot, then two feet of powder. I watch Fiske, who ignores me. The weather rages and we turn inward; the times of silence are natural for them. This spiritual hibernation makes me edgy, though my bread-baking improves. Two days pass.

On the third morning, Gabrielle vanishes.

I SLEEP. I wake with a start, furious with my failed vigil. Today Leon, Xavier, and I search outside for Gabrielle, but our efforts were thwarted by the storm's bluster. She disappeared in the night, like Praxades. The spirits of the nuns are visibly leadened, even Fiske's. My mind is groggy; confused speculations stick in my skull. Why is everyone so resigned about Praxades, now Gabrielle? Why does Reverend Mother appear fatigued? She walks hesitantly, as if movement is an effort. Is Fiske poisoning Reverend Mother? Has Fiske killed Gabrielle?

A distant sound travels from the corridor. I sit up. Was that the timbers creaking? I toss off the comforter; chill seeps through my habit, cold slipping like spiders under the thermal underwear. In a few seconds I light the hurricane lamp, pull on my insulated boots, and tiptoe into the dark hall. All but one of the cell doors are closed. I peer into that room and my candlelight glows to an empty pallet. Seeing the tidy vacant room is a blow. I run to the kitchen, the dining room, the infirmary, the sitting room, the chapel, my search as fruitless as I feared. At the entryway door, I yank on anorak, gloves, cap and let myself out into the clear, breezy night, the cold so sharp my lungs inhale reflexively with the shock. It is always like this after a storm, as though fierce weather hones winter to better express its nature. The northerly has swept the entryway clear of all but a half-foot of powder, though drifts smooth the side wall clear up to the eaves. I round the building and find wind and deep snow . . . and heartache.

A figure glows in the frosty moonlight, skin gleaming whitely, a wide sweep of black and jiggling buttocks. "Leon!" I cry. She turns, a statue of salt, merging into the colorless world except for dark thatches of hair at crotch and head. My boots sink deep into the fresh powder as I struggle to her side.

"Please don't worry," Leon said. "I have faith." Syllables slur from frozen lips. "I'm getting warmer. My feet—"

"Leon, for the love of God, *please.*" Unshed tears chill my eyes. "You're not getting warmer. You're freezing."

My own face is ice. My stiff fingers won't grip. I loop my arm under hers and guide her toward the building. She resists; her red-lashed eyes blink sleepily under the narcotic of hypothermia.

"Damn you, Leon, *walk.*"

Her pale mouth opens in a semblance of a smile, the muscles of her jaw stiff with cold. "I'm walking, Ellen," she mumbles. "I'll come back. Reverend Mother did." Her arm slips like mist from mine and she stumbles away, wading through fresh snow, moving with speed I wouldn't have thought possible. But she is numb. My legs drag through thigh-deep drifts and, trailing her, I fall, flounder deep in powdery whiteness. My freezing arms thrash for purchase in a substance as unstable as flour. Snow blankets my vision. I regain my footing, breathing hard, brushing ice from my face. Every muscle trembles so violently, my body straining to produce heat, that I can barely stand. I am alone in a landscape as pale and barren as the moon, and I suddenly understand who the murderer is.

I RACE THROUGH the corridor to Reverend Mother's room and enter without knocking, throat parched from cold and panic. A single candle flickers from the floor. Reverend Mother lies on her bed in full habit, fingers laced at her waist, thick black socks on her feet. The down comforter and blankets have been kicked to the floor. I lean over her. "I don't know what rot you've been telling these women, but Leon's out there and you're going to help me get her inside. If she hears you calling, she'll come in." Part of me says it's already too late for Leon, but I can't listen to that.

Reverend Mother stares at me, eyes glittering as though a fire blazes inside her skull. "It's Lent. The Lord calls her. She's being tested."

I pull her to a sitting position and her heat radiates like a furnace. Fever has glossed her skin with perspiration. "This is not Christ asking the apostles to walk on water, damn it. This is Alaska and she'll die out there. No one can survive that cold."

Her hands clutch my shoulders with a frenzied strength. "I did."

An odor pierces my hysteria, a fetid smell. It isn't a chamberpot stink, but a scent of putrefaction and decay. With horror, I look at her feet, which she suddenly tucks under her skirts, a childlike gesture. I pull back the material. She isn't wearing thick, dark socks; frost-bitten toes and heels have swelled, rotted, and blackened. I slide up the polypro of her long underwear. Dark streaks on the calves disappear under the fabric, infection spreading toward her groin. Sickened, I cover her legs. Reverend Mother lies back against her pallet, and whispers a few words in German, the gist of which I understand. "Yes," I nod sadly, "you have faith."

*   *   *

THE PILOT AND I haven't spoken. I'm his only passenger and wear heavy, insulated ear muffs to dull the engine noise; conversation is impossible. I'm also wearing a thin gauze mask that Sister Xavier fashioned at my request before I left the cloister. The pilot didn't ask about it. He probably thinks the mask is a religious garment. Below us is Anchorage, refreshingly green in its springtime mantle.

Xavier and I hunted but never found Leon's body. We speculated that she must have entered an abandoned mine shaft. After the start of the thaw, I found Gabrielle not far from the tunnel where the others had barricaded Praxades, and where we had entombed the corpse of Reverend Mother. I spent the last four months meditating on my own considerable responsibility in these terrible deaths. At first I raged at the twisted beliefs that corralled this small, insular society into suicidal behaviors. After talking awhile with Fiske and Xavier, though, I saw that I could have played a part in bringing a sort of heathen reasoning to their lives. However, my goal was self-protection and isolation, not involvement. Perversely, I managed to neither protect myself nor remain uninvolved. Guilt will always reside within me, a hard, frozen shard of northern Alaska.

After the pilot lands, I step down from the plane, pull the mask below my chin, and walk toward the terminal.

Travelers at the airport stare, but I've taken a gift—and a lesson—from my months in the cloister. In my soul spreads a vast emptiness, images and ideas bright stars with light-years of distance in between.

Ian Rankin's last appearance with us was in *The Year's 25 Finest Crime & Mystery Stories,* Fourth Annual Edition. Usually his novels and stories center around John Rebus, a Scottish police inspector, and are becoming increasingly more popular, having been translated into Italian and Japanese. However, he doesn't need to rely on a series character to write gripping, tightly plotted mysteries. "Principles of Accounts" is a fine example.

Principles of Accounts
IAN RANKIN

It began as a hobby.

But then quite quickly the hobby became a career, and now he was a professional, taking a professional's care in the details of his craft. True, something had been lost; that was the trouble when a hobby became mere business. But at least he had the consolation of knowing that business was good. He saw himself as a value assessor. He assessed the value of an item, then collected on it, the money being insurance against loss. He had always been good at accounts, economics, business studies. He loved those subjects at school, hardly believing the sheer thrill of balancing books. The sums *always came out the same,* either side of the thick vertical centre line. He used similar skills now when assessing each item: value of item balanced against risk involved.

Not that he ever damaged an item. It hadn't been necessary so far. But he was very good at pretending he would damage them. He could reduce tough fathers to pleas and weeping, and all via the telephone. The telephone was his friend—not any one particular telephone, but *all* phones, spread across the country in a matrix of elegantly anonymous paybooths. He made a point of spending not more than a minute in each phone box he used, timing each call. Single-mindedness was his real strength. Determination of purpose. The sixty-second calls had become his trademark. People knew when they were dealing with the Minute Man.

The media, who had coined the nickname, they too were his friends, stirring up fear, building him into a figure of terror. He rewarded them with increased circulation and viewing figures, while the police held increasingly ineffectual press conferences requesting information, playing tapes they'd made of his voices.

He used several voices, none his own. He hadn't spoken more than six words to any of his four young items, and even then had disguised his voice. Actually, he'd used more than six words with the last one, the one whose value now sat before him on the table. She had been a talker, a good talker, too. She'd recited stories and anecdotes—even when she couldn't be sure he was there. Occasionally he'd asked a question, something to help him get the story straight in his mind. She had given him her stories, and now her father had given him all this money.

Tonight, with an open bottle of cheapish Australian Chardonnay on the floor beside his chair, with his belly full from the meal he'd eaten at the Indian on the High Street, tonight was for reflection. At the top of the hour, he hit the remote to catch the Channel 4 news and saw with some pride that he was the main story. Or rather, the item was.

She blinked a lot. Nervousness, or perhaps the glare of the lights and flashguns. Her hair had been washed, but she wore no makeup, and her face looked pale. She had lost a little weight, her own fault for not eating everything he'd given her.

She'd worked out pretty quickly—they usually did—that the food was laced with tranqs, crushed-up sleeping pills. But like the others, she'd given in and eaten anyway. Sensible, when the only other alternative was force-feeding by rubber tube and plastic funnel.

She stayed onscreen only half a minute, refusing to answer the yelled questions. Now she was replaced by a policeman. A captain appeared along the bottom of the screen: Ch. Supt. Thomas Lancaster. Ah yes, Tom Lancaster. He raised his glass, toasting his adversary, even though the police's inefficiency was a constant source of irritation to him.

"... and I must praise Miss Webster's calm and her bravery," Lancaster was saying. "After her release, she was able to help us compile this composite photograph of her kidnapper."

He put down his glass. The photo was onscreen now.

"The man we're looking for is five feet seven or eight, stocky, with blue eyes. As you can see, he has a round face, full lips, and thick, slightly curly hair, either black or very dark brown."

He whooped. He got up and danced. She'd never set eyes on him! He never allowed his items the luxury. He looked at himself in the mirror. He was six feet tall, certainly not stocky. He had brown eyes, short, straight, light-brown hair. Full lips? No. Round face? No. She'd given the police a wholly fictitious account. Tomorrow the photo would be in every newspaper, pinned up outside every police station. This was better than he could ever have imagined. . . .

But why had she done it? What was she playing at? He didn't like puzzles, didn't like it when the accounts failed to balance at the bottom. He switched off the TV and put aside his wine. One thing was obvious: She didn't want him caught. Only two people could be certain her description was a fiction: the item, and the Minute Man. He was still deep in thought when ten o'clock came round. He switched on the TV news again, and was thrown into fresh confusion.

"There has been an arrest tonight after the latest Minute Man kidnap victim was released."

Sitting up, he kicked over the wine bottle. It poured out its contents unchecked.

"A man, believed to be a business acquaintance of Gillian Webster's father, has been taken to Castle Lane police station for questioning. We now go over live to Castle Lane, where Martin Brockman is waiting to speak to us. Martin, any more details?"

Now the reporter was on the screen, looking cold against a damp nighttime street, headlamps flashing past him. He wore a sheepskin coat and had one hand pressed to his ear, holding in place the earphone. He began to speak.

"All police will say is that a man is being questioned in connection with the kidnapping of Gillian Webster, who was released unharmed this morning. There's no word yet of whether or not the man will be asked to take part in an identity parade, but rumour has it that the man police are questioning is actually *known* to Miss Webster's father, the millionaire Duncan Webster, and that it was Mr. Webster himself who first noticed the resemblance between the photofit and the man police are currently questioning."

"Let's get this right, Martin, you're saying Mr. Webster *identified* his daughter's kidnapper?"

"I don't think we can go that far just yet, but . . ."

But he had switched off the television.

"What's your game, little Gillian?" he said quietly. "Your game . . . or your father's?" He felt dizzy, confused. There had to be a reason for all of this. The wine was thumping in his head.

"I hate puzzles!" he yelled at the blank TV screen. "I hate puzzles!"

IN CASTLE LANE POLICE STATION, Chief Superintendent Tom Lancaster was about to get some sleep. He'd phoned his wife to explain that he wouldn't be home. He kept a fresh suit, shirt, and tie in the office anyway, and now there was a camp bed there too, with an army-quality sleeping bag. Nothing to the comforts of home, but it would have to do. Tomorrow might be even busier than today. He was comforted to know that the press weren't going home either. Some had crawled off to hotels and boardinghouses, but others were camping out in cars and vans outside the station.

Lancaster slipped off his clothes and into the chilled sleeping bag. He wriggled for a few seconds, getting warm, then reached to the floor, where several bulging files lay. The transcript of Gillian Webster's conversations with the Minute Man had been typed up. He read through them again. It was one-way traffic. The Minute Man had said only a couple of dozen words, mostly in the form of abrupt questions.

His second victim, Elaine Chatham, had managed a longer utterance from him. She'd asked if she could have a book of crosswords to pass the time. She'd kept on asking until she'd forced from him a gruff confession (in his Geordie accent this time). Three important little words. Tom Lancaster whispered them to himself.

" 'I hate puzzles.' "

Then, smiling, he reached for the anglepoise and turned off the light.

IT WAS NEARLY MIDDAY when Mrs. Angelo heard the bell tinkling at the front desk.

"Coming!" she called, trying to sound calm. Her husband, Tony, should have been helping her, but he had the flu and was upstairs asleep. It was his third bout of flu this year; he never wanted the doctor called in. The man standing at the desk carried a sports holdall and a sheaf of the morning papers. He wore a new-smelling sheepskin jacket and a harassed grin.

"I'd like a room, please," he announced.

"Just the one night, is it?"

"Well . . ."

"You're a journalist," Mrs. Angelo stated. "You're reporting on that kidnapping, and you don't know how long you'll need the room. Am I right?"

"You could write our astrology column."

She checked the rack of room keys on the wall. "Number 6 has a wash basin, or there's number 11, but it doesn't. Those are the only two I've got." She turned to him. "We're busy all of a sudden."

"You've already got reporters staying?"

"One's been here all the way through, the others moved in yesterday. And I've a very nice cameraman and soundman from the BBC, only they complain because *their* reporter is in some posh hotel. I told them, posh just means expensive. Number six or number eleven?"

"Six, please."

"Only the best, eh? I dare say you're on expenses." She unhooked the key, then swivelled the register around for him to sign. "So which paper are you from?"

He didn't look up from his writing. "I'm freelance. A few magazines are interested, so I thought I'd . . . you know."

She swivelled the register back towards her. "Well, Mr. Beattie, let's hope you get your story, eh?"

"Yes," he agreed, taking the key from her warm, damp fingers. "Let's hope."

HE THREW THE PAPERS ONTO THE FLOOR beside the single bed. The mattress was softer than he liked, but the room was clean and fresh. It worried him that there were other reporters here. He didn't want them asking him questions. He unzipped the holdall, taking his Gillian Webster case notes from it. Included in the file was a packet of black and white photographs he'd taken during the weeks leading up to the snatch. He looked through them again.

The Websters lived in a large detached house set in a few acres of rambling grounds. He'd gone out there one Sunday with his camera. He'd been out that way several times before in his car, stopping once with engine trouble near the house. About a hundred yards from the house there was a clump of bushes and saplings, big enough for him to hide in. On that particular Sunday, he'd taken his very best zoom lenses for the Canon camera. Then he went strolling with camera and binoculars and a bird identification book.

What he hadn't expected was that Gillian Webster would not be home. He also had not expected the Websters to be entertaining. They'd invited a dozen or so people for late-afternoon drinks. He was lucky the weather was cool: Nobody seemed inclined to wander down into the garden towards where he was hiding. But a verandah ran the length of the back of the house, and some of the guests wandered out onto it; so, occasionally, did the host and hostess. He shot off a single roll of film, concentrating on Webster and his wife. She was younger than her husband by at least ten years; even so, she was showing her age. The skin sagged from her face and neck, and her short blonde hair looked brittle.

Lying on the bed, he paused at one particular photograph. A man had been standing alone on the verandah, then had been joined by Mrs. Webster. It looked as though she were greeting the man. They were kissing. The man, who was holding a champagne flute, held Mrs. Webster's arm with his free hand, drawing her towards him. The kiss was no perfunctory peck. Their lips met, were maybe even parted. The kiss had seemed to last quite a while. He searched through the other photos for a better one of the man. Yes, here he was with Mr. Webster and another guest. They looked serious, as though discussing business. The man was caught face-on. He was shorter than Webster, heavily built, with dark wavy hair just covering his ears. Early on in the party, he had loosened his tie and shirt collar. Did he merely look serious in this photo, or did he looked worried? There were dark bags under his eyes. . . .

He lifted a newspaper and stared at the photofit police had issued, the one made up from Gillian Webster's description. It was the guest from the party. He was sure of that.

THE LOCAL RADIO STATION had set up a van in the police station car park, with a tell antenna flexing from its roof. It looked as though the journalists had been made to move into the car park. Probably their cars had been holding up traffic in Castle Lane. As he arrived, they were milling around, drinking beakers of tea, talking into portable phones, reading from sheets of paper.

He looked around. One young man stood apart from the others. He looked shy and uncomfortable, and was wearing cheap clothes. There were spots around his mouth and on his neck, and he kept pushing slippery glasses back up his nose as he read from his own sheets of paper, glancing up from time to time to see what the other journalists were doing.

He was perfect.

"Local are you, chief?"

The young man looked up in surprise at the man with the southeast accent, the man wearing the expensive jacket.

"Sorry?"

"You look like the local press."

The young man twitched. "I'm from the *Post.*"

"Thought so." The sheets of paper were plucked from the young man's hands. They detailed the morning's media briefing. There would be a conference at three o'clock, and another at seven. Otherwise, the only news was that the man they'd been questioning was to be held for another twenty-four hours.

"What do you think, chief?" The young man looked dazed. "Come on, you can tell Uncle Des."

"There's not much *to* think."

He wrinkled his nose, folding the press release and shoving it into the young man's anorak pocket. "Don't give me that. That's the *official* line, but this is between you and me. You're *local,* my son, you've got the edge on all of us." He nodded towards the scattering of journalists, none of whom was taking any notice of this conversation.

"Who are you?"

"I thought I told you, Des Beattie."

"Beattie?"

"How long have you been in this game, son?" He shook his head sadly. "The Ripper case, I covered it for the *Telegraph.* Freelance now, of course. I can pick and choose my crime stories. A *certain magazine* has asked me to see if there's an angle in all this." He looked the young man up and down. "You might be in for half the byline. Could be your ticket out of here, chief. We all had to start somewhere."

"Stefan's my name, Stefan Duniec."

"Pleased to meet you, Stefan." They shook hands. "What's that, Russian is it?"

"Polish."

"Well, I'm Des Beattie and I'm from Walthamstow. Only I live in Docklands now." He winked. "Handy for the newspaper officers. So what've you got?"

"Well . . ." Duniec looked around. "It's not really *my* idea . . ." Beattie shrugged this aside. There was no copyright on news. "But' I've heard that someone's got a name."

"For the sod they're questioning?" Duniec nodded. Beattie seemed thoughtful. "Maybe it'll tie in with my own ideas. What's the name, Stefan?"

"Bernard Cooke."

Beattie nodded slowly. "Bernie Cooke. The businessman, right?"

Now Duniec nodded. "Does it tie in?"

Beattie puckered his mouth. "Might well do. I need to check a few facts first."

"I could help." The kid was keen all right. He didn't want to wear that anorak forever. Beattie patted his shoulder.

"Stick around here, Stefan. Keep your ears open. I'll go make a couple of calls." Duniec glanced down at the large pockets of Beattie's sheepskin. Beattie grinned. "We can't all afford cell phones. Meantime . . ." He nodded towards the other reporters. "You might try writing this up. You know, something wry about the long wait. Eight hundred words, who knows, there's always a market for filler. The Sundays are nothing but filler these days."

"Eight hundred?"

Beattie nodded, then reconsidered. "Seven-fifty," he said, heading out of the car park.

A SMALL ENGINEERING WORKS on a purpose-built estate.

A helpful sign at the site entrance told him he was looking for Unit 32, Cooke Engineering Ltd. He drove his rented Fiesta slowly through the narrow winding roads, giving way to lorries and delivery vans. Half a dozen cars were parked outside Unit 32 in tightly marked bays. The building was grey corrugated steel, shared by two companies. Unit 31 manufactured frozen foods. Driving past it, he sized up Unit 32. There was a door which would lead to the reception area or offices, and a loading bay door near it. Both were closed. Parked in the loading bay was a sporty Ford Sierra, one of the custom jobs. In the driver's seat, a man was talking on a car phone. In the back seat were two more large pasty-faced men. They looked like reporters. Well, if a dolt like Duniec knew about Cooke, the professionals would know too. And though Cooke himself wasn't here, though he was sweating and dog-tired in one of Castle Lane's interview rooms, a team had been sent to stake the place out.

He gnawed at his bottom lip, and decided to take a calculated risk. He drove to the next lot of units, parked, and walked back towards Cooke Engineering. The door he was approaching, having ignored the carful of staring eyes, had OFFICE printed on it. He knocked and entered, closing the door behind him. He'd expected noise: After all, only a partition wall separated this part of the unit from the actual production line. But there was silence, punctuated by the slow clack of fingers on a word processor keyboard.

"Can I help you?" She sat behind a desk, but also behind huge red-rimmed spectacles, which magnified her already large eyes. Her tone was hardly welcoming.

"Mr. Cooke?" he said nervously. "Wondered if I could have a—"

"Do you have an appointment?"

"No, well I . . ."

"Are you a reporter?" She examined him, hunched over as he was, shuffling and twitching and awkward. "You don't look like one." She sighed. "No cold calling, reps by appointment only. I take it you *are* a rep?"

"Well, as it happens I—"

"Sorry," she said, seeming to take pity on this particularly pitiful example of an unlovely breed. "Mr. Cooke's not here anyway."

He looked around. "Place looks dead."

"Dead about sums it up."

"Business bad?"

"Let's just say you shouldn't look for too many orders."

"Ah . . ." He seemed to think of something. "But the cars outside . . . ?"

"We let the guys from the frozen-food place park their excess cars there."

"Oh dear." He nodded towards where he assumed the production line would be, just through the wall. "Then you're not . . . ?"

"We're not producing. So unless you're selling jobs in the light engineering sector, I shouldn't bother."

He smiled. "But you're still here."

"Only till the weekend. No pay by Friday, I'm off." She went back to her typing, her fingers hammering the keys.

He turned to leave, his back and shoulders more hunched than ever. Then he stopped and half-turned. "What made you think I was a reporter?"

"You'll read about it."

Only after he'd gone did she pause in her work. She'd seen them all in her time, all the types of rep you could imagine. But she'd never come across one who didn't even bother to bring samples with him. . . .

ACROSS FROM THE INDUSTRIAL ESTATE was a recently built pub, doubtless put there by a canny brewing concern who knew there would be plenty of clients from an estate of eighty-odd units.

"That was the idea anyway," the barman admitted, pouring a pint of beer, "before times got hard. What gets me is that none of these *financial projections*—" he said the words with distaste "—ever *projected* hard times ahead. And let me tell you, there's no money-back guarantee with these things." He had handed over the drink, received a five-pound note, and now pressed a key on the till.

"Accountants aren't all bad," said the customer.

As the barman handed over the change, the customer asked a question. "Does a man called Bernard Cooke drink in here?"

There was a snort from further down the bar, where a man on a stool was doing the crossword in the local paper.

"Why do you ask?" asked the barman.

"I was supposed to be seeing him today. Drove all the way down from bloody Lancaster." The barman didn't seem about to doubt his northwest accent. "Only there's no bugger about except some right rough types in a car parked outside."

"Reporters," said the crossword solver.

"Oh aye?"

"You won't be seeing Cooke for a while." The crossword solver tipped back the dregs of a half-pint.

"We don't know that," snapped the barman. "Don't go jumping to bloody conclusions, Arthur."

Arthur merely shrugged in compliance, staring down at his paper.

"He's in trouble, is he?" asked the traveller.

"Maybe."

"Bang goes my bloody contract."

"You're lucky, then," said Arthur.

"How do you mean?" He nodded towards the empty glass. "Get you another?"

"Thanks, I will."

The barman refilled the glass, but wouldn't take one himself. Arthur sipped and swallowed. "I mean," he said at last, "Bernie's been in trouble for yonks, money trouble. Chances are, if you were buying from him, you wouldn't have got what you ordered, and if you were selling, you wouldn't have seen the money."

"Thanks for the tip."

"I've known for months he was in trouble. Used to be, he'd nip in here Friday lunchtime for something to eat and a couple of brandies. Then it got to be twice a week and four brandies, and three times a week and six. Somebody drinks like that, it's not because they're flush, it's that they're worried."

"I know what you mean."

"All *I* know," chipped in the barman, "is that he always paid . . . and that's more than some."

Arthur winked at Beattie. "That's a dig at me."

Beattie finished his drink and eased himself off the barstool.

"Back to Lancaster?"

He shook his head. "Couple more calls first."

After he'd gone, the bar was silent a few moments, then Arthur cleared his throat.

"What do you think?"

"Well," said the barman, "he wasn't a reporter. I'm not even sure he's in business."

"How do you make that out?"

"No expense account—didn't ask for a receipt for the drinks."

"Maybe he doesn't need receipts, Sherlock."

"Maybe." The barman lifted away the empty glass and washed it, placing it on the rack to dry. Then he wiped the bartop where the man had been sitting, and put down a fresh beermat. Now there was no sign anyone had ever been there.

"Just be a second," the barman told Arthur. Then he disappeared into the alcove where the telephone was kept.

At THREE-FORTY, the journalists slouched out of the press room carrying the latest news release. They were talkative, if they weren't too busy drawing in cigarette smoke. Some were making calls on their telephones, or going off to their cars to make calls. They squeezed from the police station's double doors and fanned out across the car park. A camera unit had been readied for the TV reporter called Martin Brockman, who was now checking his script while a makeup girl tried to get his hair to stop flying into a vertical peak every time a gust blew.

Stefan Duniec walked slowly across the car park, not heading towards his car—he did not have a car—but just keeping moving, so he looked as busy and important as the other reporters. He was staring down at his notebook and didn't notice the figure blocking his way until he'd practically bumped into it.

"Hello, Mr. Beattie, you missed the conference."

"Couldn't be helped, Stef. Anything to report?"

"I got you a copy of the press release."

"Good lad." Beattie started to read from the two stapled sheets. Gillian Webster, he read, had now given a description of the room she'd been kept in during her "ten-day ordeal." Not so much a room, more a cupboard, kept in darkness. She could hear distant traffic, as though heavy lorries were passing outside. But she was tied up, mouth taped shut, and couldn't cry out.

Beattie read it again. Well, it was true he'd kept her mouth taped shut occasionally, but everything else was a fabrication, another false account.

"Interesting," he said. "Are they still questioning Cooke?" Duniec nodded. "And I suppose they'll be giving his factory the once-over?"

"How do you mean?"

"Stands to reason, Stef. This cupboard could be in Cooke's factory. I've just come from there. He's been laying off staff. The only person left is a secretary, and I doubt she goes anywhere near the shop floor— she might get her hands mucky." He glanced again at the paper. "Lorries going past . . . sounds just like an industrial estate."

"I suppose it does," Duniec said quietly.

"And if he's been laying off men, what does that tell you?"

"His company's in trouble."

"Dead right. So tell me, young Stef, is Cooke wealthy or skint?"

"Skint, I suppose."

"And desperate."

"So he kidnaps someone he knows. . . . How could he hope to get away with it?"

"All we know is that he knew the parents; we don't know Gillian knew him."

"But he let her see him," Duniec protested. "He must've known she'd give a description—that her father would see it. . . ."

Beattie nodded. Precisely. That was just one of the flaws. Would Cooke really have kept her in his factory, with someone else on the premises all day? How could he feed Gillian without the secretary becoming suspicious? Gillian's story was badly flawed. But Beattie wondered if the police would see that. *He* could see what Gillian Webster was doing, and how she was doing it. He just couldn't account for the why. But he had an idea now, a good idea. He only needed to study the photographs again.

Meantime, Stefan had obviously been considering all the flaws too.

"Like you say, he must have been desperate."

"He was desperate all right, he just wasn't very bright." He tapped Duniec's shoulder with the rolled-up press release. "I'll see you later." He winked. "Remember the byline."

"And the seventy-five words!" Duniec called after him. "I've already made a start!"

Without looking back, Beattie gave a raised thumbs-up. Duniec watched till he was out of sight, then turned back towards the reporters' cars. Three men were in a huddle next to a red Porsche.

"Excuse me," he said, interrupting them. One man, the one with a proprietorial hand resting on the Porsche's roof, spoke for all of them.

"What is it?"

"You're Terry Greig, aren't you?"

Greig puffed out his chest. Of course he was Terry Greig, king of the tabloid newsroom, scourge of copy-takers. And here was another tyro looking to make his acquaintance.

"What can I do for you, lad?"

Duniec didn't like that "lad," but like Beattie's "Stef" he let it lie. "Did you see that man I was talking to?" he asked instead. "In the sheepskin jacket?"

Greig nodded. Little escaped him. "I saw him earlier," he confirmed.

"Right," said Duniec. "And have you seen him before? I mean, do you know who he is?"

"Don't know him from Adam. Football manager, is he? Third Division? They're the only buggers would wear a coat like that."

"Except for Brockman," added one of the other reporters.

"Except for old Brockie," Greig agreed. Then they all laughed, all except Stefan Duniec. When the laughter had died and they were waiting for him to leave, he turned his gaze once more to Greig.

"He wrote up the Ripper case for the *Telegraph.*"

"No he didn't, not unless he meant the *Belfast Telegraph.*" They all laughed again. Even Duniec's lips were bent slightly in what might have passed for a smile.

"What's it all about, lad?" asked Greig.

"Could we step inside the station, sir?" Duniec said. To anyone standing within earshot, it didn't sound much like a question. . . .

THE MAN WHO called himself Des Beattie was packing his bag.

He tore the ring-pull from another can of McEwan's and gulped from the can. The photographs were lying on the bed. He paused in his packing and studied the photos again. Cooke with Duncan Webster. Cooke with Mrs. Webster. Cooke looking *very* comfortable with Mrs. Webster. Cooke looking *extremely* uncomfortable with Duncan Webster, looking like maybe he owned the man money, money he couldn't hope to repay. But that wasn't Cooke's problem. No, Cooke's problem was the wife. Look at the two of them: touching, kissing. With Mr. Webster, Cooke looked more like a business acquaintance than anything; but with Mrs. Webster he looked like a very close friend indeed.

Whether Webster knew or not, he couldn't tell. But the daughter had known. Gillian Webster had found out about Cooke and her mother, about their affair. Christ, and she was Daddy's little daughter, wasn't she? When she'd spoken to him of her home life, hoping to ingratiate herself, hoping he wouldn't harm someone he knew as a *real person* rather than an item (yes, she'd been clever all right), when she had done this, she had spoken always of her father first, her mother second. Daddy, Daddy, Daddy: It had always been Daddy. While Mother had remained just that: "Mother."

All those hours she'd been alone, those hours with little to do but struggle against her bonds, little to think about but . . . but how to turn this little adventure to her own advantage. She would set up Bernard Cooke. She must have known his company was in trouble, giving him the motive. Who would suspect she'd lie about something like this? No one, no one would know excepting three people: Cooke himself, the mother, and the real kidnapper. Cooke would protest his innocence, but it was his word against Gillian's. Mrs. Webster . . . what would *she* say without revealing the extent of her ties to Cooke? And as for the kidnapper . . . well, was he going to come forward to help Cooke? Of course not!

It was true, wasn't it? He wasn't going to do anything. He was going to leave this town and never return. With Cooke inside, the heat would be off, the police would stop checking airports and seaports. Yes, a foreign holiday, somewhere sunny and dry, not like this cold miserable island where he worked. He could stop by a travel agent's tomorrow. On the plane out, he'd order champagne and drink to poor Bernard Cooke.

That was that.

He opened another can and picked up the photo, the one of Cooke and Mrs. Webster kissing. The more he looked at it, the more he saw that he could be wrong. What if it *was* just a friendly kiss? These types, types like Mrs. Webster, they could get overfamiliar. What if it had nothing to do with the mother? What if . . . what if it had to do with *Gillian* instead? She'd told him, "Daddy doesn't like it when I bring home older men." Could there have been something between Gillian and Bernard Cooke? Maybe he'd broken it off and she was out for his blood. . . .

Wait, think a bit. If Cooke was single, it wouldn't work. It only worked if he was married and had to hide the relationship. His head began spinning, and he tried to stand up. How could he be sure? How could he be sure that Cooke and Mrs. Webster or Cooke and Gillian had been an item?

He caught that word "item" and smiled. If they'd been an item, people would have seen them together, somewhere they felt safe from Mr. Webster. Maybe that was why Cooke started using the pub across from the estate more often; nothing to do with his financial troubles. It should be easy enough to check. He'd go there now, on his way out of town. He thought of Stefan Duniec. Stefan, who probably wasn't fit to report on a flower show, never mind a police inquiry. There were some real thick bastards in the world, when you thought about it.

Jesus, weren't there just.

IT WAS FIVE O'LOCK when he walked into the bar. As he'd hoped, the shift had changed. The barman was new. What's more, Arthur had moved on. Good: They'd have thought it more than a little off, the Lancastrian returning to ask questions about Cooke and some woman.

The beer he'd drunk in his room had given him a taste, so he ordered a double Armagnac with a half of lager to chase it down. Fuel for the long drive ahead. The bar was medium-busy with workers on their way home from the estate. He sat on the same stool as earlier, and made a show of checking his watch and keeping an eye on the door.

"Waiting on someone?" the new barman dutifully asked.

"Bernard Cooke. I thought we arranged to meet at five."

The barman tried the name. "Don't think I know him."

"He's a lunchtime regular."

"I never do lunchtime."

He nodded miserably and finished the Armagnac. It burned him all the way down. One last time then: "He usually has a woman with him, a bit of posh."

The barman shrugged and went back to wiping glasses.

"Thanks anyway." He finished the lager and had another idea. It was a bit late, but worth a try. As he pushed open the door to the outside world, he met resistance. It was Arthur, coming in. Arthur looked surprised. Beattie switched to a northwest accent.

"Hello, Arthur."

"Thought you were off to the wide blue yonder."

"Just heading back now. I've been hearing Cooke has a fancy piece." He winked. "That's an expensive hobby, no wonder he's gone broke."

Arthur just stared, as though listening to a ghost. There was almost . . . it wasn't shock, it was more like *fear* in his eyes.

Beattie persisted. "Nice looker, by the sound of her."

"Eh?"

"They used to come in here."

"Did they?"

Was the man pissed? Maybe those crosswords had addled his brain. Beattie felt good and mellow.

"Never mind," he said. "See you around."

Arthur seemed to perk up. "Oh, right you are. Take care now."

"I will, Arthur, I will."

THE SECRETARY, having faithfully placed a dustcover over the computer, was putting on her coat when he arrived. She looked daggers at him, and he raised his hands in surrender.

"I'll only take a minute," he said. He hadn't really expected her to still be here. How much paperwork could an empty factory produce?

The reporters had vanished from outside, along with most of the cars on the estate.

"You're persistent," she said. "He's not here."

"It was you I wanted to speak to."

"Oh?"

He stepped forward and produced the photo from his pocket, the one of Cooke and Mrs. Webster kissing.

"Is your boss married?" he asked.

She smiled sourly. "I knew you weren't a rep."

"Did I say I was? So what's the answer? A simple yes or no."

"What business is it of yours?"

He gave a fumey sigh. "I can't find out. It's not difficult."

"Off you go then and find out."

"Did you know he was having an affair?"

"It's only an affair if the person's married."

"Oh? So Cooke's a bachelor then?"

"That's not what I said."

"Mrs. Webster's married though." He was seeking a reaction, *any* reaction. "Her daughter's single."

"Get out." Her voice was colder than the lager he'd just consumed.

"Let me guess," he persisted. "You had the hots for him yourself, maybe he was stringing you along. . . ."

She picked up the receiver.

"All right, I'm going." He put the photo back in his pocket. "But remember, you don't owe him anything. It's him that owes you. Just give me a yes or no: Is he married?"

She started punching telephone buttons, so he left. She was breathing hard, but didn't let it show. She stared at the door, willing it to stay closed. Then she was connected. "Police?" she said. "I want to speak to Chief Superintendent Lancaster. . . ."

Outside, he sat in his car, thinking about the man called Arthur, the secretary, and Stefan Duniec. Then he got out again and started looking for another car. Any car would do, so long as it had a car phone.

LANCASTER PUT DOWN THE RECEIVER and looked towards the two people sitting across the desk from him.

"That was your secretary, Mr. Cooke." Bernard Cooke nodded: He'd gathered as much already. "Our man has just turned up again, asking if you're married and implying you've been having an affair with Mrs. Webster." He looked at the young woman next to Cooke. "Or even with you, Gillian."

Gillian Webster snorted. Lancaster was smiling.

"Looks like it's worked," he said. *I hate puzzles.* Those three words had set the whole game in motion. And the game was about to end:

right result, right team. "He had a photo with him," he went on, turning back to Bernard Cooke. "You and Gillian's mother on the verandah at her home."

"That Sunday drinks party," Cooke decided.

"The Minute Man was watching."

"He thinks Cora and I are lovers?"

"He's putting two and two together and making five, luckily for us. If that photo had just shown the two of you talking, he might not have suspected anything."

"Whereas as it is . . ."

"He thinks he knows why Gillian's set you up. It couldn't have worked out better."

Gillian Webster turned to Cooke. "Kissing my mother on the verandah?"

Cooke tried a nervous smile. Lancaster shifted in his chair. He was nervous for all sorts of reasons. The Minute Man *had* to solve puzzles, even if that meant conjuring an answer out of the thinnest stuff. Lancaster had invented a conundrum, hoping his adversary would be irritated by it . . . and drawn towards it. Someone even suggested the Minute Man might pose as a reporter—a suitable disguise for showing interest in the case. . . .

There was a knock at the door, and a young man came in. Lancaster introduced him.

"I don't think either of you has met Detective Constable Duniec." Duniec nodded a greeting, but Gillian's mind was on the idea of Cooke and her mother. "Well, Stefan?" Lancaster asked.

The look on Duniec's face was bad news.

"He paid his bill and left over an hour ago."

Lancaster nodded. "He's been back to the Forester's, a regular called Arthur just phoned to tell me. And he paid another visit to the factory."

"We know his car, sir, red Fiesta, there's a call out for it."

"All exit roads are covered, aren't they?"

Duniec nodded.

"Then all we can do is wait."

Lancaster tried to look relaxed. Bernard Cooke had been doubtful of the plan at first, but as a friend of Gillian's he'd gone along with it. After all, partly it had been her idea. She was looking pale again. She'd been ordered to rest by the doctors, but had insisted on sticking around. The phone rang again. Lancaster snatched the call.

"Red Fiesta," he said afterwards. "Sighted heading for Lower Traherne." He fixed his eyes on Gillian. "Looks like he's heading out to your home." Then he turned to Duniec. "Get onto it, Stefan." Duniec nodded and left the room.

This eventuality, too, had been covered. The Websters were in a local hotel, under plainclothes protection. A driver and unmarked car were waiting outside to take Gillian back there. The Minute Man was driving into a trap.

The phone rang yet again, and Lancaster picked it up, glad of something to do. He listened for a moment, a muscle going rigid in his jaw. When he spoke, it was in a dry voice. "Put him through, will you? And try to get a trace." He then pushed a button on the telephone and replaced the receiver. A small integral speaker crackled into life. A female voice said, "You're through, caller." Lancaster swallowed and spoke.

"Hello?"

"Superintendent Lancaster?"

"Speaking."

Lancaster watched Gillian. She was staring at the telephone. What little colour she had vanished from her face.

"Don't bother with a trace, Tom. I won't be on long, you know that."

"We get a dozen cranks a day saying they're the Minute Man."

"You know who I am, Tom."

"Why are you phoning?"

"Because you've got the wrong man."

Lancaster looked to Gillian and Cooke. She looked ready to leap from her seat, while Cooke seemed pinned against the back of his as if by G-force.

"Have we?"

"Yes. She's set him up."

"Who has?"

"The girl."

"Why would she do that?"

"He's been having an affair with her mother. She wants revenge."

Lancaster forced a laugh. "How can you possibly know that?"

"I know. I know all of it now."

The line went dead.

"Christ," Cooke said. Lancaster checked with the switchboard, but the Minute Man hadn't been on long enough to give them a chance. In fact, he'd been on the line for scarcely a minute. . . .

Lancaster got to his feet. "I wonder if he still plans to visit Lower Traherne? One way to find out . . ."

"I'm coming too," said Cooke, rising shakily to his feet. Gillian was still staring at the telephone. Neither man needed confirmation that she had recognised the voice. When Lancaster touched her shoulder she flinched.

"Come on, Gillian," he said. "Let's get you back to the hotel."

THEY OPENED THE BACK DOOR of the car for her and she got in. The engine was running and the car moved off at once, through the car park, past the usual ruck of reporters and cameras, and out of the iron gates of Castle Lane police station. She didn't want to go to the hotel, not really. She wanted to go home, to Lower Traherne. But she doubted the police driver could be persuaded to take her there. She noticed a walkie-talkie on the floor by his feet. Or maybe it was a portable phone. Whatever happened at the house, she'd hear of it. He was looking at her in the rearview mirror. When she looked back, he gave her a reassuring smile. Then she noticed they'd passed the regular turning.

"We should have gone left there."

He was still smiling. The car was building up speed. Gillian felt a lump swell in her throat, the fear nearly choking her.

"I know it all now," he said quietly. "The way Lancaster spoke, that conformed it. Oh yes, that balanced both sides of the ledger quite nicely."

She swallowed, shifting the blockage. "Where's the driver?"

"*I'm* the driver."

"The policeman."

"You think he's in the boot?" He shook his head. "I told him his chief wanted him in the press room."

She was relaxing a little. His voice was calm. It had been calm all the time she'd been his captive. "Where are we going?" she asked.

"Lower Traherne."

"What?"

"I'm taking you home, Gillian."

"But why?"

He shrugged. "Just to show them I can."

She thought for a moment. While she was thinking, he spoke again.

"It was good, very good, nearly had me fooled. Except for one scared bloke in a pub . . ."

She felt the words tumble from her mouth, like someone else was speaking. "They've got the exit roads covered, and there are police at the house, inside and outside. You'll never—"

"It's all right, Gillian. You'll see, both sides will balance."

"What do you mean, balance?"

So for the rest of the journey, the Minute Man tried to explain to her his own particular theories of the principles of accounts.

Max Allan Collins is the first one to admit his writing is primarily in the "hard-boiled" tradition, so at first the idea behind this story may seem to be a departure from his usual work. However, once its true nature becomes apparent, this story rivals anything Chandler or Thompson could have done. More of his short fiction can be found in *Murder Is My Business, Werewolves,* and *Vampire Detectives.* His current novel series features Nate Heller, a private eye in the 1940s.

Mommy
MAX ALLAN COLLINS

The mother and daughter in the hallway of John F. Kennedy Grade School were each other's picture-perfect reflection.

Mommy wore a tailored pink suit with high heels, her blond hair short and perfectly coifed; pearls caressed the shapely little woman's pale throat, and a big black purse was tucked under her arm. Daughter, in a frilly white blouse with a pink skirt and matching tights, was petite, too, a head smaller than her mother. Their faces were almost identical—heart-shaped, with luminous china-blue eyes, long lashes, cupid's bow mouths, and creamy complexions.

The only difference between them was Mommy's serene, madonna-like countenance; the little girl was frowning. The frown was not one of disobedience—Jessica Ann Sterling was as well-behaved a modern child as you might hope to find—but a frown of frustration.

"Please don't, Mommy," she said. "I don't want you to make Mrs. Withers mad at me. . . ."

"It's only a matter of what's fair," Mommy said. "You have better grades than that little foreign student."

"He's not foreign, Mommy. Eduardo is Hispanic, and he's a good student, too. . . ."

"Not as good as you." Mommy's smile was a beautiful thing; it could warm up a room. "The award is for 'Outstanding Student of the Year.' You have straight A's, perfect attendance, you're the best student in the 'Talented and Gifted' group."

95

"Yes, Mommy, but . . ."

"No 'buts,' dear. *You* deserve the 'Outstanding Student' award. Not this little Mexican."

"But Mommy, it's just a stupid plaque. I don't need another. I got one last year . . ."

"And the year before, and the year before that—and you deserve it again this year. Perhaps it's best you go out and wait in the car for Mommy." She looked toward the closed door of the fifth-grade classroom. "Perhaps this should be a private conference . . ."

"Mommy, please don't embarrass me . . ."

"I would never do that. Now. Who's your best friend?"

"You are, Mommy."

"Who loves you more than anything on God's green earth?"

"You do, Mommy."

The little girl, head lowered, shuffled down the hall.

"Jessica Ann . . ."

She turned, hope springing. "Yes, Mommy?"

Mommy shook her finger in the air, gently. "Posture."

"Yes, Mommy . . ."

And the little girl went out to wait in their car.

THELMA WITHERS KNEW THAT trimming her room with Christmas decorations probably wasn't politically correct, but she was doing it, anyway. She had checked with Levi's parents, to see if they objected, and they said as long as there were no Christian symbols displayed, it was okay.

For that reason, she had avoided images of Santa Claus—technically, at least, he was Saint Nicholas, after all—but what harm could a little silver tinsel around the blackboard do?

The portly, fiftyish teacher was on a stepladder stapling the ropes of tinsel above the blackboard when Mrs. Sterling came in.

Looking over her shoulder, Mrs. Withers said, "Good afternoon, Mrs. Sterling. I hope you don't mind if I continue with my decorating . . ."

"We did have an appointment for a conference."

What a pain this woman was. The child, Jessica Ann, was a wonderful little girl, and a perfect student, but the mother—what a monster! In almost thirty years of teaching, Thelma had never had one like her—constantly pestering her about imagined slights to her precious child.

"Mrs. Sterling, we had our conference for the quarter just last week. I really want to have these decorations up for the children, and if you don't mind, we'll just talk while . . ."

"I don't mind," the woman said coldly. She was standing at the desk, staring at the shining gold wall plaque for "Outstanding Student of the Year" that was resting there. Her face was expressionless, yet there was something about the woman's eyes that told Thelma Withers just how covetous of the award she was.

Shaking her head, Mrs. Withers turned back to her work, stapling the tinsel in place.

The click clack of the woman's high heels punctuated the sound of stapling as Mrs. Sterling approached.

"You're presenting that plaque tonight, at the PTA meeting," she said.

"That's right," Mrs. Withers said, her back still to the woman.

"You *know* that my daughter deserves that award."

"Your daughter is a wonderful student, but so is Eduardo Melindez."

"Are his grades as good as Jessica Ann's?"

Mrs. Withers stopped stapling and glanced back at the woman, literally looking down her nose at Jessica Ann's mother.

"Actually, Mrs. Sterling, that's none of your business. How I arrive at who the 'Outstanding Student' is is my affair."

"Really."

"Really. Eduardo faces certain obstacles your daughter does not. When someone like Eduardo excels, it's important to give him recognition."

"Because he's a Mexican, you're taking the award away from my daughter? You're punishing her for being white, and for coming from a nice family?"

"That's not how I look at it. A person of color like Eduardo—"

"You're not going to give the award to Jessica, are you?"

"It's been decided."

"There's no name engraved on the plaque. It's not too late."

With a disgusted sigh, Mrs. Withers turned and glared at the woman. "It is too late. What are you teaching your daughter with this behavior, Mrs. Sterling?"

"What are you teaching her, when you take what's rightfully hers and give it to somebody because he's a 'person of color'?"

"I don't have anything else to say to you, Mrs. Sterling. Good afternoon." And Mrs. Withers turned back to her stapling, wishing she were stapling this awful woman's head to the wall.

It was at that moment that the ladder moved, suddenly, and the teacher felt herself losing balance, and falling, and she tumbled through the air and landed on her side, hard, the wind knocked out of her.

Moaning, Mrs. Withers opened her eyes, trying to push herself up. Her eyes were filled with the sight of Mrs. Sterling leaning over her, to help her up.

She thought.

JESSICA ANN WATCHED as one of the JFK front doors opened and Mommy walked from the building to the BMW, her big purse snugged tightly to her. Mommy wore a very serious expression, almost a frown.

Mommy opened the car door and leaned in.

"Is something wrong?" Jessica Ann asked.

"Yes," she said. "There's been a terrible accident . . . when I went to speak to Mrs. Withers, she was lying on the floor."

"On the floor?"

"She'd been up a ladder, decorating the room for you children. She must have been a very thoughtful teacher."

"Mommy—you make it sound like . . ."

"She's dead, dear. I think she may have broken her neck."

"Mommy . . ." Tears began to well up. Jessica Ann thought the world of Mrs. Withers.

"I stopped at the office and had the secretary phone for an ambulance. I think we should stay around until help comes, don't you?"

"Yes, Mommy. . . ."

AN AMBULANCE CAME, very soon, its siren screaming, but for no reason: when Mrs. Withers was wheeled out on a stretcher, she was all covered up. Jessica bit her finger and watched and tried not to cry. Mommy stood beside her, patting her shoulder.

"People die, dear," Mommy said. "It's a natural thing."

"What's natural about falling off a ladder, Mommy?"

"Is that a smarty tone?"

"No, Mommy."

"I don't think Mrs. Withers would want you speaking to your mother in a smarty tone."

"No, Mommy."

"Anyway, people fall off ladders all the time. You know, more accidents occur at home than anywhere else."

"Mrs. Withers wasn't at home."

"The workplace is the next most frequent."

"Can we go now?"

"No. I'll need to speak to these gentlemen."

A police car was pulling up; they hadn't bothered with a siren. Maybe somebody called ahead to tell them Mrs. Withers was dead.

Two uniformed policeman questioned Mommy, and then another policeman, in a wrinkled suit and loose tie, talked to Mommy, too. Jessica Ann didn't see him arrive; they were all sitting at tables in the school library, now. Jessica Ann was seated by herself, away from them, but she could hear some of the conversation.

The man in the suit and tie was old—probably forty—and he didn't have much hair on the top of his head, though he did have a mustache. He was kind of pudgy and seemed grouchy.

He said to Mommy, "You didn't speak to Mrs. Withers at all?"

"How could I? She was on the floor with her neck broken."

"You had an appointment . . ."

"Yes. A parent/teacher conference. Anything else, Lieutenant March?"

"No. Not right now, ma'am."

"Thank you," Mommy said. She stood. "You have my address, and my number."

"Yeah," he said. "I got your number."

He was giving Mommy a mean look but she just smiled as she gathered her purse and left.

Soon they were driving home. Mommy was humming a song, but Jessica Ann didn't recognize it. One of the those old songs, from the '80s.

It was funny—her mother didn't seem very upset about Mrs. Withers' accident at all.

But sometimes Mommy was that way about things.

JESSICA ANN LOVED THEIR HOUSE on Rockwell Road. It had been built a long time ago—1957, Mommy said—but it was really cool: light brick and dark wood and a lot of neat angles—a split-level ranch style was how she'd heard her Mommy describe it. They had lived here for two years, ever since Mommy married Mr. Sterling.

Mr. Sterling had been really old—fifty-one, it said in the paper when he died—but Mommy loved him a lot. He had an insurance agency, and was kind of rich—or so they had thought.

She had overheard her mommy talking to Aunt Beth about it. Aunt Beth was a little older than Mommy, and she was pretty too, but she had dark hair. They reminded Jessica Ann of Betty and Veronica in the Archie comic books.

Anyway, one time Jessica Ann heard Mommy in an odd voice, almost a mean voice, complaining that Mr. Sterling hadn't been as rich as he pretended to be. Plus, a lot of his money and property and stuff wound up with his children by (and Mommy didn't usually talk this way, certainly not in front of Jessica Ann) "the first two bitches he was married to."

Still, they had wound up with this cool house.

Jessica Ann missed Mr. Sterling. He was a nice man, before he had his heart attack and died. The only thing was, she didn't like having to call him "Daddy." Her real daddy—who died in the boating accident when she was six—was the only one who deserved being called that.

She kept Daddy's picture by her bed and talked to him every night. She remembered him very well—he was a big, handsome man with shoulders so wide you couldn't look at them both at the same time. He was old, too—even older than Mr. Sterling—and had left them "well off" (as Mommy put it).

Jessica Ann didn't know what had happened to Daddy's money—a few times Mommy talked about "bad investments"—but fortunately Mr. Sterling had come along about the time Daddy's money ran out.

When Jessica Ann and her mother got home from the school, Aunt Beth—who lived a few blocks from them, alone, because she was divorced from Uncle Bob—was waiting dinner. Mommy had called her from JFK and asked if she'd help.

As Jessica Ann came in, Aunt Beth was all over her, bending down, putting her arm around her. It made Jessica Ann uneasy. She wasn't used to displays of affection like that—Mommy talked about loving her a lot, but mostly kept her distance.

"You poor dear," Aunt Beth said. "Poor dear." She looked up at Mommy, who was hanging up both their coats in the closet. "Did she see . . . ?"

"No," Mommy said, shutting the closet door. "I discovered the body. Jessica Ann was in the car."

"Thank God!" Aunt Beth said. "Do either of you even feel like eating?"

"I don't know," Jessica Ann said.

"Sure," Mommy said. "Smells like spaghetti."

"That's what it is," Aunt Beth said. "I made a big bowl of salad, too . . ."

"I think I'll go to my room," Jessica Ann said.

"No!" Mommy said. "A little unpleasantness isn't going to stand in the way of proper nutrition."

Aunt Beth was frowning, but it was a sad frown. "Please . . . if she doesn't want . . ."

Mommy gave Aunt Beth the "mind your own business" look. Then she turned to Jessica Ann, and pointed to the kitchen. "Now, march in there, young lady. . . ."

"Yes, Mommy."

"Your salad, too."

"Yes, Mommy."

AFTER DINNER, Jessica Ann went to her room, a pink world of stuffed animals and Barbie dolls; she had a frilly four-poster bed that Mommy got in an antique shop. She flopped onto it and thought about Mrs. Withers. Thought about what a nice lady Mrs. Withers was. . . .

She was crying into her pillow when Aunt Beth came in.

"There, there," Aunt Beth said, sitting on the edge of the bed, patting the girl's back. "Get it out of your system."

"Do . . . do you think Mrs. Withers had any children?"

"Probably. Maybe even grandchildren."

"Do you . . . do you think I should write them a letter, about what a good teacher she was?"

Aunt Beth's eyes filled up with tears and she clutched Jessica Ann to her. This time Jessica Ann didn't mind. She clutched back, crying into her aunt's blouse.

"I think that's a wonderful idea."

"I'll write it tonight, and add their names later, when I find them out."

"Fine. Jessy . . ." Aunt Beth was the only grown-up who ever called her that; Mommy didn't like nicknames ". . . you know, your mother . . . she's kind of a . . . special person."

"What do you mean?"

"Well . . . it's just that . . . she has some wonderful qualities."

"She's very smart. And pretty."

"Yes."

"She does everything for me."

"She does a lot for you. But . . . she doesn't always *feel* things like she should."

"What do you mean, Aunt Beth?"

"It's hard to explain. She was babied a lot . . . there were four of us, you know, and she was the youngest. Your grandparents, rest their souls, gave her everything. And why not? She was so pretty, so perfect—"

"She always got her way, didn't she?"

"How did you know that, Jessica Ann?"

"I just do. 'Cause she still does, I guess."

"Jessy . . . I always kind of looked after your mother . . . protected her."

"What do you mean?"

"Just . . . as you grow older, try to understand . . . try to forgive her when she seems . . . if she seems . . ."

"Cold?"

Aunt Beth nodded. Smiled sadly. "Cold," she said. "In her way, she loves you very much."

"I know."

"I have dessert downstairs. You too blue for chocolate cake?"

"Is Mark here? I thought I heard his car."

"He's here," Aunt Beth said, smiling. "And he's asking for you. Mark and chocolate cake—that's quite a combo."

Jessica Ann grinned, took a tissue from the box on her nightstand, dried her eyes, took her aunt's hand, and allowed herself to be led from her room down the half-stairs.

MOMMY'S NEW BOYFRIEND, Mark Jeffries, was in the living room sitting in Mr. Sterling's recliner, sipping an iced tea.

"There's my girl!" he said, as Jessica Ann came into the room; Aunt Beth was in the kitchen with Mommy.

Mark sat forward in the chair, then stood—he was younger than either

Mr. Sterling or Daddy, and really good looking, like a soap opera actor with his sandy hair and gray sideburns and deep tan. He wore a green sweater and new jeans and a big white smile. Also, a Rolex watch.

She went quickly to him, and he bent down and hugged her. He smelled good—like lime.

He pushed her gently away and looked at her with concern in his blue-gray eyes. "Are you okay, angel?"

"Sure."

"Your mommy told me about today. Awful rough." He took her by the hand and led her to the couch. He sat down and nodded for her to join him. She did.

"Angel, if you need somebody to talk to . . ."

"I'm fine, Mark. Really."

"You know . . . when I was ten, my Boy Scout leader died. He was killed in an automobile accident. I didn't have a dad around . . . he and Mom were divorced . . . and my Scout leader was kind of a . . . surrogate father to me. You know what that is?"

"Sure. He kind of took the place of a dad."

"Right. Anyway, when he died, I felt . . . empty. Then I started to get afraid."

"Afraid, Mark?"

"I started to think about dying for the first time. I had trouble. I had nightmares. For the first time I realized nobody lives forever. . . ."

Jessica Ann had known that for a long time. First Daddy, then Mr. Sterling. . . .

"I hope you don't have trouble like that," he said. "But if you do—I just want you to know . . . I'm here for you."

She didn't say anything—just beamed at him.

She was crazy about Mark. Jessica Ann hoped he and Mommy would get married. She thought she could even feel comfortable calling him Daddy. Maybe.

Mommy had met Mark at a country club dance last month. He had his own business—some kind of mail-order thing that was making a lot of money, she heard Mommy say—and had moved to Ferndale to get away from the urban blight where he used to live.

Jessica Ann found she could talk to Mark better than to any grown-up she'd ever met. Even better than Aunt Beth. And as much as Jessica Ann loved her mommy, they didn't really *talk*—no shared secrets, or problems.

But Mark put Jessica Ann at ease. She could talk to him about problems at school or even at home.

"Who wants dessert?" Aunt Beth called.

Soon Jessica Ann and Mark were sitting at the kitchen table while

Mommy, in her perfect white apron (she never got anything on it, so why did she wear it?) was serving up big pieces of chocolate cake.

"I'll just have the ice cream," Aunt Beth told Mommy.

"What's *wrong* with me?" Mommy said. "You're allergic to chocolate! How thoughtless of me."

"Don't be silly. . . ."

"How about some strawberry compote on that ice cream?"

"That does sound good."

"There's a jar in the fridge," Mommy said.

Aunt Beth found the jar, but was having trouble opening it.

"Let me have a crack at that," Mark said, and took it, but he must not have been as strong as he looked; he couldn't budge the lid.

"Here," Mommy said, impatiently, and took the jar, and with a quick thrust, opened the lid with a loud *pop*. Aunt Beth thanked her and spooned on the strawberry compote herself.

Mommy sure was strong, Jessica Ann thought. She'd seen her do the same thing with catsup bottles and pickle jars.

"Pretty powerful for a little girl," Mark said teasingly, patting Mommy's rear end when he thought Jessica Ann couldn't see. "Remind me not to cross you."

"Don't cross me," Mommy said, and smiled her beautiful smile.

AT SCHOOL THE NEXT DAY, Jessica Ann was called to the principal's office.

But the principal wasn't there—waiting for her was the pudgy policeman, the one with the mustache. He had on a different wrinkled suit today. He didn't seem so grouchy now; he was all smiles.

"Jessica Ann?" he said, bending down. "Remember me? I'm Lieutenant March. Could we talk for a while?"

"Okay."

"I have permission for us to use Mr. Davis' office."

Mr. Davis was the principal.

"All right."

Lieutenant March didn't sit at Mr. Davis' desk; he put two chairs facing each other and sat right across from Jessica Ann.

"Jessica Ann, why did your mother want to see Mrs. Withers yesterday?"

"They had a conference."

"Parent/teacher conference."

"Yes, sir."

"You don't have to call me sir, Jessica Ann. I want us to be friends."

She didn't say anything.

He seemed to be trying to think of what to say next; then finally he said, "Do you know how your teacher died?"

"She fell off a ladder."

"She did fall off a ladder. But Jessica Ann—your teacher's neck was broken. . . ."

"When she fell off the ladder."

"We have a man called the medical examiner who says that it didn't happen that way. He says it's very likely a pair of hands did that."

Suddenly Jessica Ann remembered the jar of strawberry compote, and the other bottles and jars Mommy had twisted caps off, so easily.

"Jessica Ann . . . something was missing from Mrs. Withers' desk."

Jessica Ann's tummy started jumping.

"A plaque, Jessica Ann. A plaque for 'Outstanding Student of the Year.' You won last year, didn't you?"

"Yes, sir."

"Mrs. Withers told several friends that your mother called her, complaining about you not winning this year."

Jessica Ann said nothing.

"Jessica Ann . . . the mother of the boy who won the plaque, Eduardo's mother, Mrs. Melindez, would like to have that plaque. Means a lot to her. If you should happen to find it, would you tell me?"

"Why would *I* find it?"

"You just might. Could your mother have picked it up when she went into the classroom?"

"If she did," Jessica Ann said, "that doesn't prove anything."

"Who said anything about proving anything, Jessica Ann?"

She stood. "I think if you have any more questions for me, Lieutenant March, you should talk to my mother."

"Jessica Ann . . ."

But the little girl didn't hear anything else; not anything the policeman said, or what any of her friends said the rest of the day, or even the substitute teacher.

All she could hear was the sound of the lid on the strawberry compote jar popping open.

WHEN JESSICA ANN GOT HOME, she found the house empty. A note from Mommy said she had gone grocery shopping. The girl got herself some milk and cookies but neither drank nor ate. She sat at the kitchen table staring at nothing. Then she got up and began searching her mother's room.

In the middle drawer of a dresser, amid slips and panties, she found the plaque.

Her fingers flew off the object as if it were a burner on a hot stove. Then she saw her own fingerprints glowing on the brass and rubbed them off with a slick pair of panties, and put the shining plaque back, buried it in Mommy's underthings.

She went to her room and found the largest stuffed animal she could and hugged it close; the animal—a bear—had wide button eyes. So did she.

Her thoughts raced; awful possibilities presented themselves, possibilities that she may have already considered, in some corner of her mind, but had banished.

Why did Mr. Sterling die of that heart attack?

What really happened that afternoon Mommy and Daddy went boating?

She was too frightened to cry. Instead she hugged the bear and shivered as if freezing and put pieces together that fit too well. If she was right, then someone *else* she thought the world of was in danger....

MARK JEFFRIES KNEW SOMETHING WAS WRONG, but he couldn't be sure what.

He and Jessica Ann had hit it off from the very start, but for the last week, whenever he'd come over to see her mother, the little girl had avoided and even snubbed him.

It had been a week since the death of Mrs. Winters—he had accompanied both Jessica Ann and her mother to the funeral—and the child had been uncharacteristically brooding ever since.

Not that Jessica Ann was ever talkative: She was a quiet child, intelligent, contemplative even, but when she opened up (as she did for Mark so often) she was warm and funny and fun.

Maybe it was because he had started to stay over at the house, on occasion ... maybe she was threatened because he had started to share her mother's bedroom.

He'd been lying awake in the mother's bed, thinking these thoughts as the woman slept soundly beside him, when nature called him, and he arose, slipped on a robe, and answered the call. In the hallway, he noticed the little girl's light on in her room. He stopped at the child's room and knocked, gently.

"Yes?" came her voice, softly.

"Are you awake, angel?"

"Yes."

He cracked the door. She was under the covers, wide awake, the ruffly pink shade of her nightstand lamp glowing; a stuffed bear was under there with her, hugged to her.

"What's wrong, angel?" he asked, and shut the door behind him, and sat on the edge of her bed.

"Nothing."

"You've barely spoken to me for days."

She said nothing.

"You know you're number one on my personal chart, don't you?"

She nodded.

"Do you not like my sleeping over?"

She shrugged.

"Don't you ... don't you think I'd make a good daddy?"

Tears were welling in her eyes.

"Angel."

She burst into tears, clutching him, bawling like the baby she had been, not so long ago.

"I ... I wanted to chase you away...."

"Chase me away! Why on earth?"

"Because ... because you *would* make a good daddy, and I don't want you to die...."

And she poured it all out, her fears that her mother was a murderer, that Mommy had killed her teacher and her daddy and even Mr. Sterling.

He glanced behind him at the closed door. He gently pushed the girl away and, a hand on her shoulder, looked at her hard.

"How grown-up can you be?" he asked.

"Real grown-up, if I have to."

"Good. Because I want to level with you about something. You might be mad at me...."

"Why, Mark?"

"Because I haven't been honest with you. In fact ... I've lied."

"Lied?"

And he told her. Told her about being an investigator for the insurance company that was looking into the latest suspicious death linked to her mother, that of her stepfather, Phillip Sterling (at least, the latest one before Mrs. Withers).

Calmly, quietly, he told the little girl that he had come to believe, like her, that her mother was a murderer.

"But you ... you slept with her...."

"It's not very nice. I know. I had to get close to her, to get the truth. With your help, if you can think back and tell me about things you've seen, we might be ..."

But that was all he got out.

The door flew open, slapping the wall like a spurned suitor, and there she was, the beautiful little blonde in the babydoll nightie, a woman with a sweet body that he hadn't been able to resist even though he knew what she most likely was.

There she was with the .38 in her hand and firing it at him, again and again; he felt the bullets hitting his body, punching him, burning into him like lasers, he thought, then one entered his right eye and put an end to all thought, and to him.

*   *   *

JESSICA ANN WAS SCREAMING, the bloody body of Mark Jeffries sprawled on the bed before her, scorched bleeding holes on the front of his robe, one of his eyes an awful black hole leaking red.

Mommy sat beside her daughter and hugged her little girl to her, slipping a hand over her mouth, stifling Jessica Ann's screams.

"Hush, dear. Hush."

Jessica Ann started to choke, and that stopped the screaming, and Mommy took her hand away. The girl looked at her mother and was startled to see tears in Mommy's eyes. She couldn't ever remember Mommy crying, not even at the funerals of Daddy and Mr. Sterling, although she had seemed to cry. Jessica Ann had always thought Mommy was faking ... that Mommy couldn't cry ... but now ...

"We have to call the police, dear," Mommy said, "and when they come, we have to tell them things that fit together. Like a puzzle fits together. Do you understand?"

"Yes, Mommy," Jessica, trembling, wanted to pull away from her mother, but somehow couldn't.

"Otherwise, Mommy will be in trouble. We don't want that, do we?"

"No, Mommy."

"Mark did bad things to Mommy. *Bedroom* things. Do you understand?"

"Yes, Mommy."

"When I heard him in here, I thought he might be doing the same kind of things to you. Or trying to."

"But he didn't—"

"That doesn't matter. And you don't have to say he did. I don't want you to lie. But those things he told you ... about being an investigator ... *forget* them. He never said them."

"Oh ... okay, Mommy."

"If you tell, Mommy would be in trouble. We don't want that."

"No, Mommy."

"Now. Who's your best friend?"

"You ... you are, Mommy."

"Who loves you more than anything on God's green earth?"

"You do, Mommy."

"Good girl."

THERE WERE A LOT OF MEN AND WOMEN IN THE HOUSE, throughout the night, some of them police, in uniform, some of them in white, some in regular clothes, some using cameras, others carrying out Mark in a big black zippered bag.

Lieutenant March questioned Mommy for a long time; when all the others had left, he was still there, taking notes. Mommy sat on a couch in the living room, wearing a robe, her arms folded tight to her, her expression as blank as a doll's. Just behind her was the Christmas tree, in the front window, which Mommy had so beautifully trimmed.

Aunt Beth had been called and sat with Jessica Ann in the kitchen, but there was no doorway, just an archway separating the rooms, so Jessica could see Mommy as Lieutenant March questioned her. Jessica Ann couldn't hear what they were saying, most of the time.

Then she saw Mommy smile at Lieutenant March, a funny, making-fun sort of smile, and that seemed to make Lieutenant March angry. He stood and almost shouted.

"No, you're not under arrest," he said, "and yes, you should contact your attorney."

He tromped out to the kitchen, to bring the empty coffee cup (Aunt Beth had given him some coffee) and he looked very grouchy.

"Thank you," he said to Aunt Beth, handing her the cup.

"Don't you believe my sister?" Aunt Beth asked.

"Do you?" He glanced at Jessica Ann, but spoke to Aunt Beth. "I'll talk to the girl tomorrow. Maybe she should stay with you tonight."

"That's not my decision," Aunt Beth said.

"Maybe it should be," he said, and excused himself and left.

Aunt Beth looked very tired when she sat at the table with Jessica Ann. She spoke quietly, almost a whisper.

"What you told me . . . is that what really happened, Jessica Ann?"

"Mommy thought Mark was going to do something bad to me."

"You love your mommy, don't you?"

"Yes."

"But you're also afraid of her."

"Yes." She shrugged. "All kids are afraid of their parents."

"Beth," Mommy said, suddenly in the archway, "you better go now."

Aunt Beth rose. She wet her lips. "Maybe I should take Jessica Ann tonight."

Mommy came over and put her hand on Jessica Ann's shoulder. "We appreciate your concern. But we've been through a lot of tragedy together, Jessica Ann and I. We'll make it through tonight, just fine. Won't we, dear?"

"Yes, Mommy."

BOTH JESSICA ANN AND HER MOTHER were questioned, separately and individually, at police headquarters in downtown Ferndale the next afternoon. Mommy's lawyer, Mr. Ekhardt, a handsome gray-haired older man, was with them; sometimes he told Mommy not to answer certain questions.

Afterward, in the hall, Jessica Ann heard Mommy ask Mr. Ekhardt if they had enough to hold her.

"Not yet," he said. "But I don't think this is going to let up. From the looks of that lieutenant, I'd say this is just starting."

Mommy touched Mr. Ekhardt's hand with both of hers. "Thank you, Neal. With you in our corner, I'm sure we'll be just fine."

"You never give up, do you?" Mr. Ekhardt said with a funny smile. "Gotta give you that much."

Mr. Ekhardt shook his head and walked away.

JESSICA ANN WATCHED as her Mommy pulled suitcases from a closet, and then went to another closet and began packing her nicest things into one of the suitcases.

"We're going on a vacation, dear," Mommy said, folding several dresses over her arm, "to a foreign land—you'll love it there. It'll be Christmas every day."

"But I have school . . ."

"Your break starts next week, anyway. And then we'll put you in a wonderful new school."

"What about my friends?"

"You'll make new friends."

Mommy was packing so quickly, and it was all happening so fast, Jessica Ann couldn't even find the words to protest further. What could she do about it? Every kid knew that when your parents decided to move, the kid had no part of it. A kid's opinion had no weight on such matters. You just went where your parents went.

"Take this," Mommy said, handing her the smaller suitcase, "and pack your own things."

"What about my animals?"

"Take your favorite. Aunt Beth will send the others on, later."

"Okay, Mommy."

"Who's your best friend?"

"You are."

"Who loves you more than—"

"You do."

The girl packed her bag. She put the framed picture of Daddy in the middle of the clothes, so it wouldn't get broken.

THEY DROVE FOR SEVERAL HOURS. Mommy turned the radio on to a station playing Christmas music—"White Christmas" and the one about chestnuts roasting. Now and then Mommy looked over at her, and Jessica Ann noticed Mommy's expression was . . . different. Blank, but Mommy's eyes seemed . . . was Mommy frightened, too?

When Mommy noticed Jessica Ann had caught her gaze, Mommy smiled that beautiful smile. But it wasn't real. Jessica Ann wasn't sure Mommy knew how to *really* smile.

The motel wasn't very nice. It wasn't like the Holiday Inns and Marriotts and Ramada Inns they usually stayed in on vacation. It was just a white row of doorways on the edge of some small town and a junkyard was looming in back of it, like some scary Disneyland.

Jessica Ann put on her jammies and brushed her teeth and Mommy tucked her in, even gave her a kiss. The girl was very, very tired and fell asleep quickly.

She wasn't sure how long she'd been asleep, but when she woke up, Mommy was sitting on the edge of Jessica Ann's bed. Mommy wasn't dressed for bed; she still had on the clothes she'd been driving in.

Mommy was sitting there, in the dark, staring, her hands raised in the air. It was like Mommy was trying to choke a ghost.

'Sometimes Mommys have to make hard decisions," Mommy whispered. "If they take Mommy away, who would look after you?"

But Jessica Ann knew Mommy wasn't saying this to her, at least not to the awake her. Maybe to the sleeping Jessica Ann, only Jessica Ann wasn't sleeping.

The child bolted out of the bed with a squealing scream and Mommy ran after her. Jessica Ann got to the door, which had a nightlatch, but her fingers fumbled with the chain, and then her mommy was on top of her. Mommy's hands were on her, but the child squeezed through, and bounded over one of the twin beds and ran into the bathroom and slammed and locked the door.

"Mommy! Mommy, don't!"

"Let me in, Jessica Ann. You just had a bad dream. Just a nightmare. We'll go back to sleep now."

"No!"

The child looked around the small bathroom and saw the window; she stood on the toilet seat lid and unlocked the window and slipped out, onto the tall grass. Behind her, she heard the splintering of the door as her mother pushed it open.

Jessica Ann was running, running toward the dark shapes that were the junkyard; she glanced back and saw her mother's face framed in the bathroom window. Her mother's eyes were wild; Jessica Ann had never seen her mother like that.

"Come back here this *instant!*" her mother said.

But Jessica Ann ran, screaming as she went, hoping to attract attention. The moon was full and high and like a spotlight on the child. Maybe someone would see!

"Help! Please, help!"

Her voice seemed to echo through the night. The other windows in the motel were dark and the highway out front was deserted; there was no one else in the world but Jessica Ann and Mommy.

And Mommy was climbing out the bathroom window.

Jessica Ann climbed over the wire fence—there was some barbed wire at the top, and her jammies got caught, and tore a little, but she didn't cut herself. Then she was on the other side, in the junkyard, but her bare feet hurt from the cinders beneath them.

Mommy was coming.

The child ran, hearing the rattle of the fence behind her, knowing Mommy was climbing, climbing over, then dropping to the other side.

"Jessica Ann!"

Piles of crushed cars were on either side of Jessica Ann, as she streaked down a cinder path between them, her feet hurting, bleeding, tears streaming, her crying mixed with gasping for air as she ran, ran hard as she could.

Then she fell and she skinned her knee and her yelp echoed.

She got up, quickly, and ran around the corner, and ran right into her mother.

"What do you think you're doing, young lady?"

Her mother's hands gripped the girl's shoulders.

Jessica Ann backed up quickly, bumping into a rusted-out steel drum. A wall of crushed cars, scrap metal, old tires, broken-down appliances, and other things that must have had value once was behind her.

"Mommy . . ."

Mommy's hands were like claws reaching out for the girl's neck. "This is for your own good, dear. . . ."

Then Mommy's hands were on Jessica Ann's throat, and the look in Mommy's eyes was so very cold, and the child tried to cry out but she couldn't, though she tried to twist away and moonlight fell on her face.

And Mommy gazed at her child, and her eyes narrowed, and softened, and she loosened her hands.

"Put your hands *up,* Mrs. Sterling!"

Mommy stepped away and looked behind her. Jessica Ann, touching her throat where Mommy had been choking her, could see him standing there, Lieutenant March. He was pointing a gun at Mommy.

Mommy put her head down and her hands up.

Then Aunt Beth was there, and took Jessica Ann into her arms and held her, and said, "You're a brave little girl."

"What . . . what are you *doing* here, Aunt Beth?"

"I came along with the lieutenant. He was keeping your mother under surveillance. I'm glad you have good lungs, or we wouldn't have heard you back here. We were out front, and I'd fallen asleep. . . ."

"Aunt Beth . . . can I live with you now? I don't want to go to a new school."

Aunt Beth's laugh was surprised and sort of sad. "You can live with me. You can stay in your school." She stroked Jessica Ann's forehead. "It's over now, Jessy. It's over."

"She couldn't do it, Aunt Beth," Jessica Ann said, crying, but feeling strangely happy, somehow. Not to be rescued: but to know Mommy couldn't bring herself to do it! Mommy couldn't kill Jessica Ann!

"I know, honey," Aunt Beth said, holding the girl.

"Mommy *does* love me! More than anything on God's green earth."

The child didn't hear when Lieutenant March, cuffing her hands behind her, asked the woman, "Why didn't you do it? Why'd you hesitate?"

"For a moment there, in the moonlight," Mommy said, "she looked like *me*. . . ."

And the cop walked the handcuffed woman to his unmarked car, while the aunt took her niece into the motel room to retrieve a stuffed bear and a framed photo of Daddy.

J. N. Williamson has had more than 150 short stories published in a variety of genres and anthologies. Recent work by him appears in *White House Horrors, Murder Most Delicious,* and *Holmes for the Holidays.* His most recent novel is *Bloodline* (Byron Preiss, 1994). "Beasts in Buildings," Turning 'Round is a study in locked room terror, made all the more unnerving by its setting, cut straight from today's headlines.

Beasts in Buildings, Turning 'Round
J. N. WILLIAMSON

If she'd had a premonition that morning that she was going to die that day, it probably wouldn't have occurred to her that her life would end in the bomb shelter.

Certainly not with her throat cut.

Three people with her in the old, reopened shelter saw the start of the woman's death if not, in all cases, the cause of it. They were among those who weren't praying for the missiles to pass by the hotel again that afternoon, though they certainly wished for another miracle. One of them merely happened to turn his head in her direction at the moment it appeared that the taut skin at the front of her neck and just above the collarbone was splitting, opening up of its own accord. Fascinated, he had the impression as well that the gap immediately began to widen—as though something inside her was pushing out, trying to escape. But that was only the blood.

A second person saw the death start, too, but looked away. He was too frightened by the noise above the hotel to allow anything to register in his mind except his personal terror.

The third person who observed the arrival of death and had not been praying was the murderer. By the time the dead woman was pitching forward with no sound escaping her lips—moving for an instant as if she might be on the verge of standing—that person was already sitting alone in a concave hollow of the shelter even more steeped in shadow than the rest of the bare and colorless, utterly functional room.

He didn't point, cry out, or rise until the first witness was already emitting piteous cries, which drew the complete attention of the other fifteen living people present, and by then, an unsuppressed smile didn't matter much.

Under the circumstances, it was safe to consider himself successful.

Safe, successful, and self-satisfied for the third time running.

Three women murdered inside a stale and poorly illumined bomb shelter built to fend off the weapons of other, half-forgotten wars and taking up less than half the cellar of the modest old hotel. Just one exit, too! Three, during a total of nine raids spread over four days—let the foreign army devil see a pattern in that! Three down, fourteen to go, some men, some women—it was delicious to picture them trying to decide whether the males were to be spared, and only the females stalked and slaughtered! Fourteen human beings of varying faiths and several nations, the imbeciles huddled together because they already feared for their worthless lives—incapable of going anywhere else from terror of the bombs!—and they had no way to discover who was cutting their throats!

His solitary risk lay in the likelihood that they'd no longer think, after this, that two or more nationals were killing each other; they'd *know* there was just one murderer. But that added another element of challenge, of delight! The trick was to take them when they least expected it, and to destroy as many of them as possible prior to the eventual evacuation.

So, since they wouldn't anticipate consecutive attacks, the next victim must die during the next sortie of planes and missiles. Perhaps—if they were rattled badly enough—his total might climb to five or six, even more.

And they would never discover the motive behind the killings in ten thousand risings of the sun—in one hundred thousand!

Because there was none.

THE THREE MEN from the embassy had taken the best table in the restaurant of the besieged hotel with as little to-do as if magnetized by it, and the headwaiter had passed out menus without giving a thought to their right to the table. There was that kind of dignity to the graying ambassador, whether anyone else in the place knew his profession or not. His aide was trying hard—fine-haired mustache meant to age him, twitching whenever he wiggled his upper lip—to do a good impression of the old man.

As to the uniformed man with the short-cropped, wiry hair, he had his own sort of dignity, but would have felt badly about his small group commandeering the big table if the ranks of people staying at the hotel hadn't been thinned. In addition to the trio of women killed in the basement shelter, a number of frightened individuals had run off into the war-torn city to vanish, and some patrons, obviously, had stayed in their rooms tonight.

Not that he blamed them. He'd been stunned when the latest victim's throat was slashed. *Dead bodies work up very little appetite,* he thought, and began to survey the other tables, counting those who were present until it was time to place his order. *"That,"* he said, blindly jabbing an index finger at the menu. He wouldn't be in the dining room at all except the ambassador desired the views of his attaché.

Three of them, seven other customers scattered around the sizable, candlelit room. The hotel was trying to conserve the generator. Since only three employees remained—the maids had taken off so there was the dark-skinned cook, an aged runt of a bellhop, and the hotel manager obliged to double as headwaiter—that meant two folks were alone now in their rooms. The captain remembered. An exotic-looking woman who reminded him of some fifties actress, and an Alexandrian business type; they were not present and accounted for.

It dawned on him with distaste that he was beginning to look at the others as if one was the worst kind of murderer he'd ever imagined and, with a shock akin to a minor electrical jolt, that one of them undoubtedly was.

"My money's on a terrorist," said the ambassador. His voice and chin were low; he seemed to be addressing his silverware. "Who else could manage such a thing in the midst of other people?"

The young aide bobbed his head. "That's a given." He didn't admit he was contradicting his own first impression that there were conflicting groups of nationals.

"Well, how hard is it to imagine a psycho at work," the captain said slowly, "considering the shelter is half-dark and folks are already terrified by bombs? No nation or race is free of madness." He let his gaze wander. Counting the actress-type in her room, there were only four women left. With surprise, he saw that one of them was seeking his gaze. "This fellow's a planner who takes his time."

"Terrorists can calculate matters down to the fine details," the aide argued, appealing to his employer with a glance. "There may be some clever *pattern* that—"

"Planners of terrorism plan," the captain told him. "They send emotional types to get the job done. Expendable fanatics full of passion, high as kites."

The distinguished ambassador remarked, "I find that most interesting."

"Thank you, sir." He broke eye contact with the young woman. It was a night of surprises. This old man in the gray, perfectly tailored suit rarely offered a compliment. "I have my ideas, but their only value is that they are mine."

A crinkled smile. The ambassador peered up with a disturbingly challenging expression. "They're about to acquire added weight, Captain. No one else in this place can get to the bottom of things but you. Not so far as I know."

The captain frowned, sat back. He had just walked straight into one of the old diplomat's famous traps. "I have no authority here if you mean I should conduct an investigation." He really meant that none of them did. Suddenly, he felt quite tired. The embassy had been closed with little prior notice. Everyone had piled into vehicles headed for the airport, and their own car hadn't made it. Only decent luck had gotten them to this hotel in one piece. Their driver hadn't been that fortunate.

The old man's blue eyes had a way of frosting out to colorlessness when he'd gotten into something; they were like that now. "I doubt anyone will raise an objection if you stop the son of a bitch. Look. The phone lines are down, even if we could persuade a policeman to jeopardize his life in coming here. I know your record, Captain. A hitch in Intelligence. You are the best man for the job."

Sensing an approach, he leaned forward to reply, just above a whisper. "All right. Because he probably *will* do it again if no one volunteers. What else is there to it, sir?"

"Shrewd question." The old man's voice was scarcely audible. "Before losing the phones, we were informed that command will provide a little lift for us in the morning, whenever it looks clear. The hotel will be evacuated."

"Keep it quiet," the aide added. "There'd be panic if the bird couldn't land for any reason."

Yet if an Apache *did* make it in tomorrow morning, thought the captain, everybody there would be airlifted out, ultimately dispersed to God knew how many nations—

And the damned killer would get by with the vilest crimes he had ever heard of. He would be free to go on slicing up innocents whenever and wherever he—

"Please," said the standing woman, "pardon me. But if you're the best man to find the murderer, we should get acquainted."

He stared up, startled that she was speaking flawless English. "How did you hear what we were saying?"

"I didn't." She gave him a fleeting smile. "I read lips. As to what was discussed, don't worry. I'll keep it quiet about the helicopter."

She was in her late twenties, her auburn hair tousled as if she'd brushed at instead of brushing it, and very, very short. The captain had the impression that her mammoth purse with the strap was far too large for her

... of demureness, and mental gears furiously shifting ... of Western dress hastily assembled over a figure that was probably cute (a type he'd never much appreciated) ... and of an icy challenge with the same flinty self-confidence he associated—loved and hated—with the ambassador.

"If we can have a moment," she went on, "at my table"—she lifted her head—"I'll have my say before your meals arrive."

Irritation flared, but the ambassador answered her before he could. "We'll excuse you, Captain," he said, rising to nod at their petite intruder. He smiled down, benignly. "Perhaps the young lady believes she knows the identity of the murderer." Everything in his face but the smile asked the captain to take over, and be discreet.

Fuming, he followed her to her table, saw her seated, went around to face her. "Under the circumstances, I don't see how I can shout to make myself understood."

"You needn't." She watched him lower himself to a chair. "My hearing is excellent. I learned to lip-read to deal better with patients suffering psychosomatic deafness."

"You're a doctor, then?"

"No." Her way of staring directly at him and seldom blinking was unnerving, and it made him glance down at her hands. Folded on the edge of the table, they might have been those of a small, tiny child. "I'm a clinical psychologist with a background in experimental, comparative, and social psychology as well as criminology."

"How impressive, *Ms.*—?"

"Sister," she said. "Sister Bethany will do." His lips parted, she saw and giggled like a five-year-old. "A nun, that's correct."

The captain sat up straight. "Forgive me for asking, but what are you doing in this part of the world?"

"And, 'Why in heaven's name would *I* want to talk with the best man to find a killer?' " She closed and opened her eyes. "A clinical psychologist not only diagnoses and tries to treat mental disorders, but does research into the subject of mental illnesses."

"And these days there's no better place for you to come," he said, smiling.

"Captain," she said—"I'm the best *woman* for the job. The murders."

"Why?" He put the question before thinking.

"Perhaps it's crossed your mind that a possible motivation of the person killing these women is religious." A shrug. "I'm a psychologist *and* a nun."

"And a woman."

"How perceptive," she said. "But I won't take the killer's work personally."

"As a nun?"

"No," Sister Bethany said, "as a psychologist." Something turned her eyes to green flame for an instant. "As a nun, I'm afraid I take it quite personally."

"Criminology, too," he noted. He lifted the tips of his fingers to suggest the others in the restaurant. "What do you deduce, looking around you, Sister?"

She shook her head, and a faint line appeared between her eyes, above her small nose. "Such remarks will lead us nowhere, Captain. Sherlock Holmes might study the faces, hands, clothing of the others present to determine where they came from, their vocations, why they came here—and that's quite pointless to us now."

He asked bluntly, "Why?"

"Because, sir, you and I could simply stand, and go *ask* them!" Her cheeks reddened. "The murderer in this case lives life as an ordinary person who won't even lie if there's no need for it. You'll find no fangs sank into the women's throats."

Annoyed, the captain motioned to the waiter for coffee, turned up a cup the nun had not used, pointed. "Some of us at my table believe the murderer is a terrorist. After all, the victims were very neatly, efficiently executed. As if the man had practice."

She waited until the swarthy hotel manager doubling as maître d' filled both their cups. His thick mustache a work of patience and the passage of years, he paused, lips moving nervously, but Sister Bethany waved him away. "Isn't it possible that what you cite as practiced efficiency is necessary speed? Even in a shelter that size, there's no time for admiring his handiwork."

Her forthrightness was off-putting. "I suppose. But—"

"But you neither believe he's a terrorist or care for that reasoning," she interposed, "and neither do I." She smiled charmingly, stunningly. "As James Thurber said, 'The conclusion you jump to may be your own.' The individual we intend to stop, Captain, isn't a terrorist, not in the usual sense. He or she is either a psychopath or a sociopath."

"If I have to choose, as a working theory," he said, "I think of the psycho as a man compelled to—well, destroy his victim. Maul, disfigure, annihilate." He realized his curiosity about this little woman's ability was growing in pace with his annoyance. His meal and the meals of the ambassador and his aide were being put on a tray by the headwaiter, and he might be wasting time on the nun. But he wasn't Catholic, was military, and his training prompted him to be properly courteous. "Am I mistaken in that?"

"Not is one assumes he's acting at the crest of his rage. At that moment, he definitely would be out of control." Her smile was gone. She seemed to peer at him above the rim of her cup with a new respect. "And it's difficult to imagine the psychopathic personality regaining his control the next second after he's killed. In time to move away from the victim's body before she even slumps to the floor."

She was telling him he was right, and that flustered him. "I must rejoin the others in a moment," he said. "Tell me, Sister. What is it you intend to do to help me stop this lunatic?"

Sister Bethany replaced her cup in its saucer demurely. For the first time it occurred to him to wonder how natural diffidence and humility were to her. And how much justification there was for the self-assurance he was beginning to pick up from her attitude and comments.

"Gradually, I'm developing a profile of the troubled and terrible person who is stalking us even as we finally start to stalk him. With no undue modesty, I'm quite good at this kind of thing." Her face was heart-shaped, he realized; it occurred to him she was the prettiest unpretty woman he had met. "If we had the time, I might be able to pick the killer out of such a limited number of suspects and talk with him, *reach* the person on one level or another, forestall an early attack."

"We don't have the time." He said it under his breath while he stood. A "troubled" person!

"Then, all I can promise," Sister Bethany said quietly, "is that even if the murderer kills one of us during the next raid, I'll determine his identity—and there'll be no further killings after the helicopter has evacuated us."

A promise! Feeling enormous and clumsy looking down at her, he bent slightly. "Most people here heard that the first two victims were Jews, and that this afternoon's victim had a British passport and name. Before you rule a terrorist out completely, Sister, you'd better know that her maiden name was Epstein."

She sighed sadly. "Alas, Captain, that only stresses a factor for which we simply do not have the time."

He opened his mouth, astonished. "But a fact is a fact."

"Those." She spoke with disdain. "Modern people, in trying to be better than nature, or not a part of it, have used facts to make the devastating weapons that military men then bend over backward to refrain from using! We handpick the facts that serve us, ignore the rest. Well, that's what *I'll* do. It's just that I belong to realms of nature and authority which fail to conform with the realms you prefer."

He saw the mustached manager with the food at his table. "I think you're talking about the supernatural," he corrected her gently, "not the natural."

"Oh? Your logic would force us to see that the killer has a means of identifying the victims. You might find he knew them all before coming to the hotel or that they were all familiar with each other. You might— *if* we all remained in this place indefinitely. Where's your logic, your appreciation of facts, in that?"

"Such information may be instrumental in learning the monster's identity."

Her expression pitied him. "I've learned that it's under conditions of great difficulty that people may bypass the bothersome facts and fears, and realize we're conscious creatures primarily for the purpose of discovering how to direct our own lives. We're never free until then. Cows *think* they have the liberty to go where they please."

"Sister Bethany—"

"If we didn't have a good chance to improve ourselves by learning ways to deal with crises, God would give us neither the wit to achieve nor the problems!" She, too, stood. "There would be no utter failure like mass killers, then. But we'd be nothing more than erect beasts in buildings, and God alone could truly shelter us. Captain, we can't have it both ways—the opportunity to cope with our problems, and the godlike indulgence of comprehending every conceivable *aspect* of them."

Well, he hadn't gotten a dressing-down in a long time. "You equate opportunity with crisis, intelligence with ordinary decency? Studying all the facts thoroughly with self-indulgence?"

Sister Bethany took her check. And his, for the coffee. "Thurber also wrote, 'The noblest study of mankind is Man, says Man.' When I said we'll learn who the killer is even if he attacks again, I told you that as a clinical psychologist. I also said the murders will stop then." She patted his wrist just before the sirens began anew. "That was a pledge of faith—because an element of what I'm saying to you is definitely supernatural!"

He hadn't cut the throat of a celebrity before, and the foreign slut actress was the most interesting of his remaining possibilities, but she was a luxury for a later time. The devil in the uniform would be expecting Four to be another woman. Additionally, the captain might think her an Israeli and expect her to be next.

His selection was neither Jewish nor female.

With no doubt, he was making the right choice. Everyone in the shelter was frightened that the missiles would crush or burn them to death, and most—particularly the females and Jews left—were equally terrified, at least, of him.

But a few obviously thought they were invulnerable, unassailable—immune to any attack within the bomb shelter, certainly. And those foreign fools were actually doing their best to *watch out for* the four remaining women! It was clear to see!

Fleetingly—so briefly only the blood racing in the veins took note—there was enough of a break in the cacophony of war raging in the air above the hotel for the majority of people uncomfortably huddled in the badly lit room to catch a sigh of relief. He moved then, in the silence—in his perfectly controlled composure—to cross a space of no more than ten meters to his favored victim. Not while the sound was all but deafening and they waited in tense expectancy. He crossed it at a normal, suitable speed with neither nonchalance nor stealth. He went to the elderly man appearing concerned but bravely reassuring, he went to him with an air that said he was one of them, he belonged—and he was! Then, clear as lake water about what was customary and what wasn't, displaying no sign of disjoined stress or passion, he paused ...

Until, automatically, the distinguished gentlemen sat erect and looked up expectantly from where he sat on the wooden bench.

Just as the blue eyes focused upon him and immediately before the ambassador could say "Yes?" he drove the knife into the soft folds of flesh under the prominent jaw. The blade's tip stopped short of the bone that might have pinioned it in marrow and came out cleanly on a line like a red kite tail.

Neither the young aide nor the body of the diplomat moved until he was three paces away, raising his bare hands to the unseen skies as if beseeching the gods to halt the new torrents of sound, the screams of death-dealing missiles.

Then when the youth cried out about his murdered leader, *he* was sitting next to a woman on the other side of the shelter, pretending to comfort her. Later and luxury were now.

The actress from another world rested her head gratefully, momentarily, against his arm.

"Are you from Israel?" He appeared to be trying to soothe and distract her. He had to repeat the question in two other languages before she understood, but that could have been terror.

"I am not." She stared at him blankly without turning her head, eyes midnight smudges of confusion and fear. They were breathtakingly beautiful.

"It doesn't matter," he said, bringing his hand up from where it had dangled between his knees. The hand was not empty now.

In the darkness he wasn't able to judge just where the blade entered, but he was able to drag the knife around, in a sawing motion, and to withdraw it before either his hand or cuff were soaked.

Now, perhaps, she understood what was happening. If not, the matter was of no interest to him. He kissed Five on the side of the cheek because he could, and then jumped up to join the others in a general uproar of shouts at the foreign devil in the captain's uniform to "do something."

There were twelve to go. Excluding, of course, himself.

The actress's body fell rather noisily to the shelter floor, and it was another instant of triumph when he saw from their faces that no one at all imagined she had fainted.

If only for this wonderful interval, he had become more terrible than war.

*   *   *

BECAUSE THEY'D TURNED TO HIM in the shelter, the captain had fulfilled half the ambassador's order. He had taken command of the investigation.

The main part, stopping the son of a bitch, was already a washout.

He had thought of confining the last dozen people to their rooms until morning, then dismissed the plan for various reasons. As a group, they'd still be in greater danger from missiles than from the murderer; they'd be sitting ducks, since there were no men to post as guards in front of their rooms; it would garner him no more information via interrogation than it would in the restaurant, which was nearer to the bomb shelter; and they probably wouldn't stay put anyway. Civilians didn't understand the necessity of orders or obey them faithfully regardless of nationality, and that went for the nun, too.

He turned his head to check on Sister Bethany where she sat at the same table she'd had before the last two deaths, rubbed his burr head with the palm of one hand, sighed. In the end, he'd rounded all the survivors up where they could at least get something to eat or drink, make believe the world wasn't changing. Candles provided sparse light to save the almost-drained generator, and the restaurant looked both romantic and eerie as the anteroom to hell. He'd come to have feeling for the ambassador, and that rather surprised him. He supposed he should be pleased about that, even if the feeling wasn't pure, or purely affectionate. A long while back—when he decided to stay in, make a career of it— there'd been feeling for every goddamn thing that moved. Even when that altered, he'd felt for anything on his side. Anybody. This was the first time in decades there was enough to be bothered by, and he wished detesting the politician in the old man was not a big part of the feeling.

The first person he'd questioned had been the businessman from Alexandria. He didn't know why. Probably because he and the actress had been the only ones to remain in their rooms during the dinner hour. Maybe they'd used only one room, it was a sexual thing, maybe her death had been unconnected with the other murders (since this was the only time two were killed); maybe the Egyptian had remembered a wife.

But the man (in textiles, he said) offered nothing to work with, and neither did the rest who followed him. As the manger/maître d' walked off muttering to himself, the captain realized there probably weren't a dozen suspects, not bonafide. He himself had killed nobody, the boyish aide was in a state of useless shock, and the surrender of the Allied coalition to Saddam Hussein would not have surprised the captain more than discovering the tiny nun was sprinting around in the cellar with a razor-sharp knife.

Leaving nine viable suspects. Nine who could become victims of the pervert before the bird showed up eight or nine hours from then. One who was the murderer.

Two women (other than Sister Bethany), both fifty if a day and only one conceivably attractive to a sighted man; a journalist from New Zealand, a Tel Aviv native who turned out to be a rabbi, two Turkish brothers who claimed to be importers; and the three men still working in the hotel: the bellhop, smaller than the nun and as old a some sins she fretted about. Another, the dark-skinned cook who was so heavyset and stank so much it was hard to believe anybody in a shelter could fail to see his movements. And the manager, lips always working under his mustache, hands shaking so badly he couldn't pour water.

Which left *her* to interrogate. That word, this context, was absurd. He wondered if her promises were, too—if the deaths would stop, the madman's identity be known before the morning evac. Also absurd was thinking she could be right. But like the stalker, Sister Bethany wouldn't be around to crow over him when they were airlifted out; she'd go her own way, too.

He was wondering why he disliked the thought of that when, before he could rise and walk to her table, she was heading toward his. Fast, like the answer to a short and reasonable prayer.

"You're ready for me."

"Sit down." It wasn't a question, and he was glad since he couldn't have answered it. Other women sat down in segments, as if hiding things or emphasizing things. Sister Bethany just sat. "The actress wasn't a Jew. Neither was the ambassador."

"Black Elk remarked that Native Americans did everything in circles and was asked why. 'That is because the Power of the World always works in circles, and everything tries to be round.' "

"And that means?"

"If one begins with Jews and isn't stopped, he'll proceed to the rest, but come back to Jews. He's trying to be the Power; to be round. Wherever one starts, he circles, returns." She drew herself to her seated height, little hands in her lap clasped. "I agreed that the murderer wasn't a terrorist or a psychopath. That left you with a sociopath to stop."

"What goes around comes around, I follow that. Go on."

"Unlike the psycho, this person cannot be broken emotionally by questioning him. He has no impossible dreams, he suffers no guilt, he can't be ruffled by authority or by his own emotions—for the very sound reason that he may have none."

"No feelings sounds as crazy to me as having fantasies or delusions."

"It can be, but you don't follow me." She placed her fingertips on the table edge, tablecloth and candlelight painting the nails red. "In his delusions, the psycho can't distinguish between reality and unreality. Everyone fantasizes except, perhaps, the sociopath. He makes painstaking plans, enacts them with full knowledge. You and I can't imagine what it would be like to have absolute control of our acts regardless of *what* we were doing. Automatically, we consider what others think and, unlike him, how they may feel.''

His mind was wandering and he blamed the hour, the lighting. What this woman said sounded like meaningless philosophizing, and he had to remind himself that, in fact, he had nowhere else to look for help. "The socio does none of that?"

"He *tries* to do so, at times," Sister Bethany said, "in my opinion. But because he has only the intellectual capacity to estimate how we'll react, it's just when we pin a label to him that he can start forming a clear picture of us, or of himself, Captain, he *cannot care.*"

He leaned back. "Please don't tell me he feels unloved."

"But he does—and unhated, too!" The hollows of her face were darkened by light from their candle. "He sees no reason why we should detest him until he has individually attacked us. However, because he's usually very bright and knows *about* feelings, he believes he would be fine and content if he was given enough *attention.* It's my theory that since he is incapable himself of loving, he comes to see our observance and scrutiny—our *notice—as the range of emotions we call love!*"

He was so startled, he threw out his hand and nearly knocked the candle off the table. "You're talking about notoriety, being in the *spotlight!*"

"And having enough of it." She nodded. "We see it in many leaders who are sociopathic, yet never take a life. They *have* enough time in the limelight. When they do kill, it's because someone whom they imagine loved *them* died, so that person is symbolically both punished and avenged in some way and replaced by another admirer. Captain, you looked askance when I called this man—a sociopath is almost always male—troubled; but how else can I see someone who must content himself with apparent regard, the look of being cherished or admired?" She shuddered. "To never feel or know *love* ..."

He sat forward. "Forgive me for wanting even more to stop him."

"I would," Sister Bethany said, "except you really mean—to kill him. I will stop both of you."

For one heartbeat he didn't grasp what she had said so matter-of-factly. "In the morning, Sister," he said tightly, "he'll be gone."

"So shall we all, one morning." Abruptly, her girlish giggle escaped. "James Thurber pointed out, 'Where most of us end up there is no knowing, but the hell-bent get where they are going.' I just can't let you do what you plan to yourself. The sociopath, to put it in the vernacular, doesn't give a damn. I mean that literally, Captain—but you don't get the gravity of what I'm saying. Which is why he and his kind are usually undetected in an open society. And why he seized the chance to do what he pleased in this artificially closed one."

"I suppose maybe I *don't* get it," he retorted. He made sure he was wearing his sidearm. "I suppose *I* don't care what makes him the way he is. Sister—why should I?"

"He looks no different, utters no word to indicate the presence of an abnormal mind," she went on as if he hadn't spoken, "he thinks logically—and he is incredibly dangerous to your soul, because he will do *anything* at all."

"My soul?"

"Yours, mine." The candlelight flickered. "With no treasured memories, no beloved family, no law or moral principle dear to him—no childhood crony, no pet, not even the psychopath's release when he's killed—the man we seek may possess the kind of secret knowledge that often summons . . ." She broke off.

"Supernatural powers?"

Sister Bethany beamed so happily it was as if he'd strolled into one of the old ambassador's little traps. "I'm so glad you chose those words."

"I?" he repeated with a scowl.

"I won't let you harm your soul to punish a person who has none."

"What was that?" he demanded. "*No* soul?"

"Perhaps not. But *especially*," she finished her original remark, "when he'd think you were showing you cared for him. That's an obscenity." Impulsively, she put out her hand, tried to take his. Grudgingly, he gave her the tips of his fingers. "About the mistake he makes in taking recognition for emotions we can experience, imagine this: the man who has no feeling for society will end by accepting society's opinion of him."

"You're remarkable, Sister." He extricated his fingers gently. "Yet nothing you said suggests to me you can keep the promises you made."

"True. But don't be concerned." She drew a mirror from her purse, brushed a straying auburn wave back into place. "If the bombs fall again, that will mark the end of the murders." That second her eyes provided no more light than the candle. "I know the identity of this sociopath, and I'll point him out to you."

ALL HELL BURST OUT IN THE SKIES. And though he did not much like the expression, it would burst out again, now, in the cellar shelter.

Missiles were soaring into the city at such a rate that combined with return fire, it sounded like a machine gun war. He had heard every kind of explosive except the atomic bomb, but one could not remember the music those weapons made. Not with one's ears. Possibly in the part of the mind that lingered, hovered.

He had selected his target before this raid began. Killing two again had seemed a child's dream. However, this sortie was so powerful that most of the dozen people with him were wrapping their arms around their heads or staring blankly straight ahead, teeth chattering. Only a coward would utterly rule out an unexpected opportunity.

It occurred to him as he shifted his hips in apparent nervous discomfort, but in readiness to rise and begin, that a direct hit could cave in the ceiling of the shelter in such a way that seven or eight mightn't die, could merely be badly wounded. If so, *he*—

The building tremored as if the earth itself had quaked in fear, but the danger was not from beneath them. When he saw the hotel would stand, he willed himself erect, willed his heart to be calm, his brain to operate efficiently, willed his feet to carry him—a terror-stricken-appearing man, arm upraised, lips mutely moving—toward Six.

His victim's sex, race, age, religion were no more and so less evident to him than they would have been to any normal person; they did not hypnotize or revulse him. The victims, the numbers, meant nothing except as the details physically delineating themselves individually helped fix them in memory. Not that he'd have a sexual climax, a nostalgic chill, even a sense of satisfying revenge when he recalled them and their deaths someday.

He would know just that he had fully outsmarted—bested—some of the many people who'd ordered him about and stared through him as if intuiting his essential substancelessness. And had acquired an image of *his* face—his drab, unexciting, normal face—in their memories forever.

Since no one told how long that was, a fraction of one second was enough.

"*El qounboulas,*" he complained, whining. *The bombs.* Twisting his head right to left, he seemed to be speaking to nobody in particular; like them, he was only scared, weary, seeking human contact at an instant when death confronted them all. And so he was, but *he functioned.*

Six, scarcely raising his head, scarcely saw him.

Beside the intended target, however, the young woman was lifting her head to stare into his eyes ... and bringing her palms together in a quickening beat he could not for another second understand.

She kept the rhythm up—smiling, at him, green eyes seeming to flash her approval, admiration—as he realized with amazement that *she was applauding him!*

She recognized and was *cheering* him. "Bravo!" she cried, breaking off long enough to touch the top of his hand where it clutched a knife inside his unbuttoned suit coat. Her fingers—warm, *warm.* "Bravo!"

Next to her, after a moment, the foreign devil in uniform joined her—clapped for him, too! Across the shelter, the youth who'd sat next to Number Four also acknowledged and greeted him with applause.

But the captain stopped clapping long enough to touch his hand as the woman had—and the masculine, businesslike fingers spread as if to ensnare his wrist.

Flushed, filled with confusion, he spun on his heel and raced toward the door in a bewildered daze.

—And was through it, mentally searching for a place to hide in the building he knew better than any other, when he realized tears were streaming down his cheeks into his mustache.

"YOU TRIED TO TRICK HIM, to capture him!" Sister Bethany and the captain had rushed after the murderer, but he'd slammed the shelter door in their faces. By the time they were emerging from the basement stairwell and were stepping into a deserted lobby, the hotel manager was nowhere to be seen. "You have no *trust*. Another moment and everyone present would have been applauding!"

"And then what?" Sidearm drawn, the captain proceeded carefully across the lobby to the doors. One stood wide. "Would he have had to cut the throats of the Third Armored Division for an encore?"

Realizing they hadn't needed to shout to be heard, staring through the open door at a smoke-filled but otherwise clear sky, they turned to each other. "You won't find him out there."

"There'll only be looters in those streets," he said, "except him."

She saw the sudden, horizon-eating flash of missiles miles in the distance.

"Stay here," he commanded, paused. "How did you spot him?"

Shrugging, she began to walk slowly back across the lobby. "He kept referring to *mawt*, Arabic for death, even while he was serving us. When you questioned him and let him go, he muttered *gharib*—foreign—and *qatzir*—dirty. Then a term I would rather not repeat. He promised you 'mawt,' Captain."

He stared dumbfounded from the door. "He didn't say a damn word like that," he called. "I was listening."

"You forget. I read lips. And they definitely were *damning* words."

She was at an alcove leading off the lobby. He had to raise his voice, and the tremor he heard in it made him aware of some problems his conscious mind hadn't confided clearly. "Where are you going, Sister?"

"I didn't question your ability to find him in the city, Captain. I only meant that a man who regards himself as infinitely superior wouldn't have gone out among looters to hide." She was small as a speck across the long lobby. "Neither you nor he would've had to open those doors, Captain. The glass was already shattered by the blasts."

He glanced down at the floor and saw that he was crunching shards under his feet. Looking up, he saw that the speck had vanished.

SHE REMEMBERED READING THE SIGN indicating the *lukanda* manager's office when she checked in, and she wasn't surprised when the door yielded to her slight weight and opened. The only reason she hesitated in the entrance was to let her vision adjust to the darkness.

"Hiding can be rather demeaning, I think." The office door went back all the way to the wall with a light push. "I really do believe your timing and planning have been brilliant." No reply. "Between the two of us, your hotel is being evacuated in a few hours. You can see for yourself, it *is* over."

Yellow as urine, his face materialized in a flare of dim light. When he put the lantern down, his eyes still had a uremic cast to them, and the mustache that managed to conceal and distort the lower part of his face looked as if he had pulled his head out of a toilet. No startlement, no apprehension in the eyes. They didn't even swing to a position beyond her to search for the uniformed man.

He stood in a corner of his office—not crouching but bracing himself on the wall with one hand, idly. The knife in the other hand was gripped as if he'd just completed a business call and hadn't put the phone back in its cradle. Sirens screeched above the hotel, and a low hum began building with such incremental steadiness that it suggested to Sister Bethany an abnormally swift growth of tissue around the building. He glanced up, casually curious, as though trying to gauge distances with astronomical precision. "Gounod's *Ave Maria* is lovely."

"I think so." She went in, closed the door quietly behind her. There were other marked offices along the corridor, and the captain couldn't read Arabic. "I didn't write it, of course. Neither the music nor the words." A flag hung from one wall, framed photographs of other mustache-wearing men from another. "You're aware of my vocation, then." The humming grew much closer now; the cocoon around the *lukanda* was hardening.

"I saw that you were intelligent. You were to be one of the last." He didn't quite imply it, but she inferred his belief that she could still be. His gaze dropped from the heavens, came at her like tracer fire. "It may be of *faida*—interest—to know I hoped to keep you awhile, with me. Now," his eyelids went back to show tears standing in them, "I must decide swiftly the degree of your sincerity, your touch. Were you really appreciative or, filled with your churchly arrogance, just pretending and hungry to watch me at work?"

She raised her arms slightly and walked nearer. *Bypass the bothersome facts and fears,* she thought. "I think it wouldn't be quite reasonable to question my sincerity. Other qualities, perhaps." She thought she heard the captain cautiously trying other doors outside the office but couldn't be sure with the *qounboulas* falling again. "You see that I noticed you, singled you out."

"Naam," he agreed, appearing curious.

"I am prepared now to tell you what I think about you—if it matters."

He didn't move. He considered that. "How can I know if it matters until I have heard what it is?" he said. "Come; tell me. And I"—he left the wall, outstretched both his arms, the knife no more unconventional to him than a wristwatch or a belt—"I shall tell you what is in my heart."

God alone can comprehend all aspects at times of crisis, Sister Bethany told herself. It wouldn't be possible to forget how he looked then, or the feeling that she might have grown vain in her knowledge. *Direct your life, Sister!*

One framed photo shot across the room. Simultaneously, the wall behind him collapsed, a missile hitting the corner of the hotel directly. The noise for an instant was too varied, too consuming, to be bearable. It was all there was.

. . . She was kneeling with no notion how she had gotten there—

And the sociopath seemed to have been obliterated.

Something, partly slithering; the sound of cloth and bone worming free. A clenched fist, the blade of a knife raked against suddenly visible bursts of explosive in the midnight sky. He, he was wrenching himself out of the rubble into a sitting position. His mustache was a smoky remnant, yet the smile was beneath it.

Sister Bethany realized he either had no legs or they were crushed under him.

"A hug." He said it plainly, neither plea nor command. It was what he wanted. Gouts of blood were on his teeth, others snapped out when he spoke. "Hug me, and I shall speak my heart."

She got to her feet. Pain somewhere. She walked toward the man with no legs.

The sharp sound like something cracking made her turn her head, and the captain stood in the doorway, partly crouching, aiming. He did not seem to see her.

She whirled and tried to run the rest of the distance to the partly buried man. "I think God—"

"Muzlim," he bit off the word. Eyes roved from her to the captain, back. And when she stood in the captain's line of sight and was inches away from her goal, she saw nothing in the eyes for her to recognize. "You—I—we're all *muzlim,* all is."

He dragged the edge of the knife across his throat, deeply.

It stayed in his hand, was covered with blood immediately, and his eyes weren't appreciably dimmer than they had been in life.

"Darkness." Sister Bethany touched his cheek, then herself. The captain was attempting to draw her away. "He said everyone is—darkness."

Because the war went on, she allowed herself to be guided into the undamaged portion of the hotel, wishing the man who had managed it had allowed her to say what she'd meant to tell him.

That she thought God loved him.

"WE MUST REMEMBER that one is able to see only to the limits permitted by one's structure, for the instrument of seeing is oneself."
—James Wyckoff, 1975

Susan B. Kelly is a British writer primarily known for her novels, which include *Hope Against Hope,* and *Time of Hope,* both featuring businesswoman-turned-sleuth Alison Hope. Her short fiction, although rare, is just as well received, as shown by this story, which placed third in the Mystery Writers of America's short story contest. In "The Best Sort of Husband," she examines the lengths that men in the Victorian Age would go to for a wife.

The Best Sort of Husband
SUSAN B. KELLY

A single woman with a very narrow income must be a ridiculous, disagreeable old maid.

Emma

"My brothers, as you know, Jane, are quite desperate to be rid of me."

I nodded. I did know. I could see their point. There is no condition worse than impoverished gentility. A lesser man might take himself into trade, forging his own vulgar riches and buying Nottingham lace by the yard for his wife. But a *gentleman*—one who has been to a good school and kept his terms at Oxford—is restricted in his choice of career: the army, the church, the law. None of these pays well since they are professions for gentlemen and assume a modest—or, preferably, immodest—private income.

It is, in short, a circular problem, since a gentleman without family money and property cannot earn a living as a gentleman—not if he wants to hunt.

It's a paradox which has vexed finer minds than mine and I do not intend to waste any more time on it.

It brings us, however, to the Crampton family and my visitor that day, Miss (Margaret) Crampton. She was the eldest of the four Crampton children and the only girl. Colonel Crampton had died ten years ago— an incident with a shotgun which had made the coroner harrumph a lot before returning an "Accidental" verdict. He had left some impressive debts of honour of which Mrs. Crampton had, until that moment, been happily oblivious.

Her family had reluctantly and meanly rallied round, obliging that lady, who was not a good manager at the best of times, to provide as well as she could for Mr. John, Mr. Richard, and Mr. George and—bottom of the pile, left to the sweepings, the gleanings, when all the rest had been seen to—poor dear Margaret.

Margaret, who had never had much hope of a husband, even before her father's disgrace.

It was not that she was exactly plain: Indeed, I found it hard to account for the fact that she was not at least as handsome as myself. Her features were regular enough—her nose not too long and sharp, as mine is, her eyes a soft and pretty grey, her mouth large and gentle and disinclined to sarcastic remarks, which is a good thing in a woman in need of a husband—but there was something undistinguished about the ensemble, something that made sure no eligible gentleman looked twice.

She had a good, fresh colour to her cheeks that morning and her soft, if overly fine, hair of that pale shade which is not unlike straw, and which was always inclined to escape from her bonnet at ill-timed moments of agitation and exertion, was threatening almost to tumble about her shoulders.

She had taken her bonnet off altogether, since we were old friends and very confidential. She looked sadly at it as it lay on her lap like a dead dog; it was old and shabby, although she dutifully trimmed it anew each spring.

We were sitting in the front parlour, the one with the creaking door which gives me warning of sudden eavesdroppers—maids coming in to shake dusters about ineffectually or Mama fretting over what to order from the butcher for dinner.

In fact, Mama and Dear Cassandra had gone out to bully some of the local poor into being less feckless—indeed, less *poor*—and my guest and I were alone in the house—except for the servants, obviously.

She had agreed to take a dish of tea with me.

"It's not that I have anything against Mr. Bailey," she went on. "He is a gentleman of good fortune, it seems, and refined education. His manners are not objectionable. He has a good address."

"He lives in Curzon Street, I understand, and in Dorset."

"I meant," she said witheringly, "that he has a good upright bearing."

"Oh."

Well, it's an easy mistake to make. And Curzon Street *is* a good address, all the same. As is several hundred acres of Dorset.

"He's not even all that bad-looking," I ventured, "or so I've heard."

She shrugged. "In fact there is much to be said for him and his offer."

And single women have such a dreadful propensity for being poor, as I remarked to dear Cassandra just the other day, possibly not for the first time, since a well-turned phrase bears repeating.

"But we know so little of him," Margaret went on, "and now he turns up asking me to marry him, and John and Richard and George are determined to make sure I say 'Yes,' and will make my life a misery if I refuse him, unless I can come up with a really *sound* reason for doing so.

"You see, Jane," she concluded. "I *like* being single."

I sighed in sympathy, although I wasn't sure whom—principally—with. I can see that there is no greater burden for a young man than a plain and fading spinster sister, raised to do nothing useful but know a little French and point out India on a globe, draw a passable imitation of a landscape with three-legged cows, and bang out a few tunes on a twenty-guinea pianoforte.

It was hardly surprising, therefore, that John (etc.) had seized on Mr. Thomas Bailey like a good angel from heaven. Margaret was twenty-nine, after all, and getting to that time of life when ladies are assumed to be fast gathering dust on the shelf.

Gentlemen, I have noticed, seem to think that one husband is as good to their sister as another, so long as he's got money in the bank and the right sort of relations and doesn't spit in the street. They do not think a woman should have irrational prejudices in preferring Mr. James to Mr. Henry, or sandy hair to black, or a cavalry moustache to a clean lip.

Still, the temptation was always there: one's own home, a dress allowance, the superior title of "Mrs."; with the right sort of husband it was not to be lightly spurned. With the best sort of husband.

The question was, though: What was in it for Mr. Thomas Bailey?

"You are lucky, Jane," Margaret was saying, "in not being in such a precarious position."

Which I was, I readily admit. True, my sainted father had also died early (although not by his own hand!) and I had as fair a share of brothers as a girl might wish—rather more than Margaret, indeed—in addition to my elder sister Cassandra.

Like Margaret, I had no money of my own with which to buy a husband and, also like her, no real wish to possess such a commodity.

The crucial difference between us was that my brother Edward had been adopted in infancy by my rich and childless cousin, Mr. Knight, and had now come into his inheritance and was in a position, therefore, to offer Mama and us two spinster girls this small but comfortable cottage in the village of Chawton for as long as we should require it, and to guarantee us against starvation.

Which was just as well, since anybody less well equipped than I to go a-governessing is hard to imagine. I can see myself running amok and laying about me with a stick at all the Miss Julias and Miss Matildas that are inflicted on me; then being sent home on the first post chaise in disgrace, having broken Master Peter's pate when he answered me back.

"He is thirty-five," Margaret continued, musing almost to herself, "claims to have a clear four thousand a year. There are two children, of course. A boy and a girl."

"Yes," I said, since this was partly the point at issue. "What exactly did happen to his first two wives?"

IT'S NOT AT ALL UNUSUAL, of course, to lose one wife in childbed, or to consumption, or any one of the thousand natural shocks that flesh is heir to, which is why middle-aged spinsters never lose hope, since there are always gentlemen coming back, as it were, on the market, only slightly shop-soiled. Occasionally they take the opportunity to marry some pretty young flibbertigibbet, but usually they want someone older and steadier, someone who will be a housekeeper and mother to their little orphans without producing more mouths to feed and backs to clothe and brains to cram with useless facts.

Two, though? Bad luck at the very least. And yet . . . if Margaret had been an heiress it would make sense, but she was not, far from it.

"He has gone on to Bath," my friend said, "and is coming back at the end of the month for my answer."

I began to see.

"I thought that since you, my dear Jane, are leaving for Bath at the end of the week . . . " She broke out suddenly, quite wringing her poor bonnet with her hands. "Oh, how I wish I could go to Bath! To spend the winter there in gaiety! What I would give!"

"But what am I to do? I'm not some sort of *spy*, Margaret."

"Just talk to his acquaintance. Watch him. Observe him at your leisure, and at his. Find out for me what measure of man this is that I am to tie myself to on such slight knowledge. Or, better still, give me a good reason—some vice, some sordid secret—" she lowered her eyes and her voice demurely, keeping up the seemly pretence that we single women know nothing of such matters "—some *woman* of the lower orders living under his protection—that will allow me to hang onto my respectable spinster state without fraternal reproach."

Well, I could hardly say no, could I?

But are they all horrid, are you sure they are all horrid?
Northanger Abbey

AS CHANCE WOULD HAVE IT, I found myself that Friday being gallantly escorted to Bath by Mr. Richard Crampton, who had business at the Assize session the following week. Mr. Dick was the middle son, now twenty-four and a barrister, having qualified for this role in life by taking a degree at Oxford and eating the requisite amount of dinners at Gray's Inn.

I prayed earnestly that I would never have need of his services. It was to be hoped, for the sake of his future progress in his sphere, that he stood far enough away from the judge to spare him his bad breath.

Me, he did not spare.

Like all the brothers, Dick was a thickset, florid, somewhat *lumbering* young man of not above middle height. His sandy hair limped out from under his hat and hung over his meagre eyes with their invisible lashes. He had little conversation beyond horses, politics, and the recent wars against the French. Of the poems of Sir Walter Scott and the novels of Mrs. Fanny Burney or Mrs. Radcliffe, he had no opinion.

Of himself, he had a very good opinion.

He was a commonplace young man; like every young man I have ever met, except perhaps one, and he is dead. I am glad that, at almost forty, I may finally be considered safe from any matrimonial consideration whatsoever and may assume the chaperone's role by the fire with a glass of warm wine, although there was a time, when we first moved to Chawton, when I might have been induced to marry the Reverend Mr. Papillon, purely for the pleasure of being Mrs. Butterfly.

I was never put to the test, however, Mr. Papillon being very set on maintaining his bachelor state.

And all of which is quite beside the point.

Mr. Dick drove competently. The journey seemed to take forever.

He was inordinately proud of the fact that Captain John Crampton had been wounded in the leg at the battle of Vitoria three months earlier. I couldn't help thinking that Master Jack, had he been quicker on his feet, and a bit less *lumbering,* might have dodged the French sabre or musket or whatever it was, but I did not say so.

It was hardly *new* news, anyway. I know the latest excitement often taken a long time to reach our quiet corner of Hampshire, but John Crampton had been sitting at home with his leg up on a stool since mid-July and it was now early September. I had already heard several times how he had personally put Buonaparté's forces to rout and had had to throw a fake faint last time the story threatened.

Luckily, the Crampton brothers are the sort of men who are always expecting women to faint on them. Except for maidservants, obviously.

We finally lapsed into silence and I was able to peruse the volume of Cowper I had brought along with me for the journey in peace.

Young Mr. George, by the way, had opted for the church and had become positively unctuous since being ordained the previous summer. If all three brothers had gone into the same profession, of course, they might have helped each other on, but were they bright enough to think of that?

Were they—!

Although I suppose, between the three of them, they had everything pretty well covered.

Dear Margaret was worth more than all of them put together, and I was determined to help her out of her predicament if I could.

I LOATHE BATH, as everybody knows, but I had not been in the best of health all summer and Mama would simply not hear of my turning down the invitation to spend a few weeks in Queen Square with my brother Edward, and with Fanny, Lizzy, Marianne, and the rest of his girls, to bathe and drink daily in the spa.

At least this time I had something to keep me occupied. So no sooner had I settled in and supervised the unpacking of my trunk and the disposition of my gowns, than I donned a pair of pattens as insurance against mud, took my new pelisse in case it turned cold and a parasol against sudden sun, and thus prepared for all eventualities, announced that I was just taking a brisk walk to the Pump Room to see if any of my acquaintance was in town.

I successfully fended off all offers to accompany me ... except those of my brother Henry, who was still mourning the loss of his wife Eliza six months earlier and whom I had not the heart to gainsay.

Henry was no trouble as an escort, in fact, having little to say for himself these days and a great deal of sighting to do, which enabled us to proceed on our way in companionable silence. I was slightly surprised that he had chosen to bring his wounded heart to a bustling social place like Bath, but I knew that since Eliza's death he had been besieged by eager spinsters who could spot a well-to-do, gentlemanlike widower across thirty miles and without spectacles and who had no compunction about moving in for the kill. No doubt he had left Chelsea to escape from a particularly persistent specimen.

I had no difficulty in spotting Mr. Bailey at the Pump Room, since he was in the company of Richard Crampton, the two seeming very confidential. They were together too at the concert at the Assembly Rooms that evening and to be seen walking arm in arm in the Circus the following morning. They were like Mary and her wretched lamb, in that everywhere Mr. Bailey went, Mr. Dick was sure to go.

Presumably he was making sure that Bailey didn't change his mind about marrying Margaret or get entrapped by some widow of a certain age and uncertain income while no one was looking.

I contrived an introduction in the Lower Rooms the next afternoon, although Mr. Dick looked as if he would have avoided it if he could, mumbling my name and the apologetic, "A neighbour in Chawton." I then had a strained conversation with Mr. Bailey about the latest uses of electricity to treat gout, from which ailment, he hastened to assure me, he did not suffer. As I did not suffer from it either, the subject did not seem to be leading anywhere very fruitful.

An everyday sort of man, I concluded, as would make a respectable husband for a poor spinster and leave a bit over. His complexion was a little pockmarked when you got close up, but you would cease to notice that by the end of the wedding journey. He might be growing a little stout under his waistcoat, but what can you expect at five and thirty? At least the waistcoat itself was tastefully restrained—plain white marcella—which is by no means guaranteed these days, what with HRH the Prince Regent and his ornate friend Mr. Brummell setting the fashion.

He didn't have the ruddy complexion or well-veined nose of a two-bottles-of-claret-a-day man, and his hands, as he offered to lead me back to my seat after the interval, were the pale, soft, well-kept sort you don't associate with vice. I was beginning to think that I could be of no use to my friend in discovering Mr. Bailey's guilty secret.

Where so many hours have been spent in convincing myself that I am right, is there not some reason to fear I may be wrong?
Sense and Sensibility

HENRY SEEMED TO TAKE A FANCY to him, though, and soon the two of them were swopping gloomy stories of dead wives over the foul-tasting water in the Pump Room every morning. I had not taken my brother into my confidence, but took the opportunity every evening to pump *him* in turn about what his new friend had said to him.

Henry's opinion was that Tom Bailey was a lonely, affectionate man, unlucky to have lost two wives in only ten years, who just wanted a nice woman to share his house and sit at the foot of his table, who needn't be handsome as long as she was good-natured and kind to his children and brought a few thousand pounds in the four percents to pay for her own keep.

Which was part of the problem: Margaret would be lucky to have two hundred pounds of her own and that not until Mrs. Crampton was dead. I did not mention this to Henry, who was not acquainted with the Crampton family or their situation.

So it was in his capacity as Henry's friend that Mr. Bailey was invited to a small private ball at Queen Square about ten days later. Mr. Richard Crampton, who was still in Bath despite the Assize being long over, was also invited as a Chawton man and my friend's brother. The Reverend George Crampton, who had recently arrived in town and who did not allow his clerical orders to prevent him from dancing (*lumberingly*) and drinking, had apparently invited himself.

Henry threw his head into his hands at the very mention of dancing and gaiety and determined not to attend, but Edward wasn't going to let that spoil anyone else's fun, and I personally was looking forward to tripping a measure and showing off my new spotted muslin ... and exposing my bosom with the best of them.

I CANNOT IMAGINE what it is like to lose a beloved spouse, of course, although I grieved long and hard for my father in the year five, but it seemed to me that Henry, who is of a naturally optimistic disposition, was beginning to show signs of recovering spirits and might have been badgered into attending the festivities had anyone tried hard enough, but as no one could be bothered, he was stuck with his original insistence that it would be too painful for him.

I was not particularly surprised, therefore, to find him hanging around in the anteroom to the best drawing room halfway through the evening, sipping punch and observing without being observed from behind a purple velvet curtain. I had danced every dance and was feeling tired, especially having had my left ankle repeatedly kicked by The Rev. George in the quadrille, so took the chance to sit with him for a while.

So it was in this manner, as in all the best novels of Mrs. Fanny Burney and Mrs. Radcliffe, that we came to overhear one of those odd and illuminating conversations that seem to occur only in books, this one being between Richard and George Crampton, carried out with the utmost safety—as they thought—under cover of the hubbub.

"HAS MARGARET BEEN BROUGHT TO CONSENT?" asked Dick.

"Not yet, but she will, with promises of new bonnets and threats of our displeasure. It is for her own good, after all, and it's not as if she will have to tolerate him for very long."

"But she doesn't know that, and must not. My sister is a woman of such high moral principle, such refined and truly delicate and feminine sensibilities—"

"Yes, yes," George interrupted him. "How is the groom, more to the point?"

"Happily convinced that my father secreted a large fortune in gold and gems before his ..."

"Accident."

"Quite. In a place where his creditors would never find them."

"Thus enabling us to provide Margaret with a suitable marriage portion. Have you drawn up the settlement?"

"I have."

"And is it watertight?"

"It is. The children will have to be provided for on his death, of course, but my sister will still be a very wealthy widow. He has no close family to kick up a fuss, as you know."

(I have noticed that these sorts of conversations in books always usefully have people telling other people things they already know.)

"Splendid!" George rubbed his hands together and I could hear the slap of sweat. Wet-palmed George the Cramptons' maidservants called him when they thought no one was listening, and they should know. "Then I shall carry out the wedding service, quietly and discreetly as befits a double widower and an ageing spinster, then—"

"Then," Dick concluded for him, "the lawyer will have done his bit and the rector will have done his bit and it remains only for the 'wounded' soldier to do his bit."

"Which no one will suspect since our hero is laid up at home with a bad cut in the leg from the cowardly Frenchies and cannot leave the house."

They both laughed, and a few minutes later I heard them move off, back into the dance.

Well, I did say they had everything covered between the three of them. Pity there wasn't a fourth brother who was a doctor, to attest that there had been no foul play, and a fifth who was an undertaker—not that either of those was a suitable career for a *gentleman.*

I glanced at Henry to see how much he had heard or understood, but he was miles away.

"Eliza was always at her loveliest at social gatherings," he bleated. "I fell in love with her at such a private ball as this, all dressed in white, her glorious hair in those . . . curl things women used to wear in the nineties."

He began to cry.

"Henry?"

He hiccupped. "Yes, Jane?"

Too much punch.

I wrote to Margaret by the next post, laying all before her. I did feel rather pleased with myself at having succeeded in carrying out my commission and with such speed, although naturally I played down the role of good fortune in revealing the plot to me and emphasised my own skill and wit. Margaret could now confront her brothers with their iniquity or, perhaps, just rid herself of Mr. Bailey by letting drop the fact that there was no secret treasure, no dowry.

The confrontation need not be long delayed since the Crampton brothers left Bath four days later, taking Mr. Bailey with them to get their sister's answer. I rather wished he might know to whom he owed his deliverance, but there was no real hope of that, and I got on with my holiday-cum-rest-cure, walking about with Henry and visiting the theatre and taking a little chaise out to Clifton one day.

I was surprised to receive a letter from Cassandra two weeks later, arriving the very day of my own departure from Bath. I thought any news she had to convey might have awaited my return. But this was too new, too exciting; she could not contain herself.

I learnt to my astonishment that Margaret Crampton and Mr. Bailey had been married by special license just five days earlier. So my dear friend had come to like him after all, chosen to accept his offer and link her destiny with his.

Of all the dreadful luck.

It was with sinking heart that I read on. I was sadly not at all astonished to learn that Mr. Bailey had met with a fatal accident while out riding the very next day. He had been quite alone, according to Cassandra, taking an early run on one of Mr. Jack's best hunters, which was in sore need of exercise with its master laid up.

"The poor creature must have bolted and stumbled into a rabbit hole," my sister wrote, "throwing its rider unconscious onto his head.

"If anyone had been with him, of course, something might have been done, but it was several hours before anyone feared for his safety and set out to look for him, and by then it was too late."

Cassandra, my dear kindhearted sister, was distraught on Margaret's behalf. Imagining her sorrow and dismay, widowed not four and twenty hours after her wedding breakfast.

How, I wondered, could my letter have so tragically miscarried? The post was usually reliable. I blamed myself; I was in anguish. By what cruel fate had Margaret not been warned in time?

A large income is the best recipe for happiness I ever heard of. It certainly may secure all the myrtle and turkey part of it.
Mansfield Park

THE HASTY FUNERAL WAS OVER and the new widow away in London by the time I reached home, so I was none the wiser and still full of self-doubt. I watched the post daily as it come to the Cramptons' mean house along the Winchester Road, expecting to see my letter, inexplicably delayed, arriving too horribly late. I wondered if there was any means of intercepting it, since for her to read it now ...

It was not to be thought of.

She was dealing with the house in Curzon Street—although one would have expected Richard to volunteer for this sad task—consulting her husband's bankers and men of law and disposing sensibly of the poor children to boarding school.

She did not return for a month, and when she did I scarcely knew my friend, so stiff and formal had she become, actually *curtseying* to me instead of shaking my hand.

I remembered to call her Mrs. Bailey, although she hardly seemed entitled to the name after such a short tenure, and noticed that her gown, while obviously the deepest mourning, was also the latest style and the best silk. She had equipped herself with a little carriage, too, with the prettiest pair of ponies you ever saw and a footman in scarlet livery.

"Dear Jane." She unbent a little and took my hand as I murmured my shocked condolences. "How good it is to see you again. Always the dearest friend, always the best of *correspondents.*"

She moved to Bath herself soon after, and I occasionally see her there in the distance, out of mourning now and dressed in the height of fashion, surrounded by beaus and sycophants and flatterers, dining with the best people, reserving the most expensive box at the theatre for her exclusive use.

She has a new bonnet every week.

She has not remarried since she was, as she had told me, very satisfied with the unmarried state, and since widows, unlike spinsters, were not so very inclined to be poor. She seemed more than satisfied with her lot, having procured for herself the very best sort of husband.

She always waves if she sees me, although often she does not seem to see me, which is just as well, I think, since I am the only one outside the family who knows the truth and she is the only one who knows that I know and I value my skin as much as the next woman.

I HAVE NOTHING MORE TO SAY on this subject. I have novels to write. I think I shall set one in Bath one day, although there will not be any murders in it since murders are not my thing.

Fiction, whatever anyone says, is always much stranger than truth.

William F. Nolan is best known for his science fiction trilogy *Logan's Run, Logan's World,* and *Logan's Search,* which detail a future world ruled by the young, where the most deadly crime is growing old. However, during his more than forty years as a professional writer, he has produced more than a thousand short stories and nonfiction works, as well as dozens of novels, scripts, and teleplays. He has also been recognized for excellence in various genres, winning two Edgar awards and an Academy of Science Fiction and Fantasy award for fiction and film. He is at his best when writing stories like "An Act of Violence," holding off until the last possible moment to reveal the final twist on an already uncommon scenario.

An Act of Violence
WILLIAM F. NOLAN

June 20, 1994

To Janice Coral Olinger,

Having read every word you've written, I feel I know you well enough to address you as "Dearest Janice," but of course this would not be socially appropriate. I'm a fellow writer who stands in your very tall shadow—but (to my honor and delight) we *have* shared many an anthology contents page together. Thus far, nine of my humble tales have been selected for anthologies in which your fine work has appeared. But I doubt that you read my contributions or even know I exist, since you probably have no time for the work of obscure writers such as myself. (I know how busy you are: *Conversations with Janice Coral Olinger* lists 98 books in a 30-year career span, and at least 25 of these are major novels. Amazing output!) But, hey, you don't have to know me because this letter will serve to introduce me to you.

My reason for writing at this time is to extend my sincere and heartfelt condolences on the very recent death of your husband, Theodore N. Olinger. I know that you and "Ted" were both very devoted to one another and that his sad passing (isn't cancer a bitch!) was a severe blow to you emotionally. Ted (if I may so refer to him) was a wonderful poet and an astute critic, and I realize that you both shared an intellectual and creative seedground as well as an abiding physical attraction. Your sex life with Ted is naturally none of my business, but a strong sexual bond was evident from your mutual behavior in public. The way you held hands and *touched* each other at that P.E.N. awards dinner made this very clear to me. (Yeah, I was there.)

Anyhow, please accept my deepest sympathy at this immense and tragic loss in your life. I trust that once you have weathered your period of mourning you will again return to the role you were born for: that of a supreme artist of the written word.

With profound respect and good wishes,
Alex Edward

P.S. My address is on the envelope in case you wish to reply—and I *do* hope you will wish to do so.

July 30, 1994

Dear Janice Coral Olinger,

Well, the Great Wheel of Time grinds ever onward and I see that more than a full month has gone by without a reply from you to my missive of 20 June. That's fine, really it is. I had, of course, hoped for a reply, but I am certainly not surprised that I failed to receive one. In view of your personal family loss, this is quite understandable, and I bear you no malice. I'm sure your mail has been piling up from many other devoted readers and that you simply have not been up to answering it. (Bet you get a *ton* of letters!)

However, now that you have been granted suitable time to pull yourself together, I *would* ask that you be kind enough to honor me with a personal reply.

I'm excited about your latest novel, WHOSE BLOOD IS IT, ANY-HOW? (what a bold and splendid title!) which I have had the pleasure of reading as they say "cover to cover." (In fact, I was up most of last night lost in those final, dynamic chapters!) May I say that I am truly awestruck at the passion and artistry evident on every page of this epic work. Your short stories are marvelous watercolors, but your novels are many-layered oil paintings. (At least, that's how I think of them.) And your dialogue . . . wow! No one in America today handles dialogue with your deft, incisive touch. Just one example (of oh, so many!): when your dying politician, Arthur (invoking shades of Camelot, right?) bids his final farewell to Morgana (a clever reversal of character names in terms of darkness and light), their exchange left me literally breathless. The entire scene was illuminated by your brilliant dialogue. Viva! Bravissimo!

I could go on for pages about BLOOD, but I'll let the critics rave for me—as they most certainly will. Let me just say how much your work has inspired my own, how your fire and passion have transformed my life. I am a better man, a better human being, because of Janice Coral Olinger. Salud!

By the way, to prove whereof I speak, I have every one of your books in mint first editions, with each dust jacket carefully protected by a clear plastic cover.

As a writer, you are numero uno. No one else has your heart, your spirit, your expansive imagination. I stand in humble awe of your powers.

Enough. Write to me soon and let me know your reaction to this letter. I eagerly await your response.

With sincere admiration,
Alex Edward

August 25, 1994

Dear Janice Coral Olinger,

I'm frankly perplexed. All these weeks have gone by and I haven't heard a peep out of you. I know you received my letters since my return address was plain on each and I never got them back from the post office. Have you been ill? On a trip? Away on a lecture tour? What's the problem? All I have asked is that you take a few minutes to reply to someone who has shown his deep and sincere respect for your boundless creative gifts? Truly, I don't see why you can't write me a letter (however brief) acknowledging my existence. Why do you continue to ignore me in this disturbing fashion when it is obvious I so greatly admire you? (It seems that common courtesy alone would dictate a reply.) I repeat, what's the problem?

Last night I reread your short story, "The River Incident"—which rightfully earned the O. Henry prize in '82 (go, Janice!). And once again I was struck with your employment of raw violence within the context of a higher sense of morality. Your characters *transcend* death, even though they may themselves die or cause others to die. In "The River Incident," when Cara shoots her father on the river bank, her act is not an act of violence, but of release. (Obviously, this is what the O. Henry judges realized.) Knowing there is no hope for the old man's future, knowing that life has become a terrible burden on him, Cara sends a .45 slug into his brain, allowing him ultimate freedom and a release from the crippling cage of his body. (Which is exactly what the great lady poet Sylvia Plath accomplished with her suicide; I *know* you agree.) "Go, my father, go," she says, pressing the barrel against his temple and pulling the trigger. She is sending him on a wondrous journey. Thus, her act is one of great compassion.

I am curious. What was your motivation for this story? Did it come out of your own life—or did you hear about an incident like this when you were growing up in that house by the river in Maryland? (The story has a ring of stark truth which cannot be denied.) Or did it all flow from your incredible imagination? Please, write and let me know.

Devotedly yours,
Alex Edward

September 2, 1994

Dear (silent) Janice Coral Olinger,

Here we are into September and I've had *no* word of any kind from you. I am baffled (and, I must confess, somewhat hurt) by your continued silence and lack of human response. Why are you treating me in this manner? Why are my letters to you being ignored? Why am *I* being ignored? It is obvious from what I've written how much I admire you and your works. I have made this abundantly clear. Why, then, have you chosen to bypass me utterly, as if I don't exist? I simply do not understand why you cannot spare a few random minutes for me (no matter *how* busy you may be).

This is not like you, not in character with your work. Your books, for all their overt violence, are extremely humanistic at their core, and I know you to be a gentle, caring person, a creature of warm compassion. (What was it Ted said of you in that *Newsweek* piece? ... that you were "a vessel of tenderness.") One look into those round dark luminous eyes of yours clearly reveals your compassionate soul. Well, what about sending some of that compassion in my direction? I could *use* a little. All I'm asking of you is a simple note, after all. A few kind words, letting me know you appreciate my devotion as a dedicated reader. Is this too much to ask? I think not. Right now, with my letter before you, write and let me know you *care.*

Vaya con Dios!
Alex Edward

October 15, 1994

Janice Coral Olinger,

I find that I can no longer address you as "Dear." Your cold, unresponsive silence has rendered such a salutation impossible. I checked my files today and find that I first wrote you a letter (and a fine, warm one it was!) on 20 June—almost *four full months ago*! I followed up this initial missive with those of 30 July, 25 August, and 2 September, all without a *single word* back from you. There is no excuse for this kind of rudeness.

You insult me with your stubborn refusal to respond to my letters. It is no longer possible for me to maintain positive feelings toward you. Your cruelty has also tainted your work, and this is most unfortunate. I now look at your shelved books and mourn the past. You have wounded me deeply. Additionally, you have made me look like a fool. I wrote to praise you and got nothing back. I'm becoming very angry at you Ms. Olinger—or however the hell you like to be addressed. Just who do you think you are, some Goddess living up in the clouds? You live right here on good ole Mother Earth, just like I do. We both breathe, eat, and shit, like everybody else on this lousy planet. You're no Goddess, lady. You may know how to write novels and stories, but you sure don't know much about common courtesy.

And what do you say to this?

In frustration,
Alex Edward

December 10, 1994

Olinger bitch ...

Again, you have chosen to callously ignore my letter of 15 October. You obviously don't give a flying fuck about me, or my opinions, or my words, or anything else having to do with Alex Edward. Normally, I'm a real easygoing guy, patient, reasonable, quick to forgive and forget— but you've gone over the line. Your snotty silence is just too fucking much. I will *not* be treated this way. Not by you or by anybody. Let me state my position loud and clear: either I get a letter of apology from you within the next ten days or I'll be over to your house in Baltimore to give you a Christmas present you *won't* like. Remember what the witch said to Dorothy in that Oz film ... "and your little dog, too!" Well, I'll also have a present for that witless little pansy poodle you lug around in your arms for all those dust jacket photos. I think you should know that what you are doing is directly promoting an act of violence. You are really one rude bitch and if I don't hear from you this time, I'm sure as hell going to pay you a personal visit.

Think I'm bluffing? Just blowing off steam? Think I won't act? Then think again, sister, because you are dealing with a guy who has your number. The way you mistreat people means you don't *deserve* to go on living.

It's like in that *Harper's* story of yours, "Dark Angel." Take my word, unless your apology is in my mailbox by 20 December I'm *your* Dark Angel come Christmas.

This is one letter you better not ignore.

Alex E.

PRESS ANNOUNCEMENT—FOR IMMEDIATE RELEASE

On the morning of December 26, 1994, in the den of a private home at 6000 Roland Avenue, Baltimore, Maryland, the body of noted writer Janice Coral Olinger was discovered by neighbors. She had been shot once in the left temple and had died instantly. Her white poodle, "Snowball," was found lying beside her. The dog had also been shot to death.

Local police were called to the scene. Lieutenant Angus Campbell of Baltimore Homicide has issued this public statement:

"Several handwritten letters, dated from June into December of this year, were found on the desk of the deceased. They were all signed 'Alex Edward.'

"Ms. Olinger's father, A. E. Coral, was for many years a prominent Baltimore banker, and was known to have a violent temper. Police records show that he had frequently been cited for physically abusive incidents involving his wife, Barbara, as well as Janice Coral (later Janice Coral Olinger), their daughter. Records indicate that Janice Coral left the family home as a teenager and apparently never saw her father again. His initials, A.E., stand for Alexander Edward, which correlate with the signatures on the letters.

"In the opinion of Dr. Thomas F. O'Rourke, a respected Baltimore psychiatrist, the emotionally shattering death of her husband, noted poet Theodore Olinger, caused a fracture in Janice Coral Olinger's personality. She took on a second, wholly separate identity based on the male persona of her violent father and, as 'Alex Edward,' wrote the series of deranged letters leading to the tragedy.

"Her death, by gunshot, was apparently self-inflicted. The police department theorizes that she first shot her pet, then put the weapon to her own head. Dr. O'Rourke explained it as an 'acting out of what her father might have done to her had she remained in the family home.' (The banker was later jailed for attempting to murder his wife, Barbara Coral, and is now serving a term in the Maryland state prison.)

"The death of Janice Coral Olinger is tragic and senseless, the product of what Dr. O'Rourke describes as 'a lingering and ultimately fatal childhood trauma.' Funeral arrangements are pending."

Regarding the following novella, *Publishers Weekly* said it "has enough plot twists to fill a novel." The MPC *Journal Tribune* said, "it is the most remarkable crime novella since the heyday of James M. Cain." Britain's *Interzone* remarked that it will "remind readers of what Quentin Tarentino has been doing on film." When the author is Ed Gorman, it's no surprise his work draws comments like these. Called "the modern master of the lean mean thriller," he has written more than a dozen novels and numerous short stories. The best of his recent short fiction has been collected in *Moonchasers*. He is especially effective in this tale of love, murder, and revenge.

The End of It All
ED GORMAN

Sometimes the only thing worse than
losing the woman is winning the woman.
     —French saying

Embrace your fate.
     —French saying

I guess the first thing I should tell you about is the plastic surgery. I mean, I didn't always look this good. In fact, if you saw me in my college yearbook, you wouldn't even recognize me. I was thirty pounds heavier and my hair had enough grease on it to irrigate a few acres of droughted farmland. And the glasses I wore could easily have substituted for the viewing instruments they use at Mt. Palomar. I wanted to lose my virginity back in second grade, on the very first day I saw Amy Towers. But I didn't lose my virginity until I was twenty-three years old and even then it was no easy task. She was a prostitute and just as I was guiding my sex into her she said, "I'm sorry, I must be coming down with the flu or something. I've got to puke." And puke she did.

This was how I lived my life until I was forty-two years old—as the kind of guy cruel people smirk at and decent people feel sorry for. I was the uncle nobody ever wanted to claim. I was the blind date women discussed for years after. I was the guy in the record shop the cute girl at the cash register always rolls her eyes at. But despite all that I somehow managed to marry an attractive woman whose husband had been killed in Vietnam, and I inherited a stepson who always whispered about me behind my back to his friends. They snickered mysteriously whenever they were around me. The marriage lasted eleven years, ending on a rainy Tuesday night several weeks after we'd moved into our elegant new Tudor in the city's most attractive yuppie enclave. After dinner, David up in his room smoking dope and listening to his Prince CDs, Annette said, "Would you take it personally if I told you I'd fallen in love with somebody?" Shortly thereafter we were divorced, and shortly after that I moved to Southern California, where I supposed there was plenty of room for one more misfit. At least, more room than there had been in an Ohio city of 150,000.

By profession I was a stockbroker, and at this particular time there were plenty of opportunities in California for somebody who'd managed his own shop as I had. Problem was, I was tired of trying to motivate eight other brokers into making their monthly goals. I found an old and prestigious firm in Beverly Hills and went to work there as a simple and unhassled broker. It took me several months, but I finally got over being dazzled by having movie stars as clients. It helped that most of them were jerks.

I tried to improve my sex life by touring all the singles bars that my better-looking friends recommended, and by circumspectly scanning many of the Personals columns in the numerous newspapers that infest L.A. But I found nothing to my taste. None of the women who described themselves as straight and in good shape ever mentioned the word that interested me most—romance. They spoke of hiking and biking and surfing; they spoke of symphonies and movies and art galleries; they spoke of equality and empowerment and liberation. But never romance and it was romance I most devoutly desired. There were other options, of course. But while I felt sorry for homosexuals and bisexuals and hated people who persecuted them, I didn't want to be one of them; and try as I might to be understanding of sado-masochism and cross-dressing and transsexualism, there was about it something—for all its sadness—comic and incomprehensible. Fear of disease kept me from whores. The women I met in ordinary circumstances—at the office, supermarket, laundry facilities in my expensive apartment house—treated me as women usually did, with tireless sisterly kindness.

Then some crazy bastards had a gunfight on the San Diego Freeway, and my life changed utterly.

This was on a smoggy Friday afternoon. I was returning home from work, tired, facing a long, lonely weekend when I suddenly saw two cars pull up on either side of me. They were, it seemed, exchanging gunfire. This was no doubt because of their deprived childhoods. They continued to fire at each other, not seeming to notice that I was caught in their crossfire. My windshield shattered. My two back tires blew out. I careened off the freeway and went halfway up a hill, where I smashed into the base of a stout scrub pine. That was the last thing I remember about the episode.

MY RECUPERATION TOOK FIVE MONTHS. It would have been much shorter, but one sunny day a plastic surgeon came into my room and explained what he'd need to do to put my face back to normal and I said, "I don't want it back to normal."

"Pardon me?"

"I don't want it back to normal. I want to be handsome. Movie-star handsome."

"Ah." He said this as if I'd just told him that I wanted to fly. "Perhaps we need to talk to Dr. Schlatter."

Dr. Schlatter too said "Ah" when I told him what I wanted, but it was not quite the "Ah" of the original doctor. In Dr. Schlatter's "Ah" there was at least a little vague hope.

He told me everything in advance, Dr. Schlatter did, even making it interesting, how plastic surgery actually dated back to the ancient Egyptians, and Italians as early as the 1400s were performing quite impressive transformations. He showed me sketches of how he hoped I'd look, he acquainted me with some of the tools so I wouldn't be intimidated when I saw them—scalpel and retractor and chisel—and he told me how to prepare myself for my new face.

Sixteen days later, I looked at myself in the mirror and was happy to see that I no longer existed. Not the former me anyway. Surgery, diet, liposuction, and hair dye had produced somebody who should appeal to a wide variety of women—not that I cared, of course. Only one woman mattered to me, only one woman had ever mattered to me, and during my time in the hospital she was all I thought about, all I planned for. I was not going to waste my physical beauty on dalliances. I was going to use it to win the hand and heart of Amy Towers Carson, the woman I'd loved since second grade.

IT WAS FIVE WEEKS BEFORE I SAW HER. I'd spent that time getting established in a brokerage firm, setting up some contacts, and learning how to use a new live phone hookup that gave me continuous stock analysis. Impressive, for a small Ohio city such as this one, the one where I'd grown up and first fallen in love with Amy.

I had some fun meeting former acquaintances. Most of them didn't believe me when I said I was Roger Daye. A few of them even laughed, implying that Roger Daye, no matter what had happened to him, could never look this good.

My parents living in Florida retirement, I had the old homestead—a nice white Colonial in an Ozzie and Harriet section of the city—to myself, where I invited a few ladies to hone my skills. Amazing how much self-confidence the new me gave the old me. I just took it for granted that we'd end up in bed, and so we did, virtually every single time. One woman whispered that she'd even fallen in love with me. I wanted to ask her to repeat that on tape. Not even my wife had ever told me she loved me, not exactly anyway.

Amy came into my life again at a country club dance two nights before Thanksgiving.

I sat at a table watching couples of all ages box-step around the dance floor. Lots of evening gowns. Lots of tuxedos. And lots of saxophone music from the eight-piece band, the bandstand being the only light, everybody on the floor in intimate boozy shadow. She was still beautiful, Amy was, not as young-looking, true, but with that regal, obstinate beauty nonetheless and that small, trim body that had inspired ten or twenty thousand of my youthful melancholy erections. I felt that old giddy high school thrill that was in equal parts shyness, lust, and a romantic love that only F. Scott Fitzgerald—my favorite writer—would ever have understood. In her arms I would find the purpose of my entire existence. I had felt this since I'd first walked home with her through the smoky autumn afternoons of third and fourth and fifth grade. I felt it still.

Randy was with her. There had long been rumors that they had a troubled marriage that would inevitably disintegrate. Randy, former Big Ten wide receiver and Rose Bowl star, had been one of the star entrepreneurs of the local eighties—building condos had been his specialty—but his success waned with the end of the decade and word was he'd taken up the harsh solace of whiskey and whores.

They still looked like everybody's dream of the perfect romantic couple, and more than one person on the dance floor nodded to them as the band swung into a Bobby Vinton medly, at which point Randy began dancing Amy around with Technicolor theatrics. Lots of onlooker grins and even a bit of applause. Amy and Randy would be the king and queen of every prom they ever attended. Their dentures might clack when they spoke, Randy's prostate might make him wince every thirty seconds, but by God the spotlight would always find its ineluctable way to them. And they'd be rich—Randy came from a long line of steel money and was one of the wealthiest men in the state.

When Randy went to the john—walking right meant the bar; walking left meant the john—I went over to her.

She sat alone at a table, pert and gorgeous and preoccupied. She didn't notice me at first, but when her eyes met mine, she smiled.

"Hi."

"Hi," I said.

"Are you a friend of Randy's?"

I shook my head. "No, I'm a friend of yours. From high school."

She looked baffled a moment and then said, "Oh, my God. Betty Anne said she saw you and—oh, my God."

"Roger Daye."

She fled her seat and came to me and stood on her tiptoes and took my warm face in her cold hands and kissed me and said, "You're so handsome."

I smiled. "Quite a change, huh?"

"Well, you weren't that—"

"Of course I was—a dip, a dweeb—"

"But not a nerd."

"Of course a nerd."

"Well, not a complete nerd."

"At least ninety-five percent," I said.

"Eighty percent maybe but—" She exulted over me again, bare shoulders in her wine-red evening gown shiny and sexy in the shadow. "The boy who used to walk me home—"

"All the way up to tenth grade when you met—"

"Randy."

"Right. Randy."

"He really is sorry about beating you up that time. Did your arm heal all right? I guess we sort of lost track of each other, didn't we?"

"My arm healed just fine. Would you care to dance?"

"Would I care to? God, I'd love to."

We danced. I tried not to think of all the times I'd dreamed about this moment, Amy in my arms so beautiful and—

"You're in great shape, too," she said.

"Thank you."

"Weights?"

"Weights and running and swimming."

"God, that's so great. You'll break every heart at our next class reunion."

I held her closer. Her breasts touched my chest. A stout and stern erection filled my pants. I was dizzy. I wanted to take her over into a corner and do it on the spot. She was the sweet smell of clean, wonderful woman flesh, and the even sweeter sight of dazzling white smile against tanned, taut cheeks.

"That bitch."

I'd been so far gone into my fantasies that I wasn't sure I'd heard her properly.

"Pardon?"

"Her. Over there. That bitch."

I saw Randy before I saw the woman. Hard to forget a guy who'd once broken your arm—he'd had considerable expertise with hammer locks—right in front of the girl you loved.

Then I saw the woman and I forgot all about Randy.

I didn't think anybody could ever make Amy seem drab, but the woman presently dancing with Randy did just that. There was a radiance about her that was more important than her good looks, a mixture of pluck and intelligence that made me vulnerable to her even from here. In her white strapless gown, she was so fetching that men simply stood and stared at her, the way they would at a low-flying UFO or some other extraordinary phenomenon.

Randy started to twirl her as he had Amy, but this young woman—she couldn't have been much more than twenty—was a far better dancer. She was so smooth, in fact, I wondered if she'd had ballet training.

Randy kept her captive in his muscular embrace for the next three dances.

Because the girl so obviously upset Amy, I tried not to look at her—not even a stolen glance—but it wasn't easy.

"Bitch," Amy said.

And for the first time in my life, I felt sorry for her. She'd always been my goddess, and here she was feeling something as ungoddesslike as jealousy.

"I need a drink."

"So do I."

"Would you be a darling and get us one, then?"

"Of course," I said.

"Black and White, please. Straight up."

She was at her table smoking a cigarette when I brought the drinks back. She exhaled in long, ragged plumes.

Randy and his princess were still on the dance floor.

"She thinks she's so goddamned beautiful," Amy said.

"Who is she?"

But before Amy could tell me, Randy and the young woman deserted the floor and came over to the table.

Randy didn't look especially happy to see me. He glanced first at Amy and then at me and said, "I suppose there's a perfectly good reason for you to be sitting at our table."

Here he was flaunting his latest girlfriend in front of his wife, and he was angry that she had a friend sitting with her.

Amy smirked. "I didn't recognize him, either."

"Recognize who?" Randy snapped.

"Him. The handsome one."

By now I wasn't looking at either of them. I was staring at the young woman. She was even more lovely up close. She seemed amused by us older folks.

"Remember a boy named Roger Daye?" Amy said.

"That candy-ass who used to walk you home?"

"Randy. Meet Roger Daye."

"No way," Randy said, "this is Roger Daye."

"Well, I'm sorry, but he is."

I knew better than to put my hand out. He wouldn't have shaken it.

"Where's a goddamned waiter?" Randy said. Only now did I realize he was drunk.

He bellowed even above the din of the crowd.

He and the young woman sat down just as a waiter appeared.

"It's about goddamned time," Randy said to the older man with the tray.

"Sorry, we're just very busy tonight, sir."

"Is that supposed to be my problem or something?"

"Please, Randy," Amy said.

"Yes, please, Dad," the gorgeous young woman said.

At first I thought she might be joking, making a reference to Randy's age. But she didn't smile, nor did Roger, nor did Amy.

I guess I just kind of sat there and thought about why Randy would squire his own daughter around as if she were his new beau, and why Amy would be so jealous.

Six drinks and many tales of Southern California later—Midwesterners dote on Southern California tales the way people will someday dote on tales of Jupiter and Pluto—Randy said, "Didn't I break your arm one time?" He was the only guy I'd ever met who could swagger while sitting down.

"I'm afraid you did."

"You had it coming. Sniffing around Amy that way."

"Randy," Amy said.

"Daddy," Kendra said.

"Well, it's true, right, Roger? You had the hots for Amy and you probably still goddamned do."

"Randy," Amy said.

"Daddy," Kendra said.

But I didn't want him to stop. He was jealous of me and it made me feel great. Randy Carson, Rose Bowl star, was jealous of me.

"Would you like to dance, Mr. Daye?"

I'd tried hard not to pay any attention to her because I knew if I paid her a little I'd pay her a lot. Wouldn't be able to wrench my eyes or my heart away. She was pure meltdown, the young lady was.

"I'd love to," I said.

I was just standing up when Amy looked at Kendra and said, "He already promised me this one, dear."

And before I knew what to do, Amy took my hand and guided me to the floor.

Neither of us said anything for a long time. Just danced. The good old box step. Same as in seventh grade.

"I know you wanted to dance with her," Amy said.

"She's very attractive."

"Oh, Jesus. That's all I need."

"Did I say something wrong?"

"No—it's just that nobody notices me anymore. I know that's a shitty thing to say about my own daughter, but it's true."

"You're a very beautiful woman."

"For my age."

"Oh, come on now."

"But not vibrant, not fresh the way Kendra is."

"That's a great name, Kendra."

"I chose it."

"You chose well."

"I wish I'd called her Judy or Jake."

"Jake?"

She laughed. "Aren't I awful? Talking about my own daughter this way? That little bitch."

She slurred the last two words. She'd gunned her drinks—Black and White straight up—and now they were taking their toll.

We danced some more. She stepped on my foot a couple of times. Every once in a while I'd find myself looking over at the table for a glimpse of Kendra. All my life I'd waited to dance like this with Amy Towers. And now it didn't seem to matter much.

"I've been a naughty girl, Roger."

"Oh?"

"I really have been. About Kendra, I mean."

"I suppose a little rivalry between mother and daughter isn't unheard of."

"It's more than that. I slept with her boyfriend last year."

"I see."

"You should see your face. Your very handsome face. You're embarrassed."

"Does she know?"

"About her boyfriend?"

"Uh-huh."

"Of course. I planned it so she'd walk in on us. I just wanted to show her—well, that even some of her own friends might find me attractive."

"You felt real bad about it, I suppose?"

"Oh, no. I felt real good. She naturally told Randy and he made a big thing over it—smashed up furniture and hit me in the face a few times—and it was really great. I felt young again, and desirable. Does that make sense?"

"Not really."

"But they got back at me."

"Oh?"

"Sure. Didn't you see them tonight on the dance floor?"

"Pretty harmless. I mean, she's his daughter."

"Well, then you haven't had a talk with good old Randy lately."

"Oh?"

"He read this article in *Penthouse* about how incest was actually a very natural drive and how it was actually perfectly all right to bop your family members if it was mutual consent and if you practiced safe sex."

"God."

"So now she walks around the house practically naked, and he rubs her and pats her and gives her big, long squeezes."

"And she doesn't mind?"

"That's the whole point. They're in on this together. To pay me back for sleeping with Bobby."

"Bobby being—"

"Her boyfriend. Well, ex-boyfriend I guess."

Kendra and Randy came back on the floor next dance. If any attention had been paid to Amy and me, it was now transferred to Kendra and Randy. But this time, instead of the theatrical, they embraced the intimate. I was waiting for Randy to start grinding his hips into Kendra dry-hump style, the way high school boys always do when the lights are turned down.

"God, they're sickening," Amy said.

And I pretty much agreed with her.

"She's going to try to seduce you, you know," Amy said.

"Oh, come on now."

"God, are you kidding? She'll want to make you a trophy as soon as she can."

"She's what? Twenty? Twenty-one?"

"Twenty-two. But that doesn't matter, anyway. You just wait and see."

At our table again, I had two more drinks. None of this was as planned. Handsome Roger would return to his hometown and beguile the former homecoming queen into his arms. Technicolor dreams. But this was different, dark and comic and sweaty, and not a little bit sinister. I could see Roger touching his nearly nude daughter all over her wonderful body, and I could see Amy—not a little bit pathetic—hurtling herself at some strapping college student majoring in gonads.

Jesus, all I'd wanted to do was a little old-fashioned home wrecking ... and look what I'd gotten myself into.

Kendra and Randy came back. Randy abused a couple more waiters and then said to me, "You having all that plastic surgery—surprised you didn't have them change you into a broad. You always were a little flitty. Nothing personal, you understand."

"Randy," Amy said.

"Daddy," Kendra said.

But for me this was the supreme compliment. Randy Big Ten Carson was jealous of me again.

I wasn't sure where Kendra was going when she stood up, but then she was next to me and said, "Why don't we dance?"

"I'm sure Roger's tired, dear," Amy said.

Kendra smiled. "Oh, I think he's probably got a little bit of energy left, don't you, Mr. Daye?"

On the floor, in my arms, sexy, soft, sweet, gentle, cunning, and altogether self-possessed, Kendra said, "She's going to try to seduce you, you know."

"Who is?"

"Amy. My mother."

"You may not have noticed, but she'd married."

"Like that would really make a difference."

"We're old friends. That's all."

"I've read some of your love letters."

"God, she kept them?"

"All of them. From all the boys who were in love with her. She's got them all up in the attic. In storage boxes. Alphabetized. Whenever she starts to feel old, she drags them out and reads them. When I was a little girl, she'd read them out loud to me."

"I imagine mine were very corny."

"Very sweet. That's how yours were."

Our gazes met, as they like to say in novels. But that wasn't all that met. The back of her hand somehow passed across the front of my trousers, and an erection the goatiest of fifteen-year-olds would envy sprang to life. Then her hand returned to proper dancing position.

"You're really a great-looking man."

"Thank you. But did you ever see my Before picture?"

She smiled. "If you mean your high school yearbook photo, yes, I did. I guess I like the After photo a little better."

"You're very skilled at diplomacy."

"That's not all I'm skilled at, Mr. Daye."

"How about calling me Roger?"

"I'd like that."

I wish I had a big capper for the rest of the evening at the country club, but I don't. By the time Kendra and I got back to the table, Amy and Randy were both resolutely drunk and even a bit incoherent. I excused myself to the john for a time, and as I came back I saw Amy out on the veranda talking to a guy who looked not unlike a very successful gigolo, macho variety. Later, I'd learn that his name was Vic. Back at the table good old Randy insulted a few more waiters and threatened to punch me out if "I didn't keep my goddamned paws" off his wife and his daughter, but he was slurring his words so badly that the effect was sort of lost, especially when he started sloshing his drink around and the glass fell from his hand and smashed all over the table.

"Maybe this is a good time to leave," Kendra said, and began the difficult process of packing her parents up and getting them out to their new Mercedes, which, fortunately, she happened to be driving.

Just as they were leaving, Kendra said, "I may see you later," leaving me to contemplate what, exactly, "later" meant.

AFTER ONE SHOWER, one nightcap, most of a David Letterman show, and a slow fall into sleep, I found out what "later" meant.

She was at the door, behind a sharp knock in the windy night, adorned in a London Fog trench coat that was, I soon learned, all she wore.

She said nothing, just stood on tiptoes, wonderful lips puckered, waiting to be kissed. I obliged her, sliding an arm around her and leading her inside, feeling a little self-conscious in my pajamas and robe.

We didn't make it to the bedroom. She gently pushed me into a huge leather armchair before the guttering fireplace and eased herself gently atop me. That was when I found out she was naked beneath her London Fog. Her wise and lovely fingers quickly got me properly hard, and then I was inside her and my gasp was exultant pleasure but it was also fear.

I imagine heroin addicts feel this way the first time they use—pleasure from the exquisite kick of it all but fear of becoming a total slave to something they can never again control.

I was going to fall disastrously in love with Kendra, and I knew it that very first moment in the armchair when I tasted the soft, sweet rush of her breath and felt the warm, silken splendor of her sex.

When we were done for the first time, I built the fire again, and got us wine and cheese, and we lay beneath her trench coat staring into the flames crackling behind the glass.

"God, I can't believe it," she said.

"Believe what?"

"How good I feel with you. I really do."

I didn't say anything for a long time. "Kendra."

"I know what you want to ask."

"About your mother."

"I was right."

"If you slept with me only because—"

"—because she slept with Bobby Lane?"

"Right. Because she slept with Bobby Lane."

"Do you want me to be honest?"

I didn't really, but what was I going to say? No, I want you to be dishonest? "Of course."

"That's what first put the thought in my mind, I guess. I mean coming over here and sleeping with you." She laughed. "My mom is seriously smitten with you. I watched her face tonight. Wow. Anyway, I thought that would be a good way to pay her back. By sleeping with you, I mean. But by the end of the evening—God, this is really crazy, Roger, but I've got like this really incredible crush on you."

I wanted to say that I did, too. But I couldn't. I might be a new Roger on the outside but inside I was strictly the old model—shy, nervous, and terrified that I was going to get my heart decimated.

By dawn, we'd made love three times, the last time in my large bed with a jay and a cardinal perched on the window watching us, and soft morning wind soughing through the windbreak pines.

After we finished that last time, we lay in each other's arms for maybe twenty minutes until she said, "I have to be unromantic."

"Be my guest."

"Goose bumps."

"Goose bumps?"

"And bladder."

"And bladder?"

"And morning breath."

"You've lost me."

"A, I'm freezing. B, I really have to pee. And C, may I use your toothbrush?"

In the following three weeks, she spent at least a dozen nights at my place, and on those nights when one or both of us had business to attend to, we had those lengthy phone conversations that new lovers always have. Makes no difference what you say as long as you get to hear her voice and she gets to hear yours.

Only occasionally did I pause and let dread come over me like a drowning wave. I would lose her and be forever bereft afterward. I was suffused with her tastes and smells and sounds and textures—and yet someday all these things would be taken from me and I would be forever alone, and unutterably sad. But what the hell could I do? Walk away? Impossible. She was succor, and life source, and all I could do was cling till my fingers fell away and I was left floating on the vast, dark ocean.

THE EIGHTH OF DECEMBER that year was one of those ridiculously sunny days that try to trick you into believing that spring is near. I spent two hours that afternoon cutting firewood in the back and then hauling it inside. Fuel for more trysts. On one of my trips inside, the doorbell rang. When I peeked out, I saw Amy. She looked very good—indeed, much better than she had that night at the country club—except for her black eye.

I let her in and asked her if she wanted a cup of coffee, which she declined. She took the leather couch, I the leather armchair that Kendra and I still used on occasion.

"I need to talk to you, Roger." She wore a white turtleneck beneath a camel hair car coat and designer jeans. There was a blue ribbon in her blond hair, and she looked very sexy in a suburban sort of way.

"All right."

"And I need you to be honest with me."

"If you'll be honest with me."

"The black eye?"

"The black eye."

"Who else? Randy. He came home drunk the other night and I wouldn't sleep with him so he hit me. He sleeps around so much I'm afraid he's going to pick up something." She shook her head with a solemnity I would never have thought her capable of.

"Does he do this often?"

"Sleep around?"

"And hit you."

She shrugged. "Pretty often. Both, I mean."

"Why don't you leave him?"

"Because he'd kill me."

"God, Amy, that's ridiculous. You can get an injunction."

"You think an injunction would stop Randy? Especially when he's been drinking?" She sighed. "I don't know what to do anymore."

This was the woman I'd come back to steal, but now I didn't want to steal her. I didn't even want to borrow her. I just felt sorry for her, and the notion was disorienting.

"Now, I want you to tell me about Kendra."

"I love her."

"Oh, just fucking great, Roger. Just fucking great."

"I'm know I'm a lot older than she is but—"

"Oh, for God's sake, Roger, it's not that."

"It isn't?"

"Of course it isn't. Come over here and sit down."

"Next to you?"

"That's the general idea."

I went over and sat down. Next to her. She smelled great. Same cologne Kendra wore.

She took my hand. "Roger, I want to sleep with you."

"I don't think that would be a good idea."

"All those years you were in love with me. It's not fair."

"What's not fair?"

"You should have gone on loving me. That's how it's supposed to work."

"What's supposed to work?"

"You know, lifelong romance. We're both romantics, Roger, you and I. Kendra is more like her father. Everything's sex."

"You slept with her boyfriend."

"Only because I was afraid and lonely. Randy had just beaten me up pretty badly. I felt so vulnerable. I just needed some kind of reassurance. You know, that I was a woman. That somebody would want me." She took both my hands and brought them to her lips and kissed them tenderly. I couldn't help it. She was starting to have the effect on me she wanted. "I want you to be in love with me again. I can help you forget Kendra. I really can."

"I don't want to forget Kendra."

"Deep down she's like Randy. A whore. She'll break your heart. She really will."

She put two of my fingers in her mouth and began sucking.

She was quite good in bed, maybe even better technically than Kendra. But she wasn't Kendra. There was the rub.

We lay in the last of the gray afternoon and the wind came up, a harsh and wintry wind suddenly, and she tried to get me up for a second time, but it was no good. I wanted Kendra and she knew I wanted Kendra.

There was something very sad about it all. She was right. Romance—the kind of Technicolor romance I'd dreamed of—should last forever, despite any and all odds, the way it did in F. Scott Fitzgerald stories. And yet it hadn't. She was just another woman to me now, with more wrinkles than I had suspected, and a little tummy that was both sweet and comic, and veins like faded blue snakes against the pale flesh of her legs.

And then she started crying and all I could do was hold her and she tried in vain to get me up again and saw the failure not mine but her own.

"I don't know how I ever got here," she said finally to the dusk that was rolling across the drab, cold midwestern land.

"My house, you mean?"

"No. Here. Forty-two goddamned years old. With a daughter who steals the one man who truly loved me." A gaze icy as the winter moon then as she said, "But maybe things won't be quite as hunky-fucking-dory as she thinks they'll be."

Later on, I was to remember what she said vividly, the hunky-fucking-dory thing, I mean.

Kendra appeared at nine that same night. I spent the first half hour making love to her and the second half trying to decide if I should tell her about her mother's visit.

Later, in front of the fireplace, a wonderful old film noir called *Odds*

Against Tomorrow on cable, we made love a second time and then, lying in the sweet, cool hollow of her arms, our juices and odors as one now, I said, "Amy was here today."

She stiffened. Her entire body. "Why?"

"It's not easy to explain."

"That bitch. I knew she'd do it."

"Come here, you mean?"

"Come here and put the shot on you. Which she did, right?"

"Right."

"But you didn't—"

I'd never had to lie to her before and it was far more difficult than I'd imagined it might be.

"Things get so crazy sometimes—"

"Oh, shit."

"I mean you don't intend for things to happen but—"

"Oh, shit," she said again. "You fucked her, didn't you?"

"—with all the best intentions, you—"

"Quit fucking babbling. Just say it. Say you fucked her."

"I fucked her."

"How could you do it?"

"I didn't want to."

"Right."

"And I could only do it once. No second time."

"How noble."

"And I regretted it immediately."

"Amy told me that when you were real geeky-looking that you were one of the sweetest people she ever knew."

She stood up, all beautiful, brash nakedness, and stalked back toward the bedroom. "You should have kept your face ugly, Roger. Then your soul would still be beautiful."

I lay there thinking about what she said a moment, and then I stalked back to the bedroom.

She was dressing in a frenzy. She didn't as yet have her bra on completely. Just one breast was cupped. The other looked lone and dear as anything I'd ever seen. I wanted to kiss it and coo baby talk to it.

Then I remembered why I'd come in here. "That's bullshit, you know."

"What's bullshit?" she said, pulling up the second cup of her bra. She wore panty hose but hadn't as yet put on her skirt.

"All that crap about keeping my face ugly so my soul would remain beautiful. If I hadn't had plastic surgery, neither you nor your mother would have given me a second glance."

"That's not true."

I smiled. "God, face it, Kendra, you're a beautiful woman. You're not going to go out with some geek."

"You make me sound as if I've really got a lot of depth."

"Oh, Kendra, this is stupid. I shouldn't have slept with Amy and I'm sorry."

"I'm just surprised she hasn't managed to tell me about it yet. She's probably waiting for the right dramatic moment. And in her version, I'm sure you threw her on the bed and raped her. That's what my father told her the night she caught us together. That I was the one who'd wanted to do it—"

"My God, you mean you—"

"Oh, not all the way. They had one of their country club parties, and both Randy and I were pretty loaded and somehow we ended up on the bed wrestling around and she walked in and—well, I guess I tried very hard to give her the impression that we'd just been about to make it when she walked in and—"

"That's some great relationship you've got there."

"It's pretty sick and believe me, I know it."

I felt tired standing in the shadowy bedroom, the only light the December quarter moon above the shaggy pines.

"Kendra—"

"Could we just lie down together?" She sounded tired, too.

"Of course."

"And not do anything, I mean?"

"I know what you mean. And I think that's a wonderful idea."

We must have lain there six, seven minutes before we started making love, and then it was the most violent love we'd ever made, her hurling herself at me, inflicting pleasure and pain in equal parts. It was a purgation I badly needed.

"She's always been like this."

"Your mother?"

"Uh-huh."

"Competitive, you mean?"

"Uh-huh. Even when I was little. If somebody gave me a compliment, she'd get mad and say, 'Well, it's not hard for little girls to look good. The trick is to stay beautiful as you get older.' "

"Didn't your dad ever notice?"

She laughed bitterly. "My father? Are you kidding? He'd usually come home late and then finish getting bombed and then climb in bed next to me and feel me up."

"God."

Bitter sigh. "But I don't give a shit. Not anymore. Fuck them. I come into my own inheritance in six months—from my paternal grandfather—and then I'm moving out of the manse and leaving them to all their silly fucking games."

"Is now a good time to tell you I love you?"

"You know the crazy goddamned thing, Roger?"

"What's that?"

"I really love you, too. For the first time in my life, I actually love somebody."

ON THE NIGHT OF 20 JAN, six weeks later, I went to bed early with a new Sue Grafton novel. Kendra had begged off our date because of a head cold. I'm enough of a hypochondriac that I wasn't unhappy about not seeing her.

The call came just before 2 A.M., long after I was sleeping and just at the point where waking is difficult.

But get up I did and listen at length to Amy's wailing. It took me a long time to understand what the exact message her sobs meant to convey.

THE FUNERAL TOOK PLACE on a grim snowy day when the harsh, numbing winds rocked the pallbearers as they carried the gleaming silver coffin from hearse to graveside. The land lay bleak as a tundra.

Later, in the country club where a luncheon was being served, an old high school friend came up and said, "I bet when they catch him he's a nigger."

"I guess it wouldn't surprise me."

"Oh, hell, yes. Poor goddamned guy is sleeping in his own bed when some jig comes in and blasts the hell out of him and then goes down the hall and shoots poor Kendra, too. They say she'll never be able to walk or talk again. Just sit in a frigging wheelchair all the time. I used to be a liberal back in the sixties or seventies, but I've had enough of their bullshit by now. I'll tell you that I've had their bullshit right up to here, in fact."

Amy came late. In the old days one might have accused her of doing so so she could make an entrance. But now she had a perfectly good reason. She walked with a cane, and walked slowly. The intruder who'd shot up the place that night, and stolen more than $75,000 in jewelry, had shot her in the shoulder and the leg, apparently leaving her for dead. Just as he'd left Kendra for dead.

Amy looked pretty damned good in her black dress and veil. The black gave her a mourning kind of sexiness.

A line formed. She spent the next hour receiving the members of that line just as she'd done at the mortuary the night before. There were tears and laughter with tears and curses with tears. The very old looked perplexed by it all—the world made no sense anymore; here you were a rich person and people still broke into your house and killed you right in your bed—and middle-aged people looked angry (i.e., damned niggers) and the young looked bored (Randy being the drunk who'd always wobbled around pinching all the little girls on their bottoms—who cared he was dead, the pervert?).

I was the last person to go through the line, and when she saw me, Amy shook her head and began sobbing. "Poor, poor Kendra," she said. "I know how much she means to you, Roger."

"I'd like to visit her tonight if I could. At the hospital."

Beneath her veil, she sniffled some more. "I'm not sure that's a good idea. The doctor says she really needs her rest. And Vic said she looked very tired this morning."

The bullet had entered her head just below her left temple. By rights she should have died instantly. But the gods were playful and let her live—paralyzed.

"Vic? Who's Vic?"

"Our nurse. Oh, I forgot. I guess you've never met him, have you? He just started Sunday. He's really a dear. One of the surgeons recommended him. You'll meet him sometime."

I met him four nights later at Kendra's bedside.

He was strapping arrogant was our blond Vic, born to a body and face that no amount of surgery or training could ever duplicate, a natural Tarzan to my own tricked-up one. He looked as if he wanted to tear off his dark and expensive suit and head directly back to the jungle to beat up a lion or two. He was also the proud owner of a sneer that was every bit as imposing as his body.

"Roger, this is Vic."

He made a point of crushing my hand. I made a point of not grimacing.

The three of us then stared down at Kendra in her bed, Amy leaning over and kissing Kendra tenderly on the forehead. "My poor baby. If only I could have saved her—"

That was the first time I ever saw Vic touch her, and I knew instantly, in the proprietary way he did, that something was wrong. He probably was a nurse, but to Amy he was also something far more special and intimate.

They must have sensed my curiosity because Vic dropped his hand from her shoulder and stood proper as an altar boy staring down at Kendra.

Amy shot me a quick smile, obviously trying to read my thoughts.

But I lost interest quickly. It was Kendra I wanted to see. I bent over the bed and took her hand and touched it to my lips. I was self-conscious at first, Amy and Vic watching me, but then I didn't give a damn. I loved her and I didn't give a damn at all. She was pale and her eyes were closed and there was a fine sheen of sweat on her forehead. Her head was swathed in white bandages of the kind they always used in Bogart movies, the same ones that Karloff also used in *The Mummy*. I kissed her lips and I froze there because the enormity of it struck me. Here was the woman I loved, nearly dead, indeed should have been dead given the nature of her wound, and behind me, paying only a kind of lip service to her grief, was her mother.

A doctor came in and told Amy about some tests that had been run today. Despite her coma, she seemed to be responding to certain stimuli that had had no effect on her even last week.

Amy started crying, presumably in a kind of gratitude, and then the doctor asked to be alone with Kendra, and so we went out into the hall to wait.

"Vic is moving in with us," Amy said. "He'll be there when Kendra gets home. She'll have help twenty-four hours a day. Won't that be wonderful?"

Vic watched me carefully. The sneer never left his face. He looked the way he might if he'd just noticed a piece of dog mess on the heel of his shoe. It was not easy being a big blond god. There were certain difficulties with staying humble.

"So you know Kendra's surgeon," I said to Vic.

"What?"

"Amy said that the surgeon had recommended you to her."

They glanced at each other and then Vic said, "Oh, right, the surgeon, yes." He gibbered like a Miss America contestant answering a question about patriotism.

"And you're moving in?"

He nodded with what he imagined was solemnity. If only he could do something about the sneer. "I want to help in any way I can."

"How sweet."

If he detected my sarcasm, he didn't let on.

The doctor came out and spoke in soft, whispered sentences filled with jargon. Amy cried some more tears of gratitude.

"Well," I said. "I guess I'd better be going. Give you some quality time with Kendra."

I kissed Amy on the cheek and shook Vic's proffered hand. He notched his grip down to midlevel. Even hulks have sentimental moments. He even tried a little acting, our Vic. "The trick will be to get her to leave before midnight."

"She stays later, eh?" I said.

Amy kept her eyes downcast, as befitted a saint who was being discussed.

"Late? She'd stay all night if they'd let her. You can't tear her away."

"Well, she and Kendra have a very special relationship."

Amy caught the sarcasm. Anger flashed in her eyes but then subsided. "I want to get back to her," she said. And Mother Teresa couldn't have said it any more believably.

I took the elevator down to the ground floor, then took the emergency stairs back up to the fourth floor. I waited in an alcove down the hall. I could see Kendra's door, but if I was careful neither Amy nor Vic would be able to see me.

They left ten minutes after I did. Couldn't drag Amy away from her daughter's bedside, eh?

IN THE NEXT SIX WEEKS, Kendra regained consciousness, learned how to manipulate a pencil haltingly with her right hand, and got tears in her eyes every time I came through the door. She still couldn't speak or move her lower body or left side, but I didn't care. I loved her more than ever and in so doing proved to myself that I wasn't half as superficial as I'd always suspected. That's a good thing to know about yourself—that at age forty-four you have at least the potential for becoming an adult.

She came home in May, after three intense months of physical rehab and deep depression over her fate, a May of butterflies and cherry blossoms and the smells of steak on the grill on the sprawling grounds behind the vast English Tudor. The grounds ran four acres of prime land, and the house, divided into three levels, included eight bedrooms, five full baths, three half baths, a library, and a solarium. There was also a long, straight staircase directly off the main entrance. Amy had it outfitted with tracks so Kendra could get up and down in her wheelchair.

We became quite a cheery little foursome, Kendra and I, Amy and Vic. Four or five nights a week we cooked out and then went inside to watch a movie on the big-screen television set in the party room. Three nurses alternated eight-hour shifts so that whenever Kendra—sitting silently in her wheelchair in one of her half-dozen pastel-colored quilted robes—needed anything, she had it. Amy made a cursory fuss over Kendra at least twice an evening, and Vic went to fetch something unimportant, apparently in an attempt to convince me he really was a working male nurse.

More and more I slipped out early from the brokerage, spending the last of the day with Kendra in her room. She did various kinds of physical therapy with the afternoon nurse, but she never forgot to draw me something and then offer it up to me with the pride of a little girl pleasing her daddy. It always touched me, this gesture, and despite some early doubts that I'd be able to be her husband—I'd run away and find somebody strong and sound of limb; I hadn't had all that plastic surgery for nothing, had I?—I learned that I loved her more than ever. She brought out a tenderness in me that I rather liked. Once again I felt there was at least some vague hope that I'd someday become an adult. We watched TV or I read her interesting items from the newspaper (she liked the nostalgia pieces the papers sometimes ran) or I just told her how much I loved her. "Not good for you," she wrote on her tablet one day and then pointed at her paralyzed legs. And then broke into tears. I knelt at her feet for a full hour, till the shadows were long and purple, and thought how crazy it all was. I used to be afraid that she'd leave me—too young, too good-looking, too strong-willed, only using me to get back at her mother—and now she had to worry about some of the same things. In every way I could, I tried to assure her that I'd never leave her, that I loved her in ways that gave me meaning and dignity for the first time in my life.

Hot summer came, the grass scorching brown, night fires like the aftermath of bombing sorties in the dark hills behind the mansion. It was on one of these nights, extremely hot, Vic gone someplace, the easily tired Kendra just put to bed, that I found Amy waiting for me in my car.

She wore startling white short-shorts and a skimpy halter that barely contained her chewy-looking breasts. She sat on the passenger side. She had a martini in one hand and a cigarette in the other.

"Remember me, sailor?"

"Where's lover boy?"

"You don't like him, do you?"

"Not much."

"He thinks you're afraid of him."

"I'm afraid of rattlesnakes, too."

"How poetic." She inhaled her cigarette, exhaled a plume of blue against the moonlit sky. I'd parked at the far end of the pavement down by the three-stall garage. It was a cul-de-sac of sorts, protected from view by pines. "You don't like me anymore, do you?"

"No."

"Why?"

"I really don't want to go into it, Amy."

"You know what I did this afternoon?"

"What?"

"Masturbated."

"I'm happy for you."

"And you know who I thought of?"

I said nothing.

"I thought about you. About that night we were together over at your house."

"I'm in love with your daughter, Amy."

"I know you don't think I'm worth a shit as a mother."

"Gee, whatever gave you that idea?"

"I love her in my way. I mean, maybe I'm not the perfect mother, but I do love her."

"Is that why you won't put any makeup on her? She's in a fucking wheelchair, and you're still afraid she'll steal the limelight."

She surprised me. Rather than deny it, she laughed. "You're a perceptive bastard."

"Sometimes I wish I weren't."

She put her head back. Stared out the open window. "I wish they hadn't gone to the moon."

I didn't say anything.

"They spoiled the whole fucking thing. The moon used to be so romantic. There were so many myths about it, and it was so much fun thinking about. Now it's just another fucking rock." She drained her drink. "I'm lonely, Roger. I'm lonely for you."

"I'm sure Vic wouldn't want to hear that."

"Vic's got other women."

I looked at her. I'd never seen her express real anguish before. I took a terrible delight in it. "After what you and Vic did, you two deserve each other."

She was quick about it, throwing her drink in my face, then getting out of the car and slamming the door shut. "You bastard! You think I don't know what you meant by that? You think I killed Randy, don't you?"

"Randy—and tried to kill Kendra. But she didn't die the way she was supposed to when Vic shot her."

"You bastard!"

"You're going to pay for it someday, Amy. I promise you that."

She still had the glass in her hand. She smashed it against my windshield. The safety glass spiderwebbed. She stalked off, up past the pines, into invisibility.

I DIDN'T BRING IT UP. Kendra did. I'd hoped she'd never figure out who was really the intruder that night. She had a difficult enough time living. That kind of knowledge would only make it harder.

But figure it out she did. Once cool day in August, the first hint of autumn on the air, she handed me what I assumed would be her daily love note.

VIC
CHECK
FIGHT
$

I looked at the note and then at her.

"I guess I don't understand. You want me to check something about Vic?"

Her darting blue eyes said no.

I thought a moment: Vic, check. All I could think of was checking Vic out. Then, "Oh, a check? Vic gets some kind of check?"

The darting blue eyes said yes.

"Vic was having an argument about a check?"

Yes.

"With your mother?"

Yes.

"About the amount of the check?"

Yes.

"About it not being enough?"

Yes.

And then she started crying. And I knew then that she knew. Who'd killed her father. And who'd tried to kill her.

I sat with her a long time that afternoon. At one point a fawn came to the edge of the pines. Kendra made a cooing sound when she saw it, tender and excited. Starry night came and through the open window we could hear a barn owl and later a dog that sounded almost like a coyote. She slept sometimes, and sometimes I just told her the stories she liked to hear, "Goldilocks and the Three Bears" and "Rapunzel," stories, she'd once confided, that neither her mother nor her father had ever told her. But this night I was distracted and I think she sensed it. I wanted her to understand how much I loved her. I wanted her to understand that even if there were no justice in the universe at large, at least there was justice in our little corner of it.

ON A RAINY FRIDAY NIGHT in September, at an apartment Vic kept so he could rendezvous with a number of the young women Amy had mentioned, a tall and chunky man, described as black by two neighbors who got a glimpse of him, broke in and shot him to death. Three bullets. Two directly to the brain. The thief then took more than $5,000 in cash and traveler's checks (Vic having planned to leave for a European vacation in four days).

The police inquired of Amy, of course, as to how Vic had been acting lately. They weren't as yet quite convinced that his death had been the result of a simple burglary. The police are suspicious people but not, alas, suspicious enough. Just as they ultimately put Randy's death down to a robbery and murder, so they ultimately ruled that Vic had died at the hand of a burglar, too.

On the day Amy returned from the funeral, I had a little surprise for her, just to show her that things were going to be different from now on.

That morning I'd brought in a hair stylist and a makeup woman. They spent three hours with Kendra and when they were finished, she was as beautiful as she'd ever been.

We greeted Amy at the vaulted front door—dressing in black was becoming a habit with her—and when she saw Kendra, she looked at me and said, "She looks pathetic. I hope you know that." She went directly to the den, where she spent most of the day drinking scotch and screaming at the servants.

Kendra spent an hour in her room, crying. She wrote the word *pathetic* several times on her paper. I held her hand and tried to assure her that she indeed looked beautiful, which she did.

That night as I was leaving—we'd taken dinner in Kendra's room, neither of us wanting to see Amy any more than we needed to—she was waiting in my car again, even drunker than she'd been the first time. She had her inevitable drink in her hand. She wore a dark turtleneck and white jeans with a wide, sashlike leather belt. She looked a lot better than I wanted her to.

"You prick, you think I don't know what you did?"

"Welcome to the club."

"I happened to have fucking loved him."

"I'm tired, Amy. I want to go home."

In the pine-smelling night, a silver October moon looked ancient and fierce as an Aztec icon.

"You killed Vic," she said.

"Sure, I did. And I also assassinated JFK."

"You killed Vic, you bastard."

"Vic shot Kendra."

"You can't prove that."

"Well, you can't prove that I shot Vic, either. So please remove your ass from my car."

"I really never thought you'd have the balls. I always figured you for the faggot type."

"Just get out, Amy."

"You think you've won this, Roger. But you haven't. You're fucking with the wrong person, believe me."

"Good night, Amy."

She got out of the car and then put her head back in the open window. "Well, at least there's one woman you can satisfy, anyway. I'm sure Kendra thinks you're a great lover. Now that she's paralyzed, anyway."

I couldn't help it. I got out of the car and walked over to her across the dewy grass. I ripped the drink from her hand and then said, "You leave Kendra and me alone, do you understand?"

"Big, brave man," she said. "Big, brave man."

I hurled her drink into the bushes and then walked back to the car.

IN THE MORNING, the idea was there waiting for me.

I called work and told them I wouldn't be in and then spent the next three hours making phone calls to various doctors and medical supply houses as to exactly what I'd need and what I'd need to do. I even set up a temporary plan for private-duty nurses. I'd have to dig into my inheritance, but this was certainly worth it. Then I drove downtown to a jeweler's, stopping by a travel agency on my way back.

I didn't phone. I wanted to surprise her.

The Australian groundsman was covering some tulips when I got there. Frost was predicted. "G'day," he said, smiling. If he hadn't been over sixty with a potbelly and white hair, I would have suspected Amy of using him for her personal pleasure.

The maid let me in. I went out to the back terrace, where she said I'd find Kendra.

I tiptoed up behind her, flicked open the ring case, and held it in front of her eyes. She made that exultant cooing sound in her throat, and then I walked around in front of her and leaned over and gave her a gentle, tender kiss. "I love you," I said. "And I want to marry you right away and have you move in with me."

She was crying but then so was I. I knelt down beside her and put my head on her lap, on the cool surface of her pink quilted housecoat. I let it lie there for a long time as I watched a dark, graceful bird ride the wind currents above, gliding down the long, sunny autumn day. I even dozed off for a time.

At dinnertime, I rolled Kendra to the front of the house, where Amy was entertaining one of the Ken-doll men she'd taken up with these days. She was already slurring her words. "We came up here to tell you that we're going to get married."

The doll-man, not understanding the human politics here, said in a Hollywood kind of way, "Well, congratulations to both of you. That's wonderful." He even toasted us with his martini glass.

Amy said, "He's actually in love with me."

Doll-man looked at me and then back at Amy and then down at Kendra.

I turned her chair sharply from the room and began pushing it quickly over the parquet floor toward the hallway.

"He's been in love with me since second grade, and he's only marrying her because he knows he can't have me!"

And then she hurled her glass against the wall, smashing it, and I heard, in the ensuing silence, doll-man cough anxiously and say, "Maybe I'd better be going, Amy. Maybe another night would be better."

"You sit right where you fucking are," Amy said, "and don't fucking move."

I locked Kendra's door behind us on the unlikely chance that Amy would come down to apologize.

Around ten, she began to snore quietly. The nurse knocked softly on the door. "I need to get in there, sir. The missus is upstairs sleeping."

I leaned over and kissed Kendra tenderly on the mouth.

*   *   *

WE SET THE DATE TWO WEEKS HENCE. I didn't ask Amy for any help at all. In fact, I avoided her as much as possible. She seemed similarly inclined. I was always let in and out by one of the servants.

Kendra grew more excited each day. We were going to be married in my living room by a minister I knew vaguely from the country club. I sent Amy a handwritten note inviting her, but she didn't respond in any way.

I suppose I didn't qualify as closest kin. I suppose that's why I had to hear it on the radio that overcast morning as I drove to work.

It seemed that one of the city's most prominent families had been visited yet again by tragedy—first the father dying in a robbery attempt a year earlier, and now the wheelchair-confined daughter falling down the long staircase in the family mansion. Apparently she'd come too close to the top of the stairs and simply lost control. She'd broken her neck. The mother was said to be under heavy sedation.

I MUST HAVE CALLED AMY TWENTY TIMES that day, but she never took my calls. The Aussie gardener usually picked up. "Very sad here today, mate. She was certainly a lovely lass, she was. You have my condolences."

I cried till I could cry no more and then I took down a bottle of Black and White scotch and proceeded to do it considerable damage as I sat in the gray gloom of my den.

The liquor dragged me through a Wagnerian opera of moods—forlorn, melancholy, sentimental, enraged—and finally left me wrapped around my cold, hard toilet bowl, vomiting. I was not exactly a world-class drinker.

She called just before midnight, as I stared dully at CNN. Nothing they said registered on my conscious mind.

"Now you know how I felt when you killed Vic."

"She was your own daughter."

"What kind of life would she have had in that wheelchair?"

"You put her there!" And then I was up, frantic, crazed animal, walking in small, tight circles, screaming names at her.

"Tomorrow I'm going to the police," I said.

"You do that. Then I'll go there after you do and tell them about Vic."

"You can't prove a damned thing."

"Maybe not. But I can make them awfully suspicious. I'd remember that if I were you."

She hung up.

It was November then, and the radio was filled with tinny, cynical messages of Christmas. I went to the cemetery once a day and talked to her, and then I came home and put myself to sleep with Black and White and Valium. I knew it was Russian roulette, that particular combination, but I thought I might get lucky and lose.

The day after Thanksgiving, she called again. I hadn't heard from her since the funeral.

"I'm going away."

"So?"

"So. I just thought I'd tell you that in case you wanted to get hold of me."

"And why would I want to do that?"

"Because we're joined at the hip, darling, so to speak. You can put me in the electric chair, and I can do the same for you."

"Maybe I don't give a damn."

"Now you're being dramatic. If you truly didn't give a damn, you would've gone to the police two months ago."

"You bitch."

"I'm going to bring you a little surprise when I come back from my trip. A Christmas gift, I guess you'd call it."

I TRIED WORKING but I couldn't concentrate. I took an extended leave. The booze was becoming a problem. There was alcoholism on both sides of my family, so my ever increasing reliance on blackouts wasn't totally unexpected, I suppose. I stopped going out. I learned that virtually anything you needed would happily be brought you if you had the money, everything from groceries to liquor. A cleaning woman came in one day a week and bulldozed her way through the mess. I watched old movies on cable, trying to lose myself especially in the frivolity of the musicals. Kendra would have loved them. I found myself waking, many mornings, in the middle of the den, splayed on the floor, after apparently trying to make it to the door but failing. One morning I found that I'd wet myself. I didn't much care, actually. I tried not to think of Kendra, and yet she was all I did want to think about. I must have wept six or seven times a day. I dropped twelve pounds in two weeks.

I got sentimental about Christmas Eve, decided to try to stay reasonably sober and clean myself up a little bit. I told myself I was doing this in honor of Kendra. It would have been our first Christmas Eve together.

The cleaning lady was also a good cook and had left a fine roast beef with vegetable and potato fixings in the refrigerator. All I had to do was heat it up in the microwave.

I had just set my place at the dining room table—with an identical place setting to my right for Kendra—when the doorbell rang.

I answered it, opening the door and looking out into the snow-whipped darkness.

I know I made a loud and harsh sound, though if it was a scream exactly, I'm not sure.

I stepped back from the doorway and let her come in. She'd even changed her walk a little, to make it more like her daughter's. The clothes, too, the long double-breasted camel hair coat and the wine-colored beret, were more Kendra's style than her own. Beneath was a four-button empire dress that matched the color of the beret—the exact dress Kendra had often worn.

But the clothes were only props.

It was the face that possessed me.

The surgeon had done a damned good job, whoever he or she was, a damned good job. The nose was smaller and the chin was now heart-shaped and the cheekbones were more pronounced and perhaps a half inch higher. And with her blue blue contacts—

Kendra. She was Kendra.

"You're properly impressed, Roger, and I'm grateful for that," she said, walking past me to the dry bar. "I mean, this was not without pain, believe me. But then you know that firsthand, don't you, being an old hand at plastic surgery yourself."

She dropped her coat in an armchair and fixed herself a drink.

"You bitch," I said, slapping the drink from her hand, hearing it shatter against the stone of the fireplace. "You're a goddamned ghoul."

"Maybe I'm Kendra reincarnated." She smiled. "Have you ever thought of that?"

"I want you out of here."

She stood on tiptoes, just as Kendra had once done, and touched my lips to hers. "I knew you'd be gruff the first time you saw me. But you'll come around. You'll get curious about me. If I taste any different, or feel any different. If I'm—Kendra."

I went over to the door, grabbing her coat as I did so. Then I yanked her by the wrist and spun her out into the snowy cold night, throwing her coat after her. I slammed the door.

Twenty minutes later, the knock came again. I opened the door, knowing just who it would be. There were drinks, hours of drinks, and then, quite before I knew what was happening and much against all I held sacred and dear, we were somehow in bed, and as she slid her arms around me there in the darkness, she said, "You always knew I'd fall in love with you someday, didn't you, Roger?"

Edward D. Hoch occupies two unique niches in the world of mystery fiction. First, he is one of the few, perhaps the only writer to make his living solely by writing short fiction. Second, he has also had, with very few exceptions, a story in every issue of *Ellery Queen's Mystery Magazine* since the early 1970s. His series characters include Captain Leopold, a brilliant police detective whose appearance in "The Oblong Room" won his creator an Edgar in 1968. Other unusual protagonists include Simon Ark, a man claiming to be two thousand years old. Adept at the mystery story in all periods, genres, and shapes, here he is up to his usual high standards in "The Hudson Chain," a tale of honor and espionage during the Revolutionary War.

The Hudson Chain
EDWARD D. HOCH

The rough mountain trails that connected West Point with the furnace and forge at Sterling Pond were still drifted with snow in spots, even though it was the end of March in this year of Our Lord 1778. Spurring his horse over the uncertain terrain, Alexander Swift was reminded again that the colonies fighting their war of independence had just suffered through one of the harshest winters of the century. General George Washington was still encamped at Valley Forge with his army, awaiting the arrival of spring, and word of their suffering had traveled north with the couriers who traversed the snowy countryside to keep open the lines of communication.

It was a twenty-five-mile ride over the mountains to Sterling, but Swift preferred it to the longer, if easier, route through Central Valley. His horse was well up to the mountain journey, which they'd already made a few times during breaks in the harsh winter. When the Sterling hearths themselves finally came into view, showering sparks by the edge of the great pond, the horse seemed to pick up speed for the final moments of the journey.

It was Chester Hayborne, the foreman, who came out to greet him. "Have you ridden up from Camp West Point?" he asked as Swift dismounted.

"I have. The day seemed right for it, and General Washington is nervous for word on the chain. He had hoped it would be in place by the first week of April."

"We will not miss that deadline by much. Come in, and I will show you our progress. How is the snow through the mountains?"

"Still deep in spots but quite passable. We will soon have this bloody winter behind us."

Hayborne was a man in his thirties, with muscles hardened from working at the forge. His face and arms were blackened by soot from the wood and charcoal used to heat the iron ore to a molten state. Alexander Swift followed him into the nearest of the buildings, feeling the intense heat as it flowed over his body in waves. Foundrymen were busy pounding red-hot bars of iron into shape, then bending them into links around a mandrel.

"Hot work," Swift remarked.

"The hottest. We welcome the cold winter here, even though there were days in recent months when the depth of the snow kept us from our labor. Here, look at what we have for George Washington's watch chain."

It was a name Swift had heard used before in referring to the gigantic chain being forged to stretch across the Hudson at West Point. It would have 750 giant links of two-inch-thick bar iron, with eight swivels and eighty clevises to yoke the sections of the chain together. Seeing the finished sections of nine links each, with a single clevis and pin, stretched out and ready for transport by ox sledges and water, he couldn't help but be impressed.

He tried to lift just one of the links. "In God's name, how much do these weigh?"

"The average weight is about one hundred fourteen pounds each, though we have one link that weighed in at one hundred thirty pounds. Each section of chain weighs more than half a ton. As you can see, they are formed from bar iron two inches square, with each link being about twelve inches wide by eighteen inches long. We trust it is much stronger than the chain at Fort Montgomery last year."

Alexander Swift still remembered General Washington's fury at that debacle, when the British outflanked the fort with an overland attack and then sailed up to the chain and filed away one link to break the barrier and open the river. Washington wanted the new chain to be strong enough to withstand a ramming by several of His Majesty's warships.

"When will you deliver it?" he asked the foreman.

"One of your officers, Colonel Clay, is here now working out the schedule."

The news surprised Swift. He had not seen Colonel Clay since arriving at West Point. He knew there was a feeling that as a civilian working directly for General Washington he'd come north to prepare reports critical of the garrison at Camp West Point. In truth, Washington only wanted the chain in position. He was not seeking to place blame.

"I should see the colonel," Swift said. "Take me to him."

Colonel Jeremy Clay was a Pennsylvania farmer who'd been one of the first to take up arms against the British. He was a gaunt man with sandy hair and the appearance of an outdoorsman. Swift had known him in New York before the British capture of the city in 1776. They found him in the foundry office going over the timetable for transporting the chain to West Point. He glanced up from the papers on the desk, showing a flicker of annoyance when he recognized Alexander.

"Ah, Swift, isn't it? I haven't seen you since before the hostilities began. You were getting married then. How's your wife?"

"She died," Swift replied without emotion.

"Oh. Sorry to hear that." He immediately dismissed the unpleasant thought. "Have you been in contact with General Washington?"

"I visited him at Valley Forge a fortnight ago."

"I know he is concerned about the chain, but you can assure him it will be solidly in place soon."

"How soon?" Swift asked.

"I told him you were working on it," Chester Hayborne said.

"I'll handle this now, Chester. You can leave us alone."

The foreman nodded and left them in the office.

"The chain was to be in place by next week," Alexander Swift said when they were alone.

"There will be a slight delay with no harm done. The winter weather is still with us and it will be another month before any skipper would be foolish enough to sail this far up the Hudson."

"Hayborne says the sections of chain are all but complete."

"That they are," Jeremy Clay confirmed. "The ironworks has been operating twenty-four hours a day for the past two months to fill the government order in record time. Sledges pulled by oxen will begin hauling the sections of chain down to the river tomorrow. The chain has eighty-four sections in all, which means eighty-four trips with the ox sledges. Then the chain will have to be assembled at a small foundry at the water's edge and floated down the river to West Point on pitch-covered log rafts. We'll have it in place, with its protective boom, within weeks."

Swift studied again the now-familiar chart of that portion of the Hudson, with its narrow S-shaped curve. He had to agree with General Washington that it was the most effective place to block the river, with gun positions able to target any ships approaching the chain. Still, "Do you think it will work, Clay? The one at Fort Montgomery—"

"This one is far thicker and stronger. The only problem might be its removal each fall and replacement the following spring. The frozen river would play havoc with the chain if we left it in place during the winter. Besides, the log platforms that buoy it up will need to be replaced each year to keep them afloat."

Swift nodded. "The general is resigned to that fact, and will issue the orders himself at the proper time each year. Is there any danger of Camp West Point and Fort Constitution across the river being outflanked as was Fort Montgomery?"

"Very little. Our main threat comes from Loyalist spies who are thick in the countryside."

"Spies? What could they do?"

"Keep the British advised of our progress." He reached into the deer-skin knapsack at his side and brought forth a letter which he passed to Alexander.

"It seems to be a message from a daughter to her mother in New York," Swift said, skimming the lengthy letter.

"But look!" The colonel held the paper up to the light from the window and pointed out a number of tiny pinpricks. "These indicate certain letters which spell out the real message: *Rebels have six 32-pounders and twenty small cannon at Camp West Point. Chain across river in place by late April.*"

Swift could hardly believe his ears. He took back the letter and examined the pinpricks, spelling out each word. "Where did you find this?"

"In the pouch of a traveler trying to cross enemy lines north of New York. You can see it is dated March twenty-second, just last week."

"It seems there is a spy operating at West Point."

"Very likely. While this message did not get through, there will certainly be others."

"Do you think the British will attack the chain?"

Colonel Clay nodded. "At the first opportunity, if only because it is General Washington's personal project."

Alexander Swift made a decision. "I will remain at West Point until the chain is secure across the Hudson."

"Do what you wish, but the spy is my affair. When I find him I will enjoy watching him hanged from the nearest tree."

CAMP WEST POINT was a relatively small garrison, established to guard the river at this narrow bend. The British had long felt that the Hudson, with its passage into Canada via Lake George and Lake Champlain, was the key to splitting the Colonies. Only a year earlier Washington had said, "The importance of the Hudson River in the present contest, and the necessity of defending it, are subjects which have been so frequently and fully discussed, and are so well understood, that it is unnecessary to enlarge upon them. These facts at once appear when it is considered that the river runs through a whole state; that it is the only passage by which the enemy from New York, or any part of our coast, can ever hope to cooperate with an army from Canada; that the possession of it is indispensably essential to preserve the communication between the Eastern, Middle, and Southern States; and further, that upon its security, ii a great measure, depend our chief supplies of flour for the subsistence of such forces as we may have occasion for in the course of the War."

Washington had tried other methods of blocking the river. The chain at Fort Montgomery had failed, as had the chevaux-defrise at Fort Washington. These were a submerged shallow-water version of an old Dutch anti-cavalry device, using sunken timbers with projecting iron spears to puncture the hulls of the enemy's wooden ships. But the Hudson was too deep for them to be effective, and its powerful tides played havoc with the devices. Fire ships and fire rafts against enemy ships also proved ineffective and too easy to avoid.

Since he was not a military man, Swift did not stay at the camp itself, but at a small nearby settlement which had sprung up almost overnight to cater to the needs of the soldiers on duty at West Point and other nearby forts. On prior visits he'd stayed at a tavern called the Nugget of Gold. He returned there now and was pleased to see the same man behind the bar. Norb Flander was the owner of the place, a red-faced man in his fifties who'd worked at a tavern on Manhattan Island until the British came in '76. He'd moved north along the river like a great many others, finally pausing near West Point to build his own place. He'd bought an old barn for its wood, torn it down, and built the Nugget of Gold.

"Good to see you again, Mr. Swift," he said by way of greeting. "I got your room waiting for you. Want your usual bourbon?"

"That will be fine, Norb."

"I think the weather's finally beginning to warm up."

"It should. It's been a long winter."

A couple of off-duty soldiers from the camp were standing at the other end of the bar, but Swift didn't recognize them. He drank the bourbon down quickly and ordered another. After a bit more small talk he asked Flander, "You get many strangers around here?"

"Hardly at all. With the war going on, every stranger might be a Loyalist spy."

Swift sipped his second drink, having no intention of finishing it. "How's Molly? I don't see her around." Molly McVey was a barmaid who worked there occasionally. Swift had become friendly with her on his previous trips to the camp.

"Probably with one of the officers. You know how it is."

"Tell her I was asking for her." He left the rest of his drink and went around to his room at the back of the tavern.

He almost hoped Molly would visit him later, but finally he fell asleep alone.

THE WEATHER WAS DAMP AND CHILLY during the first week in April, but ice was breaking up in the river. Alexander Swift watched it each day and thought about the great chain—George Washington's watch chain. On April 7, when half the chain had been assembled upstream, it was loaded on rafts of pitch-covered logs for the final leg of its journey to Camp West Point. Swift met Chester Hayborne and his crew at New Windsor, about fifteen miles upriver, where the chain-laden rafts were being launched.

"We'll keep them close to shore," the foreman told Swift. "If there is an accident we don't want to lose the chain in the deepest part of the river." He wore a sealskin jacket and cap as protection against the damp mist over the water, and watched carefully as his men poled the rafts along the shoreline.

"Colonel Clay is concerned about Tory spies," Swift told him. "Have you seen any strangers about?"

"Just the usual townsfolk. I've known them most of my life."

"Keep an eye out," Swift cautioned him.

"Are you in charge of the chain project now?"

"No, I'm just observing the progress for General Washington. Colonel Clay and Captain Machin are the military people in charge, and, of course, General McDougall." He was the senior officer in charge of all the highland posts. "When do you expect the remainder of the chain will be ready for us?"'

The muscular foreman shrugged. "A week, ten days. No longer than that."

Alexander Swift nodded. "I'll be back then."

Returning to West Point, Swift found Captain Machin, the officer who had designed the chain and arranged for its construction, watching with Clay as the first half of it was made fast to the shoreline. "Soon it will be in place," Clay said happily. "If the enemy lets us alone two weeks longer, the job will be done."

Two nights later, as Alexander Swift drank with Norb Flander in the bar at the Nugget of Gold, he noticed a curly-haired stranger at one of the tables. "Who is that?" he asked Flander.

"A fur merchant named Rowland, down from Canada."

"Ever seen him before?"

Norb Flander shook his head. "He's new to these parts."

Swift picked up his drink and joined the man at the table, introducing himself. "Pleased to meet you," Rowland said, extending his hand. Up close, the mass of curly blond locks seemed almost too large for the man's head. Swift wondered if it might be a wig.

"Flander tells me you're a fur merchant from Canada."

"That's right."

"This is a dangerous place to sell your goods, in the midst of a revolution."

"I feel safe in this area," the man said. "Since the British defeat at Saratoga last October they have stayed away. The French in Canada are now supporting your struggle."

"They stayed away only because of the harsh winter," Swift reasoned. "Now that spring is coming you will see their sails once more on the Hudson."

The merchant, who appeared not much older than Swift's own twenty-eight years, replied, "But your chain will stop them."

"Which chain would that be?" Swift asked innocently.

" 'Tis no secret in these parts. I see it lying down by the water's edge like some sun-basking serpent."

"It's not wise to pass such observations along to others," Swift warned him.

"I would not," the merchant assured him. He finished his drink and made a nervous exit from the tavern.

"Watch that one," Swift advised Norb Flander. "I do not like the look of him."

It was the following night when Molly McVey returned to West Point. Alexander saw her as soon as he walked into the Nugget of Gold. Oddly, she was standing by a table where the Canadian fur merchant, Rowland, sat whittling on a piece of wood, his left hand using a sharp hunting knife to carve out the shape of a rough wooden chain with three inter-locked links. Swift watched him finish the task and pass it to Molly. "There you are. It's my gift to you," he told her with a smile.

"How clever you are!" She tucked it away in her dress and then seemed to notice Swift for the first time. "Hello, Alex. It's good to see you again." She was the only one, other than his wife, who had ever called him Alex.

"You've been away," he said.

She turned and said good-bye to the fur merchant, then followed Swift to a table near the opposite end of the bar. Norb Flander came over with a bourbon for him and a beer for Molly. "I was visiting a friend in Albany," she said. "How long have you been here?"

"Ten days."

Molly McVey was a slender, dark-haired woman with a creamy white complexion and a way of wearing dresses a bit tighter than the fashion allowed. She was probably a bit older than Swift. She was certainly wiser in many things. "You're looking good," she told him. "Most of my friends are pale and worn after this hard winter."

"I've made a few trips to Valley Forge through the deep snow in New Jersey. That ride will keep any man in shape."

"How is General Washington?"

"Vigorous and aching for combat. It's amazing how he's kept up the spirits of his troops through this winter, despite the terrible conditions and the death of so many from starvation."

"How long will he remain there?"

Alexander shrugged. "Perhaps till June if the British do not attack. He has Baron von Steuben with him, training and reorganizing the army."

"At least this winter is at an end," she said.

They had another drink and then he followed her up the creaking stairs to her room above the bar. When he looked back, the man named Rowland was carving out another of his little wooden chains.

HE FOUND HIMSELF DRIFTING in and out of sleep until it was nearly dawn. At one point Molly said to him, "The chain is a big secret, isn't it?"

"We hope so, until it's in place. General Washington never mentions it directly in his letters."

She held up the wooden links that Rowland had given her. "Do you think the Canadian is a spy?"

"He could be."

And later, "Alex?"

"What is it, my love?"

"I heard something about you in Albany. People gossip, you know."

"What did you hear?"

"That your wife isn't dead at all. That she ran off with a British officer in New York."

He didn't answer, only lay there feeling the weight of the sheets. "Do you still love her?" Molly asked, but he didn't reply. Finally she asked, "If you found them, would you kill him?"

"Perhaps," he said, more to himself than to Molly.

"Would you kill her?"

He didn't answer. After a time he slept.

By April 16 the second half of the chain had been assembled at New Windsor. It was another damp day full of gray clouds and misty rain. When Alexander Swift reached the place, he saw Hayborne in the shallow water with his workers, trying to hoist a pair of giant links back onto their raft. Finally they succeeded and he came out of the water to dry off, fanning himself with his sealskin cap.

"That's hard work, Swift. Work for younger men than me."

"It'll soon be over."

The foreman shouted at his men to keep the rafts out of deep water as they began their journey downriver. Then he put the cap back on and strolled along with Alexander. "Over till the next job. They get harder in the summer with all that heat at the foundry."

Suddenly Swift saw someone on the hill above them. He recognized the mop of curly blond hair at once, even though he hadn't seen Rowland around for several days. "See that man? Do you know him?"

"I don't think so."

"Be careful. He may be a Tory spy."

"Glad you warned me."

Swift mounted up, preparing to ride back along the river, following the rafts in their progress downstream. Chester Hayborne disappeared from view among the pine trees, and he could no longer see Rowland anywhere. He'd ridden about fifty yards when some noise made him turn and look back. Hayborne had emerged from the trees and was walking along a raised bluff that commanded a good view of the river to the south. Perhaps he was checking the progress of the rafts, though the visibility through the mist had grown poorer.

Almost at once a second figure burst forth from the trees, running after Hayborne. Swift recognized Rowland's curly blond hair at once, and saw the hunting knife in his raised right hand.

"Rowland! Don't!" Hayborne shouted, and turned to face his attacker.

The knife plunged in again and again, through the sealskin jacket. The foreman fell to the ground at the edge of the bluff even as Swift spurred his mount forward. Rowland pushed the body with his foot and it rolled off the edge of the bluff, falling a dozen feet to the water.

The current was swift at this point and Alexander saw the body turning over and over as it was swept along. He tried to reach it, urging his horse into the shallow water near shore, but the body was moving too fast, sweeping toward the river's center. The hat came off, bobbed a moment, and then vanished with the body. Chester Hayborne was gone, and his killer had vanished as well. There was no sign of Rowland among the trees.

IMMEDIATELY UPON HIS RETURN Swift sought out Colonel Clay. He was not among the men working at the water's edge under the command of Captain Machin. "Where is Clay?" he asked the captain.

"I haven't seen him lately. Try his quarters."

Swift finally found him talking with Flander at the Nugget of Gold. He reported what had happened to Chester Hayborne. "You actually witnessed this murder?" he asked.

"I did, Colonel. Rowland stabbed him to death while I watched."

"Is there any possibility he might have survived?"

"None. I saw the body being swept away by the river."

"I don't believe I ever saw this man Rowland. Do we have an artist in the camp who might sketch him from your description?"

Norb Flander had been listening at the bar. "Molly's something of an artist, and she talked to him a couple of times. She could probably do it."

Norb found Molly in her room and brought her down. Her eyes moved from Swift to Clay while they explained what they needed. "You think he's a spy?" she repeated. Swift saw that she was fingering the little links of wooden chain as she spoke.

"And a murderer," Alexander added. "He killed Hayborne from the foundry."

"Why would he do that?"

"The British want to destroy the chain and make certain we can't replace it."

She went upstairs for her paper and sketching pencils. Swift had seen some of her drawings before, but he wondered about her ability to capture an accurate likeness of Rowland. Seated at the bar, she did a quick sketch and then began to fill in the shadings of the face and hair.

"Did you think he was wearing a wig?" Swift asked her.

"He could have been. If so, I'll have to draw him with it on because I never saw him any other way."

Flander peered over her shoulder, offering comments and suggestions. "I think the eyes are a little off, Molly. Weren't they a bit closer together?"

Alexander made suggestions, too, based on his memory, and before long they had a passable likeness of the man who called himself Rowland. Colonel Clay took it and assured them it would be seen by every man at the camp. "I'll post it at mess," he promised.

"Let Molly make a copy," Flander suggested, "and I'll post it here at the bar as well."

Swift had personal doubts that it would do any good. If Rowland had been wearing a wig his appearance could be quite different already.

TWO DAYS LATER, on the twentieth, Captain Machin reported to General McDougall. Seventeen hundred feet of the great chain was ready for use, more than enough to cross the Hudson at West Point. They only needed to wait for favorable weather to fix it in place. On the slack tide of April 30, the weather finally broke. One end of the chain was made fast to a huge rock crib some ten feet high and eight feet wide, then slowly winched across the river to a similar crate filled with stone on the opposite bank. With both ends secure and the massive chain stapled to pine log rafts, the Hudson was finally effectively blocked.

"This is a great day," Swift told Colonel Clay as they stood on the shore surveying the scene.

"Tell that to General Washington. His wild dream has come true."

"I still wonder if a large ship, with a metal prow, might strike the chain at full sail and break it."

It was a thought that had obviously bothered the colonel as well. "The foundry is turning out a smaller chain for a boom. The work was slowed by the killing of Chester Hayborne but it proceeds at a good pace now."

The boom, designed to float slightly downstream from the chain, was a series of foot-thick logs, fifteen feet long, spaced four feet apart and parallel to the water's flow, linked by sections of chain and iron bolts. The idea was that the boom would help absorb the shock of a ramming by an enemy warship, protecting the great chain from breaking. When the weather was favorable, loosely laid planks could turn the boom into a footbridge.

Swift spoke of it again that night with Molly. "It seems like a great deal of money for a chain across the river," she said. "And one man has died for it."

"Others may, too, if the British attempt to ram it."

"Is the Hudson that important?"

"It is our new nation's lifeline, as General Washington has pointed out many times. In the land east of the river there is no flour, to the west there is no meat. The two parts of our struggling nation have an absolute need for each other."

"When will the boom be in place?"

"In a few days, we hope."

"You'll be leaving then?"

"I expect so, yes."

"With Rowland still at large?"

"Colonel Clay and the others can deal with him, should he return. By now he's probably in Canada."

She fingered the chain of rough wood that Rowland had carved for her. "Where will you go next?"

"General Washington will have a place for me."

"You'd rather do this than serve in the regular army? If you're caught behind enemy lines, couldn't you be hanged as a spy?"

"I try to avoid enemy lines as much as possible."

"Don't you ever want to sneak into New York, to see her? Do you know where she is?"

"I know the street, I know the house. I can see her in my mind right now." He had turned away as he spoke.

Molly reached out to touch his face in the darkness. "Will I ever see you after you leave here?"

"I'm sure I'll be back. Washington will want periodic reports on his watch chain."

"It's different when you're here. This whole place is different. These few weeks have made everything else bearable."

"Sleep now," he told her softly. "I'm here. I won't be going away quite yet."

BY THE TIME THE BOOM was finally in place, the hills of the Hudson Valley were alive with mayflowers. The harsh winter had been forgotten with the arrival of spring. Alexander took Molly for a walk on the plank bridge across the river, and she marveled at her first close look at the giant chain.

"It's enormous, Alex! Even seeing it on the shore didn't prepare me for this. It would hold back Caesar's army!"

"But will it hold back King George's navy? That is the question. They still command the Hudson south of Peekskill."

Back on shore she held tight to his arm. "You took me out there because you're leaving tomorrow, aren't you?"

"We each have work to do."

"My work can wait," she replied with a touch of bitterness. "There are always soldiers to be comforted."

"Let us stop at the Nugget for a drink."

Norb Flander brought them their drinks and said, "We're all feeling better now that the boom is in place."

"Any sign of Rowland?"

The proprietor glanced back at Molly's sketch posted on the wall. "Not a bit. If he's been here he's a different person."

"He just might be that," Swift agreed, remembering the curly blond hair.

While she drank, Molly had taken out the carved wooden chain again and was playing with it. There were times when Swift wanted to take it from her and hurl it far away into the night. It was the gift of a spy and a murderer. Now, staring at it as if hypnotized, his mind suddenly cleared. "What is it?" she asked, noting the strange expression on his face.

"I've been a fool," he said.

"What—?"

"Flander, what night is the new moon this month?"

"Soon now. The night sky is already dark as pitch."

"But what night will it be darkest?"

"Thursday—two nights from now."

He nodded, then said to Molly, "I'll be staying through Thursday night."

THE FOLLOWING DAY Alexander Swift spoke privately with Captain Machin, because the Hudson chain was ultimately his responsibility. Certain preparations were made, though he could see the captain thought him just a bit crazy.

He sat up Wednesday night watching the water, because he could not afford to be wrong. Once, after midnight, Molly came down to where he sat in the darkness. "Nothing's going to happen tonight," she said. "Come up to bed."

"I'll be up shortly. I suppose you're right. If the British were coming they'd be here by now."

On Thursday morning the chain still held, floating serenely on the unusually calm water. He went down to the boom and walked carefully across to the other side, watching for anything unusual. The chain was undamaged, exactly as it had been. When he reached the opposite side, at Fort Constitution, he inspected the large pile of wood he'd instructed Captain Machin to build on either shore. Then he walked back across the footbridge to the West Point side.

"You look worried," Norb Flander told him later when he stopped in the Nugget of Gold.

"Just apprehensive."

Norb poured him a drink. "Why do you think the British might attack tonight?"

"It's darkest with a new moon, and the current is moving slowly. If they're coming by night to try filing through a link as they did at Fort Montgomery, this is when they'll do it."

"But our chain is stronger."

"I hope so."

Even on the darkest night it was impossible to move a large British warship up the river without attracting attention. Progress would be slowed by the danger of running aground, and if spies tried to guide it from the riverbanks their torches would be seen from the forts. Swift knew the attack, if it came at all, would come by small boats sneaking silently up the river.

As it happened, it was Molly who spotted them first. It was just before midnight when she tugged on his sleeve. "Alex! There's something moving on the river!"

He saw it then, but couldn't make out what it was. "Stay here," he whispered. "I'm going out on the boom. If you hear a shot, have them light the fires."

He hurried onto the wooden footbridge, drawing a loaded flintlock pistol from his belt. If they were bent on cutting the chain—

Then he heard soft voices, and knew they were up ahead, climbing out of their boats and onto the boom. Some would be swimming under the boom to the chain itself. He aimed into the darkness ahead and fired the pistol. There was an immediate scurry and splashing as the men on the boom dove for safety. Then, behind him on the shore, a torch blazed and the pile of wood caught fire. The guards at Fort Constitution lit their bonfire as well.

Now suddenly the river was alive with light, the waters reflecting the twin fires growing by the minute into towers of flame. Swift saw now that there were two boats ahead, rowed upstream against the current. Men were in the water, dark figures whose faces reflected the red glow of the sky. Then he saw something that sent a chill through him. One of the swimmers was on the giant chain, clinging to a bobbing raft while he crammed a package inside a link.

Gunpowder.

They were trying to blow up the chain.

The man pulled out a long fuse and struck a large-headed friction match to light it. Swift hurled his single-shot pistol at him, missed, and leaped from the boom onto the nearest raft. From both shores came the scattered chatter of musket fire.

"Don't light it!" Alexander Swift warned.

The fuse sputtered into life. "You're too late," came the reply.

Swift leaped the four feet onto the adjoining raft and grabbed for the fuse. The other pulled out a hunting knife—the same one, surely—and raised it to strike.

"Not this time," Swift shouted. "No more killings, no more escapes." He went in under the knife and slammed the man down onto the giant chain. Then he grabbed for the fuse and pulled it free of the gunpowder.

There was more firing and an oarsman in one of the boats toppled into the water. The others swam to shore where soldiers were waiting. Colonel Clay and his men came running out with torches along the foot-bridge as Swift hauled up his prisoner.

"Here's your man!" Swift told them, and the torchlight fell on the face of the foundry foreman, Chester Hayborne.

WHEN THE TORY FORCES had been rounded up and the gunpowder bomb safely removed, Alexander Swift found himself with Colonel Clay and Captain Machin at the Nugget of Gold. Drinks were on the house, Flander said, and Molly served them.

"You knew it was Hayborne?" Colonel Clay asked, incredulous. "You knew he was still alive?"

Swift nodded. "See this little chain Molly has? I watched the stranger, Rowland, carve it with the knife in his left hand. That day on the river, the curly-haired man who stabbed Hayborne and pushed the body into the river struck with his right hand. When I remembered that the other night I was sure of one thing—the murderer had not been Rowland. Yet how was that possible? I myself heard Hayborne's voice shout out 'Row-land! Don't!' an instant before the stabbing. But then I remembered something else. That shouted plea came just *before* the man in the seal-skin cap turned to confront his attacker! It was the attacker who shouted those words, not the victim. And if the attacker was not Rowland, it had to be Hayborne because I'd recognized his voice."

"Why would he shout out at all?" Clay wondered.

"To attract my attention, of course. He needed a witness to swear the victim had been Hayborne, and the killer Rowland. I should have been suspicious right away, because to my knowledge Hayborne didn't even know Rowland when he shouted the name. If you read over that inter-cepted secret message again you will see that it implies the spy has a knowledge of the great chain and its timing, yet is probably not someone stationed or living at West Point. Otherwise he or she would long ago have sent word on the number of cannons at the camp. It suggested that the spy might be a foundry worker who went to West Point only occasionally."

"Then Rowland came here to meet with Hayborne?"

"Exactly. By that time, however, I'd mentioned the possibility of spies. Hayborne was nervous and must have guessed his message had been intercepted. He decided to fake his death and make his way south to the British lines. Rowland afforded the perfect opportunity with that curly blond wig. Hayborne must have persuaded him to change clothes to avoid capture as a spy. Rowland donned the sealskin jacket and cap while Hayborne put on the wig and Rowland's coat. Then, after attracting my attention, Hayborne stabbed Rowland and pushed him into the Hudson. With the switched clothing and the poor visibility that day, he thought he could fool me. The body lost its cap, but since I'd never seen Rowland without his wig I still didn't recognize him. So far as I knew, the foreman was dead and Rowland had killed him. Hayborne was safe in assuming the body wouldn't be recovered from the swift-flowing river. He joined the British forces and led a raiding party back tonight to sever the chain with a gunpowder bomb, choosing a night they knew the sky would be at its darkest."

Clay finished his drink and stood up. "Chester Hayborne will be properly dealt with, and I will personally commend your actions to General McDougall and the commander in chief."

Swift shook his hand. "I leave in the morning for Valley Forge. Guard the chain, Colonel. Guard it well. Its links are holding this new nation together."

When he rode out at dawn the next day only Molly was there to see him, waving from her upstairs window at the Nugget of Gold.

Marcia Muller holds many titles in the mystery fiction field, most notably that of the first American author to write a detective series with a female protagonist. Fifteen novels later, Sharon McCone is still going strong, having updated her business to a new office near the waterfront of San Francisco. A collection of the McCone short stories, *The McCone Files,* was recently published, and it looks like the first modern female sleuth will be cracking cases for many more years.

"The Holes in the System," however, relegates McCone to the role of peripheral character, focusing instead on her assistant, Rae Kelleher. If Kelleher follows in her mentor's footsteps, she should have an excellent career ahead of her. It's certainly off to a mysterious start with this case of lost boys and found optimism.

The Holes in the System
MARCIA MULLER

There are some days that just ought to be called off. Mondays are always hideous: The trouble starts when I dribble toothpaste all over my clothes or lock my keys in the car and doesn't let up till I stub my toe on the bedstand at night. Tuesdays are usually when the morning paper doesn't get delivered. Wednesdays are better, but if I get to feeling optimistic and go to aerobics class at the Y, chances are ten to one that I'll wrench my back. Thursdays—forget it. And by five on Friday, all I want to do is crawl under the covers and hide.

You can see why I love weekends.

The day I got assigned to the Boydston case was a Tuesday.

Cautious optimism, that was what I was nursing. The paper lay folded tidily on the front steps of All Souls Legal Cooperative—where I both live and work as a private investigator. I read it and drank my coffee, not even burning my tongue. Nobody I knew had died, and there was even a cheerful story below the fold in the Metro section. By the time I'd looked at the comics and found all five strips that I bother to read were funny, I was feeling downright perky.

Well, why not? I wasn't making a lot of money, but my job was secure. The attic room I occupied was snug and comfy. I had a boyfriend, and even if the relationship was about as deep as a desert stream on the Fourth of July, he could be taken most anyplace. And to top it off, this wasn't a bad hair day.

All that smug reflection made me feel charitable toward my fellow humans—or at least my coworkers and their clients—so I refolded the paper and carried it from the kitchen of our big Victorian to the front parlor and waiting room so others could partake. A man was sitting on the shabby maroon sofa: bald and chubby, dressed in lime green polyester pants and a strangely patterned green, blue, and yellow shirt that reminded me of drawings of sperm cells. One thing for sure, he'd never get run over by a bus while he was wearing that getup.

He looked at me as I set the paper on the coffee table and said, "How ya doin', little lady?"

Now, there's some contention that the word "lady" is demeaning. Frankly, it doesn't bother me; when I hear it I know I'm looking halfway presentable and haven't got something disgusting caught between my front teeth. No, what rankled was the word "little." When you're five foot three the word reminds you of things you'd just as soon not dwell on—like being unable to see over people's heads at parades, or the little-girly clothes that designers of petite sizes are always trying to foist on you. "Little," especially at nine in the morning, doesn't cut it.

I glared at the guy. Unfortunately, he'd gotten to his feet and I had to look up.

He didn't notice I was annoyed; maybe he was nearsighted. "Sure looks like it's gonna be a fine day," he said.

Now I identified his accent—pure Texas. Another strike against him, because of Uncle Roy, but that's another story.

"It *would've* been a nice day," I muttered.

"Ma'am?"

That did it! The first—and last—time somebody had gotten away with calling me "ma'am" was on my twenty-eighth birthday two weeks before, when a bagboy tried to help me out of Safeway with my two feather-light sacks of groceries. It was not a precedent I wanted followed.

Speaking more clearly, I said, "It would've been a nice day, except for you."

He frowned. "What'd I do?"

"Try 'little,' a Texas accent, and 'ma'am'!"

"Ma'am, are you all right?"

"Aaargh!" I fled the parlor and ran up the stairs to the office of my boss, Sharon McCone.

*   *   *

SHARON IS MY FRIEND, mentor, and sometimes—heaven help me—custodian of my honesty. She's been all those things since she hired me a few years ago to assist her at the co-op. Not that our association is always smooth sailing: She can be a stern taskmaster and she harbors a devilish sense of humor that surfaces at inconvenient times. But she's always been there for me, even during the death throes of my marriage to my pig-selfish, perpetual-student husband, Doug Grayson. And ever since I've stopped referring to him as "that bastard Doug" she's decided I'm a grown-up who can be trusted to manage her own life—within limits.

That morning she was sitting behind her desk with her chair swiveled around so she could look out the bay window at the front of the Victorian. I've found her in that pose hundreds of times: sunk low on her spine, long legs crossed, dark eyes brooding. The view is of dowdy houses across the triangular park that divides the street, and usually hazed by San Francisco fog, but it doesn't matter; whatever she's seeing is strictly inside her head, and she says she gets her best insights into her cases that way.

I stepped into the office and cleared my throat. Slowly Shar turned, looking at me as if I were a stranger. Then her eyes cleared. "Rae, hi. Nice work on closing the Anderson file so soon."

"Thanks. I found the others you left on my desk; they're pretty routine. You have anything else for me?"

"As a matter of fact, yes.'" She smiled slyly and slid a manila folder across the desk. "Why don't you take this client?"

I opened the folder and studied the information sheet stapled inside. All it gave was a name—Darrin Boydston—and an address on Mission Street. Under the job description Shar had noted "background check."

"Another one?" I asked, letting my voice telegraph my disappointment.

"Uh-huh. I think you'll find it interesting."

"Why?"

She waved a slender hand at me. "Go! It'll be a challenge."

Now, that *did* make me suspicious. "If it's such a challenge, how come you're not handling it?"

For an instant her eyes sparkled. She doesn't like it when I hint that she skims the best cases for herself—although that's exactly what she does, and I don't blame her. "Just go see him."

"He'll be at this address?"

"No, he's downstairs. I got done talking with him ten minutes ago."

"Downstairs? *Where* downstairs?"

"In the parlor."

Oh, God!

She smiled again. "Lime green, with a Texas accent."

"So," DARRIN BOYDSTON SAID, "did y'all come back down to chew me out some more?"

"I'm sorry about that." I handed him my card. "Ms. McCone has assigned me to your case."

He studied it and looked me up and down. "You promise to keep a civil tongue in your head?"

"I said I was sorry."

"Well, you damn near ruint my morning."

How many more times was I going to have to apologize?

"Let's get goin', little lady." He started for the door.

I winced and asked, "Where?"

"My place. I got somebody I want you to meet."

BOYDSTON'S CAR WAS A WHITE Lincoln Continental—beautiful machine, except for the bull's horns mounted on the front grille. I stared at them in horror.

"Pretty, aren't they?" he said, opening the passenger's door.

"I'll follow you in my car," I told him.

He shrugged. "Suit yourself."

As I got into the Ramblin' Wreck—my ancient, exhaust-belching Rambler American—I looked back and saw Boydston staring at *it* in horror.

BOYDSTON'S PLACE WAS A STOREFRONT on Mission a few blocks down from my Safeway—an area that could do with some urban renewal and just might get it, if the upwardly mobile ethnic groups that're moving into the neighborhood get their way. It shared the building with a Thai restaurant and a Filipino travel agency. In its front window red neon tubing spelled out THE CASH COW, but the bucking outline below the letters was a bull. I imagined Boydston trying to reach a decision: call it the Cash Cow and have a good name but a dumb graphic; call it the Cash Bull and have a dumb name but a good graphic; or just say the hell with it and mix genders.

But what kind of establishment was this?

My client took the first available parking space, leaving me to fend for myself. When I finally found another and walked back two blocks he'd already gone inside.

Chivalry is dead. Sometimes I think common courtesy's obit is about to be published, too.

When I went into the store, the first thing I noticed was a huge potted barrel cactus, and the second was dozens of guitars hanging from the ceiling. A rack of worn cowboy boots completed the picture.

Texas again. The state that spawned the likes of Uncle Roy was going to keep getting in my face all day long.

The room was full of glass showcases that displayed an amazing assortment of stuff: rings, watches, guns, cameras, fishing reels, kitchen gadgets, small tools, knickknacks, silverware, even a metronome. There was a whole section of electronic equipment like TVs and VCRs, a jumble of probably obsolete computer gear, a fleet of vacuum cleaners poised to roar to life and tidy the world, enough exercise equipment to trim down half the population, and a jukebox that just then was playing a country song by Shar's brother-in-law, Ricky Savage. Delicacy prevents me from describing what his voice does to my libido.

Darrin Boydston stood behind a high counter, tapping on a keyboard. On the wall behind him a sign warned CUSTOMER: MUST PRESENT TICKET TO CLAIM MERCHANDISE. I'm not too quick most mornings, but I did manage to figure out that the Cash Cow was a pawnshop.

"Y'all took long enough," my client said. "You gonna charge me for the time you spent parking?"

I sighed. "Your billable hours start now." Then I looked at my watch and made a mental note of the time.

He turned the computer off, motioned for me to come around the counter, and led me through a door into a warehouse area. Its shelves were crammed with more of the kind of stuff he had out front. Halfway down the center aisle he made a right turn and took me past small appliances: blenders, food processors, toasters, electric woks, pasta makers, even an ancient pressure cooker. It reminded me of the one the grandmother who raised me used to have, and I wrinkled my nose at it, thinking of those sweltering late-summer days when she'd make me help her with the yearly canning. No wonder I resist the womanly household arts!

Boydston said, "They buy these gizmos 'cause they think they need 'em. Then they find out they don't need and can't afford 'em. And then it all ends up in my lap." He sounded exceptionally cheerful about this particular brand of human folly, and I supposed he had good reason.

He led me at a fast clip toward the back of the warehouse—so fast that I had to trot to keep up with him. One of the other problems with being short is that you're forever running along behind taller people. Since I'd already decided to hate Darrin Boydston, I also decided he was walking fast to spite me.

At the end of the next-to-last aisle we came upon a thin man in a white T-shirt and black work pants who was moving boxes from the shelves to a dolly. Although Boydston and I were making plenty of noise, he didn't hear us come up. My client put his hand on the man's shoulder, and he stiffened. When he turned I saw he was only a boy, no more than twelve or thirteen, with the fine features and thick black hair of a Eurasian. The look in his eyes reminded me of an abused kitten my boyfriend Willie had taken in: afraid and resigned to further terrible experiences. He glanced from me to Boydston, and when my client nodded reassuringly, the fear faded to remoteness.

Boydston said to me, "Meet Daniel."

"Hello, Daniel." I held out my hand. He looked at it, then at Boydston. He nodded again, and Daniel touched my fingers, moving back quickly as if they were hot.

"Daniel," Boydston said, "doesn't speak or hear. Speech therapist I know met him, says he's prob'ly been deaf and mute since he was born."

The boy was watching his face intently. I said, "He reads lips or understands signing, though."

"Does some lipreading, yeah. But no signing. For that you gotta have schooling. Far as I can tell, Daniel hasn't. But him and me, we worked out a personal kind of language to get by."

Daniel tugged at Boydston's sleeve and motioned at the shelves, eyebrows raised. Boydston nodded, then pointed to his watch, held up five fingers, and pointed to the front of the building. Daniel nodded and turned back to his work. Boydston said, "You see?"

"Uh-huh. You two communicate pretty well. How'd he come to work for you?"

My client began leading me back to the store—walking slower now. "The way it went, I found him all huddled up in the back doorway one morning 'bout six weeks ago when I opened up. He was damn near froze but dressed in clean clothes and a new jacket. Was in good shape, 'cept for some healed-over cuts on his face. And he had this laminated card . . . wait, I'll show you." He held the door for me, then rummaged through a drawer below the counter.

The card was a blue three-by-five encased in clear plastic; on it somebody had typed I WILL WORK FOR FOOD AND A PLACE TO SLEEP. I DO NOT SPEAK OR HEAR, BUT I AM A GOOD WORKER. PLEASE HELP ME.

"So you gave him a job?"

Boydston sat down on a stool. "Yeah. He sleeps in a little room off the warehouse and cooks on a hot plate. Mostly stuff outta cans. Every week I give him cash; he brings back the change—won't take any more than what his food costs, and that's not much."

I turned the card over. Turned over my opinion of Darrin Boydston, too. "How d'you know his name's Daniel?"

"I don't. That's just what I call him."

"Why Daniel?"

He looked embarrassed and brushed at a speck of lint on the leg of his pants. "Had a best buddy in high school down in Amarillo. Daniel Atkins. Got killed in 'Nam." He paused. "Funny, me giving his name to a slope kid when they were the ones that killed him." Another pause.

"Of course, this Daniel wasn't even born then, none of that business was his fault. And there's something about him ... I don't know, he just reminds me of my buddy. Don't suppose old Danny would mind none."

"I'm sure he wouldn't." Damn, it was getting harder and harder to hate Boydston! I decided to let go of it. "Okay," I said, "my case file calls for a background check. I take it you want me to find out who Daniel is."

"Yeah. Right now he doesn't exist—officially, I mean. He hasn't got a birth certificate, can't get a Social Security number. That means I can't put him on the payroll, and he can't get government help. No classes where he can learn the stuff I can't teach him. No SSI payments or Medicaid, either. My therapist friend says he's one of the people that slip through the cracks in the system."

The cracks are more like yawning holes, if you ask me. I said, "I've got to warn you, Mr. Boydston: Daniel may be in the country illegally."

"You think I haven't thought of that? Hell, I'm one of the people that voted for Prop One-eighty-seven. Keep those foreigners from coming here and taking jobs from decent citizens. Don't give 'em nothin' and maybe they'll go home and quit using up my tax dollar. That was before I met Daniel." He scowled. "*Damn,* I hate moral dilemmas! I'll tell you one thing, though: This is a good kid, he deserves a chance. If he's here illegally ... well, I'll deal with it somehow."

I liked his approach to his moral dilemma; I'd used it myself a time or ten. "Okay," I said, "tell me everything you know about him."

"Well, there're the clothes he had on when I found him. They're in this sack; take a look." He hauled a grocery bag from under the counter and handed it to me.

I pulled the clothing out: rugby shirt in white, green, and navy; navy cords; navy-and-tan down jacket. They were practically new, but the labels had been cut out.

"Lands' End?" I said. "Eddie Bauer?"

"One of those, but who can tell which?"

I couldn't, but I had a friend who could. "Can I take these?"

"Sure, but don't let Daniel see you got them. He's real attached to 'em, cried when I took 'em away to be cleaned the first time."

"Somebody cared about him, to dress him well and have this card made up. Laminating like that is a simple process, though; you can get it done in print shops."

"Hell, you could get it done *here.* I got in one of those laminating gizmos a week ago; belongs to a printer who's having a hard time of it, checks his shop equipment in and out like this was a lending library."

"What else can you tell me about Daniel? What's he like?"

Boydston considered. "Well, he's proud—the way he brings back the change from the money I give him tells me that. He's smart; he picked up on the warehouse routine easy, and he already knew how to cook. Whoever his people are, they don't have much; he knew what a hot plate was, but when I showed him a microwave it scared him. And he's got a tic about labels—cuts 'em out of the clothes I give him. There's more, too." He looked toward the door; Daniel was peeking hesitantly around its jamb. Boydston waved for him to come in and added, "I'll let Daniel do the telling."

The boy came into the room, eyes lowered shyly—or fearfully. Boydston looked at him till he looked back. Speaking very slowly and mouthing the words carefully, he asked, "Where are you from?"

Daniel pointed at the floor.

"San Francisco?"

Nod.

"This district?"

Frown.

"Mission district? Mis-sion?"

Nod.

"Your momma, where is she?"

Daniel bit his lip.

"Your momma?"

He raised his hand and waved.

"Gone away?" I asked Boydston.

"Gone away or dead. How long, Daniel?" When the boy didn't respond, he repeated, "How long?"

Shrug.

"Time confuses him," Boydston said. "Daniel, your daddy—where is he?"

The boy's eyes narrowed and he made a sudden violent gesture toward the door.

"Gone away?"

Curt nod.

"How long?"

Shrug.

"How long, Daniel?"

After a moment he held up two fingers.

"Days?"

Headshake.

"Weeks?"

Frown.

"Months?"

Another frown.

"Years?"

Nod.

"Thanks, Daniel." Boydston smiled at him and motioned to the door.

"You can go back to work now." He watched the boy leave, eyes troubled, then asked me, "So what d'you think?"

"Well, he's got good linguistic abilities; somebody bothered to teach him words—probably the mother. His recollections seem scrambled. He's fairly sure when the father left, less sure about the mother. That could mean she went away or died recently and he hasn't found a way to mesh it with the rest of his personal history. Whatever happened, he was left to fend for himself."

"Can you do anything for him?"

"I'm sure going to try."

MY BEST LEAD ON DANIEL'S IDENTITY was the clothing. There had to be a reason for the labels being cut out—and I didn't think it was because of a tic on the boy's part. No, somebody had wanted to conceal the origins of the duds, and when I found out where they'd come from I could pursue my investigation from that angle. I left the Cash Cow, got in the Ramblin' Wreck, and when it finally stopped coughing, drove to the six-story building on Brannan Street south of Market where my friend Janie labors in what she calls the rag trade. Right now she works for a T-shirt manufacturer—and there've been years when I would've gone naked without her gifts of overruns—but during her career she's touched on every area of the business; if anybody could steer me toward the manufacturer of Daniel's clothes, she was the one. I gave them to her and she told me to call later. Then I set out on the trail of a Mission district printer who had a laminating machine.

Print and copy shops were in abundant supply there. A fair number of them did laminating work, but none recognized—or would own up to recognizing—Daniel's three-by-five card. It took me nearly all day to canvass them, except for the half hour when I had a beer and a burrito at La Tacqueria, and by four o'clock I was totally discouraged. So I stopped at my favorite ice-cream shop, called Janie and found she was in a meeting, and to ease my frustration had a double-scoop caramel swirl in a chocolate chip cookie cone.

No wonder I'm usually carrying five spare pounds!

The shop had a section of little plastic tables and chairs, and I rested my weary feet there, planning to check in at the office and then call it a day. If turning the facts of the case over and over in my mind all evening could be considered calling it a day. . . .

Shar warned me about that right off the bat. "If you like this business and stick with it," she'd said, "you'll work twenty-four hours a day, seven days a week. You'll think you're not working because you'll be at a party or watching TV or even in bed with your husband. And then all of a sudden you'll realize that half your mind's thinking about your current case and searching for a solution. Frankly, it doesn't make for much of a life."

Actually it makes for more than one life. Sometimes I think the time I spend on stakeouts or questioning people or prowling the city belongs to another Rae, one who has no connection to the Rae who goes to parties and watches TV and—now—sleeps with her boyfriend. I'm divided, but I don't mind it. And if Rae-the-investigator intrudes on the off-duty Rae's time, that's okay. Because the off-duty Rae gets to watch Rae-the-investigator make her moves—fascinated and a little envious.

Schizoid? Maybe. But I can't help but live and breathe the business. By now that's as natural as breathing air.

So I sat on the little plastic chair savoring my caramel swirl and chocolate chips and realized that the half of my mind that wasn't on sweets had come up with a weird little coincidence. Licking ice-cream dribbles off my fingers, I went back to the phone and called Darrin Boydston. The printer who had hocked his laminating machine was named Jason Hill, he told me, and his shop was Quik Prints, on Mission near Geneva.

I'd gone there earlier this afternoon. When I showed Jason Hill the laminated card he'd looked kind of funny but claimed he didn't do that kind of work, and there hadn't been any equipment in evidence to brand him a liar. Actually, he wasn't a liar; he didn't do that kind of work *anymore*.

HILL WAS CLOSING UP when I got to Quik Prints, and he looked damned unhappy to see me again. I took the laminated card from my pocket and slapped it into his hand. "The machine you made this on is living at the Cash Cow right now," I said. "You want to tell me about it?"

Hill—one of those bony-thin guys that you want to take home and fatten up—sighed. "You from Child Welfare or what?"

"I'm working for your pawnbroker, Darrin Boydston." I showed him the ID he hadn't bothered to look at earlier. "Who had the card made up?"

"I did."

"Why?"

"For the kid's sake." He switched the Open sign in the window to Closed and came out onto the sidewalk. "Mind if we walk to my bus stop while we talk?"

I shook my head and fell in next to him. The famous San Francisco fog was in, gray and dirty, making the gray and dirty Outer Mission even more depressing than usual. As we headed toward the intersection of Mission and Geneva, Hill told me his story.

"I found the kid on the sidewalk about seven weeks ago. It was five in the morning—I'd come in early for a rush job—and he was dazed and banged up and bleeding. Looked like he'd been mugged. I took him into the shop and was going to call the cops, but he started crying—upset about the blood on his down jacket. I sponged it off, and by the time I got back from the rest room, he was sweeping the print-room floor. I really didn't have time to deal with the cops, so I just let him sweep. He kind of made himself indispensable."

"And then?"

"He cried when I tried to put him outside that night, so I got him some food and let him sleep in the shop. He had coffee ready the next morning and helped me take out the trash. I still thought I should call the cops, but I was worried: He couldn't tell them who he was or where he lived; he'd end up in some detention center or foster home and his folks might never find him. I grew up in foster homes myself; I know all about the system. He was a sweet kid and deserved better than that. You know?"

"I know."

"Well, I couldn't figure *what* to do with him. I couldn't keep him at the shop much longer—the landlord's nosy and always on the premises. And I couldn't take him home—I live in a tiny studio with my girlfriend and three dogs. So after a week I got an idea: I'd park him someplace with a laminated card asking for a job; I knew he wouldn't lose it or throw it away, because he loved the laminated stuff and saved all the discards."

"Why'd you leave him at the Cash Cow?"

"Mr. Boydston's got a reputation for taking care of people. He's helped me out plenty of times."

"How?"

"Well, when he sends out the sixty-day notices saying you should claim your stuff or it'll be sold, as long as you go in and make a token payment, he'll hang onto it. He sees you're hurting, he'll give you more than the stuff's worth. He bends over backwards to make a loan." We got to the bus stop and Hill joined the rush-hour line. "And I was right about Mr. Boydston helping the kid, too," he added. "When I took the machine in last week, there he was, sweeping the sidewalk."

"He recognize you?"

"Didn't see me. Before I crossed the street, Mr. Boydston sent him on some errand. The kid's in good hands."

Funny how every now and then when you think the whole city's gone to hell, you discover there're a few good people left. . . .

WEDNESDAY MORNING: CAUTIOUS OPTIMISM AGAIN, but I wasn't going to push my luck by attending an aerobics class. Today I'd put all my energy into the Boydston case.

First, a call to Janie, whom I hadn't been able to reach at home the night before.

"The clothes were manufactured by a company called Casuals, Incorporated," she told me. "They only sell by catalogue, and their offices and factory are on Third Street."

"Any idea why the labels were cut out?"

"Well, at first I thought they might've been overstocks that were sold through one of the discounters like Ross, but that doesn't happen often with the catalogue outfits. So I took a close look at the garments and saw they've got defects—nothing major, but they wouldn't want to pass them off as first quality."

"Where would somebody get hold of them?"

"A factory store, if the company has one. I didn't have time to check."

It wasn't much of a lead, but even a little lead's better than nothing at all. I promised Janie I'd buy her a beer sometime soon and headed for the industrial corridor along Third Street.

CASUALS, INC., DIDN'T HAVE AN ON-SITE FACTORY STORE, so I went into the front office to ask if there was one in another location. No, the receptionist told me, they didn't sell garments found to be defective.

"What happens to them?"

"Usually they're offered at a discount to employees and their families."

That gave me an idea, and five minutes later I was talking with a Mr. Fong in personnel. "A single mother with a deaf-mute son? That would be Mae Jones. She worked here as a seamstress for ... let's see ... a little under a year."

"But she's not employed here anymore?"

"No. We had to lay off a number of people, and those with the least seniority are the first to go."

"Do you know where she's working now?"

"Sorry, I don't."

"Mr. Fong, is Mae Jones a documented worker?"

"Green card was in order. We don't hire illegals."

"And you have an address for her?"

"Yes, but I'm afraid I can't give that out."

"I understand, but I think you'll want to make an exception in this case. You see, Mae's son was found wandering the Mission seven weeks ago, the victim of a mugging. I'm trying to reunite them."

Mr. Fong didn't hesitate to fetch her file and give me the address, on Lucky Street in the Mission. Maybe, I thought, this was my lucky break.

THE HOUSE WAS A VICTORIAN that had been sided with concrete block and painted a weird shade of purple. Sagging steps led to a porch where six mailboxes hung. None of the names on them was Jones. I rang all the bells and got no answer. Now what? "Can I help you?" an Asian-accented voice said behind me. It belonged to a stooped old woman carrying a fishnet bag full of vegetables. Her eyes, surrounded by deep wrinkles, were kind. "I'm looking for Mae Jones." The woman had been taking out a keyring. Now she jammed it into the pocket of her loose-fitting trousers and backed up against the porch railing. Fear made her nostrils flare.

"What?" I asked. "What's wrong?"

"You are from them!"

"Them? Who?"

"I know nothing."

"Please don't be scared. I'm trying to help Mrs. Jones's son."

"Tommy? Where is Tommy?"

I explained about Jason Hill finding him and Darrin Boydston taking him in.

When I finished the woman had relaxed a little. "I am so happy one of them is safe."

"Please, tell me about the Joneses."

She hesitated, looking me over. Then she nodded as if I'd passed some kind of test and took me inside to a small apartment furnished with things that made the thrift-shop junk in my nest at All Souls look like Chippendale. Although I would've rather she tell her story quickly, she insisted on making tea. When we were finally settled with little cups like the ones I'd bought years ago at Bargain Bazaar in Chinatown, she began.

"Mae went away eight weeks ago today. I thought Tommy was with her. When she did not pay her rent, the landlord went inside the apartment. He said they left everything."

"Has the apartment been rented to someone else?"

She nodded. "Mae and Tommy's things are stored in the garage. Did you say it was seven weeks ago that Tommy was found?"

"Give or take a few days."

"Poor boy. He must have stayed in the apartment waiting for his mother. He is so quiet and can take care of himself."

"What d'you suppose he was doing on Mission Street near Geneva, then?"

"Maybe looking for her." The woman's face was frightened again.

"Why there?" I asked.

She stared down into her teacup. After a bit she said, "You know Mae lost her job at the sewing factory?"

I nodded.

"It was a good job, and she is a good seamstress, but times are bad and she could not find another job."

"And then?"

"... There is a place on Geneva Avenue. It looks like an apartment house, but it is really a sewing factory. The owners advertise by word of mouth among the Asian immigrants. They say they pay high wages, give employees meals and a place to live, and do not ask questions. They hire many who are here illegally."

"Is Mae an illegal?"

"No. She was married to an American serviceman and has her permanent green card. Tommy was born in San Francisco. But a few years ago her husband divorced her and she lost her medical benefits. She is in poor health, she has tuberculosis. Her money was running out, and she was desperate. I warned her, but she wouldn't listen."

"Warned her against what?"

"There is talk about that factory. The building is fenced and the fences are topped with razor wire. The windows are boarded and barred. They say that once a worker enters she is not allowed to leave. They say workers are forced to sew eighteen hours a day for very low wages. They say that the cost of food is taken out of their pay, and that ten people sleep in a room large enough for two."

"That's slavery! Why doesn't the city do something?"

The old woman shrugged. "The city has no proof and does not care. The workers are only immigrants. They are not important."

I felt a real rant coming on and fought to control it. I've lived in San Francisco for seven years, since I graduated from Berkeley, a few miles and light-years across the Bay, and I'm getting sick and tired of the so-called important people. The city is beautiful and lively and tolerant, but there's a core of citizens who think nobody and nothing counts but them and their concerns. Someday when I'm in charge of the world (an event I fully expect to happen, especially when I've had a few beers), they'll have to answer to *me* for their high-handed behavior.

"Okay," I said, "tell me exactly where this place is, and we'll see what we can do about it."

"SLAVERY, PLAIN AND SIMPLE," Shar said.

"Right."

"Something's got to be done about it."

"Right."

We were sitting in a booth at the Remedy Lounge, our favorite tavern down the hill from All Souls on Mission Street. She was drinking white wine, I was drinking beer, and it wasn't but three in the afternoon. But McCone and I have found that some of our best ideas come to us when we tilt a couple. I'd spent the last four hours casing—oops, I'm not supposed to call it that—conducting a surveillance on the building on Geneva Avenue. Sure looked suspicious—trucks coming and going, but no workers leaving at lunchtime.

"But what can be done?" I asked. "Who do we contact?"

She considered. "Illegals? U.S. Immigration and Naturalization Service. False imprisonment? City police and district attorney's office. Substandard working conditions? OSHA, Department of Labor, State Employment Development Division. Take your pick."

"Which is best to start with?"

"None—yet. You've got no proof of what's going on there."

"Then we'll just have to get proof, won't we?"

"Uh-huh."

"You and I both used to work in security. Ought to be a snap to get into that building."

"Maybe."

"All we need is access. Take some pictures. Tape a statement from one of the workers. Are you with me?"

She nodded. "I'm with you. And as backup, why don't we take Willie?"

"*My* Willie? The diamond king of northern California? Shar, this is an investigation, not a date!"

"Before he opened those discount jewelry stores Willie was a professional fence, as you may recall. And although he won't admit it, I happen to know he personally stole a lot of the items he moved. Willie has talents we can use."

"MY TENNIS ELBOW HURTS! Why're you making me do this?"

I glared at Willie. "Shh! You've never played tennis in your life."

"The doc told me most people who've got it have never played."

"Just be quiet and cut that wire."

"How d'you know there isn't an alarm?"

"Shar and I have checked. Trust us."

"I trust you two, I'll probably end up in San Quentin."

"Cut!"

Willie snipped a fair segment out of the razor wire topping the chain-link fence. I climbed over first, nearly doing myself grievous personal injury as I swung over the top. Shar followed, and then the diamond king—making unseemly grunting noises. His tall frame was encased in dark sweats tonight, and they accentuated the beginnings of a beer belly.

As we each dropped to the ground, we quickly moved into the shadow of the three-story frame building and flattened against its wall. Willie wheezed and pushed his longish hair out of his eyes. I gave Shar a look that said, *Some asset you invited along.* She shrugged apologetically.

According to plan we began inching around the building, searching for a point of entry. We didn't see any guards. If the factory employed them, it would be for keeping people in; it had probably never occurred to the owners that someone might actually *want* in.

After about three minutes Shar came to a stop and I bumped into her. She steadied me and pointed down. A foot off the ground was an opening that had been boarded up; the plywood was splintered and coming loose. I squatted and took a look at it. Some kind of duct—maybe people-size. Together we pulled the board off.

Yep, a duct. But not very big. Willie wouldn't fit through it—which was fine by me, because I didn't want him alerting everybody in the place with his groaning. I'd fit, but Shar would fit better still.

I motioned for her to go first.

She made an after-you gesture.

I shook my head.

It's your case, she mouthed.

I sighed, handed her the camera loaded with infrared film that I carried, and started squeezing through.

I've got to admit that I have all sorts of mild phobias. I get witchy in crowds, and I'm not fond of heights, and I hate to fly, and small places make my skin crawl. This duct was a *very* small space. I pushed onward, trying to keep my mind on other things—such as Tommy and Mae Jones.

When my hands reached the end of the duct I pulled hard, then moved them around till I felt a concrete floor about two feet below. I wriggled forward, felt my foot kick something, and heard Shar grunt. *Sorry.* The room I slid down into was pitch black. I waited till Shar was crouched beside me, then whispered, "D'you have your flashlight?"

She handed me the camera, fumbled in her pocket, and then I saw streaks of light bleeding around the fingers she placed over its bulb. We waited, listening. No one stirred, no one spoke. After a moment Shar took her hand away from the flash and began shining its beam around. A storage room full of sealed cardboard boxes, with a door at the far side. We exchanged glances and began moving through the stacked cartons.

When we got to the door I put my ear to it and listened. No sound. I turned the knob slowly. Unlocked. I eased the door open. A dimly lighted hallway. There was another door with a lighted window set into it at the far end. Shar and I moved along opposite walls and stopped on either side of the door. I went up on tiptoe and peeked through the corner of the glass.

Inside was a factory: row after row of sewing machines, all making jittery up-and-down motions and clacking away. Each was operated by an Asian woman. Each woman slumped wearily as she fed the fabric through.

It was twelve-thirty in the morning, and they still had them sewing!

I drew back and motioned for Shar to have a look. She did, then turned to me, lips tight, eyes ablaze.

Pictures? she mouthed.

I shook my head. *Can't risk being seen.*

Now what?

I shrugged.

She frowned and started back the other way, slipping from door to door and trying each knob. Finally she stopped and pointed to one with a placard that said STAIRWAY. I followed her through it and we started up. The next floor was offices—locked up and dark. We went back to the stairwell, climbed another flight. On the landing I almost tripped over a small, huddled figure.

It was tiny gray-haired woman, crouching there with a dirty thermal blanket wrapped around her. She shivered repeatedly. Sick and hiding from the foreman. I squatted beside her.

The woman started and her eyes got big with terror. She scrambled backwards toward the steps, almost falling over. I grabbed her arm and steadied her; her flesh felt as if it was burning up. "Don't be scared," I said.

Her eyes moved from me to Shar. Little cornered bunny-rabbit eyes, red and full of the awful knowledge that there's no place left to hide. She babbled something in a tongue that I couldn't understand. I put my arms around her and patted her back—universal language. After a bit she stopped trying to pull away.

I whispered, "Do you know Mae Jones?"

She drew back and blinked.

"Mae Jones?" I repeated.

Slowly she nodded and pointed to the door off the next landing.

So Tommy's mother *was* here. If we could get her out, we'd have an English-speaking witness who, because she had her permanent green card, wouldn't be afraid to go to the authorities and file charges against the owners of this place. But there was no telling who or what was beyond that door. I glanced at Shar. She shook her head.

The sick woman was watching me. I thought back to yesterday morning and the way Darrin Boydston had communicated with the boy he called Daniel. It was worth a try.

I pointed to the woman. Pointed to the door. "Mae Jones." I pointed to the door again, then pointed to the floor.

The woman was straining to understand. I went through the routine twice more. She nodded and struggled to her feet. Trailing the ratty blanket behind her, she climbed the stairs and went through the door.

Shar and I released sighs at the same time. Then we sat down on the steps and waited.

IT WASN'T FIVE MINUTES BEFORE THE DOOR OPENED. We both ducked down, just in case. An overly thin woman of about thirty-five rushed through so quickly that she stumbled on the top step and caught herself on the railing. She would have been beautiful, but lines of worry and pain cut deep into her face; her hair had been lopped off short and stood up in dirty spikes. Her eyes were jumpy, alternately glancing at us and behind her. She hurried down the stairs.

"You want me?"

"If you're Mae Jones." Already I was guiding her down the steps.

"I am. Who are—"

"We're going to get you out of here, take you to Tommy."

"Tommy! Is he—"

"He's all right, yes."

Her face brightened, but then was taken over by fear. "We must hurry. Lan faked a faint, but they will notice I'm gone very soon."

We rushed down the stairs, along the hall toward the storage room. We were at its door when a man called out behind us. He was coming from the sewing room at the far end.

Mae froze. I shoved her, and then we were weaving through the stacked cartons. Shar got down on her knees, helped Mae into the duct, and dove in behind her. The door banged open.

The man was yelling in a strange language. I slid into the duct, pulling myself along on its riveted sides. Hands grabbed for my ankles and got the left one. I kicked out with my right foot. He grabbed for it and missed. I kicked upward, hard, and heard a satisfying yelp of pain. His hand let go of my ankle and I wriggled forward and fell to the ground outside. Shar and Mae were already running for the fence.

But where the hell was Willie?

Then I saw him: a shadowy figure, motioning with both arms as if he were guiding an airplane up to the jetway. There was an enormous hole in the chain-link fence. Shar and Mae ducked through it.

I started running. Lights went on on the corners of the building. Men came outside, shouting. I heard a whine, then a crack.

Rifle, firing at us!

Willie and I hurled ourselves to the ground. We moved on elbows and knees through the hole in the fence and across the sidewalk to the shelter of a van parked there. Shar and Mae huddled behind it. Willie and I collapsed beside them just as sirens began to go off.

"Like 'Nam, all over again," he said.

I stared at him in astonishment. Willie had spent most of the war hanging out in a bar in Cam Ranh Bay.

Shar said, "Thank God you cut the hole in the fence!"

Modestly he replied, "Yeah, well, you gotta do something when you're bored out of your skull."

BECAUSE A SHOT HAD BEEN FIRED, the SFPD had probable cause to search the building. Inside they found some sixty Asian women—most of them illegals—who had been imprisoned there, some as long as five years, as well as evidence of other sweatshops the owners were running, both here and in Southern California. The INS was called in, statements were taken, and finally at around five that morning Mae Jones was permitted to go with us to be reunited with her son.

Darrin Boydston greeted us at the Cash Cow, wearing electric-blue pants and a western-style shirt with the bucking-bull emblem embroidered over its pockets. A polyester cowboy. He stood watching as Tommy and Mae hugged and kissed, wiped a sentimental tear from his eye, and offered Mae a job. She accepted, and then he drove them to the house of a friend who would put them up until they found a place of their own. I waited around the pawnshop till he returned.

When Boydston came through the door he looked down in the mouth. He pulled up a stool next to the one I sat on and said,

"Sure am gonna miss that boy."

"Well, you'll probably be seeing a lot of him, with Mae working here."

"Yeah." He brightened some. "And I'm gonna help her get him into classes, stuff like that. After she lost her Navy benefits when that skunk of a husband walked out on her, she didn't know about all the other stuff that's available." He paused, then added, "So what's the damage?"

"You mean, what do you owe us? We'll bill you."

"Better be an honest accounting, little lady," he said. "Ma'am, I mean," he added in his twangiest Texas accent. And smiled.

I smiled, too.

L. J. Washburn's short fiction also appears in *New Amazons* and *Careless Whispers*. She lives in Texas with her husband, author James Reasoner. Her series character, Lucas Hallam, is a private detective/stuntman/cowboy who lives in the dual worlds of fantasy and reality that is Hollywood of the 1930s. Here, Hallam discovers how deadly it can be when those worlds overlap.

Double Take
L. J. WASHBURN

The voice on the other end of the phone was frantic enough to make Hallam forget for a moment the other things on his mind. "You've got to help me, Lucas," it said. "I've got a movie half in the can, and I can't go on without Allen!"

"Take it easy, Cal," Hallam drawled. "Just slow down and tell me what happened." He covered the mouthpiece of the phone with his right hand and hissed, "Beth! Get down from there right now, you little—"

"I don't *know* what happened," Calvin Forrester said into Hallam's left ear. "All I know is that Allen didn't show up for this morning's shooting, and now the schedule's ruined!"

The producer was an excitable sort, Hallam knew, and it would probably take a while to drag a coherent story out of him. Hallam wouldn't be able to concentrate on that while he was worrying about his daughter breaking her fool neck, so he put the sternest expression possible on his craggy, gray-mustached face and pointed down at the floor. The redheaded five-year-old, who had somehow managed to stack three chairs on top of each other in the middle of the apartment's living room, looked disappointed as she perched on top of the swaying, makeshift tower. She began to climb down, however, and Hallam stood tensely beside the phone table, ready to leap and catch her if she fell.

He wondered where in blazes Beth had gotten the idea that it was all right to take such damn-fool chances.

"Settle down, Cal," he went on into the phone. "From what I hear about the feller, it ain't unusual for Hathaway to show up late for work."

The producer heaved a sigh. "You're right, you're right. He's undependable, even more so than actors usually are. Everybody in Hollywood knows that. If his pictures didn't make so damned much money, nobody would put up with him. But I'm still stuck with him."

"You call his place?" As he asked the question, Hallam nodded at Beth, who had reached the floor safely. She reached up and grabbed the top chair, obviously intending to try to take it down. Hallam shook his head and motioned curtly with his hand, telling her to leave the chairs alone. He jerked a thumb toward the arched entrance that led out of the living room and into the combination dining room and kitchen. Beth pouted, but she went.

"First thing," Forrester replied. "There was no answer. I kept trying to call. Nothing. So I sent one of the gofers over there to check on him. Allen's got a temper, you know, so I didn't want to bother him myself if he was just too drunk to answer the phone or involved with, ah, a young lady. . . ."

"What'd the feller find, Cal?"

"Allen didn't come to the door, so the boy used the key I gave him. He said the place looked like there had been a fight. Chairs turned over, things scattered around, stuff like that. I don't mind telling you, Lucas, when I heard that a chill went right down my back. Something's happened to Allen. I'm sure of it."

Hallam was inclined to take the matter a mite more seriously now himself. Allen Hathaway was a star, and as such he had money. He was also very important to the studio he worked for, especially with his current picture only half completed. Those things made him an attractive target for kidnappers.

Or maybe, knowing Hathaway, he had wrecked the place himself during a drunken rampage, then gone out to continue his bender. Either way, Hallam could understand Calvin Forrester's concern. He said, "Have you called the cops?"

"Allen hasn't been missing long enough to interest them, and there were no real signs of foul play at his apartment, no bloodstains or anything like that. Besides, I'd rather keep this quiet if I can."

That was typical; the studios covered up everything they could about their stars that might be the least bit unflattering. Hallam understood how the system worked, whether he agreed with it or not.

"All right," he said into the phone. "I'll look into it for you. If Hathaway's been snatched, is the studio willing to pay to get him back?"

"God, yes! Anything reasonable. We've got too much money tied up in him and his pictures not to."

"I'll give you a call or stop by the studio later in the day to let you know what I've found out. Try to take it easy, Cal. It ain't goin' to help nothing for you to pop a blood vessel."

"I'll try. Thank you, Lucas. I can't tell you how much I appreciate this."

"Don't thank me yet. I ain't done nothin'. So long, Cal."

He hung the earpiece in its cradle, then looked around for Beth. She hadn't come back from the kitchen. Hallam started in that direction, but he had only taken a couple of steps when he heard the crash. Something had shattered in there, but Beth wasn't howling, so it was likely she was unhurt. Hallam sighed.

Finding a vanished movie star might be difficult, or it might not. But he knew an even more formidable task was in front of him.

He had to find somebody willing to baby-sit the little hellion.

"NO, NO, NO!" Mrs. Martinez said vehemently. "The last time you left her here, she like to scare me out of five years of my life. And those are five years I cannot spare, Señor Hallam!"

"I promise Beth won't climb out on that balcony railin' again," Hallam said, his expression solemn. He had Beth's left hand held tightly in his right, her little fist swallowed up by his massive palm.

Mrs. Martinez lived right down the hall in the Fountain Avenue apartment house, and she was the handiest baby-sitter Hallam knew. But she'd had her fill of Beth's mischief, and Hallam couldn't blame her for that. He had trouble keeping up with the little girl himself, and he was her father.

That concept still threw him for a loop if he thought about it too much. He hadn't known he had a daughter, probably never would have known if Liz Fletcher, Beth's mother, hadn't died suddenly a few years earlier. Hallam and Liz had been together for a while—long enough for Beth to get started—and then Liz had left, feeling that there wasn't enough room in Hallam's life for her.

It was true that Hallam stayed busy. He had his one-man private detective agency, as well as his work as a riding extra and occasional stuntman in the herd of B Westerns that came stampeding out of Gower Gulch every year. The advent of sound had slowed down production of Westerns for a while, since it was difficult to hide the microphones during all the location shooting Western pictures required, but as always, the movie crews had come up with ways to get around the problem. Now, a couple of years into the sound era, Westerns were as popular as ever, which meant Hallam had all the work he could want.

He'd started turning some of it away, however, since Liz's sister had showed up during the middle of a particularly worrisome case and shoved a redheaded, squalling little bundle into his arms and informed him that he was responsible for it. Yep, having a daughter had changed his life a whole heap, Hallam reflected, but he wouldn't go back to the way it had been before. No sir.

"You promise she won't do nothin' crazy?" Mrs. Martinez asked dubiously.

"You got my word on it," Hallam assured her. He looked down at Beth and said firmly, "No gags while you're stayin' with Mrs. Martinez, you got it?"

"Got it," Beth muttered unhappily.

"Okay," Mrs. Martinez said, but her attitude made it clear she would believe Beth could behave only when she saw it with her own eyes. She stepped back and Beth went into the apartment carrying the stuffed horse she had brought from home. She sat down cross-legged in the middle of the living-room floor.

"All right now, you be good, hear?" Hallam said as he stepped over to her and reached down to stroke her short red hair. "Mind Mrs. Martinez, and I'll be back in a while."

"Sure," Beth said without looking up. She began to move the toy horse across the floor as if it were galloping, then she pressed its front legs down suddenly and made it tumble head over heels. "Running W!" she exclaimed.

Hallam just sighed and turned around in time to see Mrs. Martinez rolling her eyes heavenward. He smiled weakly and got out of there while he still could.

HIS FIRST STEP WAS THE STUDIO, where he picked up a key to Allen Hathaway's bungalow apartment. A very worried Calvin Forrester told him Hathaway still hadn't shown up at the studio. Hallam hadn't really expected that he would have. Hathaway was either off on a toot—or he really had been kidnapped.

There was another possibility, Hallam realized after he had paid a visit to Hathaway's place and found it just as Forrester had described it: disheveled, but with no sign of real violence. Something bad, but purely accidental, could have happened to the actor. People died in Southern California every day, and they weren't all murders. It just sometimes *seemed* that way. Hallam headed for downtown Los Angeles and the L.A. County morgue.

"Unidentified bodies?" the attendant on duty, who knew Hallam slightly, said in response to a question from the big detective. "Sure we got 'em. What kind you want?"

The fellow sounded entirely too cheerful for his job, Hallam thought, but he supposed you got used to being around dead folks. Hallam himself never had, though.

"Male, about thirty years old," Hallam said. "Dark hair, well built, handsome . . . or at least he started out that way. If something fatal happened to him, ain't no tellin' what he looks like now."

"Sounds familiar. This gink you're looking for got a name?" asked the attendant.

Hallam hesitated. He knew Forrester didn't want publicity; that was one of the reasons the producer hadn't called the cops in the first place. For the time being, Hallam figured he ought to keep the missing man's identity under the broad-brimmed Stetson he wore.

"Ain't at liberty to say."

The attendant frowned. "If you can identify one of these John Does we got here, you got to do it. It's the law."

"If the feller's who I'm lookin' for, I'll tell you," Hallam said. "You got my word on it."

"Well, I suppose that's good enough for me. Come on."

Hallam followed the man into the depths of the building, feeling a chill that had little or nothing to do with the actual temperature growing inside him with every step. The attendant led him into a large room with rows of doors stacked one above the other on both walls, and Hallam knew that behind many of those doors rested the bodies of people who had met their Maker in all the varied ways that universal passage was possible. He supposed that somebody like him, who had seen more than sixty years come and go, ought to be more comfortable with the idea of death. He had never come around to that point, though.

"Here we go," the attendant said as he consulted a piece of paper in his hand and then paused in front of one of the square doors. He took hold of its handle and slid out the drawer behind it. A long, white-shrouded figure lay on the table. Carefully, the attendant folded back the sheet. "This the guy? He's the only unidentified body I've got that fits the description you gave me."

The corpse didn't fit all of that description, Hallam thought. Nobody would ever consider those bloated features handsome. But the approximate age and the hair color were right, and Hallam could tell from the shape of the body under the sheet that this man and Allen Hathaway had been about the same size. "Could be," Hallam said grimly. "What happened to him?"

The attendant consulted the paper in his hand again. "Drowned. But the M.E. says he also got quite a bump on the back of the head. Looks like somebody clouted him and then dumped him in the ocean. That makes it murder."

Hallam's jaw was a tight line as he looked down at the corpse. Although he didn't know the why of it, he was about halfway convinced the dead man was indeed Allen Hathaway. But . . .

"How long was he in the water?"

"You'd have to ask the M.E. about that. I'd guess a day or two anyway, long enough for the fish to get at him a little. What about it, Lucas? You know this guy?"

"Maybe. But first I've got to use your phone."

*   *   *

"OH, NO. Allan was here yesterday," Forrester said. "As uncooperative with the director as usual, but definitely here."

"Then he didn't float up on the beach this morning, because the feller I just took a gander at had been in the water longer'n that. Sorry, Cal. I sure thought for a minute I'd found him. This gent here in the morgue could pass for Hathaway without a lick of trouble."

"Oh, my God." Hallam heard the stunned realization in Forrester's voice. The producer went on, "You say that man looks just like Allen?"

"Well, not like they was twins or anything, but from a distance, or if you just looked at this feller quick-like—" Hallam stopped, and his fingers tightened on the earpiece of the phone. "Aw, hell. Has Hathaway got a stunt double?"

"Of course he does. His name is Lonnie Vinson. But he hasn't been here on the lot for several days. We already shot all the gags for this picture. Lucas, you don't think the man in the morgue could be ..."

"I reckon we'd better find out," Hallam said.

HALLAM KNEW MANY OF THE STUNTMEN working in Hollywood, but not all of them. He had never met Lonnie Vinson. But once he had gone upstairs from the morgue to police headquarters and talked to a pair of homicide detectives—still keeping Allen Hathaway's name out of the conversation—it didn't take long for the cops to come up with somebody to identify the body. Hallam stood to one side of the door to the morgue as the detectives led a weeping young woman out of the place and took her up to their office to make a statement.

The attendant who had shown Hallam the body sauntered up, chewing gum now, which was something else Hallam couldn't understand. "That's the girlfriend," the attendant said, nodding toward the back of the sobbing woman. "Vinson didn't have any family out here; he's from back in Iowa or someplace like that. But she identified him, all right. I heard her tellin' those homicide bulls that it was him."

"She have any idea what happened to him?"

The attendant shrugged. "Who knows? That ain't my department."

Maybe not, Hallam thought, but it was his. Could be it was just coincidence that Allen Hathaway had vanished and his stunt double, Lonnie Vinson, had turned up dead on the same day. Could be ... but Hallam didn't think so.

He put in another call to the studio to let Calvin Forrester know that the dead man was indeed Lonnie Vinson. It was a little past noon, but Hallam wasn't hungry. The past hour had taken care of his appetite for a while. He was waiting on the steps outside city Hall, where the police department and the morgue were located, when the young woman with blond hair and red, swollen eyes emerged.

"Ma'am?" he said, stepping up to her and taking off his hat. "My name's Lucas Hallam, and I'm mighty sorry about your loss."

She looked up at him, blinking in surprise, obviously wondering why this big, rugged-looking cowboy was talking to her. Then the confusion drained out of her eyes along with another tear or two, and she nodded. "You're the man who told the police that ... that it might be Lonnie down there in the ... in the ..."

"Yes, ma'am," Hallam said.

"You ... Did you know Lonnie?"

"No, ma'am. I do some stunt work, too, but we never ran into each other. The reason I happened to be here is that I'm a private detective, and I'm workin' on a case that, well, that Lonnie's death might have something to do with."

She shook her head. "I'm afraid I don't understand at all."

Hallam decided to tell her the truth. "You know who Allen Hathaway is?"

"Of course, the movie star. Lonnie is ... was his stunt double."

"Well, Hathaway's missin', and I got to thinkin', what if somebody was after him, meanin' to grab him for ransom or something, and they made a mistake ..."

The young woman put her hand to her mouth. "You think they might have mistaken Lonnie for Allen Hathaway?"

"That's what a double is for. And when they figured out they'd snatched the wrong feller—"

"They killed him and threw him in the ocean," she finished for him. A low moan came from her lips. "Oh God! Lonnie may have died because he looked like Allan Hathaway!"

"It's a possibility," Hallam told her. "Unless you know something that says otherwise. That's why I figured I'd better talk to you. Can I buy you a cup of coffee?"

"I ... Of course, Mr. ... Hallam, was it?"

"Yes, ma'am. Lucas Hallam."

"I'm Marjorie Grant."

"There's a lunch counter right down the street."

"Oh, I couldn't possibly eat. But I think I could manage a cup of coffee, Mr. Hallam. Are ... are you going to try to find out who killed Lonnie?"

"If I do, it might lead me to whoever's got Hathaway, so I reckon I'll do my best."

"Then I definitely want to talk to you. I want whoever did this awful thing caught and punished."

There was an unexpected ferocity in her voice. Marjorie Grant, Hallam thought, was probably not a good woman to cross.

*   *   *

"THE MAN'S NAME IS ARNOLD MOSS. I distinctly remember Lonnie telling me about him." Marjorie Grant looked at Hallam over her cup of coffee, then sipped some of the strong black brew.

"The name's familiar," Hallam said with a nod. "He's a gambler, I think. Pretty shady character. You're sure of what your friend Lonnie said about him?"

"I'm certain. Mr. Hathaway had told Lonnie all about it. They were sort of friends, you know, not in any close way, but because they shared so much. Playing the same characters onscreen and all."

Hallam nodded. Some stars were indeed friendly with their stunt doubles, knowing that the doubles kept them from having to perform any dangerous gags. Others, as if wanting to maintain in their own minds the illusion that was created on the screen, had nothing to do with the stuntmen who passed for them.

"Lonnie said that Mr. Hathaway owed a lot of money to Arnold Moss because of some bets he lost. Mr. Hathaway didn't want to pay, even though he could afford to, and Moss threatened to get the money one way or another."

That way could be by holding up the studio for ransom, Hallam thought. And if Moss had snatched Lonnie Vinson by mistake, thinking he was Hathaway . . .

"Reckon I'll have to look up this feller Moss and have a talk with him," Hallam said quietly.

Marjorie gave him a solemn nod. "I think that would be a good idea. You might be able to save Mr. Hathaway, even if Lonnie is already . . . already *dead.*" Her voice broke a little, and she set her cup back in its saucer with a rattle of china. Fresh tears welled from her eyes. She rested her elbows on the Formica-topped diner table between her and Hallam and put her hands over her face as she sobbed.

Hallam glanced around uncomfortably. None of the other customers in the busy lunch counter seemed to be paying any attention to Marjorie's quiet crying, and he was glad of that. He said, "If Moss is responsible for Lonnie's death, I'll see that he pays for it, ma'am. You got my word on that."

She sniffled a few more times, wiped her nose on the back of her hand, and summoned up a feeble smile. "I believe you, Mr. Hallam. You . . . you seem to be the kind of man who does what he says he's going to do."

"Yes, ma'am. Right now, I'm going to see if I can find Moss." He hesitated, then asked one more time, "You're sure Lonnie was tellin' you the straight of it?"

"I'm positive. There were no secrets between us." Her smile grew a little stronger with the memory. "You see, we were going to be married next month. Lonnie would never have lied to me."

It had been Hallam's experience that anybody would lie about just about anything, if they had a good enough motive, but he couldn't see any reason for Lonnie Vinson to lie about Allen Hathaway being threatened by Moss. For one thing, Hallam knew from what he had heard around town that Arnold Moss was not only a gambler, but he was pretty ruthless about collecting when someone tried to welsh on him. For another, he had also heard rumors about Hathaway's gambling. There had been enough gossip to make Hallam believe that the actor was capable of running up a big debt, then refusing to pay it. Hathaway had always been arrogant, thinking himself above the rules.

Maybe he had found out the hard way that some people took rules mighty seriously.

HALLAM DROVE SOUTH through Inglewood to Hollywood Park. He didn't follow horse racing that closely, but a glance at a newspaper had told him the ponies were running today, and that would be the most likely place to either find Arnold Moss or get a lead on him.

The horses were just coming to the post for the second race when Hallam strolled along the sun-splashed gallery next to the track. The grandstand lifted to his right, row after row of benches filled with spectators. Someone called his name, and he turned to wave at a grinning Buck Jones, an acquaintance from the studios who was most likely between pictures since he was at the track in the middle of the afternoon. Hallam saw other people he knew from the studios, mostly front-office types. He didn't pause to chew the fat with anyone, however, since he was here on business.

After a few minutes, he spotted the man he was looking for, a small, flashily dressed gent who called himself Hopper. As far as Hallam was concerned, Hopper spent way too much time reading stories by some New York sportswriter named Runyon, because he had it in his head that he ought to dress and act like all the racetrack touts in those yarns. But Hopper knew just about everybody who bet on horse races in this town, and Hallam intended to pick his brain.

"Howdy, Hopper," he said as he came up to the man.

"Hallam!" exclaimed Hopper. "I didn't know you played the nags. Hey, I got a tip for you, Buffalo Gal in the fifth race. She can't lose!"

"Much obliged, but I reckon I already lost enough money over the years."

"But this isn't even a bet, Hallam! It's a sure thing! Would I steer you wrong?"

"I hope not," Hallam said. "I'm lookin' for Arnold Moss."

Instantly, a frown appeared on the tout's face. "What do you want with Moss? There's plenty of other guys who'll take your action. You don't want to mess with Moss these days."

"Oh? Why's that?"

Hopper glanced around apprehensively. "It ain't always safe to talk, you know, even with all this noise around. Somebody could overhear...."

Hallam let him see the corner of the sawbuck in his hand, and it disappeared smoother than Houdini.

"But I'm always glad to do a favor for an old friend," Hopper went on without missing a beat. "Word around the track has it that Moss is really on edge, like he's got something going that's making him nervous. I wouldn't deal with him if I was you."

"Is he here?" Hallam asked.

"Oh yeah, he's here, all right. I seen him down by the paddock a little while ago. Hey, they're at the post!" Hopper held up the ten-spot Hallam had just given him. "I got to get a bet down!"

With that he scurried away, and Hallam let him go. He had found out what he wanted to know. A moment later the bell rang and a full-throated roar went up from the crowd as the horses burst away from the post. Hallam hoped Hopper had had time to place that bet.

So, Hallam thought as he made his way through the crowd toward the paddock, Arnold Moss was jumpy about something, was he? Kidnapping a movie star and holding him for ransom was enough to make anybody nervous. Hallam might have enough right now to go to the cops and let them deal with Moss. They could sweat the gambler, get the truth about Hathaway—and Lonnie Vinson's murder—out of him.

But Hallam preferred to talk to Moss himself. He wanted some real proof, so that the cops wouldn't have to beat a confession out of the gambler.

Hallam didn't really notice the noise from the crowd swelling even more as the race neared its conclusion. Seeing which horse could run around in a circle the fastest didn't interest him. During the days when he had still been cowboying, before he'd pinned on first a Texas Ranger's badge and then a Pinkerton's shield, he had been to plenty of races, although he had never ridden in one because he was too big. Back then, at every county fair, the local cowboys had gotten together to see who had the fastest pony. *Those* races meant something. Hallam couldn't get too excited about this modern kind.

He circled the grandstand and approached the paddock. The stables were beyond the fence enclosure where quite a few horses were currently being saddled for the next race. Several men leaned on the fence. Hallam looked them over, didn't recognize any of them as Arnold Moss. The gambler had been pointed out to him in various speakeasies, and Hallam was confident he would recognize the man.

He nodded to one of the gents watching the horses and asked, "Arnold Moss around?"

The man jerked his chin toward the stables. "Saw him going that way just a little while ago."

"Thanks," Hallam said. He frowned a little as he started toward the stables. Technically, nobody was supposed to be back there except owners, trainers, jockeys, exercise boys, and people who worked for the track. Other folks, especially gamblers, weren't supposed to be that close to the horses. But Hallam supposed that money could get a feller around those rules, too.

He was close enough to the stables to smell the familiar blend of odors that was common to any barn when a man sauntered out coming in his direction. The man wore an expensive suit, a Panama hat, and the kind of Italian shoes that would make anybody think twice about wearing them into a stable. Evidently Arnold Moss had been careful about where he stepped, though, because his shoes were still clean and brightly polished. He had a hand-rolled cigarette in the corner of his mouth. His eyes, set deeply in his narrow face, flicked over Hallam without recognition or interest.

Hallam recognized him, though, and Moss had no choice but to stop when Hallam stepped in front of him. "Howdy, Moss," Hallam said.

The gambler glared at him, irritated at being stopped. "Do I know you, cowboy?"

"I don't reckon you do. But I know you, Moss." Hallam decided to go ahead and prod the man to see what would happen. "I know all about that bad debt and what you intend to do to collect on it, too."

Moss's eyes widened, and he breathed, "Son of a bitch!" Despite all the people around, his hand moved instinctively under his coat as he reached for a gun. Hallam's left hand darted out, clamped on Moss's wrist, and squeezed. Moss let out a squeak of pain and hunched over. Hallam had been ready for just such a reaction when he confronted Moss.

He wasn't ready for the two men who came out of the barn behind Moss and charged toward him when the gambler yelped, "Get this guy!"

Both of the newcomers were big and ugly, just the type that a gambler like Moss would have hanging around to take care of any rough stuff. As they came toward him, Hallam shoved Moss at them as hard as he could. Moss went backward, arms windmilling as he yelled. One of the bruisers managed to avoid him, but he crashed into the other one, getting their feet tangled up. Moss and the flunky went down.

The other man swung a roundhouse punch that Hallam saw coming a mile away. He ducked under the blow, stepped in, and hooked a hard right into the man's midsection. It felt almost like punching a washboard, but Hallam saw a tiny flash of pain in the man's eyes. Hallam's hand hurt, that was for sure. And he had made the mistake of getting inside the circle of the man's arms.

Those arms locked around Hallam in a brutal bear hug, making his ribs creak. Hallam brought his knee up into his opponent's groin, and that caused more than a flash of pain. The man's eyes widened and he groaned. His grip slipped a little enough for Hallam to get one hand loose and slam his fist into the man's jaw. That rocked him a little more, and Hallam was able to tear himself free. Now that he had some room, he swung two more punches, a left and a right that jerked the bruiser's head back and forth. The gent's jaw might not be glass, but it was more fragile than his stomach. His eyes rolled up in his head and he slumped to his knees.

The other man was on his feet by now. Hallam heard him coming, twisted aside, and stuck out a booted foot. The man tripped over it and fell, and on the way to the dirt in front of the stable, Hallam brought his clubbed fists down hard on the back of his neck. The man groaned once, tried to push himself back up, then slumped down again.

Hallam was breathing hard. These boys were pretty tough, he thought, but they hadn't ever broken up a fight in a saloon and then had to take on both bunches of cowboys who had started the brawl. Hallam had.

He turned toward Arnold Moss in time to see the gambler scrambling back to his feet, a little nickel-plated pistol in his hand. Hallam muttered, "Oh, hell," then took one long stride that brought him within reach of Moss. The gambler was still lifting the gun when Hallam backhanded him, knocking him off his feet. The gun skittered away.

Moss propped himself up on an elbow and put his other hand to his bloody mouth. "You didn't have to do that!" he said through lips that were puffing up. "You didn't have to stick your nose in! Nobody would've gotten hurt!"

"What about Lonnie Vinson?" Hallam demanded. "And for all I know, you planned to kill Hathaway, too, once you'd collected the ransom on him."

A sizable crowd had gathered, drawn by the brief fight, and one man said, "Holy cow! The big galoot's talking about murder and kidnapping. I'm getting the cops!"

Hallam glanced over his shoulder. Several of the racetrack's guards were already on their way to check out the commotion, he saw. He turned back to Moss and said, "Talk fast, mister. Where are you holdin' Hathaway?"

Moss just stared at him for a few seconds as blood continued to drip from his lips. Finally, he said frantically, "What the *hell* are you talking about? Who's Lonnie Vinson? And if you're talking about Allan Hathaway, I don't want anything more to do with that damned welsher!"

"Yeah, you just stick with that story," Hallam advised him grimly. "I reckon the cops'll enjoy gettin' the truth out of you."

"Look," Moss said desperately as he sat up. "I don't know anybody named Vinson, and I sure didn't kill or kidnap anybody!"

He looked and sounded like he was telling the truth, Hallam thought. "What about the money Hathaway owes you?"

"Hell, everybody gets stuck with some bad debts now and then. I don't like it, but I wouldn't kill anybody over it, no matter what you've heard."

"Then why'd you try to pull a gun on me?"

"Because I thought you knew about—" Moss fell silent abruptly.

Hallam stepped closer to him, looming over him. "Knew about what?"

Moss muttered a few more curses, then said, "I got the fix in on the sixth race. The favorite's been doped. The trainer played ball with me because he's into me for ten grand. But if you're going to start throwing charges around like murder and kidnapping, I'll admit to the fix. I don't want any cops trying to sweat a confession out of me for something I didn't do."

Moss could still be lying, of course, but Hallam didn't think so. The words had the ring of truth. Hallam said, "You haven't seen Hathaway last night or today?"

"I haven't seen him in a week, I swear to God. I don't want to see him!"

Hallam took a deep breath, let it out in a long sigh. He believed Moss. And that left him right back where he had started.

A PHONE CALL TO THE STUDIO from the track offices after the business with Moss had been cleaned up told Hallam that not only had Allen Hathaway not put in an appearance, but there had been no ransom demand of any kind, either.

"Maybe the kidnappers are just trying to draw things out and make us more eager to pay once they get in touch with us," Calvin Forrester suggested.

"If Hathaway was kidnapped at all," Hallam muttered. "He still could have gone off on his own."

"Oh, Lord. What are we going to do, Lucas?"

"I'll do some more lookin' around," Hallam promised. "Don't give up yet."

But that was just about what Hallam was ready to do a couple of hours later. He had checked the railroad station and the bus terminal— although he couldn't imagine a star of Hathaway's magnitude slipping out of town on a bus—with no luck. Hathaway could have disguised himself, of course. No ships had sailed today, so Hathaway hadn't left Los Angeles that way. Hallam knew most of the speakeasies in town and was acquainted with the bartenders. None of them had seen Hathaway, and Hallam checked from the swankiest private club to the dingiest hole-in-the-wall dive. Hathaway had been known to frequent all of them when he was drinking.

But now he seemed to have dropped off the face of the earth.

The last place Hallam stopped was the Waterhole, the speak where the cowboy stuntmen and riding extras spent their days when they weren't working. It was unlikely that an urbane movie star like Hathaway would have let himself be caught dead in a place like the Waterhole, surrounded by cowboys, but Hallam was getting desperate. Besides, he had an appetite now, and he intended to visit the free-lunch counter and wash down some hard-boiled eggs and ham and pickles with a mug of cold beer. It had been a long, frustrating day.

Several of his friends called him over to a table. Hallam sat down and returned their greetings. The young man called Pecos, who was as dare-devil a rider as Hallam had ever seen, grinned and said, "You look like you been rode hard and put up wet, Lucas. Working on a case?"

Hallam nodded. "Yep. Any of you boys know a feller named Lonnie Vinson?"

Several of the men nodded, including Pecos. "Sure, I knew Lonnie," the young man said. "Heard he got himself killed. Damn shame. You tryin' to find out who did him in, Lucas?"

"That's right. I made a promise to a pretty little gal who got her heart broke earlier today."

Pecos frowned. "I didn't know Lonnie had a sister."

"Not his sister. His fiancée. Gal named Marjorie Grant."

"Somebody's told you wrong, Lucas," Pecos said, shaking his head. "I met Marjorie a few times. Pretty little nurse who works over at the county hospital. But Lonnie broke up with her two weeks ago. He never asked her to marry him. Shoot, *she* was the one who wanted to get married, but Lonnie, he wanted to stay footloose and fancy-free."

Hallam stared across the table at Pecos. "You sure about that?"

"You bet. Lonnie himself told me about it. Said Marjorie took it awful hard when he told her it was over. She even kept calling him later, he said, wanting to get together and see if they could patch things up."

The beer and the free food were forgotten. Hallam sat there in silence for a long moment, then said slowly and quietly, "Well, hell . . ."

DUSK WAS SETTLING DOWN by the time Hallam found Marjorie Grant's house, a cottage in Glendale that she rented. It had taken Hallam more time than he liked to think about to find out where she lived, since the woman in the office at the county hospital hadn't wanted to give him the address. He had finally persuaded her that it was a matter of life and death.

Maybe not for Allen Hathaway, Hallam thought as he approached the house—but Lonnie Vinson was sure enough dead. And Hathaway might be sooner or later, when things didn't work out to suit Marjorie.

He circled the cottage, hoping to discover where she was keeping Ha-thaway before he went hustling in. The shadows outside were thick enough now to conceal him. He found a kitchen window at the rear of the house. Hearing someone humming inside, he took off his hat and decided to risk a glance.

Marjorie was coming out of a narrow door on the other side of the room. She turned quickly, as soon as she was through the door, and shut it behind her. Hallam heard a lock click into place. A faint smile tugged at his mouth. Sometimes a feller got lucky, and he was overdue. He moved clear of the window, straightened, and went to the back door.

Marjorie answered his soft knock almost immediately. "Mr. Hallam!" she said, obviously surprised to see him. "Did you . . . did you find out what happened to Lonnie?"

"As a matter of fact, I sure did," he told her. "Reckon I could come in and tell you about it?"

"Of course. Please, come in." She stepped back. "Can I get you some coffee?"

"That'd be fine." Hallam put his hat on the kitchen table and sat down.

While she fussed with the coffee, she said, "Was . . . was it that awful man Moss? Was it like you thought, he meant to kidnap Mr. Hathaway but got my Lonnie by mistake?"

"Well, Moss is mixed up in plenty of crooked stuff, but he ain't to blame for what happened to your feller."

"My fiancé," Marjorie said as she turned away from the stove and put a cup of coffee on the table beside Hallam. "Remember, Lonnie and I were going to get married. There you are, drink up."

"In a minute," Hallam said, pushing the cup aside. "First I want to tell you what happened to Lonnie."

"All right." She sat down in one of the other chairs at the kitchen table. "Go ahead."

"Somebody called him and talked him into meetin' 'em," Hallam said. "Probably down by the ocean somewhere. They had an argument, and I reckon Lonnie must've made the mistake of turnin' his back on this person, 'cause he got hit on the head hard enough to knock him out. Then the one who'd called him and got him to come there shoved him into the water, and he drowned." Hallam shook his head. "Lonnie never should've turned his back. But I reckon he still trusted her, even though he shouldn't have."

Marjorie's face was still placid, but her voice was brittle as she said, "Her?"

"You, Marjorie," Hallam said quietly. "You killed Lonnie because he wouldn't marry you. Then, since you couldn't have him, you went out and got the next best thing. You kidnapped Allen Hathaway."

"That's utterly insane," Marjorie murmured. "How could I kidnap someone like Allen Hathaway, a big strong movie star like that?"

"By shootin' him with a hypo full of the stuff you stole from the hospital where you work, the same stuff that's likely in that coffee you just fixed me." Hallam pointed at the cup with his thumb. "Did you plan to stash me in the basement, too?"

"You don't know what you're talking about," Marjorie told him calmly. "I never heard of such a thing. You think I have a movie star in my basement?"

"Yes, ma'am." Hallam pushed himself to his feet. "And if you don't mind, I reckon I'll go have me a look on the other side of that door."

He took a step toward the locked door and she came at him, exploding up from the chair and bringing up the knife she had hidden in the folds of her dress in case the knockout drops in the coffee didn't work. Hallam twisted toward her, saw the blade coming at him, and blocked her arm with his. All he meant to do was keep her from stabbing him, but he must have hit her harder than he had intended. He heard the bone in her forearm snap, and she gave a thin little scream as she dropped the knife. Hallam kicked it away. Marjorie fell to her knees, clutching her broken arm against her body.

"Leave him alone," she said, her voice ragged. "He's not the man you're looking for. He's got Allen Hathaway. He's Lonnie. He's Lonnie, and he's going to marry me. He swore he would, and now he's going to do it. He's Lonnie, I tell you. He looks just *like* Lonnie."

Hallam didn't bother asking her for the key to the basement door. He just kicked it open and looked down the steps. The light from the kitchen fell in a long rectangle that showed him the man lying on the cement floor, hands tied behind him. The man looked up at Hallam, blinking against the light. His voice was thick with the drug as he said, "Who . . . what . . . what am I . . . doing here?"

"Doublin'," Hallam told Allen Hathaway. "Doublin' for Lonnie Vinson."

HALLAM ALMOST FELT CHEERFUL as he walked down the hallway toward Mrs. Martinez's apartment. Allen Hathaway was in the hospital and would be all right in time, and Hallam had a check from a very grateful Calvin Forrester in his pocket.

But Marjorie Grant was also in the hospital, under a police guard, and while her broken arm would heal, she would never really be all right again. And Lonnie Vinson was still in the morgue. Those were reasons enough for Hallam not to feel too good about how everything had worked out.

On the other hand, Arnold Moss's little race-fixing scheme had been exposed, too, so that was a little more to be considered on the good side, even though it had only happened because Marjorie wanted to divert suspicion from herself by steering Hallam to Moss.

Hallam knocked on the door of the apartment, and it was jerked open almost before his knuckles bounced off the wood the last time. Mrs. Martinez stood there, her hair askew, her eyes wide. A torrent of angry Spanish poured out of her mouth, and for an awful moment, Hallam was afraid something had happened to Beth.

Then he heard laughter coming from inside the apartment, little-girl laughter, and he sighed with relief.

"Do you know what she did this time?" Mrs. Martinez demanded in English.

"No, ma'am, but I'm sure you'll tell me," Hallam said as he slid his hand inside his pocket and touched that check from the movie studio. It was a good thing he had it, he thought.

He might need it to pay for the damages.

Along with Sue Grafton's Kinsey Millhone and Marcia Muller's Sharon McCone, Sara Paretsky's Chicago detective V. I. Warshawski is one of the most prominent female detective characters in modern mystery fiction. In addition to her novels, Paretsky is also an accomplished anthologist. Her first collection of crime fiction by women writers, *A Woman's Eye*, won the Anthony Award for best anthology. The second, *Women on the Case*, was published in 1996 by Delacorte Press. Also, a collection of V. I. Warshawski short fiction, *Windy City Blues*, was published in 1995. "Grace Notes" is from that collection, a tour de force of Warshawski's family, history, and, of course, Chicago.

Grace Notes
SARA PARETESKY

I

GABRIELLA SESTIERI OF PITIGLIANO.
Anyone with knowledge of her whereabouts should contact the office of Malcolm Ranier.

I was reading the *Herald-Star* at breakfast when the notice jumped out at me from the personal section. I put my coffee down with extreme care, as if I were in a dream and all my actions moved with the slowness of dream time. I shut the paper with the same slow motion, then opened it again. The notice was still there. I spelled out the headline letter by letter, in case my unconscious mind had substituted one name for another, but the text remained the same. There could not be more than one Gabriella Sestieri from Pitigliano. My mother, who died of cancer in 1968 at the age of forty-six.

"Who could want her all these years later?" I said aloud.

Peppy, the golden retriever I share with my downstairs neighbor, raised a sympathetic eyebrow. We had just come back from a run on a dreary November morning and she was waiting hopefully for toast.

"It can't be her father." His mind had cracked after six months in a German concentration camp, and he refused to acknowledge Gabriella's death when my father wrote to inform him of it. I'd had to translate the letter, in which he said he was too old to travel but wished Gabriella well on her concert tour. Anyway, if he was alive still he'd be almost a hundred.

Maybe Gabriella's brother Italo was searching for her: He had disappeared in the maelstrom of the war, but Gabriella always hoped he survived. Or her first voice teacher, Francesca Salvini, whom Gabriella longed to see again, to explain why she had never fulfilled Salvini's hopes for her professional career. As Gabriella lay in her final bed in Jackson Park Hospital with tubes ringing her wasted body, her last messages had been for me and for Salvini. This morning it dawned on me for the first time how hurtful my father must have found that. He adored my mother, but for him she had only the quiet fondness of an old friend.

I realized my hands around the newspaper were wet with sweat, that paper and print were clinging to my palms. With an embarrassed laugh I put the paper down and washed off the ink under the kitchen tap. It was ludicrous to spin my mind with conjectures when all I had to do was phone Malcolm Ranier. I went to the living room and pawed through the papers on the piano for the phone book. Ranier seemed to be a lawyer with offices on La Salle Street, at the north end where the pricey new buildings stand.

His was apparently a solo practice. The woman who answered the phone assured me she was Mr. Ranier's assistant and conversant with his files. Mr. Ranier couldn't speak with me himself now, because he was in conference. Or court. Or the john.

"I'm calling about the notice in this morning's paper, wanting to know the whereabouts of Gabriella Sestieri."

"What is your name, please, and your relationship with Mrs. Sestieri?" The assistant left out the second syllable so that the name came out as "Sistery."

"I'll be glad to tell you that if you tell me why you're trying to find her."

"I'm afraid I can't give out confidential client business over the phone. But if you tell me your name and what you know about Mrs. Sestieri we'll get back to you when we've discussed the matter with our client."

I thought we could keep this conversation going all day. "The person you're looking for may not be the same one I know, and I don't want to violate a family's privacy. But I'll be in a meeting on La Salle Street this morning; I can stop by to discuss the matter with Mr. Ranier."

The woman finally decided that Mr. Ranier had ten minutes free at twelve-thirty. I gave her my name and hung up. Sitting at the piano, I crashed out chords, as if the sound could bury the wildness of my feelings.

I never could remember whether I knew how ill my mother was the last six months of her life. Had she told me and I couldn't—or didn't wish to—comprehend it? Or had she decided to shelter me from the knowledge? Gabriella usually made me face bad news, but perhaps not the worst of all possible news, our final separation.

Why did I never work on my singing? It was one thing I could have done for her. I didn't have a Voice, as Gabriella put it, but I had a serviceable contralto, and of course she insisted I acquire some musicianship. I stood up and began working on a few vocal stretches, then suddenly became wild with the desire to find my mother's music, the old exercise books she had me learn from.

I burrowed through the hall closet for the trunk that held her books. I finally found it in the farthest corner, under a carton holding my old case files, a baseball bat, a box of clothes I no longer wore but couldn't bring myself to give way.... I sat on the closet floor in misery, with a sense of having buried her so deep I couldn't find her.

Peppy's whimpering pulled me back to the present. She had followed me into the closet and was pushing her nose into my arm. I fondled her ears.

At length it occurred to me that if someone was trying to find my mother I'd need documents to prove the relationship. I got up from the floor and pulled the trunk into the hall. On top lay her black silk concert gown; I'd forgotten wrapping that in tissue and storing it. In the end I found my parents' marriage license and Gabriella's death certificate tucked into the score of *Don Giovanni.*

When I returned the score to the trunk another old envelope floated out. I picked it up and recognized Mr. Fortieri's spiky writing. Carlo Fortieri repaired musical instruments and sold, or at least used to sell, music. He was the person Gabriella went to for Italian conversation, musical conversation, advice. He still sometimes tuned my own piano out of affection for her.

When Gabriella met him, he'd been a widower for years, also with one child, also a girl. Gabriella thought I ought to play with her while she sang or discussed music with Mr. Fortieri, but Barbara was ten years or so my senior and we'd never had much to say to each other.

I pulled out the yellowed paper. It was written in Italian, and hard for me to decipher, but apparently dated from 1965.

Addressing her as *"Cara signora Warshawski,"* Mr. Fortieri sent his regrets that she was forced to cancel her May 14 concert. "I shall, of course, respect your wishes and not reveal the nature of your indisposition to anyone else. And, *cara signora,* you should know by now that I regard any confidence of yours as a sacred trust: you need not fear an indiscretion." It was signed with his full name.

I wondered now if he'd been my mother's lover. My stomach tightened, as it does when you think of your parents stepping outside their pre-scribed roles, and I folded the paper back into the envelope. Fifteen years ago the same notion must have prompted me to put his letter inside *Don Giovanni*. For want of a better idea I stuck it back in the score and returned everything to the trunk. I needed to rummage through a different carton to find my own birth certificate, and it was getting too late in the morning for me to indulge in nostalgia.

II

Malcolm Ranier's office overlooked the Chicago River and all the new glass and marble flanking it. It was a spectacular view—if you squinted to shut out the burnt-out waste of Chicago's west side that lay beyond. I arrived just at twelve-thirty, dressed in my one good suit, black, with a white crepe-dechine blouse. I looked feminine, but austere—or at least that was my intention.

Ranier's assistant-rum-receptionist was buried in Danielle Steel. When I handed her my card, she marked her page without haste and took the card into an inner office. After a ten-minute wait to let me understand his importance, Ranier came out to greet me in person. He was a soft round man of about sixty, with gray eyes that lay like pebbles above an apparently jovial smile.

"Ms. Warshawski. Good of you to stop by. I understand you can help us with our inquiry into Mrs. Sestieri." He gave my mother's name a genuine Italian lilt, but his voice was as hard as his eyes.

"Hold my calls, Cindy." He put a hand on the nape of my neck to steer me into his office.

Before we'd shut the door Cindy was reabsorbed into Danielle. I moved away from the hand—I didn't want grease on my five-hundred-dollar jacket—and went to admire a bronze nymph on a shelf at the window.

"Beautiful, isn't it." Ranier might have been commenting on the weather. "One of my clients brought it from France."

"It looks as though it should be in a museum."

A call to the bar association before I left my apartment told me he was an import-export lawyer. Various imports seemed to have attached themselves to him on their way into the country. The room was dominated by a slab of rose marble, presumably a work table, but several antique chairs were also worth a second glance. A marquetry credenza stood against the far wall. The Modigliani above it was probably an original.

"Coffee, Ms."—he glanced at my card again—"Warshawski?"

"No, thank you. I understand you're very busy, and so am I. So let's talk about Gabriella Sestieri."

"D'accordo." He motioned me to one of the spindly antiques near the marble slab. "You know where she is?"

The chair didn't look as though it could support my hundred and forty pounds, but when Ranier perched on a similar one I sat, with a wariness that made me think he had them to keep people deliberately off balance. I leaned back and crossed my legs. The woman at ease.

"I'd like to make sure we're talking about the same person. And that I know why you want to find her."

A smile crossed his full lips, again not touching the slate chips of his eyes. "We could fence all day, Ms. Warshawski, but as you say, time is valuable to us both. The Gabriella Sestieri I seek was born in Pitigliano on October thirtieth, 1921. She left Italy sometime early in 1941, no one knows exactly when, but she was last heard of in Siena that February. And there's some belief she came to Chicago. As to why I want to find her, a relative of hers, now in Florence, but from the Pitigliano family, is interested in locating her. My specialty is import-export law, particularly with Italy: I'm no expert in finding missing persons, but I agreed to assist as a favor to a client. The relative—Mrs. Sestieri's relative—has a professional connection to my client. And now it is your turn, Ms. Warshawski."

"Ms. Sestieri died in March 1968." My blood was racing; I was pleased to hear my voice come out without a tremor. "She married a Chicago police officer in April 1942. They had one child. Me."

"And your father? Officer Warshawski?"

"Died in 1979. Now may I have the name of my mother's relative? I've known only one member of her family, my grandmother's sister who lives here in Chicago, and am eager to find others." Actually, if they bore any resemblance to my embittered Aunt Rosa I'd just as soon not meet the remaining Verazi clan.

"You were cautious, Ms. Warshawski, so you will forgive my caution: Do you have proof of your identity?"

"You make it sound as though treasure awaits the missing heir, Mr. Ranier." I pulled out the copies of my legal documents and handed them over. "Who or what is looking for my mother?"

Ranier ignored my question. He studied the documents briefly, then put them on the marble slab while condoling me on losing my parents. His voice had the same soft flat cadence as when he'd discussed the nymph.

"You've no doubt remained close to your grandmother's sister? If she's the person who brought your mother to Chicago it might be helpful for me to have her name and address."

"My aunt is a difficult woman to be close to, but I can check with her, to see if she doesn't mind my giving you her name and address."

"And the rest of your mother's family?"

I held out my hands, empty. "I don't know any of them. I don't even know how many there are. Who is my mystery relative? What does he—she—want?"

He paused, looking at the file in his hands. "I actually don't know. I ran the ad merely as a favor to my client. But I'll pass your name and address along, Ms. Warshawski, and when he's been in touch with the person I'm sure you'll hear."

This runaround was starting to irritate me. "You're a heck of a poker player, Mr. Ranier. But you know as well as I that you're lying like a rug."

I spoke lightly, smiling as I got to my feet and crossed to the door, snatching my documents from the marble slab as I passed. For once his feeling reached his eyes, turning the slate to molten rock. As I waited for the elevator I wondered if answering that ad meant I was going to be sucker-punched.

OVER DINNER THAT NIGHT with Dr. Lotty Herschel I went through my conversation with Ranier, trying to sort out my confused feelings. Trying, too, to figure out who in Gabriella's family might want to find her, if the inquiry was genuine.

"They surely know she's dead," Lotty said.

"That's what I thought at first, but it's not that simple. See, my grand-mother converted to Judaism when she married Nonno Mattia—sorry, that's Gabriella's father—Grandpa Matthias—Gabriella usually spoke Ital-ian to me. Anyway, my grandmother died in Auschwitz when the Italian Jews were rounded up in 1944. Then, my grandfather didn't go back to Piti-gliano, the little town they were from, after he was liberated—the Jewish community there had been decimated and he didn't have any family left. So he was sent to a Jewish-run sanatorium in Turin, but Gabriella only found that out after years of writing letters to relief agencies."

I stared into my wineglass, as though the claret could reveal the secrets of my family. "There was one cousin who she was really close to, from the Christian side of her family, named Frederica. Frederica had a baby out of wedlock the year before Gabriella came to Chicago, and got sent away in disgrace. After the war Gabriella kept trying to find her, but Frederica's family wouldn't forward the letters—they really didn't want to be in touch with her. Gabriella might have saved enough money to go back to Italy to look for herself, but then she started to be ill. She had a miscarriage the summer of '65 and bled and bled. Tony and I thought she was dying then."

My voice trailed away as I thought of that hot unhappy summer, the summer the city burst into riot-spawned flames and my mother lay in the stifling front bedroom oozing blood. She and Tony had one of their infrequent fights. I'd been on my paper route and they didn't hear me come in. He wanted her to sell something which she said wasn't hers to dispose of.

"And your life," my father shouted. "You can give that away as a gift? Even if she was still alive—" He broke off then, seeing me, and neither of them talked about the matter again, at least when I was around to hear.

Lotty squeezed my hand. "What about your aunt, great-aunt in Melrose Park? She might have told her siblings, don't you think? Was she close to any of them?"

I grimaced. "I can't imagine Rosa being close to anyone. See, she was the last child, and Gabriella's grandmother died giving birth to her. So some cousins adopted her, and when they emigrated in the twenties Rosa came to Chicago with them. She didn't really feel like she was part of the Verazi family. I know it seems strange, but with all the uprootings the war caused, and all the disconnections, it's possible that the main part of Gabriella's mother's family didn't know what became of her."

Lotty nodded, her face twisted in sympathy; much of her family had been destroyed in those death camps also. "There wasn't a schism when your grandmother converted?"

I shrugged. "I don't know. It's frustrating to think how little I know about those people. Gabriella says—said—the Verazis weren't crazy about it, and they didn't get together much except for weddings or funerals—except for the one cousin. But Pitigliano was a Jewish cultural center before the war and Nonno was considered a real catch. I guess he was rich until the Fascists confiscated his property." Fantasies of reparations danced through my head.

"Not too likely," Lotty said. "You're imagining someone overcome with guilt sixty years after the fact coming to make you a present of some land?"

I blushed. "Factory, actually: the Sestieris were harness makers who switched to automobile interiors in the twenties. I suppose if the place is even still standing, it's part of Fiat or Mercedes. You know, all day long I've been swinging between wild fantasies—about Nonno's factory, or Gabriella's brother surfacing—and then I start getting terrified, wondering if it's all some kind of terrible trap. Although who'd want to trap me, or why, is beyond me. I know this Malcolm Ranier knows. It would be so easy—"

"No! Not to set your mind at rest, not to prove you can bypass the security of a modern high rise—for no reason whatsoever are you to break into that man's office."

"Oh, very well." I tried not to sound like a sulky child denied a treat.

"You promise, Victoria?" Lotty sounded ferocious.

I held up my right hand. "On my honor, I promise not to break into his office."

III

It was six days later that the phone call came to my office. A young man, with an Italian accent so thick that his English was almost incomprehensible, called up and gaily asked if I was his "Cousin Vittoria."

"Parliamo italiano," I suggested, and the gaiety in his voice increased as he switched thankfully to his own language.

He was my cousin Ludovico, the great-great-grandson of our mutual Verazi ancestors, he had arrived in Chicago from Milan only last night, terribly excited at finding someone from his mother's family, thrilled that I knew Italian, my accent was quite good, really, only a tinge of America in it, could we get together, any place, he would find me—just name the time as long as it was soon.

I couldn't help laughing as the words tumbled out, although I had to ask him to slow down and repeat. It had been a long time since I'd spoken Italian, and it took time for my mind to adjust. Ludovico was staying at the Garibaldi, a small hotel on the fringe of the Gold Coast, and would be thrilled if I met him there for a drink at six. Oh, yes, his last name—that was Verazi, the same as our great-grandfather.

I bustled through my business with greater efficiency than usual so that I had time to run the dogs and change before meeting him. I laughed at myself for dressing with care, in a pantsuit of crushed lavender velvet which could take me dancing if the evening ended that way, but no self-mockery could suppress my excitement. I'd been an only child with one cousin from each of my parents' families as my only relations. My cousin Boom-Boom, whom I adored, had been dead these ten years and more, while Rosa's son Albert was such a mass of twisted fears that I preferred not to be around him. Now I was meeting a whole new family.

I tap-danced around the dog in my excitement. Peppy gave me a long-suffering look and demanded that I return her to my downstairs neighbor: Mitch, her son, had stopped there on our way home from running.

"You look slick, doll," Mr. Contreras told me, torn between approval and jealousy. "New date?"

"New cousin." I continued to tap-dance in the hall outside his door. "Yep. The mystery relative finally surfaced. Ludovico Verazi."

"You be careful, doll," the old man said severely. "Plenty of con artists out there to pretend they're your cousins, you know, and next thing—phht."

"What'll he con me out of? My dirty laundry?" I planted a kiss on his nose and danced down the sidewalk to my car.

Three men were waiting in the Garibaldi's small lobby, but I knew my cousin at once. His hair was amber, instead of black, but his face was my mother's, from the high rounded forehead to his wide sensuous mouth. He leapt up at my approach, seized my hands, and kissed me in the European style—sort of touching the air beside each ear.

"Bellissima!" Still holding my hands he stepped back to scrutinize me. My astonishment must have been written large on my face, because he laughed a little guiltily.

"I know it, I know it, I should have told you of the resemblance, but I didn't realize it was *so* strong: The only picture I've seen of Cousin Gabriella is a stage photo from 1940 when she starred in Jommelli's *Iphigenia.*"

"Jommelli!" I interrupted. "I thought it was Gluck!"

"No, no, *cugina,* Jommelli. Surely Gabriella knew what she sang?" Laughing happily he moved to the armchair where he'd been sitting and took up a brown leather case. He pulled out a handful of papers and thumbed through them, then extracted a yellowing photograph for me to examine.

It was my mother, dressed as Iphigenia for her one stage role, the one that gave me my middle name. She was made up, her dark hair in an elaborate coil, but she looked absurdly young, like a little girl playing dress-up. At the bottom of the picture was the name of the studio, in Siena where she had sung, and on the back someone had lettered, *"Gabriella Sestieri fa la parte d'Iphigenia nella produzione d'Iphigenia da Jommelli."* The resemblance to Ludovico was clear, despite the blurring of time and cosmetics to the lines of her face. I felt a stab of jealousy: I inherited her olive skin, but my face is my father's.

"You know this photograph?" Ludovico asked.

I shook my head. "She left Italy in such a hurry: All she brought with her were some Venetian wineglasses that had been a wedding present to Nonna Laura. I never saw her onstage."

"I've made you sad, cousin Vittoria, by no means my intention. Perhaps you would like to keep this photograph?"

"I would, very much. Now—a drink? Or dinner?"

He laughed again. "I have been in America only twenty-four hours, not long enough to be accustomed to dinner in the middle of the afternoon. So—a drink, by all means. Take me to a typical American bar."

I collected my Trans Am from the doorman and drove down to the Golden Glow, the bar at the south end of the Loop owned by my friend Sal Barthele. My appearance with a good-looking stranger caused a stir among the regulars—as I'd hoped. Murray Ryerson, an investigative reporter whose relationship with me is compounded of friendship, competition, and a disastrous romantic episode, put down his beer with a snap and came over to our table. Sal Barthele emerged from her famous mahogany horseshoe bar. Under cover of Murray's greetings and Ludovico's accented English she muttered, "Girl, you are strutting. You look indecent! Anyway, isn't this cradle snatching? Boy looks *young!*"

I was glad the glow from the Tiffany table lamps was too dim for her to see me blushing. In the car coming over I had been calculating degrees of consanguinity and decided that as second cousins we were eugenically safe; I was embarrassed to show it so obviously. Anyway, he was only seven years younger than me.

"My newfound cousin," I said, too abruptly. "Ludovico Verazi—Sal Barthele, owner of the Glow."

Ludovico shook her hand. "So, you are an old friend of this cousin of mine. You know her more than I do—give me ideas about her character."

"Dangerous," Murray said. "She breaks men in her soup like crackers."

"Only if they're crackers to begin with," I snapped, annoyed to be presented to my cousin in such a light.

"Crackers to begin with?" Ludovico asked.

"Slang—*gergo*—for '*pazzo,*' " I explained. "Also a cracker is an oaf— a *cretino.*"

Murray put an arm around me. "Ah, Vic—the sparkle in your eyes lights a fire in my heart."

"It's just the third beer, Murray—that's heartburn," Sal put in. "Ludovico, what do you drink—whiskey, like your cousin? Or something nice and Italian like Campari?"

"Whiskey before dinner, Cousin Vittoria? No, no, by the time you eat you have no—no tasting sensation. For me, Signora, a glass of wine please."

Later over dinner at Filigree we became "Vic" and "Vico"—"Please, Veek, no one is calling me 'Ludovico' since the time I am a little boy in trouble—" And later still, after two bottles of Barolo, he asked me how much I knew about the Verazi family.

"*Niente,*" I said. "I don't even know how many brothers and sisters Gabriella's mother had. Or where you come into the picture. Or where I do, for that matter."

His eyebrows shot up in surprise. "So your mother was never in touch with her own family after she moved here?"

I told him what I'd told Lotty, about the war, my grandmother's estrangement from her family, and Gabriella's depression on learning of her cousin Frederica's death.

"But I am the grandson of that naughty Frederica, that girl who would have a baby with no father." Vico shouted in such excitement that the wait staff rushed over to make sure he wasn't choking to death. "This is remarkable, Vic, this is amazing, that the one person in our family *your* mother is close to turns out to be *my* grandmother.

"Ah, it was sad, very sad, what happened to her. The family is moved to Florence during the war, my grandmother has a baby, maybe the father is a partisan, my grandmother was the one person in the family to be supporting the partisans. My great-grandparents, they are very prudish, they say, this is a disgrace, never mind there is a war on and much bigger disgraces are happening all the time, so—poof!—off goes this naughty Frederica with her baby to Milano. And the baby becomes my mother, but she and my grandmother both die when I am ten, so these most respectable Verazi cousins, finally they decide the war is over, the grandson is after all far enough removed from the taint of original sin, they come fetch me and raise me with all due respectability in Florence."

He broke off to order a cognac. I took another espresso: Somehow after forty I no longer can manage the amount of alcohol I used to. I'd only drunk half of one of the bottles of wine.

"So how did you learn about Gabriella? And why did you want to try to find her?"

"Well, *cara cugina,* it is wonderful to meet you, but I have a confession I must make: It was in the hopes of finding—something—-that I am coming to Chicago looking for my cousin Gabriella."

"What kind of something?"

"You say you know nothing about our great-grandmother, Claudia Fortezza? So you are not knowing even that she is in a small way a composer?"

I couldn't believe Gabriella never mentioned such a thing. If she didn't know about it, the rift with the Verazis must have been more severe than she led me to believe. "But maybe that explains why she was given early musical training," I added aloud. "You know my mother was quite a gifted singer. Although, alas, she never had the professional career she should have."

"Yes, yes, she trained with Francesca Salvini. I know all about that! Salvini was an important teacher, even in a little town like Pitigliano people came from Siena and Florence to train with her, and she had a connection to the Siena Opera. But anyway, Vic, I am wanting to collect Claudia Fortezza's music. The work of women composers is coming into vogue. I can find an ensemble to perform it, maybe to record it, so I am hoping Gabriella, too, has some of this music."

I shook my head. "'I don't think so. I kept all her music in a trunk, and I don't think there's anything from that period."

"But you don't know definitely, do you, so maybe we can look together." He was leaning across the table, his voice vibrating with urgency.

I moved backward, the strength of his feelings making me uneasy. "I suppose so."

"Then let us pay the bill and go."

"Now? But, Vico, it's almost midnight. If it's been there all this while it will still be there in the morning."

"Ah: I am being the cracker, I see." We had been speaking in Italian all evening, but for this mangled idiom Vico switched to English. "*Mi scusi, cara cugina:* I have been so engaged in my hunt, through the papers of old aunts, through attics in Pitigliano, in used bookstores in Florence, that I forget not everyone shares my enthusiasm. And then last month, I find a diary of my grandmother's, and the writes of the special love her cousin Gabriella has for music, her special gift, and I think—ah-ah, if this music lies anywhere, it is with this Gabriella."

He picked up my right hand and started playing with my fingers. "Besides, confess to me, Vic: In your mind's eye you are at home feverishly through your mother's music, whether I am present or not."

I laughed, a little shakily; the intensity in his face made him look so like Gabriella when she was swept up in music that my heart turned over with yearning.

"So I am right? We can pay the bill and leave?"

The wait staff, hoping to close the restaurant, had left the bill on our table some time earlier. I tried to pay it, but Vico snatched it from me. He took a thick stack of bills from his billfold. Counting under his breath he peeled off two hundreds and a fifty and laid them on the check. Like many Europeans he'd assumed the tip was included in the total: I added four tens and went to retrieve the Trans Am.

IV

As we got out of the car I warned Vico not to talk in the stairwell. "We don't want the dogs to hear me and wake Mr. Contreras."

"He is a malevolent neighbor? You need me perhaps to guard you?"

"He's the best-natured neighbor in the world. Unfortunately, he sees his role in my life as Cerberus, with a whiff of Othello thrown in. It's late enough without spending an hour on why I'm bringing you home with me."

We managed to tiptoe up the stairs without rousing anyone. Inside my apartment we collapsed with the giggles of teenagers who've walked past a cop after curfew. Somehow it seemed natural to fall from laughter into each other's arms. I was the first to break away. Vico gave me a look I couldn't interpret—mockery seemed to dominate.

My cheeks stinging, I went to the hall closet and pulled out Gabriella's trunk once more. I lifted out her evening gown again, fingering the lace panels in the bodice. They were silver, carefully edged in black. Shortly before her final illness Gabriella managed to organize a series of concerts that she hoped would launch her career again, at least in a small way, and it was for these that she had the dress made. Tony and I sat in the front row of Mandel Hall, almost swooning with our passion for her. The gown cost her two years of free lessons for the couturier's daughter, the last few given when she had gone bald from chemotherapy.

As I stared at the dress, wrapped in melancholy, I realized Vico was pulling books and scores from the trunk and going through them with quick careful fingers. I'd saved dozens of Gabriella's books of operas and lieder, but nothing like her whole collection. I wasn't going to tell Vico that, though: he'd probably demand that we break into old Mr. Fortieri's shop to see if any of the scores were still lying about.

At one point Vico thought he had found something, a handwritten score tucked into the pages of *Idomeneo*. I came to look. Someone, not my mother, had meticulously copied out a concerto. As I bent to look more closely, Vico pulled a small magnifying glass from his wallet and began to scrutinize the paper.

I eyed him thoughtfully. "Does the music or the notation look anything like our great-grandmother's?"

He didn't answer me, but held the score up to the light to inspect the margins. I finally took the pages from him and scanned the clarinet line.

"I'm no musicologist, but this sounds baroque to me." I flipped to the end, where the initials "CF" were inscribed with a flourish: Carlo Fortieri might have copied this for my mother—a true labor of love; copying music is a slow, painful business.

"Baroque?" Vico grabbed the score back from me and looked at it more intensely. "But this paper is not that old, I think."

"I think not, also. I have a feeling it's something one of my mother's friends copied out for a chamber group they played in: She sometimes took the piano part."

He put the score to one side and continued burrowing in the trunk. Near the bottom he came on a polished wooden box, big enough to fit snugly against the short side of the drunk. He grunted as he prised it free, then gave a little crow of delight as he saw it was filled with old papers.

"Take it easy, cowboy," I said as he started tossing them to the floor. "This isn't the city dump."

He gave me a look of startling rage at my reproof, then covered it so quickly with a laugh that I couldn't be sure I'd seen it. "This old wood is beautiful. You should keep this out where you can look at it."

"It was Gabriella's, from Pitigliano." In it, carefully wrapped in her winter underwear, she'd laid the eight Venetian glasses that were her sole legacy of home. Fleeing in haste in the night, she had chosen to transport a fragile load, as if that gained her control of her own fragile destiny.

Vico ran his long fingers over the velvet lining the case. The green had turned yellow and black along the creases. I took the box away from him, and began replacing my school essays and report cards—my mother used to put my best school reports in the case.

At two Vico had to admit defeat. "You have no idea where it is? You didn't sell it, perhaps to meet some emergency bill or pay for that beautiful sports car?"

"Vico! What on earth are you talking about? Putting aside the insult, what do you think a score by an unknown nineteenth-century woman is worth?"

"Ah, *mi scusi,* Vic—I forget that everyone doesn't value these Verazi pieces as I do."

"Yes, my dear cousin, and I didn't just fall off a turnip truck, either." I switched to English in my annoyance. "Not even the most enthusiastic grandson would fly around the world with this much mystery. What's the story—are the Verazis making you their heir if you produce her music? Or are you looking for something else altogether?"

"Turnip truck? What is this turnip truck?"

"Forget the linguistic excursion and come clean, Vico. Meaning, confession is good for the soul, so speak up. What are you really looking for?"

He studied his fingers, grimy from paging through the music, then looked at me with a quick frank smile. "The truth is, Fortunato Magi may have seen some of her music. He was Puccini's uncle, you know, and very influential among the Italian composers of the end of the century. My great-grandmother used to talk about Magi reading Claudia Fortezza's music. She was only a daughter-in-law, and anyway, Claudia Fortezza was dead years before she married into the family, so I never paid any attention to it. But then when I found my grandmother's diaries, it seemed possible that there was some truth to it. It's even possible that Puccini used some of Claudia Fortezza's music, so if we can find it, it might be valuable."

I thought the whole idea was ludicrous—it wasn't even as though the Puccini estate were collecting royalties that one might try to sue for. And even if they were—you could believe almost any highly melodic vocal music sounded like Puccini. I didn't want to get into a fight with Vico about it, though: I had to be at work early in the morning.

"There wasn't any time you can remember Gabriella talking about something very valuable in the house?" he persisted.

I was about to shut him off completely when I suddenly remembered my parents' argument that I'd interrupted. Reluctantly, because he saw I'd thought of something, I told Vico about it.

"She was saying it wasn't hers to dispose of. I suppose that might include her grandmother's music. But there wasn't anything like that in the house when my father died. And believe me, I went through all the papers." Hoping for some kind of living memento of my mother, something more than her Venetian wineglasses.

Vico seized my arm in his excitement. "You see! She did have it, she must have sold it anyway. Or your father did, after she died. Who would they have gone to?"

I refused to give him Mr. Fortieri as a gift. If Gabriella had been worried about the ethics of disposing of someone else's belongings she probably would have consulted him. Maybe even asked him to sell it, if she came to that in the end, but Vico didn't need to know that.

"You know someone, I can tell," he cried.

"No. I was a child. She didn't confide in me. If my father sold it he would have been embarrassed to let me know. It's going on three in the morning, Vico, and I have to work in a few hours. I'm going to call you a cab and get you back to the Garibaldi."

"You work? Your long lost cousin Vico comes to Chicago for the first time and you cannot kiss off your boss?" He blew across his fingers expressively.

"I work for myself." I could hear the brusqueness creep into my voice—his exigency was taking away some of his charm. "And I have one job that won't wait past tomorrow morning."

"What kind of work is it you do that cannot be deferred?"

"Detective. Private investigator. And I have to be on a—a—"—I couldn't think of the Italian, so I used English—"shipping dock in four hours."

"Ah, a detective." He pursed his lips. "I see now why this Murray was warning me about you. You and me are lovers? Or is that a shocking question to ask an American woman?"

"Murray's a reporter. His path crosses mine from time to time." I went to the phone and summoned a cab.

"And, cousin, I may take this handwritten score with me? To study more leisurely?"

"If you return it."

"I will be here with it tomorrow afternoon—when you return from your detecting."

I went to the kitchen for some newspaper to wrap it in, wondering about Vico. He didn't seem to have much musical knowledge. Perhaps he was ashamed to tell me he couldn't read music and was going to take it to some third party who could give him a stylistic comparison between this score and something of our grandmother's.

The cab honked under the window a few minutes later. I sent him off on his own with a chaste cousinly kiss. He took my retreat from passion with the same mockery that had made me squirm earlier.

V

All during the next day, as I huddled behind a truck taking pictures of a handoff between the vice president of an electronics firm and a driver, as I tailed the driver south to Kankakee and photographed another hand-off to a man in a sports car, traced the car to its owner in Libertyville, and reported back to the electronics firm in Naperville, I wondered about Vico and the score. What was he really looking for?

Last night I hadn't questioned his story too closely—the late night and pleasure in my new cousin had both muted my suspicions. Today the bleak air chilled my euphoria. A quest for a great-grandmother's music might bring one pleasure, but surely not inspire such avidity as Vico displayed. He'd grown up in poverty in Milan without knowing who was his father, or even his grandfather were. Maybe it was a quest for roots that was driving my cousin so passionately.

I wondered, too, what item of value my mother had refused to sell thirty summers ago. What wasn't *hers* to sell, that she would stubbornly sacrifice better medical care for it? I realized I felt hurt: I thought I was so dear to her that she told me everything. The idea that she'd kept a secret from me made it hard for me to think clearly.

When my dad died, I'd gone through everything in the little house on Houston before selling it. I'd never found anything that seemed worth that much agony, so either she did sell it in the end—or my dad had done so—or she had given it to someone else. Of course, she might have buried it deep in the house. The only place I could imagine her hiding something was in her piano, and if that was the case I was out of luck: The piano had been lost in the fire that destroyed my apartment ten years ago.

But if it—whatever it was—was the same thing Vico was looking for, some old piece of music—Gabriella would have consulted Mr. Fortieri. If she hadn't gone to him, he might know who else she would have turned to. While I waited in a Naperville mall for my prints to be developed I tried phoning him. He was eighty now, but still actively working, so I wasn't surprised when he didn't answer the phone.

I snoozed in the president's antechamber until he could finally snatch ten minutes for my report. When I finished, a little after five, I stopped in his secretary's office to try Mr. Fortieri again. Still no answer.

With only three hours' sleep, my skin was twitching as though I'd put it on inside out. Since seven this morning I'd logged a hundred and ninety miles. I wanted nothing now more than my bed. Instead I rode the packed expressway all the way northwest to the O'Hare cutoff.

Mr. Fortieri lived in the Italian enclave along North Harlem Avenue. It used to be a day's excursion to go there with Gabriella: we would ride the Number Six bus to the Loop, transfer to the Douglas line of the el, and at its end take yet another bus west to Harlem. After lunch in one of the storefront restaurants, my mother stopped at Mr. Fortieri's to sing or talk while I was given and old clarinet to take apart to keep me amused. On our way back to the bus we bought polenta and olive oil in Frescobaldi's Deli. Old Mrs. Frescobaldi would let me run my hands through the bags of cardamom, the voluptuous scent making me stomp around the store in an exaggerated imitation of the drunks along Commercial Avenue. Gabriella would hiss embarrassed invectives at me, and threaten to withhold my gelato if I didn't behave.

The street today has lost much of its charm. Some of the old stores remain, but the chains have set out tendrils here as elsewhere. Mrs. Frescobaldi couldn't stand up to Jewel, and Vespucci's, where Gabriella bought all her shoes, was swallowed by the nearby mall.

Mr. Fortieri's shop, on the ground floor of his dark-shuttered house, looked forlorn now, as though it missed the lively commerce of the street. I rang the bell without much hope: No lights shone from either story.

"I don't think he's home," a woman called from the neighboring walk.

She was just setting out with a laundry-laden shopping cart. I asked her if she'd seen Mr. Fortieri at all today. She'd noticed his bedroom light when she was getting ready for work—he was an early riser, just like her, and this time of year she always noticed his bedroom light. In fact, she'd just been thinking it was strange she didn't see his kitchen light on—he was usually preparing his supper about now, but maybe he'd gone off to see his married daughter in Wilmette.

I remembered Barbara Fortieri's wedding. Gabriella had been too sick to attend, and had sent me by myself. The music had been sensational, but I had been angry and uncomfortable and hadn't paid much attention to anything—including the groom. I asked the woman if she knew Barbara's married name—I might try to call her father there.

"Oh, you know her?"

"My mother was a friend of Mr. Fortieri's—Gabriella Sestieri—Warshawski, I mean." Talking to my cousin had sunk me too deep in my mother's past.

"Sorry, honey, never met her. She married a boy she met at college, I can't think of his name, just about the time my husband and I moved in here, and they went off to those lakefront suburbs together."

She made it sound like as daring a trip as any her ancestors had undertaken braving the Atlantic. Fatigue made it sound funny to me and I found myself doubling over to keep the woman from seeing me shake with wild laughter. The thought of Gabriella telling me "No gelato if you do not behave this minute" only made it seem funnier and I had to bend over, clutching my side.

"You okay there, honey?" The woman hesitated, not wanting to be involved with a stranger.

"Long day," I gasped. "Sudden—cramp—in my side."

I waved her on, unable to speak further. Losing my balance, I reeled against the door. It swung open behind me and I fell hard into the open shop, banging my elbow against a chair.

The fall sobered me. I rubbed my elbow, crooning slightly from pain.

Bracing against the chair I hoisted myself to my feet. It was only then that it dawned on me that the chair was overturned—alarming in any shop, but especially that of someone as fastidious as Mr. Fortieri.

Without stopping to reason I backed out the door, closing it by wrapping my hand in my jacket before touching the knob. The woman with the laundry cart had gone on down the street. I hunted in my glove compartment for my flashlight, then ran back up the walk and into the shop.

I found the old man in the back, in the middle of his workshop. He lay amid his tools, the stem of an oboe still in his left hand. I fumbled for his pulse. Maybe it was the nervous beating of my own heart, but I thought I felt a faint trace of life. I found the phone on the far side of the room, buried under a heap of books that had been taken from the shelves and left where they landed.

VI

"Damn it, Warshawski, what were you doing here anyway?" Sergeant John McGonnigal and I were talking to the back room of Mr. Fortieri's shop while evidence technicians ravaged the front.

I was as surprised to see him as he was me: I'd worked with him, or around him, anyway, for years downtown at the Central District. No one down there had told me he'd transferred—kind of surprising, because he'd been the right-hand man of my dad's oldest friend on the force, Bobby Mallory. Bobby was nearing retirement now; I was guessing McGonnigal had moved out to Montclare to establish a power base independent of his protector. Bobby doesn't like me messing with murder, and McGonnigal sometimes apes his boss, or used to.

Even at his most irritable, when he's inhaling Bobby's frustration, McGonnigal realizes he can trust me, if not to tell the whole truth, at least not to lead him astray or blow a police operation. Tonight he was exasperated simply by the coincidence of mine being the voice that summoned him to a crime scene—the nature of their work makes most cops a little superstitious. He wasn't willing to believe I'd come out to the Montclare neighborhood just to ask about music. As a sop, I threw in my long-lost cousin who was trying to track down a really obscure score.

"And what is that?"

"Sonatas by Claudia Fortezza Verazi." Okay, maybe I sometimes led him a little bit astray.

"Someone tore this place up pretty good for a while before the old guy showed up. It looks as though he surprised the intruder and thought he could defend himself with—what did you say he was holding? An oboe? You think your cousin did that? Because the old guy didn't have any Claudia whoever whoever sonatas?"

I tried not to jump at the question. "I don't think so." My voice came from far away, in a small thread, but at least it didn't quaver.

I was worrying about Vico myself. I hadn't told him about Mr. Fortieri, I was sure of that. But maybe he'd found the letter Fortieri wrote Gabriella, the one I'd tucked into the score of *Don Giovanni*. And then came out here, looking for—whatever he was really hunting—and found it, so he stabbed Mr. Fortieri to hide his— Had he come to Chicago to make a fool of me in his search for something valuable? And how had McGonnigal leaped on that so neatly? I must be tired beyond measure to have revealed my fears.

"Let's get this cousin's name. . . . Damn it, Vic, you can't sit on that. I move to this district three months ago. The first serious assault I bag who should be here but little Miss Muppet right under my tuffet. You'd have to be on drugs to put a knife into the guy, but you know something or you wouldn't be here minutes after it happened."

"Is that the timing? Minutes before my arrival?"

McGonnigal hunched his shoulders impatiently. "The medics didn't stop to figure out that kind of stuff—his blood pressure was too low. Take it as read that the old man'd be dead if you hadn't shown so pat—you'll get your citizen's citation the next time the mayor's handing out medals. Maybe Fortieri'd been bleeding half an hour, but no more. So, I want to talk to your cousin. And then I'll talk to someone else, and someone else and someone else after that. You know how a police investigation runs."

"Yes, I know how they run." I felt unbearably tired as I gave him Vico's name, letter by slow letter, to relay to a patrolman. "Did your guys track down Mr. Fortieri's daughter?"

"She's with him at the hospital. And what does *she* know that you're not sharing with me?"

"She knew my mother. I should go see her. It's hard to wait in a hospital while people you don't know cut on your folks."

He studied me narrowly, then said roughly that he'd seen a lot of that himself, lately, his sister had just lost a kidney to lupus, and I should get some sleep instead of hanging around a hospital waiting room all night.

I longed to follow his advice, but beneath the rolling waves of fatigue that crashed against my brain was a sense of urgency. If Vico had been here, had found what he was looking for, he might be on his way to Italy right now.

The phone rang. McGonnigal stuck an arm around the corner and took it from the patrolman who answered it. After a few grunts he hung up.

"Your cousin hasn't checked out of the Garibaldi, but he's not in his room. As far as the hall staff know he hasn't been there since breakfast this morning, but of course guests don't sign in and out as they go. You got a picture of him?"

"I met him yesterday for the first time. We didn't exchange high school yearbooks. He's in his midthirties, maybe an inch or two taller than me, slim, reddish-brown hair that's a little long on the sides and combed forward in front, and eyes almost the same color."

I swayed and almost fell as I walked to the door. In the outer room the chaos was greater than when I'd arrived. On top of the tumbled books and instruments lay gray print powder and yellow crime-scene tape. I skirted the mess as best I could, but when I climbed into the Trans Am I left a streak of gray powder on the floor mats.

VII

Although her thick hair now held more gray than black, I knew Barbara Fortieri as soon as I stepped into the surgical waiting room (now Barbara Carmichael, now fifty-two, summoned away from flute lessons to her father's bedside). She didn't recognize me at first: I'd been a teenager when she last saw me, and twenty-seven years had passed.

After the usual exclamations of surprise, of worry, she told me her father had briefly opened his eyes at the hospital, just before they began running the anesthetic, and had uttered Gabriella's name.

"Why was he thinking about your mother? Had you been to see him recently? He talks about you sometimes. And about her."

I shook my head. "I wanted to see him, to find out if Gabriella had consulted him about selling something valuable the summer she got sick, the summer of 1965."

Of course Barbara didn't know a thing about the matter. She'd been in her twenties then, engaged to be married, doing her masters in performance at Northwestern in flute and piano, with no attention to spare for the women who were in and out of her father's shop.

I recoiled from her tone as much as her words, the sense of Gabriella as one of an adoring harem. I uttered a stiff sentence of regret over her father's attack and turned to leave.

She put a hand on my arm. "Forgive me, Victoria: I liked your mother. All the same, it used to bug me, all the time he spent with her. I thought he was being disloyal to the memory of my own mother ... anyway, my husband is out of town. The thought of staying here alone, waiting on news. . . ."

So I stayed with her. We talked emptily, to fill the time, of her classes, the recitals she and her husband gave together, the fact that I wasn't married, and, no, I didn't keep up with my music. Around nine one of the surgeons came in to say that Mr. Fortieri had made it through surgery. The knife had pierced his lung and he had lost a lot of blood. To make sure he didn't suffer heart damage they were putting him on a ventilator, in a drug-induced coma, for a few days. If we were his daughters we could go see him, but it would be a shock and he wanted us to be prepared.

We both grimaced at the assumption that we were sisters. I left Barbara at the door of the intensive care waiting room and dragged myself to the Trans Am. A fine mist was falling, outlining street lamps with a gauzy halo. I tilted the rearview mirror so that I could see my face in the silver light. Those angular cheekbones were surely Slavic, and my eyes Tony's clear deep gray. Surely. I was surely Tony Warshawski's daughter.

The streets were slippery. I drove with extreme care, frightened of my own fatigue. Safe at home the desire for sleep consumed me like a ravening appetite. My fingers trembled on the keys with my longing for my bed.

Mr. Contreras surged into the hall when he heard me open the stairwell door. "Oh, there you are, doll. I found your cousin hanging around the entrance waiting for you, least, I don't know he was your cousin, but he explained it all, and I thought you wouldn't want him standing out there, not knowing how long it was gonna be before you came home."

"Ah, *cara cugina!*" Vico appeared behind my neighbor, but before he could launch into his recitative the chorus of dogs drowned him, barking and squeaking as they barreled past him to greet me.

I stared at him speechless.

"How are you? Your working it was good?"

"My working was difficult. I'm tired."

"So, maybe I take you to dinner, to the dancing, you are lively." He was speaking English in difference to Mr. Contreras, whose only word of Italian is "grappa."

"Dinner and dancing and I'll feel like a corpse. Why don't you go back to your hotel and let me get some sleep."

"Naturally, naturally. You are working hard all the day and I am playing. I have your—your *partitura*—"

"Score."

"*Buono.* Score. I have her. I will take her upstairs and put her away very neat for you and leave you to your resting."

"I'll take it with me." I held out my hand.

"No, no. We are leaving one big mess last night, I know that, and I am greedy last night, making you stay up when today you work. So I come with you, clean—*il disordine*—disorderliness?, then you rest without worry. You smell flowers while *I* work."

Before I could protest further he ducked back into Mr. Contreras's living room and popped out with a large portmanteau. With a flourish he extracted a bouquet of spring flowers, and the score, wrapped this time in a cream envelope, and put his arm around me to shepherd me up the stairs. The dogs and the old man followed him, all four making so much racket that the medical resident who'd moved in across the hall from Mr. Contreras came out.

"Please! I just got off a thirty-six-hour shift and I'm trying to sleep. If you can't control those damned dogs I'm going to issue a complaint to the city."

Vico butted in just as Mr. Contreras, drawing a deep breath, prepared to unleash a major aria in defense of his beloved animals. "*Mi scusa, Signora, mi scusa.* It is all my doing. I am here from Italy to meet my cousin for the first time. I am so excited I am not thinking. I am making noise, I am disturbing the rest your beautiful eyes require. . . .*"

I stomped up the stairs without waiting for the rest of the flow. Vico caught up with me as I was closing the door. "This building attracts hardworking ladies who need to sleep. Your poor neighbor. She is at a hospital where they work her night and day. What is it about America, that ladies must work so hard? I gave her some of your flowers; I knew you wouldn't mind, and they made her so happy, she will give you no more complaints about the ferocious beasts."

He had switched to Italian, much easier to understand on his lips than English. Flinging himself on the couch he launched happily into a discussion of his day with the "partitura." He had found, though our mutual acquaintance Mr. Ranier, someone who could interpret the music for him. I was right: It was from the Baroque, and not only that, most likely by Pergolesi.

"So not at all possibly by our great-grandmother. Why would your mother have a handwritten score by a composer she could find in any music store?"

I was too tired for finesse. "Vico, where were you at five this afternoon?"

He flung up his hands. "Why are you like a policeman all of a sudden, eh, *cugina?*"

"It's a question the police may ask you. I'd like to know, myself."

A wary look came into his eyes—not anger, which would have been natural, or even bewilderment—although he used the language of a puzzled man: I couldn't be jealous of him, although it was a compliment when we had only just met, so what on earth was I talking about? And why the police? But if I really wanted to know, he was downstairs, with my neighbor.

"And for that matter, Vic, where were you at five o'clock?"

"On the Kennedy Expressway. Heading toward North Harlem Avenue."

He paused a second too long before opening his hands wide again. "I don't know your city, cousin, so that tells me nothing."

"*Bene.* Thank you for going to so much trouble over the score. Now you must let me rest."

I put a hand out for it, but he ignored me and rushed over to the mound of papers we'd left in the hall last night with a cry that I was to rest, he was to work now.

He took the Pergolesi from its envelope. "The music is signed at the end, with the initials 'CF.' Who would that be?"

"Probably whoever copied it for her. I don't know."

He laid it on the bottom of the trunk and placed a stack of operas on top of it. My lips tight with anger I lifted the libretti out in order to get at the Pergolesi. Vico rushed to assist me but only succeeded in dropping everything, so that music and old papers both fluttered to the floor. I was too tired to feel anything except a tightening of the screws in my forehead. Without speaking I took the score from him and retreated to the couch.

Was this the same concerto Vico had taken with him the night before? I'd been naive to let hm walk off with a document without some kind of proper safeguard. I held it up to the light, but saw nothing remarkable in the six pages, no signs that a secret code had been erased, or brought to light, nothing beyond a few carefully corrected notes in measure 168. I turned to the end where the initials "CF" were written in the same careful black ink as the notes.

Vico must have found Fortieri's letter to my mother stuffed inside *Don Giovanni* and tracked him down. No, he'd been here at five. So the lawyer, Ranier, was involved. Vico had spent the day with him: Together they'd traced Mr. Fortieri. Vico came here for an alibi while the lawyer searched the shop. I remembered Ranier's eyes, granite chips in his soft face. He could stab an old man without a second's compunction.

Vico, a satisfied smile on his face, came to the couch for Gabriella's evening gown. "This goes on top, right, this beautiful concert dress. And now, *cugina*, all is tidy. I will leave you to your dreams. May they be happy ones."

He scooped up his portmanteau and danced into the night, blowing me a kiss as he went.

VIII

I fell heavily into sleep, and then into dreams about my mother. At first I was watching her with Mr. Fortieri as they laughed over their coffee in the little room behind the shop where McGonnigal and I had spoken. Impatient with my mother for her absorption in someone else's company I started smearing strawberry gelato over the oboe Mr. Fortieri was repairing. Bobby Mallory and John McGonnigal appeared, wearing their uniforms, and carried me away. I was screaming with rage or fear as Bobby told me my naughtiness was killing my mother.

And then suddenly I was with her in the hospital as she was dying, her dark eyes huge behind a network of tubes and bottles. She was whispering my name through her parched lips, mine and Francesca Salvini's. *"Maestra Salvini . . . nella cassa . . . Vittora, mia carissima, dale . . ."* she croaked. My father, holding her hands, demanded of me what she was saying.

I woke as I always did at this point in the dream, my hair matted with sweat. "Maestra Salvini is in the box," I had told Tony helplessly at the time. "She wants me to give her something."

I always thought my mother was struggling with the idea that her voice teacher might be dead, that that was why her letters were returned unopened. Francesca Salvini on the Voice had filled my ears from my earliest childhood. As Gabriella staged her aborted comeback, she longed to hear some affirmation from her teacher. She wrote her at her old address in Pitigliano, and in care of the Siena Opera, as well as through her cousin Frederica—not knowing that Frederica herself had died two years earlier.

Cassa—box—isn't the usual Italian word for coffin, but it could be used as a crude figure just as it is in English. It had always jarred on me to hear it from my mother—her speech was precise, refined, and she tolerated no obscenities. And as part of her last words—she lapsed into a coma later that afternoon from which she never awoke—it always made me shudder to think that was on her mind, Salvini in a box, buried, as Gabriella was about to be.

But my mother's urgency was for the pulse of life. As though she had given me explicit instructions in my sleep I rose from the bed, walked to the hall without stopping to dress, and pulled open the trunk once more. I took out everything and sifted through it over and over, but nowhere could I see the olivewood box that had held Gabriella's glasses on the voyage to America. I hunted all though the living room, and then, in desperation, went through every surface in the apartment.

I remembered the smug smile Vico had given me on his way out the door last night. He'd stuffed the box into his portmanteau and disappeared with it.

IX

Vico hadn't left Chicago, or at least he hadn't settled his hotel bill. I got into his room at the Garibaldi by calling room service from the hall phone and ordering champagne. When the service trolley appeared from the bar I followed the waiter into the elevator, saw which room he knocked on as I sauntered past him down the hall, then let myself in with my picklocks when he'd taken off again in frustration. I knew my cousin wasn't in, or at least he wasn't answering his phone—I'd already called from across the street.

I didn't try to be subtle in my search. I tossed everything from the drawers onto the floor, pulled the mattress from the bed, and pried the furniture away from the wall. Fury was making me wanton: By the time

I'd made sure the box wasn't in the room the place looked like the remains of a shipwreck.

If Vico didn't have the box he must have handed it off to Ranier. The import-export lawyer, who specialized in remarkable *objets,* doubtless knew the value of an old musical score and how to dispose of it.

The bedside clock was buried somewhere under the linens. I looked at my watch—it was past four now. I let myself out of the room, trying to decide whether Ranier would store the box at his office or his home. There wasn't any way of telling, but it would be easier to break into his office, especially at this time of day.

I took a cab to the west Loop rather than trying to drive and park in the rush-hour maelstrom. The November daylight was almost gone. Last night's mist had turned into a biting sleet. People fled for their home-bound transportation, heads bent into the wind. I paid off the cab and ran out of the ice into the Caleb Building's coffee shop to use the phone. When Ranier answered I gave myself a high nasal voice and asked for Cindy.

"She's left for the day. Who is this?"

"Amanda Parton. I'm in her book group and I wanted to know if she remembered—"

"You'll have to call her at home. I don't want this kind of personal drivel discussed in my office." He hung up.

Good, good. No personal drivel on company time. Only theft. I mixed with the swarm of people in the Caleb's lobby and rode up to the thirty-seventh floor. A metal door without any letters or numbers on it might lead to a supply closet. Working quickly, while the hall was briefly empty, I unpicked the lock. Behind lay a mass of wires, the phone and signal lines for the floor, and a space just wide enough for me to stand in. I pulled the door almost shut and stared through the crack.

A laughing group of men floated past on their way to a Blackhawks game. A solitary woman, hunched over a briefcase, scowled at me. I thought for a nervous moment that she was going to test the door, but she was apparently lost in unpleasant thoughts all her own. Finally, around six, Ranier emerged, talking in Italian with Vico. My cousin looked as debonair as ever, with a marigold tucked in his lapel. Where he'd found one in mid-November I don't know but it looked quite jaunty against his brown worsted. The fragment of conversation I caught seemed to be about a favorite restaurant in Florence, not about my mother and music.

I waited another ten minutes, to make sure they weren't standing at the elevator, or returning for a forgotten umbrella, then slipped out of the closet and down to Ranier's import-export law office. Someone leaving an adjacent firm looked at me curiously as I slid the catch back. I flashed a smile, said I hated working nights. He grunted in commiseration and went on to the elevator.

Cindy's chair was tucked against her desk, a white cardigan draped primly about the arms. I didn't bother with her area but went to work on the inner door. Here Ranier had been more careful. It took me ten minutes to undo it. I was angry and impatient and my fingers kept slipping on the hafts.

Lights in these modern buildings are set on master times for quadrants of a story, so that they all turn on or off at the same time. Outside full night had arrived; the high harsh lamps reflected my wavering outline in the black windows. I might have another hour of fluorescence flooding my search before the building masters decided most of the denizens had gone home for the day.

When I reached the inner office my anger mounted to murderous levels: My mother's olivewood box lay in pieces in the garbage. I pulled it out. They had pried it apart, and torn out the velvet lining. One shred of pale green lay on the floor. I scrabbled through the garbage for the rest of the velvet and saw a crumpled page in my mother's writing.

Gasping for air I stuck my hand in to get it. The whole wastebasket rose to greet me. I clutched at the edge of the desk but it seemed to whirl past me and the roar of a giant wind deafened me.

I managed to get my head between my knees and hold it there until the dizziness subsided. Weak from my emotional storm, I moved slowly to Ranier's couch to read Gabriella's words. The page was dated the 30th of October 1967, her last birthday, and the writing wasn't in her usual bold, upright script. Pain medication had made all her movements shaky at that point.

The letter began *"Carissima,"* without any other address, but it was clearly meant for me. My cheeks burned with embarrassment that her farewell note would be to her daughter, not her husband. "At least not to a lover, either," I muttered, thinking with more embarrassment of Mr. Fortieri, and my explicit dream.

My dearest,

I have tried to put this where you may someday find it. As you travel through life you will discard that which has no meaning for you, but I believe—hope—this box and my glasses will always stay with you in your journey. You must return this valuable score to Francesca Salvini if she is still alive. If she is dead, you must do with it as the circumstances of the time dictate to you. You must under no circumstances sell it for your own gain. If it has the value that Maestra Salvini attached to it it should perhaps be in a museum.

It hung always in a frame next to the piano in Maestra Salvini's music room, on the ground floor of her house. I went to her in the middle of the night, just before I left Italy, to bid her farewell. She feared she, too, might be arrested—she had been an uncompromising opponent of the Fascists. She gave it to me to safeguard in America, lest it fall into lesser hands, and I cannot agree to sell it only to buy medicine. So I am hiding this from your papa, who would violate my trust to feed more money to the doctors. And there is no need. Already, after all, these drugs they give me make me ill and destroy my voice. Should I use her treasure to add six months to my life, with only the addition of much more pain? You, my beloved child, will understand that that is not living, that mere survival of the organism.

Oh, my darling one, my greatest pain is that I must leave you alone in a world full of dangers and temptations. Always strive for justice, never accept the second-rate in yourself, my darling, even though you must accept it from the world around you. I grieve that I shall not live to see you grown, in your own life, but remember: *Il mio amore per te è l'amor che muove il sole e l'altre stelle.*

My love for you is the love that moves the sun and all the other stars. She used to croon that to me as a child. It was only in college I learned that Dante said it first.

I could see her cloudy with pain, obsessed with her commitment to save Salvini's music, scoring open the velvet of the box and sealing it in the belief I would find it. Only the pain and the drugs could have led her to something so improbable. For I would never have searched unless Vico had come looking for it. No matter how many times I recalled the pain of those last words, *"nella cassa,"* I wouldn't have made the connection to this box. This lining. This letter.

I smoothed the letter and put it in a flat side compartment of my case. With the sense that my mother was with me in the room some of my anger calmed. I was able to begin the search for Francesca Salvini's treasure with a degree of rationality.

Fortunately Ranier relied for security on the building's limited access: I'd been afraid he might have a safe. Instead he housed his papers in the antique credenza. Inside the original decorative lock he'd installed a small modern one, but it didn't take long to undo it. My anger at the destruction of Gabriella's box made me pleased when the picklocks ran a deep scratch across the marquetry front of the cabinet.

I found the score in a file labeled "Sestieri-Verazi." The paper was old, parchment that had frayed and discolored at the edges, and the writing on it—clearly done by hand—had faded in places to a pale brown. Scored for oboe, two horns, a violin, and a viola, the piece was eight pages long. The notes were drawn with exquisite care. On the second, third, and sixth pages someone had scribbled another set of bar lines above the horn part and written in notes in a fast careless hand, much different from the painstaking care of the rest of the score. In two places he'd scrawled "da capo" in such haste that the letters were barely distinguishable. The same impatient writer had scrawled some notes in the margin, and at the end. I couldn't read the script, although I thought it might be German. Nowhere could I find a signature on the document to tell me who the author was.

I placed the manuscript on the top of the credenza and continued to inspect the file. A letter from a Signor Arnoldo Piave in Florence introduced Vico to Ranier as someone on the trail of a valuable musical document in Chicago. Signor Ranier's help in locating the parties involved would be greatly appreciated. Ranier had written in turn to a man in Germany "well-known to interested in 18th-century musical manuscripts," to let him know Ranier might soon have something "unusual" to show him.

I had read that far when I heard a key in the outer door. The cleaning crew I could face down, but if Ranier had returned ... I swept the score from the credenza and tucked it in the first place that met my eye—behind the Modigliani that hung above it. A second later Ranier and Vico stormed into the room. Ranier was holding a pistol, which he trained on me.

"I knew it!" Vico cried in Italian. "As soon as I saw the state of my hotel room I knew you had come to steal the score."

"Steal the score? My dear Vico!" I was pleased to hear a tone of light contempt in my voice.

Vico started toward me but backed off at a sharp word from Ranier. The lawyer told me to put my hands on top of my head and sit on the couch. The impersonal chill in his eyes was more frightening than anger. I obeyed.

"Now what?" Vico demanded of Ranier.

"Now we had better take her out to—well, the place name won't mean anything to you. A forest west of town. One of the sheriff's deputies will take care of her."

There are sheriff's deputies who will do murder for hire in unincorporated parts of Cook County. My body would be found by dogs or children under a heap of rotted leaves in the spring.

"So you have Mob connections," I said in English. "Do you pay them, or they you?"

"I don't think it matters." Ranier was still indifferent. "Let's get going. ... Oh, Verazi," he added in Italian, "before we leave, just check for the score, will you?"

"What is this precious score?" I asked.

"It's not important for you to know."

"You steal it from my apartment, but I don't need to know about it? I think the state will take a different view."

Before Ranier finished another cold response Vico cried out that the manuscript was missing.

"Then search her bag," Ranier ordered.

Vico crossed behind him to snatch my case from the couch. He dumped the contents on the floor. A Shawn Colwin tape, a tampon that had come partially free of its container, loose receipts, and a handful of dog biscuits joined my work notebook, miniature camera, and binoculars in an unprofessional heap. Vico opened the case wide and shook it. The letter from my mother remained in the inner compartment.

"Where is it?" Ranier demanded.

"Don't ask, don't tell," I said, using English again.

"Verazi, get behind her and tie her hands. You'll find some rope in the bottom of my desk."

Ranier wasn't going to shoot me in his office: too much to explain to the building management. I fought hard. When Ranier kicked me in the stomach I lost my breath, though, and Vico caught my arms roughly behind me. His marigold was crushed, and he would have a black eye before tomorrow morning. He was panting with fury, and smacked me again across the face when he finished tying me. Blood dripped from my nose onto my shirt. I wanted to blot it and momentarily gave way to rage at my helplessness. I thought of Gabriella, of the love that moves the sun and all the other stars, and tried to avoid the emptiness of Ranier's eyes.

"Now tell me where the manuscript is," Ranier said in the same impersonal voice.

I leaned back in the couch and shut my eyes. Vico hit me again.

"Okay, okay," I muttered. "I'll tell you where the damned thing is. But I have one question first."

"You're in no position to bargain," Ranier intoned.

I ignored him. "Are you really my cousin?"

Vico bared his teeth in a canine grin. "Oh, yes, *cara cugina,* be assured, we are relatives. That naughty Frederica whom everyone in the family despised was truly my grandmother. Yes, she slunk off to Milan to have a baby in the slums without a father. And my mother was so impressed by her example that she did the same. Then when those two worthy women died, the one of tuberculosis, the other of excess heroin, the noble Verazis rescued the poor gutter child and brought him up in splendor in Florence. They packed all my grandmother's letters into a box and swept them up with me and my one toy, a horse that someone else had thrown in the garbage, and that my mother brought home from one of her nights out. My aunt discarded the horse and replaced it with some very hygienic toys, but the papers she stored in her attic.

"Then when my so-worthy uncle, who could never thank himself enough for rescuing this worthless brat, died, I found all my grandmother's papers. Including letters from your mother, and her plea for help in finding Francesca Salvini so that she could return this most precious musical score. And I thought, what have these Verazis ever done for me, but rubbed my nose in dirt? And you, that same beautiful blood flows in you as in them. And as in me!"

"And Claudia Fortezza, our great-grandmother? Did she write music, or was that all a fiction?"

"Oh, no doubt she dabbled in music as all the ladies in our family like to, even you, looking at that score the other night and asking me about the notation! Oh, yes, like all those stuck-up Verazi cousins, laughing at me because I'd never seen a piano before! I thought you would fall for such a tale, and it amused me to have you hunting for her music when it never existed."

His eyes glittered amber and flecks of spit covered his mouth by the time he finished. The idea that he looked like Gabriella seemed obscene. Ranier slapped him hard and ordered him to calm down.

"She wants us excited. It's her only hope for disarming me." He tapped the handle of the gun lightly on my left kneecap. "Now tell me where the score is, or I'll smash your kneecap and make you walk on it."

My hands turned clammy. "I hid it down the hall. There's a wiring closet.... The metal door near the elevators...."

"Go see," Ranier ordered Verazi.

My cousin returned a few minutes later with the news that the door was locked.

"Are you lying?" Ranier growled at me. "How did you get into it?"

"Same as into here," I muttered. "Picklocks. In my hip pocket."

Ranier had Vico take them from me, then seemed disgusted that my cousin didn't know how to use them. He decided to take me down to unlock the closet myself.

"No one's working late on this side of the floor tonight, and the cleaning staff don't arrive until nine. We should be clear."

They frog-marched me down the hall to the closet before untying my hands. I knelt to work the lock. As it clicked free Vico grabbed the door and yanked it open. I fell forward into the wires. Grabbing a large armful I pulled with all my strength. The hall turned black and an alarm began to blare.

Vico grabbed my left leg. I kicked him in the head with my right. He let go. I turned and grabbed him by the throat and pounded his head against the floor. He got hold of my left arm and pulled it free. Before he could hit me I rolled clear and kicked again at his head. I hit only air. My eyes adjusted to the dark: I could make out his shape as a darker shape against the floor, squirming out of reach.

"Roll clear and call out!" Ranier shouted at him. "On the count of five I'm going to shoot."

I dove for Ranier's legs and knocked him flat. The gun went off as he hit the floor. I slammed my fist into the bridge of his nose and he lost consciousness. Vico reached for the gun. Suddenly the hall lights came on. I blinked in the brightness and rolled toward Vico, hoping to kick the gun free before he could focus and fire.

"Enough! Hands behind your heads, all of you." It was a city cop. Behind him stood one of the Caleb's security force.

X

It didn't take me as long to sort out my legal problems as I'd feared. Ranier's claim, that I'd broken into his office and he was protecting himself, didn't impress the cops: if Ranier was defending his office why was he shooting at me out in the hall? Besides, the city cops had long had an eye on him: They had a pretty good idea he was connected to the Mob, but no real evidence. I had to do some fancy tap dancing on why I'd been in his office to begin with, but I was helped by Bobby Mallory's arrival on the scene. Assaults in the Loop went across his desk, and one with his oldest friend's daughter on the rap sheet brought him into the holding cells on the double.

For once I told him everything I knew. And for once he was not only empathetic, but helpful: He retrieved the score for me—himself—from behind the Modigliani, along with the fragments of the olivewood box. Without talking to the state's attorney, or even suggesting that it should be impounded to make part of the state's case. It was when he started blowing his nose as someone translated Gabriella's letter for him—he didn't trust me to do it myself—that I figured he'd come through for me.

"But what is it?" he asked, when he'd handed me the score.

I hunched a shoulder. "I don't know. It's old music that belonged to my mother's voice teacher. I figure Max Loewenthal can sort it out."

Max is the executive director of Beth Israel, the hospital where Lotty Herschel is chief of perinatology, but he collects antiques and knows a lot about music. I told him the story later that day and gave the score to him. Max is usually imperturbably urbane, but when he inspected the music his face flushed and his eyes glittered unnaturally.

"What is it?" I cried.

"If it's what I think—no, I'd better not say. I have a friend who can tell us. Let me give it to her."

Vico's blows to my stomach made it hard for me to move, otherwise I might have started pounding on Max. The glitter in his eyes made me demand a receipt for the document before I parted with it.

At that his native humor returned. "You're right, Victoria: I'm not immune from cupidity. I won't abscond with this, I promise, but maybe I'd better give you a receipt just the same."

XI

It was two weeks later that Max's music expert was ready to give us a verdict. I figured Bobby Mallory and Barbara Carmichael deserved to hear the news firsthand, so I invited them all to dinner, along with Lotty. Of course, that meant I had to include Mr. Contreras and the dogs. My neighbor decided the occasion was important enough to justify digging his one suit out of mothballs.

Bobby arrived early, with his wife, Eileen, just as Barbara showed up. She told me her father had recovered sufficiently from his attack to be revived from his drug-induced coma, but he was still too weak to answer questions. Bobby added that they'd found a witness to the forced entry of Fortieri's house. A boy hiding in the alley had seen two men going in through the back. Since he was smoking a reefer behind a garage he hadn't come forward earlier, but when John McGonnigal assured him they didn't care about his dope—this one time—he picked Ranier's face out of a collection of photos.

"And the big guy promptly donated his muscle to us—a part-time deputy, who's singing like a bird, on account of he's p-o'd about being fingered." He hesitated, then added, "If you won't press charges they're going to send Verazi home, you know."

I smiled unhappily. "I know."

Eileen patted his arm. "That's enough shop for now. Victoria, who is it who's coming tonight?"

Max rang the bell just then, arriving with both Lotty and his music expert. A short skinny brunette, she looked like a street urchin in her jeans and outsize sweater. Max introduced her as Isabel Thompson, an authority on rare music from the Newberry Library.

"I hope we haven't kept dinner waiting—Lotty was late getting out of surgery," Max added.

"Let's eat later," I said. "Enough suspense. What have I been lugging unknowing around Chicago all this time?"

"She wouldn't tell us anything until you were here to listen," Max said. "So we are as impatient as you."

Ms. Thompson grinned. "Of course, this is only a preliminary opinion, but it looks like a concerto by Marianne Martines."

"But the insertions, the writing at the end," Max began, when Bobby demanded to know who Marianne Martines was.

"She was an eighteenth-century Viennese composer. She was known to have written over four hundred compositions, but only about sixty have survived, so it's exciting to find a new one." She folded her hands in her lap, a look of mischief in her eyes.

"And the writing, Isabel?" Max demanded.

She grinned. "You were right, Max: It is Mozart's. A suggestion for changes in the horn line. He started to describe them, then decided just to write them in above her original notation. He added a reminder that the two were going to play together the following Monday—they often played piano duets, sometimes privately, sometimes for an audience."

"Hah! I knew it! I was sure!" Max was almost dancing in ecstasy. "So I put some Krugs down to chill. Liquid gold to toast the moment I held in my hand a manuscript that Mozart held."

He pulled a couple of bottles of champagne from his briefcase. I fetched my mother's Venetian glasses from the dining room. Only five remained whole of the eight she had transported so carefully. One had shattered in the fire that destroyed my old apartment, and another when some thugs broke into it one night. A third had been repaired and could still be used. How could I have been so careless with my little legacy?

"But whose is it now?" Lotty asked, when we'd all drunk and exclaimed enough to calm down.

"That's a good question," I said. "I've been making some inquiries through the Italian government. Francesca Salvini died in 1943 and she didn't leave any heirs. She wanted Gabriella to dispose of it in the event of her death. In the absence of a formal will the Italian government might make a claim, but her intention as expressed in Gabriella's letter might give me the right to it, as long as I didn't keep it or sell it just for my own gain."

"We'd be glad to house it," Ms. Thompson offered.

"Seems to me your ma would have wanted someone in trouble to benefit." Bobby was speaking gruffly to hide his embarrassment. "What's something like this worth?"

Ms. Thompson pursed her lips. "A private collector might pay a quarter of a million. We couldn't match that, but we'd probably go to a hundred or hundred and fifty thousand."

"So what mattered most to your ma, Vicki, besides you? Music. Music and victims of injustice. You probably can't do much about the second, but you ought to be able to help some kids learn some music."

Barbara Carmichael nodded in approval. "A scholarship fund to provide Chicago kids with music lessons. It's a great idea, Vic."

We launched the Gabriella-Salvini program some months later with a concert at the Newberry. Mr. Fortieri attended, fully recovered from his wounds. He told me that Gabriella had come to consult him the summer before she died, but she hadn't brought the score with her. Since she'd never mentioned it to him before he thought her illness and medications had made her delusional.

"I'm sorry, Victoria: it was the last time she was well enough to travel to the northwest side, and I'm sorry that I disappointed her. It's been troubling me ever since Barbara told me the news."

I longed to ask him whether he'd been my mother's lover. But did I want to know? What if he, too, had moved the sun and all the other stars for her—I'd hate to know that. I sent him to a front-row chair and went to sit next to Lotty.

In Gabriella's honor the Cellini Wind Ensemble had come from London to play the benefit. They played the Martines score first as the composer had written it, and then as Mozart revised it. I have to confess I liked the original better, but as Gabriella often told me, I'm no musician.

Peter Crowther is adept at writing in many genres of fiction, including fantasy and science fiction. His short fiction can also be found in *White House Horrors, Cat Crimes III,* and *Careless Whispers.* His mystery novels and short stories usually involve Koko Tate, the New York City, based private eye. Here Koko investigates a crime that affects him and his family most of all.

Keepsakes
PETER CROWTHER

The man stared at me, checking me over.

He looked like he'd been made by a poorly coordinated kid who got bored easy and had no sense of design. He was carrying about thirty pounds more than he should, stood around six foot in shoes, and his general demeanour was a complex mixture of hard and soft, aggression and compassion, warmth and coolness. His disarming and yet authoritative air probably made people forgive him almost anything. Almost.

The face itself was straight from *Sesame Street,* shaped over time by fist, blackjack, the occasional knife and even a razor or two . . . plus other assorted objects. It was a thick wedge of tan skin-coloured modelling clay with two bushy, almost-Neanderthal brows—a bullet had burned a gap in the right one—and large green-brown eyes, bordered by lines and underscored with overnight bags. Right now, the eyes were narrowed tightly, appraising me.

This was a curious man.

Above the eyes was a thick tuft of sagebrush hair, cut unfashionably short and so black it was almost purple. On one cheek was a small dark circle which looked like stubble missed by the morning shave. It was actually a healed-over bullet hole. Below it, and to the side, his lips looked like they were welded together so they'd never smile. But that was just a pose, and one of many. Perfectly on cue he allowed a small smile. This was not a man to do what was expected of him.

He wore a brown Polo shirt beneath a light-green tweed sportscoat, beige canvas pants and a pair of lace-up sensible brogue shoes, thick-soled and bearing the soft look that shoe leather can only get over years of painstaking cleaning and polishing. He lifted one leg so that the sock became exposed. It was bright yellow with green vertical flashes.

This man was not a slave to fashion.

We'd known each other a long time, him and me. I was used to him, familiar with his ways and always comfortable with his decisions. I bent down and hoisted up my travel bag. He did the same. He also copied me when I checked my side pocket for my car keys, my inside pocket for my wallet and my holster for my .38. What else does any man need?

I checked behind me in the room to see if I'd left anything. I hadn't. I turned back in time to see him turning back from checking *his* room. It looked a lot like mine. He looked a lot like me. I had one advantage though: When I looked at him, I saw only what I wanted to see. When he looked at me, he saw the truth.

But out of all the similarities, the reflected echoes, we did have one very important thing in common: Our mom loved us. And we loved our mom.

It was only three weeks since Easter but already the threat of New York summer hung heavy in the air, its muggy ninety-degree days sending out an advance guard of thin whispy tendrils of heat, snaking along the sidewalks by the delis and the art shops, and in the park beside the bushes and around the bandshell.

I felt a mixture of excitement and apprehension. The excitement came from the prospect of leaving the city for a few days, the apprehension from spending those few days with my mom. When I looked at my other self, I saw that the guy in the mirror showed only the apprehension, carved deep in a long line across his forehead. As I watched, he relaxed. Gave me a smile that said, *It'll be okay.* Maybe it would. I took a final look around the apartment and walked out, slamming the door. Hard.

Out in the street, my Toyota waited, breathless, ready to move. I threw in my bag and my jacket, unclipped my holster and tossed it onto the passenger seat, climbed in behind the wheel. We set off, man and machine—both sluggish at first—heading for Broadway and parts beyond.

It was one of those days when I wished I had a convertible, but I made the Toyota into the next best thing and rolled down all the windows. The finishing touch was a cassette of Vivaldi's *The Four Seasons* ... all I needed now was Alan Alda sitting beside me and we'd be fine.

Broadway parallels the Hudson River and, if you ever want to go north out of New York, it's the best route of escape ... straight, colorful and interesting. I crossed the Harlem into the Bronx, drove past Van Cortlandt Park into Yonkers and the start of Westchester County. Somewhere over left of me, fortunes were being made and lost, and reputations manipulated, along the lush tees of St. Andrews. Golf had never been a game I could come to terms with but it ranked second against Big Business. Maybe the two of them deserved each other.

Along the way, Broadway changes its name a few times—Albany Post Road and U.S. 9 being the most common—but it will always be Broadway to me.

The Toyota had got its wind now and it gulped both the oncoming countrified air and the endless blacktop with impressive ease. I leaned my arm out of the window and enjoyed the flattening landscape and the lush compositions of Vivaldi as we moved through small towns whose names ended with on-Hudson—Hastings, Ardsley and Croton—over the Tappan Zee Bridge and into whimsical Tarrytown, one time home of Washington Irving.

From there into Ossining where, glancing across at the ghost town of Sing Sing, I turned down the sound to see if I could hear the spectral echoes of metal mugs on steel bars that so characterised the old prison-break movies. But there was only the soft soughing of the wind and the smells of defeat, failure and incarceration.

Before long, following State 9D, we drifted through Garrison, Boscobel and Cold Spring. For old times' sakes, I stopped the car in Cold Springs and, amidst the heady perfume of roses—maybe more imagined than real—I thought of Mom and Dad and, more recently, of Philippa Tamidge and Rodney Millerchap. I made a mental note to bring Ella Thornley out here sometime.

When I got back to the car, I had butterflies in my stomach.

Back on the road, we re-joined U.S.9 into Rhinebeck before branching off onto State 9G—less traffic, nearer the river and air redolent with the smell of apples. I stopped at a little roadstand and bought a bag from a towheaded kid, dressed in faded denims and sporting the biggest booger of dried snot on his top lip that I'd ever seen. "You ought to see about getting that amputated," I said. Who needed Alan Alda?

"Huh?" he said.

"Doesn't matter," I told him, taking the apples. I held out a five-dollar bill and he snatched it, keeping his eyes on me all the time. Those same eyes looked set to fall right out of his head when I waved away his offer of change. Koko Tate, Big Spender.

Munching my McIntosh, I drove on through Hudson itself, switched to State 9J to keep next to the river, and onwards to Kinderhook, Resselaer and the dusty state capital, Albany. Out of Albany and into Troy—where, sparing a thought for Herman Melville, I bellowed "Thar she blows!" out of the window, scaring an old man who was busy scything his lawn out of any growing he still had left to do—then onto U.S. 4 back over the Hudson into Waterford and across the Mohawk to Cohoes. By this time, the butterflies in my stomach had put on boots and were busy working out to Michael Jackson.

Crescent road followed the Mohawk through Crescent, Vischer Ferry and Rexford, then it became State 146 and took us on into Niskayuna and Schenectady.

Our destination.

Schenectady is home to two formidable institutions: General Electric's research and development center and my mom.

Although New York's heartland is generally considered to begin west of the industrial triangle of Albany, Troy and Schenectady, north of the Catskills and south of the Adirondacks, there's still a lot of small-town soul in Schenectady itself ... along with some of the prettiest picket-fenced smallholdings you'll see this side of a Rockwell calendar or the pages of an old Archie comic book. Eleanor Alice Tate lived at one of them, 421 Fenimore Street.

I pulled the Toyota up against her front lawn and turned off the engine. The car breathed a clink of relief and began to settle itself onto its chassis for a well-earned rest. I got out and stretched, winding my head around to bring some feeling back into my shoulders, breathing in the heady scent of roses and night stocks that wouldn't even begin doing their real work until the sun went down and the air cooled off. Just as I was thinking of opening the back door and getting my jacket, the little old lady that used to protect Tweety and smack Sylvestor with a broom walked out onto the step of the house, holding the screen door ajar with her shoulder and wiping her hands on a blue-and-yellow floral apron. Shielding her eyes with her right hand, she stared at me across the grass. "Koko?"

"Hi, Mom," I shouted. The butterflies had tuned in to a metal-rock station. I walked towards her, the years falling away from me with every step, the sounds of the Toyota's hot metal ticking behind me, the gentle breeze lifting the branches of a huge sycamore that probably looked down in the same benevolent way when the American Locomotive Company opened for business back in 1851. Two houses along, a guy in a Hawaiian shirt stopped mowing his lawn and leaned on the machine handle.

The smell of freshly cut grass drifted across and around me and, by the time I got up to her, I was 14 years old, knees scuffed and hands dirty, looking behind her small frame for a sign of Dad standing in the doorway, rolled-up copy of *The New York Times* grasped firmly in one hand. But he didn't appear. I hadn't seen him—except in my dreams and one time during a scary hypnotism session with Jim Garnett—since 1972 when we'd lad him to rest in a small graveyard in Lawnswood where, on a still clear night, you could hear the shouts of kids reaching for the brass rings on the Palisades rides and smell the sweet, cloying drift of cotton candy.

My mom took hold of my arms and held me there, eyes moistening.

Behind me, the guy in the shirt started up his mower. She shook her head and when she spoke it was with a mixture of pride and loss, her voice shaky and unsure. "Koko," she said, "it's real good to see you."

"You too, Mom," I said, and I bent forward and hugged her to me and bit my lip to stop from crying, squeezing my eyes tightly closed and breathing in her smells so that I could call on them those times when I felt scared or lonely. She patted my back and shook her head again, pushing me back to arms' length and taking another look. "My, but you're so *tall*," she said with just a hint of a smile.

"Six feet is all, Mom," I said, "same as ever."

She nodded her head and then lifted a hand to tuck a strand of hair beneath a silver clip. "It's me, I guess. Shrinking," she said. Then, with a dismissive wave, "Go get your things, now. I've got hot blueberry muffins and a fresh pot of coffee."

"Hot dog," I said, immediately wondering where those words had come from, and I jogged back, up through the years, to the disappointment of adulthood and the promise of decay and obsolescence offered by my slumbering Toyota.

As THE AFTERNOON DRIFTED into early evening and the first night flies took to the air waves, my mom and I brought each other up to date with news and stories, rediscovering each other again after long months of unnecessary separation.

I told her about "Lonesome" Pines—missing out the shooting—and Philippa Tamidge, and about the Bible murder and my trip down to Louisiana with Jeff Sandusky. She liked that story a lot, always having been partial to cats. I didn't tell her about the little old ladies from last Christmas. Too close to home.

And as she stood at her sink, washing our plates and cups and staring out into the colours of the evening, I told her about Ella Thornley, and about how much she'd like her. My mom told me that Ella sounded just fine and that I had to bring her up to visit. In her voice I could hear her silent prayers that God should keep me well and make me settle down and marry and, maybe, just so's she could see them one time, bless me and this Ella Thornley with kids that could run bare-assed through the long grasses that she still thought existed off the main roads of New York City.

Sitting in Dad's old chair, smoking a stale Pall Mall from a pack that Mom kept around for emergencies, I flicked through an old copy of *Vogue*. Mom turned on a side lamp and settled down into the chair next to me, picked up her sewing. I felt like I was in an off-Broadway play, maybe something by Arthur Miller, set back in the mid-1950s. We were building up to moving into the second stage of our conversations when the knock on the door interrupted the thought flows.

"Just hold a minute," Mom said, straining out of the chair. "Now who could that be at this time?" she muttered, aside to me. I watched her walk to the door, arthritis pulling her knees outwards, and wondered where all the time had gone.

She pulled the door open and gave a small yelp of delight. "Tyrone Daniels, what are you doing out here at this time?"

A tall, thin man in his late fifties ambled through into the living room, nodding to Mom and smiling across at me. "I couldn't get out here until now, Eleanor, I truly am sorry."

Mom waved him nevermind.

"We had all manner of things going on today and I did promise I'd get out here and talk to you about the missing hosepipe and . . ." Tyrone Daniels let his voice drift and fixed his eyes on me the way any lawman would.

"This is my son, Koko," Mom said grandly. "Koko, this is Tyrone."

I nodded and held out a hand. "Tyrone, how you doing?"

He took it and shook it hard. "Doing just fine," he said, "just fine." He removed his hand and jammed it into his jacket pocket. "Koko you say?" he said to Mom.

"It's short for Kokorian," I explained over Mom's nod. "Mom always wanted me to be a ballet dancer, but I never did make it."

"Oh, Koko!" she said with a laugh, and struggled back to her chair, landing with a *plump* and a sigh into the cushions.

Tyrone Daniels gave out the kind of smile that people reserve for when they don't know what the hell's going on. I shook my head and waved him free.

"Sit down, Tyrone," Mom said. She turned around to me and said, "Tyrone works out at the sheriff's office."

'Oh?" I said, like I hadn't already guessed. The big man nodded and sat on the edge of a high-backed chair. "What you been doing, Mom? Not speeding again?"

"Land sakes, no," she said, treating me to another of those old-time phrases—like "Gee" and "Swell"—that have all but disappeared . . . though nobody knows why. Mom shook her head, allowed her beaming smile to spread still further across her face and pushed her glasses further back on her nose.

"There's been a whole spate of burglaries along this road, Mr. Tate," Tyrone Daniels said.

"That's Koko," I corrected.

He smiled and gave a quick nod.

"Burglaries? You didn't mention this to me, Mom."

"Didn't see that I needed to, son. They didn't get away with much at all, just some old hosepipe I had curled up outside the back porch."

"Any ideas on who was responsible?"

"Kids most likely," Daniels said in an easy voice that covered up his strength and sharpness admirably. I was impressed. "Stole junk and bric-a-brac mostly," he went on. "No offence, Eleanor."

Mom shook her head and resumed her sewing. "None taken, Tyrone."

"Junk? Like what?"

"Well, your mom's hosepipe, some barbecue equipment—tools and the like, you know—a couple of garden pixies from Mrs. Berryman's place . . ." Mom sniggered and Tyrone shot her a glance before continuing. "A garden fork left out overnight . . . that kind of thing. Nothing important but it's just the fact that there's someone prowling around that . . . well, it just causes folks some discomfort."

"When was this, Mom?"

"Couple of nights ago, now. It's not all that important, now, so stop your worrying," she said, patting my arm. Then to Tyrone, "I'm really grateful you came around, Tyrone, but everything's all right now Koko's here."

I flexed my muscles and put on one of my toughest expressions. "Koko Tate, scourge of pixie thieves!" The lawman laughed dutifully.

"So what line of business you in?" he said, getting to his feet. "Seeing as how you didn't make the Bolshoi."

"Same as you," I said, "but private."

"A pee eye, huh." He didn't sound impressed. Nobody ever did. "How's it pay?"

I shrugged. "I eat every other day and sleep at the Y on Saturdays. What was it the animals used to say on *The Flintstones?* 'It's a living!' "

"Yeah, right," he said. He didn't know what the hell I was talking about. He turned to my mom and gave her the big warm smile he had so successfully kept from me. "You let me know if you hear anything now, Eleanor," he said, "and keep those doors locked." Mom started to get out of the chair but stopped when he placed a firm hand on her shoulder. "I'll see myself out." He turned around and walked to the door. "Good meeting you, Mr. Tate," he said.

"You too, Tyrone," I answered. I walked over to him and pulled open the door, walked out onto the step with him. He paused and looked up into the steadily darkening sky. "Gonna be another hot one," he said.

I followed his gaze . . . Fredric March and Spencer Tracy out on the front porch in *Inherit the Wind.* "Yep," I said, fighting off the need to hitch up my pants. "Looks that way."

"You staying long?"

"Over the weekend," I said. "Mother's Day."

"Right. My mom died few years back." I nodded and just managed to stop from telling him I was sorry to hear that. "Well, gotta get along now." He ambled off across the grass towards a waiting Dodge Rambler with its sides on. "Be seeing you."

I waited until he got into his car and gave a wave as he pulled off. Somewhere up behind the nighttime clouds, a god that must've had a soft spot for Steven Spielberg sent a comet searing across the treetops on the other side of the road, flying high enough to make Toledo. Its trail flashed bright and then disappeared, leaving a dark scratch, like a kid's uneven scrawl or an old woman's signature, etched on the blackness.

When I looked down and turned around, the guy in the Hawaiian shirt was watching me, standing out on the sidewalk smoking a cigarette. I nodded to him. "Hello there."

"Hello yourself," he said. "You Ellie's boy?"

"I guess so," I laughed, "but 'boy' might be a bit ambitious." I held out my hand and walked over to him. "Koko Tate," I said.

He took the hand, limply, held it for a second or two, like it was fresh dog turd, and then let it drop. "Jerry Parmenter. So how's she doing?"

"My mom? She's doing just fine far as I can make out. But maybe it's me should be asking you."

"Me? Hell, we never hardly see hide nor hair of Ellie. Keeps herself to herself," he said, pulling on his cigarette. "And that's just fine with me's what I say." He raised his eyebrows and nodded at me, as if to say it was a pity more folks along the street didn't follow my mom's example.

"Yeah," I said, mainly because I couldn't think of anything else to say, and looked around at the street and my Toyota. "It sure is quiet along here."

He pulled again on the cigarette and threw it to the grass, ground it in with his foot and blew out a cloud of smoke. "We were worried about her a while back, me and Doreen—Doreen's my wife."

I smiled. "Worried?"

"Yeah, she didn't seem herself."

"How's that?"

"Oh, I don't know." He pulled a bent-looking pack of Kool out of his shirt pocket and shook one out. I didn't even know they still made menthol cigarettes. He put his cigarette in his mouth and said, "Walking around the lawn late at night, muttering . . . like she was talking to somebody." He looked sheepish, embarrassed to be telling me this about my mother.

I glanced back at my mom's house, saw the curtain twitch at the window. "How late is late?"

"This time, maybe a little later. I always come out round about now. For a smoke, you know? Doreen, she doesn't like me smoking in the house."

"She do it often?"

"Most every night," he said emphatically.

"When was the last time?"

He frowned. "Night before last, I think."

"Well, I'm grateful for you telling me, Jerry. I don't see how there's a whole lot I can do about it but I do appreciate you telling me."

"Where're you from ... Koko?"

"New York City. Born and bred. Mom moved a few years after dad died."

"You staying long?"

"Just over Mother's Day, going back Monday morning."

He threw the cigarette down on top of the first one, ground it in the same way. "Well, gotta be getting back. Only supposed to have one." He slapped the pack of Kool through his shirt pocket like a teenager checking his trusty Trojans. "You give her my best, now," he said as he walked across the grass to his house.

"Will do," I shouted after him. When I turned around, the curtain twitched again.

Back inside the house, Mom was making a fresh pot of coffee and there was a plate of cookies all laid out on the table. "Who was that?" she said.

"One of your neighbors, Jerry Parmenter."

She sniffed her disapproval. "He's new. Been here around four months ... never speaks to me, neither him nor Doreen—she's his wife."

"I know."

"You shake his hand?"

I laughed. "Like a dog's paw."

She joined in with the laughter. "He's out there every single night, smoking those mint cigarettes." She tutted and stirred the coffee. "You'd never catch anyone who was anyone smoking those things."

Mom had always been the ad man's dream come true. For most things, but particularly for cigarettes. She smoked Chesterfield because Ronald Reagan said he sent all his friends a box at Christmas and then Luckies when Marlene Dietrich advertised them in the early fifties. It was Camel when John Wayne told the nation "It's kind of gratifying to see that *my* cigarette is America's choice, too," then Philip Morris when Lucy Ball told everyone to "Call for Philip Morris." Mom stayed with Philip Morris right up until Lucy and Desi got their divorce, then switched back to Chesterfield when they advertised that they were actually air-softened and because the ads said that two out of every three smokers smoked them. Now she smoked hardly any at all and she only bought what was cheapest in the store.

"He say anything about me?" She handed me a pot of steaming coffee that smelled strong enough to climb right out and walk around the floor.

I took the coffee and frowned, shook my head thoughtfully. "Uh, he said for me to give you his best." I slipped.

"Mmmm." She flopped into her chair and winced in pain.

"Bad?"

"They're always bad around nighttime, honey. There's not a single thing you can do about it." She rubbed her swollen knee joints tenderly and I felt suddenly sorry that she had to do it for herself. No one around to give her sympathy, show her affection, tell her she looked nice.

"You look great in that dress, mom," I said.

"This?!" she took hold of the collar like it was an old sooty rag, and laughed a short sharp snort. But deep down, I knew, she liked me saying.

I NEVER SLEEP LATE.

So it was a surprise to find it was almost 10 o'clock when I came downstairs in the morning, the house silent and empty, a bowl and packet of Cheerios left out on the table for me. A note in Mom's careful hand said she'd gone out to church and would be back around 11:30.

The slowed-down country air had furred my head cogs and left me feeling thick, couldn't-care-less and young. I wandered around the rooms rediscovering pieces of my youth, all preserved just the way I remembered them. My heart ached with the memories and the silence. I felt like I was waiting for something to happen.

I went down to the Toyota and brought up the flowers and candies I'd bought before I left New York, put them out on the table so she'd see them as soon as she walked in the house. Then I decided to cut the grass. Out in the garage, jammed down behind the mower, is where I saw the hosepipe. To one side of it were too brightly colored pixies that could have been identical twins. Behind an old washtub cabinet that I remembered Dad taking the mechanical guts out of I found the pitchfork. Everything else was there, too. It seemed like I could solve cases without even trying.

By the time she got home, I'd finished the grass and used the telephone. The first thing I said to her when she walked in was, "Happy Mother's Day, Mom." The second was, "Cute move stealing your own hosepipe. The last person to be a suspect is one of the victims."

Her mouth dropped open, then snapped shut. Years tumbled down out of the ceiling and landed squarely on her shoulders, bending her almost double by the time she'd made it to the chair.

I lifted the flowers and placed them on her lap, gave her a big kiss on the cheek and knelt beside her. "You want to tell me about it?"

The world has a lot of sights that just take hold of your heart and wring the life right out of it. One of the worst of those is seeing your mom cry. Only seniority can truly console and when you get on up towards seventy years old, there's not too many folks left around who qualify for the task. She sobbed and shook her head, holding onto her flowers like a mother with her baby. Which made an awful lot of sense.

"You feeling lonely out here?"

The tears subsided a little and she nodded. "Very," she said, making such a short simple word into a huge weight of despair.

"So you took the things to draw attention to yourself."

She looked at me in horror. "No! I did no such thing. I didn't want people to know it was me."

I stroked her arm and shook my head. "No, I know you didn't want people to know it was you, but, deep down, maybe you thought they'd find out. Then wonder why you did such a thing."

"No, it wasn't a cry for help, son." She gave the phrase a dose of disdain and licked her lips. "They were keepsakes."

"Keepsakes?"

"Yes, mementoes of life I suppose."

I watched her face, waiting for it to make some sense to me.

"The pixies and the barbecue things . . . they're all things that people have, that people make a noise around. I guess I just wanted to bring some of that life inside." Her face was bright now, animated with trying to make me see. "There's no life around me anymore. Everything's so still and so slow, everybody treats me so soft and gentle . . . I don't want that, Koko. I remember the days when . . . when everything was so active around me." Her eyes misted up again and I held onto her hand tighter now. When she spoke again it was so soft I almost couldn't hear her. "I miss him so much, son," she said. "I get so lonely."

"I know, Mom, I know."

The knock came right before the door opened and Tyrone Daniels stood there, a sky-gray Stetson Whippet clasped tightly in his hand, a big beaming Sunday smile on his face. When he saw Mom his smile dropped.

"It's okay, Tyrone," I said, "she hates it when I give her things."

Tyrone looked a little confused and cleared his throat. "I just came to say I got all the things back to their owners, Koko."

I squeezed Mom's hand twice. "Glad to hear it. You figure you'll ever catch who left the stuff over in those bushes?"

He shook his head. "Kids. Like I said. Leastways nothing was broken."

"Yeah, nothing was broken." I stood up and moved towards the door.

"I just came around to thank you again, Koko," he said, following me. "Seems like we country folks could learn a thing or two from you big city slickers."

I smiled awkwardly and slowly pushed the screen door open.

"Well, you take care now, Eleanor," he said over his shoulder, and I saw Mom's eyes twinkle in surprise. "I'll be in touch Monday or Tuesday. There's a recital at the church on Thursday, thought you'd like to go. I'll give you a call. Thought you might be lonely when Koko goes back."

Mom nodded in amazement.

I followed Tyrone outside where it had started to rain. I'd cut the grass just in time. Halfway down the path, he said, "How was I?"

"Don't give up the day job."

He sniggered.

"You laid on the country bumpkin act with a trowel," I said. "And what the hell are city *clickers*?"

"Huh?"

Maybe he hadn't laid it on all that much.

Waving him off, relishing the refreshing coolness of the rain on my head and shoulders, I felt undeniably good. The first warmth of the year's summer. Mom would never know that I had told Tyrone Daniels the truth, told him what she'd done and what I believed had caused her to do it. That was the *real* present right there. Real presents aren't always things you can see or buy, like candies and flowers . . . they're things you *know,* and things you *do.*

I turned around just in time to see the garish strains of a Hawaiian shirt disappear into mom's house.

When I got back inside, she was pouring hot water into three mugs. The cookies were already laid out on a plate and Jerry Parmenter was halfway through his first Kool.

Before I got the chance to say anything, Mom said, "Jerry asked if he could duck in here for a cigarette. Doreen doesn't like him smoking in the house."

"Yeah," I said.

"It's raining," Jerry Parmenter said.

"Yeah," I said again.

"I told him it was okay to call in any time, particularly when it's raining. I love the smell of tobacco."

I looked across at the man with the dullest handshake this side of a cemetery and saw him wink at me. Some neighbours are like that. They don't miss a trick. He'd seen Tyrone Daniels and me loading the things into Tyrone's trunk, put two and two together.

Mom handed out the mugs of coffee and plopped into her chair. She looked as fresh as mountain air. "We'll just drink this down and then I'll fix us some lunch," she said, taking a sip.

"And I'll just have another cigarette," Jerry Parmenter said. "You want to try one of these?" he asked my mom, holding the pack of Kool out to her.

Mom reached for them and looked up at me with that old mischievous gleam. "Mmm, menthol. Don't mind if I do, thank you."

Jerry Parmenter lifted his mug towards the ceiling. "Here's to mothers . . . everywhere," he announced.

"Amen to that," I said, hoisting my own mug into the air.

My mom laughed her *aw, shucks* laugh, and the sound of it made the world smile.

Carole Nelson Douglas is the author of more than thirty novels, covering such diverse genres as mainstream, historical, mystery, and science fiction. Her rise in the mystery field began with her quartet of historical mysteries featuring Irene Adler, the female counterpart to Sherlock Holmes, and the only character to outwit him. Recently, her novel series involving the feline detective Midnight Louie has been occupying her time, but not enough that she can't turn out first-rate stories like this one.

Dirty Dancing
CAROLE NELSON DOUGLAS

The orange flyer featured drawings of balloons, cocktail glasses, and confetti, its centerpiece a crude picture of a fifties-vintage convertible. Words angled here and there: "Drinks" "Dancing" "Disco."

" 'Portnoy's.' Sounds like a place my kids would go against my best advice," I complained when the girls at work flourished the flyer for the monthly employees' club outing. "What is it?"

"Oh, a singles' bar, really," said Mary Lou, "but our group booked it earlier in the evening, before the rush." She is an outgoing bottle redhead who is becoming pleasantly plump now that menopause has come and gone. "It'll be fun. They have a huge buffet, and drinks, of course, and pool tables and stuff."

"Sounds like a blast," Connie said, her choice of words revealing her own fifties generation and taking me back to my single years, which had suddenly come again.

Connie was younger than Mary Lou and I, a thin, forbidding-looking fashion plate who was actually a cream puff at heart.

"Why not the usual daytime outing?" I wondered. "I don't even know what to wear to that kind of place."

"Oh, we'll dress up, I imagine," said Mary Lou. "You know, something middle-aged-respectable but a little kicky. Listen, we old broads would never dare go to a place like that if it weren't under company auspices. Some guy in accounting is program chair and he set it up. We can see how the aerobic set lives."

"You make it sound like a strip bar," I fussed. My upbringing always inclined me to step wide around the unrespectable.

"It's not," Mary Lou assured me. "My kids have been there. Do you think I'd let them go anyplace tacky?"

I wasn't keen on going to a place that appealed to my friends' kids: Unlike many parents, I knew that kids like to do things that their parents would never approve of.

But I'd never missed a company outing, so I went.

I didn't expect to be nervous, any more than I had expected to be suddenly single. And I know I'm out of touch with the modern-day cult of the deliberately crass, but the smooth, unexceptional course of my life has isolated me from the ruder realities. I grew up in the Midwest, and attended college long enough to acquire a degree and a fiancé.

His name was Jim, and he was, of course, a gentleman.

We had two children, who never gave us more than the expected minor trouble. When they were both in high school, I entered the working world. College loomed, and while Jim was doing well working for the city, additional income was nothing to sniff at. Besides, we wanted other things than the necessities; we weren't getting any younger.

I was as giddy as a girl graduate to win my first paid position at a large bank in town, and while the ins and outs of finance are more arcane than most, I thrived on the challenge and a new circle of work friends, many women like myself, either single parents or working wives.

Despite one or two women vice presidents—who avoided fraternizing with the other women employees, not wanting to be mistaken for less than what they were—women filled most of the firm's support jobs and had the sort of easy camaraderie that made going to work stimulating.

The kids moved on to college in that smooth slipstream all middle-class families dream of. Everything was wonderful. Jim and I were even planning a modest cruise for Christmas.

Then he died. Suddenly, at work. I was notified at my desk, but my rush to the hospital was a mere formality. The heart attack had been unheralded and immediate.

At fifty-two, I was a widow, a bewildered widow who'd had no warning. Everything I'd done, everything I'd assumed, had been Jim and I. Now "I" was at sea. The cruise seemed pointless, although the kids urged me to go anyway. The kids were always urging me to do something atypical after Jim died, as if they worried that I would wither if not exposed to stimuli.

Work proved to be a blessing, of course, especially my women co-workers. Women form a certain sisterhood because of the unspoken fact that they expect to last the longest, and live alone the longest.

So Mary Lou and Connie, my middle-aged girlfriends, made sure I went now and then to movies I didn't really like, and out shopping for clothes, and to the monthly office outings.

We met at Connie's house at seven-thirty, then she drove us in her Taurus to the highway that looped the city. We moved through a river of black asphalt shimmering with the head- and taillights of heavy traffic.

"I had no idea the Loop was so clogged this far past rush hour," I said from the front passenger seat.

"You've been in a rut, Linda." Mary Lou, in the backseat, sat forward to talk to me, bracing her hand on Connie's headrest. "This section of the Loop is teeming with superstores and trendy restaurants. That's a pretty dress; where did you get it?"

"Mallow's." I touched the full chiffon skirt figured in a floral swirl of dusky rose, purple, and green. "I bought it for the cruise."

They were silent for a bit. I noticed the streetlights glinting off of Mary Lou's wedding ring as we passed under them. I still wore mine, of course; it had never occurred to me to take it off.

Portnoy's announced itself with racy outlines of red and lavender neon. Except for that garish decoration, it resembled the nearby upscale franchise restaurants that squatted on black islands of asphalt parking lots all along the freeway—a one-story sprawling building tricked out with ersatz Art Deco architectural details. The facade's wavy glass block windows reflected the red neon, making it look as if bloody, agitated water washed against them.

Inside the place was dim and barnlike, the bar a neon-outlined altar winking with glassware and bottles. A wooden dance floor adjoined the bar, and the only other seating was the far banquettes that rimmed the perimeter and a few tiny round tables on stilts.

I recognized a sprinkle of faces there as we headed for the banquettes. Unused to wearing high heels except to weddings, I stepped gingerly over the polished parquet dance floor.

Everyday faces had altered in that lurid nightclub atmosphere. The other women had chosen dressy clothes as well, thank God; the men, of course, looked the same. Suits are suits.

After the women complimented each other on their outfits, our group hunted for a table. I realized that the banquettes had to be mounted by a step, and that the only occasional chairs were actually high stools.

"This is silly." Mary Lou giggled, hopping up on a stool despite her high heels. "I'm too old to do this without jiggling like a bowlful of jelly in all the wrong places."

"Maybe this is the wrong place," I suggested.

A willowy woman definitely young enough to hop on and off a hundred barstools without jiggling anywhere but where it draws applause passed our table. "Drinks, ladies?"

We eyed each other. "A margarita," Connie ordered with aplomb. Mary Lou rolled her lively eyes. "I can never make up my mind—how about a . . . lite beer?"

The girl nodded, then eyed me with the bright, expectant look of a begging squirrel that I assumed was her workaday mask. I can never decide either.

"A Bloody Mary," I finally said.

She sashayed off with the round brown empty tray and I noticed then that her skirt barely covered her bottom.

"The men will love this place," Mary Lou predicted in a low, laughing voice.

"I like the family outings better," I said. "With our failing eyes, we can hardly see in this barn. Wasn't the sleigh ride in December fun? Or that June trip to the water park? What are we going to do here, except drink and talk to only the people we know?"

"It's good to see how the other half lives," Mary Lou said. "And I hated wearing a bathing suit in front of all my coworkers. Some things are meant to be kept between an older woman and her Maker, like cellulite. Gosh, look at this place. I forgot what it was like, being meat on the hoof and single."

A few young customers were edging into the cavernous space, all dressed with casual care and all wearing a wary, hopeful look in their eyes. The place was otherwise deserted except for our group, but suddenly the music system shuddered into loud life.

"Goll-y." Mary Lou clapped her palms over the red curls covering her ears. "I thought our hearing was supposed to be going, too."

Already the cigarette smoke from a banquette behind us was drifting into my nostrils, tickling my allergies. The pounding bass beat made the stool legs and the tabletop vibrate, a slight, shrilly annoying sensation that made me move my hands to the boxy black satin evening bag sitting on my perilously slanted lap.

Then an odd thing happened. I found my feet tapping the stool's wooden rail to the thunderous beat. Jim and I used to dance when we were dating, standing apart but near, gyrating to music not quite as loud but just as insistent. Married life and responsibilities had made that phase less than a memory. Now, here, unexpectedly, it came back. The Jim of those days came back—tall, thin, a bit raw, but so likable . . . and ultimately, so lovable.

I would not dissolve into more widow's tears; not in public. Jim's death had shown me now repressive the fifties had been: A public place was nowhere to display affection, fears, tears, or even opinions that might ruffle someone.

I wished that I had been less inhibited, and had gone to work sooner, had not neglected myself while I fulfilled the roles of wife and mother.

Now husband and kids were gone, and I was like some gawky, awkward spinster despite my devotion to husband, home, and family. I was alone and aging, linked by telephones to my nearest and dearest. If I hadn't had work . . .

A new song—if you can call contemporary music that—came on. No, not a new one—an old one. The forgotten but familiar guitar twangs snapped my senses like a barrage of rubber bands. "Johnny Be Good."

"Oh," I said impulsively to Mary Lou. "Jim and I used to dance to that all the time when we were young. That rhythm makes me want to beat my feet on some floor all night."

Mary Lou glanced around the dim room. "Too bad there aren't any suitable partners in the employees' club—unless you want to ask the night security guard to dance," she added with a snicker. "He's here alone."

Harvey was a retiree past seventy—genial and paunchy, with a slight limp.

I jerked an elbow into her side. "Shhh!" With the music so blaring, I had to talk loud even to urge discretion. "I wouldn't ask anyone to dance, but I sure love that music. Uh! Listen to it! Doesn't it get your blood pumping? I loved to dance to that song." The deserted dance floor begged for some young people gyrating on it, even if they were only ghosts.

"Say," came a voice from the nearest banquette. "Jerry likes to dance and I don't. Why don't you two hit the floor?"

She was a beautiful young woman—dark-haired with classic features, and more, a kind face. Startled, I eyed her escort, a man I'd never seen at the company. He was perfectly presentable, a classic thirtysomething with curly blond hair and the eager, energetic smile of a born salesman. Maybe his slight buckteeth enhanced that notion.

"I couldn't! I haven't danced in years."

"Go ahead," the young woman urged. "I hate to deprive Jerry."

He was getting up and coming toward me, his friendly grin as unwelcome to me as a sinister leer. I was appalled. I wasn't used to making an unrespectable spectacle of myself: For thirty years, not doing that had been my vocation. How was I going to untangle myself gracefully from the damn high chair?

And still, at my back, the music's beat beckoned, making me giddy, making me reckless.

Who cared what a woman past fifty did? Jim and I had planned to dance again, a little, on the cruise. This unknown young man couldn't possibly be construed as anything but a "safe" sexless partner for a woman my age.

Besides, he was pulling back my stool. Before I knew it, I was tipped onto my tottery feet—the shoes were new—and we were threading past the empty tables to that empty, garishly lit dance floor where a ghost of a me I'd forgotten was urging, *Hurry up, the song will end. This is your last chance.*

"Do you whoosh dance?" he asked from behind me.

"What? I can't hear over the music."

"Push dance?"

"Push? No, I never heard of it—"

We were on the floor and I turned to my providential partner, hoping I wouldn't look too silly doing the gyrations of thirty years ago, the Swim and the Jerk. Maybe I would pick up some updated moves from my dance-loving partner.

He grabbed my hand.

No! We danced alone, in the old days, without touching, without accommodating ourselves to a partner. Didn't they still do that? Isn't that what was on MTV all the time nowadays?

He swung me behind him, his strength, unexpected in such a wiry short man, jerking me around like a Raggedy Ann doll. I turned, dazed, and he jerked me in the opposite direction. I was dizzy already, and disoriented, and the soles of my untried high heels skidded over the slick floor.

He never let me go. He never let me stand in one place. It didn't matter what I did, I was an object he manipulated. He twirled me under his arm and I felt the underarm seam of my new dress rip. I wasn't dressed for this kind of workout, this kind of wrenching.

Around me, the seductively throbbing music had become a relentless care of lyrics and never-ending beat.

Way down yonder in New Orleans ...

Spun, turned, twisted, jerked in an unanticipated directions, then snapped in the opposite direction ... dizzy ... as if trapped for endless minutes on a state fair ride you regret going on the moment it starts hurtling you in some unnatural motion....

This wasn't dancing as I knew it, as I had expected, where I stood alone on my own two feet and was in control of myself. This was like a French Apache dance. The only hand-holding dance I had ever done was the sedate lindy hop as a preteen; this was a frenetic jitterbug. I could only hope he wouldn't lift me off the floor and throw me around like they used to.

Then, midway through a powerful jerk, his fingers released mine. I saw his grinning face. In the lurid light it looked demonic.

He had released me in midmotion. Like any thrown object, I kept moving, out of control. My shoe slipped on the floor. I was spinning, downward. To the floor. Hard.

The music—I had thought it was a short song, but perhaps it had been a shorter dance than the forever it felt like—twanged on. I was sitting on the floor looking like a fool, an incompetent old fool, breathless with the shock of the fall.

He came to help me up, but I pulled away, feeling my face redden as it hadn't in years, and struggled gracelessly to my feet, my high heels snagging in the full chiffon skirt.

When I turned, trying not to look beyond the dance floor to my watching coworkers, I saw him waiting for me.

"I wanted to dance alone," I shouted over the scream of the sound system. "Separately." My arms gestured apart.

He grabbed one.

I couldn't believe that he wouldn't stop, wouldn't let me go.

Jerk. I was pulled beyond him into the dark, noisy outer space beyond the shining neon planet of the dance floor, where people I knew and didn't know were grinning at the spectacle I made.

Just when I thought I would hurl into merciful darkness, his arm jerked me back into the vortex of noise and neon and his grinning face. Twirl. Pull. Spin. Jerk.

Dizziness had escalated to utter disorientation. I didn't know where dance floor or watchers were, where dark and light began and ended. I just tried to keep on my feet until the damn, driving music ended and freed me.

It did just that far too late. He released my hand.

"What were you doing?" I demanded in the quiet moment before another selection began.

"Dancing," he said, still grinning.

"I didn't know that dance."

He shrugged. Was it a matter of pride with him, that he was a short man strong enough to jerk even an inexperienced partner around the floor? You would think a good dancer, a gentleman, would not want to try anything so athletic with an unknown partner that it would send her to the floor. You would think.

I was steady enough to walk back to my table, imagining what my friends thought, or would say, but I was too numb to say anything more. Our drinks had arrived. Connie and Mary Lou were studiously sipping away before their sympathetic eyes met mine.

"We'll have to try it again sometime," he said blandly in parting. I couldn't believe his nonchalance about it all, like he tossed women to the floor every day.

"I don't think so."

He smiled again, grinned. "Sometime when we haven't been drinking."

"I was perfectly sober," I said indignantly, knowing that such assertions always sounded like their opposite, but my Bloody Mary hadn't even arrived until now.

His smile smug and disbelieving, he vanished back to his young woman, who was also smiling. I understood now why the lovely young lady with the kind face wouldn't dance with him.

*   *   *

"FORGET IT," Mary Lou said in the ladies' room at work the next day, fluffing her moussed curls with a metal pick. "He's just a jerk."

"But he made me look like a fool! Why? And then he acted as if it was *my* fault, like I was a lush or something."

She shrugged. "Nobody will remember that you fell in a few days."

"Everybody will think I'd been drinking."

"Maybe. But hey, you've got reason to let loose a little. They've all done something like that."

"I don't even know who that young couple was, where they work."

"Accounting, I think, both of them. Those people come and go."

"Not soon enough."

MARTHA IN PERSONNEL was an elevator friend of mine; we only chatted going up or down together, but we did a lot of that.

"Jerry in Accounting?" She frowned, her darkly penciled brows drawing together. She had the lacquered hair and nails of a woman groomed to greet the public, a longtime receptionist. "We've got more than one. Why are you interested?"

I lowered my voice and told her. Martha was about my age. She raised an irked eyebrow.

"What a dirty trick! And you didn't even know that push dancing is a cousin to slam dancing. You don't do that kind of a dance with a partner you haven't practiced with, or who doesn't know the dance pretty well."

"Slam dancing," I said in horror, for even I had heard of that violent exercise. "How do you know about this push dancing?"

"My kids, of course," she said. "It's like jitterbug, and it's getting popular again, but it's not for amateurs. Tell you what, I'll look him up in the computer."

Her nails clicked on her clacking keyboard. "Got a Jerry Snyder . . . or a Kimball."

Inspired, I asked, "Which one is on the employee club board?"

"That info wouldn't be in here."

"I don't suppose his description is in his file."

"This ain't police headquarters, honey. But . . ." She glanced around. "You could always go down to Accounting and check it out."

"I don't want to see him again," I said between tight teeth. "I just want to tell him off from a safe distance, so I don't kill him. If I had his phone number, I'd tell him what he did so he doesn't do it again to anyone else."

"Don't you think he knows what he did?"

"No! I think he's a thoughtless creep without any manners who imagines himself God's gift to dancing women."

"Tell you what." Martha's lethally long crimson fingernail tapped the edge of her keyboard. "You make sure it's the right Jerry, and I'll get you his home phone number."

ACCOUNTING WAS FOREIGN TERRITORY TO ME; my work never called me down there. The place was a maze of the latest office cubicles, sleek, neutral-colored, and impersonal. I wandered through, feeling like an awkward intruder, ready to jump if my particular bogeyman popped up from a cubicle like a jack-in-the-box. Every cubicle I peeked into was a potential bomb of unwanted recognition for me.

"Oh."

I had not found him, but I had found her. The nameplate on her inner cubicle wall read "Misty Weatherall."

"Hi." She looked as surprised as I did.

"I'm . . . looking for your young man."

"Jerry?"

"Yeah."

"He's not my young man. I just went out with him a couple of times. I won't anymore."

"Why not?"

"He's kind of . . . got a chip on his shoulder."

"Why did you suggest I dance with him?"

"I overheard you saying you wanted to dance, and I don't dance."

"You don't push dance?"

"No."

"Have you ever danced with Jerry?"

"Once. The second time we went out."

"And?"

Her eyes evaded mine. "I didn't fall, but I didn't like it."

"Is that why you sicced him on me?"

"Listen, you said you wanted to dance. I thought you knew how, that you could handle that kind of thing. And I sure didn't want to dance with him."

"Is that the only reason you aren't going out with him again?"

"Well, there's you. Once you two hit the floor, it was obvious that you weren't up to his speed. He should have stopped."

"Thanks."

"And he's awfully bitter about his ex-wife. It gets tiresome hearing him going on about it. Actually, I dated him because I felt sorry for him; then I felt sorry for me." She frowned. "He doesn't take no for an answer. He's going to be hard to cut loose. I guess we both made a mistake."

"Do you have his phone number?"

"Never needed it."

"What's his last name, anyway."

"Snyder."

"Is he on the employee club committee?"

"Sure, he's program chairman now. Why do you think we all ended up in his favorite venue?"

"Wait a minute, if you overheard me wishing I could dance, did you both overhear me complaining that a singles' nightclub wasn't a great place for a meeting?"

Her dark eyes shifted to her computer screen, where a complex table of numbers stood frozen in their amber rankings. She tapped a key and the screen went black. "I heard it."

"Could he have?"

"I guess, but it was my idea to suggest the two of you dance."

"You didn't suggest the kind of dance, though."

She shrugged again and looked at me. "Jerry doesn't do any other kind of dancing."

I went back to Martha and got the phone number.

IT DID ME NO GOOD.

I called it in the evenings, several evenings. All I ever got was an answering machine and a smarmy recorded message that "Jerry was out having fun."

I never left a message. I wanted to hear him respond when I told him what he had done; how irresponsible he had been. How my dress was too fragile and my shoes too new for such gymnastics, how boorish it was to hurl a strange woman old enough to be his mother around a dance floor in such a violent manner. I wanted to tell him what a cad he was to blame my fall on alcohol. All right, "cad" was a melodrama word. I wanted to tell him what a jerk he was.

"He never answers his phone himself," I complained to Connie one day. "Probably people are standing in line to tell him off."

"Why not confront him at work?"

"I've made enough scenes in front of my coworkers."

Mary Lou had overheard us and bustled over, waving papers. "I told her to forget the jerk," she explained to Connie. "He doesn't care anyway."

"Yeah." Connie's smooth blond head nodded without disturbing a hair. "Some guys are like that; they get a kick out of rattling women's cages."

"That's just it. I felt like I was caged with a wild animal out there on the dance floor. I could have seriously injured myself when I fell, broken a leg. It was ... social assault."

"God, you women." Gene, the assistant manager, was suddenly behind me. "Everything's rape nowadays."

Speechless, I watched him walk away before I could answer, feeling rage boil over.

"He's a jerk, too," Connie said softly. "Mary Lou's right. Forget it. There isn't anything you can do about it."

SOME ACTS IN LIFE ARE TOO UNCIVIL to be borne, and sometimes they seem very small things on the surface.

I can't help feeling that way. I was reared in a generation in which children were to be seen and not heard, when politeness was an expected feature of daily life, and when most people were assumed to mean well. If knighthood was no longer in flower (I'm not that old), men—except for the most illiterate types who still spat in the street—were expected to behave like gentlemen.

I began calling Jerry Snyder impolitely early in the morning when he would be getting ready for the office, and even on weekends. Always the answering machine. Jerry was out having "fun." I even tried calling at three in the morning, one night when I couldn't sleep. I was having trouble sleeping; I kept going over and over the incident in my mind, wondering if he did it deliberately because I had criticized his idea of entertainment, deciding what I would say to him when I finally cornered the rat. He deserved a good dressing down.

Martha got me his address as well, with only a lift of her eyebrow for comment.

I looked it up on the city map: deep in a nest of new apartment complexes for young singles on the city fringes.

I drove by one Saturday, looking for his unit. The buildings suggested Swiss chalets. A flashy fountain spit high into the air in an artificial pond near the complex's center. Complex was the name for the place, although it was pretentiously called Woodwinds. Laid out at angles, each building's numbers hid discreetly. I finally found number 66—a second-story unit reached by both exterior stairs and an internal elevator.

If all else failed, I could waylay him; confront him in person at his door. That meant I had to park our '85 gray Honda Civic and wait. He would have to come back to that apartment sometime.

But he didn't, not all day Saturday, and not as late as ten o'clock, when I finally gave up and left.

I needed more information than Martha's user-friendly personnel files would provide. I thought about it. With his car license and description, I could find his car in the employee section of the parking ramp and follow him home after work, just like a lost dog.

The telephone again. Stomach fluttering, I called the Motor Vehicles department.

"I have a problem," I told the woman who answered, wanting to sound flustered and innocent and having no trouble doing that. I wasn't used to extracting possibly confidential information. "A gentleman and I got into a fender bender the other day. He gave me his card, but I'm in sales and call on a lot of people who give me cards, and the accident shook me up. Now my insurance company needs the information. I think I know which card it is, and have a likely name. Could you tell me what the car looks like from your records, and then I'll be sure it's the right person?"

The pause made my heart beat triple time. "I'll transfer you to someone who can help."

I repeated my spiel to a man this time, my nervousness all the more genuine. I'm sure he was thinking, "just like a woman," when he looked up the name. The computer, he told me, would take a few moments to sift through all those names for the right one in the right town.

"Two cars, ma'am. A yellow '86 Corvette and a black '72 Chevrolet Impala."

"Oh, it was the black Chevrolet. I remember it was an older car," I exclaimed with honest relief. "I certainly would have remembered the Corvair."

"Corvette," he corrected in a weary, condescending tone.

Good. I had been made to look like a fool on the dance floor, and now I was discovering that it could serve my purpose to look like one elsewhere. The clerk would never be suspicious of such a ditsy middle-aged woman.

I didn't have the license numbers—I didn't want to stir doubts by asking for too much. Better safe than sorry; I knew that from recent experience.

On my lunch hour I prowled the employee parking levels. Parking ramps are eerie, echoing places. Women are always urged to be wary in them, but now I relished the deserted air, the scrape of my shoes on cement and the squeal of cars turning down the exit ramp the only sounds. Our employees invariably ate at their desks or downtown.

Not being an expert in cars, I had purchased a Blue Book and went down the rows, proud when I stood before the broad black rear of the correct-vintage car. I jotted down the license number on my notepad.

I always got off half an hour earlier than Accounting employees. All I would have to do is drive out and park on the street near the exit—not easy during rush hour with limited spots, but if I went round and round until something turned up, it should work. And I should . . . wear a hat or scarf, so he wouldn't recognize me. Tonight. I would put the plan into operation right after work tonight.

Everything went perfectly. I bought a nondescript scarf on my lunch hour. I looked like a grandmother, but all the better. *Oh, what big eyes you have, Grandmother!* I thanked God now that Jim and I hadn't been able to afford a flashy new car someone might notice. My hands gripped the Civic's wheel, even though I was parked; the motor was running and I was ready.

As cars poured in a relentless stream from the parking ramp's mouth, I had only a moment to identify the right vehicle. This was the hardest part. Cars all looked alike to me, except for the most flagrant. And so many people had black, gray, and white cars these days. With dirt and dust, they all faded into one monotonous neutral stream.

Then—a large, dusty-black silhouette, a flash of blond curly hair. I wrenched the steering wheel and checked the traffic stream in my left mirror—a truck coming fast in my entry lane.

I pressed the accelerator and spun out of the parking place. Behind me an angry trucker honked. I didn't care; I was only a car behind the black '72 Chevrolet.

I stayed behind, but it never went onto the Loop towards Woodwinds. That unnerved me. I knew how to get there. I didn't know where the car would take me now.

Then, after we left the crowded downtown and I did get an idea, I didn't like where it was leading me—out to the dingy circle of deteriorating neighborhoods that ringed the downtown, we drove. Out where makeshift Vietnamese restaurants stand next door to pawnshops and Laundromats and missions, and even big, belching city buses drive by fast. Out where gangs wage war and men lie like the dead in alleyways, drunk or drugged or even really dead.

It was still broad daylight, but driving through that area dimmed my vision; I was as nervous as if nightfall veiled my senses.

Jerry stopped his car before a seedy-looking three-story brick apartment building from the twenties. He vanished inside. Too scared to venture after him, I decided to wait for him to come out again.

And, again, he didn't, at least not by eight o'clock, which was as long as I dared stay, even with all the car doors locked.

I decided I had to follow him again, and I needed more protection than locks. I was able to purchase a can of pepper spray from the gun section of the local mall's sports outlet. Standing at the glass counter with all the mechanical black and silver weapons laid out on shelves beneath me was ... nerve-racking. The young man behind the counter even assumed I wanted to buy a gun.

"Can just anybody do that?" I asked with an uneasy laugh.

"Yes, ma'am. Just fill out a form and wait a few days. Want to see anything?"

I eyed the foreign instruments. That's what they looked like, instruments for some strange manufacturing process. "No, thanks. The human bug spray should do it."

*   *   *

"How about a movie tonight? *Jurassic Park* should be running out of hordes of kids by now at the cheapie theaters."

Connie and Mary Lou stood beside my desk like the Bobbsey Twins, radiating innocent eagerness.

"No . . . uh, thanks. I have to volunteer at the old folks' home tonight."

They finally left, after more idle chitchat, which I had no time for. I had things to do.

Driving behind Jerry after work that day was a picnic. In fact, I had brought along a thermos of coffee and had packed a sandwich and raw veggies with a cookie in an Igloo cooler—I hadn't made lunches like that since the kids were in grade school. I was prepared for the long haul. He was not going to elude me this time. Besides, it was so fascinating to watch the smartly suited young accountant vanish into that disreputable building. Why?

This time I didn't park the moment he went in. I drove around the block, undeterred by overflowing Dumpsters and a ragged man shuffling down the alley behind Jerry's place. Alley! On the next cruise through, I turned down that narrow way lined with dented silver garbage cans and littered with trash.

I counted the buildings as I drove and—yes! A shambling wooden garage for four cars hunkered behind Jerry's building. The alley was narrower, dimmer, meaner than the street, but I found a deserted garage to park by. Then I slumped behind the wheel and waited.

None too soon. A dirty door in Jerry's garage began crawling upward on its tracks, screeching with age. Shortly after, a sleek, low yellow rear edged out. Jerry backed the Corvette in the absolutely wrong direction to the way I was facing. Frantic, I balled up my fists, then started the car and seesawed it out of the cramped spot. The Corvette was gone when I was once more pointed down the alley, but I hit the accelerator and sped at forty miles an hour down the lane. One wasn't supposed to drive more than twenty in an alley, I remembered from my long-ago driver's test, but this was an emergency.

My car paused for the side street as I peered right and left. A yellow glint at my right made me jerk the wheel that way. The old car squealed at such treatment; Jim would know why a steering wheel always did that when cranked too hard. I didn't care. I followed the car back onto the street in front of the apartment buildings.

The Corvette was attracting greedy street glances now, but Jerry was impervious, fleeing this sad neighborhood. My car attracted no notice, from the street men or from Jerry.

We headed for the Loop at last, and I was mentally rehearsing my diatribe against him, which by now had become quite a production. He would finally face what he had done and realize his behavior had been thoughtless at best and caddish at worst.

But the yellow Corvette did not take the exit for Woodwinds.

Instead of entering an affluent apartment complex, I finally found my car sitting in the parking lot before a big, boxy building identified only by a big, boxy, cheap-looking sign high on a pole beside it.

"Foxy Chic," it read, none too legibly. "Topless dancing. Beautiful babes."

I sighed, and set about eating dinner and drinking coffee and waiting for dark, which no longer scared me, because then I would be invisible.

With the proper spray in my right hand, I waited past eleven. The yellow—atrocious color for a car, and yet how fitting to his poisonous personality!—Corvette was impossible to miss, even at night in the dimly lit parking lot. Sinister customized vans hiding who-knows-what in their roomy, secret interiors, pickup trucks, junkers and sports cars whose names I didn't know, and massive motorcycles sprinkled the lot around me. It was only a weeknight, after all.

About eleven-thirty I noticed movement by the Corvette and sat up straight.

I dared to roll down the window a bit. Voices, abrading voices, drifted in through it. A man's and a woman's.

"I told you to leave me alone, Jerry! Damn it, why do you come here!" Her voice was ragged, raw and on the verge of sobs. "I'm working."

"I pay for my drinks like anybody else. I can watch you like anybody else, Tiffany." He sneered the name, obvious pseudonym that it was.

"I don't want to see you anymore."

"But I can see you any time I want, all of you. Come on, get in the car."

"No! I just want you out of here. Get a life, get another girl, get one who wants you. I don't."

Something rang in the air, the clap of a hand on a face. I started the motor, thinking of my own two daughters, who would never be caught dead in a place like this, yet . . .

I shifted into gear. I didn't want to . . . to blow my cover, but I could see the two figures interlocked, and this time the push dancing was serious.

I pulled on my headlights and pointed my car at them. They were framed and frozen by lights like deer on the highway.

Jerry's face wore the same leer/sneer I knew so well from my one nightmarish dance with him. The girl who was shaken in his grasp, being pulled this way and that, now suddenly jerked to face the lights. Her expression was unforgettable, fear and struggle masking her pretty, made-up features. I was aware of long, bare legs and arms, of white boots and some skimpy sort of cover-up, of flying long red hair etched into flaming tendrils against the car's garish yellow background.

"Let me go, Jerry," she begged as she saw her opportunity. "Just let go and don't come back."

He glared into the corona of my headlights, looking for someone to blame behind the wheel. Then he released her so quickly that she fell, fell hard against the car. My foot pressed the accelerator as he jumped into the Corvette's low front seat.

In a moment he had roared away with taillights as red as the devil's eyes glaring back at us. I slowed to cruise past the dazed and shaken girl. She stared mindlessly into my driver's window as I passed. I knew that in the dark it was only a blank, black grease-blob of glass, and that I was nameless and faceless, just another passerby in the night.

THE PHONE WAS RINGING when I got home.

"Linda! Mary Lou and I were worried sick! If you're going to be out so late, let us know."

"What did you call for?"

"Well, we wanted to take you out to dinner. You've been keeping to yourself so much lately. You dash out of work every night like a rabbit scurrying home to its burrow. We're worried that silly incident at Portnoy's is turning you into a hermit."

I tried not to laugh.

THE NEXT DAY, I decided my investigation needed to take a new tack. Martha could help me again.

"Ex-wife?" She frowned at her computer screen. "I doubt we'd have that."

"She wasn't always 'ex.' Maybe she was listed as next of kin when he applied for work here."

"Why do you want it?"

"Oh, it's silly, but I thought . . . maybe if I understood him, if I knew why he was so hostile to women that he took it out on me, a complete stranger—old enough to be his mother, for heaven's sake—I'd be a little more understanding of what happened."

Martha grinned up at me. "*Cherchez le* shrink, huh?"

"Who knows a man better than an ex-wife?"

I LOOKED SO RESPECTABLE that she let me into her apartment almost immediately. Her name was Karen. She was a tiny woman almost overwhelmed by her cloud of bouffant brown hair, the painfully thin kind who always look cold, hunched somehow, but pretty if habitual anxiety hadn't sharpened her face. When I told her I was there about Jerry, her haunted features grew even starker, all cheekbones and big eyes and soft, scared mouth.

"Oh, God, I can't even stand to hear his name. I just want to forget him, I just want him to—please, God—forget me."

I told her why I couldn't forget him, and she just nodded. "Listen . . ."

"Linda."

"Listen, Linda, he is such bad news. You're lucky that all he threw you around was a dance floor. And his hate just escalates."

I glanced at the impressive battery of locks and chains on the front door.

She nodded. "My name's not on the mailbox and I have an unpublished number. Every time it rings I'm afraid it might be him anyway. I'm just grateful he found that stripper. I had a lawyer who was trying to represent my rights in the divorce, but Jerry got so ugly that I finally just took the divorce papers and ran, left him everything. God, I am so glad to be out of there."

"So now she's got him," I mused. "Looks like the only way to escape him is if he finds another victim."

"Look, it's not like that. I wouldn't wish him on anybody. But he doesn't let go easily." She shook her head and bit her already raw lip. "And I don't understand the creepy apartment near downtown, the two cars . . . although I get he got the 'Vette with what would have been my part of the divorce settlement. All I know is that he was meaner than a junkyard dog, abusive, obsessive, and he was just getting worse. I'm lucky to be alive."

I stood to leave. "Thanks for the insight. I'm shocked but not surprised. This puts my dance from hell into a different light."

WHEN I LEFT I KEEP SEEING Karen's old-young face and hearing her soft, tremulous voice. I thought about my two distant, happily married, wholesome daughters and their dull textbook husbands and suburban houses. I thanked God, and I knew I couldn't stop now.

The sleazy street in front of Jerry Snyder's apartment building was never deserted. I wore an old raincoat I'd kept for yard work in cold weather and the dowdy scarf and tennis shoes. I parked a half block away and shuffled toward his building, ignoring the men on the street, my pepper spray clutched in a fist tucked into a pocket.

The building's deserted lobby was like a movie set: peeling gray paint, cigarette butts and advertising flyers stuck to the vinyl tile floor, a battered rank of painted gray metal mailboxes. Tattered pieces of paper identified some of the units as occupied; last names were the only clue to who lived there. Once this tawdry puzzle-board with half the words missing would have stymied me, brought me to the brink of tears with rustration. Now I wasn't so easily put off. Of course, "Jerry Snyder" was nowhere listed. One word caught my eye. Rider. It rhymed with Snyder and sounded like a c.b. radio handle, a second, secret self-identity a macho-man would take. Rider. Maybe a man with two cars and two lives.

The landlady was what I'd expected—buxom, blowsy, indifferent, her television baby-sitting four fussing kids in the background. Her aquiline nose and challenging eyes didn't promise easy cooperation, but I softly told her that I'd come to town to tell my son that his daddy had died and I didn't know anywhere else to reach him and who knows where he was during the day. . . .

My sad tale didn't soften her heard-it-all facade, but she didn't care about apartment house rules anyway. When I told her my name was Rider, she nodded.

"He doesn't hang around here much anyway, but he always pays his rent on time."

"Oh, I'm glad to hear that, about the rent, I mean."

She looked at me as if I were the most naive mother in the world. Obviously she found Rider's long absences suspiciously criminal, as did I. But she gave me the extra key. I trudged up three flights of filthy stairs and finally stood before door number nine.

The place was as grim inside as the untended hall outside. An ugly plaid sofa on its last legs was the only furniture in the living room. The tiny kitchen beyond was relatively clean, and equipped with a small microwave. The cupboards were sparsely stocked with instant coffee and discount-store eating utensils, glasses, cups, and dishes. The microwave dishes looked new. A bottom cupboard had an extensive if purely functional bar. In the ancient white refrigerator frozen meals crammed the frost-caked freezer—all trendy, low-fat entrées with angel hair pasta and the like. I thought of Jerry's curly blond cherub hair and shook my head.

Besides a front-room closet, mostly empty, only one other room opened off the living area. I opened the bedroom door and felt my knees go weak.

The room was wallpapered with women, women frozen in photographic pornography—some of the soft-core, soft-focus images seen in shrink-wrapped magazines; most of it vile, sadistic stuff I'd never imagined. Ordinary, innocent snapshots of Jerry's ex-wife, Karen, were tacked up among the raw stuff, and lots of black-and-white photos of the girl I'd seen him arguing with outside Foxy Chix, obviously taken while she was performing. I inched along the photo-papered walls.

Stark black-and-white photos of other real women punctuated the lushly colored and brutal images of anonymous, writhing women: women spread-eagled, women bound, whipped, chained, raped. One small photo of a smiling, pretty young girl had obviously been cut from a high school yearbook. Another subject of a "real" photo, I saw with a shudder, was just a child. I forced myself to study the pornography, the women's faces contorted in pain passing for passion. Then, between the spread thighs of a leather-masked woman, I spotted a small black-and-white photo of myself. Self-recognition was a body blow; my heart pounded, even harder when I realized the photo's source. The employees' club monthly newslet-

ter. I had been cited as a top employee of my department *two* years
before. I was a trophy, too, carefully recorded, though a small one.

In the bedroom closet I waded past sadomasochistic props to find boxes
of copper-tipped bullets, huge heavy-handled knives, hunting knives, I
think. No gun here, but I found lots of the same used, nondescript clothing I wore now, suspended from cheap wire hangers like empty carcasses.

I returned the key and left, wondering if the landlady would bother to
tell Rider his mother had called.

I CALLED THE POLICE, like a good citizen. Finally referred to a harried-
sounding woman detective, I was told that until Jerry did something
provable and punishable, nothing in his behavior or his lifestyle was a
crime. They could watch him to see if he was involved in a pornography
ring if I would give them his name.... She addressed me as "ma'am"
every other sentence. I hung up.

KAREN WAS EASY TO DISGUISE; just slap some makeup on her white-
washed face and draw her hair back into a sleek ponytail. We bought
her a black leather jacket so she would look a little tougher. I wore a
blond wig my second daughter had to have when she was eighteen and
left behind when she married, and junked up my clothes as best I could.

The taped hard rock music inside Foxy Chix was earsplitting. It made
Portnoy's seem like a wake. I identified Jerry's latest girl the moment
the stage spotlights hit her long red hair. The show didn't shock me.
What these women did was pretty tame, and even playful, compared to
the wall of photographs, even though they both fed the same sick needs
in a working woman's simple quest to survive....

It was easy to talk to Tiffany—after finishing their acts, the women
strolled topless among the tables of men. I hooked her attention with a
fifty-dollar bill. Maybe lesbians came in here occasionally, but I doubted
that. It didn't bother me if anyone thought that's what I was, anyway.

Karen and I took her to an all-night diner nearby, where we huddled
in a back booth and everybody had hot fudge sundaes on me.

We told her what Jerry had done to us. She told us what Jerry had
done to her, which was worse, much worse. She didn't have to tell us
how scared she was. She would leave the planet to escape him, if she
could, but she had to work, she had to live somewhere. She could be
found. I told her what I'd already told Karen—about Jerry's secret life
and how his sanctuary was equipped for bloody murder.

"He's got to be stopped," I said.

Tiffany slurped the last sweet liquid from the bottom of her glass. "Do
you mean what I think you do? I don't have the nerve—"

"I'll buy the gun," I said quickly. "I know just where to go. The young man behind the counter said he'd 'walk me through it,' whatever that means. A woman my age, a widow suddenly living alone, logically feels the need for home protection. We should clean out his hole. Mama Rider can do it. The landlady won't care if he ever comes back as long as the apartment is empty and clean. The police may ask you two some questions. Have good answers."

"But ..." Karen's thin face showed hope for the first time. "What about that incident with Jerry on the dance floor? You could be a suspect if something happened to him."

I shook my head to dismiss that objection. I had finally put that sad little episode into the proper proportion.

"Don't worry about that. Like my friends kept telling me, I was making a mountain out of a molehill. Dancing with intent to humiliate is not a killing offense, for heaven's sake. Everybody's forgotten about it. Everybody."

Julian Rathbone has been writing full-time since 1973, and in the past two decades achieved a reputation for creating taut international thrillers involving global politics and crime. His short fiction, at least this piece, is vastly different, showing a slice of life in rural London. What he does, and does marvelously in this story, is weave together the unrelated threads of seemingly innocuous events into a tight, cohesive look at everyday lust, life, and death.

Of Mice, Men and Two Women
JULIAN RATHBONE

Ranjit Singh owned a tiny corner shop in Walthamstow, one of the more run down suburbs of northeast London. Since he was some distance behind the high street and a good half mile from the nearest superstore and another good mile from the nearest street market it was a handy little business. His shop closed for eight hours in every twenty-four and during the other sixteen sold bread, milk, cakes, biscuits, crisps, newspapers, pork pies and sausage rolls, condoms, aspirin, and from a cold cabinet with a steel grill which was meant to be kept locked, Lambrusco wines, halfs of scotch and vodka, blue thunderbird wine, strong lagers, and Kinder eggs.

Through a variety of means, including extortion with menaces, bribery, and other malpractices, a property firm called Casby, Casby, Casby, and Sun had acquired ninety-nine-year leases on the three terraced properties next to the shop and planning permission to convert them not just into the usual six flats but, through cunning exploitation of the fact they owned three linked shells rather than three separate buildings, ten. There were actually no Casbys extant in the firm and Sun was Kai Won Sun late of Victoria Island, Hong Kong.

When he read the request for planning permission Ranjit had been delighted: ten families instead of six would mean that much more custom. He had been far less pleased though when the first skip arrived on his doorstep and the banging and crashing got under way as the dwellings were gutted, and planks and piles of wet cement appeared on the pavement. Worst of all the progress of his regular customers to his shop door was impeded by trundling wheelbarrows and a startlingly beautiful Afro-Caribbean male who stood in the pocket handkerchief gardens of the houses and heaved into the skips the timber and plaster his mates chucked down to him. His name was Lennie Enfield.

Not that Ranjit was much bothered personally. He was rarely in the shop these days, leaving the work to his wife, Amirya, and a succession of ill-paid school-leavers. A thin, dried-up man, prematurely aged at sixty, he was now deeply into study of the seven gurus of his religion and confined his shopkeeping to examining the accounts less attentively than he did the scriptures.

About Lennie Enfield's beauty let's just say it reminded elderly white females of Harry Belanfonte in *Island in the Sun,* and while we're at it we might add that Amirya's recalled in the hearts of elderly white males the transcendent loveliness of Ava Gardner in *Pandora and the Flying Dutchman,* but a Gardner with an all-over tan. Amirya herself came from Trinidad and was well-Westernized in her ways. However, her parents maintained the formalities of Sikh culture, and her marriage to Ranjit, who did indeed hail from the Punjab, had been arranged.

Lennie was twenty, she was thirty and the oldest of the three children of her loveless marriage was already fourteen years old. All right, we all know that most arranged marriages are not loveless, but hers was. She was unlikely to have any more children since Ranjit had given up on sex as well as commerce.

Lennie fell in love at first sight. There was nothing romantic about it in the Mills and Boon sense of the word though Byron might not have found the cosmic energy of his lust alien to the Romantic Imagination. Nor would elderly white males who still remember Ava Gardner.

He waited, though, after his first sight of her, not for seven centuries nor for seven years but seven minutes, until the shop was empty; then he swung through the chiming door and stood in front of the low glass-topped counter and looked across at her. His thumbs were hooked in the wide belt of his tight jeans, his biceps stretched the short sleeves of his green sweatshirt. Outside the late April sunshine danced through the motes above his skip and made an aureole round his bronze head, silvered the sweat, glanced off his shining skin, glittered in his single earring.

He flexed his pectorals and said: "Twenty Embassy, and please, woman, would you fuck with me?"

Since this precisely fitted the fantasy she had been working on ever since she clapped eyes on his torso through the shop window above the video poster for *Basic Instinct* just six minutes earlier, a fantasy that had caused her to give change for a placido when the customer had tended her a fiver, she was not surprised, or frightened. Indeed, the fact that he

had said "would you" and "with me," and "please," though that probably
related to the cigarettes, added tenderness to passion.

She smiled, those teeth, those full, plum-coloured lips, and sighed—
that large heavy but well-shaped bosom—leant across the counter and,
in a gesture that was almost maternal, brushed white plaster dust from
his chest, letting her hand discover the hardness of the muscle beneath.

"That would be nice, man. But where?"

"Woman," he said, and she fancied it was more a growl, the sort of
growl a tomcat makes prior to the moment of truth, than any noise
Belafonte ever emitted, "next door we have twenty-eight empty rooms.
An' some of thems still 'as beds in."

THE AFFAIR WAS BRAZEN. Ranjit was not popular in the neighbourhood:
He gave tick to no one, not to Afros finding themselves out of bread of
both sorts on a Sunday morning, nor to old cockney ladies who claimed
they had been mugged on his very doorstep. When the children of BBC
(Radio) producers came for adult videos he sent them back and made
their parents collect the videos in person. Moreover, there was no Sikh
community in the area: Ranjit had picked the shop from an *Evening
Standard* advertisement and had not minded moving the five miles or so
from Tower Hamlets. So no one in the near neighbourhood was going
to tell him his wife was having it away with an Afro stud ten years
her junior.

She found plenty of excuses to get out while the teenagers and school-
leavers minded the shop: Down the cash and carry for something he had
forgotten, an open afternoon at the primary school, aromatherapy and
reflexology classes, and the Asian Women for Peace Association were
already on her list for calls in the few hours he allowed her to be out
each afternoon. Once clear of the shop she had only to duck down a
service entry and into the tiny alley that ran behind the terrace to where
Lennie would be waiting for her at one of three gates, alone.

The old biddies told her: "Go on ducks, get it while yer can, they
won't look at yer'n ten years' time, we won't tell, and I think I'll 'ave a
packet of the Belgian meat paste while I'm at it, my goodness 'e can't
really want 87p for a sliver like that, can 'e?" And she sold the Afro
kiddies ciggies, but still whacked them over the earhole if they tried to
steal, which they respected her for, and when Ben, from opposite,
wrapped a copy of *Penthouse* inside his *Independent* just as his wife came
in to remind him to get some green lentils, she didn't let on at all. She
charged him though, of course. And in return for these little favours
everyone kept quiet about her.

Lennie's mates really were mates, even the foreman was only twenty-
five and had not yet turned class traitor: when the contractor came round

at an inopportune moment he always said that Lennie was the reliable one, the one he sent out for a kilo of nails or a five litre can of paint stripper if they'd run short, when actually he was bonking Amirya in the upstairs back of number eight. And once, when the contractor, a podgy grey man whose car component business in the north Midlands had gone into liquidation two years earlier, questioned the rhythmic beat on the ceiling above, the foreman explained that it was a minor plumbing problem they were getting on the top of; indeed, Lennie was down B and Q looking for some washers right now.

And so in upstairs rooms, filled with dust, lit from open curtainless windows, often with only a bare mattress considerately left for them to lie on, they made rapturous sunlit love in just about every way you can think of. The air around them was laden with the perfume of narcissi, then lilac and finally roses; outside lascivious sparrows chirped rhythmically while the blackbirds sang smugly of territory held and eggs hatched in the depths of untended privet. Occasionally Lennie would bring a joint of best Colombian red, and once or twice, knowing her husband would be out way beyond when Lennie would have to go, and breath fresheners would have time to remove the evidence, she brought up a half of Bell's with nan bread and a wedge of dolcelatte. These extra delights were not there to stimulate exhausted desire but rather to celebrate its happy satiation. No one had ever told them that sadness follows copulation, so for them it did not.

But one by one the mattresses went, new doorways smaller even than before were made good, and the heavy smell of modern gloss paints poisoned air that had been redolent with the sour sharpness of fresh wood shavings. Amirya longed for decent comfort. And so one Sunday evening late in May she told Lennie that since nine o'clock next morning Ranjit would be out, she expected Lennie to be in, and dammit, she'd close the shop. He, for his part, had come to tell her that since the full skips could not be collected until the late morning he and his mates would be down Hackney Marshes on another job until one o'clock, but he agreed they'd cover for him.

AMONG THE SHOP'S MOST FAITHFUL customers were Ben and Amanda, who lived across the road on the ground floor of a terrace house just like all the rest apart from its lilac door. Amanda was a social worker who moonlighted counselling the terminally ill. She could spot an abused child from fifty paces, inoperable cancer from forty. Ben was an assistant producer for BBC Radio Five. They had many friends, gave small barbecue parties on Sundays in summer when they could use the strip of lawn at the back, and attended various action groups supporting the more obviously deprived or endangered human subspecies, but drawing the line at the elderly who are difficult, depressing, and live next door. And occasionally, when she had a manuscript to deliver to her publisher, Amanda's sister Beatrice came to stay.

Beatrice, whose given name was Veronica, wrote detective stories set in mid-Victorian London and against the background of the Pre-Raphaelite Movement, which she had researched to the bone and beyond. Her publisher, who ran a small but flourishing business with a cheerful efficiency quite alien to the industry in general, and all from a couple of rooms just two stops down the Victoria Line, believed that if only she would settle on the one detective, Thomas Carlyle say or Ford Madox Ford, he'd have the next Ellis Peters on his hands.

And on that Sunday evening Beatrice walked into Ranjit Singh's shop and asked for a bottle of wine. Always she forgot, until the very last minute, to bring a bottle. Amirya remembered that it was Sunday, checked that it was past seven, unlocked the cabinet. Beatrice, fumbling inside, found a Lambrusco medium white; Amirya gave her change for a five-pound note, and watched the thin rather drab middle-aged lady cross the road. Beatrice bumped into the skip and coming out from behind it she was almost knocked down by a pick-up truck that swung into the kerb and parked between the skip and Ranjit's Transit van.

"Daft bat," Amirya said to herself, but already her heart was beating faster, for the pickup was Lennie's.

MONDAY MORNINGS ARE THE DEADEST part of the week for corner shops. Consequently when his fellow students (themselves mostly shopkeepers in the same mould) proposed to him they should meet Monday mornings in the Sikh temple in Tower Hamlets to attempt to fathom their fathomless scriptures, Ranjit willingly agreed. Thus Amirya was able at least to compound the last betrayal: she took Lennie into the matrimonial bed.

It did not suit him. It was too soft and it creaked. The room was dark and cluttered with furniture Lennie stumbled over, it was filled with smells more alien than those of paint. For the first time in his life, the organ they had nicknamed "Marley" refused to perform. Poor Lennie. He was upset.

"Every little thing goin' to be all right," Amirya murmured as she gently but ineffectually caressed it. It stirred, thickened, but as soon as she pulled him in towards her, or attempted to mount him, flop it went again.

Lennie was humiliated, hurt, deeply bothered, and finally, as macho-men do (and really he was not much more than a lad), when something they can't explain interferes with their manhood, became very angry. He smashed his fist in the bedhead, stormed round the room shaking and scolding the recalcitrant member, and let out a howl of frustrated pains as inadvertently he hurt himself.

Neither heard the return of Ranjit's Transit, the click of the multiple

locks, the dull rattle of a chain, the squeak of his foot on the stairs, but
Lennie saw the door handle turn and got in behind it just as it opened.
Amirya sat up in bed, holding the sheet in front of her breasts.

"Ranjit, why have you come back so soon, my dear?"

"I forgot to take with me my copy of the holy writings of the sixth
guru. But Amirya, what are you doing in bed, my dear, and why is the
shop below closed?"

A heavy brass vase presented itself to Lennie's hand, or so it seemed
to him, and he used it to hit Ranjit on the head. Ranjit sank to his knees,
shook his head, attempted to get up. Lennie lifted off Ranjit's turban
and hit him again, this time from above and with more conviction.

THE NIGHT BEFORE, at supper, with the Lambrusco safely in the fridge
and the single candle glowing sweetly over a bottle of Tesco's Corbières,
Ben had asked Beatrice one of the three questions authors always get
asked: "And what's the next one going to be about?"

(The other two are: *And what name do you write under?* to which I
always answer: *Frederick Forsyth,* and *Where do you get your ideas
from?*)

Now the other two are boring, but this one touches a chord: You've
just finished what you knew was going to be a masterpiece, but now
you're not so sure, while the idea that lies behind the next one is a
surefire all the way winner. Beatrice expounded, attempting to sling
whole-wheat spaghetti with green lentil Bolognese onto her fork:

"I have cats, you know that. . . . No, don't laugh. And what has always
of course made me sad about them, is the way they play with mice." She
spoke in the clipped, controlled way she usually adopted after two glasses
of wine. "So like prolonged torture, although of course they don't know
that. Now the other day Molly, my silver tabby, brought in a mouse. I
intervened of course and as a result the mouse escaped and hid under
the piano. I can't move the piano, and Molly can't get under it. The
mouse was safe. But it did not stay there. It came out and allowed itself
to be caught again. . . . In short, and this is what my book will be about,
the mouse was a willing victim. Seeking to renew the pleasure of being
hunted and toyed with, out it came again."

"You mean, some species are willingly preyed on because they enjoy
it?" asked Ben. "And you are going to write a detective story about
someone who wills her or himself to be a victim? Because they enjoy it."

"Something like that. It goes like this, I think. The mouse gets a huge
adrenaline rush, then it's caught, and carried the way a cat carries a
kitten, and at that time I think it probably feels secure, loved. Then the
cat puts it down and tries to make it run again, and when the cat at last
hurts it, it does run. Then the whole pleasurable sequence all through

again. But if the mouse does get away to a spot where the cat can't get it, it has to come out again. . . ."

"You may have something here," said her sister. "It makes evolutionary sense, too. The lemming impulse. Rodents are terribly successful survivors. Pleasurable death at the hands of the hunter eases their overcrowding problem . . . and on the other side it helps to keep the not too successful predators fed, who in turn play their part in keeping rodent numbers down to a viable level. . . ."

Clearly she was not going to stop if no one made the effort: That's a training in social sciences for you. Ben made it with the wine, but not too much, they might be forced back on to the Lambrusco, and asked what was for dessert.

"Rhubarb crumble: our first picking of the year. I'll go and get it. But really, Vron, I think that's a jolly good idea."*

As they were going to bed Beatrice overheard Amanda say: "It'll be autobiographical, you know. Vron was born a victim, such a wimp."

The following morning Ben and Amanda, already dressed for work (he in check shirt and jeans, she in business suit, high heels, and frothy blouse), cleared away the muesli bowls and instructed Beatrice on how she should let herself out when the time came for her to leave. Unpressured by clocks she sat at the table, dressed in a long cotton dressing-gown over Viyella pyjamas, nursing a mug of Sainsbury's Keemun.

"When do you have to be at your publisher?" Amanda asked.

"Eleven o'clock."

"Lucky for some," she glanced at her watch. "Oh, come on, Ben."

"Please leave the dishes. I've got plenty of time," Veronica murmured.

But Ben had no intention of leaving any unnecessary opportunity for his sister-in-law to break anything. Whenever she came to stay she broke something: Last time it had been an Art Deco teacup, quite rare, a wedding present.

"Now, I'll leave the spare keys on the table by the front door just in case you want to go out and come back in again. . . ."

"I shan't."

"But you may," said Amanda with uncalled for sharpness.

"But if you don't, then you don't have to touch them. Simply pull our front door to behind you, and then the outer front door, making sure that in both cases they are properly latched. All right?"

"Of course. I'm not an idiot, and I have done it twice before."

"Come on, Ben, don't just stand there. Vron, have a bath if you want, make yourself coffee or whatever if you feel up to it, we must dash."

*So do I, and it's mine! J.R.

Swift kisses all round, and the double closing of outer doors. Even from the tiny kitchen at the back Beatrice (who hated to be called Vron or Veronica, even by her sister) could hear the repeated chugging of the Lada, but at last it fired, and they were gone. Yes, she thought, a bath would be nice. But first she must attempt to reconstruct a large armchair out of the put-u-up she had slept on. It was the sort of task she found particularly difficult.

AMIRYA WAS SHOCKED AND FRIGHTENED, but the contemplation of her husband's brains sharpened her very capable intellect and in twenty minutes she had worked out a plan. Lennie, of course, once he had washed human tissue, some of it still palpitating, from his naked torso, could do nothing but sit on the edge of the bed and, head in his hands, rock and moan.

"Lennie love, here's what you must do. Lenn-ee, kill that row or I call the police right now, all right? Listen. I'm going to take the van down to near Tower Hamlets and dump it, then I'll go to my sister's in Leyton, where she'll tell the pigs when they come I've been there since nine o'clock. While I'm gone you bag the ol' man up in plastic bin liners an' out him in one of those skips. Then you clear off right out of here. . . . No, no. You stay until the skip's been took, then you clear off out. . . ."

Lennie was not devoid of imagination and various unwelcome scenarios scrolled down his inner eye. "But what if when they get to the dump the plastic tears, or . . . or anything?"

"Listen, love. It'll be on the top of the skip, so when they tip it off, first in the pit, first to be covered. Anyway once the skip's gone you buzz me at my sister's and then you sod off."

"What'll you do?"

"I'll come back here and clean up so no forensic scientist in the world will get the least littlest clue as to what happened. One thing I do know is cleaning. One good thing . . . you were naked when you did it, nothing on your clothes."

"An' after that?"

"I stay at my sister's an' from there I sell the shop: It's half in my name anyway. Then I move up north, with the kiddies, but another shop and then I ask you to come, like if you still want to. All you got to do, lover, is get that on the top of a skip. OK? Now I'm gwine to get dressed and you should do, too. No, honey, I'm not interested in Marley right now. You shot the sheriff and it's a question of first things first. Oh, oh . . . oh. All right."

Later she murmured: "Honey, I reckon you just shot the deputy, too. Now. Get dressed."

TIME FLEW FOR BEATRICE. She pottered unsteadily about the ground floor flat, reconstructed the armchair, folded the duvet, had a bath, made herself a coffee, and by the time she had done all that it was a quarter past ten. She checked her overnight bag for her washing things, her pyjamas and dressing gown, and above all for the manuscript she was about to deliver (*Murder on Denmark Hill* by Beatrice Burne-Jones), picked up the keys, remembered what she had been told, and put them down again. She let herself out into the tiny lobby, paused for a moment, thought really hard: Had she left anything behind? No, she had not, and she pulled the inner front door to, made the latch click, then leant against it to make doubly sure it was properly locked. Then she turned to the outer door, put up the catch, turned the knob of the Yale lock, and pulled. Nothing. She pulled again. It must be stuck. She bent down and found by the doorknob a second brassy keyhole: Writers of detective stories know a thing or two about locks—she recognized a mortice. She turned, hammered on the second front door, the one that led to stairs and the upstairs flatlet, but knew it was useless. The occupant had left shortly after Ben and Amanda for the primary school where she taught, and against all her usual habits, had double locked the outer door.

Writers of detective stories also know a thing or two about locked room mysteries, but for the life of her Beatrice could not see how she was going to get out of this one.

LENNIE WAS STRONG, and after the initial shock had worn off, not naturally squeamish. Ranjit was small and slight of build and it was not much of a problem to get his legs and lower torso into one big black bin liner. The top half was messy, but he got over that by pulling a white swingbin liner over the old man's crushed skull. Then he found some parcel tape, and used it clumsily and in large amounts to fasten the two bin liners together. This was the worst part really: the tape stuck to itself, and to the wrong bits of the bags, to his fingers. He found it almost impossible to hold the edges of the plastic where he wanted them to be, and manipulate the tape at the same time. But he managed.

Then he humped his five-foot-long parcel over his shoulder and got it down into the shop. The next problem was getting it on to the top of the nearest skip without anyone seeing him: Amirya had been adamant about that. He went back upstairs, and peeping round the lace curtain waited until the coast was clear, the street empty. He did not have to wait long. Monday morning, half-past ten, everyone was at work or school, or almost everyone. Only a young woman, part ethnic, was across the road and for some reason bending down over the letter-box of the house opposite. It did not occur to Lennie to wonder why. The young woman straightened and walked briskly away, round the corner, was gone, leaving the street to a large and ugly ginger tom who sidled along the low garden walls opposite.

*   *   *

"HELP! I SAY HELP! I need help."

Five minutes earlier the young part ethnic lady who worked flextime as a cashier and shelf filler at Tesco's half a mile away, had heard the plaintive cry. But she could not work out where it was coming from.

"Over here. I'm behind the front door of number five, speaking through the letter box." The flap was sprung and very difficult to lift from inside and keep open. But Beatrice had managed using her Parker pen, which she had now wedged in the gap so it kept the flap open. "I'm locked in the lobby and I can't get out."

"How did that happen then?"

"The upstairs tenant must have double-locked, using the mortice. She never has before. And I'd already pulled my sister's front door shut, leaving the key inside. It's what they told me to do."

"I don't see how I can help."

"Well, I think you can. This is my address book. It has my brother-in-law's work number at the BBC, Broadcasting House, and I'm sure if you could get through to him they'll let him come home to release me...."

"No, miss. I can't do that. I'm late for work already, you keep calling and I'm sure you'll find someone soon." And she hurried away. Damn, thought Beatrice.

ON THE OTHER SIDE OF THE ROAD Lennie opened the shop door and was in and out with his awful black parcel in ten seconds flat, draping it across the high pile of rubble that more than filled the skip. He locked the doors behind him again and went back to the upstairs bedroom to wait for the skip truck to come.

Presently the large ginger tom leapt up on to the skip and began scratching round what Lennie knew very well was the head end of the parcel. Presently he could see the white of the inner bag, then hair and ...

"Oh, shit!" cried Lennie, aloud, and grabbing up the parcel tape again he shot back out into the street. The cat hissed and scatted, and he hurled lumps of cement after it trying desperately for the sort of accuracy that might make it reluctant to come back. Then he got to work again with the tape that seemed more unbiddable than ever and absolutely refused to stick to anything wet.... And apart from the blood, it had begun to rain....

"Help, I say. Help. Please."

He looked all round, up and down the empty street. Even the cat had gone.

"Over here. I'm locked in behind the front door of number five."

Heart thudding now, Lennie came between the skip and the back of his pickup, crossed the road. He stooped, looked beneath the wedged letter flap. He couldn't believe it. He could not believe it. There was a woman behind the door, a grey thin middle-aged biddy, just the sort that spies on everything that happens. Peering through the slit, she must have seen everything.

"How long you bin 'ere?"

"Oh, about twenty minutes I think, not more...." Lennie groaned inwardly: She had, he thought, she had seen everything. "Listen, here's what I want you to do...."

But Lennie was not listening. He ran back into the shop, setting the bell jangling behind him, locking himself in again. What to do, what could he do? He was done for unless ... he'd killed once, could he kill again? Yes. He'd have to, it was the only way, but how? How? He paced about the shop, banging his forehead, wringing his big black hands, racking his brains, then, Sunny Jim, it came to him.

BEATRICE COULD NOT BELIEVE her bad luck. Only two passersby in twenty minutes had appeared to hear her, and neither seemed prepared to help. She was beginning to feel desperate, claustrophobic, it was after all a tiny space she was in, little more than a metre square and two metres high, trapped between three locked doors. She tried bracing her back against the wall and her feet against her sister's door, but soon realized it was quite useless. She was nowhere near strong enough. Every time she heard footsteps she got back on her knees and cried out through the slit again, help, help. She could hear the footsteps stop, she could guess how they looked around for her, and then hurried on from the ghost-like cry before she could tell them where she was.

But now, at last, someone seemed to be coming, was it the man who had come from the other side of the road? She rather thought it was. And what's this, has he thought of some ingenious way of getting her out, a black plastic spout through the letter box, fluid from a red plastic can splashed about her feet, the smell of petrol, and what's he doing now? A packet of Sunny Jim firelighters? Is he mad, am I mad?

"Stop it, please stop it," she cried, as he fed the white waxy rectangles one by one through the slit, each one burning on a corner. She managed to extinguish the first three, but on the fourth the petrol exploded with a dull whumph. Bracing her feet against her sister's door once more and her back against the wall opposite, she forced herself up, foot by foot, inch by inch above the flames, but into the smoke. She realized she was not shouting, screaming, and she wondered why not. She realized that she had never been so excited in her whole life, that never before had she felt so alive, so at one with an elemental universe whose existence she had suspected but never before experienced. The fumes drugged her, she breathed them in with a welcoming abandon, fell dizzy, and dropped fainting into the tiny inferno three feet below. Almost her fall was enough to put out the flames, almost. . . . Never had she felt so happy and her last thought was: I'm right about mice.

"WHY, I DON'T UNDERSTAND WHY?" her sister wailed later that evening. The policeman tried to explain.

"We think she must have seen something she shouldn't have seen out in the street. A mugging maybe, something like that."

"But that's not possible. She had terrible eyesight, tunnel vision, could only see properly with glasses that made her eyes look like oysters. She only wore them to read. She can't have *seen* anything. . . ."

Richard T. Chizmar's fiction has been called "always effective, notable for its clarity of style and originality of concept," and "[his work] should concern anyone interested in exceptional writing talent." Some of his more than forty published short stories appear in *Frankenstein: The Monster Wakes, White House Horrors,* and his own collection, *Midnight Promises,* published in 1995. "The Silence of Sorrow" examines how, if possible, the grief over a loved one's death can be compounded.

The Silence of Sorrow
RICHARD T. CHIZMAR

I

He stood there for a long time, just staring out the upstairs bedroom window, listening to the sounds of a lazy spring afternoon. A dog barking somewhere in the distance; a chorus of lawn mowers; the sweet music of a child's laughter; the soft hum of neighborhood traffic.

He stood there, unable to move, unable to breathe, unable to make sense of the thoughts whirling madly within his head. The sheer curtains, nudged by a gentle breeze, fluttered inward and brushed against his arms and the scent of cut grass and fresh flowers was thick and rich in the air. It filled the room with the promise of summer.

He looked at the photos again, just a quick glance, and suddenly the sun felt unbearably hot on his face; blistering; suffocating. He took a step backward into the room. Closed his eyes. And it was then that his hands began to shake, and he discovered he could not stop them.

The photos slipped from his fingertips, tumbled soundlessly in a stream onto the carpet. Piled there like discards from a poker game. One by one they fell until his hands were empty.

Then he began to weep.

2

He hadn't wept since the funeral service—a cloudless June morning six days earlier—and now the tears streamed hot and angry down his cheeks. He sobbed with great force, but silently, afraid the others would hear, terrified they would rush to comfort him. He sat down on the edge of the bed and took in deep, whistling gulps of air. After a time, the pressure on his chest eased and he felt less light-headed, but his stomach remained cramped and tight.

He had come here, to this house of death, with a mixture of dread and sorrow. It was such a horrible task—the toughest he had ever faced, in fact—but it was his duty. And he was not the only one. There were eight of them in total. Three (his daughters; all married and living in distant cities) were downstairs talking on the back porch, resting from a long morning of backbreaking work. The others (a son-in-law and three longtime neighbors) had gone downtown twenty minutes earlier in search of drink reinforcements and pizza and sandwiches. And so he was left alone in the house.

3

He'd found them in the bedroom closet. Hidden inside a shoebox, the box carefully tucked away beneath a tangled clutter of clothes hangers and worn-out jogging shoes. There were other things inside the box, but the photos were the worst. And there were dozens of them.

4

The accident had made the papers and the television news as far west as Emittsburg and as far east as Baltimore. Yes, sir; it was a pretty big story for a slow week in June. Nine cars and two trucks involved. A series of spectacular explosions. Seven gut-wrenching fatalities, including the owner of the Hagerstown Baysox (a local minor league ballclub; currently four games out of first), a twenty-year veteran of the D.C. police force, a young retarded boy, and a hometown hero.

It was inside this hometown hero's bedroom that Frank Martin sat alone with a pile of photos and his troubled thoughts.

5

Frank, back in his midtwenties, had once worked as a maintenance man at an apartment complex just outside of Pittsburgh. During his first month on the job, he'd been forced to help clean out a woman's one-bedroom apartment after she'd committed suicide. The woman had had no family, no friends; no one to carry on her name, much less collect her memories. So the job had fallen to the employees.

Frank had hated it.

All morning and afternoon, while he boxed her personal belongings and piled them in the hallway for the others to carry outside to the truck, he'd felt as if the walls were closing in on him. He'd felt dirty, like a trespasser.

Even then, while he struggled with the cardboard boxes and the packing tape, he'd clearly known that the details of the day would haunt him forever; he would never be able to forget what kind of plates and utensils the woman had in her kitchen, the titles of the books on her shelves, the simple prints and paintings on the walls, her favorite color of shoes, the style of dress she preferred, what her handwriting looked like on a grocery list magneted to the refrigerator door. And so many other little things he had no right to possess knowledge of.

For days after the job, Frank had experienced such a profound feeling of sorrow that he'd broken down in tears several times with the memory, and his nightly routine of seven hours' sleep became five hours, then three, then almost nothing. When his appetite began to diminish, Sarah (his wife of just over a year at the time) convinced him to take a weekend off and they'd snuck away to the country for two days of rest, relaxation, and magic.

6

Frank thought of that long-ago day and immediately realized the sad irony. Here he was, after all these years, once again cleaning up after the dead.

His hands still trembled, but just enough now to make picking up the color Polaroids a slow process. He crouched to one knee and snatched them up with his right hand and collected them with his left. He did this without looking at the pictures. He had seen enough.

When he was finished he tossed them into the shoebox, which was now resting on the bed, and returned the box to the clutter at the bottom of the closet. He dropped a pair of folded sweaters on top, closed the door, and went downstairs.

7

Lunch was a club sandwich, corn chips, and a frosty can of Coke. They ate outside at the picnic table and Frank forced himself to clean his plate; he knew they were concerned about him and would be watching. In fact, he didn't doubt for a moment that Sarah had asked one—or even all three—of the girls to make sure he didn't skip his lunch. *He'll need the energy,* she probably told them. *So you make certain he eats something, even if it's just a candy bar.*

My God, he thought, watching two squirrels play chase in an ancient weeping willow, he had himself one wonderful old lady.

As they'd done the day before, everyone remained in the backyard sunshine after lunch was finished, planning which are of the house to clear next and discussing which boxes needed to be moved where. Frank said very little. Instead, he found himself studying the faces of his friends and family, listening to each of their voices, watching their gestures and expressions, and he was surprised when he was almost moved to tears. God, how he loved these people. Loved their strengths, their weaknesses. Loved what they stood for after all these long years. He would have gladly faced death for each and every one of them—traded his breath for theirs—and he knew the feeling was mutual . . . yet at no other time in his life had he felt so utterly helpless.

So completely alone.

8

Eventually, as it had done so many other times during the past week, the conversation turned to fond reminiscing and favorite memories. Frank sat back in the tall grass, stretched his legs, and listened to the familiar stories:

The day when Chuck was six years old and he fell face-first into the wishing fountain at the Gateway Shopping Mall . . .

The summer day, a year later, when he ran away from home and ended up being sprayed by an angry skunk in the old Hanson woods . . .

The time he was almost suspended from school for freeing the frogs from the biology lab . . .

The summer he saved that woman's life at the beach, springing to action and starting CPR when the teenaged lifeguard froze in terror . . .

The fine spring day he graduated from law school with honors and at the top of his class . . .

The afternoon he was married to his wonderful Mary Ellen . . .

The magical night the twins were born . . .

The day he was elected mayor of their small ("but growing") town, the
youngest ever at the age of thirty-three, and a hometown boy to boot . . .
Despite the midday sun, Frank's hands felt clammy, his chest ice-cold.
He listened halfheartedly, nodding when he felt it was appropriate,
feigning laughter several times, mainly just smiling sadly.

Soon he found his thoughts drifting away from the conversation to one
memory in particular: *It had been Chuck's eleventh birthday, and the two*
of them had spent the day together. That had been Chuck's only birthday
wish that year: to spend the entire day with his Dad; just the two of them.
They'd planned the day for weeks, and when it finally arrived, they'd
attacked it head-on like a pair of young brothers, instead of a father and
son. First thing in the morning, they'd fished for catfish down at the big
bend in Hanson's Creek (and been quite lucky with their catch). Next,
after a quick shower and a pizza lunch at the mall, they'd watched their
Orioles and the Red Sox battle it out in an afternoon doubleheader at
Memorial Stadium. It had been a perfect day, capped off by a postgame
photo of father and son and Brooks Robinson, their favorite ballplayer. . . .

Frank, to his amazement and horror, felt a smile forming, and he
choked it back in immediately. An enlarged and framed print of the
birthday photo hung proudly in his den, a surprise retirement gift from
Chuck two years earlier. In his mind's eye, Frank imagined seeing the
photo hanging side-by-side next to an enlargement of one of the photos
from upstairs—a "that was then, this is now" comparison of his son.

His brain flashed this image in grim detail and, for one frightening
moment, he thought he might be sick.

9

They were photos of naked children. Glossy, full-color Polaroids.

Solo shots. Couples. Group shots.

Frank thought of the photos—images so perverse and unspeakable that
nothing in his sixty-four years of life had prepared him for the sight of
them—and for a moment he was sure that he had to be dreaming. That
the feel of the grass and the sun and the breeze had to be part of the
dream. That the faraway voices and faces around him were imagined,
not real.

He closed his eyes and rested his head.

Felt the grass tickle the back of his neck.

Listened to the beating of his heart.

But he knew he wasn't dreaming.

And he knew what he had seen: a brown shoebox full of shiny magazines filled with disgusting pictures, a worn datebook full of mysterious
addresses and phone numbers and cryptic appointment notes, a pair of

unlabeled video cassettes, and dozen and dozens of photos ... several of them capturing the smiling image of his only son. . . .

And in these photos Chuck was not alone.

10

Frank Martin stretched out in the cool grass and listened to the silence. The entire neighborhood seemed to be taking a midday break, and he was alone again with his thoughts. The others had all gone back inside, and from time to time, he could hear a muffled voice or the echo of footsteps or the soft thud of a box being moved. But mostly he heard nothing at all.

He sat there, staring up at the bedroom window, and soon his hands began to twitch. He clasped them together and squeezed, and it occurred to him that he was probably losing his mind.

A tornado of thoughts touched down in his head:

He thought of Sarah and the others. What would he—or could he—tell them? That Chuck was not the son, the brother, the friend they all thought him to be?

He thought of Mary Ellen, Chuck's young wife, also lost in the accident. Had she been suspicious? Had she seen the warning signs?

And then he thought of the very worst ... the twins. Two bundles of joy and energy and hope, safe at home with their grandma. What would their futures have held if not for the accident? Would he *(sweet Jesus please please don't let it be true!)* find them upstairs in those photos? On those videos?

He felt smothered by these dark questions, but he ran them through slowly and carefully, a small piece of his heart breaking off and dying with each thought. After a long time, he got up and walked into the house, into a world that suddenly made no sense. No sense at all.

Joan Hess first started out writing romances, but switched to mysteries on the advice of her agent, and has never looked back. Her novels, usually set in small Arklansas towns, have won the Agatha, American Mystery, and Macavity awards. Her shorter fiction has appeared in *Cat Crimes* and *Crimes of Passion*. Currently she is editing a collection of humorous fiction along the lines of her own books. In "All That Glitters," she takes a break from the population of Maggody, Arkansas, to look in on a different kind of love triangle.

All That Glitters
JOAN HESS

Welcome to the home of Remmington Boles and his mother, Audrey Antoinette (née Tattlinger) Boles. It is a small yet gracious house in the center of the historic district. At one time it was the site of fancy luncheons and elegant dinner parties. There have been no parties of any significance since the timely and unremarkable demise of Ralph Edward Boles. I believe this was in 1962, but it may have been the following year.

Remmington, who is called Remmie by his mother and few remaining relatives, is forty-one years old, reasonably tall, reasonably attractive. There is little else to say about his physical presence. It's likely you would trust him on first sight. He has never been unkind to animals or children.

Audrey is of an age that falls between sixty and seventy. She was once attractive in an antebellum sort of way. In her heyday thirty years ago, she was president of the Junior League and almost single-handedly raised the money for a children's cancer wing at the regional hospital.

At this moment, Audrey is in her bedroom at the top of the stairs. Although we cannot see her, we can deduce from her vaguely querulous tone that she is no longer in robust health.

"Remmie? Do you have time to find my slippers before you leave? It seems so damp and chilly this morning. I hope there's nothing wrong with the furnace."

Her son's voice is patient and, for the most part, imbued with affection. He is not a candidate for sainthood, but he is a good son.

"There's nothing wrong with the furnace," he says as he comes into her bedroom. "Let me raise the blinds so you can enjoy the sunshine."

He takes two steps, then pauses as he does every morning. The micro-drama has been performed for many years. Very rarely does anything happen to disrupt it, and there is nothing in the air to lead Remmie to suspect this day will be extraordinary.

"No, leave them down. I can't tolerate the glare. Oh, Remmie, I pray every night that you'll never face the specter of blindness. It's so very frightening."

Two steps to her side; two squeezes of her hand. "Now, Mother, Dr. Whitbread found no symptoms of retinopathy, and he said you shouldn't worry. The ophthalmologist said the same thing only a few months ago."

Her eyes are bleached and rimmed with red, but they regard him with birdlike acuity. "You're so good to me. I don't know how I could ever get along without you."

"I'm late for work, Mother. Here are your slippers right beside the bed. I'll be home at noon to fix your lunch." He bends down to kiss her forehead, then waits to be dismissed.

"Bless you, Remmie."

Remmie Boles goes downstairs to the kitchen, rinses out his coffee cup, and props it in the rack, then makes sure his mother's tray is ready for her midmorning snack; tea bag, porcelain cup and saucer, two sugar cookies in a cellophane bag. The teapot, filled with a precise quantity of water, is on the back burner.

He enjoys the six-block walk to Boles Discount Furniture Warehouse, and produces a smile for his secretary, who is filing her fingernails. She is not overly bright, but she is very dependable—a trait much valued in small business concerns.

"Good morning, Ailene," Remmie says, collecting the mail from the corner of her desk.

"Some guy from your church called, Mr. Boles. He wants to know if you're gonna be on the bowling team this year. He says they'll take you back as long as you promise not to quit in the middle of the season like you did last year." Having been an employee for ten years, she feels entitled to make unseemly comments. "You really should get out and meet people. You're not all that old, you know, and kinda cute. There are a lot of women who'd jump at the chance to go out with a guy like you."

"Please bring me the sales tax figures from the last quarter." Remmie goes into his office and closes the door before he allows himself to react.

Ailene has made a point. Remmie is not a recluse. He has dated over the year, albeit infrequently and for no great duration. Alas, he has not been out since the fiasco that was responsible for his abandonment of the First Methodist Holy Rollers in midseason.

Yes, even Methodists can evince a sense of humor.

Lucinda was (and still is, as far as I know) a waitress at the bowling alley. He'd been dazzled by her bright red hair, mischievous grin, and body that rippled like a field of ripe wheat when she walked. She agreed to go out for drinks. One thing had led to another, first in the front seat of his car, then on the waterbed in her apartment.

The very idea of experiencing such sexual bliss every night left Remmie giddy, and he found himself pondering marriage. After a series of increasingly erotic encounters, he invited Lucinda to meet his mother.

It was a ghastly idea. Lucinda arrived in a tight purple dress that scarcely covered the tops of her thighs, and brought a bottle of whiskey as a present. In the harsh light of his living room, he could see the bags under her eyes and the slackness of her jowls. Her voice was coarse, her laugh a bray, her ripple nothing more than a cheap, seductive wiggle. He quit the bowling team immediately.

Back to work, Remmie.

He ignores the message and settles down with the figures. At eleven, he goes out to the showroom to make sure his salesmen aren't gossiping in the break room. He is heading for the counter when a woman comes through the main door and halts, her expression wary, as if she's worried that ravenous beasts are lurking under oak veneer tables and behind plaid recliners.

If Ailene hadn't made her presumptuous comments, perhaps Remmie would not have given this particular customer more than a cursory assessment. As it is, he notices she's a tiny bit plump, several inches shorter than he, and of a similar age. Her hair, short and curly, is the color of milk chocolate. She is wearing a dark skirt and white blouse, and carrying a shiny black handbag.

"May I help you?" he says.

"I'm just looking. It's hard to know where to start, isn't it?"

"Are you in the market for living room furniture? We have a good assortment on sale right now."

"I need all sorts of things, but I don't have much of a budget," she says rather sadly. "Then again, I don't have much of a house."

To his horror, her eyes fill with tears.

Remmie persuades her to accept a cup of coffee in his office, and within a half hour, possesses her story. Crystal Ambler grew up on the seedy side of the city, attended the junior college, and is now the office manager of a small medical clinic. A childless marriage ended in divorce more than five years ago. She spends her free time reading, gardening, and occasionally playing bridge with her parents and sister. She once had a cat; but it ran away and now she lives alone.

"Not very exciting, is it?" she says with a self-deprecatory laugh. "It's hard being single these days, and almost impossible to meet someone who isn't burdened with a psychosis and an outstanding warrant or two."

"Mr. Boles," Ailene says from the doorway, "your mother called to remind you to pick up syringes on your way home for lunch."

"Is your mother ill?" asks Crystal with appropriate sympathy.

"She was diagnosed with diabetes the year I graduated from college. It's manageable with daily insulin injections and a strict diet."

"It must be awfully hard on you and your wife," she begins, then gasps and rises unsteadily. "I'm sorry. It's none of my business and I shouldn't have—"

"It's perfectly all right." Remmie catches her hands between his and studies her contrite expression, spotting for the first time a little dimple on her chin. "I should be the one to apologize. You came here to look for furniture, and I've wasted your time with my questions. I do hope you'll allow me to help you find a bargain."

Crystal is amenable.

REMMIE SMILES THOUGHTFULLY as he walks home for lunch. There is something charmingly quaint about Miss Ambler. She is by no means a hapless maiden awaiting rescue by a knight; when she selected the sofa, she did so with no hint of indecision or tacit plea for his approval. But at the same time, she is soft-spoken and modest. He's certain she would never wear a tight purple dress or drink whiskey. He doubts she drinks anything more potent than white wine.

He's halfway across the living room when he realizes something is acutely wrong. His mother never fails to call his name when he enters the house. It is an inviolate part of their script.

"Mother?" he calls as he hurries upstairs to her bedroom. The room is dim; the television, invariably set on a game show, is silent. The figure on the bed is motionless. "Mother?" he repeats with a growing sense of panic.

"Remmie, thank God you're here. I feel so weak. I tried to call you, but I couldn't even lift the receiver."

"Shall I call for an ambulance?"

"No, I simply need something to nibble on to elevate my blood sugar. If it's not too much trouble, would you please bring the cookies from this morning?"

"You skipped your snack? Dr. Whitbread stressed how very vital it is that you stay on your schedule. Maybe I should call him."

"All I need are the cookies, Remmie." Despite her avowed weakness, she picks up the clock and squints at it. "My goodness, you're almost an hour late. Was there an emergency at the store?"

"A minor one," he murmurs.

REMMIE CALLS CRYSTAL that evening to make sure she is pleased with her selection. She shyly invites him to come by some time and see how well the sofa goes with the drapes. Remmie professes eagerness to do so, and suggests Saturday morning. Although Crystal sounds disappointed, she promises coffee and cake.

The week progresses uneventfully. Whatever has caused Audrey's bout of weakness has not recurred, although she has noticed a disturbing new symptom and broaches it after the evening news is over.

She holds out a hand. "Feel my fingers, Remmie. They're so swollen I haven't been able to wear any of my rings. Perhaps you should take all my jewelry down to the bank tomorrow morning and put it in the safe-deposit box. If it's not too much bother, of course. It's so maddening not to be able to do things for myself. I know I'm such a terrible burden on you."

"I'll do it Saturday morning," Remmie says. "I have some other errands, and I'll be in that neighborhood."

"Errands? I hate to think of you spending your weekend driving all over town instead of having a chance to relax around the house. You work so hard all week."

"I enjoy getting out." He picks up her tray and heads for the kitchen.

SATURDAY.

Remmie grimaces as he pulls into the driveway. His mother's jewelry is still in the glove compartment, and the bank closes at noon on Saturdays. His mother will spend the weekend fretting if she finds out about his negligence, but there's no reason why she will. A good son does not cause his mother unnecessary concern.

He sits in the car and replays his visit. Upon opening the door, Crystal hadn't thrown herself into his arms, but she'd held his hand several seconds longer than decorum dictates. Their conversation had been lively. They'd parted with yet another warm handshake.

He locks the glove compartment and goes inside. And freezes as he sees his mother slumped on the sofa, her hands splayed across her chest and her eyes closed.

"Mother!" he says as he sinks to her side. "Can you hear me?"

"I'm conscious," Audrey says dully. "I was on my way to the kitchen when I felt so dizzy I almost fell."

"Let me help you back to bed, and then I'll call the doctor." Remmie picks her up and carries her to her bedroom, settles her on the bed, and reaches for the telephone.

"No, don't disturb Dr. Whitbread. He's entitled to his weekends, just as you are. If I'm not better on Monday, you can call him then."

"Are you sure?" asks Remmie, alarmed at the thinness of her voice.

"It's very dear of you to be so concerned about me, Remmie. Most children put their ailing parents in nursing homes and try to forget about them. The poor old things lose what wits they have and spend their last days drooling and being tormented by sadistic nurses."

"This is your home, Mother. Why don't you take a little nap while I fix your lunch?"

"Bless you," she says with a sigh. He's almost to the door when she adds, "There was a call for you half an hour ago. A woman with a trailer park sort of name said you'd left your gloves at her house. I tried to catch you at the bank to relay the message, but they said you hadn't come in. I hope they weren't your suede gloves, Remmie. I ordered them from Italy, you know."

"I know." He urges himself back into motion. Had he subconsciously chosen to leave his gloves at Crystal's house so he'd have another excuse to call her? He ponders the possibility as he washes lettuce and slices a tomato.

AUDREY IS STRANGELY QUIET all afternoon and declines his offer to play gin rummy after dinner. Remmie finally breaks down and tells her about Crystal Ambler.

"She sounds very nice," says Audrey. "She lives in that neighborhood beyond the interstate, you said? Your father and I made a point of never driving through that area after dark, even if it meant going miles out of our way." She pauses as if reliving a long and torturous detour, then says, "What exactly does this woman do?"

Audrey listens as Remmie describes Crystal's job, her clean, if somewhat Spartan, house, her garden, even her new sofa. "She sounds very nice," is all she says as she limps across the dining room and down the hall. "Very nice."

SUNDAY, SUNDAY.

Remmie calls Crystal while his mother is napping. After he apologizes for leaving his gloves, he invites her to meet him after work on Monday for a glass of wine.

MONDAY.

Remmie tells his mother he'll be working late in preparation for the inventory-reduction sale. He uses the same excuse when he takes Crystal to dinner later that week. On Saturday afternoon, he makes an ambiguous reference to the hardware store and takes Crystal for a drive in the country. Afterward, he feels foolish when Audrey not only brings up Crystal's name, but encourages him to ask her out. He admits they have plans.

"Dinner on Wednesday?" murmurs Audrey, carefully folding her napkin and placing it on the table. "What a lovely idea, Remmie. I'm sure she'll be thrilled to have a meal in a proper restaurant."

"Would you like me to see if Miss McCloud can sit with you while I'm out?"

"I wouldn't dream of bothering her. After all, I'm here by myself every day. I'm so used to being alone that I'll scarcely notice that you're out with this woman."

"I'D LIKE TO MEET YOUR MOTHER," Crystal says as they dally over coffee in her living room. "You're obviously devoted to her."

"My father left a very small estate. My mother insisted on working at a clothing shop to put me through college, then used the last of the insurance money to finance the store. Before her illness grew more debilitating, she came down to the showroom at night and dusted the displays." Remmie smiles gently. "I'd like you to meet her. She's asked me all about you, and I think she's beginning to suspect I might be ..."

"Be what?"

"Falling in love," he says, then leans forward and kisses her. When she responds, he slides his arm behind her back and marvels at the supple contours. Their kisses intensify, as do Remmie's caresses and her tiny moans. His hand finds its way beneath her sweater to her round breasts. His mind swirls with deliciously impure images.

Therefore, he's startled when she pulls back and moves to the far end of the sofa. For an alarming moment, she looks close to tears, but she takes a shuddery breath and says, "No, Remmie, I'm not going to have an affair. I shouldn't have gone out with you in the first place. I'm too old to get into another pointless relationship. I'd rather get a cat."

Remmie bites back a groan. "Crystal, darling, I'd never do anything to hurt you. I don't want a pointless relationship, either."

"Then take me home to meet your mother."

He frowns at the obstinate edge in her voice. "I will when the time's right. Mother's been fretting about her blood pressure lately, and I don't want to excite her more than necessary."

"Maybe you'd better go home and check on her," Crystal says as she stands up. However, rather than hurrying him out the door, she presses her body against his and kisses him with such fierce passion that he nearly loses his balance. "There'll be more of this when we're engaged," she promises in a warm, moist whisper. She goes on to describe what lies in store after they're married.

The constraints of the genre prevent me from providing details.

TIME FLIES.

"Does your friend drive an old white Honda?" Audrey asks Remmie while he's massaging her feet to stimulate circulation.

He gives her a surprised look. "Why do you ask?"

"Someone who matches he description has driven by here several times. It most likely wasn't her, though. This woman had the predatory gleam of a real estate appraiser trying to decide how much our house is worth." Audrey manages a weak chuckle. "And of course I can barely see the street from my window these days. It's all a matter of time before I'm no longer a burden, Remmie, and you'll be free to get on with your life."

"Don't say that, Mother," he says as he strokes her wispy gray hair. A sudden vision of the future floods his mind: his mother's bedroom is unlit and empty, but farther down the hall, Crystal smiles from his bed, her arms outstretched and her breasts heaving beneath a silky black gown.

He realizes his mother is staring at him and wipes a sheen of perspiration off his forehead. "Don't say that," he repeats.

SEVERAL MORE WEEKS PASS, and then back to Boles Discount Furniture Warehouse we go.

This morning Ailene is typing slowly but steadily. "Crystal called," she says without looking up. "She said to tell you that she can't go to the movies tonight."

"Did she say why?"

"Something about baby-sitting for her sister. Oh, and your mother called right before you got here. She wants you to pick up some ointment for her blisters. She said you'd know what kind and where to get it."

Remmie closes his office door, reaches for the telephone, and then lowers his hand. Crystal has made it clear that he's not to call her at the clinic. But this is the second time this week she's canceled their date to do a favor for her sister. Last week she met him at the door and announced she was going out with some friends from the clinic. Remmie had not been invited to join them.

Can he be losing her? When they're together on the sofa, her passion seems to rival his own. Although she continues to refuse to make love, she has found ways to soften his frustration. She swears she has never loved anyone as deeply.

He collapses in his chair, cradles his head in his hands, and silently mouths her name.

WHEN REMMIE COMES INTO THE LIVING ROOM, he is shocked. He is stunned, bewildered, and profoundly inarticulate. The one thing he is not prepared to see is his mother sitting at one end of the sofa and Crystal at the other. A tray with teacups and saucers resides on the coffee table, a few crumbs indicative that cookies have been consumed.

"Crystal," he gasps.

"Remmie, dear," his mother says chidingly, "that's no way to welcome a guest into our home. Have you forgotten your manners?"

Crystal's smile is as sweet as the sugar granules on the tray. "I was in the neighborhood, and it seemed like time to stop by and meet your mother. We've been having a lovely chat."

"Oh, yes," says Audrey. "A lovely chat."

Remmie sinks down on the edge of the recliner, aware his mouth is slack. "That's good," he says at last.

Audrey nods. "Crystal and I discovered a most amazing coincidence. It seems her mother used to clean house for Laetitia Whimsey, who was in my garden club for years."

"Amazing," Remmie says, glaring at Crystal. He's angry at he effrontery in coming, but she refuses to acknowledge him and listens attentively as Audrey reminisces about her garden club.

Out on the porch, however, Crystal crosses her arms and gazes defiantly at him. "This meeting was long overdue," she says, "and you've been stalling. Well, now I've met her. She seems to like me well enough, and I'm sure we'll get along just fine in the future. We do have a future, don't we?"

"Of course we do," he says, shocked by her vehemence. "I was only waiting until Mother . . ."

"Dies?"

Remmie steps back and clutches the rail. "Don't be ridiculous. She's experiencing numbness in her lower legs and feet, and the doctor recommended tests for arteriosclerosis. Mother is always distraught about going into the hospital."

"And then what, Remmie? Will she have problems with her kidneys? Will her blood pressure fluctuate?"

"I don't know, Crystal. Her condition is very delicate, but the doctor seems to feel that in general her prognosis is good."

"Then what's the delay?" she counters. "I believed you when you told me that you love me. Otherwise, I would have broken off our relationship long before I became emotionally involved. There are plenty of women who'll sleep with you, Remmie—if that's all you want."

He stares as she marches down the steps and across the street to her little white car. He remains on the porch even after she has driven away without so much as a glance in his direction.

"Remmie?" calls his mother. "Could you be a dear and help me upstairs? I wasn't expecting any visitors, and now I'm exhausted. There's no rush, of course. I'll just sit here in the dark until you have a moment."

JANUARY PROVES TO BE the cruelest month.

Crystal allows Remmie to take her out several times, and permits him a few more liberties on the sofa, for which he is grateful. On the other hand, he senses a reticence on her part to abandon herself to his embraces. They both avoid any references to Audrey, who continues to encourage him to go out with Crystal.

Remmie begins to feel as if he's losing his mind. He's obsessed with Crystal; his waking hours are haunted by memories of how she feels in his arms. His dreams are so explicit that he awakens drenched with sweat and shivering with frustration.

The obvious question arises: Why does he not propose marriage? If he could answer this, he would. For the most part, Crystal is the girl of his dreams (if he and I may employ the cliché). She has shown a flicker of annoyance now and then, but she is quick to apologize and kiss away his injured feelings. She has joined his church. On two occasions she has brought Audrey flowers and perky greeting cards.

When Audrey mentions Crystal's name, Remmie listens intently for any nuances in her voice. He's perceptive enough to anticipate a petty display of jealousy, but thus far he has not seen it. Audrey maintains that she is fond of Crystal, that she enjoys their infrequent but pleasant conversations.

Why is he incapable of proposing?

MERCIFULLY, January ends and we ease into February, a month fraught with significance for young and old lovers alike.

"Does Crystal have a brother?" asks Audrey one morning as Remmie is straightening her blanket.

"I don't think so."

"How odd," she says under her breath.

"Why would you think she has a brother, Mother?"

"It's so silly that I hate to confess." Audrey sighs and looks away, then adds, "I called her house yesterday morning to thank her for the romance novel she sent. A man answered the telephone, and I was so unnerved that I hung up without saying a word. It was quite early; you'd just left for work."

Remmie is aware that two days ago Crystal canceled their plans for dinner, saying that she needed to work on files from the clinic. He has not spoken to her since then, although he has left messages for her to call.

"It must have been a plumber," Audrey says dismissively. "Would you check the thermostat, dear? I can hardly wiggle my toes."

AS VALENTINE'S DAY APPROACHES, Remmie becomes more and more distracted. Crystal denies having a brother; he's too embarrassed to say anything further. He feels as if he's driving down a steep mountain road, tires skidding, brakes smoking and squealing, gravel spewing behind him.

He is staring at the calendar when Ailene comes into his office.

"Here's the candy," she says, putting down a plain white box that has come in the morning mail. "You should get a medal or something for going to all this trouble every year. It must cost twice as much as regular candy."

"It's one of our little traditions. I've told Mother she can have sugar-free chocolate all year, but she says it's sweeter because it's a Valentine's Day gift."

"You doing something special with Crystal?" asks Ailene, who has been monitoring the relationship with a healthy curiosity.

Remmie comes to a decision. "Yes, I am," he says without taking his eyes off the white box.

LATE IN THE MORNING, he calls Audrey and tells her that he is unable to come home to prepare her lunch, citing the need to run errands. She wishes him a profitable hour and assures him she will have a nice bowl of soup.

Remmie goes to the bank and gains access to the safe deposit box. The jewelry is in a brown felt pouch. He spreads it open and finds the diamond engagement ring given to his mother fifty-odd years ago. If he wished, he could buy a bigger and more impressive one, but he hopes Crystal will accept this as a loving tribute to his mother.

At the drugstore, he buys two heart-shaped boxes of candy. One is red, the other white, and both have glittery bows. He finds a sentimental card for his mother, who will reread it many times before adding it to the collection in her dresser drawer.

When he returns to the office, he opens the white box and dumps the sumptuous chocolates on Ailene's desk. He then refills the box with the sugar-free chocolates made especially for diabetics, writes a loving message to his mother, and tucks the card under the pink ribbon.

Gnawing his lip, he dials the telephone number of a cozy country inn that is a hundred miles away. He makes reservations for dinner for the evening of February 14.

Despite a sudden dryness in his mouth, he also reserves a room with a fireplace and a double bed.

Crystal agrees to dinner. Remmie does not mention the room reservation. He will wait until they are sipping wine and savoring whatever decadently rich dessert the inn has prepared for the event, then slip the ring on her finger and ask her to marry him. He feels a warm tingle as he envisions what will follow.

"HOW ROMANTIC," murmurs Audrey as he describes the plans he has made, although he alludes only obliquely to what he hopes will transpire after his proposal. He's aware that she disapproves of sexual activity outside of wedlock, but he is over forty, after all.

He realizes he is blushing and wills himself to stop behaving like a bashful adolescent. "I'll call Miss McCloud and ask her to stay with you. That way, if you feel dizzy or need extra insulin, she'll be there to help you."

"Don't be absurd," she responds curtly.

"But I'll worry about you if you're here alone all night."

"I can take care of myself—and don't call her against my wishes. If she shows up at the front door, I'll send her away. Now please stop dithering and bring me another blanket. My feet feel as though they're frozen."

He goes to the linen closet in the hallway. As he takes a blanket from the shelf, he hears a peculiar thump. He dashes to his mother's bedroom and finds her lying on the floor like a discarded rag doll.

"DID SHE BREAK ANY BONES?" asks Crystal.

Remmie puts down his coffee cup and shrugs. "No, she just has some bad bruises. They kept her overnight at the hospital for observation, but Dr. Whitbread insisted she'd be more comfortable in her own bed. I took her home after I got off work."

"And left her alone?"

"Of course not," he says, appalled that she would even ask. "Miss McCloud stopped by with a plant, and I took the opportunity to come see you for a few minutes." He looks at his watch and stands up. "I'd better go."

Crystal stands up but does not move toward him. "Does this mean our Valentine dinner date is off? If you're afraid to leave your mother for more than thirty minutes, I'd like to know it right now. There's a new doctor at the clinic who's asked me out a couple of times. He's single, and he doesn't make plans around his mother."

"We're still going," he says hastily.

She goes to the door and opens it. "You'd better go home, Remmie. I hear your mother calling."

Oddly enough, Remmie almost hears her, too.

AUDREY IS UNABLE TO SLEEP because of her pain. At least once a night she calls out for Remmie, who hurries into her room with a glass of water and a white pill. Each time she apologizes at length for disturbing him.

YOU KNOW WHO CRYSTAL REMINDS ME OF?" asks Audrey as Remmie pauses. He is reading the newspaper to her because her eyesight has worsened. It has become a new addition to their evening ritual.

"Who?"

"That woman from the bowling alley. They both have a certain hardness about their eyes. Not that Crystal is anything like . . . what was her name?"

"Lucinda," supplies Remmie. He zeroes in on a story concerning a charity fund-raiser and begins to read.

Too loudly, I'm afraid.

* * *

VALENTINE'S DAY.

Remmie hands his mother a notebook. Names and telephone numbers are written in a heavy black hand; surely she can make them out should an emergency arise. "It's not too late to call Miss McCloud, Mother. She said she will be delighted to stay with you. If you prefer, she can stay downstairs and you won't even known she's here."

"Absolutely not."

"If you're sure," he says. He has already made his decision, but it is not too late for Audrey to change the course of her destiny. He looks down at her. Her lower lip is extended and her jaw is rigid.

He realizes that when next he sees her, she will be at peace. Blinking back tears, he bends down to brush his lips across her forehead. "Good-bye, Mother," he whispers.

"Good-bye, Mrs. Boles," Crystal says from the doorway. She is holding something behind her back and scuffling her feet as if she were a small child. She gives Remmie a conspiratorial smile. "Aren't you forgetting to give your mother something?"

Remmie's face is bloodless as he takes the white heart-shaped box and presents it to Audrey. "I didn't forget," he says. "Special candy for a special person. Don't eat so much you get a tummy ache."

"Don't condescend to me," Audrey says coldly, but her expression softens as she reaches up to squeeze his hand. "I love these chocolates almost as much as I love you, Remmie. One of the days you won't have to go to all the bother to order them just for me."

Remmie stumbles as he leaves the room, brushing past Crystal as if she were nothing more substantial than a shadow.

Unamused, she follows him downstairs to the kitchen, where a second box of chocolates sits on the table. "Did you order them just for me?" she says, mimicking Audrey's simpery voice.

THE TRIP HAS NOT STARTED on a happy note, obviously. Remmie curses as he fights traffic until they are clear of the city, and only then does he loosen his grip on the steering wheel and glance at Crystal.

"You look nervous," he comments.

"So do you." She opens the box of chocolates and offers it to him.

He recoils, then regains control of himself. "Maybe later," he mumbles unhappily.

"Are you worried about your mother?"

"Of course I am. What if she has a dizzy spell and takes another fall? She could break her hip this time and be in such pain that she's unable to call for help."

"She'll be all right," Crystal says as she selects a chocolate and pops it in her mouth. A surprised expression crosses her face, but Remmie is in the mist of passing a truck and does not notice.

In fact, he is so distracted that he fails to respond when she comments on the scenery, and again when she cautions him to slow down as they approach a small town.

She finally taps him on the shoulder. "What's the matter with you, Remmie? Do you want to turn around and go home to check on your mother?"

Sweat dribbles down his forehead. His breathing is irregular, his lips quivering, his eyes darting, his hands once again gripping the steering wheel so tightly that his fingers are unnaturally pale.

"Remmie!" Crystal says, suddenly frightened. "What's wrong?"

He pulls to the shoulder, stops, and leans his head against the steering wheel. "I can't go through with it," he says with a whimper. "I thought I could, but I just can't do it. I'll have to find a telephone and call her before it's too late—even if it means she'll hate me for the rest of her life." He begins to cry. "How could I have betrayed her like this?"

"What are you talking about?"

"I switched the candy. The sugar will put her in a diabetic coma, and it's likely to be fatal unless she gets emergency treatment. I have to call her. If she doesn't answer, I'll call Dr. Whitbread and have him go to the house." He sits up and wipes his cheeks. "Maybe it's not too late. We've only been gone half—"

"It's not too late," Crystals snaps, "and you don't need to call anyone, especially this doctor. You'll be confessing to attempted murder. I doubt the jury will feel much sympathy."

"I don't deserve any sympathy, and I don't care what happens to me. We've got to find a telephone."

She reaches over to take the key from the ignition. After a moment of reflection, she sais, "Your mother is not in danger. While I was waiting in the kitchen, I opened both boxes and figured out what you'd done. I switched them back, Remmie. Audrey is contentedly eating sugar-free chocolates."

"She is?" he says numbly.

Crystal's nod lacks enthusiasm and her smile is strained. "Yes, she sure is. I knew you couldn't live with yourself if you did something so terrible."

Remmie finally convinces himself that she is telling the truth and his mother is not in danger. "I suppose I'd better take you home."

"Why?"

"You must loathe me."

"I'll get over it," Crystal says, shrugging. "What I think we'll do is have our dinner and spend the night at this inn. Tomorrow morning we can go to the local courthouse and get a marriage license, and find a justice of the peace. Audrey will be surprised, of course, but she'll get over it more quickly if it's a done deal."

Remmie is more surprised than Audrey will ever be. "You want to get married—knowing that I tried to murder my mother? Don't you want some time to think about it?"

"I assumed you were going to propose this evening, and I'd decided to accept. I've already given my notice at the clinic so that I can stay home and take care of your mother."

Remmie attempts to decipher the odd determination in her voice, but finally gives up and leans over to kiss her. "I brought a ring to give you over dinner," he admits. "It's the one my father presented to my mother on their second date."

"How thoughtful," she says. "You really must call your mother as soon as we check in and reassure yourself that she's perfectly fine."

AND SO REMMIE AND CRYSTAL DINE by candlelight and make love under a ruffled canopy. The following morning, a license is procured and a justice of the peace conducts a brief ceremony. The witnesses find it remarkably romantic and are teary as the groom kisses the bride.

Only later, as Remmie catches sight of the white heart-shaped box on his mother's bedside table, does he ask himself the obvious question: How did Crystal know to switch back the chocolates?

He does not ask her, however. He is a good husband as well as a good son.

And there is always next year.

Peter Lovesey is well known to mystery readers the world over as the creator of Victorian age police offices Sergeant Cribb and Constable Thackeray. Other creations include using King Edward VII as a sleuth in another take on the Victorian age. In between these series he has also written dozens of short stories, as well as several television plays. A winner of both the Silver and Gold Dagger awards from the Crime Writers' Association, he can now add another laurel to his list of honors, having won the Mystery Writers' of America story contest with "The Pushover."

The Pushover
PETER LOVESEY

During the singing of the Twenty-third Psalm, the man next to me gave me a nudge and said, "What do you think of the wooden overcoat?"

Uncertain what he meant, I lifted an eyebrow.

"The coffin," he said.

I swayed to my left for a view along the aisle. I could see nothing worth interrupting the service for. Danny Fox's coffin stood on trestles in front of the altar looking no different from others I had seen. On the top was the wreath from his widow, Merle, in the shape of a large heart of red roses with Danny's name picked out in white. Not to my taste, but I wasn't so churlish as to mention this to anyone else.

"No handles," my informant explained.

So what? I thought. Who needs handles? Coffins are hardly ever carried by the handles. I gave a nod and continued singing.

"That isn't oak," the man persisted. "That's a veneer. Underneath, it's chipboard."

I pretended not to have heard, and joined in the singing of the third verse—the one beginning "Perverse and foolish oft I strayed"—with such commitment that I drew shocked glances from the people in front.

"She's going to bury Danny in the cheapest box she could buy."

This baboon was ruining the service. I sat for the sermon in a twisted position, presenting most of my back to him.

324

But the damage had been done. My response to what was said was blighted. If John Wesley in his prime had been giving the address, I would still have found concentration difficult. Actually it was spoken by a callow curate with a nervous grin who revealed a lamentable ignorance about the Danny I had known. "A decent man" was a questionable epithet in Danny's case; "a loyal husband" extremely doubtful; "generous to a fault" a gross misrepresentation. I couldn't remember a time when the departed one had bought a round of drinks. If the curate felt obliged to say something positive, he might reasonably have told us that the man in the coffin had been funny and a charmer capable of selling sand to a sheik. I cared a lot about Danny, or I wouldn't be here, but just because he was dead we didn't have to award him a halo.

My contacts with the old rogue went back thirty years. Danny and I first met back in the sixties, the days of National Service, in the air force, at a desolate camp on Salisbury Plain called Nether-avon, and even so early in his career, still in his teens, Danny had got life running the way he wanted. He'd formed a poker school with a scale of duties as the stakes and, so far as I know, served his two years without ever polishing a floor, raking out a stove, or doing a guard duty. No one ever caught him cheating, but his silky handling of the cards should have taught anyone not to play with him. He seduced (an old-fashioned word that gives a flavour of the time) the only WRAF officer on the roll and had the use of her pale blue Morris Minor on Saturdays to support his favourite football team, Bristol Rovers. Weekend passes were no problem. You had to smile at Danny.

I came across him again twelve years later, in 1973, on the sea front at Brighton dressed in a striped blazer, white flannels, and a straw hat and doing a soft-shoe dance to an old Fred Astaire number on an ancient windup Gramophone with a huge brass horn. I had no idea Danny was such a beautiful mover. So many people had stopped to watch that you couldn't get past without walking on the shingle. It was a deeply serious performance that refused to be serious at all. At a tempo so slow that any awkwardness would have been obvious, he shuffled and glided and turned about, tossing in casual gull turns and toe taps, dipping, swaying, and twisting with the beat, his arms windmilling one second, seesawing the next, and never suggesting strain. After he'd passed the hat around, we went for a drink and talked about old times and former comrades. I paid, of course. After that we promised to stay in touch. We met a few times. I went to his second wedding in 1988—a big affair, because Merle had a sister and five brothers, all with families. They were a crazy bunch. The reception, on a river steamer, was a riot. I've never laughed so much.

Danny was fifty-seven when he died.

We sang another hymn and the curate said a prayer and led us out for the committal. The pallbearers hoisted the coffin and brought it along the aisle. I didn't need the nudge I got from my companion as they passed. I could see for myself that the wood was a cheap veneer. I wasn't judgmental. Quite possibly Danny had left Merle with nothing except his antique Gramophone and some debts.

"She had him insured for a hundred and fifty K," Mean-mouth insisted on telling me as we followed the coffin along a path between the graves. "She could have given him a decent send-off."

I told him curtly that I wasn't interested. God knows, I was trying not to be. At the graveside, I stepped away from him and took a position opposite. Let him bend someone else's ear with his malice.

Young sheep were bleating in the field beside the churchyard as the coffin was lowered. The clouds parted and we felt warmth on our skins. I remembered Danny dancing on the front that summer evening at Brighton. *Bon voyage,* old buccaneer, I thought. You robbed all of us of something, sometime, but we came in numbers to see you off. You left us glittering memories, and that wasn't a bad exchange.

A few tears were shed around that grave.

As the Grace was spoken I became conscious of those joyless eyes sizing me up for another approach, so I gave him one back, raised my chin to the required level, and stared like one of those stone figures on Easter Island. My twenty years of teaching fifteen-year-olds haven't been totally wasted. Then I turned away, said "Amen," and smiled benignly at the curate.

Mean-mouth walked directly through the lych gate, got into his car, and drove off. Why do people like that bother to come to funerals?

Most of us converged on the Red Lion across the street. A pub lunch. A corrective to nostalgia. It fitted my picture of Danny that his mourners should be forced to dip into their pockets to buy their own drinks. The only food on offer was microwaved meat pies with soggy crusts. Mean-mouth must have known. He would have told me that Merle was the skinflint, and on sober reflection it is difficult to believe otherwise. It seemed Danny had ended up with a tightwad wife. A nice irony.

And the family weren't partying at the house. They joined us, Merle leading them in while "Happy Days Are Here Again" came over the music system. Her choice of clothes left no one in any doubt that she was the principal lady in the party—a black cashmere coat and matching hat with a vast brim like a manta that flapped as she moved. She was a good ten years younger than Danny, a tall, triumphantly slim, talkative woman who chain-smoked. I'd heard that she knew a lot about antiques; at their wedding, Danny had got in first with the obvious joke about his antiquity, and frankly the way Merle had eyed him all through the reception, you'd have thought he was a piece of Wedgwood. Yet we all knew he was out of the reject basket. Slightly chipped. Well, extensively, to be truthful. He'd lived the kind of free-ranging life he'd wanted, busking, bartending, running a stall at a fairground, a bit of chauffeuring, leading guided walks around the East End, and for a time acting as a croupier. Enjoyable, undemanding jobs on the fringe of the entertainment industry, but never likely to earn much of a bank balance. With his innocent-looking eyes and deep-etched laughter lines, he had a well-known attraction for women that must have played a part in the romance, but Merle didn't look the sort to go starry-eyed into marriage.

Someone bought her a cocktail in a tall glass and she began the rounds of the funeral party, cigarette in one hand, drink in the other, giving and receiving kisses. The mood of forced bonhomie that gets people through funerals was well established. I overheard one formidably fat woman telling Merle, "Never mind, love, you're not bad-looking. Keep your 'air nice and you'll be all right. Won't 'appen at once, mind. I 'ad to wait four years. But you'll be all right."

Merle's hat quivered.

She moved towards me and I gave her the obligatory kiss and muttered sympathetic words. She said, "Good of you to come. We never really got to know each other, did we? You and Danny go back a long way."

"To his air force days," I said.

"Oh, he used to tell wonderful tales of the RAF," she said, calling it the "raff" and clasping my hand so firmly that I could feel every one of her rings. "I don't know if half of them are true. The night exercises."

"Night exercises at Netheravon?" said I, not remembering any.

She took hold of my hand and squeezed it. "Come on, you know Danny. That was his name for that pilot officer whose car he used."

"Oh, her."

"Night exercises. Wicked man." She chuckled. "I couldn't be jealous when he put it like that. To Danny, she was just an easy lay. I envy you, knowing him when he was young. He must have been a right tearaway. Anyway, sweetie, I'd better not gossip. So many old mates to see." She moved on, leaving me in a cloud of cigarette smoke.

Another woman holding a gin and tonic sidled close and said, "What's she on, do you think? She's frisky for a widow."

"I've no idea."

"Danny's brother Ben must have given her some pills."

"Which one is Ben?"

"In the blue suit and black Polo neck. Handy having a doctor for your brother-in-law."

"Yes." I glanced across at brother-in-law Ben, a taller, slimmer version of Danny. "He looks young."

"Fourteen years younger than Danny. They were stepbrothers, I think."

On an impulse I asked, "Was he Danny's doctor also?"

She nodded. "They never paid a bean for medicines."

Malice must be infectious. This wasn't Mean-mouth speaking. This was a short, chunky woman in a grey suit. She introduced herself as their neighbour. Not for much longer, it seemed. "Merle told me she'll be off to warmer climes now. She was always complaining about the winters here, was Merle."

"To live, you mean?"

She nodded. "Spain, I expect."

I remembered the life insurance payout. Merle's antique had, after all, turned out to be worth something if she was emigrating. Watching the newlyweds at their wedding reception, only four years ago, it hadn't crossed my mind to rate Danny as an insurance claim. Had it occurred to Merle?

What a sour thought to have at a funeral! I banished it. Instead I talked to the neighbour about the weather until she got bored and wandered off.

I did some circulating of my own and joined a crowd at a table in the main bar I recognised as more of Danny's close family. They all had large teeth and lopsided grins like his. A man who looked like another younger brother was saying what a shock his death had been. "Fifty-seven. It's no age, is it? He was always so fit. I never knew Dan had a dicky heart."

"He didn't look after himself," a woman said.

"What do you mean—didn't look after himself?" the brother retorted. "He wasn't overweight."

"He didn't exercise. He avoided all forms of sport. Never learned to swim, hold a tennis racket, swing a golf club. He thought jogging was insane."

"He danced like a dream."

"Call that exercise? He never worked up a sweat. I tell you, he didn't look after himself."

"He had two wives," one of the men chipped in.

"Not at the same time," another woman said, giggling.

"What are you saying—that two wives strained his vital powers?"

There was some amusement at this. "No," said the man. *"You* said he didn't look after himself and I was pointing out that he had two women to do the job."

"That's what marriage is for, is it, Charlie?" the woman came back at him. "So that the man's got someone to look after him?"

"Hello, hello. Have you turned into one of those feminists?" retorted Charlie.

"I'm sure being looked after wasn't in Danny's mind when he married Merle," said the giggly woman.

"We all know what was in Danny's mind when he married Merle," said the feminist.

Resisting the temptation to widen the debate by asking what had been

in Merle's mind, I went back to the bar for a white wine. When I picked
it up, my hand shook. A disturbing possibility had crept into *my* mind.
The law allows a doctor considerable discretion in dealing with the death
of a patient in his care. Provided that he has seen the patient in the two
weeks prior to the death, and the cause of death is known to him and
was not the result of an accident, or suspicious circumstances, he may
sign the death certificate without reporting the matter to the coroner.
Merle's brother-in-law Ben had treated Danny.

Across the bar, Ben was talking affably to some people who hadn't
attended the funeral. This was his village, his local. Most of the family
lived around here. He was at ease. Yet there was something more about
his manner, a sense of relief; or perhaps it was triumph.

As for Merle, she was remarkably animated for a woman who had
only just buried her husband. It must be an act, a brave attempt to get
through the day without weeping, I tried telling myself. Watching her, I
wasn't convinced. Her eyes shone like a bride's.

Another curious thing I noticed was that Merle spent time with everyone in that bar except her doctor brother-in-law, Ben. She kept away
from him as if he were radioactive. Yet they were keenly aware of each
other. Each time Merle moved, Ben would look across and check her
position. Occasionally their eyes locked briefly. I was increasingly convinced that they had agreed not to be seen talking together. They weren't
being hostile; they shared a secret.

When I left about six, the party was still going on. I didn't blame
anyone for turning it into a wake. I was sure Danny would have ap-
proved. He would have been in the thick of the junketing, well pickled
by this time, full of good humour, just as long as he didn't have to buy
a round.

MY UNEASE ABOUT THE CIRCUMSTANCES of Danny's death dispersed
within a week. I had more urgent things going on in my life that don't
play any part in these events except that by February, six months after
the funeral, I was tired and depressed. Then someone made things worse
by breaking into my car and stealing my credit cards. The police were
useless. The only positive thing they suggested was that I inform the
people who issued the cards. When my shiny and pristine replacement
cards arrived, I had an impulse to use them right away to give myself
a boost. I walked into a travel agent's and booked two weeks in the
sun. Immediately.

In Florida, I spotted Merle Fox. By pure chance, or fate, I walked into
the Guild Hall Gallery on Duval Street in Key West and there she was,
looking at stained-glass pictures of fish. She'd bleached her hair and cut
it short and she was deeply tanned and wearing a skimpy top and white
trousers that fitted like a second skin. Something new in widow's weeds,

I thought unkindly—for I recognised her straightaway. Of course, she hadn't altered her features, but her stance was the giveaway, the suggestion of swagger in the shoulders. It was no different from the way she'd swanned around the bar of the Red Lion after Danny's funeral.

I didn't speak to Merle. In fact, I moved out of range, hidden from her view by a rotating card-stand. But when she came out of the shop I followed, intrigued, you may say, if you don't call me nosy. I was pretty inconspicuous in T-shirt and shorts, like most of the tourists strolling along the street.

Halfway along Duval Street she turned up a side road that was mainly residential and lined with two-story Bahamian-style wood-frame buildings shaded by palms and wild purple orchid trees and fronted by white picket fences. She walked two blocks (with me in discreet attendance) and let herself into an elegant three-bay house with a porch and—more irony here—a widow's walk. Had I really seen Merle? The moment she'd stepped out of my view I became doubtful. It isn't the custom in Key West to have one's name on the mailbox, so it was difficult to make certain without speaking to the woman. I wasn't sure I wanted a face-to-face.

I crossed the street for a longer view of the house. The shutters were open, but the louvred windows effectively screened the interior.

You wouldn't believe that a leafy street bathed in sunlight could make you feel uneasy. After the crowds on Duval Street, this was eerie in its quietness.

A cat leaned against my shin and made a plaintive sound. I stooped to stroke it.

A voice startled me. "We call him Rocky, after the boxer. He has the most formidable front paws."

I looked behind me. This elderly woman had been sitting unnoticed in her porch swing in front of a small white house.

"He's a champion," I remarked, wondering if my luck was still running. "I was looking for a friend of mine who came to live in Key West. Mrs. Fox. Do you know her?"

She paused some seconds before answering, "I can't say I do."

"She must have arrived sometime in the last three months," I ventured. "She's a widow."

"The only lady who came to Southard Street since the summer is Mrs. Finch in the house across the street, and she's no widow," she informed me.

My confidence ebbed. "Mrs. Finch, you said?"

"Mrs. Merle Finch, from England. They're both from England."

"Ah. That wouldn't be the lady I know," I said, mentally turning a back-flip of triumph. "But thank you for your help, ma'am. Rocky is a cat in a million." I walked away, reflecting that Merle must have kept her hair extra nice to have charmed Mr. Finch, whoever he was, into such a quick marriage. A little over six months since she had buried

Danny, she was remarried, settled in her new home. If her tan was any guide, she had already been in Florida some time.

The big insurance payout, the death certificate provided by her brother-in-law, the quick marriage, and the escape to Florida. Had they all been planned? Was it any wonder I felt suspicious?

My holiday routine altered. Next morning I made sure of passing the house on my way to the shops. I lingered across the street for ten minutes or so. Wherever I went in Key West I was hawk-eyed for another sighting.

It came the next evening. Merle stepped out of Fausto's Food Palace on Fleming Street, crossed my path to a moped, and put her bag on the pannier. My heart rate stepped up. The hours of watching out for her, passing the house and so on, had made me feel furtive. Now I was ready to panic. Ridiculous.

I don't like being sneaky. That isn't my nature. I like to be straight with people. Confrontation is the honest way. So I steeled my nerves, stepped towards her, and said, "Hi, Merle."

She stopped and stared.

"Remember me?" I said. "Danny's oppo from his air force days. Isn't this amazing? I must buy you a drink."

She couldn't deny her identity. Recovering her poise, she said in her very British accent that she would have been delighted, but she had to get back to the apartment. She had something cooking.

I almost laughed out loud at the phrase. Instead I insisted we must meet and suggested a nightcap later at one of the quieter open-air bars. She had a hunted look, but she agreed to see me there at ten.

"You got your wish, then," I said when we shared a table in a dark corner of the bar, drinking margaritas.

"What do you mean?" She was tense.

"A warm place to live. I presume you live here."

"Yes, I do."

"And not alone. You're Mrs. Finch now."

She frowned. "How did you know that?"

"I was told. Is he British, your husband?"

She gave a nod.

"Anyone I know?"

She said, "Why are you asking me these things?"

I said, "What's the matter? Don't you want to talk about them?"

She said, "I left all that behind. It's painful. I don't want to be reminded."

"I wasn't reminding you about the past, Merle. I was enquiring about the present. Your present husband. What's his name?"

She took a long sip of her drink. "Have you seen him?"

"No. But I'd love to meet him—if you let him out."

She pushed aside the drink. "I'll pay for these. I'm leaving."

I put a hand on her arm. "I'm sorry. That was insensitive. Don't take offence."

She brushed my hand away and got up. I didn't follow. I knew it would be no use. I *had* been insensitive. But she had fuelled my suspicions. She had behaved like a guilty woman. Meeting me had been an unpleasant shock. The geography of the Florida Keys—the long drive south from Miami over bridges that span the sea—fosters a feeling of escape, of reaching a haven in Key West bathed in sun and goodwill. You don't expect sharp questions about your conduct.

I believed Merle and her brother-in-law Ben had conspired to murder Danny. A lethal injection seemed the most likely means. Ben had written something innocuous on the death certificate and Merle had claimed the insurance, paid Ben for his services, and escaped to Florida to marry her lover, the fascinating Mr. Finch.

I believed this, yes. But it was only belief so far. The evidence I had was circumstantial. A cheap funeral, an alleged insurance payout, some sly glances, and a quick marriage. None of this was sufficient to justify fingering Merle for murder.

Unable to sleep that night, I asked myself why I wanted to pursue the matter, for it was taking over my holiday. Was it anything as high-minded as a concern for justice? Or was it morbid curiosity?

No.

It was more personal. Danny had been important in my life. The link between us was stronger than I'd admit to anyone. I was angry, deeply angry, at what I believed had happened. Our lives had touched only intermittently since 1961, and I regretted that. Face it, I thought. His murder killed a part of you.

Yet I knew if I pursued this, I was putting myself at risk. If I threatened Merle with exposure, I would give her a reason for killing me. Or having me killed.

These were the thoughts I grappled with the next day. They made me sick with self-disgust because I had discovered I was a coward. I was scared to do any more about my suspicions. I despised myself.

So I became a tourist again, instead of a snoop. I lounged by the hotel pool in the morning and later took a trip to the coral reef in a glass-bottomed boat. I spent an hour in the cemetery. Morbid, you may think, but the gravestones are on the tourist trail. I found the famous epitaph *"I told you I was sick."* It didn't seem funny when I saw it.

Late in the afternoon, I had a quiet drink in one of the smaller bars on Duval Street, watching the movement of people towards Mallory Square. There's a tradition in Key West that people converge on the dock to celebrate the sunset. When I'd finished my drink, I joined them.

I didn't expect to meet Merle there. As a resident, she'd regard the sunset spectacle as a sideshow for tourists. Even so, as I sidled through the good-natured crowd I caught myself looking more than once at women who resembled her and the men they were with. I still wanted keenly to catch a glimpse of Mr. Finch, the new husband.

The sky became pastel blue and the sun dipped towards the sea, becoming ever more red. The heads of some of the crowd were in silhouette. At one end a tightrope was slung between tripod posts and the performer was teasing his audience, keeping *them* in suspense with patter and juggling. I ambled on, past a guitarist and a dog trainer. Ahead, someone else had drawn a fair crowd. A fire-eater, I guessed. There's something hypnotic about the sight of a flame, particularly in the fading light. But I decided the aerialist would be better value and I turned back. I was actually retracing my steps when I heard a scratchy sound that froze my blood, an old 78 record of a band playing some song from way back. It was coming from behind the crowd at the end.

I returned, fast.

I couldn't see for the tightly packed people. I circled the crowd in frustration while that infernal tune blared out. Unable to contain my feelings, I scythed through the crowd saying, "I'm sorry, I have to get through"—until I had a view.

Danny was wowing them in his straw hat, blazer, and flannels, hoofing it just as smoothly as he had in the old days. Far from dead, he had a better colour than most of his audience. The old Gramophone was behind him on the ledge, grinding out "Let's Face and Music and Dance."

He saw me and winked.

I stared back, stunned. Maybe I should have rejoiced, but I'd grieved for this fraudster. I was more angry than relieved. It was a kind of betrayal.

Coward that I am, afterwards, when the sun had set and the crowds had dispersed, I sat tamely with Danny on a ledge of the sea wall at the south end of the dock, our backs to the sea. He had a six-pack of Coors that he systematically emptied. Dancing, he explained, was thirsty work. He offered me some, and I declined.

"Merle told me she met you," he admitted. "She didn't want me to come out tonight, but I'm a performer, damnit. The show goes on. She doesn't understand that you and I go back a long way. You wouldn't blow the whistle on your old RAF buddy."

I didn't rise to that. "You've played some cool poker hands in your time, Danny, but this beats everything. I don't know how you managed it."

He grinned. "No problem. My stepbrother Ben is my doctor. He signed the death certificate. Merle picked up the life insurance and here we are—Mr. and Mrs. Finch. The fake passports cost us a packet, but we could afford them. Isn't this a great place to retire?"

"But there was a funeral."

"That didn't cost much."

"Too true."

"A lot of them were in on this," he confessed. "My cousin Jerry runs an undertaking business in the next village. He supplied the coffin."

"And a corpse?" I said, appalled.

"A couple of sandbags."

"You're a prize bastard, Danny Fox."

He chuckled at that. "Aren't I just? And the prize is in the bank."

"What you did is sick."

"Oh, come on," he said. "Who loses out? Only the insurance company. I had to pay huge premiums."

"There were people in that church who genuinely grieved for you."

"Horseshit."

That hurt. "I grieved."

"Jesus—what for?" His eyebrows jutted in genuine puzzlement.

I started to say, "If you don't remember—"

Danny cut me off with, "All that was thirty years ago. And then it was only—"

"Night exercises," I completed the statement for him.

"What?"

"Night exercises. That's what you thought of me, didn't you?" I stood up and faced him. "Admit it. Say it to my face, you skunk."

There was a pause. The night had virtually closed in. Danny upended his last can of beer. "All right, if that's what you heard from Merle, it must be true." He laughed. "Let's face it, Susan—that's what you were. P.O. didn't stand for Pilot Officer in your case, it stood for pushover."

I said, "That's unbelievably cruel."

Unmoved, Danny told me, "If you really want to know, I couldn't even remember your name that day we met in Brighton. I remembered your car, though."

That was one injury too many—even for a coward like me. The precious flame I'd guarded for thirty years was out. Our relationship had been the one experience in my life that I thought I could call truly romantic. Nothing since had compared to it. Danny had made me feel beautiful, desired, a woman fulfilled.

He knew the pain he had just inflicted. He *must* have known.

"Danny."

"Yes?" He looked up.

By that time Mallory Dock was deserted except for us. The water there is deep enough to moor a cruise liner.

The body of the middle-aged male washed up on Key West Bight a week or so later was identified as that of the man who sometimes danced on the dock at sunset. Nobody knew his name and nobody claimed the body for burial.

Ever since Lawrence Block started writing about Keller, perhaps the most gentlemanly hitman in crime fiction today, his stories have been appearing in The Year's 25 Finest Crime and Mystery Stories as well. In 1994 Keller appeared here in "Keller on Horseback." The year before that it was "Keller's Therapy." But melancholy assassins aren't all he writes about. Matthew Scudder, a policeman turned private eye, and Bernie Rhodenbarr, a gentleman thief who's always getting in over his head, are the two series currently being written. Along with fantastic novellas about Keller, of course. He has won awards from both the Mystery Writers of America and the Private Eye Writers of America. Recently he was named Grand Master of Mystery Fiction by the MWA. After reading this story, it should come as no surprise.

Keller in Shining Armor
LAWRENCE BLOCK

When the phone rang, Keller was just finishing up the *Times* crossword puzzle. It looked as though this was going to be one of those days when he was able to fill in all the squares. That happened more often than not, but once or twice a week he'd come a cropper. A Brazilian tree in four letters would intersect with a Down Under marsupial in five, and he would be stumped.

He put down his pencil and picked up the phone, and Dot said, "Keller, I haven't seen you in ages."

"I'll be right over," he said and broke the connection. She was right, he thought, she hadn't seen him in ages, and it was about time he paid a visit to White Plains. The old man hadn't given him work in months, and you could get rusty just sitting around with nothing better to do than crossword puzzles.

There was still plenty of money. Keller lived well—a good apartment on First Avenue with a view of the Queensboro Bridge, nice clothes, decent restaurants. But no one had ever taken him for a drunken sailor, and in fact he tended to squirrel away money, stuffing it in safe-deposit boxes, opening savings accounts under other names. If a rainy day came along, he had an umbrella at hand.

Still, just because you had Blue Cross didn't mean you couldn't wait to get sick.

"Good boy," he told Nelson, reaching to scratch the dog behind the ears. "You wait right here. Guard the house, huh?"

He had the door open when the phone rang. Let it ring? No, better answer it.

Dot again. "Keller," she said, "did you hang up on me?"

"I thought you were done."

"Why would you think that? I said hello, not good-bye."

"You didn't say hello. You said you hadn't seen me in ages."

"That's closer to hello than good-bye. Well, let it go. The important thing is I caught you before you left the house."

"Just," he said. "I had one foot out the door."

"I'd have called back right away," she said, "but I had a hell of a time getting quarters. You ask for change of a dollar around here, people look at you like you've got a hidden agenda."

Quarters? What did she need with quarters?

"I'll tell you what," she said. "There's this little Italian place about four blocks from you called Giusèppe Joe's. Don't ask me what street it's on."

"I know where it is."

"They've got tables set up outside under the awning. It's a beautiful spring day. Why don't you take your dog for a walk, swing by Giusèppe Joe's. See if there's anybody there you recognize."

"So this is the famous Nelson," Dot said. "He's a handsome devil, isn't he? I think he likes me."

"The only person he doesn't like," Keller said, "is the delivery boy for the Chinese restaurant."

"It's probably the MSG."

"He barks at him, and Nelson almost never barks. The breed is part dingo, and that makes him the silent type."

"Nelson the Wonder Dog. What's the matter, Nelson? Don't you like moo shoo pork?" She gave the dog a pat. "I thought he'd be bigger. An Australian cattle dog, and you think how big sheepdogs are, and cows are bigger than sheep, etc., etc. But he's just the right size."

If he hadn't come looking for her, Keller might not have recognized Dot. He'd never seen her away from the old man's house on Taunton Place, where she'd always lounged around in a Mother Hubbard or a housedress. This afternoon she wore a tailored suit and she'd done something to her hair. She looked like a suburban matron, Keller thought, in town on a shopping spree.

"He thinks I'm shopping for summer clothes," she said, as if reading his mind. "I shouldn't be here at all, Keller."

"Oh?"

"I've been doing things that I shouldn't do," she said. "Idle hands and all that. What about you, Keller? Been a long dry spell. What have your idle hands been up to?"

Keller looked at his hands. "Nothing much," he said.

"How are you fixed for dough?"

"I'll get by."

"You wouldn't mind work, though."

"No, of course not."

"That's why you couldn't wait to hang up on me and hop on a train." She drank some iced tea and wrinkled her nose. "Two bucks a glass for this crap and they make it from a mix. You wonder why I don't come to the city often? It's nice, though, sitting at an outside table like this."

"Pleasant."

"You probably do this all the time. Walk the dog, pick up a newspaper, stop and have a cup of coffee. While away the hours. Right?"

"Sometimes."

"You're patient, Keller, I'll give you that. I take all day to come to the point and you sit there like you've got nothing better to do. But in a way that's the whole point, isn't it? You don't have anything better to do, and neither do I."

"Sometimes there's no work," he said. "If nothing comes in——"

"Things have been coming in."

"Oh?"

"I'm not here, you never saw me and we never had this conversation. Do you understand?"

"Understood."

"I don't know what's the matter with him, Keller. He's going through something, and I don't know what it is. It's like he's lost his taste for it. There have been calls, people with work that would have been right up your alley. He tells them no. He tells them that he hasn't got anybody available at the moment. He tells them to call somebody else."

"Does he say why?"

"Sure, there's always a reason. This one he doesn't want to deal with, that one won't pay enough, the other one, something doesn't sound kosher about it. I know of three jobs he's turned down since the first of the year."

"No kidding."

And who knows what came in that I don't know about?"

"I wonder what's wrong."

"I figure it'll pass," she said. "But who knows when? So I did something crazy."

"Oh?"

"Don't laugh, all right?"

"I won't."

"You familiar with a magazine called *Mercenary Times?*"

"Like *Soldier of Fortune,*" he said.

"Like it, but more homemade and reckless." She drew a copy from her handbag, handed it to him. "Page 47. It's circled, you can't miss it."

It was in the classifieds, under Situations Wanted, circled in red Magic Marker. *Odd Jobs Wanted,* he read. *Removals a specialty. Write to Toxic Waste, P.O. Box 1149, Yonkers, N.Y.*

He said, "Toxic Waste?"

"That may have been a mistake," she acknowledged. "I thought it sounded good, cold, lethal and up to here with attitude. I got a couple of letters from people with chemicals to dump and swamps to drain, who wanted someone to help them do an end run around the environmentalists. Plus I managed to get myself on some damn mailing list where I get invitations to subscribe to waste management newsletters."

"But that's not all you got."

"It's not, because I also got half a dozen letters from people who knew what kind of removals I had in mind. I was wondering what kind of idiot would answer a blind ad like that, and they were about what you would expect. I burned five of them."

"And the sixth?"

"Was neatly typed," she said, "on printed letterhead, if you please. And written in English, God help us. But here, read it yourself."

" 'Cressida Wallace, 411 Fairview Avenue, Muscatine, Iowa 52761. Dear Sir or——' "

"Not out loud, Keller."

Dear Sir or Madam, he read. *I can only hope the removal service you provide is of the sort I require. If so, I am in urgent need of your services. My name is Cressida Wallace and I am a 41-year-old author and illustrator of books for children. I have been divorced for 15 years and have no children.*

While my life was never dramatically exciting, I have always found fulfillment in my work and quiet satisfaction in my personal life. Then, four years ago, a stranger began to transform my life into a living hell.

I will simply state that I have become the innocent target of a stalker. Why this man singled me out is quite unfathomable to me. I am neither a talk show host nor a teenage tennis champion. While presentable, I am by no means a raving beauty. I had never met him, nor had I done anything to arouse his interest or his ill will. Yet he will not leave me alone.

He parks his car across the street and watches my house through binoculars. He follows me when I leave the house. He calls me at all hours. I have long since stopped answering the phone, but this does not stop him from leaving horribly obscene and threatening messages on my answering machine.

I was living in Missouri when this began, in a suburb of St. Louis. I have moved four times, and each time he has managed to find me. I cannot tell you how many times I have changed my telephone number. He always manages to find out my new unlisted number. I don't know how. Perhaps he has a confederate at the telephone company. . . .

He read the letter on through to the end. There had been a perceptible escalation in the harassment, she reported. The stalker had begun telling her he would kill her and had taken to describing the manner in which he intended to do so. He had on several occasions broken into her house in her absence. He had stolen undergarments from the clothes hamper, slashed a painting and used her lipstick to write an obscene message on the wall. He had performed various acts of minor vandalism on her car. After one invasion of her home, she'd bought a dog; a week later she'd returned home to find the dog missing. Not long afterward there was a message on her answering machine. No human speech, just a lot of barking and yipping and whimpering, ending with what she took to be a gunshot.

"Jesus," Keller said.

"The dog, right? I figured that would get to you."

The police inform me there is nothing they can do, she continued. In two different states I obtained orders of protection, but what good does that do? He violates them at will and with apparent impunity. The police are powerless to act until he commits a crime. He has committed several but has never left sufficient evidence for them to proceed. The messages on my answering machine do not constitute evidence because he has some way of distorting his voice. Sometimes he changes his voice to that of a woman. The first time he did this I picked up the phone and said hello when I heard a female voice, sure that it was not him. The next thing I knew his awful voice was sounding in my ear, accusing me of horrible acts and promising me torture and death.

At a policeman's off-the-record suggestion, I bought a gun. Given the chance, I would shoot this man without a moment's hesitation. But when the attack comes, will I have the gun at hand? I doubt it. I feel certain he will choose his opportunity carefully and come upon me when I am helpless.

No doubt you could use this letter as an instrument of extortion. I can say only that you would be wasting your time. I won't pay blackmail. And if you are some sort of policeman and this ad is some sort of "sting"— well, sting away! I don't care.

If you are what you imply yourself to be, please call me at the following number. It is unlisted, but it is already well known to my adversary. Identify yourself with the phrase "toxic waste." I'll pick up if I'm at home. If I don't, simply ring off and call back later.

I am not wealthy, but I have had some success in my profession. I have saved my money and invested wisely. I will pay anything within my means to whomever will rid me forever of this diabolical man.

He folded the letter, returned it to its envelope and handed it across the table.

"Well, Keller?"

"You call her?"

"First I went to the library," Dot said. "She's real. Has a whole lot of books for young readers. Writes them, draws the pictures herself. *How the Bunny Lost His Ears,* that kind of thing."

"How did he lose his ears?"

"I didn't read the books, Keller, I just made sure they existed. Then I looked her up in a kind of *Who's Who* for authors. It had her old address in St. Louis. Then I went home and watched the old man work on a jigsaw puzzle. That's his favorite thing these days, jigsaw puzzles. When he's done with them, he glues cardboard to the back and mounts them on the wall like trophies."

"How long has he been doing that?"

"Long enough," she said. "I went downstairs and put on the TV, and the next day I went out to a pay phone and called Muscatine. I looked that up, too, while I was at the library. It's on the Mississippi."

"Everything has to be someplace."

"Well, what do you think so far, Keller? Tell me."

He reached down and scratched the dog. "I think it's asking for trouble," he said. "Guy goes down, they pick her up before the body's cold. She's got to sing like a songbird. I mean, she told us everything and we didn't even ask."

"Agreed. She'll fold the minute they knock on her door."

"So?"

"So she can't know anything," Dot said. "Can't tell what she doesn't know, right? That's the first thing I said to her, after I said 'toxic waste' and she picked up the phone. I laid it out for her. No names, no pack drill, I said. I told her a number, said half in advance, half on completion. Cash, fifties and hundreds, wrap 'em up good and FedEx the package to John Smith at Mail Boxes Etc. in Scarsdale."

"John Smith?"

"First name that came to me. Soon as I got off the phone I went over and rented a box under that name. The owner's Afghan, he doesn't know Smith from Shinola. It's better than the post office because you can call and find out if they've got anything for you. I called yesterday, and guess what?"

"She sent the money?"

Dot nodded. " 'Send half the money,' I said, 'and our field operative will call when he's on the scene. He'll introduce himself and get the information he requires. You'll never meet him face-to-face, but he'll coordinate with you and take care of everything. And afterward you'll get a final call telling you where to send the balance.' "

Keller thought about it. "There's stuff they could trace," he said. "The mailbox. Records of phone calls."

"There's always something."

"Uh-huh. What kind of a price did you set?"

"Just on the high side of standard."

"And you got half in front, and she hasn't a clue who she sent it to."

"Meaning I could just keep it. I thought of that, obviously. If you turn it down, that's probably what I'll do."

"You're not going to send it back?"

"No, but I could call around, try to find another shooter."

"I didn't turn it down yet," he said.

"Take your time."

"The old man would have a fit. You know that, don't you?"

"Gee, I'm glad you told me that, Keller. It never would have occurred to me."

"What does that mean, anyway, 'No names, no pack drill'? I'm familiar with the expression, I get the sense of it, but what's a pack drill?"

"It's just an expression, for God's sake."

"Give me the letter again," he said and read it through rapidly. "Most of the time, the people who contract these jobs, there's other things they could do. They may think otherwise, but there's usually another way out."

"So?"

"So what choice has she got?"

"Nelson," Dot said, "you know what I just did? I watched your master talk himself into something."

"Muscatine," he said. "Do planes go there?"

"Not if they can help it."

"What do I do, go there and call her? 'Toxic waste,' and then I wait for her to pick up?"

"It's 'toxic shock' now," she said. "I changed the password for security reasons."

"Thank God for that," he said. "You can't be too careful."

BACK AT HIS APARTMENT, Keller made arrangements for the dog-sitter to care for Nelson. Then he found Muscatine on the map. You could probably fly there, or at least to Davenport, but Chicago wasn't that far. American had hourly nonstop flights to Chicago, and O'Hare was a nice anonymous place to rent a car.

He flew out in the morning, had a Hertz car waiting and was in Muscatine and settled in a chain motel on the edge of the city by dinnertime. He ate at a Pizza Hut down the road, came back and sat on the edge of his bed. He had used false identification to rent the car at O'Hare and had registered at the motel under a different name and paid cash in advance for a week's stay. Even so, he didn't want to call the client from the motel. He was dealing with an amateur, and there were two principles to observe in dealing with amateurs. The first was to be ultraprofessional. The second, alas, was never to deal with an amateur.

There was a pay phone next door; he'd noticed it coming back from the Pizza Hut. He spent a quarter and dialed the number, and after two rings the machine answered and a computer-generated voice repeated the last four digits of the number and invited him to leave his message at the tone.

"Toxic shock," he said.

Nothing happened. He stayed on the line for fifteen seconds and hung up.

But was that long enough? Suppose she was washing her hands, or in the kitchen making coffee. He dug out another quarter, tried again. Same story. "Toxic shock," he said again and waited for thirty seconds before hanging up.

"Great system," he said aloud and went back to the motel.

HE TURNED ON THE TELEVISION SET and watched the last half of a movie about a woman who gets her lover to kill her husband. You didn't have to have watched the first half to know what was going on, nor did you need to be a genius to know that everything was going to go wrong for them. Amateurs, he thought.

He went out and tried the number again. "Toxic shock." Nothing. Hell.

On the desk in his room, along with carryout menus from half a dozen nearby fast-food outlets and a local Board of Realtors handout on the joys of settling in Muscatine, there was a flyer inviting him to try his luck gambling on a Mississippi riverboat. It looked appealing at first. You pictured an old paddle wheeler chugging along, heading down the river to New Orleans, with women in hoopskirts and men in frock coats and string ties. But he knew it wouldn't be anything like that. The boat wouldn't move, for one thing. It would stand at anchor, and boarding it would be like crossing the threshold of a hotel in Atlantic City.

No thanks.

Unpacking, he found the morning paper he'd read on the flight to Chicago. He hadn't finished it, and did so now, saving the crossword puzzle for last. There was a step quote, a saying of some sort running like a flight of stairs from the upper left to lower right corner. He liked these, because you had the sense that solving the crossword led to a greater solution.

Often, though, the puzzles with step quotes proved difficult, and this particular puzzle was of that sort. There were a couple of areas he had trouble with, and they formed important parts of the stepquote, and in the end he couldn't work it out.

There was a 900 number you could call. They printed it with the puzzle every morning, and for seventy-five cents they'd give you any three answers.

But did people really call? Obviously they did, or the service wouldn't exist. Keller found this baffling. He could see doing a crossword puzzle— it gave your mind a light workout and passed the time—but when he'd gone as far as he could, he tossed the paper aside and got on with his life.

Anyway, if you were dying of curiosity, all you had to do was wait a day. They printed a filled-in version of the previous day's crossword in every paper. Why spend seventy-five cents for three answers when you could wait a few hours and get the whole thing for sixty?

They were immature, he decided. He'd read that the true measure of human maturity was the ability to postpone gratification.

Keller, ready to go out and try the number again, decided to postpone gratification. He took a hot shower and went to bed.

IN THE MORNING HE DROVE into downtown Muscatine and had breakfast at a diner. The crowd was almost exclusively male and most of the men wore suits. Keller, in a suit himself, read the local paper while he ate his breakfast. There was a crossword puzzle, but he took one look at it and gave it a pass. The longest word was six letters: *Our Northern Neighbor.* The way Keller figured it, when it came to crossword puzzles, it was the *Times* or nothing.

There was a pay phone at the diner, but he didn't want his conversation overheard by the movers and shakers of Greater Muscatine. Even if no one answered, he didn't want anyone to hear him say "toxic shock." He left the diner and found an outdoor pay phone at a gas station. He placed the call, said his two words, and in no time at all a woman cut in to say, "Hello? Hello?"

Tinny phone, he thought. Rinky-dink local phone company, what could you expect? But it was better than a computer-generated phone message. At least you knew you were talking to a person.

"It's all right," he said. "I'm here."

"I'm sorry I missed your call last night. I was out, I had to——"

"Let's not get into that," he said. "Let's not spend any more time on the phone than we have to."

"I'm sorry. Of course you're right."

"I need to know some things. The name of the person I'm supposed to meet with, first of all."

There was a pause. Then, tentatively, she said, "My understanding was that there wasn't to be a meeting."

"The other person," he said, "that I'm supposed to *meet* with, so to speak."

"Oh. I didn't. . . . I'm sorry. I'm not used to this."

No kidding, he thought.

"His name is Stephen Lauderheim," she said.

"How do I find him? I don't suppose you know his address."

"No, I'm afraid not. I know the license number of his car."

He copied it down, along with the information that the car was a two-year-old white Honda Civic squareback. That was useful, he told her, but he couldn't cruise around town looking for a white Honda. Where does he park this car?

"Across the street from my house," she said, "more often than I'd like."

"I don't suppose he's there now."

"No, I don't think so. Let me look. . . . No, he's not. There was a message from him last night. In between your messages. Nasty, vile."

"I wish I had a photo of him," he said. "That would help. I don't suppose——"

No photo, but she could certainly describe him. Tall, slender, light brown hair, late 30s, long face, square jaw, big white horse teeth. Oh, and he had a Kirk Douglas dimple in his chin. Oh, and she knew where he worked. At least he was working there the last time the police were involved. Would that help?

Keller rolled his eyes. "It might," he said.

"The name of the firm is Loud & Clear Software," she said. "On Tyler Boulevard just beyond Five Mile Road. He's a computer programmer or technician, something like that."

"That's how he keeps getting your phone number," Keller said.

"I beg your pardon?"

"He doesn't need a confederate at the phone company. If he knows his way around computers, he can hack into the phone company system and get unlisted numbers that way."

"It's possible to do that?"

"So they tell me."

"Well, I'm hopelessly old-fashioned," she said. "I still do all my writing on a typewriter. But it's an electric typewriter, at least."

He had the name, the address, the car and a precise description. Was there anything else he needed? He couldn't think of anything.

"This probably won't take very long," he said.

HE FOUND FIVE MILE ROAD, found Tyler Boulevard, found Loud & Clear Software. The company occupied a squat concrete-block building with its own little parking lot. There were ten or a dozen cars in the lot, many of them Japanese, two of them white. No white Honda squareback, no plate number to match the one he'd been given.

If Stephen Lauderheim wasn't working today, maybe he was stalking. Keller drove back into town and got directions to Fairview Avenue. He found it in a pleasant neighborhood of prewar houses and big shade trees. Driving slowly past number 411, he looked around unsuccessfully for a white Honda, then circled the block and parked just down the street from Cressida Wallace's house. It was a sprawling structure, three stories tall, with overgrown shrubbery obscuring the lower half of the first-floor windows. A light burned in a window on the third floor, and Keller decided that that was where Cressida was, typing up happy and instructive tales of woodland creatures on her electric typewriter.

He had lunch and drove back to Loud & Clear. No white Honda. He hung around for a while, found his way to Fairview Avenue again. No white Honda, and no light on the third floor. He returned to his motel.

THAT NIGHT THERE WAS A MOVIE he wanted to see on HBO, but the channel wasn't available on his TV. He was irritated and thought about moving to another motel a few hundred yards down the road, where the signboard promised HBO, as well as water beds in selected units. He decided that was ridiculous, that he was mature enough to postpone gratification in this area, even as he had to postpone the gratification of dispatching Stephen Lauderheim and getting the hell out of Muscatine.

He leafed through the phone book, looking for Lauderheim. There was no listing, which didn't surprise him. He tried Cressida Wallace, knowing she wouldn't be listed. There were several Wallaces, but none on Fairview and none named Cressida.

There were Kellers, one of them with the initial J, another with the initials JD. Either one could be John.

He did that sometimes. Looked up his name in the phone books of strange cities, as if he might actually find himself there. Not another person with the same name—that happened often enough since his was not an uncommon name. But find himself, his actual self, living an altogether different life in some other city.

THE NEXT MORNING Keller had breakfast at the diner, swung past the house on Fairview, then drove out to the software company. This time the white Honda was parked in the lot, and the license plate had the right letters and numbers on it. Keller parked where he could keep an eye on it and waited.

At noon, several men and women left the building, walked to their cars and drove off. None fit Stephen Lauderheim's description, and none got into the white Honda.

At 12:30, two men emerged from the building and walked along together, deep in conversation. Both wore khaki trousers and faded denim shirts and running shoes, but in other respects they looked completely different. One was short and pudgy, with dark hair combed flat across his skull. The other, well, the other just had to be Lauderheim. He fit Cressida Wallace's description to a T.

They walked together to Lauderheim's Honda. Keller followed them to an Italian restaurant, one of a national chain. Then he drove back to Loud & Clear and parked in his old spot.

At a quarter to two, the Honda returned and both men went back into the building. Keller drove off and found a supermarket, where he purchased a box of granulated sugar and a funnel. At a hardware store in the same small shopping plaza he bought a large screwdriver, a hammer and a six-foot extension cord. He drove back to Loud & Clear and went to work.

The Honda had a hatch over the gas cap. You needed a key to unlock it. He braced the screwdriver against the lock and gave it one sharp blow with the hammer, and the hatch popped. He removed the gas cap, inserted the funnel, poured in the sugar, replaced the cap, closed the hatch and wedged it shut. Then he went back to his own car and got behind the wheel.

Employees began trickling out of Loud & Clear shortly after five. By six o'clock only three cars remained in the lot. At 6:20, Lauderheim's lunch companion came out, got into a brown Buick Century and drove off. That left two cars, one of them the white Honda, and they were both still there at seven.

Keller sat behind the wheel, deferring gratification. His breakfast had been light, two doughnuts and a cup of coffee, and he'd missed lunch. He had planned to grab something to eat while he was in the supermarket, but it had slipped his mind. Now he was missing dinner.

Hunger made him irritable. Two cars in the lot, probably two people inside, three at the most. They'd already stayed two hours past quitting time and for all he knew might stay until morning. Maybe Lauderheim was waiting until the office was empty so he could make an undisturbed phone call to Cressida.

Suppose he just went in there and did them both? Element of surprise, they'd never know what hit them. Two for the price of one, do it and let's get the hell out of here. Cops would just figure a disgruntled employee went berserk. That sort of thing happened everywhere these days, not just at post offices.

Maturity, he told himself. Maturity and deferred gratification. Above all, professionalism.

By 7:30 HE WAS READY to rethink his commitment to professionalism. He no longer felt hungry but was seething with anger, all of it focused on Stephen Lauderheim.

The son of a bitch.

Why in the hell would he stalk some poor woman who spent her life in an attic writing about kitty cats and bunny rabbits? Kidnapping her dog, for God's sake, and then torturing it and killing it, and playing her a tape of the animal's death throes. Murder, Keller thought, was almost too good for the son of a bitch. Ought to stick that funnel in his mouth and pour oven cleaner down his throat.

Speak of the devil.

There he was, Stephen Fucking Lauderheim, holding the door open for a nerdy fellow wearing a lab coat and a wispy mustache. Not heading for the same car, please God. No, separate cars, with Lauderheim pausing after unlocking the Honda to exchange a final pleasantry with the nerd in the lab coat.

Good thing he hadn't counted on waylaying him in the parking lot.

The nerd drove off first. Keller sat, glaring at the Honda, until Lauderheim started it up, pulled out of the parking lot and headed back toward town.

Keller gave him a two-block lead, then took off after him.

JUST THE OTHER SIDE of Four Mile Road, Keller pulled up right behind the disabled Honda. Lauderheim already had the hood up and was frowning at the engine.

Keller got out of the car and trotted over to him.

"Heard the sound it was making," he said. "I think I know what's wrong."

"It's got to be the engine," Lauderheim said. "But I don't understand it. It never did anything like this before."

"I can fix it."

"Seriously? You mean it?"

"You got a tire iron?"

"Yeah, I suppose so," Lauderheim said and went around to open the rear of the squareback. He found the tire iron, extended it to Keller, then drew it back. "There's nothing wrong with the tires," he said.

"No kidding," Keller said. "Give me the tire iron, will you?"

"Sure, but——"

"Say, don't I know you? You're Steve Lauderheim, aren't you?"

"That's right. Have we met?"

Keller looked at him, at the cute little chin dimple, at the big white teeth. Of course he was Lauderheim. Who else could he be? But a professional made sure. Besides, it wasn't too long ago that he'd failed to make sure, and he wasn't eager to let that happen again.

"Cressida says hello," Keller said.

"Huh?"

Keller buried the tire iron in his solar plexus.

The results were encouraging. Lauderheim let out an awful sound, clapped his hands to his middle and fell to his knees. Keller grabbed him by the front of his shirt, dragged him along the gravel until the Honda screened the two of them from view. Then he raised the tire iron high and brought it down on Lauderheim's head.

The man sprawled on the ground, still conscious, moaning softly. A few more blows to finish it?

No. Stick to the script. Keller drew the extension cord from his pocket, unwound a two-foot length of it and looped it around Lauderheim's throat. He straddled the man, pinning him to the ground with a knee in the middle of his back, and choked the life out of him.

THE MISSISSIPPI, legendary Father of Waters, swallowed the tire iron, the hammer, the screwdriver, the funnel, the cord. The empty box of sugar floated off on the current.

From a pay phone, Keller called his client. "Toxic shock," he said, feeling like an idiot. No answer. He hung up.

He went back to his motel room, packed, carried his bag to the car. He didn't have to check out. He'd paid a week in advance, and when his week was up they'd take the room back.

He had to force himself to drive over to the Pizza Hut and get something to eat. All he wanted to do was drive straight to O'Hare and grab the first plane back to New York, but he knew he had to get some food into his system. Otherwise he'd start seeing things on the road north, swing the wheel to dodge something that wasn't there and wind up putting the car in a ditch. Professionalism, he told himself, and he ate an individual pan pizza and drank a medium Pepsi.

And placed the call again. "Toxic shock"—and this time she was there and picked up.

"It's all taken care of," he said.

"You mean——"

"I mean it's all taken care of."

"I can't believe it. My God, I can't believe it."

You're safe now, he wanted to say. You've got your life back.

Instead, cool and professional, he told her how to make the final payment. Cash, same as before, sent by Federal Express to Mary Jones, at another Mail Boxes Etc. location, this one in Peekskill.

"I can't thank you enough," the woman said. Keller said nothing, just smiled and rang off.

DRIVING NORTH AND EAST through Illinois, Keller went over it in his mind. He thought, *Cressida says hello.* Jesus, he couldn't believe he'd said that. What did he think he was, an avenging angel? A knight in shining armor? Jesus.

Well, nothing all day but two doughnuts and a cup of coffee. That was as far as you had to look for an explanation. Got him irritable and angry, made him take it personally.

Still, he thought after he'd turned in the car and bought his ticket, Lauderheim was unquestionably one thoroughgoing son of a bitch. No loss to anyone.

And he could still hear her saying she couldn't thank him enough, and what was so wrong with enjoying that?

EIGHT, NINE DAYS LATER, Dot called. Coincidentally, he was doing the crossword puzzle at the time.

"Keller," she said, "guess what Mary Jones didn't find in her mailbox?"

"That's strange," he said. "It's still not here? Maybe you ought to call her. Maybe FedEx lost it and it's in a back office somewhere."

"I'm way ahead of you. I called her."

"And?"

"Line's been disconnected. . . . You still there, Keller?"

"I'm trying to think. You're sure that——"

"I called back, got the same recording. 'The number you have reached, blah-blah-blah, has been disconnected.' Leaves no room for doubt."

"No."

"The money doesn't show up, and now the line's been disconnected. Does it begin to make you wonder?"

"Maybe they arrested her," he said, "before she could send the money."

"And stuck her in a cell and left her there? A quiet lady who writes about deaf rabbits?"

"Well——"

"Let me pull out and pass a few slow-moving vehicles," she said. "What I did was, I called Information in St. Louis."

"St. Louis?"

"Webster Groves is a suburb of St. Louis."

"Webster Groves."

"Where Cressida Wallace lives, according to that reference book in the library."

"But she moved," Keller said.

"You'd think so, wouldn't you? But the Information operator had a listing for her. So I called the number. Guess what?"

"Come on, Dot."

"A woman answered. No answering machine, no computer-generated horseshit. 'Hello?' 'Cressida Wallace, please.' 'This is she.' Well, it wasn't the voice I remembered. 'Is this Cressida Wallace, the author?' 'Yes.' 'The author of *How the Bunny Lost His Ears*?' "

"And she said it was?"

"Well, how many Cressida Wallaces do you figure there are? I didn't know what the hell to say next. I told her I was from the Muscatine paper and that I wanted to know her impression of the town. Keller, she didn't know what I was talking about. I had to tell her what state Muscatine is in."

"You'd think she'd at least have heard of it," he said. "It's not that far from St. Louis."

"I don't think she gets out much. I think she sits in her house and writes her stories. I found out this much. She's lived in the same house in Webster Groves for thirty years."

He took a deep breath, then said, "Where are you, Dot?"

"Where am I? I'm at an outdoor pay phone half a mile from the house. I'm getting rained on."

"Go on home," he said. "Give me an hour or so and I'll call you back."

"ALL RIGHT," he said, closer to two hours later. "Here's how it shapes up. Stephen Lauderheim wasn't some creep, stalking some innocent woman."

"We figured that."

"He was a partner in Loud & Clear Software. He and a fellow named Randall Cleary started the firm. Lauderheim and Cleary, Loud & Clear."

"Cute."

"Lauderheim was married, father of two, bowled in a league, belonged to the Rotary and the Jaycees."

"Hardly the type to kidnap a dog and torture it to death."

"You wouldn't think so."

"Who set him up? The wife?"

"I figure the partner. Company was doing great and one of the big Silicon Valley firms was looking to buy them out. My guess is one of them wanted to sell and the other didn't. Or there was some kind of partnership insurance in place. One partner dies, the other buys him out at a prearranged price, pays off the widow with the proceeds of the insurance policy. Of course, the company's now worth about twenty times what they agreed to."

"How'd you get all this, Keller?"

"Called the city room at the Muscatine paper, said I was covering the death for a computer magazine and could they fax me the obit and anything they had run on the killing."

"You've got a fax?"

"The candy store around the corner's got one. All the guy in Muscatine could tell from the number I gave him was it was in New York."

"Nice."

"After the fax came in, the stuff he sent gave me some ideas for other calls to make. I could sit on the phone for another hour and find out more, but I figure that's enough."

"More than enough," she said. "Keller, the little shit foxed us. Then he stiffed us in the bargain."

"That's what I don't get," he said. "Why stiff us? All he had to do was send the money and I'd never have thought of Iowa again unless I was flying over it. He was home free. All he had to do was pay what he owed."

"Cheap son of a bitch," Dot said.

"But where's the sense? He paid out half the money without even knowing who he was sending it to. If he could afford to do that on the come, you can imagine what kind of money was at stake here."

"It paid off."

"It paid off, but he didn't. Stupid."

"Very stupid."

"I'll tell you what I think," he said. "I think the money was the least of it. I think he wanted to feel superior to us. I mean, why go through all this Cressida Wallace crap in the first place? Does he figure I'm a Boy Scout, doing my good deed for the day?"

"He figured we were amateurs, Keller. And needed to be motivated."

"Yeah, well, he figured wrong," he said. "I have to pack. I've got a flight in an hour and a half and I have to call the dog-sitter. We're getting paid, Dot. Don't worry."

"I wasn't worried," she said.

WHICH ONE, he wondered, was Cleary? The plump one who'd gone to lunch with Lauderheim? Or the nerd in the lab coat who'd walked out to the parking lot with him?

Or someone else, someone he hadn't even seen? Cleary might well have been out of town that day, providing himself with an alibi.

Didn't matter. You didn't need to know what a man looked like to get him on the phone.

Cleary, like his late partner, had an unlisted home phone number. But the firm, Loud & Clear, had a listing. Keller called from his motel room— he was staying this time at the one with HBO. He used the electronic novelty item he'd picked up at Abercrombie & Fitch, and when a woman answered he said he wanted to speak to Randall Cleary.

"Whom shall I say is calling?"

Whom, he noted. Not bad for Muscatine, Iowa.

"Cressida Wallace," he said.

She put him on hold, but he did not languish there for long. Moments later he heard a male voice, one he could not recognize. "Cleary," the man said. "Who is this?"

"Ah, Mr. Cleary," he said. "This is Miss Cressida Wallace."

"No it's not."

"It is," Keller said. "I understand you've been using my name, and I'm frightfully upset."

Silence from Cleary. Keller unhooked the device that had altered the pitch of his voice. "Toxic shock," he said in his own voice. "You stupid son of a bitch."

"There was a problem," Cleary said. "I'm going to send you the money."

"Why didn't you get in touch?"

"I was going to. You can't believe how busy we've been around here."

"So why did you disconnect your phone?"

"I thought, you know, for security reasons."

"Right," Keller said.

"I'm going to pay."

"No question about it," Keller said. "Today. You're going to FedEx the money today. Overnight delivery, Mary Jones gets it tomorrow. Are we clear on that?"

"Absolutely."

"And the price went up. Remember what you were supposed to send?"

"Yes."

"Well, double it."

There was a silence. "That's impossible. It's extortion, for God's sake."

"Look," Keller said, "do yourself a favor. Think it through."

Another silence, but shorter. "All right," Cleary said.

"In cash, and it gets there tomorrow. Agreed?"

"Agreed."

He called Dot from a pay phone, had dinner and went back to his room. This motel had HBO, so of course there was nothing on that he wanted to watch. It figured.

In the morning he skipped the diner and had a big breakfast at a Denny's on the highway. He drove up to Davenport and made two stops, at a sporting goods store and a hardware store. He went back to his motel, and around two in the afternoon he called White Plains.

"This is Cressida Wallace," he said. "Have there been any calls for me?"

"Damned if it doesn't work," Dot said. "You sound just like a woman."

"But I break just like a little girl," Keller said.

"Very funny. Quit using that thing, will you? It sounds like a woman, but it's your way of talking, your inflections underneath it all. Let me hear the Keller I know so well."

He unhooked the gadget. "Better?"

"Yes, much better. Your pal came through."

"He got the numbers right and everything?"

"Indeed he did."

"I think the voice-change gizmo helped," he said. "It made him see we know everything."

"Oh, he'd have paid anyway," she said. "All you had to do was yank his chain a little. You just liked using your new toy, that's all. When are you coming home, Keller?"

"Not right away."

"Well, I know that."

"No, I think I'll wait a few days," he said. "Right now he's edgy, looking over his shoulder. Beginning of next week he'll have his guard down."

"Makes sense."

"Besides," he said, "it's not really a bad town."

"God, Keller."

"What's the matter?"

" 'It's not a bad town.' I bet you're the first person to say that, including the head of the chamber of commerce."

"It's not," he insisted. "The motel set gets HBO. There's a Pizza Hut down the street."

"Keep it to yourself, Keller, or everybody's going to want to move there."

"And I've got things to do."

"Like what?"

"A little metalwork project, for starters."

He hung up and used the carbide-bladed hacksaw from the hardware store to remove most of both barrels of the shotgun from the sporting goods store, then switched blades and cut away most of the stock as well. He loaded both chambers and left the gun tucked under the mattress. Then he drove along the river road until he found a good spot, and he tossed the sawed-off gun barrels, the hacksaw and the shotgun-shell box into the Mississippi. Toxic waste, he thought, and shook his head, imagining all the junk that wound up in the river.

He drove around for a while, just enjoying the day, and returned to the motel. Right now Randall Cleary was telling himself he was safe, he was in the clear, he had nothing to worry about. But he wasn't sure yet.

In a few days he'd be sure. He'd even think to himself that maybe he should have called Keller's bluff, or at least not agreed to pay double. But, what the hell, it was only money, and money was something he had a ton of.

Stupid amateur.

Which one was he, anyway? The nerd with the wispy mustache? The plump one, the dumpling? Or someone yet unseen?

Well, he'd find out.

Keller, feeling professional, feeling mature, sat back and put his feet up. It was fun, postponing gratification like this.

Barbara Paul uses her experience as a former drama and English teacher to good advantage as a novelist. Her two series are as different as night and day, one featuring the singer Enrico Caruso as an amateur sleuth, the other about a New York City policewoman named Marian Larch. Other notable novels include *He Huffed and He Puffed*, a wicked mix of larcenous characters whose only desire is to protect themselves at any cost. Her short fiction can be found in the anthologies *Future Net*, *Murder Most Delicious*, and *Santa Clues*, among many others.

Midnight Sun
BARBARA PAUL

Fur-ruffling breeze; a sniff of winter. Good and bad. Good: warm fireplaces, warm laps, warm chocolate in her saucer. Bad: feet-freezing white stuff on the ground. Playing in the snow was for kittens and humans.

The visitors grew fewer every day . . . the young ones and the old ones, the white ones and the yellow ones and the brown ones, the ones that talked funny and the ones that didn't talk at all. The ones with bad eyesight who had to look through little black boxes that flashed a light before they could see.

Ingvald hunkered down, stroked her long fur. "You smell winter coming, don't you, Takki? Hm?" Carefully he looked over the fenced-in medieval village maintained as an open-air museum, making sure everything was in order. No one lived in the village now . . . except Takki. Ingvald's house was her winter home, but the village was where she lived in summer.

The beefy-chested man approached them, Lars, who helped take care of the place. "Anything scheduled for today?"

Ingvald stood up. "A private party of six, coming by limousine from Lillehammer around three o'clock. Arne's bringing in a tourist bus at four. But that's all . . . other than the usual drop-ins."

Lars nodded. "The private party—Americans?"

"Yes, I believe so."

"They'll think this is a Viking village. Vikings, the Middle Ages ...
it's all the same to them."

"I know. But at least they come."

Lars looked at the leaden sky. "Storm. Big one."

"Not for hours yet." The two men moved off, talking.

Takki felt the breeze lift her long fur again, a little more insistent this
time. Not yet prepared for the cold, she padded toward her favorite
house in the village. Small rooms, small furniture, low ceilings ... cozy
and comforting. Ingvald had to stoop when he went through the doorways. Takki automatically avoided the wooden cradle. The one time she'd
tried to sleep there, that particular piece of furniture had proved remarkably unstable, actually rocking beneath her every time she moved.

She leapt to a wooden bench, found a patch of sunlight shining through
the window, and curled up for her after-lunch nap.

THE SOUND OF CAR DOORS slamming roused her. Instantly awake, Takki
stood up and stretched; her patch of sunlight had disappeared. She
dropped lightly from her bench and trotted outside.

All the buildings in the village had been constructed on pilings that
raised them several feet above ground level, offering some rudimentary
protection against both wild beasts and deep snows. The beasts were all
gone now, but the open spaces beneath the buildings made good hiding
places for a kitty intent on checking out these newest guests in her village.

This was an older crowd, autumn visitors who'd waited until the students and the lovers and the families with small children had all ended
their sampling of Norway's fjords and mountains and lush summer val-
leys. All six of them were dressed in colorful summer clothing, as if
determined to hang on to a season that had already served notice that
the end was in sight.

And they were a vocal bunch, talking loudly at one another even as
they spread out to see what the village had to offer. *"Smørbrød,
smørbrød,"* one man in his fifties was complaining. "If I go into one
more hotel that serves us *smørbrød*, I think I'll puke."

His wife raised an eyebrow. "You never complained about open-faced
sandwiches at home."

"At home I don't have to eat them every goddamned day."

She laughed shortly. "Vince, we haven't had them *every* day."

"Seems like it," Vince growled. 'These people don't exactly knock
themselves out for you, do they?" He glanced to where Ingvald was
courteously answering questions put to him by another of the tourists.
"Look at this guy, Millie. A cold fish if ever I saw one. Real remote,
these people."

But Millie had grown tired of his complaints. "If you wanted to be
fawned over, you should have stayed at home."

He shot a look toward her, but she had her back turned, heading toward the nearest village building. Vince muttered under his breath and went hunting for something to look at.

Another couple had heard the exchange. "Vince and Millie are at it again," the woman said with poorly concealed glee. "I don't think Vince travels well."

Her husband sighed. "Vince thought he was flying into Oslo for meetings with the Nordstrom people and then would fly straight back home again. Mr. Hysinger sprang this little vacation trip on us after we got here, remember?"

"Uh-huh. And neither one of you suspected a thing? Even when Mr. Hysinger said 'Bring your wives—I'm paying'?"

"We've talked about this before."

"Yes, we have, haven't we? I told you before we left that this trip is by way of being an audition."

"Deb, Mr. Hysinger as good as promised me the position."

"Then why is Vince here? And why is Charlotte Evers here?"

"Vince is a branch manager. Who better to advise when we're opening a new branch? And Charlotte is Mr. Hysinger's statistical analyst. He doesn't make a move without her."

Deb looked at him meaningfully.

"Oh, don't read anything into that." He laughed dismissively.

"She's your real competition, you know. I think Vince has already struck out. He's obviously having trouble adjusting to this country. Charlotte's the one you should be worrying about."

"Charlotte's administrative experience is minimal. You're seeing roadblocks where there are none," he insisted. "I'm going to be running the Norwegian branch, count on it."

She stared. "Jerry, sometimes you can be so naive I can't believe you. Don't you see? Hysinger is playing you off against each other."

"No, he's not," Jerry said firmly. "Mr. Hysinger doesn't operate that way. You've misunderstood the situation completely. Relax a little, Deb. Try to enjoy your vacation."

With an effort she bit back what she wanted to say. "All right. We'll play it your way."

"Good." He smiled. "Oh, look at that—there's a cat peeking out at us from under the house." He moved closer to the open space beneath the building. "Hello, kitty ... what are you doing under there? Come here. Here, kitty kitty!"

Takki just looked at him, didn't move.

Deb gave a will-he-never-learn sigh. "Jerry, European cats don't know *kitty kitty*. You have to say *puss puss puss puss puss*."

He tried it, but Takki still didn't move.

Ingvald came up to them. "Ah, there she is. I was wondering where she'd gone to."

"How do you call her?" Jerry asked. "I can't get her to come out."

"I usually just call her by name. Come on out, Takki."

Takki oozed up to Ingvald, butted her head against his shin.

"Takki, huh?" Jerry said. "I'm a sucker for cats myself."

"I found this one huddled by the door to my office when she was still so young she had to be fed with an eye . . . ah." Ingvald groped for the English word. "Eye dropper . . . she took milk from an eyedropper. I have no idea where she came from."

"She reminds me of a long-haired cat we once had. Deb, do you remember Mitzi?"

Deb looked at him as if he were simpleminded. "Of course I remember Mitzi. She lived with us for six years."

Ingvald changed the subject. "I'm afraid I have bad news. I just got a call from the weather station in Trondheim, and a storm is moving in faster than was expected. It would be better if you all returned to Lillehammer."

"But we just got here!"

"I know, and I'm sorry. But there's a low stretch of road about a kilometer from here where the Lågen River always overflows its banks following heavy rains. You could be cut off. And we have no facilities for overnight guests here."

The other man sighed. "Well, it will be up to Mr. Hysinger. It's his party."

"Which one is he?"

"Totally bald, you can't miss him. Last I saw him, he was going into the building over there."

Jerry was pointing toward the long hall, the communal building where those long-dead villagers had taken all their food and drink together, had met to thrash out shared problems, or just had gathered for the warmth of fellowship during the long Norwegian winters. Takki scampered ahead as Ingvald headed toward the hall.

The hall contained the largest single room in the village. Pairs of crossed iron-headed axes faced each other from opposing walls, but other than that the room was quite bare. The villagers had poured their yearning for beauty into their church and into their homes, where every lintel was meticulously carved, where every piece of furniture was decorative as well as useful, where artfully woven tapestries picturing religious and outdoor scenes were hung on the wooden walls, where every surviving box or ale-bowl or wooden chest had been lovingly painted with bold colors and vigorous lines. The whole village was a monument to folk art. But the hall where those people had spent most of their time together—

they'd left that stark and barren, even bleak. The two small windows let in only enough daylight to throw the shadows into prominence.

Ingvald walked in on what was clearly a private conversation. The bald-headed man named Hysinger was talking earnestly to a well-groomed woman in her late thirties, the youngest member of the party. "Don't tell me Nordstrom wants to keep all its personnel, I *know* that," Hysinger was saying—and then broke off to look at Ingvald. Impervious to the tension in the room, Takki jumped up on the table to see if either of the two visitors wanted to pet her.

Neither did. Ingvald apologized for interrupting and repeated his warning about the storm. "I've had to cancel a tourist bus that was due in later this afternoon. And it would be better if your party returned immediately, before the rain starts. If you're driving through the lowlands when the Lågen overflows, it could be dangerous."

Hysinger swore mildly. "Well, if the man says we gotta go, we gotta go."

"I did not see your driver," Ingvald said. "Where—"

"Jerry drove the limo," the woman interposed. "There are only the six of us."

"Round them up, will you, Charlotte?" Hysinger said casually. "I'll be along in a minute."

Charlotte clearly didn't relish being made an errand girl, but she got up to do as Hysinger asked. She passed Ingvald without a glance.

When she'd left, Hysinger cocked his head to the side. "I don't know your name."

"Ingvald Gunnarsson."

"Well, Ingvald, let me ask you something." He paused to push Takki away. "I want to build an executive retreat within driving distance of Oslo. A posh place, where we can bring potential clients. But it's gotta have a spectacular view. Anyplace like that around here?"

"Several," Ingvald answered. "But they are all part of this national preserve. Not for sale."

"Everything's for sale. But I gotta know where to look. You know this country around here, and I'd kinda like the retreat to be near some sort of tourist attraction like this little village you got here. Give the clients something to do if they get bored. Tell me a coupla places to look at."

Ingvald shrugged mentally and gave him directions to two scenic spots in the area. Hysinger pulled out a leather-bound notebook and used a gold pen to take notes.

When he'd finished, he put a hundred-dollar bill on the table. "A little something for your trouble."

Ingvald fixed his gaze on one pair of the iron-headed axes mounted on the wall. "Thank you, Mr. Hysinger, but national preserve employees are not permitted to accept gratuities."

Hysinger laughed. "A man of principle, huh? I like that." He pocketed the hundred.

Feeling patronized, Ingvald said, "Now you must excuse me. I have to see the others." He scooped up Takki from the tabletop and left.

Outside, there wasn't another person visible anywhere. Even Lars, whose help Ingvald could use just then, was nowhere in sight. He glanced up at the sky, now an ominous pewter color. When Takki started wriggling in his arms, he put her on the ground and started a systematic search of the village.

Ingvald tried the church first, as it was the most engaging building in the village. No one. He checked the rest rooms. Empty. He worked his way through the small homes, the prettiest one first. Takki's favorite. Not a sign of anyone. Where had they all disappeared to?

He finally found Vince and Millie at the *stabbur,* the storehouse for communal food and clothing that had no precise equivalent in American towns; America had had no Middle Ages. Vince and Millie were sitting on the removable steps to the second floor entrance of the *stabbur,* puffing away on cigarettes. And arguing.

"Fer gawd's sake, Millie, we'd have to *live* here. In a foreign country. Let him give the job to Charlotte."

"Or Jerry."

"Jerry's a weak sister. He'll pick the yuppie, you'll see."

"If he does, it's because you're not *trying,* Vince! You're the only one here who's ever managed a branch—you're the obvious choice! What would be so terrible about living here?"

Vince caught sight of Ingvald just in time. "Oh, er, hi there."

"Smoking is not permitted," Ingvald said expressionlessly and watched as they quickly stubbed out their cigarettes. For the third time he explained about the storm and led them back toward their limousine.

Charlotte had located Jerry and Deb. "Let's get out of here," she said nervously. "I don't like the look of that sky."

"Where's Mr. Hysinger?" Millie asked.

They all glanced around, as if expecting to spot him hiding behind a tree. "I left him in the long hall," Ingvald said.

"He's probably waiting for someone to come fetch him," Deb said. The five of them avoided one another's eyes, none of them wanting to play the sycophant before the others.

Hiding his irritation, Ingvald said, "I'll get him." Anything to be rid of these people. He took off toward the long hall at a trot.

And was surprised to find the door to the hall shut; all the doors in all the village buildings were kept propped open during tourist season. As he lifted the latch, he heard a plaintive mew from inside.

"Takki?" he said, pushing the door open. "How did you get shut up in here?"

The cat darted between his legs and disappeared.

Ingvald stepped inside and called out, "Mr. Hysinger?" As soon as his eyes adjusted to the dim light, he saw what had frightened the cat.

Hysinger lay slumped at the end of the long table, one of the iron-headed axes from the wall buried in his skull.

THE RAIN WAS A solid wall of water, pounding down hard and cold; the storm had come shrieking in just as Ingvald was telling the others that Hysinger had been murdered. Ingvald demanded the keys to the limousine from Jerry and then directed them all to take refuge in the church—a small building, but still the largest in the village after the long hall. Then he and Lars had hurried away to close all the doors and window shutters.

It was as if someone had turned off the sun. The five tourists groped their way through the darkness, getting their bearings through the brief illumination provided by the occasional flash of lightning. Inside the church was pitch black, until a new lightning flash showed four small windows open to the rain, the wooden shutters banging against the outside walls in the gale. Ducking their heads against the wind, Jerry and Deb closed and latched the shutters.

Then they were in total darkness—scant comfort for the five cold, wet, anxious people. Vince and Millie flicked their cigarette lighters, and they all made their way to the carved wooden pews that had first seen service some six hundred years earlier.

Then they sat there invisibly, listening to one another breathe. Someone's teeth were chattering. "I thought this was supposed to be the Land of the Midnight Sun," Vince complained.

"It's the storm," Deb said impatiently. "It's been light enough to read by most nights since we got here."

"Well, it's not light now."

A sound of annoyance. "Vince, you can always be counted on to state the obvious."

"Well, excuse me, Miss Know-It-All!"

Charlotte spoke up. "Oh, stop it, both of you. We've got a bigger problem than a little temporary discomfort."

"Poor Mr. Hysinger," Millie murmured.

"Poor Mr. Hysinger?" Charlotte repeated in astonishment. "Hasn't it sunk in on you yet? Someone right here killed him! We've got a murderer sitting here with us!"

That put an end to the talk for a while. Eventually Jerry cleared his throat and said, "I know we're all feeling uneasy, but I doubt we're in any danger. We can't see a thing in the dark, but neither can the killer. Surely he wouldn't attempt to, er, strike again under these conditions."

"Why would he want to?" Millie asked, bewilderment and fear in her voice.

"How do you know it's a he?" Vince said gruffly.

"Why kill Mr. Hysinger anyway?" Jerry wanted to know. "Who benefits?"

They were still mulling that over when the church door roared open, letting in a blast of rainy wind. "Why didn't you light the candles?" Ingvald asked them.

Deb laughed shortly. "Candles. We are in a church, aren't we?" No one had thought of it.

Ingvald and Lars had brought oilskin-wrapped blankets, which Ingvald distributed to the cold and wet tourists as Lars moved around the small interior, lighting the thick candles in their iron sconces. The glow of candlelight on old wood created the illusion of warmth where there was none, and the growing light revealed the five visitors sitting as far apart as possible.

"Takki," said Ingvald with a smile. "I knew you'd be all right."

Sitting majestically at the base of the altar, Takki looked out at them through slitted eyes. She was the only dry one in the place.

Vince huddled miserably in his blanket. "Some vacation."

Jerry said. "The road to Lillehammer ... where does it go in the other direction?"

Lars answered him. "It goes to small lake. No houses." Ingvald got a whiff of his breath. Lars was a good maintenance worker but not much good with people; as soon as the tourists had showed up, he'd retreated to his bottle.

Deb made a suggestion. "I say we try for Lillehammer. The longer we wait here, the more chance the river will have to flood."

Ingvald stood in front of the altar and faced them. "It has already flooded. I called the police in Lillehammer. They instructed me to keep you here until they can get through."

"Keep us here?" Jerry raised both eyebrows. "You can't keep us here if we want to leave."

This part was touchy; Ingvald had to make sure everyone understood. "Excuse me, I have the authority to make arrests," he said. "All directors of state preserves do. There have been problems elsewhere with public drunkenness and vandalism."

"Oh?" Charlotte smiled at him sweetly. "And how many arrests have *you* made?"

"None." Ingvald let his eyes travel over them. "You will be my first."

They got the message. Millie said, "Then we'll have to stay here ... until the water recedes. How long will that take?"

"We need wait only until the storm passes. Then the police will send a boat up the river."

"Well, that's not too bad," Millie said, determined to find some bright spot.

Deb asked, "Any idea how long this storm will last?"

"No. The phone went dead before I could ask." Ingvald took out a notebook and pencil he'd picked up from his office. "Please, information you give me now will save the police time later. Three of you were employees of Mr. Hysinger, is that correct? What is the name of his company?"

They all stared at him. "You've never heard of Hysinger Furnaces?" Vince demanded.

They were here to sell furnaces? "You full names and addresses, please."

True Americans, they all insisted Ingvald call them by their first names and assumed he would welcome the same familiarity in return. Hysinger Furnaces' corporate headquarters were located in Chicago, where three of the suspects lived. Ingvald no longer thought of them as tourists.

Jerry Swann was vicepresident in charge of marketing. His wife, Deb, ran an art gallery in Chicago that she oh-so-cleverly called Swann's Way. Charlotte Evers was the company's director of statistical analysis. She was married to a cellist in the Chicago Symphony Orchestra, which was currently playing in Rome—the reason Charlotte's husband had not accompanied them to Norway.

Vince Taggart managed the St. Louis branch of the company, so he and Millie were residents of Missouri. Millie Taggart was what the Americans so dismissively called a housewife. And almost unconsciously Ingvald had pretty much dismissed her as a viable suspect. Fiftyish, a little on the plump side, she walked as if her feet hurt her. Not exactly a daring ax-murderer type. Besides, Millie was the only one who seemed genuinely upset that a man had died. The others were all thinking of their own skins.

Hysinger had bought out a business called A. R. Nordstrom Company, a heating supplies concern based in Oslo. The buyout had been friendly; Nordstrom would become Hysinger's Norwegian branch.

"And possibly even more than that," Charlotte added. "Hysinger was considering making Nordstrom his European headquarters. More than just a branch of managership was involved here."

Jerry waved a hand dismissively. "That was just talk, Charlotte."

"You think so?" She smiled slyly: *I know something you don't know.*

Ingvald watched them carefully. There was more than just money at stake here. Ego, prestige. Status. "Hysinger was going to put one of you in charge of the Norwegian operation? Is that why he was killed?"

"That doesn't make any sense," Deb snapped. "Why kill the goose that lays the golden eggs?"

"Unless he had made his choice," Ingvald pointed out. "If he informed one of you that he or she was no longer on the running—ah." He corrected himself. "*In* the running. But if Hysinger were dead, then no one need know the killer had been passed over. Who will decide now who is in charge of the Norwegian branch?"

Jerry said, "That'll be up to the board of directors. Or else they'll appoint a new CEO and let *him* decide."

"Or her," Charlotte murmured.

"So the killer would still have a chance at the job, you see," Ingvald concluded. "With Hysinger out of the way, there'd still be the possibility of promotion. Perhaps Hysinger had even fired the killer. Perhaps the killer saw getting rid of Hysinger as the only way to save his career."

"That lets me out, then," Vince said. "I didn't even want the damned job."

Deb hooted. "Like hell you didn't! We've all seen you play coy before, Vince."

"I tell ya, I didn't want it," Vince insisted. "No offense, Ingvald, but I don't want to live here."

Charlotte looked thoughtful. "You didn't want the managership of the St. Louis branch either—but somehow you let Hysinger talk you into it."

Jerry's eyes widened. "That's right . . . you said you didn't want to live in Missouri. I remember."

"That was different. Hey, what is this? How come you're all fingering *me*?"

Lars was standing by the door with his arms folded; he and Ingvald exchanged a look as the five Americans quarreled among themselves. Ingvald felt a small head butting against his leg; Takki had been ignored for too long. The man sat down in the first pew; the cat jumped up on the seat next to him to make it easier for him to scratch behind her ears.

The five suspects had argued themselves into a state of sullen silence. Ingvald picked up his notebook again. From the time he'd left Hysinger in the long hall to the time they all gathered by the limousine couldn't have been more than twenty-five minutes or half an hour. He'd spent that time looking for the Americans, until he finally came upon Vince and Millie sitting on the steps of the *stabbur*. But one of them had used the time to kill Hysinger. Could Vince have murdered a man and then calmly sat down and had a cigarette with his wife?

But he hadn't been calm, Ingvald remembered. *He'd been arguing with Millie.*

The wind was rattling the wooden shutters at the windows with a violence that made all of them uneasy. Lars moved quietly from one window to the next, checking the latches.

Ingvald turned sideways in the pew so he could face the others. "Now you will please tell me where you were in the thirty minutes before I found Hysinger's body. Everyplace you went. We start with Mrs. Taggart."

"Millie," she corrected automatically. "Well, I spent some time right here, in the church."

"How long, please?"

"Oh, ten minutes, about."

"Did anyone else come in?"

"No, no one. Then I went into that funny little storage building. I was looking out at that tiny balcony when I saw Vince coming. You remember, we were having a smoke when you found us. Why does a storage building have a balcony?"

Ingvald said, "It's strictly ornamental. The people who lived here thought even a storage facility deserved to be decorative. Now then, Mr. Taggart—Vince."

"Oh, hell, I don't know where I was," Vince said. "I looked into two or three of the buildings. These people sure were small, weren't they? Small rooms, small furniture . . . I got claustrophobic and went outside and just wandered around until I saw Millie poking her head out on that balcony."

"You never went into the long hall?"

"That's were Hysinger was killed? Naw. And I didn't see anybody go in, either."

A crash of thunder made them all jump; the storm was still going strong. Ingvald quickly asked Charlotte what she had been doing during the crucial half hour.

She shrugged. "You know what I was doing. I was looking for the others. I found Jerry and Deb and you found Vince and Millie."

"Did you look in the *stabbur* . . . the storage building?"

Charlotte frowned. "I think that was one of the places I checked early. Millie must not have gotten there yet."

"Where did you find Jerry and Deb?"

"Oh, Jerry was wandering around looking lost and Deb was in one of the homes."

"I was not lost," Jerry said with irritation. "I didn't actually go into any of the buildings. I walked around the perimeter of the village—I was more interested in the architecture of the place."

"Did you see any of the others?"

"Not a soul. I must have just missed, er, everybody. Then Charlotte found me and told me we had to leave."

"But you already knew you had to leave," Ingvald pointed out. "I had told you so myself, before I went to speak to Hysinger."

"Sure, but we'd come all this way and I wanted to get a quick look before we left."

That sounded reasonable. Ingvald looked at Jerry's wife. "Deb?"

She said, "I spent all my time in the same home. I don't know how to identify it . . . it has an almost rococo mantelpiece, and a hand-carved wooden cradle. . . ."

Takki's house. "I know the one." Ingvald suppressed a smile at her use of the term *hand-carved;* how else would a cradle be carved in the Middle Ages?

"Well, I stayed there the whole time," Deb said. "That place is just full of goodies! Ingvald, are any of those items for sale? The cradle, that enormous wooden spoon with the elaborate carved handle—"

"I am sorry, nothing is for sale. Everything here is the property of the state."

Unhearing, she said, "You know I run an art gallery." Deb stood up and made her way back toward the church door, clutching her blanket around her. Lars moved aside to give her room as she ran her hand down a painted door panel that showed some mythical plant blooming out of an urn poised precariously on an abstract geometrical design, a design that was repeated in reverse at the top of the panel. "Look at that!" Deb said appreciatively. "Do you know what I could get for that in Chicago?"

Vince growled. "Fer gawd's sake, Deb, the man's trying to conduct a murder investigation!"

"Yes, Deb," Millie agreed. "This is not the time."

Ingvald asked, "Did anyone else come in while you were there?"

"Just Charlotte. I left with her."

Ingvald regarded her closely as she stood possessively by the door. "Are you sure you never left that one building?"

"Yes, of course I'm sure."

"Not even once?"

All restless movement stopped; the others sensed something in the wind. "I told you," Deb said, "I stayed there the whole time until Charlotte showed up."

Ingvald dropped a hand on the napping Takki, whom he'd been looking for as well as for the Americans. "I checked that building. No one was there. Not one."

Deb tuned white. "You must be mistaken! Did . . . did you check that room in the back? I was—oh. Wait a minute. I did leave to go to the rest room, over by the office. But I wasn't gone more than five minutes and I went right straight back to the same building."

A silence grew. Then: "You know," Charlotte drawled, "that rest-room story might be a tad more believable if you'd thought of it *before* Ingvald said he'd checked that building out."

Vince snorted. "A little credibility problem there, Deb."

"I had to pee!" Deb cried. "That makes me a murder suspect?"

Jerry exploded. "This is absurd! Do you really think Deb could swing a big heavy ax like that? That's ridiculous."

Lars surprised everyone by speaking up. "You do not have to swing the ax. Just let it fall. The iron head does all the work."

The Americans were momentarily taken aback, but then Jerry persisted. "I doubt if Deb could even lift it."

"How do you know the ax is big and heavy, Jerry?" Ingvald asked quietly. "If you never went into the long hall, as you say—then how do you know how big the ax is?"

Jerry sighed impatiently. "You're telling me the ax was tiny and light? *All* axes are big and heavy, Ingvald. I doubt that even in the Middle Ages they made them any different."

Again, a reasonable-sounding response. Jerry was quite good at that. And that made Ingvald suspicious. And while Jerry had come to his wife's defense . . . he'd not done so immediately. But that meant nothing; maybe he just enjoyed seeing her squirm.

Ingvald stood up to stretch his legs. Deb had indeed been in Takki's house; otherwise she wouldn't have known about the cradle and the other things there. But how *long* had she been there? She could have slipped in right before Charlotte found her. There would have been time to kill Hysinger first.

In fact, they all would have had time. Even Charlotte could have gone back to the long hall and done the deed while she was supposed to be looking for the others. She and Hysinger had not seemed very friendly when Ingvald walked in on them. Jerry and Vince also had the time. Even Millie, although Ingvald didn't believe she was guilty. For all his questioning, Ingvald had not been able to remove a single name from the suspects list.

"I've got a headache," Millie announced.

"Because you're hungry," Vince told her. "Hell, *I'm* hungry. Hey, Ingvald—you got any vending machines in that office of yours?"

Ingvald said no. "But we can make coffee."

"Coffee," Charlotte said, her eyes lighting up.

Lars cleared his throat. "I have *bakverk* from my wife."

"A kind of pastry," Ingvald explained.

"Oh, that sounds marvelous," Millie said.

"Yes, it does," Charlotte agreed. "We all need something on our stomachs."

That was an idiom not familiar to Ingvald, and he had a fleeting vision of the five Americans lying flat on their backs in the pews, balancing pastries on their stomachs. Lars was struggling into one of the oilskins they'd brought in wrapped around the blankets, preparing to brave the storm in search of *bakverk* and coffee.

"Thank you, Lars," Ingvald said. Lars grunted and left—probably glad to be out of there. Deb closed the paneled door behind him.

They were all on their feet now except Millie, moving around in the limited space with their blankets wrapped around them toga-style, trying to get their circulation going. It would take Lars a while to brew up enough coffee for seven people, and they were all fidgety anyway; walking was good. Millie's face was pinched; Ingvald wished he'd thought to tell Lars to bring back some aspirin.

A creaking floorboard woke Takki up. She yawned a little and stretched a little and then noticed all the people moving about. She stood up on her hind legs to get a better view, resting her front paws lightly on the back of the pew.

Ingvald moved over to a window and lifted the latch. He slowly eased one of the shutters open until he felt a blast of wet air in his face. Even so, the wind was not as strong as it had been earlier, and there'd been no sound of thunder for some time. The worst of the storm had passed. The rain was still coming down solidly; it smelled clean and good. Ingvald closed the shutter and dropped the latch.

He leaned his back against the closed shutter, watching Takki watch the Americans. There was another mystery there. The killer had closed the door when he or she left, shutting the cat inside. But what was Takki doing there in the first place? The long hall was not one of her special places in the village; she'd gone in earlier that day only because that's where Ingvald was going.

But why did she go back a second time, the time Hysinger was killed? The only notice Hysinger had taken of the cat was to push her out of the way. Takki wouldn't go back to a man who'd dismissed her like that; some cats might, but not Takki. There seemed to be only one explanation; someone had picked her up and carried her inside. Someone who liked cats. And there was only one of the Americans who had paid any attention to Takki at all.

Jerry.

Jerry the smooth talker, who always had a sensible explanation for what he did. Jerry who claimed he'd never been inside the long hall but seemed familiar with the murder weapon. Jerry who'd been led to think the Norwegian branch was his. Jerry, whom Vince had called the "weak sister" in the three-way race for the new job.

There'd been remarkably little blood; the killer either hadn't been splattered or had had time to go to the rest room and clean up. But clearly it was an impulse murder—not planned ahead of time. Had Jerry gone berserk when Hysinger told him he wasn't getting the Norwegian branch? Had he just grabbed the first thing that came to hand—the ax— and hit Hysinger? And then, realizing what he'd done, he'd wandered around outside "looking lost," as Charlotte said, until she found him. It fit; Jerry could have closed the door in a trance, automatically, not thinking about it. And Takki had been trapped inside with the dead man.

Ingvald didn't have the slightest notion of what to do about it. The police would never arrest a man because a preserve director said his cat wouldn't have gone into a certain building on her own. An impulse murderer might not have had the presence of mind to wipe fingerprints off the ax handle, but Ingvald wasn't counting much on prints. The handles of those axes had been partially wrapped with leather thongs, to make gripping easier; it was doubtful that enough smooth surface was left to take a print.

A thumping at the door announced Lars's return; Vince let him in. Lars was laden with thermos jugs, paper cups, pastry, even milk for Takki. And he'd thought to bring aspirin for Millie. "Wind's dying down," Lars said.

The Americans were soon gulping down hot coffee and devouring Lars's pastry. *You'd think they'd never missed a meal before,* Ingvald mused to himself. He fed a little piece of pastry to Takki but didn't eat any himself.

Then they waited, talking only desultorily or not at all. Ingvald and Lars kept a close watch on the weather. Once the wind was gone, the swollen Lågen River would be less dangerous to navigate; the Lillehammer police could well be here before morning. The candles were burning low in the church, but a supply of fresh ones was kept stored behind the altar.

Ingvald left the weather-watching to Lars and sat down in one of the pews, twisting sideways to stretch out his legs on the seat behind him. He'd barely got settled when Takki leaped up to his lap and kneaded his stomach with her paws a few times. Ingvald dropped a gentle hand on her back and started to stroke her—and scratched himself.

Curious, he parted her long fur and found what looked like a silver earring. Takki hissed, but Ingvald held her still until he'd worked it loose. It was an earring, all right, one of those that clamp on; Takki's fur had caught in the hinge.

Ingvald's heart thudded as he realized what that meant. One might argue that Takki could have picked up the earring anywhere, that it had been dropped on her or she'd lain on it just about anyplace. But he didn't think so; there just hadn't been time. When Ingvald had opened the door to the long hall, Takki had scooted out between his legs and out of sight. The cat would have known a storm was coming; she'd have headed straight for the nearest shelter—which was the church. The fact that Takki remained dry while all the people got soaking wet meant she didn't linger waiting for the rain to start. No, she'd acquired the earring in the long hall.

Ingvald looked at the earring cupped in his hand. Two intertwined silver spirals, a double helix; very distinctive. Casually he turned his head to look at the three women in the church. Both of Millie's pearl earrings were in place. Neither Deb nor Charlotte was wearing earrings.

Deb or Charlotte.

Charlotte had been in the long hall talking to Hysinger when Ingvald went in, so she could have lost the earring then. Ingvald closed his eyes and tried to visualize the scene, but gave up in frustration. He just couldn't remember whether she'd been wearing earrings or not. If she had lost it then, innocently, then he was back to square one, as the Americans liked to say. But if she'd gone back later and lost it then, or if the earring belonged to Deb . . .

Ingvald looked at Millie. The pinched look was gone from her face; the aspirin had done its job. He decided to take a chance on her. Easing Takki from his lap, Ingvald stood up and went back to where Millie was sitting.

He bent down and said into her ear, low, so only she could hear: "Will you please come with me to the altar, where the light is better? There's something I want to show you." She looked startled, but agreed readily enough.

The church was small enough that his speaking to Millie could not go unnoticed. All eyes were upon them as they made their way to the altar.

When they were there, Ingvald said, "Please keep your voice low." He opened his hand. "Do you know whom this belongs to?"

She didn't even have to stop to think. "Why, that's Deb's. Where did you get it?"

"Are you sure? Could it possibly belong to Charlotte?"

Millie shook her head firmly. "I have never once seen Charlotte Evers wearing earrings. Not once."

Ingvald felt like kissing her. Instead he thanked her and asked her to return to her seat. Then he went over to the window where Lars was watching and told his assistant to go stand by the church door in case anyone tried to bolt.

The Americans were all watching him expectantly. Ingvald took a deep breath, steadying himself to make his first arrest. He walked down the narrow center aisle until he reached Deb's pew. He cleared his throat and said, "Would you care to change your story about never going into the long hall?"

She was indignant. "No, of course not! Why should I?"

"Because you left a calling card behind." He held up the earring.

"That's not mine," Deb said quickly.

Charlotte got up for a closer look. "Yes, it is, Deb. You were wearing those this morning. What did you do with the other one? Throw it away?"

"You're imagining things! I ought to know my own earrings!"

Ingvald felt an enormous relief. If she'd said yes, that was her earring but she'd noticed it missing when they first got here—well, he wouldn't have a leg to stand on. But by lying, she'd only dug herself in deeper.

Ingvald said, "Two people have now identified this earring as yours. You were in the long hall and you lost your earring there. That places you at the scene of the crime. That is sufficient for an arrest."

"You're crazy!" Deb screamed. "I didn't kill him!"

Ingvald stood up straight. "I am now arresting you for murder." That didn't sound right, but he couldn't remember what words he was supposed to use.

"Jesus H. Christ." Vince's mouth was hanging open.

Frightened, Deb looked at her husband. "Jerry?"

But he was already on his feet, protesting. "Ingvald, you're out of your mind! Deb didn't kill anyone. You call that evidence, one flimsy little earring? The *real* police will laugh in your face." He turned to his wife. "Don't worry, Deb, they won't even charge you. And if they do, I'll get the best lawyer this country has to offer." Back to Ingvald. "Better think what you're doing, Ingvald."

"You'll *what*?" Deb said to Jerry, rising from her seat.

"I don't know Norwegian law," Jerry sent on, "but I'm sure you have something equivalent to our false arrest. Do you want to get sued, Ingvald?"

"Wait a minute, wait a minute," Deb interrupted. "Did you say you'd get me the best *lawyer*?"

"The very best there is. Don't worry, now, you—"

"Why, you son of a bitch," Deb said, furious. "You're going to let me be arrested?"

Jerry was making little calming gestures with his hands. "Now, Deb, don't say anything until I get the lawyer. I mean, don't say *anything*. Just keep quiet and everything will be all right."

Right then Deb looked as if she was capable of murder, with her husband as her intended victim. "Oh, no, you don't. I've put up with a lot from you, Jerry, but now you go too far! I am not going to prison for you!"

"Now, Deb, think what you're saying—"

She turned to face Ingvald. "Jerry hit Hysinger with that ax. I was there, I saw him do it, and I'll testify that I saw him do it!" Jerry moaned and sank down on a pew.

So it was Jerry after all? Well, well. Everyone was staring at the accused man. "In that case," Ingvald said to Jerry, "I am now arresting *you* for murder." He looked back at Deb. "You are still under arrest. You knew who killed Hysinger and lied about it. I'm sure there's a law against that."

"Good God," said Charlotte. "What happened?"

Jerry buried his face in his hands, didn't answer. Deb said, "We went to see if Hysinger had made up his mind about who'd get the job. He had. He told Jerry he was out of the running." She sighed. "He said the job was Vince's if he wanted it and Charlotte's if he didn't. But Jerry was out."

"I don't want the goddamned job!" Vince roared. "How many times do I have to say it?"

"Then what?" Ingvald asked Deb.

She said, "Jerry went nuts, completely nuts . . . that's the only way to describe it. I've never seen him like that. He was like a wild man. He pulled that ax off the wall and buried it in Hysinger's skull."

Millie was sniffling. "Oh, this is terrible, just terrible!"

Ingvald asked Deb, "What did you do?"

"I tried to stop him, I grabbed one arm . . . but I don't think he even knew I was there." She touched her ear. "That must be when I lost the earring, during that useless little tussle. It was all so fast . . . anyway, then I ran. I was terrified! I ran until I was out of sight of that building, and then I ducked into one of the little homes . . . the one with the cradle and the other nice things. Then I just sat there, trying to think what to do."

"You should have stuck together," Charlotte said dryly. "Alibi each other." Deb shot her a look of pure venom.

Ingvald said to Jerry, "Then what did *you* do?"

Jerry sat slumped in his pew, not looking at anyone. Unbidden, Lars had moved into the pew behind him and stood there towering over him. Jerry glanced over his shoulder at him. "I was in a daze," Jerry said to Ingvald. "I don't know where I went. I was just wandering until Charlotte found me."

Ingvald nodded, satisfied that the picture was now complete. "Then the storm intervened. When I was at last able to start questioning you, you'd had time to put your thoughts together. And Deb had decided to say nothing."

"I hadn't *completely* decided," Deb said in her own defense. "But I hadn't had a chance to talk to Jerry alone since . . . since it happened."

A silence developed. Then Jerry looked up at Ingvald, a sadly wistful smile playing around his lips. "Aren't you going to put the cuffs on me?"

Ingvald was embarrassed. "I don't have any."

"That's all right," Deb snapped. "He's not going anywhere."

There was no more to be said. The other four Americans all avoided looking at Jerry, and Charlotte was even smiling. Ingvald thought he knew why: With Jerry arrested for murder and Vince withdrawn from the competition, the new job was hers by default.

LESS THAN AN HOUR LATER, Lars opened the church door and announced, "Rain has stopped."

The three innocent Americans practically fell over themselves getting outside, freed at last. Lars planted himself in the open doorway of the church, a warning to Jerry and Deb not to try running. Outdoors, the cool air was heavy with moisture, and broken tree limbs and other detritus of the storm lay scattered on the muddy ground; the only one who minded the slippery footing was Takki. The blackness brought by the storm was completely gone; the familiar light of Norway's night sky was back.

"There's your midnight sun, Vince," Millie said.

He wrapped an arm around her and gave her a hug. "Some vacation, huh? Missouri's gonna look damned good."

Charlotte drew Ingvald aside. "I was impressed by the way you handled this problem," she said. "You had none of the resources of the police at your disposal, but you still managed to arrive at the truth. You were *very* impressive."

"Thank you." He didn't know what else to say.

"When this new branch in Oslo gears up, we're going to need a security chief. Someone who can think on his feet. I'm going to recommend you for the job. You're wasted out here, Ingvald."

He wasn't expecting anything like that. "Ah, I thank you, but I must decline. My life is here."

"Don't you ever want a little change in your life?" she asked, surprised. "You'd be making a lot of money working for us. You'd be in the city, right at the center of what's happening—not stuck out in the middle of nowhere. Do you live alone?"

Thinking the question impertinent, he nevertheless answered it. "I live with Takki."

"The cat? Way out here with nothing but a cat for company? What kind of life is that?"

"It is my kind of life. Thank you for the offer, but the answer is no."

She raised an eyebrow. "You prefer cats to people?"

Ingvald smiled. "The cat is never vulgar," he said.

Anne Perry is the writer of two series of mystery novels, both set in Victorian England. The first involves an amnesiac police inspector; the second, more long-running series is about another police inspector and his wife. Both series examine not only the Victorian age's hypocrisy and injustice but also comment on the role of women during that age. Her work is characterized by strong female characters (for the time period) and a keen attention to detail. Here, however, she returns to the Victorian age with a different protagonist who encounters a variant of the social crime so prevalent during that time.

The Blackmailer
ANNE PERRY

The butler closed the withdrawing room door behind him. "Excuse me, sir. There is a young gentleman called to see you." He held out the silver tray, offering Henry Rathbone the card on it.

Henry picked it up and read. The name James Darcy was only slightly familiar. It was half past nine on a January evening, and bitterly cold. The gas lamps in the street were haloed in fog, and the hansom cabs' wheels hissed in the damp, their horses' hooves muffled by the clinging darkness.

"He seems very agitated, sir," the butler said, watching Henry's face. "He begged me to ask if you would see him, as he is in some kind of difficulty, although of course he did not impart its nature to me."

"Then I suppose you had better show him in," Henry conceded. "I cannot imagine how he believes I may help." Nor could he. He was a mathematician and occasional inventor, a lover of fine watercolors which he collected when he could afford to, and an inveterate dabbler in shops which dealt in anything old. He liked the evidences of ordinary life, rather than the antiques of wealth.

The man who followed the butler into the room was of average height, fair coloring, and regular features. He was very well dressed. His cravat was tied to perfection, his boots gleamed, and in spite of his obvious anxiety, he bore himself with confidence.

"It is very good of you to receive me, sir," he said, extending his hand. "Most particularly since I have called at such an uncivil hour. To tell you the truth, I have been arguing with myself all afternoon as to what I should do, and whether or not I should approach you." He met Henry's eyes with disarming candor, and Henry saw the fear sharp and bright in them.

"Please sit down, Mr. Darcy," he invited. "A glass of brandy? You must be cold."

"Indeed I am. That is most kind of you." Darcy moved closer to the fire and stood for a moment. Then, as if his legs had collapsed, he sank into the chair, letting out his breath in a shaking sigh. "I am in a most terrible situation, Mr. Rathbone, and I cannot get myself out of it without the help of someone like yourself, a man of unquestioned honor. I am being blackmailed." He sat quite still, his blue eyes fixed on Henry's face, as if dreading his response, yet unable to move his gaze until he had seen it.

Henry poured the brandy and passed it across.

"I see. Do you know by whom?"

"Oh, yes," Darcy said quickly. "A man called James Albury. To my sorrow, I have a passing acquaintance with him."

Henry hesitated. He had never encountered blackmail before, but he was willing to do what he could to help this young man so obviously in distress. Whatever his weakness or failing, another man's attempt to profit from it in this manner was inexcusable. It was indelicate to ask, and yet in order to foresee the consequence of failure, he had to know the original offense.

As if reading his dilemma, Darcy spoke, leaning forward a little, the firelight warming the pallor of his face.

"I did not commit any crime, Mr. Rathbone, or I would not place you in the embarrassment of being party to it. If I tell you my story, you will understand."

Henry sat back and, without thinking, rested his feet on the fender. His slippers were already well scorched from the practice. "Please do," he said encouragingly.

Darcy sipped his brandy, cradling the glass in his hands.

"I was staying the weekend at the country house of Lord Wilbraham. There were several other guests, among them Miss Elizabeth Carlton, to whom I am betrothed." He took a deep breath and looked down. The flush in his cheeks was more than the reflection of the flames.

Henry did not interrupt.

"You will need to understand the geography of the house," Darcy continued. "The conservatory lies beyond a most agreeable morning room in which are hung some rather valuable pictures, most particularly some Persian miniatures painted upon bone. They are quite small, not more than a few inches across, most delicately wrought—with a single hair, so I have heard. There is no other door to the morning room except that into the hall."

Henry wondered where Darcy was leading. Presumably it had something to do with the miniatures.

Again Darcy seemed uncomfortable. His eyes left Henry's and he looked down at the carpet between them.

"Please believe me, Mr. Rathbone, I am devoted to Miss Carlton. She is everything a man could desire: honest, gentle, modest, of the sweetest nature. ..."

It occurred to Henry that these were euphemisms for saying that the girl was lacking in spirit or humor, and more than a little boring, but he smiled and said nothing.

Darcy bit his lip. "But I was rash enough to spend a great deal more of the evening than I should have in the company of another young lady, alone in the conservatory. I had gone in there, rather more by chance than design, and when I heard Lizzie ... Miss Carlton, through the open doors into the morning room, I did not wish to be seen coming out with Miss Bartlett. She was ... er ... in high good humor, and ... a trifle disheveled in her dress. She had caught her gown on a frond of one of the palm trees ... and ..." He opened his eyes wide and stared at Henry with wretchedness.

"I see," Henry said with considerable compassion. The truth of the matter might be as Darcy said, or it might not. It was not for him to judge. "Where do the miniatures come in to the matter?"

"Two of them were stolen," Darcy said huskily. "The alarm was raised as soon as it was noticed, and from the circumstances it was obvious that they were taken before Lizzie went into the morning room, although she said that she had not noticed their absence."

"And the blackmail?" Henry asked. "Is the suggestion that you took them as you passed through to the conservatory?"

"Yes. They were seen shortly before that!" Darcy's voice rose in anguish. "You perceive my dilemma? I was at all times with Miss Bartlett. She would swear for me that I did not, and could not, have taken them! But if she were to do so, then Lizzie would know that I was in the conservatory with Miss Bartlett ... and I confess, Mr. Rathbone, that would be most painful for her, and some considerable embarrassment for me. Miss Bartlett's reputation is ... less ..."

"You do not need to spell it out for me." Henry leaned forward and poked the fire, putting on another two or three coals.

"Added to which," Darcy went on, "if I were to prove myself innocent, then it would leave poor Lizzie with the matter of proving herself innocent also. Of course she is! She is as honest as it is possible to be, and is an heiress to a considerable sum. It would not be more than unpleasant for her. No one could imagine ... Nevertheless, I cannot ..."

"I see your predicament," Henry said with feeling. Indeed, it was very apparent, as was his conflict of emotions over the wealthy Miss Carlton, who would not take a pleasing view of his dalliance, real or imagined, with Miss Bartlett.

"But I do not know how I can help. What does Mr. Albury require of you? You have not said."

"Oh, money!" Darcy answered with contempt. "And of course if I should pay him once, then there is nothing on earth to stop him returning again and again, as often as he pleases." His voice rose close to panic and there was desperation in his eyes. "If I once give in to him, he could bleed me till I have nothing left!" His hands were clenched before him. "But if I don't, he leaves me no alternative but to permit him either to ruin me or drive me to defend myself at Lizzie's cost, and the end of my betrothal and my future happiness." He bent forward and covered his face with his hands. "God, I was a fool to stay there in that damned conservatory, but there was no harm in it, I swear to that!"

Henry felt an intense pity for him. It was a piece of very mild foolishness, such as any young man might commit. Possibly most young men had, feeling the constraints of marriage and domestic ties closing around them, and taking a last opportunity for a gentle flirtation. Darcy had been caught by an extraordinary mischance. But Henry had no idea how he could help. He sought anything to say that would at least be of comfort, and found nothing.

Darcy looked up. "Mr. Rathbone, I can think of only one way in which this blackguard might be confounded...."

"Indeed?" Henry was greatly relieved. "Pray tell me how, and I will do all I can to aid you, and with the greatest pleasure." He meant it profoundly.

Darcy straightened himself and set his shoulders square. He took another healthy sip of his brandy and then put the glass down.

"Mr. Rathbone, if you, and some highly reputable and esteemed gentleman of your acquaintance—I know there are many—were to come to my rooms and secrete yourselves in the adjoining chamber, with the door on the jar, I could face Albury and entice him to commit himself verbally to precisely what he is doing. Then he will have damned himself out of his own mouth. With witnesses against him such as yourself, a disinterested party whose reputation no man would question, then I think he will not dare to press his case further. He could have as much to lose as I, or perhaps even more. No man of honor can tolerate a blackmailer."

"Quite!" Henry said almost eagerly. "I do believe you have the answer,

Mr. Darcy. And I have half a dozen acquaintances at the very least, who would be happy to dispatch such a fellow and count it a service to humanity to do so. Lord Jesmond leaps to mind most readily. If he is agreeable to you, I shall approach him tomorrow."

"Most agreeable, sir," Darcy said quickly. "An admirable gentleman, and his condemnation could ruin Albury, or any man fool enough to earn it. I cannot begin to express to you how grateful I am. I shall be forever in your debt, as will my dear Lizzie, although she will never know it." He rose to his feet and held out his hand impulsively. "Thank you, Mr. Rathbone, with all my heart!"

IT WAS TWO DAYS LATER on a sharp, frosty afternoon, with ice cracking in the puddles and a bleached winter sky that promised a bitter night, when Henry Rathbone and Lord Jesmond alighted from their hansom cab and presented themselves at Darcy's lodgings in Mayfair. They had not used Lord Jesmond's carriage in case its presence in the mews might cause the blackmailer to suspect a witness to his dealings.

They were welcomed at the door by Darcy, who was quite understandably in a state of considerable anxiety. His eyes were bright and his color feverish. He moved jerkily, all but drawing them inside, with a hand on Henry's arm which he released with a stammered apology as soon as he realized his unwarranted familiarity. Henry introduced him to Lord Jesmond.

"I am most heartily grateful, my lord," Darcy said earnestly. "It is an inestimable kindness for you to have taken up my cause in this way. I can never repay you."

"No need, my dear fellow," Jesmond assured him, taking the offered hand and shaking it warmly. "Dastardly thing, blackmail. Fellow deserves to be horsewhipped, but I daresay a damned good fright will serve the purpose, and without jeopardizing your good name or your future happiness. Now, where may we wait so as to observe this wretch without ourselves being seen?"

"This way, my lord." Darcy turned on his heel and led them into a most agreeable room furnished with armchairs and a small carved table of Oriental style. The fireplace was after the fashion of Adam, and above the mantel was a highly individual collection of paintings of the scenery of the Cape of Good Hope. There were brass candlesticks of some elegance at either end, and a brisk fire which made the room most comfortable.

Darcy led them to a door at the farther side, and the chilly, apparently unused, bedroom beyond, in which there was no furniture except a large Chinese silk screen.

"I'm sorry," he apologized. "I know it is miserably cold in here, but were I to set a fire, Albury might wonder why, and I am desperate to get this matter over with. I fear if I do not succeed this time, I shall not have another opportunity. He is a blackguard, but he is not a fool."

"Quite, my dear fellow," Lord Jesmond said immediately. "Might choose to meet you somewhere in the open next time, what? Damn the cold and the rain! This will do very well, I assure you. Handy having the screen there, in case he should look in. Daresay you thought of that, what?" He smiled, perhaps attempting to put Darcy in good heart.

Darcy smiled back. It was a pained expression, the specter of fear too sharp in it for Henry at least to miss.

"Don't worry," he said gently. "He won't raise the issue again, once we've caught him fairly at his game. But anxiety in your manner will be all to the good. Now pull the door to, and we will wait here, behind the screen."

"Thank you again, gentlemen," Darcy said with feeling, then did as he was bid. The next moment the door was all but closed, and Henry and Jesmond were alone, seeing nothing but the delicately embroidered silk of the screen. The silence was so complete it all but crackled. There were no footsteps or voices of domestic service. Possibly whoever cared for Darcy's needs had been sent out of the house on errands of one sort or another. There was not even the hiss of flames or the settling of coals beyond the door. The whole house seemed to have held its breath.

Then at last it came, a voice which was not Darcy's, a soft, insinuating, well-bred voice of a man used to charm and ease of good manners. But Henry heard in it the higher pitch of nervousness, the added sharpness, the little space for an indrawn breath of a man who knows he is about dangerous business, and has something to win or lose.

"Right, Darcy, let us not waste time with pleasantries neither of us means. I hope you are well. You wish I would meet with lethal mischance which would free you from all risk from me. Let us assume it has been said. But I am alive and in excellent health, and look set to remain so— unless you are rash enough to try to murder me! But I have taken some precautions against that." He laughed abruptly. "And it would seem an excessive reaction to what is, after all, a fairly modest request to a man of the means you will have when you have married Miss Elizabeth Carlton." There was a moment's silence.

"Damn you!" Darcy said chokingly.

"And I know of nothing which will prevent that," Albury went on, "except your failure to oblige me."

Darcy's voice came sharply. "In what manner 'oblige you'?"

"Oh, come!" Albury said in disgust. "Don't be coy with me. You understand me very well. We have already made our positions quite plain." There was no impatience in his voice. To Henry, standing in the chill behind the Chinese screen, there was a note of pleasure in it, as if he savored his power and was in no haste to have the moment over.

The same thought must have come to Darcy, because the next instant his voice came quite clearly, raised a little.

"You are enjoying this, you wretch! I used to consider you, if not a friend, at least a person worthy of respect. My God, how wrong I was! You are not fit to cross the threshold of any decent house!"

"You are in no position to criticize, my dear Darcy, let alone to fling insults," Albury replied with amusement. "How many thresholds do you suppose you would be permitted to cross were it generally known that you pocketed two of your host's most delicate and valuable Persian miniature paintings?"

"I did not!" Darcy said desperately. "I—"

"Indeed," Albury said with disbelief. "Then no doubt you will prove it and have me for false accusation when I tell everyone what I know."

"I . . ." Darcy was all but sobbing. Henry glanced at Jesmond. Darcy was playing his part extremely well. Perhaps he had less confidence in his plan than he had seemed to have earlier. Albury had apparently robbed him of his faith. Henry's anger against him almost boiled over. Blackmail was among the most despicable of crimes, a slow and quite deliberate torture.

"You could always pay me, as agreed," Albury said distinctly. "Twenty pounds a month, I think, will keep me in the luxuries to which I would like to accustom myself, quite without beggaring you. You will have to forgo a few of the pleasantries of life you now enjoy. Your good claret may have to go, your visits to the opera, your rather regular new shirts. You will have to wear your boots a trifle longer than you do now. And I daresay, at least until your marriage, you will not be able to be quite so generous to Miss Carlton."

"Damn you!" Darcy said fiercely. "That is blackmail!"

"Of course it is!" Albury replied, his tone filled with amusement. "Do you mean to say you have only just appreciated that?"

"No." Now the confidence was back, Darcy sounded like a different man. "No, I have always known it was; I simply wanted to hear you say so. Because blackmail is a crime, quite a severe one, and I have witnesses to our conversation. And that, I think, gives me an equal advantage with you."

"What?" Albury was aghast. "Where?"

Henry moved from behind the screen just as the door was flung wide and a dark, lean young man faced them, his mouth open, his eyes filled with horror.

"Mr. Darcy is quite correct," Henry said, moving forward to allow Lord Jesmond also to be seen. "We have overheard your entire exchange, Mr. Albury, and you would be well advised to leave here and never mention the matter to anyone as long as you live. Count yourself fortunate to have escaped ruin and prosecution. You will not get a penny from Darcy. In return, neither Lord Jesmond nor myself will speak of your contemptible behavior. It will remain as secret as it is now."

Albury backed away, turning to stare at Darcy with loathing.

"Nothing," Darcy reaffirmed, pointing to the farther door and the way out. "Leave my house and do not set foot here again. Should I chance to meet you socially, I shall treat you with civility, as if nothing had happened between us, for the sake of our bargain."

Henry and Jesmond came into the sitting room, glad of the warmth. The fire crackled in the grate. Darcy had set more coals in it. There was an ease in the air, a sense of victory.

"Bargain?" Albury looked from one to the other of them in rage and frustration. "I get nothing, and you get away with theft! What are those miniatures worth? A hundred, two hundred? More? You'll sell them and do very nicely."

"I didn't take them," Darcy said earnestly. "I have never stolen a thing in my life."

"No?" Albury's eyes widened in exaggerated disbelief.

"No," Darcy said firmly.

"Then why did you not say so at the time, and tell me to go to hell?" There was a smirk on Albury's face and his eyes were bright and hard.

"Because to do so I should have to admit that I was alone in the company of a young lady other than my betrothed, and for a longer time than she might understand. Also, it would provoke speculation that—" Darcy stopped suddenly, perhaps realizing he had said far more than he needed to, and raised the very questions he wanted to avoid.

Albury smiled, showing very fine teeth, transforming his face.

"You mean that it might suggest that Miss Carlton took them herself? Of course it might! In fact it would! And there would be a certain justice in that."

"It would be monstrous!" Darcy said furiously. He took a step forward, his fists clenched by his sides. "Don't you dare say such a thing ever again. Do you hear me? Or I shall take great pleasure in thrashing you till you are obliged to eat your meals from the mantelpiece, sir."

"It would also be true," Albury returned without moving a step.

"You go too far, sir," Jesmond stepped forward at last. "To blacken a lady's name when she is not here to defend herself is inexcusable. You will retract your calumny immediately, and then leave while you still have a whole skin and can walk away with nothing but your honor injured."

Henry was staring at the two younger men and the emotions written so deeply in them. A strange thought was stirring in his mind.

"It makes no sense," Darcy protested. "Lizzie would never do such a thing. Anyone who knows her knows that! She has all the means she could wish, and she is as honest as the day."

"But a woman," Albury said, ignoring Lord Jesmond and looking only at Darcy. "And as capable of feeling jealousy as the next."

Darcy swallowed. "Jealousy?" he said hoarsely.

"Of course! Did you imagine she did not know you were in the conservatory with Belle Bartlett, or picture in her mind only too clearly what you may have been doing in between the orchids and the potted palms? Then you are a fool!"

Darcy gulped. He seemed to be shaking very slightly, as if in spite of the heat in the room he were cold within.

"She took them," Albury went on. "In order to compromise you. She knows of a surety, better than anyone else, that you did not take them. But either she will see you, or Miss Bartlett, accused of the theft, in thought if not in word, or failing that, she will hold it over your head for the rest of your life together."

"Never say that again!" Darcy said between dry lips, his voice strangled in his throat. "Never, do you hear me?"

Albury held out his hand. "Fifty pounds, once only."

Darcy turned and went to a small bureau at the far side of the room. He opened the top, and from a pigeonhole took out several Bank of England notes. Without a word, he held them out to Albury.

"Just a moment!" Henry reached across and closed his hand over Darcy's, preventing Albury from taking the money. "You do not need to pay him."

"Yes, I do!" Darcy said desperately. "God knows, I cannot marry Lizzie now. It would be a torment every day, every night. I should see this jealousy in her eyes each time I looked at her. Our life would be intolerable. Every time I spoke civilly to another woman I should fear what she might do. But one cannot kill the habit of love so easily, not in one blow, however hard. I shall protect her honor in the eyes of others. No one need know but herself and her father." He bit his lip. "I shall have to speak to him. Our understanding cannot remain. But I shall do this for her at least. Free my hand, sir."

Henry kept hold of it.

"What you wish to give Mr. Albury, or why, is your own affair, Mr. Darcy, but you do not need to pay him in order to protect Miss Carlton. She is guilty of nothing more than perhaps a misjudgment of character."

"I don't know what you mean," Darcy protested. "She has behaved despicably. She has attempted out of jealousy to brand Miss Bartlett a thief!"

"Because she knew that you and she were in the conservatory together?" Henry asked.

"Apparently."

"Then she knew that just as Miss Bartlett could swear to your innocence of theft, so you could, and would, swear to hers! That would leave her own guilt suspect, in just the manner Mr. Albury has said."

Darcy paled, glanced at Albury, then back at Henry Rathbone. He made as if to speak, but no words came.

"But my dear chap, it makes no sense," Jesmond said in utter confusion. "You must be mistaken."

"It makes perfect sense," Henry explained. "If you consider the story from the beginning, not as Mr. Darcy would have us believe. Take all the facts as he described them. A young man, betrothed to one young lady, finds himself most attracted to another, perhaps more vivacious. He cannot break his word to the first. That is legally breach of promise, and socially suicidal to one who has considerable aspirations. Also it would be unlikely to gain him the hand of the lady he desires. Her father, also wealthy and of eminent position, would not countenance it."

Darcy was ashen now.

"He must find another way out," Henry continued. "The young lady will not leave him. He must create an honorable cause to leave her, one in which he remains untarnished, free to pursue his ambitions. At a country house party the opportunity presents itself and the idea is born. He needs only the help of a clever actor." He glanced at Albury, who was now in an extremity of embarrassment. "And two witnesses of reputations above question, and by nature honorable, eager to right a wrong, and perhaps a trifle innocent in the ways of young men with too few scruples and too much appetite for success."

"Good heavens!" Jesmond was appalled.

Henry looked again at Darcy.

"Don't feel you have failed entirely, Mr. Darcy. As soon as I acquaint Miss Carlton with the facts, she will free you to pursue Miss Bartlett, or whomsoever else you wish. Although I doubt Sir George Bartlett will accept you into his family, any more than I should. I have not been the service to you that you intended, but I have indeed served a purpose. Come, Jesmond." He led the way to the door, then, with Jesmond at his heels, turned back. "Don't forget you owe Mr. Albury for an excellent piece of acting! Good day, gentlemen!"

BIBLIOGRAPHY
A 1995 Yearbook Compiled by
Edward D. Hoch

I. Collections and Single Stories

Alcott, Louisa May. *Unmasked: Collected Thrillers.* Boston: Northeastern University Press. Edited by Madeleine Stern. Twenty-nine tales, 1863–70, previously collected in five volumes.

Allingham, Margery. *The Darings of the Red Rose.* Norfolk, VA: Crippen & Landru. Eight collected stories about a female Robin Hood, first published in a London women's magazine in 1930.

Asimov, Isaac. *Magic: The Final Fantasy Collection.* New York: HarperPrism. Eleven stories, one an uncollected Black Widowers tale, and thirteen essays and introductions.

Bailey, Hilary. *The Strange Adventures of Charlotte Holmes.* London: Constable. Six connected stories about Sherlock Holmes's younger sister, narrated by Dr. Watson's wife (1994).

Bankier, William. *Fear Is a Killer.* Oakville, ON, Canada: Mosaic Press. Edited and introduced by Peter Sellers. Sixteen stories, 1962–86, mainly from *EQMM.*

Brand, Max. *The Collected Stories of Max Brand.* Lincoln, NE: University of Nebraska Press. Eighteen stories, 1918–48, mainly Westerns but including a spy story and a detective story from the pulps (1994).

Cave, Hugh B. *Death Stalks the Night.* Minneapolis: Fedogan & Bremer. Crime stories from the weird menace pulps of the 1930s, at least two with detection.

Chandler, Raymond. *Stories & Early Novels. Later Novels & Other Writings.* New York: The Library of America. A two-volume collection of all seven Chandler novels, thirteen pulp stories, the screenplay *Double Indemnity,* and selected essays and letters.

Collins, Wilkie. *The Complete Shorter Fiction.* New York: Carroll & Graf. Forty-eight stories and novelettes, mainly criminous but with some fantasy. Edited by Julian Thompson with valuable headnotes for each story.

Copper, Basil. *The Recollections of Solar Pons.* Minneapolis: Fedogan & Bremer. Four new stories about the Sherlockian sleuth created by August Derleth. One of them, "The Adventure of the Singular Sandwich," was distributed in a separate "sampler" booklet at Bouchercon 26.

Elward, Miles. *Sherlock Holmes in Canterbury.* Kenley, England: Wynne Howard Publishing. Three new Sherlockian pastiches.

Francis, Dick. *Racing Classics.* London: Penguin Books. A booklet containing the first chapter of his novel *Dead Cert* and a 1973 short story "The Gift."

Freeman, R. Austin. *The Dead Hand.* Aldershot, England: Highfield Press. A 42-page booklet containing an uncollected Dr. Thorndyke novelette later expanded into the 1925 novel *The Shadow of the Wolf.*

Gorman, Ed. *Cages.* Los Gatos, CA: Deadline Press. Introduction by F. Paul Wilson, afterword by Marcia Muller. A 1993 novelette and twenty short stories, five new. Some fantasy.

Hoch, Edward D. *The Theft of the Rusty Bookmark.* New York: The Mysterious Bookshop. A single new short story about Nick Velvet, published as a holiday gift by the Manhattan bookstore.

Jablokov, Alexander. *The Breath of Suspension.* Sauk City, WI: Arkham House. Fantasy stories with some detection.

Jesse, F. Tennyson. *The Adventures of Solange Fontaine.* London: Thomas Carnacki. Eight stories, one in two versions, from the *Premier* and *Strand* magazines, 1918–19 and 1931.

Koontz, Dean. *Strange Highways.* New York: Warner Books. Two novels, one new, plus twelve novelettes and short stories, mainly fantasy but some criminous.

Laymon, Richard. *A Good, Secret Place.* San Jose, CA: Deadine Press. Introduction by Ed Gorman. Twenty stories, five from *EQMM,* in a limited edition (1994).

Lewin, Michael Z. *Telling Tails.* Frome, England: PawPaw Press. Nine short-short stories, eight new, about a hard-boiled dog detective (1994).

Moquist, Richard W. *The Franklin Mysteries.* Salt Lake City: Northwest Publishing. Nine new stories featuring Ben Franklin as detective.

Mortimer, John. *Rumpole and the Angel of Death.* London: Viking. Six new novelettes about the British barrister.

———. *Under the Hammer.* London: Penguin Books. Six new stories about a pair of auction house sleuths (1994).

Muller, Marcia. *The McCone Files.* Norfolk, VA: Crippen & Landru. Introduction by the author. Thirteen stories about private eye Sharon McCone from various sources, plus two new "framing" stories at the beginning and end.

Niven, Larry. *Crashlander.* New York: Ballantine. Future crime stories with some detection (1994).

———. *Flatlander.* New York: Ballantine. The collected tales of Gil "The Arm" Hamilton, including a short novel and four stories, one new. Concludes with an essay on "Science/Mystery Fiction."

O'Callaghan, Maxine. *Maxine O'Callaghan Bibliography.* Mission Viejo, CA: A.S.A.P. Publications. Two stories plus bibliographic material.

Paretsky, Sara. *A Taste of Life.* London: Penguin Books. A booklet containing three nonseries stories from various sources.

———. *Windy City Blues.* New York: Delacorte. Nine stories about female private eye V. I. Warshawski, with an author's introduction about the Chicago setting. The British edition, *V. I. For Short* (Hamish Hamilton), omits the introduction.

Porter, Joyce. *Dover: The Collected Short Stories.* Woodstock, VT: Foul Play Press. Introduction by Robert Barnard. Eleven stories about the incompetent inspector, all from *EQMM.*

Rendell, Ruth. *Blood Lines: Long and Short Stories.* London: Hutchinson. A novella and ten stories, one about Inspector Wexford. Six stories were new at the time of British publication but appeared in *EQMM* prior to the 1996 American edition from Crown.

Rhea, Nicholas. *Constable Beneath the Trees.* London: Hale. Stories about a British police constable (1994).

———. *Constable Versus Greenglass.* London: Hale. More stories of a British constable.

Satterthwait, Walter. *The Gold of Mayani.* Gallup, NM: Buffalo Medicine Books. six stories from *AHMM.*

Smith, Noel E. *Stories of a Wallasey Detective.* Wallasey, Merseyside, England: Noel E. Smith. Four stories.

Starrett, Vincent. *The Eleventh Juror and Other Crime Classics.* Toronto: Metropolitan Toronto Reference Library. Ten stories from various sources, collected as volume six of the Vincent Starrett Memorial Library Series. All volumes edited and introduced by Peter Ruber.

———. *The Escape of Alice and Other Fantasies.* Toronto: Metropolitan Toronto Reference Library. Twenty-three stories, some fantasy but including a few crime tales, Sherlockian and Van Dine parodies. Volume seven of the series.

———. *The New Adventures of Jimmie Lavender.* Toronto: Metropolitan Toronto Reference Library. Twelve stories, 1944–65, about a gentleman detective. Volume four of the series.

Symons, Julian. *The Man Who Hated Television and Other Stories.* London: Macmillan. Eleven stories in the late author's final collection.

van de Wetering, Janwillem. *Mangrove Mame and Other Tropical Tales of Terror.* Tucson, AZ: Dennis McMillan. Seventeen stories, six new, from *EQMM* and elsewhere.

Wilhelm, Kate. *A Flush of Shadows.* New York: St. Martin's. Five novelettes, two new. Three are occult fantasy, two are detection.

II. Anthologies

Ashley, Mike, ed. *The Mammoth Book of Historical Detectives.* New York: Carroll & Graf. Twenty-nine stories, twelve new, ranging in setting from the ancient world to the 1920s.

Bristow, Joseph, ed. *The Oxford Book of Adventure Stories.* Oxford & New York: Oxford University Press. Twenty-three stories, 1833–1991, a few criminous.

Brownworth, Victoria A., ed. *Out For Blood.* Chicago: Third Side Press. Thirteen new suspense stories and four new ghost stories by women writers.

Clark, Mary Higgins, ed. *Bad Behavior.* San Diego: Gulliver/Harcourt Brace. Twenty-two stories, eight new, in an anthology of the International Association of Crime Writers with special appeal to young adult readers.

Cox, Michael, & Jack Adrian, eds. *The Oxford Book of Historical Stories.* Oxford & New York: Oxford University Press. Thirty-six stories, 1853–1993, a few criminous.

A Dead Giveway. London: Warner Futura. Five new detective novelettes by British writers Clare Curzon, Gillian Linscott, Peter Lovesey, Dorothy Simpson, and Margaret Yorke.

Edwards, Martin, ed. *Northern Blood 2.* Newcastle, England: Flambard Press. Twenty new stories by writers in the North of England, plus two previously unpublished talks by Ngaio Marsh.

Gorman, Ed, & Martin H. Greenberg, eds. *Night Screams.* New York: Penguin/Roc. Twenty-two mystery and horror stories, sixteen new. Some detection, some fantasy (1/96).

Greenberg, Martin H., ed. *Malice Domestic 4.* New York: Pocket Books. Introduction by Carolyn G. Hart. Twelve new stories in the fourth of an annual anthology series.

———. *Murder Most Delicious.* New York: Signet. Seventeen new mysteries involving food, with original recipes.

———. *Vampire Detectives.* New York: DAW Books. Nineteen new mystery and crime stories, mainly fantasy.

——— & Ed Gorman, eds. *Cat Crimes Takes a Vacation.* New York: Donald J. Fine. Fifteen new cat mysteries set in exotic vacation spots.

Hale, Hilary, ed. *Midwinter Mysteries 5.* London: Little, Brown. Nine new stories by British writers in an annual anthology series.

Hart, Carolyn G., ed. *Crimes of the Heart.* New York: Berkley. Fourteen new stories with themes for Valentine's Day.

Heald, Tim, ed. *A Classic Christmas Crime.* London: Pavilion. Thirteen new Christmas stories by British writers.

Hoch, Edward D. *The Year's Best Mystery and Suspense Stories 1995.* New York: Walker and Company. Fourteen of the best stories from 1994, with bibliography, necrology, and awards lists.

Hutchings, Janet, ed. *Ellery Queen Presents Readers' Choice.* New York: Bantam Doubleday Dell Magazines. A 74-page promotional booklet containing four stories from *EQMM,* 1990–92, three winners and a runner-up in the annual Readers' Award poll.

Jakubowski, Maxim, ed. *No Alibi: The Best New Crime Fiction.* London: Fourth Estate/Ringpull. Twenty-seven stories, all but two new. Also distributed in a separate edition at Bouchercon 26.

Manson, Cynthia, ed. *Murder by the Book.* New York: Carroll & Graf. Twenty literary mysteries from *EQMM* and *AHMM.*

———. *Mystery Cats 3.* New York: Signet. Sixteen cat stories, a few fantasy, mainly from *EQMM.*

——— & Cathleen Jordan, eds. *Murder Most Medical.* Fifteen stories with medical backgrounds, from *EQMM* and *AHMM.*

——— & Adam Stern, eds. *Silver Screams: Murder Goes Hollywood.* Stamford, CT: Longmeadow Press. Seventeen stories from *EQMM* and *AHMM.*

Miller, John, & Tim Smith, eds. *San Francisco Thrillers: True Crimes and Dark Mysteries from the City by the Bay.* San Francisco: Chronicle Books. Eleven stories and excerpts, plus two accounts of true crimes.

Mystery Scene, Staff of, eds. *The Year's 25 Finest Crime &Mystery Stories,* Fourth Annual Edition. New York: Carroll & Graf. Introduction by Jon L. Breen. Twenty-five of the best stories of 1994.

Pronzini, Bill, & Jack Adrian, eds. *Hard-Boiled: An Anthology of American Crime Stories.* New York: Oxford University Press. Thirty-six stories and novelettes, 1925–92, tracing the evolution of the hard-boiled crime story.

Randisi, Robert J., ed. *The Eyes Still Have It.* New York: Dutton. Twelve Shamus Award winners from the Private Eye Writers of America.

Rendell, Ruth, ed. *The Reason Why: An Anthology of the Murderous Mind.* London: Jonathan Cape. More than a hundred excerpts from prose, drama, and poetry examining the motives for murder. (U.S. edition: Crown, 1996)

Resnick, Mike, & Martin H. Greenberg, eds. *Sherlock Hollmes in Orbit.* New York: DAW Books. Twenty-six new Sherlockian stories with science fiction or fantasy themes.

Rowe, Jennifer, ed. *Love Lies Bleeding: Crimes for a Summer Christmas*

5. St. Leonards, Australia: Allen & Unwin. Thirteen new stories by Australian writers in the fifth of an annual series.

Skene-Melvin, David, ed. *Crime in a Cold Climate: An Anthology of Classic Canadian Crime.* Toronto: Simon & Pierre. Fourteen stories and four poems, 1888–1929, from various sources.

Windrath, Helen, ed. *Reader, I Murdered Him, Too.* London: The Women's Press. Fifteen stories by women writers, some new.

Woods, Paula L., ed. *Spooks, Spies, and Private Eyes: Black Mystery, Crime, and Suspense Fiction.* New York: Doubleday. Twenty-two stories, nine new, by black writers.

III. Nonfiction

Block, Lawrence, & Ernie Bulow. *After Hours: Conversations with Lawrence Block.* Albuquerque, NM: University of New Mexico Press. Interviews with Block, plus a reprint of his first published story, four essays, and a bibliography of his writings.

Bloom, Harold, ed. *Classic Crime and Suspense Writers.* New York: Chelsea Books. Brief biographies, critical extracts, and bibliographies of thirteen leading American and British suspense writers.

———. *Classic Mystery Writers.* New York: Chelsea Books. Biographical, critical, and bibliographical information on thirteen major mystery writers up to 1930.

Borcherding, David H., ed. *Mystery Writer's Source Book: Where to Sell Your Manuscript,* Second Edition. Cincinnati: Writer's Digest Books. Articles on craft and technique, interviews with leading editors, lists of book publishers, magazines, literary agents, mystery bookstores, and organizations, as well as detail on how three specific works—a short story and two novels—were developed and sold. The story and excerpts from the novels are included.

Close, Alan. *The Australian Love Letters of Raymond Chandler.* Victoria, Australia: McPhee Gribbler Publishers. A "Platonic romance" carried on in actual letters between 67-year-old Chandler and a 17-year-old Australian girl he never met, blended into a book that combines fact and fiction.

Coren, Michael. *Conan Doyle.* London: Bloomsbury. A biography of Sherlock Holmes's creator.

Corvasce, Mauro V., & Joseph R. Paglino. *Modus Operandi: A Writer's Guide to How Criminals Work.* Cincinnati: Writer's Digest Books. How criminals plan and execute various crimes.

DeMarr, Mary Jean, ed. *In the Beginning: First Novels in Mystery Series.* Bowling Green, OH: Bowling Green State University Popular Press. Fourteen essays on first novels in established mystery series.

Duran, Leopoldo. *Graham Greene: An Intimate Portrait by His Closest Friend and Confidant.* San Francisco: HarperCollins. A memoir of Green's later years by the priest who inspired *Monsignor Quixote.*

Dyer, Carolyn Stewart, & Nancy Tillman Romalov, eds. *Rediscovering Nancy Drew.* Iowa City: University of Iowa Press. Twenty-seven essays and a bibliography dealing with the girl detective, the outgrowth of a Nancy Drew Conference at the University of Iowa in 1993.

Greene, Douglas G. *John Dickson Carr: The Man Who Explained Miracles.* New York: Otto Penzler Books. A critical biography of Carr, with discussions of his novels, short stories, and radio plays. Includes photographs and a complete bibliography.

Heising, Willetta L. *Detecting Women: A Reader's Guide and Checklist for Mystery Series Written by Women.* Dearborn, MI: Purple Moon Press. Listings for more than 450 series detectives created by women.

———. *Detecting Women 2.* Dearborn, MI: Purple Moon Press. An update of the previous volume, with a pocket guide to authors and titles sold separately.

Irons, Glenwood, ed. *Feminism in Women's Detective Fiction.* Toronto: University of Toronto Press. Twelve essays on women sleuths in fiction.

Klein, Kathleen Gregory. *Women Times Three: Writers, Detectives, Readers.* Bowling Green, OH: Bowling Green State University Popular Press. Women readers comment on women writers and their female detective characters.

Kogan, Deen, ed. *The Mid-Atlantic Mystery Cookbook.* Philadelphia: Detecto Mysterioso Books. Ninety recipes from mystery writers (1994).

Lownie, Andrew. *John Buchan.* London: Constable. A new biography of the author of *The 39 Steps.*

Lycett, Andrew. *Ian Fleming: A Biography.* London: Weidenfeld. A life of James Bond's creator.

Mactire, Sean P. *Malicious Intent: A Writer's Guide to How Criminals Think.* Cincinnati: Writer's Digest Books. A study of criminal psychology.

Metess, Christopher, ed. *The Critical Response to Dashiell Hammett.* Westport, CT: Greenwood Press. Some sixty essays, reviews, and commentaries on Hammett.

Moore, Lewis D. *Meditations on America: John D. MacDonald's Travis McGee Series and Other Fiction.* Bowling Green, OH: Bowling Green State University Popular Press. A study of MacDonald's work, with emphasis on the McGee novels.

Pearsall, Jay. *Mystery & Crime: The New York Public Library Book of Answers.* New York: Fireside/Simon & Schuster. Questions and answers about mystery writers and their books.

Penzler, Otto, annotated by. *The Crown Crime Companion: The Top 100*

Mystery Novels of All Time. New York: Crown. Compiled by Mickey Friedman from a poll of members of the Mystery Writers of America, with separate essays by ten leading mystery writers on various categories of mysteries.

Polito, Robert. *Savage Art: A Biography of Jim Thompson.* New York: Knopf. The life and work of a master of *noir* fiction.

Reynolds, William, & Elizabeth Trembley, eds. *It's a Print! Detective Fiction from Page to Screen.* Bowling Green, OH: Bowling Green State University Popular Press. Essays on screen adaptations of mystery novels.

Rosenheim, Shawn, & Stephen Rachman, eds. *The American Face of Edgar Allan Poe.* Baltimore: Johns Hopkins University Press. Thirteen essays about Poe's place in American culture.

Roth, Marty. *Foul and Fair Play: Reading Genre in Classic Detective Fiction.* Athens, GA: University of Georgia Press. A structuralist approach to mystery and espionage fiction.

Smith, Myron J., Jr., & Terry White. *Cloak and Dagger Fiction: An Annotated Guide to Spy Thrillers,* Third Edition. Westport, CT: Greenwood Press. Revised and updated edition of a guide first published in 1976 and previously updated in 1982.

Stine, Kate, ed. *The Armchair Detective Book of Lists,* Revised Second Edition. New York: Otto Penzler Books. A revised and enlarged guide to the best in mystery fiction, including winners and nominees of all major awards, and lists of favorites from critics, writers, and booksellers. Lists of organizations, conventions, and publications are included.

Tallett, Dennis. *The Ruth Rendell Companion.* Glendale, CA: Companion Books. A study of all Rendell's novels and short stories, including the "Barbara Vine" books, through 1993, complete with plot synopsis and list of characters.

Whiteman, Robin. *The Cadfael Companion.* New York: Mysterious Press. An alphabetical listing of all characters and places names in the Brother Cadfael mysteries. Introduction by Cadfael's creator, Ellis Peters.

Necrology

Ted Allan (1916?–95). Coauthor (with Roger MacDougall) of a 1957 dramatic version of Roy Vickers's novelette *Double Image.*

Kingsley Amis (1922–95). Well-known British mainstream novelist who published five mystery-intrigue novels and a collection of short stories, some criminous. He also published *The James Bond Dossier*

(1965), and as Robert Markham continued the Bond saga with *Colonel Sun* (1968).

Charles Bennett (1899–1995). Dramatist and screenwriter, two of whose works were filmed by Hitchcock: *Blackmail* (1929) and *The Man Who Knew Too Much* (1934).

Ernest Borneman (1915–95). Author of a single crime novel under his own name, but best known for *The Face on the Cutting Room Floor* (1937), as by Cameron McCabe.

Russell Braddon (1920–95). Author of eight crime novels, notably *End Play* (1972).

John Brunner (1934–95). Well-known science fiction writer who published eleven mystery and crime novels, 1965–87.

Don Carpenter (1931–95). Mainstream novelist whose work included at least one crime novel, *Blade of Light* (1968).

Diane Cleaver (1941–95). Literary agent who authored a single mystery novel, *Sherbourne's Folly* (1978), under the pseudonym Nora Barry.

Thomas P. Cullinan (1919?–95). Novelist and television writer whose work included at least two mysteries, *The Besieged* (1970) and *The Eighth Sacrament* (1977).

Robertson Davies (1913–95). Mainstream Canadian author whose novels often contained elements of mystery and crime, as in *Fifth Business* (1970), *What's Bred in the Bone* (1985), and *The Cunning Man* (1995). Also published a collection of ghost stories, *High Spirits* (1982), several of which were reprinted in *EQMM*.

Bernard Victor Dryer (1917?–95). Author of three novels, notably *Port Afrique* (1949).

Elizabeth (Xavia) Ferrars (1907–95). Pseudonym of British author Morna Brown, published in America as E. X. Ferrars. Her more than sixty novels included *Give a Corpse a Bad Name* (1940), *Enough to Kill a Horse* (1955), and *Skeleton in Search of a Cupboard* (1982).

Jack Finney (1911–95). Author of four crime novels, notably *Five Against the House* (1954) and *Assault on a Queen* (1959), but best known for his fantasies *Invasion of the Body Snatchers* (1955) and *Time and Again* (1970).

Nichol Fleming (1939–95). Nephew of Ian Fleming and author of three crime novels.

William Campbell Gault (1910–95). Well-known author of some thirty mystery novels, notably the Edgar-winning *Don't Cry for Me* (1952) and *The Bloody Bokhara* (1953). Also published more than 120 short stories, mainly in the pulps, and 35 juvenile novels with sports backgrounds. Winner of Lifetime Achievement Award from Private Eye Writers of America, 1984.

Charles Gordone (1925–95). Author of a single crime play, *No Place to Be Somebody* (1969), winner of the Pulitzer Prize for Drama.

Herbert Harris (1911–95). British author of four novels and more than three thousand short-short stories in newspapers and magazines, under his own name and as by Michael Moore, Frank Bury, Peter Friday, and Jerry Regan. Past chairman of the Crime Writers Association and longtime editor of its annual anthologies.

Sylvia Theresa Haymon (1918–95). British author of seven novels since 1980, notably *Ritual Murder* (1982), all published as by S. T. Haymon. An eighth novel will appear in 1996.

Patricia Highsmith (1921–95). Well-known author of twenty crime novels, notably *Strangers on a Train* (1950) and *The Talented Mr. Ripley* (1955), as well as seven collections of short stories. Also published an early mainstream novel as Claire Morgan.

John Honeywood (1928–95). Pseudonym of British crime reporter Arthur John Owen who authored two mystery novels in 1981, both unpublished in America.

(Walter) Ryerson Johnson (1901–95). Well-known pulp writer who authored two paperback crime novels under his own name, three Doc Savage novels under the house name of Kenneth Robeson, and one or more Phantom Detective novels under the house name of Robert Wallace. Also wrote two paperback crime novels with Davis Dresser under the joint pseudonym of Matthew Blood, and authored at least two of the later Brett Halliday novels.

Sidney Kingsley (1906–95). Well-known playwright whose work included *Dead End* (1936) and *Detective Story* (1949).

Howard Koch (1902–95). Coauthor (with Julius Epstein) of the screenplay for *Casablanca,* published in book form in 1973.

Andrew Lyttle (1902–95). Author of two crime novels, *The Long Night* (1936) and *A Name for Evil* (1947).

James McCahery (1934–95). Author of two novels about Lavinia London, starting with the Anthony Award-winning paperback *Grave Undertaking* (1990).

Mike McQuay (1949–95). Science fiction writer who published four SF mysteries about private eye Matthew Swain as well as several thrillers, four of them as Jack Arnett. Also ghosted at least two of Don Pendleton's Executioner series.

Ellen Nehr (1931–95). Long active in mystery fandom, she published the *Doubleday Crime Club Compendium 1928–1991* in 1992.

Richard Pape (1916–95). British/Australian author of two 1960s crime novels, unpublished in America.

Edith Pargeter (1913–95). British author best known for her twenty Ellis Peters novels about twelfth-century Benedictine monk Brother Cadfael, starting with *A Morbid Taste for Bones* (1977). She published some seventy-five books in all, including historical novels under her own name and as by Peter Benedict, and mystery fiction as by Peters, Jolyon Carr, and John Redfern. Her most notable non-Cadfael mysteries were the Edgar-winning *Death and the Joyful Woman* (1961) and *Never Pick Up Hitch-Hikers!* (1976).

Don Pendleton (1927–95). Author of more than 80 books under his own name and as by Dan Britain and Stephen Gregory. Best known for his Executioner series of paperback originals about Mack Bolan, a former soldier battling the Mafia, which in time led to more than 250 novels and spin-offs by Pendleton and others.

Gary Provost (1944–95). Nonfiction author who published two true-crime novelizations, *Finder* (1988) and *Without Mercy* (1990), the former with Marilyn Greene.

Bob Randall (1937–95). Pseudonym of Stanley B. Goldstein, author of four novels, notably *The Fan* (1977).

W. E. Dan Ross (1912?–95). Canadian author of scores of mystery novels and thirty-four Gothic novels as by Marilyn Ross, based on the *Dark Shadows* television show. Also wrote as Dan Ross, W. E. D. Ross, Laura Frances Brooks, Lydia Colby, Rose Dana, Jan Daniels, Diana Randall, Marilyn Ross, and—with Orlando Joseph Rigóni—Leslie Ames. Also published some fifty short stories as Dan Ross and another twenty in collaboration with his wife, Charlotte, in *Mike Shayne Mystery Magazine, The Saint Magazine,* and elsewhere.

Norma Schier (1930?–95). Author of four paperback mystery novels and a collection of pastiches, *The Anagram Detectives* (1979).

R. McNair Scott (1906–95). Collaborator with T. H. White on a single mystery novel, *Dead Mr. Nixon* (1931).

Irving Shulman (1913–95). Well-known novelist and screenwriter who authored eight crime novels and a short story collection, beginning with *The Amboy Dukes* (1947). Also published one crime novel as Tabor Rawson.

Margaret St. Clair (1911?–95). Science fiction author who also wrote as Idris Seabright and who, under her own name, contributed occasional crime short stories to Mystery Book Magazine and elsewhere.

Ross Thomas (1926–95). Well-known author of some twenty political thrillers, notably his two Edgar winners *The Cold War Swap* (1966) and *Briarpatch* (1984). Also published five thrillers as Oliver Bleeck. Past president of Mystery Writers of America.

Robert Towers (1922?–95). Novelist who authored a single mystery-fantasy, *The Summoning* (1983).

Elleston Trevor (1920–95). Prolific British author of more than one hundred novels, notably *The Flight of the Phoenix* (1964) and *The Quiller Memorandum* (1965). The latter, an Edgar-winning spy novel, became the first of eighteen Quiller novels published as by Adam Hall.

Trevor also wrote suspense novels under the pseudonyms Mansell Black, Trevor Burgess, Howard North, Simon Rattray, Warwick Scott, and Caesar Smith.

Kathleen Tynan (1937–1995). Canadian/British author of a single mystery novel, *Agatha* (1978), and the screenplay for the film version the following year.

Edward Whittemore (1933?–95). Mainstream writer whose novels included at least two involving crime and espionage, *Nile Shadows* (1983) and *Jericho Mosaic* (1987).

Roger Zelazny (1937–95). Well-known science fiction writer who authored a collection of criminous novelettes, *My Name Is Legion* (1976).